Reparations

THE COMPLETE SERIES
(Omnibus Edition)

Reparations USA
Reparations Mind
Reparations Core
Reparations Maze

PHILIP WYETH

CONTENTS

Reparations
USA

(BOOK ONE)

1. THE PROGRAM

The studio audience responded to the producer's waving arms by cheering loudly. When the theme music began to fade out, they quieted down. A camera dolly crept toward the bright stage where two women sat opposite one another on red felt chairs.

"Welcome back to *Tina Talk!*"

The host was a lively woman of forty, whose sculpted brown mane flowed onto a bright yellow dress which hugged her curves and showed off much of her long legs, right down to the matching high heels.

"Our guest this segment is Kate Donohugh, and she works at the Historical Reparations Administration megabranch in Newark. Welcome, how are you?"

"Hi, Tina! Thank you so much for having me on."

Kate, who was in her thirties, wore clothing more appropriate for someone speaking on behalf of the government, but was put together in a way that showed she had enough style sense to make any outfit work.

"Now," Tina began, "it says here that you are an Assistant Regional Manager, but isn't it true that you really have to be a jack-of-all-trades considering the kind of work that goes on over at the HRA?"

"That's right. What we do tends to be cross-disciplinary, but at the same time you've got to have the right people skills to interact with the public."

Tina looked down at a pad in her lap and spun a pen in her fingers.

"I'm quite fascinated by all the fields of expertise that came together to make this project even possible. I mean, five-hundred-plus years, that's a lot of people and events to account for!"

"Oh yes, the HRA is an incredible undertaking! In fact, a whole new college career track called Reparology was recently designed to give students a rigorous background in such areas as history—of course, haha—but also accounting, social work, law enforcement, archaeology, genealogy, and—should I keep going?"

Kate gave a smile and the audience responded with a healthy round of applause.

"Hahahahaha, that's remarkable," Tina laughed. "Now, the administration officially launched just two-and-a-half years ago —"

"After nearly a decade of planning, mind you."

"Of course. So you rolled it out across the country, opening field offices for customer service, document submission, appeals... You're a veritable DMV of sorts, hahahaha..."

"Oh yes, the HRA was unprecedented in its goal of righting all the wrongs that piled up ever since that first European ship landed on Tribal American shores. We understood the importance of engaging with the public on a practical level to work toward that goal, because it is an ongoing, perpetually adapting program. At the end of each month our supercomputer network—"

"MARVIN."

"Haha, yes, which stands for Macro Aggregating Restitution Vector Input Navigator. He—it—MARVIN, conducts a rolling audit as new documents come to light, which ensures that those who owe historical debts pay their fair share."

"Fascinating. Now, this can all seem a bit abstract so why don't you give our audience some hard numbers about the results you and the HRA are achieving."

A graphic appeared and Kate began to walk viewers through the charts.

"In just a couple of years we have been able to assist one-hundred-sixty-million Historically Wronged Americans, who fall into our Beneficiary class, by recapturing seven trillion dollars from Legacy Violators, members of the Debtor class which consists of approximately two-hundred-seventy-five-million citizens."

"Is that not amazing, folks?" Tina implored the audience to stand up and clap. "A dot-GOV agency really doing its job, all right!"

After the crowd settled down, Kate continued. "The program has been such a success that—while I can't divulge any specifics

—let me just say that we are in negotiations with certain well-known international bodies to roll out sister agencies in Europe and its former colonies. This won't happen overnight, however, because compared to the rest of the world, the United States is a fairly small and well-documented country. Can you imagine the amount of work it will take to just get organized in huge landmasses like Brazil, Africa, and India?"

"Kids watching at home," Tina cackled, "if you're looking for long stable careers where you get to see the world—learn a second language now and get on the HRA career track!"

"Haha, yes, exactly…"

"Tell me, having made so much progress already, can you predict when the program might achieve its goal here at home?"

"I'd say still quite a while. New documents from the distant past are being discovered every day. These have to be uploaded into the system, processed, and then authenticated. Debit Scores adjust in each monthly spreadsheet to reflect the latest data.

"But beyond redistribution," Kate continued, "our deeper goal is for Beneficiaries to achieve competence and self-sufficiency. And I can report that a small but respectable percentage of them have been using their newfound capital to restore crumbling neighborhoods and start new businesses. Shout out to the HRA jobs training program!"

"Absolutely! Now," Tina said as she furrowed her brow, "one unfortunate by-product of these historical documents taking such a prominent role in our everyday affairs, is the rise of an underground resistance campaign by so-called debt protesters, who make no bones about destroying inconvenient archives."

"Yes, unfortunately the descendants of KKK members who once rode through the night to lynch Afrigro-Americans, now go to great lengths to shirk their responsibilities in this modern-day version of book burning. It is a crime. And not only that, it is a violation of human rights."

The audience rumbled in a low cascade of boos.

"Now, Kate," Tina said. "Let me change gears here to talk about one of the more innovative ways the HRA is spreading its message. They call it Direct Descendant Match—DDM, for short —and it's actually modeled after game shows. Can you please explain?"

"Of course. As your audience knows, our supercomputers are

constantly reanalyzing the vast historical database and making new connections. On average, for every thirty billion Certified Historical Events that MARVIN processes, it matches up two living citizens where at least ten Domination Events—DEs— have taken place between their bloodlines in the past five hundred years."

"Can more than one DE within a single lifetime count toward the total?"

"No, and that's what makes DDM so significant. We're talking about ten of Person A's ancestors involved in DEs with ten of Person B's ancestors. Usually the domination is always one-sided, but in rare cases it isn't and MARVIN takes these details into account.

"Anyway, the HRA believes that such heavily weighted bad karma should be redirected in a public forum to help cleanse our national palate. So these two people appear on the show, *DDM TV Live*, to explore the dark and violent path that led them to this dramatic moment."

"Sounds fascinating! Then what happens?"

"Well, MARVIN never stops calculating, and just before he passes assessment, he processes documents from the contestants' own lifetimes."

"Nooooo!"

"Hahaha, yes, it's amazing, I know!"

"And then what?"

"The two join hands, and as they face the screen their assessment is read."

"And it just so happens that you brought us a clip from a recent episode of the show. Let's take a look!"

A video began, showing a skinny white man in a striped v-neck t-shirt holding hands with a short woman of Northern Tribal features. A deeply suntanned host said, "Jonathan Wibble. Your blood has affronted the blood of Agnes Yazzie sixteen times. No slivers from your bank account could hope to make up for these crimes. In the name of justice and fostering goodwill, so that we can finally stop this cycle of abuse, you are remanded to HRA Garden 2-F in Champaign, Illinois, where you will grow food with Mrs. Yazzie for a period of one year. And afterward, your reduced Debit Score will reflect this honorable service."

The studio audience went wild with applause. Tina leaned

forward onto her crossed legs and brought a hand to her heart.

"My goodness," she gushed. "Is that not proof that the HRA is about more than money, and also helping to move humanity forward?"

More applause. Kate mouthed "thank you" to the crowd.

Tina sat back and said, "Kate, it's been a thrill having you here, but before I let you go, one last question. Have any love connections ever blossomed during a DDM assignment? Seems like all those months together, things could get *very* intimate!"

"Well," Kate began with a sigh, "such liaisons are discouraged—because in fact a certain percentage of DDM conflicts do involve family feuds over romantic affairs—but I am happy to report that there are three married couples out there right now thanks to the program."

"How about that, ladies and gentlemen? Kate Donohugh, thank you so much for coming on *Tina Talk*..."

After the show, Kate stepped into the brisk, overcast Manhattan streets with a jump in her step, feeling proud that she'd given the HRA a good showing. She was in no way a trained PR spokeshuman, but between her genuine smile and high school theater background, the administration felt confident in sending her out for the occasional media puff piece.

Aside from a few smaller news programs and prerecorded web spots, however, most of her previous media placements had only been quotes in press releases and news stories. This *Tina* show was by far her biggest appearance, and perhaps normally out of her league, but the HRA was celebrating the latest trillion-dollar milestone by sending out anyone who wasn't a total buffoon to tout the administration's success.

What had started nearly ten years earlier as a disorganized rabble of idealistic left-wing activist groups had tapped into a growing sentiment that beyond merely throwing government money at problems—War on Poverty, War on Drugs—the similarly abstract War for Equity required not only an organized, systematic approach but also an adaptive component. Because when holding history's conquerors to account over such a long timeline, a rigid set of rules would only hamstring the executive body and set the program up for abuse and failure.

This all coincided with the reliable political pendulum swing back to the left after nearly a decade of populist-fueled conservative rule, so that when the reinvigorated Dramacrats won a majority in both houses of Congress, their new president quickly signed into law the establishment of the Historical Reparations Administration. And contrary to the Rebellicans' snide predictions of economic doom, it turned into a jobs bonanza because so many different professions were required for the whole plan to work.

Eileen Jeffries-Lao, the ceiling-shattering candidate who became both the first female and first Chinese-American president, was called a modern-day FDR as an army of document experts, historians, social workers, and accountants all moved in to the administration's seven hundred new field offices, which had employed another thirty-eight-thousand people during construction.

Kate Donohugh's life dovetailed with all of this beautifully. Whereas so many idealistic young people find that the pull of the world's demands slowly suffocates their desire to make a difference, Kate had been among this new breed of digitally empowered activists who had never tasted the good-times wealth that the Boomers and older Gen Xers enjoyed. Children of successive economic avalanches, these late-stage Gen X, Millennial, and Gen Z visionaries used their tech savvy to circumvent the ossified policies of the status quo and mold all the disparate groups that were yelling in the streets into a legitimate political force effecting tectonic policy changes on a national level.

It was not all some hippie fantasy, however. For so many Caucmericans to willingly transform the amorphous concept of "white guilt" into an actionable platform required ruthless introspection so as not to patronize the very Minoricans they sought to help. To do so, they channeled life opportunities stemming from their privileged backgrounds toward a goal which was bigger and more noble than merely helping a homeless person or even one's local community—because the HRA, dollar by dollar, was making a rigorous public accounting of half a millennium of oppression and exploitation, both by clearing the balance sheet for the living as well as setting a tone for how business would be done moving forward. In short, equitably.

Whenever Kate felt the weight of colonialism bearing down on her shoulders, or in moments of prideful weakness, she recited a prayer from the Book of Reparations, the inspirational tome compiled during the years that this political crusade unfolded. "Although I was born into this white vessel," she would whisper, "we all bleed red. No matter how privileged I find my station in life, I extend a hand down so that one day we may all stand side by side."

These words helped Kate keep perspective whenever she felt a pang of guilt about her comfortable life: nice apartment in gentrified Brooklyn, her white husband Chris, and their two Corgis. At least they'd decided not to have kids—that was easy penance for two middle-class Caucs in their early thirties to pay.

Back to reality, Kate mused as she breezed past the retinal scanner at an employee entrance of her HRA field office across the water in Newark. She took an elevator up to the second floor and headed to her desk.

"Great job today," a voice said from below a nearby cubicle wall.

Kate shifted in mid-stride to enter the workspace and received a warm smile from TJ, a plump bearded coworker whom she also considered a friend. He was a reparatician highly skilled in document analysis, particularly in detecting pixel flaws deep within flattened forgeries. This work both reduced MARVIN's workload and kept the payments flowing.

"Everyone's got to pitch in," she said and reached to meet his high-five.

"You're telling me," TJ sighed. "I've been asked to do three radio segments and you know I *never* do these promo things— but at least one's NPR, my fave!"

"Well, it's an election year, and we've got a lot to celebrate, right?"

"On the surface, absolutely. But between you and me, I think the Old Debt Boy Network has finally started to shake off their hangover and get a bit more organized."

"Whaaaat?" Kate leaned in so they could speak discreetly— they were surrounded by wall-mounted cameras that could enable someone reviewing the footage to read their lips, as well as dozens of employee tablets that were equipped to record audio.

TJ lowered his voice and said, "You know that I ran away from the South as fast as my hiney could take me, but I still check in with my folks every so often (Lord knows they're getting up there in age). So anyway, the last time I spoke to my dad… I don't know… Just something about the tone of his voice, it sounded less down in the dumps. And some of the things he said made it seem like he'd even made his peace with me—for being gay *and* working for an organization that he once said was stealing my inheritance.

"So I asked him if he was sick and he clucked, 'No! Doc says I'm fine,' so I said, 'Well, what *is* it, Dad? Don't leave me in the dark.' And he just blew it off, 'No, no. Everything's fine. Seems like this country's headed back on the right track again, that's all.' And I was like, 'Okay, I guess…?' "

Kate made a face. "Weird."

"I know, right? So I jumped online and started poking around for negative chatter about the HRA—at home on a private browser via proxy server, of course; God forbid I did that here— and I've got to tell you, not only are the hate sites saying the usual nasty things, but vandalism on scanners and field offices is up twenty percent in the last six months alone."

"Really? I haven't heard anything about that."

"Wouldn't surprise me if they're trying to keep it all hush-hush. And you know, some people are just up and leaving. They'd rather live off the grid than pay—"

"Ah, here's our big morning show star!" an approaching voice beamed from outside the cubicle.

It was Jan, a regional manager and Kate's direct supervisor— an eighteenth-generation Afrigro-American who donated her benefits to fund summer camping trips for inner city kids who otherwise might never see the countryside.

Jan patted Kate on the back, smiled at TJ, then said, "But as great as you were out there, the trenches beckon. Got the usual drama over in disbursements: lady brought in her kids, wants more money, you know the drill. Asked for a supervisor but honestly, DC scheduled a last-minute conference call that I've got to sit in on. You're senior enough, Ms. *Tina Talk*, think you can handle that for me?"

"But of course," Kate said with a nod and twirl of her hand, smiling at TJ as she drifted away.

No time for lunch today, she thought, her stomach grumbling at each turn down the winding hallway. An elevator ride took her down to the ground floor, then she went out one security door, scanned her key card at the reception entrance, and walked past a dozen cubicles before finally turning right into a small room with a table and four chairs.

Inside, a young black woman was tending to a baby stroller while a boy explored the room.

"Hello there! I'm Kate Donohugh, I hear you asked for a supervisor?"

"Yes, thank you. I'm Myra Jenkins."

"Why don't you take a seat and let's see if I can help you."

As they sat down on opposite sides of the table, Myra pulled a folder out of her bag and began spreading papers over nearly the entire surface.

"Okay, this is the family tree that I got from y'all." She held up a printout which bore the HRA seal, then picked up a second sheet with her other hand. "Says right here I'm only entitled to six hundred dollars each month for past crimes against my people. But that just ain't enough and we used to get more. I got two little ones. Can you do anything to help us?"

While Ms. Jenkins was saying all this, Kate had removed her laptop from her work bag and opened the lid. As she booted up and logged into the HRA system, she said, "Let me just access your file—"

"The man I talked to at the counter already did that."

"Yes, well, I'd like to get up to speed before answering any of your questions."

As Kate cycled between tabs on the screen—which displayed details about Ms. Jenkins such as her age and address, ancestry, and finances—she felt something hit her foot. She looked down to see a six-year-old boy with a race car in his hand smiling from beneath the table.

"Oh, hello there, young man!"

"Tyrell," Myra sighed, "is that you under there? Please get up and let this woman do her job."

The boy crawled out and she motioned for him to sit next to her.

Kate turned her attention back to the file, which included certain tabs only visible to higher ranking employees—the first case worker did not have access to this information. She tapped a nail on the screen and looked up.

"Okay, I think I see the problem. Earlier this year the MARVIN mainframe accepted two new documents certifying that in 1822, an ancestor on your mother's side purchased two slaves."

"But what's that got to do with me?"

"While black-on-black ownership was uncommon, and oftentimes the result of freed slaves buying their own relatives—*although... actually...* that purchaser was a white farmer named Colin Evers. So it looks like you are, in fact, one-two-hundred-and-fifty-sixth Caucmerican!"

"Wow. Um... So nothing about *my* life has changed—except I had a baby last year—but you found some old piece of paper and now I get less?"

"You've done quite well under the program so far."

Myra looked down into her hands. "I know, but it's hard out there, even with your money."

"It's not *our* money—it's yours!"

"I'm just sayin', couple months back, the landlord started charging a new fee on top of the rent. Called it 'lurf' or something."

"Yes," Kate sighed, "that's the Lower Income Retainer Fee, unfortunately. Property owners have lobbyists too, and they were able to convince the legislature to collect that from many Beneficiaries who rent."

"I see."

"Oh, there's one other thing I should bring to your attention. Informally, of course."

"And what's that?"

Kate rotated her laptop and a small video player showed a black teenager spraying graffiti.

"That's your cousin Alex outside a Shell gas station two weeks ago."

"Why are you showing me this?"

"Because," Kate began, "the Joint Telecom & Penal Bureaus want to implement a new policy where all petty crimes caught on camera with definitive ID—and here we have scans of both Alex's face and eyes—they would bypass our overcrowded court system, and instead fines would be imposed automatically."

"Which means what, exactly?"

"Reduced payments, for one. And the possibility of being placed under Microscopic Protocol."

"What's that, like probation?"

"Precisely," Kate said with as friendly a smile as she could muster. "But the HRA has *begged* these bureaus not to move forward because it will disproportionately affect the people we're trying to help here. But I've heard that they're compiling a large body of evidence they want to present before Congress to try and force it through."

"When's all that gonna happen?"

"If we're lucky we'll hold them off until the beginning of next year. But maybe you can give Alex a little heads-up to be more careful out there."

"So you got these cameras everywhere and you're just watching everything people do?"

Kate pointed to a camera mounted in a protective box up in the corner of the room and winked.

"This ain't right," Myra said as she stood up and gathered her papers in a mash. "I thought the whole point of these agencies was to *help* people. C'mon, Tee, let's get out of here…"

She wheeled the stroller out through the door and Tyrell followed.

Kate eased her laptop shut, walked to the door and quietly closed it, then wedged herself into the corner directly under the camera, trying to be in as little of the frame as possible. She closed her eyes and rubbed circles around her temples while taking slow even breaths through her mouth, then began reciting the Mantra of Atonement. "Although I was born into this white vessel…"

Stressful encounters like these were the biggest cause of burnout on any HRA staff. A platoon of therapists had been trained to specifically address this pressure point, and with soothing words they attempted to reinforce the core idea that the HRA sought an incredibly lofty goal in trying to repair over five hundred years of ugly history, but human nature doesn't simply change overnight. Therefore employees were encouraged to view their role as holy humans leading pilgrims across dangerous and unfamiliar territory into the Promised Land.

A few minutes into the calming routine, Kate heard her work

phone ping from inside her bag. It was a text from Jan's assistant which said: "Boss still on conference call. Asked if you'd head over to Debts and help out. Room 114."

Kate wrote back, "Sure thing. Challenges on both sides of the spreadsheet today, what can you do?"

In addition to secure employee-only areas, the public sections of all HRA field offices had separate wings to serve Beneficiaries and Debtors. Smart scanners granted appropriate entry to each side, and armed guards posted throughout the facility helped prevent or break up any conflicts between the two groups.

For Kate to reach the Debtor wing, she had to walk through an exit-only door, wind her way down several bright corridors, then scan herself through an interior employee entrance. This side of the facility had a bit more security on hand, and Kate always felt a slight chill in the air here. Everyone understood that this was not the happiest of places, because even though the dual-purpose field offices had been set up to encourage dialogue with the public, Debtors rarely brought in authentic documents that reduced their obligations or at least warranted an extension.

Not that in-person pleas were the only or most effective means of reducing one's debt load. Legal and accounting firms had virtually tap danced with glee at the immaculate conception of a whole new revenue stream when the HRA was created. Perhaps the most opportunistic company of all was the tax firm H&R Block, which poetically rebranded itself as working to "block" historical reparations from being collected.

Between these scoundrels trying to put the brakes on one of mankind's most noble projects and several legal cases working their way up the court system hierarchy, HRA employees felt enough trepidation below the surface to keep motivated and working on an aggressive timeline. There were so many past examples of ambitious programs that had been derailed by judges or bureaucratic incompetence, that there was simply no room for hubris or believing that the righteousness of one's cause guaranteed the inevitability of its success.

For each day that passed without an injunction granted by some bench that was stacked with Rebellicans during the past two presidential terms, it meant that millions of deserving Americans had been served another small taste of justice.

With these conflicting sensations of apprehension and purpose, Kate smoothed her blouse then stepped resolutely in her pump shoes across the threshold into a room that very much resembled the one she had just left in the opposite wing of the field office. Inside sat a Caucmerican in his sixties with stringy, stark white hair and heavy eyelids over blue-gray eyes. She extended her hand.

"Kate Donohugh, how do you do?"

"Miss, my name is James. I got a bum knee, my truck needs new tires, and my job at the hardware store—which I suspect just keeps me on because I been there for so long—they cut my hours back to just twelve a week."

"I'm sorry to hear all that."

"So how do you expect me to pay?" he asked, letting the last word slowly trail off.

"Well, if you could just tell me your last name," she said while her hands automatically reached for her laptop, "I'll review your account and see what I can do."

The man leaned away and slung an arm over the back of his chair. "Here we go again."

"Full name, please?"

"It's James William Haggerston. I already went through all this. The lady outside scanned my eye with her tablet and everything."

"I know, I know, just give me a second. Yes, there you are. Hmm. It says here you only owe a hundred and thirty dollars per month, that's not so high—especially considering that your great-great-great-great-uncle killed three Choctaw Indians."

"But my actual father managed a furniture factory that hired dozens of Minoricans, as you call them, over the twenty-odd years that he was in charge there. Surely that's got to offset something a distant relative did in the 1850s."

"Thirties, actually. The 1830s."

Silence.

"And yes," Kate continued, "your father's biographical data points have all been uploaded and factored in to your cumulative Debit Score. But there's so much more: at least two ancestors worked on slave ships—granted, they only delivered human cargo to the West Indies, and I don't think the HRA has an extraction treaty there yet—but moving on, I also see theft of indigenous land, and even a case of arson against an Afrigro-American man's tractor."

"My god, are you talking about my cousin Luke? He and Albertson were friends! They used to get drunk together all the time. It was his damn wife that pressed the charges—no one really knows what actually happened!"

"The court documents in my system are pretty unambiguous."

"He said, she said, I don't know what to tell you. He had to pay them damages at the time, right?"

"The point, Mr. Haggerston, is that you felt compelled to come down here to plead your case, and so far you haven't given me much of a reason to even offer you a grace period."

He pulled out a kerchief and wiped his forehead, then said calmly, "I am tired from working my fingers to the bone just trying to survive. First they closed the factories and moved them overseas. Then they let illegal labor come in and undercut my wage. I tried to adapt by learning computers but they change faster than I can keep up. And hell, Burger Citizen started using kiosks to take your order so I can't even work there now.

"It's enough to break any man down, I don't care *what color* he is or who his second cousin, ten times removed, fought a duel with. But *you* care. Hard as it is to live in the here and now, I got the HRA with its teeth latched into my shoulder like a damned zombie on the TV. So what I'm asking for is some sort of mercy or understanding, because I cannot win by fighting this administration all by myself."

After a frozen moment, Kate turned back to her computer and clicked around. Her eyes narrowed and when she had locked onto what she was looking for, she tapped a nail onto the screen.

"Mr. Haggerston, I've got two options for you. First, I see your son Morgan earns a nice salary remodeling homes for environmental compliance, and due to several impressive maternal deductions—that being on your wife's ancestral timeline—he barely owes more than you do each month. I could request to have, say, two-thirds of your debt rotated onto his bill if you think that might be agreeable to him?"

"What's my other option?"

"That four acres of undeveloped land you own in Pennsylvania, I could put a temporary lien on it. Secured by the HRA's long-term trust, to be released when you get back on your feet."

"That's family land. Before permits and paperwork turned construction into a bureaucratic decathlon, that property was very much developed. A lot of love and memories floating above the wild grass out there."

He rose to leave and trudged to the door, looking back as he said, "No, I'll find a way to handle this business myself. Because I will *not* place another old man's burden on my son's shoulders. You have already done quite enough of that."

It was only 2 pm but Kate felt like she had worked a twelve-hour shift. Another common symptom of working at the HRA, and internal policy made generous allowances for leaving the office early. CalmTime was seen as more than a fair trade-off if it aided in employee retention, plus there was a long list of on-call temps, fully trained and ready to fill in during these minor emergencies.

Kate saw her hands moving across the laptop keyboard. The employee app opened, the mouse scrolled onto and clicked the TapOut icon, and a green capital R spun as the system sent pulses to alert some central computer that she was done for the day. She felt herself numbly moving down the hallway toward the exit, then she was on the HRA shuttle bus to the subway, somehow found herself on the right train home, and nearly crawled through the front door of her apartment.

No one was home. Chris was across town helping a client set up a new server and the dogs were at day care—was she supposed to pick them up? She'd figure that out later.

Kate moved absently into the bathroom and started to fill the tub. She closed the door and slowly peeled off her work clothes. She saw herself nude in the full-length mirror hanging on the back of the door and began to sob. When her breath caught, she leaned her head against a forearm high on the door and closed her eyes, bringing the other arm across her chest in a sort of hug. The wave of self-pity that had washed over her subsided just as quickly and was replaced by a sudden hyper-awareness.

Her left hand, which was draped across her right breast, had touched on something. She looked down but saw nothing there. She felt again—there, under the surface, something dense about the size of a pebble. Unmistakable. Terrifying. Too much to deal with on top of everything else. She climbed into the bath, draped a washcloth over her face, and went to sleep.

"Hon?" a voiced called from down the hall. "Are you home?"

The sound of dogs barking, clawing outside the bathroom door. Kate pulled the washcloth from her eyes and squinted around the room. A knock at the door.

"Helloooo?" Chris called out playfully. "Kay, are you in there?"

Mechanically, Kate climbed out of the water and put on her bathrobe. She opened the door and before Chris could say a word, she wrapped him in a wet embrace and wept.

2. THE WORKAROUND

The scanner spit out a piece of paper onto the right side collection tray. A black boy about ten years old held it up under the streetlight and inspected the top right corner. In small red letters was the printed message: "Rejected. Level 9 forgery. Please do not resubmit this document. This scanner is under surveillance. Thank you."

The boy crumpled up the paper and tossed it away, then turned to his friends and said, "Here, give me another one."

A second boy reached into his backpack, poked around, then pulled out a more weathered looking sheet. "Try this," he said. "I spent an hour putting in the wrinkles, then I dripped some soda around the edges."

The first boy took it carefully and held it up to the receiving port on the scanner's left side. The machine sucked it in and the boys waited anxiously as it made little fidgeting noises. When it gave a chirp, the second boy said, "That's good, right?"

"It didn't like the first two, spat 'em right out. It must be thinking on this one."

"Good. I put that the governor's granddaddy stole a car from us. So maybe we can get us a sweet ride."

The three other younger boys tagging along with them liked this idea, and they all crowded close to the scanner as it finished analyzing the homemade document. When the paper eased out onto the cast-iron collection tray—these machines were built tough—they nearly destroyed it fighting each other to be the one who read the verdict.

The first older boy shoutsed them down and took the sheet. "Durn," he said. "Still no good." He mashed the paper and tossed it into a pile of similar trash that surrounded the scanner. The second boy dove onto the ground and retrieved his creation, unbunching it and studying the rejection message.

"Only a level 8 fake!" he said happily. "Means I'm getting better at this. One day I'm gonna fool it and y'all be asking me for money."

But the other boys were already walking away so he stuffed the paper back into his bag and ran after them. The scanner remained stoic and inscrutable in their wake, even a few minutes later when someone ran up and spray-painted "out of order" onto its dark chrome body.

A boy in his mid-teens approached the group and called out, "Hey Tyrell, yo mama wants you back."

One of the younger boys reluctantly peeled off and said, "Hi, Clyde. Whatchu been doin'?"

"Gettin' everything ready for the Pigeon Man. He says I keep bringing him these drones, he'll let me use a few for my video."

The younger boy made a silly dance move. "DJ Clydoscope, what-what!"

"Don't you make fun now! I got skills. And eyes. I see what's goin' on up in here. Come on."

Clyde softly grabbed him by the scruff of the neck and they walked a few blocks to a rundown apartment building, then climbed up to the third floor. He pushed open the front door which was cracked, and they walked inside.

"I went in there the other day like you wanted," Myra said, facing a well-built man in white tank undershirt and matching skull cap. "But they wouldn't raise it. Maybe next month we get more."

"Man, but I need to get some of that HRA cheese," he said.

"Hold on." She walked over to the younger boy. "Tyrell, why you ain't answer your phone? Can't be out at night like this, you too young."

Clyde stepped in. "He aight. I look out for you. Right, boy?"

"Yeah," Tyrell said softly. He picked up an open bag of chips from the dining room table. "You da man, Uncle Clyde."

Myra turned back to the man and said, "Wish you'd come over here for more than just money, Octavius. Your baby sleepin' in the other room, if you even care."

"At least I'm here," he snorted. "I ain't seen Tyrell daddy face in years."

"Whateva."

"Yeah, whateva's right. Anyway, I gotta head out, handle some business. Yo, Clyde! You wanna do a little job tonight?"

"Aight," Clyde said.

"Well, come on then. Show these hoes how we do."

Myra put a hand on Clyde's shoulder. "You be careful. You know what I told you."

"Yeah, yeah. Don't get no girl pregnant. Don't get in trouble."

"You just got no idea. Tell Mama I said hi when you get home."

Clyde and Octavius put on their coats and walked outside. Octavius pulled out his phone and typed into it while they walked to his car. It was a speckled crimson early '10s Buick outfitted with custom throwback fins and gold-plated rims imprinted with dollar signs. As they entered traffic, he turned on the stereo and loud music started blasting. Clyde asked who was singing.

"DJ Above Ground," Octavius said. "The king of Bayou Rage-Hop."

"Tight."

"Hell yeah. How you doin' with the music? Got any new beats?"

Clyde looked out the window into the street. "Nah. Working on some ideas though."

"You keep at it. 'Cause you never know. But until then, let's go make some real money now!"

They parked on a side street then walked into a liquor store. Octavius waved to the Korean clerk and said, "Sup, Mr. Joon?" as they passed through to the back. He pushed open a door into the stockroom and they walked past stacks of cardboard boxes all the way to the rear exit, which opened onto an alley. Octavius checked to make sure that the slide-lock was secure.

He set up two folding chairs near the door and said, "You thirsty? Go grab us some Lectrolades."

Clyde walked back into the store and browsed in front of the beverage fridges. He picked out two neon plastic bottles and walked toward the counter, but the clerk waved a hand, saying, "It's okay, it's okay," so he turned back, grabbing a bag of pretzels as he passed into the stockroom.

About fifteen minutes later, while he and Octavius were snacking, a brisk three knocks came at the exit door. Octavius looked through the peephole and then opened the door. A lanky young black man walked in carrying a case of beer.

"You just set that on the floor," Octavius said. "You got the receipt?"

The other man put the case down and handed Octavius a sliver of curled white paper.

"You got your card?"

The man held up a credit card. Octavius glanced between it and the receipt a few times, then grabbed a pen from his ear and made a mark on the receipt. "Aight, we cool." He unzipped a pouch inside his jacket and pulled out a small plastic baggie, handing it and the receipt to the customer.

"My man! Say, you mind if I—?" He pointed at the case of beers.

"All good," Octavius said. "Clyde, get this man a chaser."

Clyde opened the box and pulled out a tall-boy of Noble Gent malt liquor, then handed it over. He heard a crisp crack outside the door just before it closed behind the customer.

"And that's how we do," Octavius said. "Full-service station."

Over the next few hours they did business with twenty other customers. Beer cases stacked up high next to the chairs. A little after 1 am, the store clerk came to the back and had a discussion with Octavius that Clyde had trouble following. He saw them count all the cases of beer, then the clerk made some notes on a small pad before pulling a zip-wallet from his back pocket. He removed several white credit cards and handed them to Octavius.

"Yo, Clyde. Grab a dolly and help this man."

The Korean brought over two dollies from a side wall, and together he and Clyde loaded up all the cases of beer and rolled them back into the front of the store, which was now mostly dark. As they put the beer back into the fridges, the clerk set aside the cases which had been opened and replaced the missing bottles and cans with matching loose beers that he pulled from the refrigerator shelves. He resealed each box with a small glue gun before sliding it across the floor to Clyde.

Octavius came in from the back and said, "Aight, Mr. Joon. See you tomorrow night."

"Okay, see you!"

On the drive back to the neighborhood, Octavius said, "Nice work tonight."

"Cool. I had a good time."

Octavius reached into his pocket and handed Clyde one of the credit cards. "Here ya go. HRA card, all loaded up!"

Clyde took the card and put it into his wallet.

A few minutes later Octavius said, "Drop you at your mom's?"

"Yeah."

"You got my number?"

"Think so."

"Okay. Maybe we do this again."

"Yeah."

When he got out of the car, Clyde turned back and said, "You going back over to my sister's?"

"Nah. Got somewhere to be."

"Oh, okay. Later."

Clyde watched as Octavius gunned the souped-up Buick around the corner and out of sight. Then he heard the buzz of a mini-drone zipping past, tracking it with his eyes by the green light casting downward as it maneuvered through the streets.

These cylindrical HRA drones were about the size of the average city bird, and equipped to record audio and video as well as summon emergency personnel. They bore a capital *R* underneath, which sent an assuring green glow down onto the residents they served in dangerous neighborhoods densely populated with Beneficiaries.

Clyde thought back to when the HRA had first been signed into law. People danced in the streets in celebration. White HRA reps ran around the neighborhood with questionnaires asking how they could help the residents improve their lives.

Over time these workers slowly disappeared, and in proportion the drones began to appear zipping through the streets. While Clyde could remember in his early childhood seeing cameras mounted high above some of the larger intersections, now you couldn't even walk down an alley without wondering if one of these "birds" wasn't secretly watching from a charging station—which were now installed more discreetly than at the beginning, because kids being kids, they had made a game out of smashing this gear.

A couple of the more enterprising older guys approached the boys and suggested that rather than destroy the drones and chargers, they could earn HRA cards loaded with twenty dollars for every intact item they brought over.

So Clyde spent the afternoons of his adolescent years after school with like-minded mercenaries trying to crack the code on how to bring down the HRA mini-drones without causing damage. It had been relatively easy—and thrilling fun—to destroy them in combat, but to knock them out of the air without breaking their fragile components was a new challenge.

First they had to figure out how to slow them down, preferably getting them to hover in place. They understood that these drones, being an auxiliary of the HRA's mission to improve Beneficiaries' lives, were programmed to respond to sensory data that indicated possible crime, danger, or injury. So Clyde and his friends began simulating robberies and bicycle accidents to get their attention. But once they appeared, the drones never dropped below twenty feet—and simply throwing objects at them wasn't any good now. The boys started to get frustrated knowing that money was sitting on the table if they could just think of a solution.

One day when they were killing time, they saw a real emergency up on someone's balcony. An old woman was screaming for help because her husband was having a heart attack. The boys watched as a mini-drone appeared at her eye level, then hovered for fifteen minutes until the paramedics arrived to take her husband away.

Clyde and his friends, in a moment of glorious abstract clarity, realized that if you targeted a drone from *above* it wouldn't see you coming—then all you had to do was control the way it came down. They started staging their own health panics —best to avoid fake assaults in case the cops actually showed up —on balconies and other places where you could get up onto the roof, and while the drone observed the situation, one of the boys standing above would cast a large blanket over top of it. Then the clump fell down softly onto a large piece of foam that another boy had rolled out to pad the landing. And just like that, they were in business.

You had to be careful handling the drones once captured—their tiny hyperblades could take your fingertip right off if you weren't careful—and some of the newer models had speakers that barked a warning message too. To secure their fresh capture, one boy slowly pulled the blanket back while another—wearing long sleeves, padded gloves, and a clear face shield—placed it into a homemade box equipped with a stolen charging station fed by battery power. Once in its "nest," the drone stopped talking and the blades shut off.

They had the free night classes to thank for this last bit of technical prowess. The HRA, for all its flaws, was at least serious about its "hand up" philosophy, and had established a new vocational program in town which offered complimentary courses to anyone who was interested in learning blue collar skills, such as engine repair, AC installation, and the fine details of working with electronics.

Among the group of student poachers, Clyde's friend Damon had a real aptitude for signal flow and soldering wires, and it was he who designed these mobile charging stations—"bird cages"—which enabled them to discreetly deliver captured drones to their customers.

The most prolific among them was a guy in his thirties they called the Pigeon Man, because he kept his fleet up on the roof of his apartment building. A military veteran who had spent more of his time in the service tinkering rather than fighting, he now reprogrammed the HRA drones to serve the needs of a poor neighborhood's underground economy. Pickup and delivery of drugs, running the numbers, and his own brand of surveillance which he called "private security."

So Clyde only got a few hours of sleep after Octavius dropped him off, because he and Damon were supposed to meet the Pigeon Man and deliver two drones they'd recently captured. They took an early morning bus a few miles down to his building —the innocuously painted plywood boxes resting on their laps— and rode the elevator up to the penthouse before walking up the last flight of stairs to the roof.

The Pigeon Man, whose real name was Nolan, sat in his work shack with sparks flying all around as he modified something.

When Clyde and Damon knocked and walked in, he lifted his welding mask and said, "Poachmaster C, Poachmaster D! Good morning."

They set the boxes down and exchanged semi-elaborate handshakes with Nolan, who couldn't contain his excitement about the new delivery and immediately opened the boxes.

"Very nice!" he said. "Newer model. Mm-hmm. Pristine. Excellent work, guys."

He opened a drawer and pulled out two HRA debit cards, slapping one into each of their hands.

"Come on," Nolan said, "let me show you something."

They walked out onto the roof, where the rising sun was shining majestically over the whole city. Nolan went to a long row of tall planter boxes and pushed one aside with his hand, sliding it over like a keyboard shelf. Hidden underneath was part of his fleet, charging silently in the dark until needed. He reached inside, grabbed a wireless controller, and said, "Watch this."

With a flick of a switch, four mini-drones slowly rose, then darted away in formation before swooping back in a swirling dance of synchronized beauty.

"You see," Nolan said over the whir of the blades, "I control all four with the same device, but each one can improv freely inside the radius that I set."

Clyde and Damon nodded their heads.

"Here, Damon. Come give it a try."

Damon took the controller and did as Nolan instructed. The birds rose and dove around them in a graceful mechanical ballet.

"You boys are getting too old to be playing in the streets, stealing these birds. Damon, you've got potential with what that trade school taught you. Probably time you started working for me for real. Serious responsibility, serious money."

While Nolan talked and Damon flew the squadron, Clyde looked out over the city that was now bathed in a soft orange light, the drones passing through his field of vision every few seconds. All this gritty work and talk about big money didn't really interest him. He had poetry inside. Still, every time he tried to open his mouth and say something, he felt like he couldn't breathe. But up here—up here on the roof was where he saw what could be. The clear sky, the endless horizon, a straight shot forward into the unknown—and nothing like the human insects fighting each other in the dingy streets below.

He wanted to say all this and more with his music. Tell the world that his neighborhood was still waist deep in shit. That the HRA was maybe a nice idea but all the Beneficiaries—himself included—had found every way to use, abuse, and milk the program, but not in any way that brought about long-term improvement. They had workarounds for the cashless system and ended up spending their stipends on the usual waste. And so once again it was only the hustlers, liquor stores, and rim shops that got ahead.

He had come into awareness of the world alongside the birth of the HRA, watching as its bubbly workers left the hood each night back to the safety of their own world. And he came of age under the shadow of the administration's high hopes succumbing to the greed and self-destructiveness that only seemed to have increased with all this newfound money floating around.

If he could make something happen with the music, it wouldn't be just so he could get rich and run away. While a lot of his favorite rappers and singers talked about making it big— living the dream life and traveling around—Clyde didn't want to leave his family or his neighbors behind in misery while he posed for pictures wearing diamonds. He wanted to see his hometown become the safe, clean, less tense place that the HRA had probably set out to make it.

But who was he? Just another kid with no dad around, committing petty crimes that no one pursued. Because the HRA couldn't very well go after the "oppressed people" it was created to help.

He'd have to do something though. Maybe finish that new song which had slowly taken shape over the past few months and was about ready now. Try to capture a snapshot of the suffering that he saw in his world each day, and which the HRA's little scouts seemed to miss as they flew by.

"Guess they got the wrong kind of sensors," he said to himself, watching as Nolan's drones soared and tumbled through the air, their green bulbs removed long ago.

3. CRIMINALS

Shortly after sunset, the family gathered around a campfire that two of the men had built up while the other members unloaded the vehicles. In addition to tents, hiker's packs, and coolers, they also removed a dozen bankers boxes which they placed near the fire pit.

Two school-aged children worked together to carry an old footlocker over to the fire. One of the men patted them on the head, then placed his foot on top of the locker and looked into the flames.

A short while later, after the tents had been assembled and some food cooked over the fire, everyone sat around the pit and began to hum softly. One of the women removed a box lid, tapped it with her fingers affectionately, then began dropping its contents into the fire.

Papers, folders, photos all went in and the flames devoured this easy fuel. When the box was empty, the woman simulated wiping a tear from her eye and bowed toward the fire. A man opened the next box, motioned for a boy to join him, then handed him a folder and nodded. The boy opened the folder and let the contents slide out to be consumed.

The humming grew more soulful as each empty box was tossed away into the darkness. When all that remained was the footlocker, a tall man wearing a plaid shirt tucked into dark jeans rose and stood beside it.

"For three hundred years our family has called this land home. From the cold shores of Massachusetts to the fertile soil of the Plains, out to the pitiless heat of the Southwestern deserts, and back again to these beautiful, tree-capped Pennsylvania hills. The adventurers, the farmers, the craftsmen, and so many more. And like any other American lineage, they rode the ups and downs of life in their time, both decent and flawed, with only God to answer to for their reckoning.

"We kept these papers and relics to remember our heritage,

the good and the bad. Whoever could have imagined that programs like the Ancestry Project would come back to bite us all so hard?

"Well, we've done what we had to do to give our children a chance to live without a millstone around their neck. The Haggerstons are survivors, so let's keep our emotions in check and get this last bit over with."

He opened the locker and removed a thick folded cloth which he unfurled in the firelight. A large felt Washington Redskins tapestry rippled in the smoky air as the family's song hit a fever pitch.

Just as the man dipped one end of the tapestry into the fire, three spotlights converged on the group. Everyone went silent and the air was filled with the buzz of three orb-shaped drones which approached, one immediately dropping to just above the fire pit and blasting a mist downward that almost instantly extinguished the flames.

The campers leaped up and scattered, some heading toward the vehicles, others aiming for the woods surrounding the small clearing, and the two other drones split up and zipped after them in pursuit.

Official tools of the History Patrol, these large but agile drones—menacing black orbs made of a durable, textured composite material—were terrorizing enforcers affectionately nicknamed S'more Stoppers by the HRA teams which served alongside and maintained them. These document preservation assets came into heavy use after the President Jeffries-Lao executive order which mandated the installation of SafePlace devices in homes nationwide—similar to smoke detectors, these cutting-edge sensors took high resolution scans of documents before they were burned in fireplaces.

People with something to hide adapted and soon found creative ways to destroy documents. Simulated camping trips were a common ruse employed by these scofflaws with large caches of incriminating data to unload. While financial penalties were harsh if caught, the gambit was seen as worth the risk if one could eliminate thousands of dollars of annual debt per family.

The drone that had put out the fire next secured the contents of the footlocker, then sifted through the ashes for any surviving fragments that could be scanned. The other S'more Stoppers were off chasing down the nine suspects. One darted to the vehicles and quickly punctured a tire on each, then retracted its pointed metallic arm and assessed the scene: there were four adults, all unarmed, scurrying around the cars.

The drone first tasered a man who had picked up a dead branch and swung it, then after he fell in a writhing mass, the orb zipped a few feet away and squirted a glowing blue gel at two of the others—this substance contained the same ingredients as pepper spray—and each only ran a dozen steps before also falling to the ground in agony.

The fourth suspect had crawled under one of the cars and was covering herself with leaves to protect against any gel that might be sprayed. The drone placed a flashing red beacon onto the car's roof and then zoomed off into the woods in pursuit of the other suspects.

At the same time, the human members of this History Patrol unit were moving in now that the drones' video feeds had established the size of the party and their, in this case, lack of firepower. While the drones were equipped with a variety of tools and non-lethal weapons, their human counterparts all carried real firearms.

Two agents—playfully called Graham Cracker and Cracker Jack—were assigned to each S'more Stopper, and now these six men dressed in dark camouflage fanned out through the clearing, the flashlights mounted on their rifles sweeping across the suddenly darkened campsite. One agent ran up to the footlocker and slammed the top shut, yelled into the radio mounted on his wrist, and watched as the drone which had secured the campfire rose and flew off in the direction of the pursuit.

Moments later a boxy black truck pulled up beside the suspects' vehicles. A passenger leaped out and ran over to the fire pit, then dragged the footlocker to the rear of the truck and hoisted it in. He ran back to the pit but was waved away by the other man, who nudged the empty bankers boxes with his boot.

Two other members of the tactical unit had meanwhile dragged the woman under the car out from her hiding place and zip-tied her hands and feet. Then they cuffed the other three who had been taken down—also applying neon yellow balm to the two suffering the effects of the blue gel, until the mixture turned green. One by one they were led into the back of the armored truck.

The pursuit in the wooded area was quickly coming to an end. Three of these five suspects were children who had scrambled behind bushes not far from the clearing, and red beacons were dropped in their vicinity. As the two other drones entered the trees, the full force of the S'more Stoppers stalked their prey, scanning and sending data packets back and forth until they had triangulated upon the two remaining adult fugitives.

Each drone was now pulsing a red light as it crept between the tree trunks. Catching a glimpse of one of the suspects through its heat and motion sensors, the first drone that had entered the woods squirted a burst of the glowing blue gel into the woman's eyes, then moved on when she howled in pain and dropped to her knees.

The last suspect had climbed a tree and now all of the drones converged, hovering around him with their spotlights shining. One drone shot a stream of gel but it had no effect because the man had put on gloves and a ski mask, and hid his face close against the bark.

Down below, several of the tactical agents surrounded the base of the tree and aimed their weapons up at him.

"You'd better come down on your own," one of the agents said. "I don't want to kill you, and if these drones taser you, you're gonna land pretty hard."

The man put out a hand in a gesture of surrender, then slowly eased himself down to the ground. Two officers came up and sprayed the parts of him that were blue with the neutralizing gel, then the team leader yanked off his ski mask and held a scanner up to his eye.

"Good evening, Mr. Morgan Haggerston. Ready to take a ride?"

The suspects were loaded into the back of the armored vehicle, which as it left the scene of the raid was joined by three black SUVs, each transporting a S'more Stopper and its human team.

The Haggerston family members sat in various stages of discomfort, worst off being the man with wild hair who had been tasered. Those who had been gelled still suffered minor irritation which was slowly subsiding. The children were frightened, as much by the raid itself as by seeing their parents so shaken. Only

Morgan seemed no worse for wear, and despite the trauma to his family, was in decent spirits.

"Say, Dad," he said. "How you doing?"

The tasered man put a hand to his forehead. "Feels like the arthritis in my knee spread through my whole body."

"It'll be worth it in the long run. Maybe a couple days in jail, higher Debit Score for a while, but the most important thing is that all those documents are gone forever."

"What about the stuff in the locker?" the older man asked, nodding at a steel mesh cage toward the front of this rear compartment, where their footlocker had been secured.

"Mostly symbolic stuff. Still allowed to own a Revolutionary War reenactor's uniform, right?"

"I guess we'll find out."

An hour later the truck came to a stop. It was the middle of the night. The double-doors opened and four armed guards escorted the suspects into an HRA facility, which was a closed police station that had been converted for use by the administration's law enforcement wing. The group staggered into a brightly lit lobby, the adults' hands still zip tied, and the children hugging their legs as they moved along.

The four men watched helplessly as the women and children were then taken out of the room, presumably to a washroom and sleeping quarters. The men did not anticipate getting any such rest tonight.

They were told to sit on a bench in the middle of the room, then a junior officer walked past and scanned each man's right eye with a small device. One by one their Citizen Profiles were projected onto the white wall behind a front counter where two other officers were typing into computers. One of these officers pushed a button on the center of the console and a door in the back of the room buzzed open.

The lead agent from the raid stepped in front of the bench and cracked open a tall soda can, taking a long swig and smacking his lips.

"God, I love the taste of carbonated shit after a camping trip." He laughed and the sound bounced around the room's high walls. "Takes the edge off not being at home with my family. But hey, for every one of you that I catch, it shaves a little bit more off my own Debit Score. Call it an employee stock option, if you will."

He paced slowly in front of the men, two of whom had dropped their heads.

"What's the matter, gentlemen? Starting to regret our latest crimes against humanity?"

"Hey, boss," Morgan said, "I hate to interrupt your big moment, but these men might need some medical attention. And besides, you didn't get a damn thing tonight."

"But I got youuuuuu," the agent said, pointing a finger.

"Then do what the law says you can do. This sad performance of yours has nothing to do with the HRA."

"Me, sad? No, no, no. It's you who's gonna be crying. Because it's off to prison for you, and say bye-bye to the kids because your wives, who acted as accomplices tonight, will be deemed unfit as mothers. I just hope the foster parents teach your children better respect for the law than you have."

"You son of a—"

"Agent Essex," the man said as he strutted away, "process, pack, and ship 'em out."

In a manner of minutes, the men were stood up, had their faces wiped clean and their hair brushed, then lined up in a tight bunch directly in front of the counter. A husky Latiza in her fifties wearing a black robe entered the room and sat on an elevated central chair behind the counter.

"All rise," a junior officer said, "the Honorable Judge Hortencia Rosales presiding."

"Good morning, gentlemen," she said. "Since you seem perplexed, let me explain what's going on. I'm one of the night magistrates. I was just awoken from a wonderful dream having something to do with water skiing—and now we are here. Bailiff, what are the charges?"

"Your Honor, these men stand accused of destroying twelve boxes of historical data, as well as possessing Stigmatized Relics and resisting arrest."

"My, my, my. Accused, what do you say to these charges?"

Morgan took a step forward. "With all due respect, Your Honor, don't we have a right to counsel?"

"Ohhh, I forgot." She pressed a button on the center console and an aqua-tinted hologram appeared beside the men. "This is your lawyer, Mr.—" She consulted her tablet. "—Lawbotov."

"What the hell is this?" Morgan said.

"Like I said, he's your counsel."

"A pastel hologram?"

"A SADA, to be precise. State Appointed Digital Attorney."

"You expect us to win this case with a fake lawyer we've never met before?"

"No, I expect to be back in bed in half an hour."

"But if our lawyer isn't real, why do we have a live judge?"

"Because I'm getting paid! 'My people, my people,' you know."

Morgan shook his head and waved a hand.

The men were found guilty of destruction of historical data, but acquitted on the other charges—their CGI lawyer had at least been competent enough to cast doubt on those allegations. But document destruction was seen as a growing threat across the nation—and the HRA wanted to send a preemptive warning to would-be arsonists living in other former colonial countries—so judges were now throwing the book at offenders.

First, the patriarchal line of the Haggerston family was added to the National Doc Offender Registry, meaning that in the future they could not so much as throw out the paper wrapper of a fast food sandwich without handing it over to an authorized Shred-It agent—this being another company forced to rebrand to survive—who would securely transport it and other documents for inspection by HRA scanners before disposal.

First-time offenders were normally put on probation, which involved enhanced home monitoring by the similarly retooled ADT, as well as weekly sensitivity training meetings. But the volume of documents the Haggerstons had destroyed, which was proven beyond a reasonable doubt by the number of empty bankers boxes found at the scene, as well as one drone's Sift n' Scan of the ashes, compelled Judge Rosales to adhere to the tougher sentencing laws dubbed "One Match Strike and You're Out."

Their punishment was to each serve a year at a former FEMA facility near the Berkshire Mountains, where they would repay their now incalculable debts to society "in a variety of creative ways," Judge Rosales said with a wink.

Before they were led away to wait for the midday transport bus, James found enough strength to ask, "Will I get to see my grandkids before we go?"

The judge laughed and said, "Did Africans who were kidnapped and bound for the plantation get to give their babies a kiss goodbye? I don't think so! Good night, gentlemen."

While it was happily back to dreamland for the judge, each of the four Haggerston men spent the few remaining hours of darkness alone in a cell, sleepless, with tears welling in their eyes. By late morning they were all shackled and loaded onto a bus that had arrived half full, and it meandered through miles of beautiful country roads, stopping twice to pick up more inmates, before arriving in late afternoon at a facility surrounded by chain-link fence topped with razor wire. Two guard towers loomed at the edges, and as the bus approached the entry booth, a large sign came into view that said:

Pennsylvania Debtors' Prison
Rehabilitation Today, Reparations Every Day

After the bus pulled through the gates, the Haggerstons could see that the prison looked more like a work camp, with a handful of narrow, one-story dormitories, two larger administration-type buildings, and ample open space peppered with a number of square concrete plots whose purpose was hard to distinguish in the fading light. A couple dozen inmates were idling around the doors of the living quarters, while others seemed to be flowing into one of the larger structures which cast bright light out of its windows and open double-doors.

The bus stopped in a cul-de-sac near the other administration building, and after the door was opened, the thirty new arrivals shuffled and clanked their way from their seats out into the cool evening air, then through the building's front entrance. None of them spoke or made any shows of bravado—they were not career criminals (not in this lifetime, at least), and it didn't occur to them that they would be watched when approaching a prison yard for the first time.

The processing area was a long open room with various desks, cabinets, and other tools for admitting new inmates. Guards maneuvered the mass of bodies into neat rows, then one by one the men were called up to the front table for the obligatory retinal scan. Each was then escorted to one of the screened off sections in the far corner, where they exchanged their street clothes for prison garb, which consisted of navy blue twill shirt and pants, each bearing a white spray-painted stencil with the letters "PDP."

When admitting was complete and the men were taken over to housing, the Haggerstons found that each had been assigned to a different dormitory. Besides James and his son Morgan, there was also James's younger brother Ed, and Morgan's brother-in-law Gary (whose last name was Olsen, so technically not a Haggerston, but most definitely in the same troubled boat with them). They all passed another restless night, this time among rows of army cots that were alive with the sound of snoring.

Wake-up call was at 6 am, and the prisoners drowsily made their way to the mess hall, which was the other large building that the new arrivals had seen people entering the previous night. The food was tolerably horrible, but the Haggerston clan was at least able to sit together and acclimate to their new surroundings in relative safety. Here they took stock of the prison population: about 250 in all, they were almost exclusively white men except for a few of mixed-race. Judging by appearances, the inmates ranged across all ages and socioeconomic backgrounds, with members of similar classes seeming to stick together. There wasn't any noticeable tension between or hierarchy within these groups either—everyone looked like they were enduring this time away from home in as familiar company as possible.

After breakfast the prisoners went out into the open yard, splitting up and gathering at the many paved squares that the Haggerstons assumed were work stations having something to do with their rehabilitation. Stepping onto the concrete edge of one, they were startled to see a group of men sitting around a table where each was intently focused on a coloring book. Brown and red crayons of various shades were littered across the tabletop, and the prisoners carefully selected each new implement before returning to their work.

James leaned over one man's shoulder and made an admiring remark, then asked, "May I?" The other man smiled and proudly handed over his book. James held it up and flipped through, and the Haggerstons saw page after page of dark brown men driving, red women dancing, milk chocolate children swimming, and crimson boys playing baseball.

James absently handed the coloring book back to the man and then the four stumbled over to another assembly nearby. Here stood a replica Aztec pyramid, about four feet in height, made out of wood and painted charcoal gray. A handful of prisoners sat cross-legged near the base, while two others stood just behind the pyramid, each holding a white and brown Ken doll in their hands.

"Oh, great sky gods of justice," the man on the left proclaimed while shaking his brown Ken, "today we honor your thirst for punishment. Commence the sacrifice!"

The other man placed his white Ken down on top of the altar, then together the two brown Kens did a violent dance which sent the doomed white doll tumbling down the front steps and clattering onto the concrete below. The men who were sitting scrambled forward and fought over the body, while the executioners above made ritual pronouncements that did not bode well for the second white doll.

The Haggerstons turned away without a word, separating as each walked over to another cluster of prisoners. Twenty minutes later they found each other and stared around in bewilderment. A voice came at them from behind.

"Don't tell me you're already shell-shocked! You haven't even heard your first sermon yet."

A muscular man of medium height with slicked-back dark hair approached, holding his hands up to indicate he was not a threat, because there were four of them and this *was* still a prison.

"My name's Aaron, but people call me Brick. I'm guessing this is your first time in rehab?"

"Morgan. How you doing? We're still stunned by what's happened in the past two days. Separated from our families, put in these prison clothes—"

"And now this," Brick said, jerking his thumb toward a group of prisoners.

"Yeah. I just saw three grown men crawl into a tepee together."

"Jesus H. Christ," James said.

"Well, gents," Brick said as he put his hands in his pockets, "that's just the appetizer. I'll look for you after the sermon to find out if you haven't seen the light." He slowly walked away on the heels of his boots.

Ed took James by the sleeve. "What the hell do you think he's talking about? Is this a prison or a loony bin?"

"Looks like we're about to find out," Gary said, pointing to the middle of the open yard.

They could see a tall flatbed cart with large wagon wheels being pulled by a team of four white men in leather harnesses and chains. All the prisoners had dropped their work and were streaming toward it. Standing atop the cart was a rotund black man holding a giant object with some sort of pointed shape.

The Haggerstons looked at each other, took a breath, then walked over to see what would happen next. By the time the cart stopped and they'd caught up to the edge of the large crowd, the black man had set down his prop and was milling around the makeshift stage, which stood about five feet above the ground. He rubbed his hands together and flexed his facial muscles back and forth. Several prisoners up front were so excited that they pretended to box with each other.

Finally the man slid his hands back across the sparse long hairs on his head, toyed with his wisp of a goatee, then commenced.

"Oh, Lord. A prison yard full of white men. Ain't that a beautiful sight?"

"Amen, yes it is, brother!" shouted one of the prisoners near the cart.

"I *had* a dream—and now it has come true! For the love of God, are *any* of you really surprised to find yourselves locked up in here?"

"No, sir!"

"For four hundred years your families have been kickin', cheatin', sellin', and killin' my people. But *you* thought you was different. 'Those are sins of the past, pal. That's not who we are.' That's what you said. No, no, no!"

He was working up into a sweaty lather of emotion and indignation, stalking around the cart surrounded by a sea of navy blue.

"Something *has* changed though. But it wasn't you, no sir. Know what it was? The law! The law is what changed. And now you are behind bars because you're just like your daddy and his daddy and his daddy before him."

"So what can we do?" another man called out.

"It's a looooong road to Reparations, my friends. But you can start by taking this first step."

"What is it? Tell us!"

The man bent over and hoisted up his prop, swinging it

around to reveal a giant check mark. He smiled.

"Check this out. You got to check it, baby. Keep yourself in check. Don't write any bad checks. But most of all, you've got to check your privileeeeeeege!!!"

This brought a roar from much of the audience.

"Come on, now! Let me see it. Show me how you check your privilege, prisoners!"

The men responded by swarming into a crowded line that extended in front of the cart. The speaker yelled, "Acolytes, forward!" and his team of human horses began to pull ahead. As the cart approached, many of the men stuck out a foot or placed their fingers in the path of the wagon wheels. One by one they turned away hobbling or squeezing their hands with a grimace. Some prisoners who had been blocked when it rolled by now ran up behind and bonked their foreheads against the cart's metal frame, staggering away with mad smiles on their faces.

The Haggerston quartet stood in silent horror as the mob chased after the cart until it reached the main gate, where armed guards stepped forward to disperse the prisoners before letting the black man roll off the property.

Brick slid into view and whistled.

"It's been *quite* a day for you boys. Anybody want to play Barbie?"

"What in the holy hell?" was all that Morgan could muster.

"You just witnessed the soul-saving spectacle of the Reverend Matthias G. Witherspoon, leader of the Foundation for Healing Colonial Guilt."

"And he comes here every day as part of our rehab?"

"My god," Gary added, "they're trying to brainwash us!"

"Depends how tough you are mentally," Brick said. "But no, he only comes here once every couple weeks. He speaks at the other HRA Debtor prisons in Pennsylvania, Ohio, Michigan, and Indiana."

"Tell me this," Morgan said. "If everyone else in here has lost their mind, why not you?"

Brick gave a little smile. "Because I'm one-thirty-second Navajo? Nah. Maybe some of the guys you see are just playing it up for the yard cameras hoping Rehabilitation Officers will let them out of here early. But hey, meet me and my crew over by the pyramid tonight after dinner." He wandered off in the direction of some of the other new arrivals.

As the day wore on, the Haggerstons fell into a daze watching the bizarre scenes unfolding out in the yard, as prisoners politely rotated from station to station every half hour. A number of inmates emerged from the processing center's side door with white bandages around their injured hands and feet, then rejoined the group activities.

Morgan and Gary took a walk while James and Ed sat down in the grass shaking their heads in disbelief. Gary wanted to talk to a few of the guards and see what their attitude was, because if they were going to live in this madhouse for a year it would be best to get the full lay of the land now.

They found a guard standing next to a water fountain who appeared to be descended from First India.

"Excuse me," Morgan said, "but do you mind if we ask you a few questions?"

"Most certainly, sir," the guard said in an upper-crust British accent.

"Wait a second, you're not American? Is that even legal, for you to work at a federal prison?"

"Funny that a man in your position would be so concerned about legalities. But to answer your query, I was brought to the States several months ago on an H-1R visa in anticipation of a similar Reparations program launching in my home country."

"Oh my god," Gary said, "they're taking this thing worldwide."

"Yes," the guard added, "and India has over one-and-a-half-billion people. The task of getting organized would be overwhelming if not for the excellent training that I and nearly three hundred other Indian team leaders are receiving in the States right now. Next month I shall be transferred to St. Louis to learn how field offices operate. I am very excited!"

"How many of the guards here are in training like you?"

"Only one or two. The rest are real-deal, American-born law enforcement personnel."

"Okay then."

Morgan and Gary made their way to a white guard and said hello. They noticed that he, like about half the other guards, was not armed with a weapon but wore a bulky gunmetal contraption on his right wrist.

"Sir," Morgan said while nodding downward, "is that some sort of weapon?"

"You got it, and then some. Taser, pepper spray, radio, panic button. And it counts my steps. Right now I'm up to... thirty-five hundred for the day."

"You worked here long?"

"This place opened up about eight months ago. I've been here since the beginning. Got my Debit Score down fifteen percent already. I figure another year and my daughter might be allowed to go to college."

Morgan and Gary exchanged a quizzical look.

"What does that mean?" Morgan asked. "I thought some states already gave free tuition to residents—and that was even before this president."

"Sir, that used to be the case, but they did a study to find out why forty percent more women go to college than men. Turns out it was *white* women who made all that difference. So now it's mandatory to fill more spaces with women of color—foreign *and* domestic."

"Well, damn. What's your daughter gonna do if she can't go?"

"Probably follow in her cousin Tammy's footsteps and join the RETC—Reparations Evading Tactical Collectors. We're talking paramilitary, JAG, boots-on-the-ground asset seizure and document preservation kind of stuff. I gotta say, the HRA is turning into a growth industry for us military types. So maybe it'll be better for her. Hell, like the posters say: See the world, save the past, and kick some ass!"

"What do you mean, 'see the world'?" Morgan said. "Don't tell me the HRA already launched overseas!"

"Nah, but you don't think the old colonies don't see it coming? Tammy told us how back in training the instructor showed them satellite temperature data from up in Canada. Buddy—fires everywhere. They're burning documents like crazy trying to protect the Queen. But not anymore. RETC is dropping in like Chuck Norris. Docu Force and shit! Yeah, Tammy!"

He raised his forearm to give a bump, but when neither Morgan nor Gary responded, he said, "C'mon guys, don't leave me hanging…"

Gary reluctantly raised his arm. The guard was so fired up that he slammed their arms together with such power that it triggered his wristband to shoot a taser blast back into his face. He fell to the ground twitching and writhing in pain, which then caused the wristband to send out a distress call to the prison's central computer system. A loud alarm sounded throughout the yard, and a robotic voice blared through speakers up on telephone poles, "Officer down! Disperse and secure!"

The other prisoners began to scatter in panic as the guards who had previously been lounging inside the administration building spread out into riot-containing formation. Several drones also fell in to assist the officers who were already in the yard. With over two hundred prisoners to contend with, their priority was to first rescue the fallen guard, and only then try to herd the men back into the dorms.

Morgan and Gary had immediately backed away from the self-tasering guard, and moments later Brick ran up to them with five other prisoners. "Quick," he said, "find your other guys and follow me. We're getting out of here!"

As they ran toward the mess hall, Morgan turned back and saw his father and uncle coming toward them as fast as they could. Behind them was a mass of men kicking up dust as they swarmed around the yard, with drones and officers trying to steer them far away from the wounded guard. "Hurry up!" he called.

The older men caught up to the group as it slowly crept around the corner of the mess hall. They froze when they reached the back of the building and saw two guards with a menacing black orb hovering between them. Brick gave them a wave.

"You told us you wanted to wait until it was dark," one of the guards said.

"Hell, an opportunity came up. We had to go for it. You ready?"

"Unlock and unload!"

The group ran toward the perimeter fence a hundred feet behind the mess hall. The drone was moving alongside them and fired something toward the barrier. The object landed a few feet short then popped and hissed, quickly filling the area with gray smoke. The men poured into the expanding cloud then watched as the drone approached the fence, lowered itself, and shot out two arms which began shredding the chain links. A few seconds later there was a hole large enough for a man to crawl through.

"Off you go," one of the guards said through the mist. "Take care of business!"

"Damn the HRA," Brick grunted.

The Haggerston men kept their mouths shut and just tried to keep pace with the other escapees, who were in shape and seemed to be coordinating silently—as if this moment had been in the works for some time. First they ran into the nearest thicket of trees before swinging around to one side, running almost parallel to the prison for a few hundred yards, before reaching a thin dirt path that was mostly overgrown.

Leading the way, Brick began to sprint down this path and the others followed rapidly one by one. After a quarter mile, it opened up onto a clearing which revealed a rocky descent, and without a word the men all began to climb down the jagged terrain, steadily working to the bottom a hundred feet below.

Once they reached flat ground, they ran another two hundred yards towards an old beige-and-wood-grain Winnebago that was parked in the shade. Brick banged on the side of the camper. Seconds later a man's head popped out of the driver's window, along with a hand aiming a pistol.

"Holy shit, you guys are way early!" he said, lowering the gun.

Brick gave a grin. "Couple of the newbies unleashed hell out on the yard. We didn't even have to set the fires."

"Good thing you told me to get a big camper. Looks like there's more than five here with you."

"Hell, I couldn't leave 'em behind, right?" Brick gave Morgan a nod.

The escapees piled into the Winnebago and fell upon a case of water bottles that was on the dining nook table. Then, as the driver pulled onto a dirt road that snaked through the valley, the men swapped out their prison uniforms for street clothes packed into suitcases. Now they began to smile and relax, lounging on couch cushions and on the floor.

Brick, who hadn't yet changed outfits, was hunkered low up front talking to the driver for the first few minutes. He sauntered to the back with a huge grin and let out a whoop. The other men responded with applause.

"Gentlemen," he said, "we did it!"

"Yeah!" they roared.

"Got out of that madhouse. But this was the easy part. Now

we're onto the real work of getting rid of the HRA!"

"Hell yeah! Woooo!"

"But," he said, turning to the Haggerstons, "there's just one question I have for the newcomers. Do you enlist?"

Morgan stood up and said, "Two days ago my wife and children were taken from me. If that's the endgame of this whole program, then the government can kiss my ass!"

The group yelled approvingly and Brick met Morgan with a high-five-forearm-handshake that ended in a chest bump.

"Let me fill you in on what you've just gotten yourselves into."

After Brick distributed several laptops to the others in back, he sat down around the nook with Morgan, James, Ed, and Gary, and told them about the underground protest movement which had been growing over the past year.

"Once everyday people started to realize that this wasn't some temporary thing like they sold it to us—you know, 'We just want to make sure everybody's water bottle is full before we keep hiking,' " he said in a nasally voice, "—and especially when the HRA itself started dropping hints that they were setting their sights on England, Spain, France... You know, where does it end? Should we really let a computer tell a guy who was born in Canada, and his ancestors came from Europe, that he owes money to people of a different skin color—even though their own families maybe didn't leave the Caribbean until fifteen years ago? It's crazy."

James spoke up. "I've tried to talk to these HRA types. For people so obsessed with small details, as individuals they're incapable of putting down the script."

"Well, you know, it's gonna fall apart and it's their own damn fault. Because there's policy, and then there's reality."

"They seem pretty confident to me. What's their weakness?"

"Law enforcement, man. The people in the big cities who cook up all this shit, they think the cops are all dumb, order-taking robots. A lot of them, yeah—but enough are awake! They've got kids, bills, and dangerous responsibilities—do that for a while and pretty soon you'll know what's what. So I'm telling you, on the surface the HRA folks are feeling pretty good —watching everything expand, they think they've never been stronger. But they're hollow inside! Got no real support where it matters, and one day—" He jabbed a finger sideways. "—pop. It'll just stop."

Gary leaned in on his elbows and said, "But won't that just leave things worse than before? The Bennies ain't ready to have their stipends cut off. And us Debtors, well, let's just say *pissed* is a nice way of describing how we feel."

"You're right. And that's why this hasn't turned into a shooting war already. If we can end this thing, we've got to replace it with something better. Which is the reason we need your help now. Because they screwed up not consulting salt-of-the-earth people the last time, and slowly all their theories are turning into a tangled up mess. Do you think seven, eight years ago these Reparations kids envisioned that they'd be sending fellow Americans to prison camps? Hell no! They thought they were just carefully arranging pillows on the couch to make everything look nice and neat."

"Amazing how much damage people who act so friendly to your face can do," Gary said.

"Ain't that the truth. People who've never done a day of manual labor in their lives, let alone had a fist fight to work something out—*they* put *you* in jail! Think about that! But like I said, enough of the good guys ain't stupid. Right now they're just biding their time, all around the country. It's almost game time and we've got a great squad."

Ed pounded his fist on the table. "Put me in, coach!"

The Winnebago moved from country roads to two-lane highways. As the fugitives lay down to sleep, Morgan Haggerston looked at the ceiling and pictured his children's faces. Whatever the underground needed him to do, he would be up to the task if it meant holding them in his arms again.

4. PRIVILEGE

The most frustrating aspect of fighting this disease was the stillness. For the past fifteen years, ever since Kate entered the world of activism as a college freshperson, life had been a wild romantic blur of dashing from scenes of environmental disaster and racial injustice to strategic meetings in rec centers and politicians' offices.

Even in later years, when the HRA concept went from pipe dream to viable to inevitable, and action shifted away from marching in the streets to endless sessions compiling and revising the seventeen hundred pages of the proposed law's guts, days sped by borne on a wing of purposeful mission. Kate could feel the transition from mere activist to bona fide change agent in every fiber of her being with each milestone.

So now, being forced to leave her coworkers and the project behind to focus on' her health left her in an existential fog. That daily injection of mental adrenaline she felt before entering the fray to interact with Beneficiaries and Debtors, coordinate with team leaders across the country, and lay the groundwork for the worldwide roll out—now unnecessary as weeks crept by at a snail's pace with seemingly nothing to do between radiation treatments. She knew she should be thankful that early detection had helped her to avoid chemotherapy, but she still found herself lethargic for days at a time.

She had resisted stepping away, of course.

"Maybe I can work remotely," she'd said to Jan. "Do as much as possible to help out."

"Girl, you're sick! Right now you've got to focus on *you* and be with your family. Besides, that next launch pad is still a long way off—get well now so we can press the button together."

"I know, I know…"

With all this down time, Kate suddenly found herself nagged by an old ghost from the early days of her awakening, when the naive, self-centered girl from the suburbs was first bombarded by the raw truth of how overwhelming the scale of world suffering was—pain that was in fact so often caused by other white people.

This new perspective had given birth to an unsparing inner voice that turned making even routine decisions into a statistical analysis ritual, which involved going down a mental checklist to consider how anything she was about to do might affect someone less fortunate than her. It was hard to be present and mindful with so many thoughts pinballing around her head, but Kate made peace with the process by assigning herself an act of contrition or charity to offset any experience or purchase that was pleasurable to herself, such as a kiss or a glass of wine.

This pestering voice went silent sometime during the HRA's planning phase, and was mostly forgotten in the busy and effective years since its launch—a fitting reward considering that Kate and her fellow visionaries had found a way to transmute the chatterbox of one's guilty conscience into applied, outcome-based altruism.

But now, laid up at home with nothing to do, the voice came back maniacally, seemingly oblivious to all that she'd accomplished, and making wild new demands about remedying problems not covered under the HRA's umbrella. She felt her mind short-circuit as it grappled with accusations that she was neglecting these other important human rights issues. How did she intend to help people with gender confusion? Was she a self-serving hypocrite for taking advantage of the HRA's generous health care plan when so many of the people she had allegedly vowed to help still only had access to woeful clinics? Maybe Myra Jenkins was right and the HRA did need to do more.

Sweating alone in bed one evening, Kate tangled her mind in knots trying to think of new ways she could eradicate her privilege. For years she and every white person she knew had done everything in their power to be conscious of their own inherent advantages, and this had guided them daily in trying to help the people who had not fared as well in life's lottery. But now she was beginning to suspect that no matter what selfless act she performed, there would always be something else to account for—and how could you sleep peacefully, let alone function, when the goalposts kept moving?

She turned on the TV to calm herself down, but the first thing she saw was an obnoxious ad by H&R Block boasting about all the archaeologists, translators, and friendly tribal leaders they'd hired to find extra deductions for Debtors. *These guys just won't stop*, she thought—and then the power abruptly cut out and she was left in complete darkness.

She should have embraced this sudden gift of quiet and stillness to go back to sleep, but the old restless Kate of indefatigable action now fighting for her life insisted upon at least getting the flashlight to keep handy until the power returned or Chris got home from the gym, whichever came first. She slid out from the sheets down onto the floor, then delicately crawled over to the TV stand where she groped around the shelves until finding the flashlight.

But she couldn't bring herself to turn it on. The instant she'd grabbed it, her mind envisioned all the people out there who didn't have a flashlight of their own. The inner voice whispered, "Don't use it. Stand in solidarity with them. Check your light privilege!"

From here her thoughts tumbled into a self-incriminating house of mirrors. What *other* comforts did she enjoy without ever acknowledging, let alone act upon to rectify? "Plumbing!" the voice yelled. "Refrigeration! Transportation! Cell phone!" And up until five minutes ago, electricity.

How could she possibly atone for all of this? What virtuous acts would serve to fully exorcise the guilt she now felt for passing decades of her life blind to the thousand micro-advantages she had taken for granted?

Falling deeper into the hallucination now, Kate's mind seized upon the fate of her remains. Although she had already decided that scattering her ashes was preferable to the environmental impact of an ornate coffin or even burying an urn, sudden panic set in when she realized that the energy expended during cremation would still add to her life's cumulative carbon footprint. She fantasized that there must be a way to eclipse the camper's motto of pack-it-in, pack-it-out, and to honor Mother Earth by disposing of a human body so efficiently as to leave no trace—even less than ashes.

Chris found her on the floor cradling the flashlight in the dark. She was paralyzed, couldn't understand what he was saying, but felt him pick her up and carry her onto the bed. She felt the blankets cover her and fell asleep as her body nestled around the unused flashlight.

That night Kate truly believed for the first time that she was going to die. In truth, it was the turning point in her recovery. Dipping a toe into the darkest corners of her subconscious had given her a sixth-sense insight into the many layers and subtle nuances crammed into that word *privilege*, and now her drive to fight for the underdog was ten times stronger than before. Once her body healed, she knew that nothing would ever slow her down again.

5. THE MENTOR

"Clyde! What the hell you looking at?"

Nolan ran up and put his arm around Clyde's shoulders.

"Come on. You got to stay focused. Every time you look over at someone, the camera sees that."

"Damn," Clyde muttered. "I'm just thinking about all this stuff. Like where I got to stand, trying to match the words, you know."

"Just remember, we're cutting this thing together piece by piece. Give me a few good seconds at a time. The action is always jumping to something else."

"Okay. Keep it simple—focus for five seconds, then do it again."

"You're the star. I'm just trying to make you look good!"

Nolan ran back to his computer setup under the tree. A couple of Clyde's friends lounging nearby were providing "security" for the set, which was a small park with an open grassy area near the playground.

"Okay, rolling…" Nolan said, then tapped the screen of his laptop. "Playback!" He reached for a tablet which was connected to speakers and a rap song began playing. "Action!"

Clyde started moving his body to the rhythm, throwing out his hands and mouthing the words while two of the HRA mini-drones cycled around in front of him. A handful of park visitors had stopped to watch, but he kept his eyes focused on one of the drones, then every few seconds pivoted to face the other.

"Just got paid, by the HRA, wish it was cash, but we work around, work around. Liquor man, double-dippin' his cans, there's a brutha out back, with the workaround, workaround…"

"Cut! Good stuff, young man!"

Throughout the whole video shoot, from early morning takes up on the roof to shots filmed at midnight in the middle of an empty street, and now here in the park, Nolan had been like a kid on his birthday playing with all his new toys. But as a man who truly loved the process as much as the final result, it was unlocking the secret of how to get DJ Clydoscope to perform in front of the camera that really hooked Nolan on making music videos. He would definitely be adding "director" to the list of services offered on his interactive business card.

He ran up to Clyde with a big smile. "We're so close, my man. A few more takes here, then we drive around the hood to pick up some B-roll, maybe grab a few still shots of you—then, I say we're done."

"Cool, cool."

One of Clyde's friends walked up. "Hey, why he ain't ever holdin' up a piece?"

"Because, Stephon," Nolan said, "this ain't that kind of song."

"But he out here representin' the neighborhood. People gonna see it and I don't want no one thinking we weak."

"My brother. You want to make a video, I will personally film it and you can wave a gun around the whole time."

"Aight! 'Cause I got one on me right now, you know."

Clyde brushed him off. "Stop being stupid, yo! Sun's going down soon, let's get back to work."

Nolan smiled. "Someone gets it. Here we go…"

Clyde had spent the past few months leading up to this music video shoot obeying Nolan's every word. One of the few men he knew who seemed to still be struggling *on top* of the bull—and not scrambling away from it down in the dirt—Nolan was part father figure, mentor, and friend to any kid who was willing to put his guard down and listen.

After Nolan had tapped fellow drone thief Damon to be one of his lieutenants, Clyde found the courage to call on him a few days later and explain what was on his mind. That he didn't want to just *talk* about doing music anymore—he'd already gone through more stage names than written actual songs—and now he had some lyrics he really cared about.

Nolan explained to Clyde some of the lessons he'd learned in the army, most importantly that to get something done you had to make a step-by-step plan and then execute it. "These guys you see on the corner," he'd said, "they get urges every five minutes and think when they chase after whatever it is, that that's a plan. Nah. Let me show you what Uncle Sam taught me."

Nolan told Clyde to send over raw demos of the new track.

He blasted back with ruthless critiques but ended each message by saying, "Don't take it personal. This is how you get better now so that one day you can be great."

Clyde resisted the instinct to lash out at Nolan for dissing his vocals, and ended up putting in ten times more effort recording it than if he'd just done it on his own. But he had to admit, the extra time spent was making the track sound closer to how he heard it in his head.

And then one day Nolan wrote back saying, "You're ready. Let me feed the birds. It's showtime!"

But Clyde started to get nervous after that. It was all theory up until now, but soon people in the hood were actually going to see his video. What would they say? That he was complaining too much about life on the street? And the chorus—the chorus. He thought it was inspiring, the whole reason for the song in the first place—but he wondered if some people might call him soft.

Again, it was Nolan who kept him on task. There were locations to scout, favors to ask from friends, and Clyde had to make a battle plan for the release. His assignment was to research not just the mainstream sites for distributing the single, but get familiar with the hip-hop podcasts in cities with big urban populations like Chicago, Atlanta, and Philadelphia. Get ready to spread the word that a new voice was dropping some unprecedented truth, because *no one* in the scene was holding the HRA's feet to the fire.

Meanwhile Nolan kept busy taking a real-time crash course in music video editing, working late into the night to bring Clyde's vision to life. Gritty street scenes during the verses transitioned to a rooftop at dawn, where Clyde sang the chorus as drones danced around him. "This is getting pretty good," Nolan said to himself.

When Clyde purchased the universal music distribution license through Tunazon, it included a Beneficiary discount, which made him laugh a little. He also prepared what Nolan called the stealth campaign: finding respected sites like Hip Hop Warfare and KeepItTrue to post streaming links, and hopefully get people discussing the song's groundbreaking message.

"Because it ain't the police or white people keeping us down anymore," Nolan had snapped. "And the damn Reparations ain't helping, just like you're saying. It created lots of office jobs for clueless Caucs, but that's about it. Patting themselves on the back with awards ceremonies and luncheons—a million miles away from understanding what's going on across town."

At first Clyde was kind of shocked to see Nolan lose his cool —not many people saw the true inner workings of this disciplined military man—but it was reassuring to know he was human. Nolan was sharp enough to get out of the hood if he really wanted to, and some people wondered why he stuck around when he could play the game. One day as they were watching a near-final cut of the video, Clyde couldn't resist the temptation to ask.

"I'm from the streets, man," Nolan said. "It's in my blood. Sure, Uncle Sam showed me the world but, you know, I care about my people here. And what you saying with this song, I've felt it for years but could never find the right words. But hey, you got the gift!"

Three weeks after the shoot and everything was ready. Clyde took out his checklist and logged into his accounts, then made the release official site by site. It was now time for DJ Clydoscope to engage.

"Okay, here we go."

6. ABSOLUTION

Morgan leaned against a railing in the walkway outside the cuisine court. He could hear the crowd in the main gallery down below, as hundreds of people gathered in front of a stage flanked by glittering blue and silver banners. He glanced back to watch them for a moment, then carefully scanned the dining area and nearby stores. His eye caught on someone stooping over a water fountain, but when that person came out from under the mesh drape, Morgan saw that it was not the man he was looking for.

The crowd stopped chattering and began to "Mmm" in unison. Someone on stage was approaching in a metallic blue-and-silver costume that rose above the head and was squared off at the top and bottom, so that it seemed as if a long cushion was waddling toward them.

As this curiosity reached the front of the stage, the hum got louder when an indentation appeared from within near the top of the costume. There was a circular movement and then a small flap dropped down, revealing a man's face. Opaque blue glasses with round lenses the size of half dollars obscured his eyes, and putty distorted the shape of his cheeks.

Arms suddenly poked out from the tight elastic holes on either side, first reaching out high then slowly settling down, and the crowd ended its incantation by breathing out, "Modesty."

The face smiled and said, "Attention, mall shoppers. There's a sale on your likeness today. Over in electronics, that video of you smoking a cigarette at a backyard barbecue will result in your health care premiums being raised by fifteen percent. We also have some nice specials over in cosmetics on Forgiveness Cream—rub it into your pores and wipe that guilt away."

"Amen!" the crowd sighed.

"Yes, my children. You bear a great burden that comes from both ends of the hourglass. Deeds once lost to the past are unearthed and presented, not as conversation pieces or cautionary tales, but as evidence against you. And that which you do tomorrow shall give rise to new chains..."

Morgan stepped away from the railing and passed through the mingled smells drifting out from the cuisine court on his way to the escalator. He'd heard plenty of sermons by the Prescient One and other wise men since first arriving here two months ago—and right now he was desperate to find someone.

He passed a small photo booth that had been converted to accommodate hasty confessions, and which afterward printed out a laminated hologram stamped with the words, "Thank you for owning up to your sins!" Noticing legs under the curtain, Morgan surreptitiously peeked inside but saw that it was not his man. He walked on.

A group of tourists from Scandinavia was browsing outside a small storefront with Tribal American mannequins in the display. Souvenir t-shirts and mugs were neatly arranged at their feet next to a fake log fire. Rather than enter, the tourists turned their attention to a nearby open space where a middle-aged man was making an elaborate show of supplication at the base of a dark chrome cube. He waved a piece of paper toward its left side, and when this sheet was suddenly accepted and sucked in, he made a praying motion before crawling away.

Morgan rode the escalator down to the second floor and glanced into The Zap, where lines of white and black people stood on opposite sides of the store. He saw a white woman bow, then a black woman grazed her shoulder with an electronic flyswatter. The white woman twitched briefly, then bowed again and withdrew.

Morgan walked into the Tears anchor chapel. A greeter stepped forward and smiled.

"Good afternoon, novice," she said. "Are you making amends?"

"Not today, sister," he said. "I need to find someone else who's already atoning."

"I see. But may I remind you that all of the redressing rooms are private?"

"Yes, um, but my fellow apprentice requested that I help him remove a nagging burden from his conscience."

"Very well. Have a modest day…"

Morgan made his way down a long walkway toward the central redressing rooms. To the left he saw a large group of pilgrims who had laid a red felt tapestry on the floor which said: Third Indiana Penance Choir. Its forty members, dressed in matching black Quaker suits with an embroidered Modidas logo on the left breast, were kneeling and weeping quietly.

He reached an area where two long rows of small doors faced each other. There was a line of people waiting at each end, and whenever someone exited one of the booths, an usher would scan the next guest's ticket and escort them in.

Morgan bypassed the line and headed directly to the stalls. A male usher caught up to him and said gently, "Sir, I'll need you to take a place in line."

"I'm not here to confess. My cloister-mate is having an atonement crisis. Stuck in 1756—please, can I help clear the blockage?"

"This is highly unusual, but if he's trapped…"

"Terribly. He's been working through this DE for weeks in our group therapy."

"Then of course…"

"Mod bless you!"

Morgan approached a door in the middle section and knocked gently. It cracked open and he could hear the hiss of a white noise machine inside. A bald man in a shimmering blue robe somewhat more ornate than Morgan's poked his head out from down below.

"What are you doing in here?" Morgan said, speaking as quietly as possible and suppressing the urge to scream. "We were supposed to meet by the cuisine court!"

"I know, brother," the bald man said. "I just got scared. Had to come back to my safe space, old lucky number 28. The thing is, he's built up such an important following here at the Mall—I don't see how he could be convinced to step away to help you."

Morgan opened the stall door wider and stuck his head inside, talking down to the other man who remained on his knees. "You let me worry about that. Just follow through on your end and get me that meeting."

"Okay, okay. One hour. Down by the entrance to Victim's Secret."

"Finish your groveling and I'll see you there."

Morgan stormed out past the dozens of people standing in line, the tassels of his robe swinging back and forth with each rapid step. Two months of his life spent trying to blend in with these lunatics, and now his main contact was losing his nerve. Looking back, the antics he'd seen at the debtors' prison were an amateur display of contrition compared to what went on here, where spectacles worthy of a sports league's championship week took place on the hour.

Although it was initially churches and later HRA-inspired organizations that took advantage of the collapsed commercial real estate market by repurposing abandoned shopping malls across the country, the Mall of Absolution now set the gold standard for community spirituality in a guilt-ridden, post-work, post-functional society.

Here at the former Mall of America in Minnesota, an enigmatic figure called the Prescient One had turned its hauntingly empty corridors into a veritable Mecca for people seeking deeper meaning while they honored the nation's commitment to Reparations. These visitors believed that the formalities of wealth transfer and jobs training could only achieve so much, instead turning to the mystical realm of prayer to manifest lasting change. At their fingertips was a diverse offering of spiritual services, as well as historical tours, interracial healing sessions, VR past-life regressions in float tanks, gift shops, pan-civilizational dining, lectures by visiting scholars, and even a wedding chapel.

The Mall had also attracted seekers who felt that the world, despite all the exciting changes and scientific breakthroughs, was actually collapsing in on them. Overwhelmed and desperate for asylum, they had entered its cavernous walkways not merely as guests but intending to make their lives here in simplicity. In response to their need, this destination-mall quickly morphed into a twenty-first-century castle complex outfitted with living quarters, a school, daycare, and rooftop gardens.

Three months ago, when the Haggerstons had first arrived in the Winnebago of fugitives at the resistance's Upstate New York compound, they underwent a strenuous few weeks of basic tactical training, learning about the nature of the mission, and ultimately specialized instruction for their upcoming assignments.

James and Ed were sent to canvass shanty tent cities to recruit homeless military veterans who still had enough fire in their bellies to fight for the America that existed in their minds. Gary had gone with Brick and a team of six other men in top physical shape to infiltrate a handful of HRA facilities, where they planned to install covert surveillance equipment.

And Morgan, having shown an ability to adapt to any number of pressure situations, was embedded with ten other underground operatives pretending to be recent converts to Modestianity who, in taking their initial vows, would live and work for two years at the Mall of Absolution. Their goal was to gain an audience with this reclusive Prescient One, a man rumored to have been one of the original designers of MARVIN's mainframe, but who'd had some sort of a breakdown and left the HRA shortly after launch.

He was said to have renounced all worldly possessions, refused to work on computers anymore, and some months later emerged from seclusion wearing a rectangular suit that looked like a blue ice cream sandwich. He began delivering inspirational, heartfelt, non-hypocritical sermons which encouraged people to be humble and forgiving, as well as advising discretion when facing the future.

Because the resistance believed that a strict repeal of the

HRA would actually harm the nation, they sought someone with deep wisdom to lead a compassionate transition out of the program. The Prescient One's journey of disillusionment and awakening seemed to have prepared him to fill that role.

Further, his obsession with modesty had also resonated with other grassroots groups that accused the HRA of extending the reach of centralized surveillance so far that the legal concept of "prior restraint" was now actually bleeding over into people's daily lives. Citizens found themselves paralyzed into inaction as they asked themselves, "Is what I'm doing being recorded? How will it come back to haunt me?"

These various factions—unaffiliated but finding common ground within the bigger picture—saw a kind of genius in the Prescient One's eccentric variation of the full-body burqa, and felt it was urgent for the country to "have that conversation" before the noose of nosiness irrevocably tightened in a dreadful trinity of paranoia, blackmail, and humiliation.

Morgan was *this close* to finally presenting their case to the Prescient One—if only his contact could find some backbone while uttering Hail Modys from a prayer bench inside a converted changing room.

In the meantime, he needed to find a quiet place to compose his thoughts before this all-important meeting. The living quarters were out of the question because his fellow novitiates, while well-meaning, were always a little too talkative back in the cloisters.

Instead he made his way down the busy length of the mall to Mercies, another converted anchor store which, while as large as Tears, was devoted to the softer side of penance. Here, people struggling with the weight of their compounded guilt were afforded a reprieve from torment at one of several pleasantry stations.

There was a waterfall so loud that devotees could scream the worst hate speech imaginable without being overheard or recorded. Elsewhere, people put on VR headsets and entered a world where everyone's Debit Score was zero. Sometimes players refused to come back to real life or immediately got back in line, so this station was forced to impose a strict once-a-week policy in the interest of fairness and preventing addiction.

Morgan found a secluded atrium where pilgrims and residents

alike sat on plush chairs, reflecting humbly under the benevolent gaze of enormous portraits of Sub-Saharan Jesus, Tribal Lincoln, and a waving Chinese train conductor.

He thought about his family, who he'd had no contact with in months, and said a little prayer while looking down at the floor. How had his life come to this moment? It seemed like only yesterday he was dropping his young daughter off at her first tee ball practice. But now he was a fugitive living incognito among people whose minds had been shattered by the psychotic philosophy that was snaking its way through the country.

Morgan had never claimed to be a saint, but also didn't think he was enough of a devil to warrant being shackled to a monthly bill that fluctuated every time MARVIN read the "D leaves." And though he was at a loss to pinpoint where things had begun to go wrong, he took heart in knowing that he was not just watching from the sidelines as events came to a head.

For people like himself who grew up in areas where the American Civil War was an intimate part of the soil, the conflict was seen as a dramatic chapter in the nation's history to be taught with respect and reverence, and without painting one side as villainous caricatures. It was a sweeping human tale full of great men and imperfect men, and common men dying tragically young in cornfields—impossibly far away from the larger narrative that said one thing in their day, and now sought to present a claim check on their lifestyle choices from out of an unearthed time capsule.

But the most palpable reason why Morgan detested the whole concept of Reparations had nothing to do with money. It was a memento most likely now sitting somewhere in an HRA evidence room: a tiny folding picture frame which had once sat on his grandfather's dresser, next to a little toy cannon and bottles of cologne. On one side was a photograph of a man with a beard wearing a dark military uniform. The other frame housed a man with a beard wearing a lighter military uniform.

Yes, blood relatives who had fought on opposite sides of the Civil War. A profound keepsake that revealed more about the complexities and mysterious paradox of life than words ever could. But in the eyes of the HRA and the pathological worldview it embodied, this heirloom was just one debt and one credit canceling each other out in two cells within a spreadsheet whose rows and columns cascaded like a cancer across a nation that was increasingly becoming so tentative and mistrustful as to not even dare to open its mouth.

The bald man was pacing nervously outside the entrance to Victim's Secret. Morgan approached and the man said, "You're sure you want to do this?"

"Now or never."

Two strongmen in satin robes opened the double doors and they walked in. The room was filled with dozens of fine blue drapes and veils, which they brushed past as they blindly went deeper inside, until coming upon an elevator. When they entered, Morgan saw that there were only two buttons—*1* and *B*—so he pressed *B* and felt the elevator descend.

Moments later the doors opened onto a sparsely lit room in which hundreds of long strips of blue cloth dangled from the ceiling, swaying gently in the cool air. As they crept slowly through this canopy of azure vines, the partially obscured figure of a man suddenly appeared a slight distance away.

"I'll be with you in one moment," he said.

Morgan turned to whisper something to the bald man but found that he had already disappeared, either into the maze of cloth or back into the elevator.

The Prescient One approached. Shed of his rectangular bodysuit and having removed the putty from his cheeks, he now wore loose-fitting silver satin shirt and pants, and from the top of his head dangled several pieces of wire that resembled blue licorice, each with a tiny rubber hand at the end which bobbed in front of his face. His eyes, no longer hidden by glasses, were nonetheless disguised by contact lenses whose speckled irises twinkled like stars in the night.

"Good evening, Mr. Walsh—or, should I say, Mr. Haggerston?"

"You're right," Morgan said. "That's my real name. How did you find me out?"

"Indeed," the Prescient One said, "you did quite well by not leaving much in the way of fingerprints. And your contact lenses, while not as effective as mine in concealing one's identity, didn't give you away either. You may take solace in knowing that you avoided detection by the HRA. But, myself feeling the need to defend this sanctuary against any potential threat, I take all of the obsessive precautions that a leader on his way out might."

"So what caught me?"

"Your toothbrush! And a hair in the shower. Oh, and—"

"I get it. How long have you known about me?"

"You *and* the others. You see, when I left the HRA—cracked up, as they say—it was my accursed foresight that drove me to establish this ark. And just as I understood the monster that we had given birth to—'He's a growing boy,' I used to warn the others about little MARVIN, 'it'll never be enough!'—so too I envisioned a time when someone on the outside would have the courage to fight back."

"We also have the strength," Morgan said, "but what we don't have is the vision to guide the nation through. We need *you* for that."

The Prescient One glided closer, though taking care to always keep some part of himself cloaked by the hanging fabric. "But *I* can't stop the HRA. Otherwise I would have done that before I lost my blue marbles."

"But you know it's about more than that. Look at how you've set up this place: on the surface it just looks like a community megachurch, but you added all these flavors around the theme of modesty. I had to think about that for a while. At first I assumed, probably like everyone else, that you were encouraging moral behavior to make better quality people, and maybe to reduce the odds of them committing crimes the HRA would punish.

"But after a while," Morgan continued, "I put it all together. You call this place an ark because you're waiting for a storm to pass—a deadly storm! All these precautions to cover people up, hide their identities in some way. You're obsessed with privacy, but I just don't know why."

"The phrase I use is 'private propriety.' We must defend it from the hungry eyes of MARVIN and his kind. To protect everyone here at the Mall, my technical team gives all security camera footage a 'dignity wipe' before it is passed along to the government—their mandate, of course.

"Consider this: if a corporation can be called amoral in its insatiable quest for profits, is the same not true for a supercomputer that craves new data? Especially now, when everything a person does has some sort of watermark attached to it, the MARVINs of this world will *never* run out of material to gather, organize, and judge. It is this shortsightedness baked into the HRA that will cause mankind to grind to a halt when his every move is put under such scrutiny."

"And that's exactly why we need you! You understand the danger and can express it so well."

"I've got my flock. They are free, they are protected here. And we are self-sufficient. When the system fails we will take our place as shepherds."

"After how many people have to die? There is a real resistance movement that has grown in just the past year—the situation now is so different from when you quit the HRA. If you ever left this cocoon maybe you'd see that it's time to strike!"

"Yes, yes," the Prescient One said with a wave, moving deeper into the blue thicket. "Everyone thinks their revolution is about to break out and win the day."

"Wait!" Morgan said. "You knew who I was, but do you know why I joined the movement?"

"I assume it has something to do with being penalized for destroying all of those antique documents."

"My wife and children were stolen from me. And if I don't turn myself in then I may never see them again. But let's say I go back and serve my time. What's stopping the HRA from grandfathering in new trumped-up charges to hang on my head later? Will I be sent back to prison again? This *will* all spin out of control, just like you said—and the only reason men like me haven't started a revolution yet is because we were told that you had the foresight to lead us over the rocky ground toward a better future. So don't you hide from us now!"

The Prescient One fiddled with one of the little blue hands bouncing in front of his face, then turned and disappeared behind a mass of blue cloth.

"If what you say is true, that an army is ready to take action, how exactly will my words be able to match your great might?"

"Because very soon we will bring your voice to the unsuspecting world."

7. SINS OF THE PAST

Several months after her dark night of the soul, Kate returned to work and a party was held in her honor. The coworkers who had visited her at home were especially happy, and everyone else was also pleased to have her back fighting the good fight. Within a week she was up to speed on all of the HRA's progress, and had personally met with the new staff hired to assist in facilitating overseas expansion. TJ had been promoted to head of his department, and Jan was the same as ever—a born leader walking confidently among the cubicles, boosting morale, offering constructive correction, and serving as feather-soother of last resort downstairs when necessary.

One afternoon a few weeks later, Jan stepped into Kate's office with a troubled expression on her face and quietly closed the door.

"Kate," she finally said, "I'm glad you're already sitting down. I just can't believe what I'm about to say."

"Okay… Has something gone wrong? Have *I* done something wrong?"

"Not you, per se. But close."

"Jan! Just tell me, what's going on?"

Jan pulled a folded piece of paper from her pocket and handed it to Kate.

"MARVIN spit this out on Sunday afternoon. I've been holding onto it trying to think of a gentle way to break the news, but there just isn't one. You came up as a DDM. Over twenty DEs."

Kate opened the printout and read the summons. It listed all of the Domination Events her ancestors had committed since the 1670s against the family of a man named Luis Ortega. At the bottom of the page it said they were required to appear on *DDM TV Live* in fourteen days.

She neatly refolded the paper and started straightening objects on her desk.

"Oh, Kate, I'm so sorry," Jan said. "If there was any way I could pull some strings to get you out of this, after all you've been through..."

"No, no," Kate replied, her face becoming serene. "It's alright. Equity means no special treatment. For anyone. Better for it to happen to me now after I've been sick, actually. I know so much more and can face the music... not with pride but... as much clarity as empathy."

The network couldn't resist advertising Kate's DDM as "the episode of the century," even though the show was only finishing its second season. The HRA also saw her appearance as a chance to cement its reputation as a truly accountable governmental organization, promoting it on the official website and with posters on field office walls.

As the show date approached, Kate began to feel that events were taking on a life of their own. Coworkers were acting weird, her face was plastered all over the place, and the show's producers were calling and emailing at all hours of the day and night. Even debt protesters got in on the action by sending around memes that mocked "the absurdity of the century" and imploring the HRA to "stop throwing stones."

Kate even started to wonder how Chris would react if she was assigned somewhere far away. He had stood by her side like a rock during treatment, but facing the prospect of being separated for over six months out of the blue definitely had *her* in shock. Currently the DDM prize package only covered a Debtor's monthly bills, with no allocation for a temporary family move or visits, and in the big scheme of things Kate understood why. The HRA was in some ways like a Silicon Valley startup that sank billions of dollars for years before seeing a profit, so between infrastructure investment, day-to-day operation costs, and its worldwide expansion plans, brief separation of DDM families was considered a small sacrifice for people already on the hook for debts to society.

She'd first met Chris during her senior year of college. He was a guitar player in an aggressive, politically charged punk rock band that had some minor success touring around the Mid-Atlantic region, but in truth it was their upper-middle class sensibilities that had drawn them together. He once joked that they were both closet anarchists, happy to protest all day long before retreating to the comforts of a clean home not overrun by unshowered, transient activists.

During their early to mid-twenties, they made the semi-long-distance relationship work as she was often on the road advocating somewhere while he stayed local building a small web design business. Deep down, despite his now-defunct band's socially conscious lyrics, Chris only agreed with about half of the issues that Kate and her crowd were passionate about—but early on in their courtship he had been so captivated by the magical beauty that nature packs into a young woman, that there may have been no limit to the number of incomprehensible things she might say before he would give her up.

A private car picked them up on the evening of the show and drove them uptown to the network. Once they arrived, Kate was quickly whisked away to hair and makeup, then a PA took her to the mobile sound cart to be outfitted with a wireless microphone. After grabbing a bottle of water at craft service, she was instructed by the assistant director to be very careful not to mess up her makeup. This AD was a frantic little woman who would appear with a question or instruction every five minutes before disappearing to handle some other aspect of this pre-show symphony that she was conducting.

Kate could now hear the audience chanting in the background and an apprehensive glaze settled over her mind as she watched the crew hustling around. The atmosphere here seemed to have more of a bite than at that somewhat scripted *Tina* show she did six months ago, and in response she felt a burst of resentment toward the crowd. They knew nothing about her at all, so how dare they think of her as a sacrificial lamb?

To stifle this selfish impulse, she took heart in the knowledge that long term, this episode would only serve to give credence to the HRA's mission. *This is good press*, she reminded herself, *and I am the poster child—at least for this week*. Because as the show boasted, "no one can ever predict what shocking DDM connection MARVIN will make next," which would push her out of the headlines.

That encouraging last thought helped clear her mind. She took a careful sip of water and looked around. Crew members were still moving gear while in the background the audience was buzzing even more loudly. And over there was Chris talking to a cameraman—she perked up on tiptoes and gave him a wave. He smiled back then returned to his conversation.

Some of the backstage lights dimmed and the AD returned to lead Kate by the elbow to a curtain beside the stage. A man with a crew cut in khaki pants was gesticulating in front of the studio audience to get them riled up. And directly across from her on the other side of the stage behind a matching curtain, Kate could see Luis Ortega, whom she recognized from the promos.

Loud music and sound effects now blasted through the sound system—and into Kate's earbud—which prompted the crew to quickly clear off the stage. The main lights dimmed in some places while getting brighter in others, and finally a distinguished-looking man with sandy blond hair and artificially tanned face stepped onto the floor. The audience greeted him with loud applause which was accepted with a gracious wave before he tilted his head down, indicating a request for silence.

"Ladies and gentlemen, boys and girls. Watching around the world on great television networks and streaming all across the internet. I'm your host, Ryan Richards, and tonight I am honored to captain this historic episode of *DDM TV Live*.

"Our mission here on the show has always been to put a human face on the sometimes overwhelming project that the Historical Reparations Administration began just three years ago. Together we've seen centuries-old family feuds end in acts of goodwill, all documented here for posterity as a testament to the power of the human heart."

He struck a dramatic pose.

"And tonight, one of the HRA's very own walks into the belly of the beast to hear the roll call of her Bloodline Crimes, and dare to face her Direct Descendant Match. Together they will explore their long-intertwined fates, before mingling them one last time to gloriously end the cycle of victimization, and mend damaged fences once and for all!"

The lights went dark and all eyes turned to a large, elevated video screen behind the stage, which displayed a picture of Kate's face and several personal details.

"Mrs. Kathleen Donohugh," the host continued. "She goes by Kate. Born and raised in Arlington, Virginia. A longtime activist who worked tirelessly with so many others to make the HRA a reality, and where she now works at their large field office in Newark, New Jersey. Who would seemingly shine as a beacon for everything noble that the HRA advocates for—but *she* has a dark secret!"

The screen flashed to display the face of a young, light-skinned Latiz-American man wearing black-rimmed glasses.

"*Twenty-two* confirmed Domination Events perpetuated against this man's bloodline!"

The crowd erupted with howls and boos.

"Yes, it's true! And we here at *DDM TV* know what that means, so say it with me now…"

Everyone in the studio audience shouted in unison, "No one expects to pay for the sins of their fathers, but for you, that bill has come due!"

All the stage lights burst back on and Kate felt a nudge from behind so she walked out to meet Ryan Richards under a barrage of cheers and boos. She put on a gracious smile and shook the host's hand.

After the audience quieted down, he put his arm around her waist and said quietly, "Kate, you more than perhaps any other Debtor we've had on this program know where this is going. Do you want to say anything before we review the offenses spiraling savagely through every double-helix in your body?"

"Thank you, Ryan. I really want this to demonstrate to our critics that the HRA applies to *all* Americans. Not only do our employees truly believe in the mission, none of us try to hide behind sneaky exemptions or play favorites as often happens in big organizations."

"That's just wonderful to hear. Now, let's bring out your DDM. Please meet Mr. Luis Ortega!"

Cheers and applause broke out as the baby-faced young man in flat-brimmed baseball cap and skinny jeans ambled toward them. He gave the crowd a modest wave, then adjusted his glasses after shaking hands with the host.

"My goodness, Mr. Ortega, everybody!"

The audience worked up to a frenzy as Richards danced around and gave him a playful high-five. Kate stood to the side and clapped her hands.

"Luis, Kate. Kate, Luis."

Richards pretended to officiate as the two shook hands.

"Now, just to confirm, you two have never met each other before this moment?"

"That's right," Kate said.

"Well, after this brief commercial break, Kate Donohugh and Luis Ortega will *very much* get acquainted. Stay tuned, folks!"

The giant video screen behind them flickered a gray interference pattern for two seconds before switching to a car commercial. Richards craned his neck back to the screen, then shrugged his shoulders at the assistant director who was running up to them.

"That was weird," the AD said. "Anyway, when we get back from break, Ryan and the announcer will go down the list of Kate's DEs. The crowd's gonna eat it up. Then the mobile MARVIN unit will pass assessment. Kate and Luis, each of you will get a minute to speak, then it's off to our second DDM pairing of the night. Sound good? Great! Looks like we're back in thirty. Hold, smile, here we go…"

In the next segment, a baritone announcer rattled off a laundry list of crimes committed by Kate's ancestors, from the petty—livestock thefts and ethnic slurs—building up to various assaults, one rape, and finally a war crime that took place somewhere on the nebulous Texas-Mexico border in 1847. The audience was livid, practically frothing at the mouth, and getting restless for the cathartic payoff soon to come.

Several times Kate put a hand on her heart and mouthed "I'm sorry," and at other moments her eyes closed as she deeply felt eons of shame purge from her soul in this cleansing fire. Meanwhile Luis toyed with the zipper pull tab of his hoodie and shuffled his weight back and forth between feet.

After all of the DEs had been announced, the lights dimmed except for a center spotlight. Richards put his arms around them both and said, "You'd think that after nearly one hundred episodes we'd be numb to history's foul deeds, but I'm pretty certain we can all say that this is *not* the case. In fact, we are appalled by what has transpired between your two bloodlines. But now—tonight—at last. Justice, healing, and yes… Reparayyy-shuuuuuns!!!"

A staggering roar surged through the studio and into the TVs, computer monitors, and phone screens of one-hundred-twenty-five-million viewers around the world. The lights came up and

Richards walked over to a machine that resembled a photocopier from the past. He pressed a red button and the machine flashed and whizzed, then spat out a red-and-black striped envelope. The host took it in his hands and walked solemnly back to center stage.

Richards pulled a silver letter opener from his jacket pocket and whipped it in front of his face with a swordsman's flourish. The crowd gasped as he proceeded to slit open the envelope with tantalizing care, then eased out a gold-rimmed card from within.

"Kathleen Donohugh," he said, "beloved HRA supervisor and guiding light of national atonement. You are hereby remanded to serve eight months at the Construction 4 Community build site in northeast Cleveland, where you and Luis Ortega will assemble low-income housing together. Standing side by side, your team will extinguish the flames of hate with every nail you hammer and each particleboard shelf you install."

In the stunned silence that followed, Richards began a slow clap which the audience built upon until the studio was pulsing with affirmation. He let them marinate in this deserved release for half a minute, then quieted them by lowering his outstretched arms. He stepped very close to Kate.

"Hi, Kate," he said softly.

"Hello, Ryan."

"Is there anything you'd like to say right now?"

She smiled, standing with hands clasped down by her waist.

"First, I want to say to you, Luis, what an honor it will be to go on this journey together as we bury history's hatchet."

Luis compressed his lips and gave a small nod.

"And what else?" Richards asked.

"I actually have a bit of a personal story to relate."

"*Oh?* Do tell."

"Well, everybody is aware of the public battles I fight each day working at the HRA. But what you don't know is that this past summer I went through a very personal struggle that taught me just how much work remains for us all.

"You see, I've just fought a battle against breast cancer. And what happened was that when I found myself betrayed by organs historically associated with what we call being a woman, I also felt my heart break for the people born into bodies that don't align with who or what is in their souls. Then I thought about all the other people in the world suffering from disease—be they cis, non-cis, trans, or straight—and I mourned for their losses as well.

"But the hardest truth I had to face was this: for all I suffered, the main reason I'm alive today is because I'm privileged in so many ways—my family, my education, my access to healthcare, and yes, my being *white*."

"Kate, that is a heartbreaking story no matter how you look at it. Just what do you propose?"

"We might have to expand the HRA's scope. Or create entirely *new* administrations tasked with meeting the needs of people who are oppressed in these other ways. Think about it— beyond the pain that came to my mind, what else must we heal? I know that the size of this potential project is enormous, but the main takeaway is that suffering exists now which lies beyond the reach of Historical Reparations, and I'll be damned if we let that need go unmet just because it was once in our collective blind spot."

Ryan Richards closed his eyes and joined his hands as if to pray. Seconds passed. Finally he said, "This is profound beyond anything we have ever gone through together here on *DDM TV*. Just now a Debtor transcended the bounds of our mission and placed a new path of responsibility before us."

Pivoting to Luis, he said with a grin, "I hate to throw all of this into *your* lap, young man, but wow! What do you say, buddy?"

Luis licked his lips and adjusted the brim of his hat, then looked around with wide, blinking eyes.

"It's pretty overwhelming, actually," he said. "My life's good right now, you know. I'm going to school in LA for electrical engineering, um, so I don't know. How's this trip to Cleveland gonna affect that?"

Just as Richards raised a finger and leaned in with a smirk, all the lights went dark and a loud buzz squawked from the sound system. The video screen above flickered a series of disjointed frames before all went quiet and a man wearing a shimmering silver Roman theater mask appeared, with bright blue dots emanating from inside the eyeholes.

"Violators and Victims," he said, "Debtors and Beneficiaries. We are the Sentinels of Jubilee. Today our moles seized control of the monstrous supercomputer called MARVIN that you beg for approval on history's box score. And I am here to declare that this misguided experiment known as the Historical Reparations Administration must come to an end."

The studio audience began to chatter while on the darkened stage below, Kate and Ryan Richards stood awkwardly in the screen's glow. She looked around and saw Luis fading away as he wandered behind a curtain.

"But we are not vindictive or bent on destruction," the masked man continued, the lights on his contacts pulsing and fading like an animated music player. "We acknowledge that the HRA was a somewhat noble effort, but this core idea of pressing pause on the future to replay old scenes is ultimately a futile endeavor.

"How can you discover the next great cure when you must constantly interrupt your concentration to pray to the god of Reparations, whose IV needle depletes all eruptions of creativity and passion? As if you could change that which can never be undone. No, it is through wisdom and teaching that you will achieve the goal of more building and less exploitation.

"But this is all a distraction from a bigger threat which looms. Consider this: if you are a Beneficiary, do you not think it possible that someday you could become a Debtor? The technology that MARVIN employs will only expand and zoom in more closely—no detail will be too small for the coming army of nanobot drones and microsensors that will monitor and upload every facet of life on Earth. You will all discover that history has indeed not ended, and your god MARVIN will pass excruciating judgment upon everyone in the sermon of his Holy Spreadsheet.

"And as each remote corner of Earth comes online, adding documents young and old, MARVIN will make deeper and deeper connections. There will be nothing you can hide, and nowhere to escape. The next frontier is not equity but total surveillance as humanity scurries in terror under the all-seeing eye of the Scrutiny State. *This* is your real enemy—not Reparations, or political parties, or even each other.

"Already this constricting existence is becoming too much to bear, always looking over your shoulder for sins committed by your ancestors in a different world—sometimes even centuries before the light bulb was invented! How can you protect *your* children and grandchildren against the acts you legally commit today but which will be reviewed, condemned, and punished tomorrow?

"This mechanism of our enslavement is already in place and that is why the HRA *must* change course before it is too late, before all trust between people is lost. We, the Sentinels of Jubilee, have drafted a plan which will remove the burden upon Debtors which has caused so much resentment, but we will not simply abandon Beneficiaries along the way. We must work together to establish codes which defend privacy and human dignity against the massive database which will surely be abused if not kept in check.

"Now, before I leave you, I have a message for this Ms. Donohugh. Kate, I sympathize deeply with anyone who faces a grave medical prognosis. But how can you think so little of yourself that in the moment of your deepest, most intimate personal sorrow, your instinct is to project it out onto anyone and everyone else? That is not compassion. Could it be that this self-effacing impulse is the same one that drives you to pick apart and micromanage every aspect of other people's lives? Is it possible that you have been brainwashed but don't even realize it? And most important of all, will the American people sit by while Kate and her millions of like-minded allies indoctrinate their own children?

"That is all for now. I will speak to you again when you are ready to take the next step. Good night."

The feed cut out and the screen switched to the *DDM TV Live* logo. The center spotlight came on and Kate saw Richards squirm as he tried to regain his composure—a producer was waving frantically at him from beside a nearby camera as the audience murmured in confusion.

"Uh, ladies and gentlemen," he said, wiping his forehead, "these impostors had *nothing* to do with our show and the important work we do. The culprits who dared to hack into our network will be caught and exposed for the cowards that they are."

He paused, put a hand to his ear, then said, "I've just been told by my producer that due to this security breach, it's in the interest of everyone's safety to end—if I may say—what had already been an unprecedented broadcast. Kate Donohugh and uh, well, I don't know where Luis has gone, but Kate, thank you for your dedicated service. We'll be checking in with you next week with an update from that housing project in Cleveland!"

The crowd gave tentative applause as Kate and Richards hugged then waved while the theme song played and show credits rolled on the screen above. As Kate began to pull away, the host whispered in her ear, "I think you're goddamned sexy. Come to my dressing room later and let's get our Reparations on."

Kate, still trying to hold a smile as the cameras circled them on stage, said, "What the hell! Is this all a big joke to you?"

"But you've got to help me, I have a sexi-medi-existential need. I'm a man that wants to feel trapped inside *your* body!"

Kate was revolted by the thick heat of his breath on her face and stumbled back, yanking away her wrist that he had taken hold of. She ran off the stage, saw Chris coming toward her, and they embraced. Tears began to stream down her cheeks and he tried to wipe them away.

"Hey, it's gonna be okay," he said tenderly. "Cleveland isn't so far away. What if they'd sent you to Phoenix?"

8. BRAINWASHED?

Immediately following the masked man's chilling declaration, HRA field offices nationwide were bombarded with phone calls, video messages, and visits from Beneficiaries terrified that they would stop receiving their deposits, as well as from Debtors eager to find out if their liability would be reduced or canceled. At the same time, Luis Ortega was nowhere to be found, and in light of the chaos at work, Kate was permitted to help out until he was located.

MARVIN was put into a protective stasis while techs scoured the millions of lines of code for any malware the hackers may have embedded. FBI security experts were brought in to help identify the moles who had infiltrated the HRA by posing as idealistic and trustworthy change agents, but were in fact bent on sabotage. The biggest challenge was that in addition to the core group of fifty thousand full-time staff, there were another eighty thousand contractors, part-timers, janitors, and volunteers to evaluate. It could take months to get an accurate picture of how compromised the HRA was. Meanwhile no one knew what the Sentinels of Jubilee intended to do next, or when.

The mood in the Donohugh household was subdued but anxious during these first days following Kate's appearance on *DDM TV Live*. Every time her phone beeped or rang it could mean that Luis Ortega had been found, and that she and Chris would then be separated for weeks or months.

After the third frantic day down at the field office, Kate came home with a case of red wine and declared that she was going to turn off her phone and force herself to relax. But even after two glasses, Chris noticed that she was still on edge and asked if something else was on her mind besides work.

"Who do you think the masked man was?" she said.

"Like, how did he end up as the mouthpiece for a group of hackers who claim they're saving the world, but he's still too afraid to show his face?"

"Sort of. I want to know what he was doing five or ten years ago. What drove him to hate the HRA so much?"

"Probably a Cauc," Chris said. "Start there."

"Obviously! But what else? How old is he?"

"I'd say late thirties to early fifties."

"Okay. But *who* is he? Seems to know a lot about tech and where it's going."

Chris took a sip from his wine glass.

"Truth is, some of what he said made a lot of sense. There is potential for abuse in the wrong hands, or worse, just losing control of it. MARVIN could be used to take cyberstalking to an insanely sophisticated level."

"But what are the wrong hands? Big scary government?"

"And corporations."

"But not you?"

"I'm a small fry. There's only so much reach an indie company like mine could have. I'm not one of these sexy startups that get huge investment capital every five years. I can't even imagine being able to do whatever I wanted with billions of dollars, then down the road just get more money because I'm big, or by telling the first investors they'll never get paid back unless they bail me out."

"But you chose to stay small. You could have found partners or approached banks for some loans, but I know you like the freedom of working from home."

"Yeah, but beyond that my life isn't very glamorous: no paid benefits, no fully stocked break room. Plus I have to deal with all the permits and fees, just like any other business. Look, I know corporations are evil and someone needs to keep an eye on them, but sometimes I just wish people who wrote policy actually did some for-profit work in the trenches. Then they'd see how hard it is to conjure up money from nothing, even without all the hoops they make us jump through."

Kate had perked up. "Which touches on another big problem. How many people of color never even find out what steps you have to take to go about starting a business?"

"Babe, just because I'm white and own a business, I still have to go out there and impress potential clients. They only care if I can get the job done for the right price, not my skin color. I'm sorry, but money talks!"

"No, there's so much more going on than just money. Countless Beneficiaries are never considered for those gigs because they're ten or fifteen years behind you in so many areas of life. What I—and the HRA—am trying to do is crack the code on how to get them up to parity with you."

"When did *I* become the official standard? There are designers, many from India—your next stop, by the way— almost half my age who have way better skills than me. And it's not like with my past client list I can just waltz in and land a big corporate contract. Don't hate me but, if you think the HRA needs to expand, why not go all the way and put *me* on the inside track with the big boys?"

"This is getting crazy. You could have gone in that direction years ago."

"I'm just saying, if you want to set some goals for helping people, then fine. But you can't pick a random person—me—and say that all Beneficiaries need to reach his level of X, Y, or Z."

Kate walked over to the curtain and looked out into the street. "What do you think he meant when he said millions of us had been brainwashed?"

"Man, this guy really got to you. I—and the dogs—am just

glad you haven't been shipped out to Cleveland."

"Me too. But it *would* have been such a valuable experience…"

"Wait! Maybe that's it right there. What that guy with the mask meant. I'm your husband, you're supposed to want to be with me. These symbolic group activities—I just don't get it."

"So I have to stay by your side like some woman of the past who had no rights?"

"Kate, that is such a mental leap."

"But it's not taking a leap to side with the freak in the mask who thinks I, your darling wife, was indoctrinated without even knowing it?"

Chris put his hands up. "Let's pick it apart then, rationally."

"Okay, how?"

"Imagine a woman," he said, "who's the exact opposite of you. Let's call her Kimberly. How is she different? Is she evil?"

"Well… She doesn't advocate for others. She doesn't fight for human rights. She doesn't consider that her every action has an expanding butterfly effect on the world. Instead she just does whatever she feels like."

"Interesting. So she doesn't rob banks or shoot people?"

"No."

"Doesn't go to cross burnings?"

"No."

"Just works a normal job, watches movies, vidchats with her friends, and *maybe* has an extra scoop of mint ice cream in secret after her husband goes to bed?"

"Hey! I thought you said we were opposites!"

"I know, I was kidding," Chris said with a smile. "But maybe not completely. Maybe this Kimberly lives a quiet, decent life not much different from yours."

"Yeah, but she's still enjoying the advantages of her privilege even if she doesn't know it."

"Okay, right there—where did *that* idea come from? You didn't think of it yourself and Kimberly certainly doesn't believe it."

"I don't know," Kate said, moving away from the window. "I'd have to think back. Sometime during middle school, maybe? Possibly at an assembly or in history class."

"Since when was the point of school to tell students how they benefited from the events being taught? I mean, pretty much everyone's lives have been improved by the invention of the wheel, right? But some people actually get run over by them and die, and there might be a remote tribe somewhere that still hasn't made first contact with the outside world. Do we somehow have to make it up to all of them?"

"Chris! Do you realize what you're saying right now and how that makes me feel?"

"You said you wanted to know if you'd been brainwashed. I'm just playing along and asking the tough questions."

"So you're saying it'd be better to live like Kimberly and just let the Beneficiaries fend for themselves for another five hundred years?"

"Did you not hear what that guy in the mask said? MARVIN may be programmed back to 1492 right now, but it's not going to stay that way forever. When did the Moors invade Spain? Way before Columbus! Are some Afrigo-Americans going to have to pay Reparations to descendants of The Conquistadors, who then just pass it right along to Tribal Americans?"

"Oh my god!" Kate screamed. "What kind of connection is that?"

Chris took a deep breath and spoke deliberately.

"I don't think any of you understand the can of worms you've opened with this. After you 'franchise' out to other former colonies and the homelands of their white invaders, it's not just going to stop there. I'll give the hacker this: he understands that the computers are going to reach not just *out* but *back*. Until every country is at each other's throats trying to get repaid for every war, every broken treaty, every sunken ship…"

Kate was in shock. She sat down against the base of the couch and pulled up her knees. Of all the people she had done intellectual battle with, she never expected that Chris would be the one to say the worst things of all.

"So the HRA has been a big mistake? You think I've wasted half my life building something that's going to stop the world? I'm just… speechless. How long have you been thinking all this?"

"Only during the last couple days since the show, really."

"And what did you think before?"

"Katie, I've always supported whatever it was you were

doing. If you were happy, then that would help make *us* work."

"My god. All this time. You never actually cared about the Victims."

"I care about you. I hope you can say that about me."

Kate stood up and walked back to the window. Some homeless people were pushing carts down the sidewalk. She knew that she should give Chris an answer but she also wanted to see if there was an extra blanket in the hall closet she could take down to help keep them warm.

Maddie, one of the Corgis, nuzzled at her feet. She squatted down and rubbed its ears, then said, "And I wuv you!" She froze and looked over at Chris, whose jaw had dropped.

"I'm going to put an asterisk beside this conversation," he said. "Everyone's stressed out right now. But I think I'll sleep in my office tonight." He got up and went into the bathroom.

Kate sat down next to the dog and stroked its neck absently.

Later that night, alone in bed while the dogs slept on the floor nearby, she couldn't stop thinking about how she'd said that she might have been brainwashed at school. It was so strange, because all of her memories from elementary school through high school graduation were of a positive place that encouraged cooperation and had no tolerance for ugly words, ignorance, or fights.

Yet somehow at college she didn't gravitate to the Greek party scene, or even a casual volunteer club, but instead fell in with righteously angry left-wing activists. She had been so happy all of her life up until they bombarded her with "the truth," and the next thing Kate knew she was their newest recruit, complete with green-dyed short hair and a nose ring. And though tempted, she could never bring herself to get a tattoo like so many of the others—because her "bourgeois soul refused to die," according to one of several regrettable dating choices she'd made during the reckless early phase that, in time, achieved balance with her former self.

Indeed, it was this coming into her own that had set the direction for the rest of Kate's life, and not the marketing degree she earned from the college. Maybe somewhere her doppelganger Kimberly had a shelf lined with advertising industry awards, but Kate was actually changing the world. And she didn't feel like a Manchurian Advocate for doing it, either!

But tonight, here in bed by herself, these affirming thoughts could not help her fall asleep. She pictured Chris scrunched up on that tiny sofa in his office. She got up and walked over to him, cramming herself up against his body under the thin blanket. She nuzzled him on the cheek.

"I looked up what 'jubilee' means," he said drowsily. "In ancient times, kings would forgive all the debts and everybody started fresh again."

"I owe you an apology, Mr. Donohugh," she said softly. "And I might know of a way to get you to forgive *my* debt…"

9. UNDER FIRE

NIFTY MINUTES – SEASON 61, EPISODE 3 – "HRA UNDER FIRE"

BEGIN SHOW TRANSCRIPT

Cheryl Li: Three years ago, the Historical Reparations Administration launched in the United States to great fanfare. It is an ambitious project which aims to right the wrongs of history and level the playing field after centuries of inequality. While any government agency can expect its share of challenges and negative press, in recent weeks two major stories have broken to cast a shadow of doubt across the young program that is so filled with hope. Our Howard Parnell reports.

Howard Parnell: Good evening, I'm Howard Parnell for *Nifty Minutes*. In this segment we will investigate why the HRA finds itself under fire from both sides of the spreadsheet, as well as explore what can be done to right the ship.

(voice-over) Our story begins in the city of Newark, New Jersey. It is one of many poor, predominantly Afrigro-American cities that the HRA targeted as a beachhead in its War for Equity. But as we will see, residents on the ground say that nearly three years in, life here has not gotten much better.

(video: A black teenager moves to the beat of hip-hop in a vacant city street at night.)

Singer: Drones fly by, money flow in. Reparations, why? Because we're victims. You got the document scan, in MARVIN we trust, but the streets still bleed, so where we at?

Parnell (voice-over): Meet fifteen-year-old Clyde Jenkins, aka DJ Clydoscope. He lives at home with his mother, has never held a real job, and admits to having stolen a number of the HRA mini-drones which patrol the city. But it's his surprise indie hit single "Fly So High," whose lyrics paint a not-so-rosy picture about the realities of life for HRA Beneficiaries, which has struck a deep chord nationwide among people dissatisfied with the program. Some are even calling Clyde the voice of the half-decade in light of this "DJ versus Goliath" phenomenon.

(on camera) Two months ago you were a complete unknown. Now your song is the hit of the year. What do you think about all that's happened?

Clyde Jenkins: It's really crazy. Like, I knew it was a good track, but I just hoped enough people would feel it to inspire me to write more.

Parnell: You didn't expect to be famous, just like that?

Jenkins: No! I mean, you dream but... how many people's dreams come true, especially where I'm from?

Parnell: What motivated you to write the song?

Jenkins: People still getting robbed, killed. So many cameras out there now, guess the HRA can see all they money being spent on drugs and all the rest.

Parnell: Does the song's popularity among other Beneficiaries encourage you in thinking that the HRA will respond by making changes?

Jenkins: Hey, I only put out the message. It's not in my hands anymore.

Parnell: Do you ever just pinch yourself and ask, "Is this even real?"

Jenkins: Well, it feels weird having all these fans, you know. Maybe in the hood, I get it. But why would someone in like, Japan, get down with my message?

Parnell (voice-over): But resonate he has. One music critic says, "The effortless turn from aggressively rapped lyrics about street life into a soulfully crooned chorus—which soars with lightness and spirituality—shows me exactly why this young man has taken the world by storm." Even the legendary rapper

MC Ergo No Mic weighed in, saying, "He's like the new Tupac. Young, fierce. Sees how things are, tells it like it is. And too young to know better than to hold back. Respect!"

One friend Clyde doesn't have? The HRA. The fact that he used stolen government property to film a no-budget video which undermines the administration's multi-million-dollar marketing campaign, isn't sitting well with management—and now their lawyers are out to seize his earnings. But DJ Clydoscope takes it all in stride.

Jenkins: I'd say it's typical, you know. Kids be out there smashing them drones the whole time. HRA could've stopped us if they wanted to. But before, I was just a poor helpless kid—a *Beneficiary*—I *needed* their help. Now that I got a voice of my own, HRA come collecting for services rendered real quick!

Parnell (voice-over): Elena Forsyth, an HRA spokeshuman, disagrees with the harsh assessment Mr. Jenkins makes, both in his interview and in the song.

Elena Forsyth: None of us have any animosity toward him. In fact, he's an empowered young person of pigment expressing himself. I'd like to think that the HRA gave him a boost, even if he doesn't see it that way.

Parnell: But what about the allegations of Beneficiaries gaming the system like the welfare abusers of old, with no oversight, and the seeming anarchy on the streets after sunset in these poor neighborhoods?

Forsyth: Some areas are worse than others. Newark historically has had a high crime rate. I don't think one song written by someone living in such a challenging place should be considered a referendum on the whole program.

Parnell: Then how do you explain the fact that it's getting airplay all over the country? There have been over eleven million downloads, countless audio streams, plus PerformTube reports sixty-five-million views. That's unprecedented for an unknown artist—something about his message *is* resonating with people from coast to coast.

Forsyth: You know, Howard, I watched the video several times—

Parnell: Oh, really?

Forsyth: Yes, we've all seen it—and it *is* a catchy tune—but my takeaway is the inspiring message of hope it sends. When you see the sun coming up over the city, the aerial ballet of the synchronized drones swirling above—

Parnell: Drones stolen from your organization, which is now threatening to slap Mr. Jenkins with legal action…

Forsyth: No one wants to take this kid to court—

Parnell: As if you haven't gotten enough bad press already…

Forsyth: Exactly. What we at the HRA would all like to do is get back to work, and we hope that this one-hit-wonder doesn't discourage people or make them impatient. We've made great strides, but admittedly there's still a lot of work to do out there.

Parnell (voice-over): But that's not all the HRA has to worry about. A much more formidable group calling itself the Sentinels of Jubilee hacked into the administration's flagship show, *DDM TV Live*, just days before this episode was scheduled to air. That "October Surprise" exposed serious vulnerabilities in the HRA's computer network which houses data on every American citizen, as well as gave troubling confirmation that disgruntled Debtors are preparing to fight back. While their plans—and masked leader—remain somewhat cryptic, the HRA has been put on notice.

I spoke with Molly Kleiner of the Thinkings Institution in our nation's capital. (on camera) Molly, what do you believe is going on out there?

Molly Kleiner: I think any time you try to roll out a large new program, people want to see immediate results. You're under a lot of scrutiny to show what good all that money is doing.

Parnell: Scrutiny. That's the same word used by the masked hacker on *DDM TV Live* the other night. Any thoughts on his fears that the technology could spin out of control?

Kleiner: Anyone who thinks the surveillance network is something new needs a brief lesson in recent history. The NSA and CIA had long been spying on American citizens by the time the Neocons took surveillance to the next level when they created the Department of Homeland Security. Not only that, people have voluntarily posted their whole lives on social media sites for years. But now that the left-wing activists are in charge, it's finally a problem? I find such fearful criticisms ironic because the HRA is actually using this data to implement policy in a forthright manner.

Parnell: But they're looking back into hundreds of years'

worth of information, not merely at people alive today.

Kleiner: It is no crime to execute laws by making use of a utility that was built before your tenure. Even if people don't like what the Dramacrats are doing to the place, they didn't build it—it's been here for quite a while.

Parnell: What would you say to those people who look at HRA failures—their word—failures like Newark, and say, "Whoa, whoa. They want to expand and one day do an accounting of the British East India Company while there are serious problems here at home?" Is the beta test maybe not over yet?

Kleiner: The program's vast scope almost guarantees that it will take many years to complete. They can't just leave Victims waiting worldwide. Besides, the system's design is sound—they just need to plug it in overseas and adapt as they go.

Parnell: Before I let *you* go, what are your thoughts on the "Fly So High" phenomenon?

Kleiner: However crude, I think the song carries an important message that the HRA should heed. Because look, if we're asking the nation to be accountable for its history, then surely the administration needs to honor that philosophy itself.

Parnell (voice-over): One interesting player in this whole drama is Nolan Simmons. A US Army veteran who's currently embedded deep within the mean streets, he also directed the "Fly So High" music video. And he's got a lot to say.

Nolan Simmons: We've got all these people who lack the life skills to keep it together, let alone compete. They've been on the government dole for decades, so giving them more money under a new name—Reparations, this time—it isn't going to help. And now you're really making white people angry! Before, they just had to pay taxes, but now someone's pointing a finger at them.

Parnell: So what is the HRA doing wrong, in your opinion?

Simmons: It's a bunch of people with master's degrees coming in and using us as guinea pigs. And when their brilliant ideas fail, there's no negative consequences for their careers or even taking a moment to ask, "Hey, what did we do wrong?" It's just a tragedy that the HRA is run by so many fools.

Parnell: Why do you call them "fools"?

Simmons: Because they think they're social workers. But their minds work like anthropologists or missionaries trying to "save the natives." They're so out of touch from our experience. They've never suffered, they've never been desperate—so the ideas that work in their world just won't take down here.

Parnell: Okay. If the HRA approached you tomorrow and said you were in charge, what would you propose?

Simmons: I'm not saying that we need to be left to our own devices, but there has to be some sort of middle ground between this going back and forth. Where one year there's more law enforcement presence, but the next year, a cop is nowhere to be found. I'm not blaming anyone, but the fact is that real bad guys fill that void.

Now, as for solutions. From my own life experience, it was the discipline of the military that made me a functional person—the consistent rules, enforcement, and consequences. So maybe we need small military academies in these poor cities—at least something like how private schools are set up—to help turn these little gang militias into an Inner City Corps of Leaders who will rebuild and protect their own neighborhoods. And no more centralized decrees! Let the communities save themselves by becoming more self-sufficient, just like the HRA wants.

Parnell: What do you say to people who would call you a hypocrite? Here you are, a former US government employee, and yet you filmed this music video with stolen HRA property.

Simmons: You know, I get it. But I help keep the corner of my hood safer, keep some of these guys out of real trouble by teaching them skills and responsibilities. I could've left town—my military experience would have opened doors for me to get a job in a safer area. But it's just like immigration: if all the smart, capable people leave to go to a nicer country, how's the old place ever gonna improve? We have got to stop the brain drain, and work to increase the pain drain!

Parnell: Well said. That actually sounds like it could be one of Clyde's lyrics.

Simmons: I'm glad you mentioned him. Because, you know, I'm taking a real risk putting my face on this show. But I think the message in his song is so important, and somehow we have this amazing opportunity to speak to the rest of the country—I owe it to the people who don't have a voice.

Parnell (in studio): Right now the HRA is reeling from a one-two punch of bad press and "technical difficulties" just weeks before the president's reelection bid. We'll learn in the coming days how well the program responds, and if Rebellican challenger Victor Dominguez—who so far has said very little about the HRA—decides to pounce. For *Nifty Minutes*, I'm Howard Parnell, giving young DJ Clydoscope the last word.

Jenkins (singing): But this ain't me, eye in the sky knows, this ain't how things supposed to be. So for all we can see, and all we can be. We got to fly, fly so high, and find a way, way outta here… alive.

END SHOW TRANSCRIPT

10. THE FUGITIVE

At a gas station along one of South Dakota's lonely highways, an infrared camera—serving as part of the national Predator Predator network, which scanned all vehicles passing through certain points on known human trafficking routes—logged the image of a person squeezed into a small crevice in the back of an old pickup truck.

A silent alarm was sent to both the FBI and the nearest police dispatch, and the truck was followed at a discreet distance by a drone paired with the camera mount. This unarmed drone sent encrypted night-vision video and GPS pings back to its charging base and out to nearby cell towers, which were then relayed to law enforcement with an impressively brief lag time.

Fifty miles west of the first sighting, near the outskirts of Rapid City, FBI agents swung into action staging a violent car crash scene involving three civilian vehicles, a fire truck, and two ambulances. Tow trucks lowered the smashed cars into place while crisis actors changed into torn clothing and applied makeup and fake blood. They, along with the paramedics, were all FBI agents trained for dangerous apprehensions such as this. The local police, whose cars were borrowed to make the scene look more realistic, were instructed to stand aside, and several agents who had put on police uniforms would make any direct contact with the vehicle of interest.

This elaborate ruse had sprung out of an Ambrosia Alert gone tragically wrong. A father who had abducted his two daughters from his ex-wife's home panicked after his car was suddenly surrounded by police on a highway. He swerved off the road near an overpass and the car plunged thirty feet into a river. It took two days to locate the bodies, and the nation mourned for a week.

Even the most stubborn FBI bureaucrats, not ones for changing agency policy in response to an exceptional circumstance, were now at least willing to consider less direct methods of engagement. Among several new concepts secretly being beta tested was the fake car crash ruse, and the bigwigs were anxious to see how tonight's exercise played out.

As a dozen FBI drones fanned out down the three miles leading up to the crash site, the original drone in pursuit was instructed to turn back and return to its charging station once it reached this perimeter. The central Predator Predator computer system notated a commendation for this camera/drone team pending the outcome of the chase.

Real civilian passenger vehicles began to line up and trickle through the modified traffic pattern, which had shifted over one lane so that eastbound cars drove on their right shoulder and westbound cars went down what would normally have been the wrong-way lane.

Because there were no convenient entry points along this wilderness highway, the FBI was not able to pull any faux-civilian vehicles directly ahead of or behind the suspect's truck. They would have to rely on a quick converging strike to simultaneously disable the vehicle and immobilize the driver— the latter being a very delicate process because saving lives had to be weighed against the risk of pricey civil rights lawsuits.

The truck slowed down into the traffic jam a half mile behind the crash site, and night-vision cameras sent back the image of an older man with a mustache wearing a cowboy hat. As the line of cars slowly moved forward, agents that had dispersed along the roadside for the last quarter mile kept radio contact, some observing through night-vision binoculars, others through the optics of their sniper rifles. All reported that the driver seemed calm and had made no movements toward the truck's camper.

The scene of the staged crash was filled with flashing lights shooting out and crisscrossing in all directions. Cars rolling past could see two overturned vehicles, shattered glass sparkling in the cascade of lights, and paramedics tending to passengers on stretchers and applying bandages outside the open rear doors of the ambulances. Police officers carefully directed traffic around the debris field while firefighters kept a wary eye on the wreckage.

Suddenly a flashbang sent a blinding burst of white light in front of an older pickup truck. Bodies seemed to rise from the dead as accident victims leaped from their stretchers and converged upon the truck.

A loud crash as the driver's window was shattered, then a quick slice through the seat belt, and four incredibly strong arms wrenched him out through the window frame. He was hustled away to the side of the road and placed on his stomach, the cowboy hat falling away into the dust as his hands were cuffed.

A team leader threw open the back of the truck with his weapon drawn. Directly behind him at the ready were three armed agents, a paramedic, and a child psychologist of each traditional gender. Slowly, the leader moved toward a false cover and then pried it open with a crowbar.

Flashlights poured into the void and up sat a terrified young man in glasses. He was pulled out of the cubby and a blanket was immediately thrown over his body. The psychologists embraced him, one putting a teddy bear into his hands, and gave assurances that everything was going to be all right.

The young man was slowly led away to the nearest ambulance for an on-site examination to make sure he had no life-threatening injuries. The FBI tactical team was giving congratulations, but kept its distance out of respect for the severe trauma this victim had endured. Other agents had already loaded the driver into one of their vehicles to be interrogated later.

When the EMT determined that the young man was in good health, he picked up a tablet and said, "Now, young fellow, I'm just going to scan your eye so we can find out where your mommy and daddy are."

"No, no, please," the young man said, waving a hand in front of his face.

"Don't be shy now, mister. We need to know who you are, now don't we?"

"Please, I just want to go back to school…"

"And you most certainly will, tough guy. You've been such a trooper already. Just… Come on… Let me see…"

"Nooooo!"

The young man bolted away from the ambulance back toward the truck, but several of the wounded crisis actors were standing nearby and quickly surrounded him.

"Say," a woman with fake blood all over her face and arm said, "he looks just like that guy who disappeared from *DDM TV* the other day."

A man in fireperson's gear said, "My god, you're right! *It's Luis!*"

"We found him! We found him!"

The young man could not comprehend this scene of crashed cars, flashing emergency lights, buzzing drones, and the joy that finding him had put on the faces of people who had seemingly suffered horrendous injuries. He brought his hands up to his face and collapsed onto the ground as FBI agents danced in a circle around him.

As the last traces of the post-World War II boom receded like a river in a drought, the United States was uncertain about how to maintain its power and standard of living. The chaotic scramble that followed, playing out on both the macro and micro stages, characterized much of early twenty-first-century American life, and is now referred to as the Great Free-for-All.

A costly series of dubious wars exhausted the military. Systemic mortgage fraud devastated millions of people when the lies woven into the corrupt financial sector also collapsed. Rampant abuse of prescription medications and illicit drugs put nearly half the population into a dependent stupor. Government bailouts to the tune of trillions of dollars were crafted in secret and siphoned off with no oversight. The dying healthcare Ponzi scheme was replaced by a compulsory national program whose bill Congress was not even allowed to read before voting on. Countless foreigners crossed the southern border without paperwork and were allowed to stay in the country indefinitely. And seemingly every other young woman posed nude online or had a sex tape.

Morale and morality were both in the gutter when the

rumblings of a more conservative attitude began to appear online, slowly percolating in an information war that culminated in 2016, when its shocking roar swept a protectionist political amateur into the White House. The Great Free-for-All is said to have officially ended early in 2021 when this president signed the pragmatic HOLA—Honoring Our Legacy as Americans—immigration bill into law.

In the interest of finally not looking the other way—cheap labor was simply no longer a valid excuse in a deindustrialized nation threatened by wandering jihadis and an increasingly automated workforce—both political parties made tremendous trade-offs in writing the legislation. No one wanted to risk the eternal political fallout of trying to round up and deport (what turned out to be) sixty-eight-million undocumented people from around the world who had entered illegally or overstayed a visa. This number did not even include their offspring born on US soil.

Jowls of indignation jiggled furiously during the historic late-night debates between career politicians who had sat idly by for decades, happily drinking mint juleps while American industry sank into a swamp of outsourcing and regulation due to their shortsightedness and blackmailable predilections. Young congresshumans begged them to consider how their grandchildren would actually live, rather than worry about what the biographers would say about them later.

In the end, the Rebellicans were willing to hold their noses and accept "Hopefully One Last Amnesty" if the Dramacrats promised not to unleash their army of civil rights attorneys when, as a condition of being granted citizenship, these immigrants were required to register for the National Biometric Identification Database—complete with fingerprinting, face and retinal scans, and submitting a DNA sample.

After the signing ceremony, the president wistfully suggested in a post to his skReacher account that the Supreme Court "just let this one go" so that America could keep moving forward. Cynical types believed that the Rebellican president had intentionally waited until winning a second term before biting the pragmatic bullet and passing amnesty, which might hand the Dramacrats power for years to come.

For the left-wing activists who had been stewing in their own juices since Inauguration Day 2017, this unexpected milestone proved to be a revelation that showed them a way forward. Instantly millions of people they had previously advocated for were now on the path to citizenship, and very likely to give their next presidential candidate enough votes to win the 2024 election in a landslide.

That the Rebellicans, under the auspices of creating a national voter ID system, would agree to support a citizen database, played right into the HRA activists' hands. First by collecting data that could be used to build comprehensive profiles of prospective Debtors and Beneficiaries, but also in helping to pave the way for an electronic currency which would transfer funds automatically. The days of hiding gold in grandma's mattress were finally coming to an end!

For the likes of Luis Ortega, who had been brought across the Mexican border as a baby and whose dreams were not nearly so lofty as the HRA founders', becoming officially legalized was an incredible weight off his shoulders. He would never have to fear returning home from school to find that his parents had been deported, and his aging grandfather was later permitted to come live with them in his final days.

He grew up near downtown Los Angeles, becoming an avid skateboarder and fan of the Dodgers baseball team. While not the best student in school, he spent a lot of his time working on old electronics which his father and uncle brought home as part of their scrap business. So in his senior year of high school he applied to some of the local community colleges, and when his DDM notice arrived from the HRA, Luis was already deep into his second semester of technology classes.

Luis and his family had never really been interested in what the Reparations program was about. While they did appreciate the modest monthly stipend, the Ortegas were still glowing in the wake of legalization and being able to make concrete plans for the future. Being called upon to appear on a national television show was a mortifying shock for the soft-spoken young man— his parents risked and sacrificed so much to give him the opportunities they'd never had, and all he wanted to do was make them proud.

The whole process of flying out to New York was a self-conscious nightmare he had just tried to endure. As a

Beneficiary, Luis was considered the guest of honor and found himself showered with attention by the press and fans of the show. He hid in the hotel suite until absolutely required to come out and go to the studio for filming.

When he first saw the white woman who was his DDM standing across the stage, he didn't understand why the audience was so angry at her. Later, as her ancestors' crimes against his family were announced, all he could think about were his cousins Umberto and Carlo, who had been brutally murdered four years ago by cartel members down in Juarez, Mexico. No news station reported on their deaths—just a drop in the bucket, sadly—and the police never found their killers.

He couldn't see why he had to go to Cleveland with this woman he didn't even know, so when everybody got confused after the lights went out, his feet started walking of their own accord and took him off stage.

First he went to the dressing room to get his phone, but when one of the PAs got in his face and asked if he was supposed to be back on stage, he realized that these people weren't going to leave him alone. He told the PA that the AD said he could take a five-minute break, then quickly ran out of the building.

Having grown up in a big city, Luis wasn't intimidated by Manhattan despite its endless rows of towering buildings. He was relieved to be away from all that craziness inside and strolled a few blocks before calling his parents back home.

"Oh my god, Luis! Is that you?" his mother screamed.

"Yeah, it's me. I'm fine."

"But what happened? Where did you go?"

"I think someone maybe hacked into the show. I didn't want to be there anymore so I left."

"But they're going to be looking for you, *mi vida*. You have to go to Cleveland!"

"I don't wanna do that stupid stuff. I need to get home, get back to my classes."

"*Dios mio!* What are we gonna do?"

When an APB with Luis's face was broadcast nationwide, the family realized that he would be apprehended if he tried to use any form of commercial travel. His father made a few phone calls and put Luis in touch with a man named Etienne Galvez, a retired coyote from back in the Great Free-for-All days who went by the nickname El Perro. The Ortegas wired him two thousand dollars to smuggle Luis from New York back to California.

It was during the long, uncomfortable hours hidden inside the secret compartment of El Perro's truck that for the first time in his life, Luis truly and profoundly understood the dangerous journey that his parents had undertaken. He had been too young at the time to remember any of it, and now whispered an emotional prayer of thanks to God for everything he had.

When the flashbang outside the truck jerked him out of the semi-meditative state he'd developed to pass the hours, Luis thought they had gotten into an accident. He hoped everyone was okay, especially El Perro, otherwise he might be forgotten in this hiding place. The frantic sequence that followed—his "liberation" and the disturbing spectacle of bloody people dancing all around—was simply too much to take, and he fell to his knees before blacking out completely.

11. SCRUTINY

Five days after the hack, Kate was called in to an early morning meeting of trusted supervisors. Jan pulled her aside before they entered the conference room.

"Kate, I want you to know how glad we are to still have you here with us. Could you imagine being trapped on the outside, walking around in a tool belt while all this was going on? At nine o'clock there'll be another hundred people lined up downstairs freaking out because they think their next payment won't get deposited."

"I'll be there to give assurances. And more autographs…"

"Yeah, everyone's got something to say about you after that speech you gave! Anyway, just keep doing what you're doing. But stay inside the building and be sure to have security walk you out tonight. There's just too many people on edge and a couple fist fights have broken out in the parking lot."

"Feels like three years ago all over again, doesn't it?"

"Mm-hmm." Jan shook her head. "Except *we* had the

momentum back then."

Kate and ten of her coworkers sat around a large table reviewing printouts as Jan led the conference call with one of the national directors.

"Hi, Peter," Jan said. "We're all here. What's the latest?"

"Good news and bad news," said the face on the large wall-mounted flat screen. "The good news is that the FBI has pinpointed the location of the rogue broadcast to within a two-mile radius in Wilmington, Delaware. Our techs and their strike team are coordinating a seize-and-shutdown raid as we speak."

"Okay! Get these guys before they cause any more panic."

"Exactly. But the bad news is that our code crawlers, after just a cursory analysis of twenty-four percent of MARVIN's software, have already detected—not any malware or viruses, per se—but suspicious footprints that suggest tampering in at least thirty-six HRA locations."

Jan looked down the table and waved to a South Korean-American man who was madly swiping and tapping on his tablet. "Tyler, any thoughts on this?"

"Yeah," he said, glancing up. "Peter, Tyler Cho from IT here. Is there any possibility that these red flags could have originated from a single source but were only placed in such a way as to make the hackers seem stronger than they really are? You know, to give them more leverage against us and public perception?"

Peter let out a long sigh. "Do I ever wish that were the case. It's possible. And we'll know a bit more as soon as we can get our team on the ground in Wilmington. But until then we're advising every field office to proceed under the assumption that they may have been compromised and that there could be a mole among them."

Everyone looked around the table at each other. Jan spoke up.

"Well, I can vouch for the people in this room, or else we've got a really big problem. Obviously, we won't say a word about this Wilmington situation until it plays out. Thanks for the update and trust, Peter."

Moments later about half of the cell phones around the table pinged at virtually the same time. People checked their screens, then looked over at Jan. She too had received a message and, after typing briefly into her phone, instructed the assistant who had run the conference call to bring up the link she had just sent him.

The picture on the screen switched from the HRA seal, which had appeared at the end of the call, to a news alert from channel KOTA, whose large logo swept away as a woman seated behind a desk began to speak.

"We have breaking news to report to you this morning. Luis Ortega, the *DDM TV Live* contestant who disappeared mysteriously during the show's recent hacked broadcast, was found alive and apprehended on a stretch of highway here in South Dakota. We go now to our reporter Gina Byles, who is at Rapid City Regional Hospital where Mr. Ortega is being held for observation. Gina, what can you tell us?"

"Good morning, Barbara. The authorities are being very tight-lipped right now, but the pieces of information we have appear to paint this picture: Mr. Ortega was attempting to flee his Cleveland DDM assignment, and instead return home to Southern California. But the FBI somehow caught wind of his daring escape while he was passing through South Dakota, and agents successfully conducted an operation to detain him."

"You say it was successful, but if so, why are you speaking to us from a hospital?"

"We in the media have been assured that no harm came to Mr. Ortega during his capture. Authorities say he collapsed due to exhaustion and has been unresponsive ever since. That was ten hours ago. Right now his condition is being monitored by medical personnel."

"Well, assuming that he's going to be okay, what sort of penalties do you think the HRA might impose when he wakes up?"

"That's a good question, Barbara. And perhaps above my pay grade. While some DDM contestants have been known to not give their best effort while on assignment, this may mark the first time someone—let alone a Beneficiary—has gone completely AWOL."

"Thanks for the update, Gina. We'll check back with you as the story develops."

All eyes slowly turned toward Kate after the segment ended. She looked at Jan, who was scrolling through her phone. Before anyone could say a word, the door opened and a man in a dark blue suit walked directly up to Kate.

"We need you on a plane right now. *DDM TV* has chartered the jet. You're going to Rapid City."

"What?" Kate said. "Luis might be in a coma. What could I possibly do to help?"

"The show wants a photo op of you comforting him at his bedside."

Kate was rushed to Teterboro Airport in a private car and arrived in Rapid City four hours later. Another executive car took her directly from the airport to the hospital, and as they pulled up outside she saw a large crowd of people on the sidewalk. Many were holding up posters of Luis's face or signs offering him well wishes. *Where did they come from?* she wondered.

Kate knew that social media had erupted after their episode, with discussions ranging from who was behind the hack to even picking apart the merits of her outfit and makeup. But the most peculiar development was the rise of a sort of Cult of Luis, "the man who dared to defy the HRA."

"Have You Seen Luis?" fan pages appeared and began posting the grainy images they received of young men in skinny jeans that, from the distance at which they were taken, could have been anyone. Three hundred skReacher accounts pretending to be Luis popped up overnight, and ranged from the silly to the perverted to the subversive. Some women even posted topless photos or said they wanted to marry the handsome young man.

But as the days passed with no sign of the reluctant *DDM TV* star, fears of foul play began to circulate. Could the HRA, believing that one of their own employees being sent on assignment was a bridge too far, have hired the CIA to assassinate the young Ortega? What *other* past show participants had the nation not heard from in a while?

Tabloids and entertainment digimags went wild trying to track down the nearly five hundred former contestants, updating their websites by replacing red question marks with green checks next to the faces of those who had been located. The process was bittersweet: while two of the love connections had young babies to show off—"our little peace accord," a proud DDM mother boasted of her daughter—it was found that several Debtors had actually committed suicide since their appearance on the program.

Kate could only assume that this large group outside the hospital had heard that Luis was being held here, and then raced from however far away they lived to greet him when he woke up. Would these people let him go to Cleveland or were they crazy enough to try and help him escape again?

Before she could go down that rabbit hole, some people in the crowd recognized her and started running aggressively toward the car. Kate yelled at the driver to move around whatever was slowing them down, and he lurched the car forward into the garage entrance before any of Luis's fans could harass her.

Once inside the hospital, Kate was escorted upstairs by armed guards, then entered a lobby bustling with staff, news types, and more law enforcement. As she rounded a corner she was mortified to see the shining white teeth of Ryan Richards grinning at her from down the hallway.

"Kate, darling!" he beamed. "I knew you couldn't stay away."

"Hello, Ryan," she said coolly. "I'm glad it's not me in that hospital bed. I doubt you'd be able to control yourself."

"Settle down, you tigress! And don't go committing any DEs against *me* now."

"Whatever. Let's just get this interview over with."

Fifteen minutes later they were led into a private room. Luis was at rest surrounded by soft studio lights and two camera stands. A PA was whispering into the ear of a camera operator, who made a motion toward the nurse adjusting Luis's sheets. Two chairs were brought in and placed near the bed, then Kate and Richards took their places.

"Good day," the host began softly, "Ryan Richards speaking to you at a very somber time. I'm at the bedside of young Luis Ortega, a recent *DDM TV* contestant who's now fighting for his life at a hospital in Rapid City, South Dakota."

The camera panned over and zoomed in onto Luis's face. Without his glasses or hat, he looked even more childlike.

"With me at his side is none other than Kate Donohugh, his twenty-second-degree DDM. Kate," he sighed, "how does it make you feel to see Luis lying there so helplessly?"

"Humbled," she replied. "And reflective. How many times throughout history did one of *my* relatives stand over the body of an Ortega? I'm just so thankful he's alive."

"What's the first thing you want to say to him when he wakes up?"

"That I understand he's scared. But DDM assignments are bigger than us as individuals—we have to make personal sacrifices for the greater good. And it's not just about national healing anymore. There are millions of Victims around the world watching, waiting for their chance at an equitable future."

Richards fell to his knees. "Please, Luis," he begged. "Wake up! You've got to start building those houses!"

After the interview ended, Kate was asked to wait in the reception area because several national reporters who had also flown in were interested in speaking to her. She sat down and grabbed a magazine, flipping through it absently while a wall-mounted TV replayed the interview in front of her. She was about to get up and look for something to drink, when a doctor frantically ran up to the nurses station and pointed at the TV. One of the nurses handed him a remote and he changed the channel to GBC.

Kate set down the magazine and turned her attention to the TV, where a middle-aged man in a gray blazer wearing a dark tactical helmet was squatting behind a car. Speaking into a mic, he said, "Yes, Leslie, I am here outside a warehouse on the east side of Wilmington, Delaware. We received an anonymous tip that SWAT teams were converging on the area, and as you can see, a number of armored trucks and tactical personnel are in place. Now, I've been advised to stay out of the way, but we have reason to believe that this raid may have something to do with the hack on *DDM TV Live* which rocked the nation nearly a week ago, so honestly, I would be doing the viewers a disservice by not bringing them the story as closely as possible in real time."

"Be careful out there, Brent," said a female voice.

"Wait! What's this? Looks like they've breached a roll-up door. Quick! Come on, let's follow them in!"

The picture jerked around as the cameraman ran after the reporter, merging with a stream of officers dressed in tactical gear as they entered the warehouse and fanned out. The picture blurred momentarily before adjusting to the lower light and resolved to reveal an array of computers running down a handful of long folding tables. The sound of voices shouting and metal clanking echoed through the warehouse.

The camera scanned around capturing the action and seconds later the reporter came running up. He removed his helmet and took a big breath, then addressed the camera formally.

"Brent Auburn, reporting live for GBC News, from what sources have just told me is the headquarters of a hacker group calling itself the Sentinels of Jubilee. Only moments ago tactical units gained entry and secured this warehouse. No one is here, there are just rows and rows of computers, each with the name of a different city floating around in the manner of a screen saver. I wonder what would happen if I tapped a key…"

"Hey! What are you doing?"

An officer leaped into frame and grabbed the reporter's arm before he could touch one of the keyboards.

Seconds later the warehouse wall behind them illuminated with the projected image of the same masked man who had interrupted the *DDM TV Live* broadcast. The cameraman adjusted his stance to better frame the wall, then steadied as the projected man spoke.

"Well done, government enforcers! Putting all your toys to good use. But we are still ahead of you and will now lead the way. The computers in front of you are loaded with files and footage from sixty different HRA facilities around the country. How did we get such access?

"Your techs who toil down in the boiler rooms, and who are creating this, the world's largest public works project—they have seen where your ship is headed. Members of law enforcement disgusted by the aggressive measures they are told to employ— they too refuse to keep paving this road to hell. So you see, our movement is not merely populated by disgruntled Debtors, and you dismiss us at your peril.

"For months we have spied on the supervisors, reparaticians, contractors, even some Beneficiaries and Debtors to prove the extent of our reach. Substance abuse in HRA parking lots, employees picking their noses while walking into the restroom, audio of private conversations secretly recorded on both personal and administration devices that were logged into unsecured public wifi networks. Innocent moments, embarrassing moments, and ambiguous moments that are all open to interpretation, misrepresentation, mockery, judgment, and yes, scrutiny.

"Today your ancestors may hang in effigy because of the crumbling documents that survived long enough to be scanned, but tomorrow *you* will be stored in a comprehensive 3D dossier and dissected without context or empathy by future historians, social scientists, judges, and jailers.

"Heaven forbid if science should ever perfect life extension technology or the ability to upload your consciousness—for they will all be waiting to interrogate you, poke you, prod you, humiliate you, sentence your digital avatar to the hellfire of eternal pixel punishment.

"Consider that if God exists, surely He has the decency not to watch while you defecate. We hold no such faith that this amoral juggernaut, which devours data like a crab scavenging the ocean floor for scraps, would ever show such discretion.

"We, the Sentinels of Jubilee, have done everything in our power to warn you about the dangers we all face. Keep your eyes on the screen, and in five minutes it will be *your* turn to take action."

The man flickered out and the picture switched to an elevated view overlooking an exterior parking lot. Text along the bottom of the image said: HRA Field Office – Houston. As two men holding coffee cups walked away from a car, a sophomoric voice mumbled, "So Ted, my daughter blah, blah, blah… Oops!" One of the men stumbled and dropped his cup, which exploded all over his companion's shoes when it hit the ground. The voice cackled hysterically. "Pardon my foible, bro!"

The picture changed again, this time showing the interior of an HRA office in Ft. Lauderdale. A heavyset woman sitting in an interview room tapped a female child on the bottom and motioned for her to sit down. A sportscaster's voice bellowed, "Ooh, a left cross to the backside! That right there is child abuse, my friend." "But Nick," another lively voice said, "did you not see what I saw just moments before the strike (which I have to say was not that hard anyway)? The child ignored repeated verbal requests and warnings to sit still." "Well, Ian. Guess we'll just have to agree to disagree, hyuk hyuk hyuk!"

The scene now switched to the exterior of a building that did not resemble an HRA facility. The text at bottom read: Manhattan Cancer Institute – New York. A young woman stepped outside leaning on the arm of a man. She faltered after taking a few steps. He caught her and helped steady her balance. A moment later she buried her face in his chest and he held her.

A harsh female voice broke in, saying, "Look at this cis scum flaunting their hetero love in public. Disgusting! What about the rest of us and *our* sensibilities? Central, this is Decency Warden 41-18C, reporting two violators of the Public Affection Code, requesting that you deploy Privilege Shields to this location and seize eighteen percent of their assets…"

The screen went black, then the following message slowly appeared:

Is This the Future You Want?
To Learn More Visit:
HRA.gov/Scrutiny

THE END.

GLOSSARY

Afrigro-American: American citizen descended from populations originating in the African continent, often brought to the Americas as slaves; term culturally agreed upon as of 2023.

Ambrosia Alert: National child abduction alert system.

Atonement Cream: Popular skincare product known for its soothing properties, inside and out.

Beneficiaries: Members of the Historically Wronged American class, who receive electronic payments from the HRA as compensation for crimes against their ancestors.

Bloodline Crimes: Roll call of confirmed Domination Events committed by a citizen's ancestors.

Book of Reparations: Holy text compiled by left-wing activists during their crusade to create the Historical Reparations Administration.

Burger Citizen: Popular fast food chain specializing in sandwiches, french fries, and soft drinks.

CalmTime: HRA-approved employee time off to recuperate after a stressful half-day at work.

Caucmerican: American citizen descended from populations originating in the European continent; also Cauc (slang, often derogatory).

Certified Historical Event: An occurrence verified by one or more authenticated documents, and included in the MARVIN database timeline.

Citizen Profile: Dossier compiled by MARVIN containing all pertinent personal, historical, criminal, and financial information.

Construction 4 Community: National volunteer organization that builds homes for low-income families.

D Leaves: Slang term, often used mockingly, to refer to MARVIN's monthly data analysis; for example, reading the D leaves.

Debit Score: A numerical expression based on an aggregated analysis of a citizen's historical and lifetime files, calculated monthly by MARVIN.

Debtors: Members of the Legacy Violator class, who reimburse Beneficiaries for ancestral crimes; electronic funds are deducted automatically by the HRA.

Debt Protesters: Informal term applied to Debtors who destroy historical documents in an effort to reduce their monthly Reparations bill.

Decency Warden: Hypothetical law enforcement officer used as a scare tactic during the second Sentinels of Jubilee broadcast.

DDM TV Live: Popular television program created by the HRA as a public forum to clear the bad karma from Direct Descendant Matches.

Dignity Wipe: Illegal removal or obscuring of personally identifying information from security footage recorded at the Mall of Absolution, before its required submission to the federal government.

Direct Descendant Match: Instance where ten or more Domination Events take place between two citizens' bloodlines, known as DDM.

Domination Event: Any affront between two humans, ranging from as little as verbal abuse all the way up to murder; known as a DE.

Extraction Treaty: Diplomatic alliance between the United States and other countries which enables the HRA to collect documents and funds held overseas.

Forgery Level: Metric used by MARVIN while analyzing inauthentic documents submitted via scanner.

Hail Mody: Traditional Modestian prayer seeking to bring about calm, propriety, and discretion.

History Patrol: Law enforcement auxiliary tasked with preventing the destruction of historical documents.

Historical Reparations Administration: National governing body which oversees the collection and distribution of restitution payments; known as the HRA.

HOLA: 2021 immigration law titled Honoring Our Legacy as Americans; referred to derogatorily as Hopefully One Last Amnesty.

Joint Telecom & Penal Bureaus: Recent alliance of two governmental bodies seeking to streamline law enforcement through enhanced communication, surveillance tools, and punishment; known as the JTPB.

Latiz-American: American citizen descended from populations originating in Central and South America, often of mixed Tribal and European ancestry; term culturally agreed upon as of 2022; the male form is Latizo, the female form is Latiza.

Lectrolade: Popular energy drink known for its bright colors, high electrolyte content, and caffeine boost.

Lower Income Retainer Fee: Surcharge added to the monthly bill of many renters across the country; first appeared early in 2028; known as LIRF.

Mall of Absolution: The former Mall of America in Minnesota; home to Modestianity, the religious community led by a former MARVIN team leader known as the Prescient One.

Mantra of Atonement: A popular prayer found within the Book of Reparations.

MARVIN: Macro Aggregating Restitution Vector Input Navigator; the HRA supercomputer whose analysis software calculates citizens' Debit Scores.

Mercies: Anchor chapel in the Mall of Absolution where acolytes go for temporary reprieve from their burdens.

Microscopic Protocol: Proposed variation of the current probation system, as sought by the JTPB.

Minoricans: Any American citizen not of Caucasian or Asian descent.

Noble Gent: Popular malt liquor brand, available in 24 oz cans and 40 oz bottles.

Modestianity: Modern religious sect founded by the Prescient One.

Modidas: Clothing manufacturer with exclusive license to all branded apparel sold at the Mall of Absolution.
Nifty Minutes: Weekly newsmagazine television program that reports on politics and topical social issues.

One Match Strike and You're Out Law: Strict sentencing guidelines established in 2027 to discourage citizens from destroying historical documents as an attempt to reduce their Debit Score.

Pardon My Foible: Slang expression, often sarcastic, used by teenagers to comment on a mistake or accident.

Pleasantry Station: Any number of attractions within the Mercies anchor chapel at the Mall of Absolution that enables a person to temporarily relieve the burdens of one's guilt.

Predator Predator Network: Nationwide surveillance system targeting human traffickers.

The Prescient One: Founder of Modestianity, a modern religious sect based out of the Mall of Absolution.

Privacy Shield: Hypothetical law enforcement tool used as a scare tactic during the second Sentinels of Jubilee broadcast.

Public Affection Code: Hypothetical ordinance used as a scare tactic during the second Sentinels of Jubilee broadcast.

Reparatician: Highly specialized document examiner trained to identify forgeries.
Reparations: United States law passed in 2025 that established the HRA, which oversees the collection and dispensation of compensatory payments to citizens descended from victims of slavery and colonialism.

Reparations Evading Tactical Collectors: Paramilitary force entrusted by the HRA with discretionary powers in apprehending suspects, preserving documents, and seizing assets; known as the RETC.

Reparology: Comprehensive, cross-disciplinary college-level curriculum designed to prepare students for HRA careers.

SafePlace: Sophisticated document scanners installed in home fireplaces, as mandated by the 2026 executive order.

Scrutiny State: Term coined by the Prescient One referring to his doomsday prediction of total surveillance.

Sentinels of Jubilee: Underground anti-HRA resistance group accused of hacking into the MARVIN computer database.

Sift n' Scan: Patented scanning technology and equipment installed in History Patrol drones to efficiently secure, preserve, and scan partially destroyed historical documents, usually by fire.

skReacher: Messaging app where users communicate by posting short blurbs.

S'more Stoppers: Nickname given to History Patrol drones that assist in document preservation and non-lethal suspect neutralization.

State Appointed Digital Attorney: Computer-generated legal counsel offered free of charge; known as a SADA.

Stigmatized Relics: Politically incorrect possessions from past cultural eras, often kept for symbolic reasons; their legality varies.

TapOut: Internal HRA computer program used by employees when signing in to CalmTime.

Tears: Penance-themed anchor chapel in the Mall of Absolution.

Thinkings Institution: Public policy research organization based in Washington, DC.

Tribal American: Descendant of the original indigenous populations which inhabited North, Central, and South America prior to European colonization.

War for Equity: Political movement spearheaded by left-wing change agents seeking to level the playing field for historically oppressed groups.

The Zap: Storefront in the Mall of Absolution which hosts interracial healing sessions.

Reparations
MIND

(BOOK TWO)

1. IN CRISIS

Several hours after the second Sentinels of Jubilee broadcast, HRA senior reparatician TJ Rowe tossed and turned in the bedroom of his Manhattan apartment.

David sat up in the dark and said, "Hey, what's wrong, guy?"

TJ brushed away the pillow that was covering his face. "I'm just really upset right now."

"You're overreacting. They'll catch those hackers. The HRA's gonna be fine."

"They're doing more than hurting us at work. They just humiliated a lot of innocent people. Including some of my friends."

TJ got up and put on his glasses. He took a pair of jeans off a chairback and started getting dressed. As he buttoned up his shirt, David said, "What are you doing?"

"I'm going out."

"At this hour? Want me to come with you?"

"No, David. Let me be, please."

TJ took the elevator down to the lobby and walked out onto Spring Street. A cold wind was blowing so he flipped the collar of his pea coat up against his beard.

He walked quickly and turned down a narrow side street. A cluster of neon signs glowed brightly halfway down the block on the left side. He approached, but then began to pace back and forth outside.

Finally, he put his hands in his pockets and trotted up the steps of a storefront whose sign said, "Ming's Thai Assuage — Home of the Not Guilty Ending."

A bell jingled as the door closed behind him. A petite woman arose from a white wicker chair and glided across the darkened front room. She took TJ's hand and caressed it.

"Ooh, you shaking," she said.

"Yeah," TJ said, "it's been a rough day."

"You in the right place then. Mama Ming set you up with

nice advocate. She give you good assuage, make you feel better."

"Yeah, that sounds real good."

"What kind of voice you like? Maybe high pitch like sweet princess?"

"No, no. Confident. Smooth."

"Oh, okay, haha! Lisa right girl for you."

The hostess went to the reception stand and started typing on a tablet screen. A door behind her clicked and she said, "Okay, room six. Go back, door on the right."

TJ eased down a dim hallway that had recessed red ceiling lights. Crimson lace hung in front of several closed doors that he passed. He reached room six and found the door ajar, so he pushed through the lace and entered.

"Have you been bad DNA?" a raspy voice cooed from the shadows.

"That's what they keep telling me."

A sultry Thai woman wearing a knee-length judge's robe approached. She rubbed TJ's back.

"Hello, Debtor," she said. "No, it's not your fault. So many peoples before you did all that bad things. You are so nice."

"Do you think so? Can you help me?"

"Yes, Miss Lisa expert at assuage. Just tell her what wrong and I try to make the reproach stop for you."

TJ slumped to the floor. "I'm so worried right now. My friend, she's in trouble. I can't help feeling like we're responsible for letting her get hurt."

Lisa dragged a tall, heavy wooden chair next to him and climbed up onto it, then slipped a blindfold over her eyes.

"There, there, Mr. Debtor. Now tell me, this girl you know, she is Afrigro?"

"No, that's not it. She's a Cauc like me."

"Hmm. I'm confused. How you think we can make this stress go bye?"

"Just tell me it's not too late to help her. I know she's really far away from us right now, but I have to do something."

"You such nice man. Big. Strong. You do good each day. You honor the world…"

"Yes, yes…"

"You will help this friend because you must."

"Yeah, that's the spot. Right there."

"She your friend. So she smart too. You reach out brave hand, she know what to do. She take it. Then she heal."

"So it's not all on my shoulders?"

"No! Now we make it official. I, Miss Lisa, hereby acquit you of this weight of the world."

"You did it. I feel like a new man!"

"See?" the woman said, giggling as she removed the blindfold. "Lisa always work out the deep issue."

"Thank you. Now I know what to do."

The next morning, TJ took a water taxi across the river to Newark. Through his earpiece he listened to NPR reports about the nationwide fallout from the latest Sentinels video manifesto.

"We've had sporadic reports," a broadcaster said, "of small-scale gatherings and vandalism in a dozen cities across the country. Authorities say they have been able to step in and get things under control without major incident. So, considering that we have witnessed two brazen attempts to undermine the Historical Reparations Administration in the last week, the nation remains in an anxious but hopeful state of calm…"

TJ looked at his fellow commuters. No one seemed particularly agitated. Most were holding coffees or staring at their phones—but what were they watching? Sports highlights or embarrassing clips on the hacked HRA web page?

After the taxi docked, TJ walked the several hundred yards from the pier to the HRA shuttle bus while trying to suppress his nerves.

The scene outside the megabranch looked as if it could boil over at any moment. First, the employee door he normally passed through was locked and a sign posted on it instructed everyone to use the main entrance. Out front he saw two armed National Guard troops keeping a wary eye on the nearby crowds.

Some anti-HRA protesters holding signs were chanting in a circle between the long lines of Debtors and Beneficiaries waiting outside their separate entrances. A handful of HRA security guards also stood watch, and TJ saw one angry man get firmly escorted back into line.

Once inside the building, he passed through the crowded Beneficiary lobby and took an employee elevator up to the second floor. He found half of his coworkers in tears. Some were sobbing while leaning into their computer screens—and most likely watching mortifying videos of themselves. Others were balled up in a group hug that grew sad new appendages as more people arrived for work.

TJ, freshly renewed after his late-night assuage session, stepped in and tried to cheer them up.

"Now, now, y'all," he said. "We've got to keep it together."

"Why should we?" one woman moaned from deep within the hug cluster.

"Yeah," a man on the floor wrapped around someone's leg said. "MARVIN's already been out of commission for days. And now this! How will we *ever* get back to work?"

This caused the whole blob to shudder and moan even more loudly. It slowly began to wriggle away down the hallway.

TJ watched it round a corner, then he stepped into his office. Jan was sitting on the edge of his desk. Her face said it all.

"Oh, Jan, don't tell me you're done for too?"

"No, TJ," she said. "Just really, really upset. And feeling pretty helpless. It's been a long time since I've been this low."

"May I?" TJ opened his arms wide.

"Of course, thank you."

Jan stood up and leaned into TJ's teddy bear hug. She wiped a tear out of the corner of her eye.

"We'll get it all back on track," he said. "Most of the people here have just never been tested before. They left college and immediately started working for the HRA. I bet if you and I show some strong leadership, we can help them calm down."

"I just don't know. But look, TJ. The real reason I'm in here is because I was looking out for when you scanned in."

"Of course. I'm touched you felt you could lean on me."

"I mean… Yes, without a doubt. But also, there's an FBI investigator in the conference room right now. And he wants to talk to you."

"Me? What on earth for?"

"I don't have the faintest idea. But this all got really serious as of last night. I've got a hundred things to do that are all marked urgent. So I've got to go. Do your best in there. I'll catch up with you maybe later in the afternoon."

"Okay, boss. Chin up."

"Thank you."

TJ began to walk toward the conference room. An icy chill was in the air. Ever since that first hack which undermined confidence in the HRA, it had been a struggle for the employees to believe that things would be okay—let alone put on a good face for the upset citizens downstairs or calling in on video chat. Now their anxiety had turned into near panic.

TJ had seen this shocked desperation firsthand as a child and again as a teenager, when the 2000 dot-com and 2008 Wall Street crashes chopped his parents and friends' families off at the knees. But being resilient Southerners, they'd battled through and rebuilt their lives stoically. TJ carried with him this dust-yourself-off attitude, even after moving far away and later joining the vanguard of a political movement that was vastly different from his family's politics. He may have been the outlier, but at his core their pragmatic values remained.

TJ was annoyed that the FBI wanted to interview him at a time when he felt he should be rallying his team. So he went into the kitchen and prepared a cup of coffee as slowly as possible, fully stirring in each packet of sugar before adding another. He also used the restroom before finally reaching the conference room, where a middle-aged man in a shimmering black suit was waiting with a stack of folders and two tablets laid out.

"Ah, Mr. Rowe," the man said. "Nice to see you at last. Please have a seat."

"And you are?"

"Agent Wynn. FBI special investigations. I'm on the national task force that's trying to figure out what the hell is going on with these hacks. And after last night's business, we've got no time to waste."

"I'm here."

"Now, TJ. I see that you're one of the lead reparaticians at this branch. Would it be safe to say that you know a lot of what goes on around here?"

"Within reason. You think I might be able to help catch the hackers?"

"Uh, not exactly. I called you in here privately because your name actually came up."

"*My* name? For what?"

"I don't quite know. It's just that your name came up and I'd like to give you a chance to explain yourself. You know, tell your side."

"Tell my side of what?"

Agent Wynn opened a folder and started flipping through the pages.

"All I know is that someone thinks you might be one of the moles that the Sentinels planted. Now, I don't know if that's true, and we're not running a kangaroo court here. So let's just chat."

"Listen, I'm a technician. What interests me are microfibers and using my expertise to toss out forgeries that might undermine the HRA's effectiveness. If I was working for the other side, I could just falsify documents on my own to cause problems. Do you have any evidence to suspect me of doing that?"

"Now, now. Don't get curt with me. I'm just doing my job. Something's wrong here at the HRA and they called in the pros to straighten things out."

TJ sat back and crossed his arms. "Oh, I get it now. We're the new kid in town so the big boys think they can drop in to get us to heel."

"Call it respect for your elders."

"Sir, let me tell you something. I'm as progressive as they come, but I *am* from the South. We remember Waco and that fishy business out in Oklahoma City—so don't look at me like some pushover sitting in awe of you guys at the FBI."

"You want to make me the bad guy? I've got the power here, bub. The power to clear your name so you can get back to fiddling with your ancient scrolls. And the power to haul you in to my district office and play hardball. Because this is no laughing matter! You wanna get cute with me about thirty-year-old cases? There's trillions of dollars on the line right now!

"I'm talking about the credibility of the US government, and respect for the office of the president! This goes way beyond party lines, ideology, even belief in Reparations itself. And yet you sit there smug, just like you have since the day of the first hack. Yeah, I know about you and your cavalier attitude. And still you wonder why I've got you in here."

TJ put his palms on the table. "I've simply been trying to keep my cool while everyone else got weak at the knees. Setbacks happen!"

"You know," Wynn said, "having a hard drive crash is a

setback. But someone hacking into the mainframe of your whole operation is a bit of a bigger deal, wouldn't you say? I'd like nothing more than to cross your name off my list so I don't waste any more time on a dead end. What do you say, can you work with me here?"

"Okay. Now that we're square."

"Tell me, then. Did you know anything about the hack beforehand?"

"Of course not."

Agent Wynn looked down at his papers.

"Have you ever been in contact with, or provided internal data to, any person you know to be a member of the Sentinels of Jubilee?"

"I told you, no. And you'll get that same answer from me all day."

"Noted. Alright, go run on back to your documents. But don't forget, I've got my eye on you."

TJ left without saying another word and stomped back into his office. He left the door open and spent the next hour collating a stack of old contracts that were backlogged because MARVIN remained in lockdown.

He briefly consulted with several of his assistants, then took the elevator to the ground level and left the building. He ignored the crowds outside and walked to a sandwich shop a few blocks away, ordering lunch to go.

With paper bag in hand he walked toward a nearby park, but ordered a taxi with his phone so that just as he reached a picnic table, he was able to quickly duck into the back seat of an approaching car.

A mile down the road he asked to be let out.

"But it says you want to go across river," the driver barked. "Come on, man! I thought I was getting nice fare!"

"Sorry. Here's lunch instead."

TJ dropped the paper bag onto the front passenger seat and got out of the cab. He heard the driver mutter something in Russian as he shut the door and walked away.

He turned down a side alley and dialed his phone. His coworker and friend Kate Donohugh answered.

"Oh my God! TJ! I'm so glad to hear from you."

"And do we ever need to talk. But first off, how are you?

Where are you now?"

"Still in South Dakota, unfortunately. They kept me here at the hospital overnight. Luis is still unconscious. I don't know what's going on or what they expect me to do."

"Things aren't any better back here either. It's crazy outside the office. And some suit just pulled me into an interrogation— as if *I* was one of the spies!"

"Please tell me that you're not. I just couldn't handle it."

"Hell no, I'm not in on the hack. Jesus! But that's not the only reason why I'm calling. Kate, as bad as that ordeal was, I've been feeling just awful for you."

"Thank you, TJ. I mean it."

"That they would specifically target you because you were on *DDM TV* during their first hack. And then to use that footage of you when you were at your weakest—disgusting."

"I couldn't even take Chris's call after it happened. I cried all night in this patient room they stuck me in."

"I'm so sorry. Now things are really getting nasty. Seems like everyone's swarming around us."

"It's sad but true," Kate sighed. "The best I could come up with to calm myself down this morning was knowing that they've got footage of everyone. It was just the worst possible luck that my life played into their narrative. For two weeks I was already the poster child for the HRA and that TV show—the Sentinels just took the baton and kept running with it."

"God, I admire your strength. Because honestly, I was so upset thinking about how we let you get dragged into everyone's nets without our support."

"Don't say that, TJ. I know you all care about me."

"We really do. Did you end up talking to Chris?"

"I finally called him a little while ago. He's just as mad as you are. He says I've given more than enough to everybody. Wants to take a vacation so we can clear our heads."

"So do it! It's been a hell of a year for you, take a break."

"I know, I know. It's just—for some reason I can't face him right now. There's this new feeling of doubt in the back of my mind that I need to understand. I mean, how did it all end up here like this? How did my life—which I spent doing everything to help others from the bottom of my heart—how did that turn into me becoming the object of ridicule in the middle of a political disaster? Not only is my whole life's work possibly falling apart, but some people are saying we're on the verge of a second civil war!"

"You can't put it all on yourself. You're just one of thousands of cogs in this machine that's behind Reparations."

"But that's exactly it. We're all willing cogs. We signed up for it. Like that famous line, 'We hold these truths to be self-evident,' and therefore we must do X. But I don't remember ever debating the merits and defects of what we believe. I mean, I always *thought* I was my own person, but now I wonder if there's some narrative or script that I've been going off the whole time."

"So, what? You don't think the Kate that I know and care about is the real you? 'Cause if that's the case, what can you even do to find her?"

"I feel like somehow I have to go to the source. Not to find out 'where it all went wrong,' but to know how I found myself on this path. Because what if I was just *put* on it, and there was never a fork in the road or a series of truly different options? Then every choice was just an illusion, and in the end we all got funneled to serve their agenda."

"And who are they?" TJ asked.

"I know, that's the trillion-dollar question. First asked by every tin-foil-hat-wearing conspiracy guy. And now by obedient little Kate Donohugh, the woman who dedicated her life to caring about the world. But I have to know, has somebody really been pulling my strings?"

"Kate, just be really careful going down that rabbit hole. Sometimes the person who comes back is so shook up by the new knowledge, that it would probably have been better to stay in the dark."

"I hear you. Any other time and I wouldn't go there. But this year I've been dragged through a lot of drama. I can't face the next forty years of my life blindly going off assumptions anymore. I've got to put the old me to the test and see who's really left standing afterwards. And… I think I have to do it alone."

"Then trust your gut. And don't be in any rush to come back here. People are so paranoid right now that this could turn into a witch-hunt. Or if the public loses confidence in the program… Who knows how bad things could get?"

"Good God."

"The National Guard was already out there this morning. Seriously, *do not* come back unless they force you to."

"But won't that also make me look suspicious? Am I just supposed to sit around my apartment while you're across the water dealing with all this stress?"

"I don't have the answers. All I know is that everything we've worked for is in jeopardy. Kate, I don't want our legacy to be that we only got in three good years before it all fell apart."

"I know! Somehow we've got to reestablish morale within our ranks. But how do you rebuild the trust when there could be a mole sitting right next to you?"

"This is like some episode of the *Twilight Zone*. Friends and allies turning against each other."

Kate paused. "Hey, TJ? I've got to get off the phone now. Something's going on and they need me."

"Okay. Just remember, you're the good guy here. Don't let them intimidate you."

"Goodbye, buddy…"

Kate set her phone down and turned to face the woman who had opened her door without knocking.

"Mrs. Donohugh? We need you out here on the double."

"What's happening? If they're putting me back on camera, I'll need to put on some makeup."

"After last night, I don't think we're on that script anymore. But Mr. Ortega just woke up and we'd like you to help put him at ease."

"If you say so. I don't think seeing *my* face will offer him much comfort though. This DDM has probably been his worst nightmare."

"Hey—are you a part of this team? Have you been watching TV this morning?"

"No. I saw more than enough yesterday, if you know what I mean."

"The point is, we're *all* in scramble mode here. We just had to arrest ten of Luis's fans when they tried to break in through the garbage facility. So can you just saddle up for us, please?"

"I'll be there in five minutes."

Luis's room was half-filled with hospital staff and business types, but Kate was relieved to see that Ryan Richards was not among them. The group parted as she approached the bed, and a nurse motioned for her to sit beside Luis.

Kate settled into a chair and smiled at him.

"Good morning. It's been quite a week for all of us. How are you feeling?"

"Hi, Kate," Luis said. "I'm okay, just really sleepy."

"Well, you may be the lucky one for having slept through everything else that's happened. Have they told you about yesterday's news?"

"No, they just keep staring at me and whispering. Am I really that sick?"

"Not in the least! And in fact," Kate said, turning toward the others, "do you all need to be in here? How about a little breathing room?"

As most of the people cleared out, one suit leaned in and whispered to Kate, "Keep leading him forward. We've got to find out if he's willing to go to that job site. Do your best to convince him. We *really* need a PR win right now."

The man retreated to a far corner chair and began typing into his phone. One nurse also remained in the room a respectful distance away. Kate turned back toward Luis.

"Now, have they even told you where you are?"

"The nurse said something about South Dakota. Guess I'm still a long way from home."

"Yeah. The Beneficiary-turned-fugitive. Not a good look for the HRA! I don't think the way they caught up to you is playing very well with the public either."

"I was just chilling in the back of the truck. Trying not to get claustrophobic, just thinking about getting home, you know. Then everything got crazy. People running around, sirens, lights —and now I wake up in here."

"So, Luis, that all happened a couple days ago. And yesterday the same hackers who took over our TV show sent another message. As you may remember, I actually work for the HRA, and honestly, we're hurting right now. I think all these people here want a picture of you and me in Cleveland smiling together wearing hard hats."

"Oh, no more, please," Luis groaned. "I'm missing my classes."

"But," Kate said quietly as she leaned in, "I don't really feel like doing that either. So if you keep refusing, I'll try to back you up."

The suit in the corner looked up from his phone and called out, "What are you two whispering about? Is he gonna play ball or not?"

"Sir, I don't think so. Mr. Ortega, who happens to be our Beneficiary guest of honor, insists that completing his studies is a more important priority."

"Is that true, young man?"

Luis adjusted himself higher in the bed. "I need to make my family proud. Some of them already do construction and stuff. I want to do more, get that degree in electrical engineering."

"So you won't go, huh?"

Luis and Kate both stared at the man defiantly. He turned and left the room. The nurse approached and offered Luis a glass of water. He gulped it down and thanked her.

A moment later the suit charged back in followed by an older, more distinguished-looking man. Kate recognized him as an HRA bigwig, whom she might have even briefly met at a function sometime in the past.

The suit dragged a chair to the opposite side of the bed and motioned for the older man to sit. Luis glanced at Kate. She gave a small shrug of her shoulders.

"Well, Luis," the man said, "it's nice to see you're up and no worse for wear."

"Thank you."

"My name's Joshua Gerber. I'm one of the HRA's national directors. Yesterday they flew me out here from DC to see what all the fuss was about. I was in the air when the latest Sentinels of Jubilee nonsense happened. The HRA brass didn't know whether to turn the plane around or what. But you know what I said? 'Let me talk to this brave man, Luis Ortega. Let us have a heart-to-heart and see if we can't come to an understanding.' They agreed, but from what I hear, you insist on not being a part of this great outreach program Construction 4 Community. Is that right?"

"Okay," Luis began, "I'll tell you the same thing I'm saying to all the other people. I'm in college. That's a big deal in my family. I think it's dumb to leave it and waste my time doing manual labor."

"Really now? You don't want poor kids to have a nice new home? Some gratitude…"

"If I may," Kate said. "I think, Mr. Gerber, what Mr. Ortega is trying to say is that his own family comes from an impoverished background. And pursuing this course of higher education is perhaps his own attempt to fulfill the American Dream."

"Is that the deal? And you're his DDM who works for us, right?"

"I know, it sounds like I'm speaking against our own interests. But is the HRA really about us or them? The organization or the Beneficiaries?"

"Of course it's ultimately for them. But there's more to it than one man's fate. There's public perception, for example, and right now we've got another bloody nose! The HRA has already helped his family out financially, so now he's got to do his part to keep the show on the road."

"Isn't there any way that he could continue his studies, but we parlay it so that the HRA still looks good? Show people that we have a heart?

"*Parlay*, did you say? Hmm…"

Gerber rubbed his temples for a moment, then looked up with a satisfied smile.

"Tell me, Luis. How long until you get your degree?"

"It's only an associate's, so like, less than two years."

"Okay, so if we let you defer your DDM assignment, you could fulfill it in 2030."

"You know, Luis," Kate added, "many people pursue a four-year bachelor's degree immediately after getting their associate's. Then there's master's and doctoral programs to consider. In theory, you could be in school for the next ten years!"

Gerber stared daggers at her.

"Thank you, Mrs. Donohugh. I'm sure Mr. Ortega will be able to make up his own mind about such matters."

"I just want him to know all his options. He *is* a Beneficiary, right?"

"Oh, yes. And I've just come up with an idea which might *benefit* all parties involved. Now listen, Luis. I'm happy to let you get back to your studies in California. All I ask is one small favor in return…"

2. WINED AND DINED

"Excuse me, sir?"

Clyde Jenkins felt a tap on his arm. He opened his eyes and saw the flight attendant smiling at him.

"Sorry to wake you," she said, "but we're going to be landing in half an hour. Can I get you anything else before we close up?"

Clyde rubbed his eyes. "Just a little orange juice. Thanks."

He glanced out the window at the patches of clouds scattered above the rocky, desert terrain below. He smiled. Months ago, back in the doldrums of his old life, the view from his mentor Nolan's rooftop in Newark was as far as he could see. But it had given him an inspirational vision, a new thread of hope that he followed until it manifested in the hip-hop song "Fly So High."

This single was a raw and youthful take on the frustrating reality of life for America's poorest, even several years into the nation's formal effort to atone for its colonial past via Reparations. And it had resonated with millions of people, becoming the surprise hit of the summer as it catapulted Clyde's life into the spotlight.

There was no telling where this whirlwind that had saved him from the aimless life of the streets would take him next, but for one moment, as the plane eased downward, Clyde sat back to take in the view. Because right now, he was flying so much higher than he ever imagined was possible for anyone.

After the plane landed and was taxiing toward the gate, the same flight attendant came back into the first-class cabin and leaned down toward him.

"Mr. Jenkins? We've been told that a bit of a crowd has gathered in the terminal. Your escort sent two bodyguards to accompany you as soon as you get off the plane."

"Oh, wow," Clyde said. "They want to see me in the flesh all the way out here?"

"I guess so! Welcome to Los Angeles…"

The scene at LAX may not have been as rabid as when The

Beatles passed through, but Clyde was nonetheless impressed to see nearly a hundred people crowded around the terminal exit. Some fans held up signs proclaiming their support or wishing him a happy sweet sixteen. Others proudly shook 3D-printed bobblehead dolls with his likeness.

A handful of people wore bulky metal harnesses equipped with a dozen selfie-stick camera mounts. They had been hired by fans who lived far away or were too socially awkward to leave home, but still wanted the experience of being there in person.

Hovering above the crowd were a few brightly colored QuietDrones which were owned by media outlets. Clyde waved up at them and chuckled. Just as a reporter angled to get a crack at an interview, the two towering bodyguards asserted themselves and briskly led Clyde along the barrier that held back the fans.

He came face to face with a short man in a business suit who was holding a small sign of his own. It read: "Happy (Belated) Birthday, Clyde!"

"There he is!" the man said. "The DJ himself. How was your flight?"

"How you doin', Mr. Pryor? It was a nice trip out."

"Great to hear, great to hear. But please, call me Eddie. We're gonna be good friends."

"Okay, Eddie. Sure thing. Man, this is wild."

Clyde pulled out his phone and started taking pictures of the crowd. One group had begun to chant, "DJC! DJC!" Another group responded with, "Clyde! Clyde! Clyde!"

"Yep," Eddie said, "they really love you. Did Mr. Simmons fly out with you?"

"Nah. Nolan's got a lot going on right now. He wanted to come, but since you and I are just talking…"

"No problem. Come on, let's head to the limo. Did you check a suitcase?"

"Nope. Got all I need in this gym bag."

They loaded up into the car a few minutes later. After the driver shut the doors, Eddie leaned back in his seat and put his hands behind his head. He grinned.

"I'm so glad you made it. First time in LA?"

"Yeah."

"You'll soon find out that the west coast is nothing like how

things are back east. Everything is so *constricting* back there!
People always on your ass about something. But—if I may
paraphrase you—*out here, out here,* people leave you the hell
alone if you go with the flow."

"Cool, cool."

The limo left the airport and Clyde watched with interest as
the West Los Angeles streets came into view. Everything was
packed together like back home, but the atmosphere still felt
more open. There were fewer tall buildings, for one thing. And
that bright sun shining on his face through the open window was
just electric.

"Is there anything you want to see before you get settled at
the hotel?" Eddie asked. "Want to put your toes in the sand? The
ocean's only fifteen minutes away!"

"No, thanks. I need to get a shower, take a little rest. Maybe
we do that tomorrow before I fly out."

"You're the boss! Here, have a sparkling water."

Clyde closed the window and relaxed, taking occasional
glances at the streets as the limo worked its way into Hollywood.
Forty-five minutes later they arrived at the Mondrian hotel,
where a sharply dressed concierge greeted them and escorted
them to the elevator.

"I hope, sir," the concierge said, after opening the doors of an
incredibly large penthouse suite, "that you have a wonderful stay
with us—up here, up here!"

The concierge walked off with a jump in his step. Clyde
shook his head and said, "Being famous is a trip."

"Haha, oh yes," Eddie said. "Everybody puts on a little show
for you. That guy wants to be a star too, you know."

Clyde walked to the window and looked out at the Sunset
Strip and Hollywood Hills behind it. Fancy houses sat
precariously on the edges, often with thin metal poles supporting
balconies and garages.

Eddie stood beside him and patted him on the back. "Nice,
huh? Some people work in the industry for a long time before
they can afford something like that. People you've never heard
of. Animators. Producer's assistants. But I tell ya what—" Eddie
rubbed his hands together "—you and I make a nice deal, you'll
be in one of those houses next week. And still keep a place back
east if you want."

"They look nice, no doubt."

"Throw some parties. Get the girls coming over. Just gotta keep writing hits…"

Clyde turned away back toward the suite.

"But anyway," Eddie said, skipping past him, "plenty of time to dive into that later. Get some rest, young man, and I'll pick you up at six-thirty. We've got reservations right down the street —and *then* we can talk turkey!"

The door clicked shut a moment later and Clyde was alone. He unpacked his bag and brought the toiletries into the bathroom. He brushed his teeth and rinsed his face, then plopped down onto the suite's enormous bed.

"Not bad," he said. "A bed fit for a king."

Clyde closed his eyes and thought about the upcoming evening. First a dinner meeting with Eddie, then a chance to explore the nightlife. See how the LA scene compared to places like Chicago and Atlanta, where the clubs had made him their darling. Little old Clyde, who'd never been on anyone's guest list, was now being comped ornate bottles of liqueur in gated-off VIP sections.

And the girls! No more pleading the neighborhood sisters for attention—they all wanted him now, even the really fine ones. But anytime he felt himself about to lose control and get swept away into the party life, his sister Myra's words of warning echoed in his head. *Don't get no girl pregnant.*

And she would know why. Knocked up at sixteen with Tyrell by a guy who Clyde barely remembered. Then Octavius got her pregnant two years ago. But at least he came around more often, even threw Clyde some odd jobs before his song blew up this past summer.

But it was really Nolan who helped Clyde keep his wits. He did give Clyde a wide berth at first, when the world suddenly opened up and it was hard to tell who was more starstruck—the fans for Clyde or vice versa.

Nolan accompanied him on trips to the big cities, keeping a cautious eye as Clyde soaked up the glitter of being the man of the hour. Sometimes Clyde ended up doing an impromptu live rendition of his song, and his spirits soared when the audience sang along with the chorus.

But one morning in September, after two days of hard

partying in Baltimore, Nolan somehow got into Clyde's suite and put his foot down. First, he told the girl in Clyde's bed to get out. When Clyde protested, Nolan poured him a cup of coffee and told him that play time was over and he should get dressed.

As annoyed as Clyde was to see What's-Her-Name with the curly hair leave, he always trusted Nolan to look out for him, so he didn't say anything and got himself ready. Nolan drove the rental car out of the nice area where they were staying and crossed over into a crumbling part of town that looked just as bad as some of the streets back home in Newark.

All Nolan said during the next hour, as they passed block after blighted block, was "Mm-hmm" and "You see?" Clyde nodded his head, because he did see. The song that had made him famous wasn't about him—it was about the people in broken-down areas across the country who lived his message: that Reparations was not achieving what it set out to do.

At one point, Nolan stopped the car at a dingy intersection and they looked around. An old woman shuffled down the sidewalk while pushing a mesh cart with a misshapen wheel. Trash and dead branches clogged a gutter grate. Guys in layers of sweats smoked cigarettes and moved from one boarded-up storefront to another. And a small makeshift memorial of glass candle, flowers, and a picture frame lay tipped over next to a stop sign.

When an HRA mini-drone came into view and hovered over the intersection like a hummingbird, Nolan tilted his head toward Clyde and raised his eyebrows. Clyde nodded. Nolan put the car in drive and took him back to the hotel.

After that Baltimore trip, Clyde found that Nolan was less and less available to act as chaperon when he traveled. But he had gotten the message, and made a point of meeting up with locals in small groups, talking to them, listening to their stories. He absorbed their praise of his song humbly and with gratitude, and found that in the evenings he didn't want to party so much anymore.

Because he had work to do. A responsibility to these people. And a new song to write.

But even after refocusing, Clyde still struggled to find a message as important as the one in "Fly So High." It wasn't even that he was afraid of being a one-hit wonder—that was a common fate in this era of instant downloads and short attention spans. But the world was actually listening to what an everyday Beneficiary had to say right now, and DJ Clydoscope did not want to squander that opportunity. Nolan often reminded him of this, and the responsibility weighed on him.

After waking up from his nap, Clyde showered and put on his maroon suit. He looked at himself in the mirror and was impressed—but couldn't help wondering if he really deserved all that Eddie Pryor was offering. This top-tier agent had a roster of professional artists that made Clyde feel way out of his league. But Eddie had been very persistent over the past month, so Nolan agreed that Clyde should at least listen to his pitch.

"Worst case," Nolan had said, "it'll open your eyes a bit more. Best case, you get to take your message big time for real."

The limo arrived promptly at six-thirty and drove them west down Sunset. The early fall twilight gave Clyde a taste of what Saturday nights on this famous strip must look like, but for now it was mostly the dinner crowd that was out.

They pulled up to a row of restaurants about a mile away from the hotel. There was fancy Italian, a sushi joint, and a brewpub with a wood-fired oven. Eddie led Clyde down the sidewalk to a place whose logo featured two capital *R*'s sitting back to back. The front of the building was brick accented by shiny brass.

As they entered, Clyde could see through the dim lighting several dozen glowing teal tubes made of frosted glass. They were spaced evenly throughout the entire establishment, from the lobby to the dining area and back into the kitchen.

A skinny man, whose jet-black hair had a green streak down the middle, glided toward them. He adjusted the keychain zipper at the top of his faux-leather shirt and beamed.

"Welcome to RestauRoom! Do you have a reservation?"

"Yes, we do," Eddie said. "Under Pryor."

"Oh, but of course! We have a private booth over in the corner, just as you requested. Follow me, please."

As they entered the seating area, Clyde saw one of the tall neon tubes swivel open. A man stepped out, and the glass closed again as he walked away.

And when Clyde's party reached their booth, the tube right

next to their table also opened, and again someone came out. Clyde watched as this woman made her way to the other side of the dining room, where she sat down at a table and joined the conversation.

He turned to the host. "What's up with all these sliding doors?"

"First time here, sir?"

Eddie patted Clyde on the back. "Visiting from back east."

"Oh, my! Welcome, then! You are in for a real treat. RestauRoom is the world's first and only all-accommodating, gender-inclusive dining establishment. We have facilities for thirty-four different pronouns, plus three rotating tubes over by the bar for wandering genders."

Clyde pointed to the monolith of curved glass beside him. "So this is a toilet right here? Next to where I'm supposed to eat?"

"It was the only way. This ain't wide-open Texas, cowboy. Between high real estate prices and limited space here on Sunset, we had to utilize absolutely every square inch. Retrofitting was simply out of the question, so we hired the legendary Toronto designer Elephon to bring our vision to life. Xe did a fabulous job intertwining the layout, don't you think? Efficient and elegant!"

"It doesn't smell bad, at least," Clyde mumbled.

"Don't be silly! Each chute is equipped with an eight-stage air filter and Bose noise-canceling technology. Belize me, what happens in tube, stays in tube!"

"So how do I know which one to use?"

"You see those girls walking around carrying shooter trays? Find one of them, order a shot—if you want, that is—and they'll help you locate the cubbyhole which best serves your current gender."

"I think he gets it," Eddie said. "Let's have a seat. Thank you."

Clyde settled into the round booth and surveyed the restaurant. He saw a man exit the tube beside the reception station and immediately shake someone's hand. He looked over at Eddie.

"You like this place?"

"Oh yeah! My clients come from *all* walks of life. And

RestauRoom has the facilities to meet their needs. As I like to say," Eddie added, tapping the glass tube beside him with a large gold ring, "the teal seals the deal!"

A moment later, this door rotated open and a woman with shaved head and giant purple ear gauges poked her head out.

"Sorry, sorry," Eddie said. The door closed again.

"How's the food here?" Clyde asked.

"It's excellent. The best!"

"What do they mean when they say this?" Clyde looked down and read from the menu, "Diversify your digestion with our ethno-fluid entrees."

"That just means they have it all, pal. You want free-range chicken, they got it. Fair-trade tofu, no problem. *And* they use separate preparation areas in case you're allergic—divided by a wall of peanuts, of course, hahaha! Just kidding, oh boy…"

"I'll probably just have a burger."

"Ahhh, here we go, right on time!"

A server had arrived with a bottle of champagne. After she poured their drinks and withdrew, Eddie raised his glass and smiled.

"A toast to the rising star. DJ Clydoscope, may all of your wishes come true!"

"Cheers, Eddie. I appreciate all the effort you're making to show me a good time."

A few minutes later, after they'd ordered their dinners, Eddie brought his fingertips together.

"Okay, young man, here's the deal. Your song, it was brilliant. As if in that golden moment of inspiration, you were touched by the hand of God. But—can you do it again?"

"I hope so," Clyde said. "I plan to."

"How long has it been now? Three, four months? What else have you written? Most guys who make it have at least a few other decent tracks ready to go."

Clyde looked down. He said, "The old ones aren't so good. I'm trying to get the lyrics right for the next song."

"Clyde, we're losing time here. With every week that passes, your window to seize on this momentum shrinks. By January people will be like, 'Clyde who?' You've got so much potential to springboard to the next level right now. We can't let it go to waste."

"I mean, I'm close. Kind of. Maybe another month, I'll be ready."

Eddie stabbed at his ice water with a straw.

"How would you feel," he said, "if I told you I've already got it all set up? Five tracks completely written. A studio at my disposal, day or night. And videographers on call. We could do this thing tomorrow!"

"Five songs? About what?"

"Oh, you know. The HRA being crap. The president being a failure. How much you love your family and hate to see them suffer."

"My family?" Clyde drew back in his seat.

"Yeah! Heartstrings stuff. But not just that. My stylists can mock up a whole new look for you—wardrobe, hats, jewelry, everything. Hey, do you like Bekki Triage?"

Clyde nodded. "She aight."

"Great!" Pryor said. "We could have you two walk down Rodeo Drive together. Maybe you even give her a peck on the cheek—it's okay, she'll be in on it—and our photographer will send some pics over to *TMZ. Then* DJ Clydoscope will get that promotional boost that only Eddie P. can deliver!"

Eddie grabbed his champagne and sat back against the booth, smirking as he gave a firm nod.

"Hold on," Clyde said. "I respect that you know how to make singers get big. It's a honor being here with you. But what does me flirtin' with Bekki have to do with my music?"

"Clyde," Eddie said, "you've been the male version of Cinderella for a little while now. The poor boy from New Jersey —the upstart, the mystery man. And Bekki is hip-hop *royalty!* This rumor of a fling will cement you as a force to be reckoned with. And right then, we hit 'em with your next track! In fact, we've got a timely little ditty that I even helped to write. It's called 'Non Compos Presidentis.' Eh?"

Clyde wiped his mouth with a napkin, then exhaled.

"I get it," he said. "You're trying to take things to the next level. But this is my actual life, Eddie. I'm just Clyde, you know? I found the people—or they found me—because what I did was real. It was genuine, from the heart. But acting like I have a famous girlfriend or singing another angry song just because? I don't know…"

Eddie shook his head quickly from side to side, then said, "How can I make you see what's there for the taking? You're gonna be at thirteen million downloads by the election. Drop the new track dissing Jeffries-Lao next week, and you'll sell a million copies out the gate! It's time to cash in on the people's rage. Come on."

"But it's so much bigger than me." Clyde gritted his teeth. "My people need more than rage. Things got to move forward. 'Cause you know, the government already gave us money, so what's more of that gonna do?"

"Clyde, Clyde. That's all well and good. I love your idealism, believe me. But we've got to think about your image. The DJC brand was built on a special kind of anger that's not blind, but righteous! Don't go soft on me and we can make this work."

" 'Go soft,' that's funny. Everything's about image, isn't it? The *impression* of who you are and how people react. Playing a part. Like the pissed-off Beneficiary, right?"

"That's what got you here." Eddie shrugged his shoulders. "And it's my job to read people's minds. I've been in the business long enough to have my finger on that pulse."

"Then why didn't you just cook up someone like me in the lab six months ago? If you already know what's up?" Clyde raised his eyebrows.

Eddie squeezed his hand into a fist and shook it. "Clyde. You erupted like a volcano out of the ocean and created a whole new island. It was a beautiful thing. But now my job is to populate the place and bring in the tourists. So unless you've already prepared a ten-year business plan that maps out your character arc…"

"Ten years? I can't think that far ahead. I don't even know what kind of inspiration I'll find at the beach tomorrow."

"My man. Here's some real talk. Every day, five million would-be artists also have their moment of inspiration. They snap a nice picture or record a homemade track, and then they throw it out into the ether. Guess what? It just floats away and fades into nothingness. To be a star with lasting power today, you need more than a dream or even a plan. You need a fully scripted identity!"

"I *do not* follow you," Clyde said. "I mean, you want to hire some ghostwriters to try to recreate my vibe? Yeah, I kinda get that. But what's up with trying to change me into something else?"

"Okay, buddy," Eddie said with a sigh. "We're getting in deep now. Maybe I shouldn't tell you all this if it's gonna burst your bubble, but if you want in on the biz—"

"Well, that I don't know. I mean, I've been havin' a good time since the summer. But like you said, I'm a new island."

"Let's pick it apart, see if you can absorb this. Here's how my world operates. You know how royal families arrange marriages to create alliances and keep up appearances?"

"I guess, maybe," Clyde said.

"Well, here in entertainment we do a similar kind of thing. Why? Because we're not just selling movie tickets! It's also celebrity lifestyles, the drama of their relationships and breakups, even their scandals. The sad fall from grace followed by the touching moment of redemption—all caught on camera for the world to see. We're talking clicks, page views, magazine readership, TV specials. We're getting people hooked on a star's brand as loyal customers for however many decades they're in the business."

"Wow..."

Eddie waved his arm across the table slowly.

"Celebrity cosmetics, clothing lines, end-of-life memoirs, all of it. You see, the side hustles pay for the big show! But the best part of it is this. Remember that concierge at the hotel earlier today? He and all the restaurant staff right here, they're banging their heads against the wall trying to figure out how to break in. And you! You just appeared like the Virgin Mary bestowing miracles on the masses. And yet from what I hear tonight, you're thinking about walking away on a technicality? Because your art has a message? That's crazy talk!"

"Well, maybe you don't know who I am then," Clyde said. " 'Cause if I'm miraculous like you say, maybe I have a bigger mission in life than being some pretty boy."

Eddie threw his hands up. "Clyde, I flew you out here because I like you. And my team wants to work with you. If I dropped too much knowledge tonight, I apologize. I don't want to scare you away. But I do want you to take the next step, whatever it may be, with eyes open. I can't be responsible if you have a mental breakdown three years from now because this whole deal wasn't what you expected it to be. Heh, you aren't supposed to freak out until *after* you turn twenty-one anyway…"

Clyde took the napkin from his lap and folded it neatly. "Mr. Pryor, thank you very much for the dinner. I think I'll go back to my hotel now."

"Oh, come on!" Eddie pleaded. "No hard feelings. But this is the Sunset Strip! Don't crash out on me, please. We've got a VIP table set up over at Club Fortuna."

"Man, I don't know. This is all getting to be too much."

"Clyde. Give 'em one hour. Some of your fans paid a pretty penny for that access. Have a little taste of what fame from coast to coast is like. No more talk about business, I promise. I just want to make sure there aren't any blind spots when you fly home."

"Alright. I'll check it out."

"That's the spirit, kid! Do you need to take a leak before we go?"

Clyde looked around the dining room from tube to tube, then smiled. "Nah… I'll just hold it til we get to the club."

"Saturday night! Hollywood! DJC in the house!"

Eddie drained his cocktail and flagged down the server.

3. THE SENTINELS

The group sat in near darkness. Two dim lamps created silhouettes of the eight men seated around the room.

The man sitting at a desk near the shaded window broke the silence. "Nine days since we announced ourselves to the world. And none of our operatives have blown their cover."

"Here, here," a voice from across the room called out.

"Now, it's three weeks until the election. New polling indicates a tightening race which the president will still likely win, so tonight we will discuss our action plan leading up to Election Day. We've already established back-channel contact with both campaigns, but beyond that it's up to the voters. Now, gentlemen, what's the first order of business?"

Another man rose from his seat and approached the window.

An outside light cast soft yellow across the edge of his face.

"Congressman," he said, "first let me offer my utmost respect for everything you've put on the line to be a part of this movement. The word 'courageous' might be used too often when a politician crosses party lines, but in your case it rings very true."

"I appreciate your kind words," the man at the desk said. "Please continue."

"When we found each other one year ago, coming together from all walks of life, our common bond was concern for the direction our country was headed. From our respective high perches, we saw lethargy and demoralization creeping across people's faces.

"Whichever way you look at it, this was a bad trend. Bad for business. Bad for our children. Bad for morale in the military. Reparations, which sought to rectify one thing, was in fact creating an enormous new tear across the fabric of this nation.

"And so we joined forces—not as a cabal or to pull off a coup —but in an attempt to take the more noble aspects of the Reparations sentiment to a more mature level. We have scored two major victories on the world stage this month, so perhaps now is a good time to assess where we are."

"If I may?" a new voice said from one of the armchairs.

"Please do, Admiral."

"My assets have been able to assemble over twenty thousand military veterans from around the country to help keep an eye on the situation. I'll admit, reports are that some of these guys are in pretty bad shape. Many were recruited from homeless encampments, in fact. But overall, they seem ready and willing to help keep the peace should things get out of hand on Main Street."

"Thank you," the man at the window said. "Who's next?"

A man seated at a small table rapped his knuckles against the surface. "Sales are down," he grumbled. "And they've been down across all industries. Who the hell wants to buy a sports car when people will look at you with suspicion for enjoying it? White or black, it doesn't matter."

"Here, here!"

"I don't care who wins the election. We need to work with whoever's president to get business moving again. Retail sales for the Holy Holidays are going to be atrocious this year. And yes, I know other factors contributed to this slump. Automation, AI, and people just holed up playing with their gadgets. But I swear, the HRA has thrown cold water into everyone's face, and people are not spending a dime because they're so tied up in knots. We gotta fix this."

"Absolutely," the congresshuman said. "Rest assured that I have been quietly discussing the economy with several of my trusted colleagues on both sides of the aisle. And when the dust settles on this election, I plan to make a passionate speech on the House floor echoing these sentiments—if not explicitly, then in words that a Dramacrat would be expected to use."

"That's all I ask. For more of the same teamwork that's gotten us so far and shocked the world already."

A man in the far corner of the room cleared his throat. "I would like to say a few words."

The man at the window stepped back into the darkness and said, "You have the floor, Your Prescience."

"Thank you. While I may not have been among your ranks this whole time, I feel that I've gotten to know you quite well over the past several months. I'm honored that you would tap me to be the... face, as it were, when announcing the existence of the Sentinels of Jubilee."

"And our judgment was validated by how well you've carried yourself. Particularly during the live broadcasts. Your mask added to the mystery, even if you wear it for your own reasons. We're all holding our breath in anticipation of your next speech."

"In truth, that is why I asked to be heard tonight. I believe that most of what needs to be done to push back against the HRA now rests with the people. They must take back control of these tools which were supposed to make our lives easier, but which have instead enslaved us to the multi-tasking treadmill.

"But until that existential declaration begins, I don't see how anything else I might say would be of use. Therefore I regrettably must use this occasion to announce my retirement from active duty, and to return to my own obligations as religious leader."

"Just like that, huh?" a man who so far had not spoken groaned. "What are we gonna do for a spokesman if he leaves?"

"Remember," the admiral said, "we have all respected the

fact that anyone who serves can only give what they are able to."

"I know, I know. But I don't understand how *he* in particular can bring himself to walk away at just this moment. Your Prescience, MARVIN is your brainchild—is it not?—and the government stole it from you. But by working with us, you've been able to take back the reins!"

"First," the Prescient One said, "I still have my own organization to run—"

"As do we all."

"And while I will neither confirm nor deny whether that operating system is my creation, the bigger point is this: the cat is already out of the bag on the idea that massive databases can enable punitive worldviews to grow to terrible proportions. It goes far beyond MARVIN now. We're too late to stop it by years! I truly hope you gentlemen are able to put your diverse experience in business and politics to good use as you try to steer the transition. But my most relevant abilities would go to waste as a technical director."

"But what are you going to do?" the man pleaded, rising from his chair. "Just wander off and live out your days in that old shopping mall?"

"I assure you that it would be impossible to return to my former life unaffected. This unique group has taught me to take my position more seriously. I promise to do my part to meet you in the middle someday soon. We all have profound work to do. Mod bless you."

"Come on, Prescient! Don't get mystical with us right at the end. We love you, buddy, and I know that Scott is in there somewhere buried under that getup of yours."

"Now, now," someone called out. "How much has he had to drink? Jesus…"

"I'm just saying, we've worked side by side but still he won't trust us enough to show his face without some sort of damn prosthetic spackled on. We're *all* complicit here. It's just, he's done an incredible job and I hate to see him go."

"This use of familiarity," the Prescient One said, "I will accept as camaraderie after serving on this secret mission together. But the Sentinels' major offensive is over, and in victory you can now map out the occupation. I have my own priorities to attend to, so forgive me if I cannot yet join you in such casual talk. Until that day, thank you one and all."

A short while later, after the meeting had adjourned and the men waited for their drivers to pull up the gravel road, the admiral felt a tap on his shoulder.

"Excuse me," the man in a long cloak and wearing an eggshell blue mask said, "I recall you saying that a number of the military veteran Sentinels are not well?"

"That's correct. Broken down bodies neglected by Veterans Affairs. Spirits thrown under the bus and crushed by the family courts. A lot of substance abuse and despair during cold nights with nowhere to stay. Thank God we've gotten them out of the shanty towns, but I doubt they'll be of any use to us tactically."

"If I may, I would like to extend an offer of a comfortable place for some of them to recuperate."

"That's very generous. But... this isn't some Modestian recruiting tactic, is it? I don't think it would do them any good to live inside that mall of yours."

"You have my word that this invitation is strictly humanitarian. Consider it a parting gift to the Sentinels. I own several properties which have been converted into convalescent homes. It would be an honor for these warriors to find some comfort after all this time out in the wilderness."

"I do appreciate your gesture. Let me make some inquiries and I'll be in touch. Ah, it looks like that's me here. Take care of yourself."

The two men shook hands and the admiral got into the back seat of a limousine. The man in the cloak watched the car drive off, then looked up at the starry night sky that was so vibrant above this isolated country estate.

After arriving at the commuter airport and embarking on his jet, the Prescient One removed his costume. Moving into the bathroom, he next took out the patterned contact lenses he habitually wore to defeat biometric cameras.

He looked at his unvarnished face in the mirror. Just another man of forty. A few wrinkles. Some stubble. More bags under the eyes than one would want to see. But the Prescient One had great responsibilities, and was under added strain trying to juggle his role as religious leader with his more recent membership among the Sentinels.

During his absence from the Mall of Absolution, which had been explained to the congregation as a spiritual sabbatical, he gave weekly sermons by video. Meanwhile, the church's high-ranking members oversaw life at the Mall.

Even prior to the first Sentinels hack, these leaders had told him that the church's ranks were starting to swell—but after that fateful initial broadcast on *DDM TV Live*, hundreds of people spooked out of their wits by the masked man's message began to arrive seeking asylum. The church was simply not equipped to handle such an influx of refugees without its leader on hand.

And though the Prescient One had not wanted to leave his post with the Sentinels until after the election, the fact that his own speeches on their behalf had put this pressure on his church, strongly influenced his decision to return home now.

As he settled into the divan on his private jet, the Prescient One wondered how long it had been since someone last addressed him by his formal name. Scott Cullen. Who the world first came to know in 2010 when he released *Thor's Tablet*, a revolutionary video game which merged all the hallmarks of fantasy lore into a modern setting, complete with real-time data gathered from cameras around the world.

This massively popular game vaulted him out of dorm-room isolation and into the arms of nerdy Comic-Con girls, as well as online fashion models whose nose for money and fame overlooked his awkward mannerisms. Several years of running with that beach-and-booze crowd served to smooth out these personality quirks.

But then, wealthy beyond his ability to spend and all partied out, Scott changed focus in time to be a prime mover in the blockchain revolution. Whereas the general population got caught up in the cryptocurrency craze looking to make a quick buck, he was obsessed with the technology's underlying premise: decentralized, permissionless information that was impervious to the kind of corruption that had enabled the Pentagon to lose track of trillions of dollars without being held accountable.

His wisdom and experience served as a beacon for people creating their own blockchain-related businesses and products, when public awareness about the technology reached a tipping point in 2019-20. Meanwhile, the prime targets of blockchain's amoral wrath—government, military, and financial institutions—

could only resist for so long. And when the American Mortgage Brokers Association later announced its intention to go "full blockchain," Scott officially declared victory and embarked on another yearlong partying binge.

Sometime during the winter of 2022-23, after he had returned from a Scandinavian backpacking expedition, he received a meeting request from a delegation of Dramacrat politicians and grassroots activists called the Colonial Amends Committee. Always up for new ideas and opportunities, Scott readily accepted. Not only did this meeting help refocus his mind on work, but one of the group's professional members sold him on their pitch.

"You've gone from cashing in on heroes and princesses," the man had said, "to battling the real-life dragon of systemic corruption. And yes, even though a lot of everyday people got rich following your lead with the cryptos, the truth is that many others are still hurting out there. Are you ready to work on something revolutionary that will help them?"

And so Scott Cullen began working on what would later become the main tool of the Historical Reparations Administration. He was hired as project leader with full supervisory powers, but soon found that operating within the government's hierarchy entailed much different nuances compared to life in the private sector. Gaming and cryptos had always been fueled by an almost standoffish, but still good-natured sense of one-upmanship—and that competitive atmosphere led to major breakthroughs that came at light speed, but often at the expense of feelings.

Scott sensed while working on Project MARVIN that programs stemming from a socially conscious viewpoint appeared to be less goal-oriented, with ample time being devoted to situational pulse-taking to ensure that everyone felt equally appreciated along the journey.

This agonizingly slow and inefficient process of patting everyone on the head resulted in numerous coding errors that later had to be fixed by the most competent techs. Delays and missed deadlines were a matter of course.

Everything came to a head for Scott in the summer of 2025. He and his development team were reviewing the latest system capabilities for several administrative types who dropped in every so often, when a seemingly innocent question about the program's termination date came up.

One of these bureaucrats paused momentarily before saying that she didn't foresee it ever ending. "If we have such a complete database, what would be the point of ever shutting it down? MARVIN will know everything, right? He can be the Alexandria Library on one hand, but also with the power to comprehensively judge. Besides, it's not like bad people have stopped committing crimes, right?"

Scott was so stunned by this unwitting admission that he could barely ask a follow-up question, let alone articulate the terrifying implications of what they were about to unleash. In the sleepless nights that followed, he began to understand how this idealistic accounting project would inevitably become a monolithic tool of vengeance, which lashed out blindly without context or other sympathetic considerations.

He foresaw that even as restitution milestones were reached over time, the system itself would never feel the human satisfaction that justice had been served. The insatiable bots would crawl on and on, perhaps going so far as to deduce more crimes within the scope of reasonable doubt when they ran out of clear-cut evidence to prosecute.

Scott went through the formal channels to voice his fears. But with the government so close to fulfilling this main campaign promise of the nation's first female president, not only were his cries of warning ignored, he was in fact forcefully removed from the project. Then a coordinated series of hit pieces against him appeared in the media. He was called "insane," accused of being a "closet racist," and the final verdict was that "this former tech wunderkind probably fears his own family's sordid past being uncovered."

Had he been younger, or had the project been closer to his heart, he might have fought back to defend his reputation. But that eagle's view which the highly successful tend to attain told him it was better to recede while he pondered all of the ramifications—rather than to simply send off a series of whiny posts on social media.

With an open heart, Scott retreated to his cabin in Colorado and contemplated the meaning of his life within the context of the macro events playing out. These meditations proved to be the seed of what blossomed into a new religion called Modestianity. He then christened himself as "the Prescient One" and dedicated his church to serve as a shield for people alienated by modern life.

This message proved timely, and the Prescient One began to grow such a large following from all walks of life, that he drew down on his fortune and paid cash for the entire former Mall of America complex. Abandoned in 2022 due to economic conditions that had wreaked havoc across the entire retail sector, the Mall had been both playground and war zone for Somali gangs until its sale to the church in 2026.

These Modestians moved into the enormous facility and went about removing graffiti, bleaching out blood stains, and laying the groundwork for the breathtaking American Mecca that it soon became. Two years later and Modestianity was a fast-growing religion that boasted nearly two hundred smaller chapels around the country.

This all gave Scott Cullen solace at the end of a roller coaster ride which had forced him to endure disgrace, cost him his identity, and nearly pushed his country to the brink of anarchy.

The plane landed at the small airport near St. Paul where the Prescient One owned a hangar. With his face fully cloaked, he quickly transferred into the church helicopter that was waiting, and was soon airborne once again. A short while later, when the Mall of Absolution came into view, he rubbed his hands together with glee.

The chopper touched down on the rooftop helipad. As the door swung open and the Prescient One stepped out wearing fresh makeup, several emissaries and proponents ran up to greet him.

"Ah, Your Prescience," they fawned. "We have missed you so!"

"And I as well. Tell me," he said to an emissary as they passed through sliding doors, "how have you all comported yourselves?"

"Most honorably, sir," the man said. "You will be so very proud of how we have maintained order in your absence."

"So, no power struggles to fill the void?"

"Heavens, no! That you would even consider the—"

"Now, now," the Prescient One said, giving the man a pat on the back. "Just a little gallows humor after so much time on the outside."

They took an elevator down to the lowest level. The doors opened onto his private sanctuary, a room where thousands of blue pieces of fabric dangled from the ceiling.

"You see," a proponent said, casting his arm out, "we've left everything as it was."

"Ah, my lovely vines! How wonderful."

The Prescient One rushed into the thicket and disappeared. The proponent chased after him, saying, "Not to spoil your private homecoming, but word has gotten out regarding your return. The people are eager to see you. Perhaps you could make an appearance this evening?"

The Prescient One poked his head out of the fabric. "Boo!" he shouted with a laugh. "My, my. Please do forgive my folly. But it feels so good to be back in my nest. As to your question, I had already planned to give several formal addresses this week. But yes, I am happy to make a brief speech later."

That evening the main amphitheater was thronged with thousands of chanting members from all stations within the church—access had been granted randomly by instant electronic lottery. For those not lucky enough to attend in person, the event was broadcast on the many large video screens located throughout the Mall.

Several prominent members made introductory remarks, then trumpets heralded the Prescient One's return. He wore a magnificent blue cape whose fifteen-foot train was carried by half a dozen female novitiates. His face was painted silver. Tiny blue fish descended from each eye.

The cheering of the crowd was overwhelming. For people who had joined the church recently, this was their first time seeing the Prescient One in person. There was, however, no way of knowing who among the many crying tears of joy were new members or old.

"Greetings from an old friend," he began. "I know that the messages I sent during my sabbatical did not have the electricity of the real experience, but it is clear to me that all is well here at home. It is a testament to you and the church leadership. I salute you all!"

The audience responded warmly as he turned and bowed to the hundred church officials also on stage.

"Perhaps you sense a more serious tone from me tonight. I

have returned from my journey a better man. Reaffirmed and more focused than ever. But I cannot take the next steps alone. I say to those of you who once came here seeking respite from the madness of this world, are you ready to apply the teachings you have absorbed?

"Because now a fresh wave of techno-refugees has arrived, and they are in worse shape than you ever were. Prove yourselves worthy of the shelter we once provided to you, by extending a hand to those now desperately in need of solace. Go out into the corridors lined with cots, or the fields of tents and RVs, and offer them food and a kind word.

"Whether you have taken formal vows or not, the Church of Modestianity has faith in you to assist your human brothers and sisters. Because this is not simply about recruiting members to our ranks—Modestianity exists today because there was a pressing need for a philosophy that looked at the present in order to face the future, rather than looking backward for guidance today.

"And while you rise to the challenge of this task, in the coming weeks and months our church shall also embark on a critical new mission. Because my recent sabbatical bore the fruit of an elegant vision of how to shine our hopeful rays across this nation which is in such pain.

"But that is all yet to come. Forgive me if I must retire so soon, but my odyssey was long and arduous. Be patient, attend to your duties, and I promise that in time your faithfulness shall be rewarded.

"The Church of Modestianity is strong, from the emissaries on down to the lay members, because of you. Whenever you honor yourself through circumspect behavior, you send a healing breath into the world. Each robust discussion about how to protect human dignity within the technological maelstrom, helps to forge the body of wisdom that is the foundation on which our religion will rise ever higher.

"It stirs my soul to not be forgotten by my acolytes. Your faith in me renews my commitment to honor you through good deeds and forthrightness. I will always strive to use my gift of prescience as a guiding light, so that we may thrive in the sweet spot between pride and humility.

"It brings me joy to finally say this in person once again. Mod bless you!"

4. GLOVES OFF

Selected excerpts from the presidential debate held at Indiana University on October 18, 2028.

Moderator: Good evening. I'm Tad Hauer, host of MBC's *News Burst*. Tonight we conduct the third and final presidential debate between Dramacrat incumbent Eileen Jeffries-Lao and Rebellican challenger Victor Dominguez. First, we will hear a brief opening statement from each candidate. Madam President, we start with you.

Jeffries-Lao: Thank you, Tad. It has been my greatest honor to serve as President of the United States. While there was much fanfare made about my gender and race during the previous election, I sincerely believe that our most significant achievements have taken place in the years since that historic victory.

The establishment of the HRA was truly a landmark moment in American history. It signified a turning point in the maturation of our nation's soul, when we finally found the courage to face our deepest historical wounds. And looking forward, perhaps the HRA can serve as a shining city on a hill—if I may paraphrase Ronald Reagan—as the concept of Reparations inspires other nations that also have imperfect track records on race.

We've already done so much, but in many ways we've only just begun. So despite the recent setbacks, you can rest assured that my administration will continue to lead the charge. Re-elect me on November seventh and let's finish the job.

Hauer: Thank you. Mr. Dominguez?

Dominguez: Ladies and gentlemen, for those of you who have followed my campaign or watched the previous debates, you might be surprised to hear me going a bit off script tonight. Sadly, the truth may be that the Rebellican Party nominated me in the spirit of past challengers like Bob Dole, Walter Mondale, and John Kerry. Candidates who were thrown into the ring to put on a decent show, but who in no way were actually going to win.

And today, that same network of Washington insiders doesn't want me evicting this incumbent and her team. Why? Because the president hasn't been in town long enough to reward all of her donors with favors!

But after the truly disturbing events we've seen these past eleven days regarding the security of the HRA, one thing has become clear to me and my trusted advisers. Beneath the Dramacrats' eternal good intentions, there has been a dangerous failure of leadership which cannot be allowed another risky four years in power. Whether you agree or disagree with the HRA, it is a massive program that has already sprouted many roots—and it is clear that the president is not capable of running it securely, transparently, and—dare I say—equitably.

Our nation suddenly finds itself on the brink of disaster due to the latest in the Left's seemingly endless series of Utopian experiments. This too threatens, in the end, to make everything worse. Thus I, Victor Dominguez, lowly first-term senator from Arizona, who many people wrote off as the Rebellicans desperately pandering for Latiz-American votes... I hereby declare my sincere intention to go for the knockout punch on Election Day!

Hauer: Our first question tonight does indeed touch on the HRA's recent troubles. Mr. Dominguez, if elected, what would be your plan to right the ship?

Dominguez: Let me first state this for the record. While most of my Rebellican colleagues did not vote in support of the HRA three-and-a-half years ago, I have no intention of disbanding the program. If I'm elected president, the first thing I would do is shore up security, both on the human and digital fronts. It's a disgrace that this centralized database of all Americans' information could be vulnerable to any hack, let alone the terrifying spectacle we've just seen. Like my plumber father, I will get down and dirty if that's what it takes to clear out this mess!

Beyond that, the negative sentiment that was festering among some Caucmericans, and which has now boiled over into this renegade group called the Sentinels of Jubilee... We must seriously consider whether the HRA is functioning as advertised, as well as do more testing and analysis before we decide how to manage the program moving forward.

Rest assured that as president, I will not take any rash steps without consulting both parties, policy analysts, and of course, the American people.

Hauer: President Jeffries-Lao, your response?

Jeffries-Lao: Yes, thank you. After months and months of just going through the motions, tonight we finally see the real Candidate Dominguez that was hiding behind the facade. Less than three weeks before the election and he springs the ultimate flip flop. Tell me, sir, who are you? No, better yet, tell the American people! Because how can you say that you won't make any rash decisions, when you've just pulled this Jekyll and Hyde on us here tonight? Frankly, I'm nervous what you might do with your finger on MARVIN's power switch.

Now, let me be clear. I take the recent troubles at the HRA very seriously. Right now, as they have been doing for the last eleven days, our technicians are working with the FBI and DHS to seal every leak, isolate every rogue actor, and bring the criminal Sentinels of Jubilee to swift justice.

Frankly, I can't believe the petty and shortsighted attitude of all these HRA critics who have popped up in droves, seemingly overnight. Only four years ago, our nation was united in the glow of defying the odds to create perhaps the most tectonic civilizational shift towards good in one hundred seventy-five years. Have we forgotten that everything in life requires fortitude to get through the gritty day-to-day process? Did Eisenhower shut down construction of the national highway network because one tractor got a flat tire? Did FDR abandon the Hoover Dam project because a worker broke his leg?

My goodness, folks. Skeptics may think that I'm so passionate because my name and legacy are forever tied to the HRA, but in my heart I'm thinking about the millions of Beneficiaries we've helped here at home, as well as future Beneficiaries around the world waiting anxiously for their governments to follow our lead. In three weeks, do the sensible thing and re-elect me to finish the job.

Dominguez: It's funny. We have a Chinese-American president overseeing and cheerleading for a program that does very little for people of her own ancestry.

Hauer: Now, now—

Jeffries-Lao: There he is, Jekyll and Hyde. I wonder how big *his* Reparations checks are…

Hauer: Please! I insist that we move on to the next question. Senator Dominguez, despite what the headlines might suggest, there's more going on in America than all things Reparations. The economy continues to sputter forward, with seemingly every new breakthrough followed by a pullback. So far, you've campaigned on a policy of embracing innovation while ensuring a safety net for the less affluent and less skilled. Does the as-of-tonight Candidate Dominguez have any new thoughts on the matter?

Dominguez: Haha, well… Yes and no.

Hauer: Do tell.

Dominguez: During my two terms as mayor of Flagstaff, I was committed to welcoming small businesses that were tired of being seen as a blood donor by fiscally irresponsible states bogged down in the swamp of debt-ridden pension plans. This policy was a net boon to our city and state. Plus, it put those Dramacrat strongholds on notice that there was an alternative to their overpromise-and-tax mentality.

In addition to my pro-business approach, I have always been aware of the delicate balance between innovation, acclimation, and obsolescence that characterizes the flow of progress in a capitalistic society. Prior to this century, workers could often expect their field of expertise to be relevant throughout their working lives. But the exponential disruption we've witnessed since 2000 makes it almost impossible for everyday people to achieve the stability necessary to live out the American Dream: homeownership, stable communities, and meaningful work.

Still, we cannot risk stunting the creative spirit that bursts forth across the country. Sacrificing the innovative spark for comfort is not the answer. So if the president wants a taste of the new me, I believe that concepts like Reparations, when taken too far, reveal an alarming truth about the Left. As if their core philosophy could be defined as an obsession with dividing up the contents of the pantry equally among all people, but at the same time completely ignoring the need to produce, adapt, and grow in preparation for the future.

Hauer: Thirty seconds…

Dominguez: Yes. The Dramacrats have long championed welfare and universal basic income as ways to protect the most economically vulnerable among us. I would also like to propose grants or setting up campuses for people born with the fire to create, so that their contributive abilities and visionary skills are not stunted by the drudgery of rote education, or even monthly bills if necessary. The nation—if not humankind itself—will surely benefit from unleashing these great minds.

Hauer: Interesting proposal. Sort of a genius career track, or something like a sports league's development system, for lack of a better metaphor. Mrs. Jeffries-Lao?

Jeffries-Lao: He's thrown so much out there, where do I begin? I assume his mention of underfunded pensions was a veiled jab at my home state of California—as if we haven't all borne the brunt of that across the nation. Nearly two dozen states have had to take similar benefits haircuts over the last decade.

And when Senator Dominguez found yet another opportunity to cast doubt upon the HRA, I have to ask where this concern has been during the past eighteen months of the campaign? Are there any *other* programs he suddenly disapproves of, and might move against as president?

Finally, I think his little "genius academy" idea is great—although it might already exist. It's called the wonderful American public school system! Where children of all races and economic backgrounds get the best education the world has to offer. Senator, if you want to privately fund this pet project, be my guest. But don't tangle the practical concept of UBI with your unspoken prejudice against our schools and their thousands of wonderful teachers.

Dominguez: Madam President, I have to hand it to you. Not only are you able to draw out my deepest secrets, you then twist my words so you can pander to the bloated teachers unions—many of which took a hit to their own pensions, I might add.

But wait, please! Let me continue. The fact of the matter is that our approach to education has been obsolete for decades. If you want to keep the elementary and university systems intact, fine. But my goodness, study after study points to the fact that imprisoning our adolescents and teenagers in the upper-middle and high school grades is perhaps the biggest cause of dysfunction, repression, crime, and unfulfilled potential across the country.

If we want any chance of keeping pace within this perpetually disruptive economy, as well as competing with other countries, for heaven's sake, unshackle our students from grades eight through twelve. They're already learning about what interests them on their phones, so why not—instead of just letting them roam free, as I'm sure the president would accuse me of advocating—offer apprenticeship tracks, so that these kids can learn the ultimate skill of focus? That crucial ability can then be applied to any number of passions after the apprenticeship ends.

Jeffries-Lao: May I get in a few words?

Hauer: Quickly, please.

Jeffries-Lao: Thank you. If this is all so important to my opponent, why has he never presented legislation of this kind in the Senate? I need not mention that his three children attend private school.

Dominguez: As did your daughter.

Hauer: Mine too, if that helps either of you score points. ... Madam President, so far we've mostly talked about the HRA and other issues in terms of the big picture, government entities and whatnot. But at the end of the day, this all boils down to real people. To use a rather crude but popular phrase, what do you say to Americans who right now are glaring at each other from opposite sides of the spreadsheet?

Jeffries-Lao: I want all Americans to know that I understand if they're feeling frustrated. If you're a Beneficiary, maybe things in your neighborhood haven't started to turn around yet. And to Debtors struggling to find a job but still forced to pay into the program, I truly sympathize. While I support the HRA's mission with all my heart, I'm not among those fringe groups that see it as a hammer of retribution. Reparations means restitution. Nothing more, nothing less. If exploring ways to help Debtors bridge the gap makes sense, perhaps my opponent can draft legislation to this effect when he's back in the Senate next January.

Dominguez: You've got to admire the president's confidence. In the six days since the Sentinels of Jubilee's second broadcast, we've seen demonstrations in thirty cities. Congress has received tens of thousands of phone calls from citizens who are scared about the safety of their personal data, as well as their children's future under a program which, in all honesty, now seems destined for failure.

With the election still weeks away, we've just seen how a lot can happen very quickly. Maybe you'll soon discover that I, and not the incumbent, am the right person for the job.

Jeffries-Lao: That was quite the cryptic remark, Victor. Does the senator from Arizona know something that the rest of us don't?

Dominguez: If I did, it would only be the latest in a succession of surprises that keep blindsiding this administration.

Hauer: I'm going to jump in here and stop you both before things get really ugly. It's time for closing statements, sixty seconds each. Senator Dominguez, you have the floor.

Dominguez: When my family came to this country fifty-eight years ago, the landscape was different in so many ways. Still, the bedrock American values of hard work, faith, and family remain. But it is now clear to me, that the founding of the HRA may very well have started a cascade of unintended consequences that pose unknown dangers to us all. Instead of harmony, we see a conflict brewing between people bent on revenge and those who nurse resentment in their hearts. The prospect of this bad blood getting out of hand could be disastrous for everyone.

When you vote for me on November seventh, you're telling Washington that you demand a more sensible policy when wielding this or any other bureaucracy. Because the stability of our nation may depend on it. And giving our children a chance to fly without tethers demands it.

Hauer: And now to you, President Jeffries-Lao.

Jeffries-Lao: I could, but I won't stoop to telling some heartfelt family anecdote in hopes of scoring cheap points. My record—first as a school board member, then as a state representative, and finally as a governor—is what put me in the White House. And it is your belief in my ability to succeed, despite all obstacles put in my way, which will send me back to Washington with a mandate not to let up, not to take my foot off the accelerator—and to fulfill the HRA's mission! Thank you, good night, and may God bless the United States of America!

Hauer: This concludes the third and final presidential debate of the 2028 campaign. Thank you both, President Eileen Jeffries-Lao and Senator Victor Dominguez. And we'll see you at the polls on November seventh. For MBC News, I'm Tad Hauer saying good night.

5. THE DISCOVERY

Kate Donohugh had taken TJ's advice and stayed away from work. Not only that, she didn't go back home to Brooklyn at all.

She tried her best to explain to Chris why she needed some time alone, and if she sounded unconvincing, it would be fair to say that Kate also didn't fully understand the reasons. But she believed everything that had happened to her this year was for a reason, so she had no choice but to follow the thread and discover what life was trying to tell her.

Kate especially wanted to prove the Sentinels' masked speaker wrong for suggesting that she had been brainwashed. She thought that revisiting the site of her political awakening might be a sensible place to start investigating—meaning that she'd have to make her way from South Dakota to Boston.

The hospital where she was staying slowly drained of its mobs of law enforcement, government bureaucrats, and *DDM TV* fans now that Luis Ortega had woken up. He too would soon return home to Los Angeles after passing some final medical tests.

Kate was told that she was free to take one of the charter flights headed back to New York, but then would be on her own getting to Boston. By chance while passing through a lobby packed with media, she recognized one camera crew's call letters as being from Boston and asked them if she might catch whatever flight they were taking home.

Some negotiations followed, with Kate ultimately agreeing to give the reporter an exclusive one-on-one interview in exchange for the ride. To her relief the questions were mostly softball, and she arrived in Boston on Saturday evening feeling like she'd taken one small step toward PR redemption.

The first thing she did was meet up with several old friends from college. They sang the night away at a karaoke bar, then ate brunch the following morning. A wave of bottomless mimosas helped to wash away the worst of Kate's South Dakota-induced anxiety, and after leaving the restaurant she felt ready to begin her quest.

She first planned to spend the afternoon quietly reminiscing on the Boston University campus, breathing in the crisp fall air as she strolled among the trees and old brick buildings, before sitting in on some classes the next day in hopes of gaining insight into her past. But when she arrived, Kate came upon a chaotic scene that was nothing like what she had envisioned.

Thousands of people were gathered in the common areas and marching around the walkways in support of the HRA. Speakers with bullhorns cursed the Sentinels of Jubilee while railing in defense of Beneficiary rights.

There were wild costumes and manic dance circles. Other people held up signs with messages such as "Free MARVIN," "Our Debt is a Badge of Honor," "United Cat Ladies of Non-England," and "Come On, Eileen!" And somewhere in the crowd a group was chanting, "Hey, hey, ho, ho, the SOJ has got to go!"

One of the speakers, a gangly white man in his late twenties decked out in jean vest and candy-striped pants, very much resembled Bjorn, the first guy Kate seriously dated after joining the world of activism. Bjorn had come from a well-to-do family, did the social justice circuit for ten years, then bowed out to fall back on his roots. The last Kate had heard, he was married with two kids and worked at a private law firm in St. Louis.

Today's speaker was riling up the audience with wild fist pumps.

"…and of course the scourge of whiteness," he was saying. "As if a devilish philosophy which operated virtually unchecked for hundreds of years would just roll over in one night. Ha! Who were we kidding? We really shouldn't be surprised that these so-called Jubileers would try to bring down the program that's finally delivering long-overdue Reparations.

"So you can't run and hide! You've got to stand up and fight back in this almighty tug-of-war for power. Because right now it's five hundred years to three. We've still got a lot of work to do to make things right. And that's why we've gathered here today —to rise up in solidarity! People of all shades, genders, and backgrounds coming together to fight for equity, to fight for the HRA, and of course, to ensure the re-election of our greatest champion, Eileen Jeffries-Lao…"

Kate walked on. At one point her path was blocked by several weeping students who were rolling around on the ground. Above them stood a weathered man in Tribal shaman costume who somberly waved a smoking branch while praising the spirit of "Soaring MARVIN." Kate worked her way around this piece of performance art and came upon a beret-wearing Latiza dressed in all black who was giving an impassioned speech.

"We tried to do it their way," she said. "Some might even say the right way. But it didn't take long for Debtors to sabotage the program. Should we really trust these Sentinels to honor their word? I say no! Should we believe that this presidential administration, which allowed the HRA to get so blindsided in the first place, is up to the task of fixing this mess? Again, I say no!

"So what can we do? What we must! There are still millions of documents out there that need to be scanned. And billions, if not trillions of dollars that still need to be turned over to their rightful inheritors. But hear me out, because I'm not calling for any kind of direct violence. We don't want all those trigger-happy NRA types to start shooting us from the bushes, now do we? We've got to be smart, just like those Sentinels.

"Tragically, the ballot box wasn't enough. But the bullet will only get a lot of us killed. We've got to create a new vision for what the word 'revolution' means in the twenty-first century. So please, join us for discussions on the commons every afternoon between now and the election. We at the Future Dream Collective have no choice but to go back to the drawing board to find a way to assert our voices with power, should the unthinkable happen and we enter a post-Reparations world.

"You still don't think it could happen? I'm sorry, but Victor Dominguez is a Latizo-in-name-only. We all know that as president he'd side with the anti-HRA forces and shut it down. So you see, we're backed into a corner with no true advocates to rely on anymore. Win or lose in this election, the responsibility rests on our shoulders to take back what is rightfully ours. Are you ready to forge Reparations 2.0?"

The crowd roared its approval. Kate kept moving. She looked over the tables covered with political pamphlets and literature. This was the type of gathering she'd been to a hundred times before—but today she just couldn't get into it. Instead she felt numbly distant from these HRA allies who, if they'd noticed her, would surely have commiserated and offered her words of encouragement.

But the instant Kate realized that it was very likely someone in this crowd would recognize her, she wanted to be as far away as possible. She did *not* have the strength to be thrust forward again and have to give any sort of speech.

Kate hastily bought a Che Guevara scarf from one of the vendors and tied it over her head, then hunched forward and slowly pushed her way through the mass of bodies. At last she got free and hurried away. She took one last look back at the spectacle and felt torn by the mixed emotions of apathy, pride, and dread.

Afterwards, she simply could not see herself going back to attend any lectures. What she really needed was a break from everything.

Kate called her parents down in Northern Virginia and asked if she could stay with them. This proved to be exactly what she needed—to fall into the arms of their unconditional love within the comfort of her childhood home. Just a few days spent marinating in this rejuvenating elixir refreshed Kate so much that, on a whim, she decided to reach out to her beloved former principal Mrs. Olney and see if she might be allowed to visit the school. The woman was delighted to hear from such a distinguished alumnus and insisted upon escorting her around personally.

So it was on Thursday, exactly one week after her whirlwind flight to South Dakota and the subsequent Sentinels of Jubilee broadcast, that Kate arrived at Washington-McKinley High School in Arlington.

She buzzed at the armor-plated front entrance, then gave her credentials and leaned in for a retinal scan. The door swung open and a police officer in full tactical gear waved her in. He silently led her from the lobby into a side hallway, with eyes alert and one hand resting on a hip holster.

"Oh, hello there, Kate!"

A woman in bright red pantsuit had popped out of a nearby doorway and was approaching quickly. The officer peeled away without a sound.

"My goodness, look at you. All grown up!"

"Thank you, Mrs. Olney. You don't look a day older than at my graduation."

"Why, thank you. The kids keep us on our toes, and I guess that makes me feel young."

"I do remember some of us being little terrors, myself excluded of course."

"I'm sure of it. Now, you said on the phone that you were trying to solve a mystery. What exactly is the problem, and how can I help? Please, sit down."

They had entered a private office past the reception desk and now took their seats.

"You see," Kate began, "I've been trying to track down where the 'me' that you see today came from. Where that all began."

"I don't quite follow. Surely you're a collection of your family, your classmates, life experiences, and—if we did our jobs—maybe you remember some of us as more than just regurgitators of textbook lessons."

"Of course! That's exactly why I'm here, in fact. My high school years were wonderful, but I have to admit that not long after going away to college, I began a bit of a wild streak. Maybe even using politics as a cover for partying, at least in the beginning before I got serious about activism."

"Oh, that tends to happen when you're on your own for the first time. We do our best to provide a controlled environment here. Help shelter children as long as possible from the bad influences that might derail them. But please, go on."

"Well, after you put it like that, I don't really know what more to ask."

"No bother then. But let me give you a little tour of the building since you've come all the way back here. Maybe it will jump-start your mind."

"That would be lovely. I'm curious to see if our field hockey team record of most goals in a season still stands."

They got up and exited through reception. Mrs. Olney first took Kate past the trophy case, then said, "So much has changed since you were here fifteen years ago. Once we were able to drop the name Lee, that's when things really started progressing."

"I remember hearing about that name change."

"Seemed only fitting to replace him with President McKinley, haha. Anyway, since we're about to pass the gymnasium, I'll show you the ingenious little setup we have there. To encourage physical activity among these digital monsters, we've got VR headsets programmed with all kinds of games to get the kids moving."

Kate watched as thirty students in yellow spandex suits jumped and ran and flashed their hands across a large open area while participating in both solo and group virtual sports. One girl, who was walking directly toward them, stopped abruptly and threw one arm up high with a big smile, then after several seconds lowered her arm and strutted away.

"Drum majorette," Olney said. "I'm surprised the software's still in there considering that we ended the football program back in 'twenty-four. For safety reasons, of course."

Kate next followed the principal across the main foyer into the library.

Olney said, "I'm so excited for you to see this! The kids, with the help of local HRA liaisons, have taken it upon themselves to add our collection to MARVIN's pipeline. Look, right there."

She pointed to a chrome HRA scanner that was in a corner rotunda. One student fed papers into its left-side collection port, while another sat at a nearby table slicing the binding off of a book.

"Volunteers," Olney said. "They get extra credit for helping upload these volumes. Working their way forward from oldest to newest."

Kate nodded. "I'm surprised you still have so many books made of actual paper. Will they recycle the ones they're scanning in right now?"

"Oh, no. We have a fancy machine that rebinds them, then it's back onto the shelf. You can't be too careful about keeping extra copies around, because you never know what one day might be considered an inconvenient archive—especially now! But pardon my…"

"It's fine, Mrs. Olney. You're doing a wonderful job here. What else can you show me?"

"Well… Do you remember the art teacher Ms. Herron? She's a bit of a star in her own right around here."

"Of course I do! She was a real task master, but we all excelled under her guidance."

"Indeed. She's still here whipping her little army into shape.

Let's drop in on her class and see what they're up to."

Kate and Mrs. Olney slipped into the back of a classroom that was dark except for a large LED screen at the front, and a small lamp on the lectern nearby.

"All art, like all ideas," the woman leading the class said, "is a weapon. But within each warhead is a seed. Because why go into battle and achieve victory if you end up leaving the land barren?"

The image of a hand holding a paintbrush appeared on the screen.

"This—and not a gun—is the most powerful weapon a person can wield. Why? Because the gun can only strike fear, coerce behavior, and kill. But the implement of artistic expression is a more subtle conqueror. As subjective ideas enter the minds of the target audience, each hair of the paintbrush snakes its way through their psyche, cleaning out the old beliefs and leaving fresh new concepts in their place.

"What? You don't believe that something as innocent as a painted canvas could be used to manipulate, redirect, or demoralize a population? Allow me!"

The next image to appear was a news website screen capture of an article titled "Modern Art was CIA 'Weapon'."

"Look at that right there. *The Independent* out of England, dated October of 1995. This article was the first to reveal—or admit—how throughout the Cold War, our own government funded the Modern Art movement to counter Soviet propaganda. But of course, our own people were exposed to these works as well.

"Now, consider the change that occurred in art from one century to the next. Look at these magnificent nineteenth century landscapes of the American wilderness. Some of these massive paintings are fifteen feet tall and twenty feet wide! Notice the attention to detail in every tree. They are masterpieces of realism!

"Compare that technique with the twentieth century works of Jackson Pollack. Utter devolution! A child, or a horse kicking over a bucket of paint, could achieve similar results. Yet Pollack's works were promoted around the world—and as we now know, not due to merit alone, but also by the hidden hand."

A sequence of movie posters and pop culture images cycled

through the screen as Herron continued. "So you see, it's everywhere. In all forms of art. The world war for your mind. Where the directors are the generals, the studios are the munitions factories, and the actors serve in the infantry. And for a long time—until about thirty years ago, when high-speed internet and digital cameras eliminated the need for costly materials—until then, we were all at the mercy of what the centralized powers wanted to show us. They told us not just what to believe, but even what to think about.

"Here is an article documenting how our own Pentagon has provided production assistance and made script recommendations for hundreds of TV shows and films. This is why, when people go on about the separation of church and state, I retort by saying that we should also keep the government's hands off of the arts.

"But when you realize that all art is political, you understand that governments are just trying to win the game. And therefore *you* have to play by those rules too."

A photograph of a mirror appeared on screen.

"Yes, you. The days of painting for enjoyment, or sculpting merely to bring something aesthetically pleasing into existence, are over. Why? Because you are the change agents in a war where the fate of the world is at stake. I know it seems like a heavy burden, but you should be thankful that you can do your part simply by using an illustration program on your computer. Would you rather be carrying a rifle and a hundred pounds of gear through some jungle? Thankfully, you *don't* have to kill anybody—only bad ideas.

"Now, normally I would say that in turn, nobody is trying to kill you. But after all that has happened in the past couple weeks with these Sentinels of Jubilee hackers, I fear that we may really have to fight to protect all the progress we've made this decade.

"So we as artists must use our vision to ensure that at the end of the day, a government program is not all we rely upon to determine the success or failure of our philosophy. It takes changing hearts, minds, and even pigment to achieve lasting victory. So everyone, grab the paint cans which I have set out on your tables, and join me as we fulfill the promise of the revolution!"

The screen came alive with a sensual cinematic tribal ritual.

Percussive dance music played as scantily clad bodies writhed against each other in torchlight. Ms. Herron raised a toddler's plastic pool above her head triumphantly, then placed it below the screen and beckoned her students forward.

One by one, silhouettes rose from their seats and approached, pouring quarts of paint into the pool while their teacher danced and swayed, stirring the different colors together with an enormous wooden spoon.

"Oh, yes!" she moaned. "The future is ours! Blend, blend, my precious proteges. Dump it all in and stir, stir them together. Oh, Keanu…"

Kate waited in the hallway while Ms. Herron cleaned herself up after the class ended. The paint ritual had gotten a little out of hand when she'd fallen into the pool and almost pulled a nearby female student in along with her. As the kids walked past her, Kate noticed how young they all looked. *These are some heavy ideas to be putting in their heads,* she thought.

But Kate and her classmates had sat through similar lectures back in her day, though perhaps not with the same wild theatrics. And there had been other teachers that were as passionate about the underlying philosophies of life as they were regarding the actual subjects being taught.

"A pan-comprehensive curriculum facilitates a fully integrated, trans-hierarchical society," Kate remembered one world history teacher as having said—or something to that effect. It sometimes took so many hyphenated slogans to encapsulate the whole progressive message, that even Kate had to smile while trying to keep up with it all. *Well, as long as one's heart is in the right place...*

The classroom door opened and out stepped Ms. Herron in all her glory: the large head of flat-topped, pepper-gray hair, thick-toothed smile behind burgundy lips, and green eyes made vivid by thick black eyeliner.

"Katie, oh my God! Did you just see all that?"

Kate gave her a hug and said, "It's so great to see you. It looks like you haven't lost a step in all these years."

"Shush! How old do you think I am? And anyway, you know me. An undulating priestess gathers no moss! So, what brings the world famous Kate Francis—excuse me, Donohugh—back to our hallowed halls?"

As they began to walk toward the teachers' lounge, Kate said, "Since I gather from the lecture that you're familiar with what's happened to the HRA, I'll get right to the point. Honestly, this whole situation has knocked me way off balance."

"How so?" Herron asked.

"I mean, I've talked about this with my husband, and had plenty of time on the plane to think as well, but I just can't shake the doubts and get back to work. So I don't know what I'm doing —searching for answers, or maybe some sort of affirmation that I'm really okay."

Herron motioned for Kate to enter the lounge. "Ah, so you've come back here as part of your journey. How fun! What's the verdict so far?"

Kate sat at a round table while Herron prepared coffees at the counter.

"On the surface," Kate said, "everything seems fine. Mrs. Olney even showed me how the kids in the library have bought into our mission and are scanning away."

"Mm-hmm."

"And you. Still a legend at taking seemingly random data, then synthesizing it into powerful ideas for the kids to digest and create new connections of their own—"

"Just like the warhead I speak of in my lectures," Herron said. "A plow clearing away the detritus in their minds, then planting new ideas in the ripe, freshly turned soil. Ah, yes…"

"But what if," Kate said, slowly stirring her coffee, "what if your students aren't quite ready at that age to have their minds blown?"

"They seem perfectly mature to me. Especially considering how much data they all consume pretty much from day one."

"But is it your place to sweep away everything they've been taught up until now? Say, by their parents or earlier schooling? Don't you worry that these ideas might send them down a path that they otherwise would never have taken?"

"But it was always there," Herron said with a wave. "I just held up a lantern at the entrance to, let's say, promote awareness of the path's existence. And besides, these kids I teach have had other art teachers before me. Think back to learning the basics of drawing and painting in the early grades. They were planting seeds too. About how to see the world, what art does to people. On and on…"

"Maybe so," Kate said, "but is anyone mentally equipped at age fifteen to make such a momentous, perhaps irrevocable decision? I mean, one day they're just trying to figure out trigonometry, or their raging hormones, and then boom—a teacher anoints them, not simply as future leaders, but as change agents. That's quite a responsibility to be assigned out of the blue."

"My goodness, Kate. Haven't you been living the bold life of an advocate for many years now? Has it not been the most fulfilling ride to see your good deeds reverberate throughout the world?"

"Ms. Herron, you know I have. And with more impact than most. But who authorized me to change the world? What qualifies me to impose my political views onto others?"

"If *you* aren't qualified to lead and help the less fortunate, then I truly don't know who is."

"I'm certainly able to do it now, but that wasn't always the case. It's as if one day at college a switch just flipped. Suddenly my mind activated into this persona that on the surface embraced progressive values, but underneath was more like a robot. Reciting the programmed catch phrases, doing all the right activities, and even wearing a sort of group-approved uniform. But what if I never actually wanted to do any of that?"

Kate felt her eyes well up and looked down in embarrassment.

"Now, now," Herron said. "It's okay to self-analyze, but you're already in pretty deep, Kate. What else would you do? Leave all the Beneficiaries on the side of the road to fend for themselves while you go pop out a bunch of kids? Ah, yes, the old cop-out and pop-out…"

Herron chuckled to herself and toyed with the lip of her coffee mug.

"You never had children of your own, right?" Kate asked.

"No, all of you are my legacy. My sacred crops, exported around the world, each year spreading these fruitful ideas far and wide."

"And do many of us come back to visit you?"

"Oh, some do," Herron said. "Now and again. But the

important thing is that they're out there doing the good work. Look at you, for example. I couldn't be any prouder than seeing what a force you've become for the HRA—and especially in knowing that I played a hand in stirring up that inner fire that has driven you this whole time."

Kate brought a hand to her forehead.

She said, "And I have marched all these miles for you obediently. To think that I entered your classroom hoping to gain an appreciation for art, and maybe to learn how to sketch… But I walked out of there as part of a sleeper cell, just waiting for my mission at some future date."

"Hmph!" Herron bristled. "I always stated it explicitly: All politics is war. All art is political. Therefore all art is a weapon of war. Don't wilt now at the first sight of your own blood. And please don't act as if you were fooled or betrayed."

"But the young mind sees these things as a kind of performance," Kate said. "Or hyperbole, at least. We're all taking in so much information about life and the world during those years. It should all just blend in, like your paints. But with teachers like you, something else lingered… took root… and it never left."

"Yes! That was my seed! I've been trying to tell you that the whole time. Forget the artists, forget the paintings. This war is a *dream* responsibility, an *honor* to fight in. How dare you get us so close to victory, and now think about bowing out or undermining the mission just because you took a little shrapnel on live TV. You want a Purple Heart for your trouble? Fine! But really, you should be thankful to end up stacked in an unmarked mass grave, if in your dying moment you know that your life was given to win the sacred War for Equity."

Kate began to shiver. She rose from the chair and absently slung her handbag over her shoulder.

"Thank you, Ms. Herron," she said softly. "Your words have been very instructive. I think I'll go home now."

She moved toward the doorway and Herron stood up behind her.

The woman said, "Get back out there, Corporal Donohugh, and make us all proud. Hail victory… Hail equity…"

Kate crept out of the lounge and slunk down the hallway as the woman's cackles echoed behind her. A soothing series of notes chimed, then a torrent of students poured into the space around her. She looked at their young faces, so bright and hopeful with shining eyes, then ran into a bathroom and sobbed in a stall.

After she got herself under control, Kate left the school building and walked to a nearby grassy area with picnic tables. She sat down under a tree and closed her eyes. Her mind was numb. She looked up and watched the rays of sunshine twinkling through the branches and leaves onto the ground beside her. She thought of the masked man's own dazzling neon blue eyes.

"You were right," she whispered. "I was brainwashed. They got inside all of our minds. But now what am I supposed to do?"

6. HOMETOWN HERO

Myra Jenkins spread a dozen vibrant fabric swatches across the tabletop that was next to an opaque glass window. One by one, she held them up against the warm yellow light that came through, then made notes on a pad.

She narrowed the swatches down to three and set the others aside. Next she pulled a tape measure from her hip and took several measurements around the window, then added to her notes.

A few minutes later, another black woman who was older than her entered the room and said, "Well, Myra, how are things going in here?"

"Hi, Ms. Wallace. I got the measurements for the windows right here. And I picked out a few color samples that I liked."

"Oh, let me see those."

Myra fanned out the swatches for Ms. Wallace, then held each one up. "See, it looks good with the daylight. Plus with these kind of beige floors, I don't know, they all just sort of fit together."

"Interesting. Now, of the three, which is your favorite?"

"Oh, I don't know."

"Come on, I want your opinion. You've already done such a good job redecorating the daycare and the lobby."

"Okay then. Thank you. At first I wanted the mint green, but then the big desk over there caught my eye. That gray, it's really dark. And when I hold up this color…"

"Wow, I see! It's very striking."

"Yeah. The royal blue makes everything come alive, but the room still seems serious. I don't think the green says 'work' like this one does."

Ms. Wallace took the blue swatch from Myra and set it on the desk. "Then it's settled. I'll have Edgar double-check your measurements—if you don't mind—and then we'll place the order."

"Oh, thank you, Ms. Wallace. This is all so fun. I never expected to be doing anything this exciting when I started working down in the daycare."

"Well, I'm just sorry these HRA trade schools lean so heavily on training people for brute blue-collar jobs. I wish we offered art classes too."

"That would be nice. I've almost got my GED done though, so this place isn't all bad."

"And who knows? After you get that diploma and do a few more of these projects, maybe your portfolio will be big enough to apply to a professional interior design program."

"Yes, ma'am. I appreciate you giving me this chance to help out."

"Of course, Myra. Give your baby girl a kiss for me now."

"I will, thank you."

Myra went into the ladies room and pulled out her phone. She scrolled to the pictures of the other rooms she had redecorated, and then envisioned how this new space would look after the curtains were installed. She smiled, then washed her hands and walked down to the daycare.

After the evening shift arrived at five-thirty, Myra clocked out and bundled up baby Sarah. As soon as they reached the sidewalk in front of the school, a sparkling crimson Buick tooted its horn and pulled up from down the block.

The engine turned off and out stepped a tall, lean man wearing a leather trench coat and white skull-cap. "Wassup, baby?" he said with a little smile.

"Right on time, Octavius. Thank you."

"Oh, you know. Only the best transportation for the most

beautiful girl in the world."

"You don't have to say that…"

"I'm talkin' about my daughter. Come here, little thing."

Octavius carefully took Sarah in his arms and placed a kiss on the child's pink beanie. Myra flipped the passenger seat forward and watched as he tenderly placed the infant into the rear car seat.

Octavius double-checked the belt fasteners, then said, "Okay, where to?"

"Home."

"You ain't hungry?"

"Mama's probably cooking something already. She loves that new kitchen. I can't believe what's got into her!"

"I'm starving," Octavius said as he revved the engine. "Let's hope she made something good!"

When they entered the condo a short while later, Octavius rubbed his hands together. "Oh, Mizz Jenkins? Something smells delicious in here. What are you cooking up for me?"

"Actually," a woman of about forty said, "I have a real surprise for both of you."

Just then, Clyde stepped out of the kitchen wearing an apron and holding up a spatula.

"Hey guys," he said with a playful lisp. "Celebrity chef here just sharing some recipes."

"My man!" Octavius said.

Myra set Sarah down in a highchair and gave Clyde a big hug.

"Hi, little brother. It's so good to see you. We love this place so much."

"Nah, forget about it. Y'all is my motivation, my inspiration."

Ms. Jenkins picked up her phone and said, "Squeeze in together. Let me get a look at you two. I'm so proud…"

While she snapped a few pictures, Octavius dropped his coat onto a chairback and moved into the living room. He sat down in the recliner and started flipping through a magazine.

"Hey," Clyde called out, "y'all didn't pick up Tee?"

"He's fine," Myra said. "This neighborhood is way better than the old place we stayed."

"Hey now," Octavius muttered.

Clyde put his arm around Myra. "It may be nice, but we ain't that far down the road from all that. I don't want him running around in the dark. He still too young."

"Alright, Uncle Clyde," Ms. Jenkins said. "You've let your voice be heard. Just wait til he gets home. The look that's gonna be on his face…"

Myra stepped into the kitchen and started preparing Sarah's bottle. She said, "So Mister DJ, tell us what's been going on this week."

Clyde took a bag of popcorn off the counter and threw a piece into his mouth. "Doing that frequent flyer thing, you know. Left LA about a week ago before heading over to—"

"Oh, how did that all go?"

"I got the royal treatment, so I can't complain too bad. The fans came out to the club for autographs and pictures. But check this out—that agent dude say he could set me up with Bekki Triage."

"Ooh," Ms. Jenkins said, "that girl is fine! Got them Indian princess eyes. Watch out!"

"Haha, I know. But they smooth out there in Cali. Pitch you a real nice deal—big money, big booties—hoping you don't see the strings attached."

"But Clyde, how much are they offering?"

"A lot. But it ain't just about the money. They kinda takin' control. Not just of what you do, but who you are. It's crazy how deep they think about this stuff and plan it all out."

"They gonna let you sing, dance, see the world? You want to go to Japan, right?"

"Of course, Mama."

"So why you playing hard to get? I know a lot of other people who can sing good, and ain't nobody knocking down their door to put them up on stage."

"I know, I know. I'm just thinking on it. Because I sign, and that's it. Locked in. I did run it by Nolan a little bit. He said to sit on it for a while. Says if they really want me, they'll reach out again."

"You better listen to what he says, then. God bless that Mr. Simmons," Ms. Jenkins said with a sigh.

Myra turned and gave her a look. "Oh, you like him now?"

"Give your mama a break. I don't know about all that business stuff. I was just looking out for my baby boy. Glad we got ours. Got mouths to feed around here."

"Yeah, well," Clyde said, "Nolan's always treated me right. Even back when we was doin' the little jobs, like catching drones for a few bucks. And also now, when we selling my track in the hundreds of thousands."

"Believe me, I am so thankful that this miracle helped get us out of the poorhouse. But I just want to make sure we covered."

"Mama, you got to chill," Myra said. "Most of that legal stuff is done by computers anyway. All the downloads, the money... Even the taxes he got to pay."

"Oh, look at you now, Miss GED. Take a couple classes and you think you know everything. But it don't take an accountant to know how human nature is. Trust is a nice idea, but I guess I've been burned too many times to feel comfortable like y'all do. Especially now that they got him paying *in* to the system."

Clyde said, "There's all these contracts out there already written up. Business, music, whatever. You just got to pick the right one."

"But what the hell's in them? How do you know someone ain't trying to pull a fast one on you?"

"Mama, thank you for watching out for me. But it's a new world out there. Everything is done on a public spreadsheet."

"Oh Lord, not another spreadsheet! That's what the HRA uses and look at the mess they're in."

"Hey, I got a new song for y'all. 'Fight the spreadsheet! Yeah, yeah. We got to... fight... fight the spreadsheet!' What you think?"

"Aw, you playin'. But that's okay. I hope you don't send that one to the agent, though. He'll delete your number!"

Clyde threw his arm around her shoulders and they all laughed.

Just then the front door opened. Tyrell walked in carrying a bookbag and a tiny football. His face lit up. "Uncle Clyde!" He ran over and jumped into Clyde's arms.

"How you do, little man?"

"I'm good. I like my new bedroom."

"Oh, you do? Finally got it all set up?"

"Yeah. It's quiet. I can't hear the people next door no more."

"That's good, real good. And how school going?"

"It's okay."

"What they teaching you now? Math? Science?"

"Kind of. The teacher put on some goggles. Then she held up this glass, and it had red stuff inside. I don't always know what she doin', though."

"That's okay. Keep at it. You'll learn things by, what they call it... Osmosis!"

"Yeah! She said that word one time."

"What about PE? They got you playing any sports?"

"Naw. But we get to go outside for recess."

"Oh yeah? What you do out there? We need to get your jump shot dialed in while you still young."

"We got a new game called 'gotcha'. All the kids get in on it."

"How it go?"

"Like, everyone at school got a tablet. If you see another kid doing something bad, you put it in there."

"I don't follow. How you mean?"

"Other day, I saw this white girl calling this white boy all these names. So I start recording all that. And when that boy cried and went away, I sent that video over."

"Wait. What?"

"Yeah, so next time we at recess, this older boy Alberto, he take out his tablet and see what in there. Then all the kids who did bad stuff got to get punished."

Clyde looked around the room. "Are y'all hearing this?"

Myra shrugged her shoulders. "Kids get up to all kinds of silly stuff. You ain't no angel, neither."

"Go on, Tee," Clyde said.

"Alberto yell out that we got to have a Revenge Event. You know, 'cause you been hittin' or stealin' from other kids."

"So what happens?"

"Whatever you did gets done back to you. 'With interest,' Alberto say. By everybody."

"Even the black kids are taking lumps?"

"Yeah. Anyone who got caught. It don't matter they color."

"And you been taking part in these Revenge Events?"

"You got to. Last week, we all put milk on this boy's head. 'Cause he tried stealing a drink from this girl. But someone got it on tape, so..."

"So you did that? And that was fun?"

"Seein' that milk go down his face, like, we laughed and

laughed! But today they got me. It wasn't no fun."

"What happened? What the hell they do to you?"

"I got bit."

"What?! Where?"

"They all got me on the leg. See, one time I bit this other girl…"

Clyde reached down and rolled up Tyrell's pant leg. He slapped his forehead when he saw a dozen small bite impressions all over the boy's calf and ankle. Myra rushed over. "Oh, my goodness…" she said.

Ms. Jenkins leaned over the sink and started muttering. "And this was supposed to be the good school!"

"Well, he ain't cut. He ain't bleeding." Myra rolled the pant leg back down.

Clyde was pacing back and forth. He said to Tyrell, "So they having little trials at school? Who's watching you during all this? Or are you kids doing it when nobody around?"

"First it was just us, but now a couple teachers help it go."

"So they got y'all spyin' and snitchin' on each other, huh? These are your classmates, your friends. This is no good. Real-time Reparations. For kids! Is this what people want? Getting the next generation working against each other, even before they understand why it was all set up? This ain't right. Tee, next time they try to make you play, you tell 'em no."

"But what if they say it's my turn? If you caught, you caught."

"You tell them your Uncle Clyde said it has to stop. Make 'em do jumping jacks or plant a damn tree instead."

Myra said, "Clyde, you're right. I had no idea they was being so rough to each other. He just kept talkin' about this fun game gotcha, but he never explained it like that before. I'm gonna talk to the school first thing tomorrow when we drop him off. Ain't that right, Octavius?"

Octavius had come in from the living room while Tyrell told his story, and now had a sour expression on his face. "No doubt," he said. "I'll back you up. But don't make me talk too much, or I'll get us all in trouble."

"No, I just want you by my side. Alright, Tee, let's get you ready for dinner."

As Myra took Tyrell upstairs and Ms. Jenkins returned to the stove, Clyde leaned toward Octavius and said quietly, "Hey, can I get a private word with you for a few?"

"Of course. Where you want to talk?"

"Let's move to the garage, shoot some pool."

Clyde set the rack while Octavius got himself a beer from the fridge.

"So what's on your mind?" Octavius said.

Clyde picked up a cue, looking at the tip intently while he applied chalk. "I see you been coming around more often lately."

"Oh, you know."

"I'm glad, is what I'm saying. I don't need you to explain your reasons."

"I do what I do. You do what you do. That's what's up."

"It's all good. We family. And, I want to keep it in the family. 'Cause money's only just one part of it."

"Money come. Money go. And that's how it goes." Octavius took a swig of beer.

"Yeah. It's just been crazy for everyone the past couple months. And you know, I look up to you. So I don't want all this DJC stuff to make things awkward."

"Clyde, I respect what you did for your sister. You did good getting her set up in a nicer place. I know I looked out for you before, threw you some jobs now and again. But I ain't coming to this house looking for no handouts. I got a kid with your sister, and I'll keep doin' whatever it takes to provide for them."

"No doubt. I'll never forget you bringin' me that work, teachin' me the hustle. But you run in a rough world. It's too hot for me. And I ain't trying to step on your feet. It's just, we ain't got no dad, so with this money I got to look out for my mom and my nephew."

"Be crazy not to. And selfish."

"So I want to make sure we square. Because something magic happened with my song to make all this possible. I can't have no bad blood mess it up, now that we got it."

"Glad you coming at me with this direct. So keep going— what do you want?"

Clyde licked his lips.

"Right now Nolan's getting pulled away to other stuff. He's a star in his own way too, kinda. So I'll be fighting off the vultures without him. You's family—your daughter is my niece. So what

I'm saying is… That world out there that loves me right now, and wants me to give them more… That's not your scene—they're not so hard on the outside, but they work on you in your mind. They try to twist you with words. But Octavius, I need a rock on my side. I know who you are. I know *what* you are. So I can trust you. And I'm asking, can I rely on you to be there? Watch my back?"

Octavius set his beer down on the pool table rail and looked Clyde dead in the eyes.

"I hear what you sayin'. I'm in this now. More than before, when it was just me and Myra. You and me, we in it together too. So what you need, protection?"

"Something like that. Call it hometown gristle. Man, those people out in LA, it's like they come from a different planet. Everyone acts kinda silly, like they putting on a show—but they ain't stupid. They' always workin' you somehow. You know, distract you with something flashy, then boom! You under they wing. It kinda scared me. So that's why I'm coming at you with this. I need someone who can look at situations with street eyes. And teach me how to spot the angle quick!"

"No doubt. Your bullshit posse."

"Ha, yeah. Keep me out of their nets so I can keep doing what I do. Make music, touch people."

"Clyde, you got an innocent soul, boy. I don't know how this all gonna play out, but if you need me to watch out for you, I do it. You keep this DJC thing rolling—you know I always wanted that for you—and we both look after your sister. Then who knows… Maybe at the end of the day, I won't have to throw so many punches."

"Then relax one of them fists right now and shake my hand."

"My brutha."

"Family. Family, yo."

Clyde and Octavius joined hands and came together for a brief hug.

A moment later, Ms. Jenkins opened the door and called them in. Dinner was served.

7. MODESTIANITY

The dancers in blue skittered across the stage. Discordant notes from a cello sent them round and round wildly, until a violin's soothing melody won the day. The troupe eased into formation, with three men swaying gently on one side and being mirrored by three women across the stage. Standing motionless on a stool in the middle was an obscured figure wearing black.

Suddenly the groups ran toward each other, meeting and pairing off in an elegant spin. The silver glitter on their faces twinkled in the spotlight. The couples moved together rhythmically, exuding the sensuous without being sensual—they were as dignified as ballet, but with the exhilaration of a river flowing toward a waterfall.

The central figure spread its arms to reveal giant wings, then stepped down and approached one of the couples. With a wide swing of the arm, this bird-human cloaked them and then pirouetted away. The audience gasped when it saw that the pair had disappeared.

This mystery figure dispatched the other couples in the same fashion, before bowing its head and closing the wings forward over its body. The stage lights cut to black and the crowd burst into applause. A moment later, the lights flashed back on and the entire cast of twenty dancers ran out and linked arms. The clapping continued for several minutes as the troupe took their bows.

One of the performers, a black man of medium complexion, gave a particularly vivid smile as he acknowledged the crowd. His journey to this moment had been even more unorthodox than the often unique life path that brought most people to the Mall of Absolution. And now he was on the cusp of moving one step closer to the inner circle of Modestianity.

The dancers waved and skipped away behind the curtain into the dressing room.

Bill Evans exchanged hugs with his fellow cast members

before washing the makeup off his face. He then removed his costume and put on his blue teal robe, which was the standard uniform worn by all novitiates during the six-month trial period that followed their first commitment.

He exited the theater and found himself floating on air as he made his way back to the cloisters. Evening feast was approaching and he didn't want to be late, but when he saw that one of his mentors was giving a lecture in the courtyard, he sat down on the edge of a fountain to listen for a few moments.

"We are flesh-and-blood animals with wild energy," Brother Salazar said. "But in order to turn our passions into brilliance, we must not simply deny that they exist. Repression only leads to pathology. Thus, Modestianity is not the religion of prudery. We do not fear embracing the earthiness of the pagans. And if we are guilty of covering ourselves out of shame, it is only away from the heartless eyes of a technology that seeks to imprison the human spirit. But to our fellow humans, we are as open to the life cycle as the leaf that shines high above in springtime, and then journeys with the wind to enrich the soil elsewhere in death…"

Bill passed through the cloister's double doors just as a three-tone bell began to chime. He joined the stream of novitiates in hooded blue robes that flowed out from the bunk rooms into a dimly lit, wood-appointed dining hall.

Each man took a bowl from an end table, then shuffled forward as servers ladled out the portions of food. The men then sat down at several long tables and waited in silence. Someone thumped his utensil against the surface and said, "Let us be circumspect in our every deed."

"Amen," the group responded.

The men quietly discussed the events of their day. Some had taken food out to the refugees living in the surrounding parking lots and fields. Others had assisted in children's reading lessons.

The man sitting next to Bill nudged his arm. "What do you think—elder or kinsman?"

"Whatever the emissaries decide, I will accept," Bill replied.

"I hear they grill you pretty hard in there. Looking for your weaknesses."

"One final test to ensure we end up in the correct role, perhaps?"

"I had a lot of responsibility back in the real world. Don't want to be spinning my wheels with the kinsmen."

"Have patience, my brother. In light of all the refugees flooding our gates, it seems likely that the need for capable church members will also increase. If you don't advance to elder in tomorrow's ceremony, surely Mod will see to it that a vacancy or new post opens up for you soon."

"Mod, I hope you're right. Thanks for your ear, brother."

"It is an anxious time for us all. But also hopeful and exciting. Keep the faith."

The other man grumbled and poked at his food.

After feast, the men slowly filed across a walkway and entered a spacious open room which had a thin layer of blue carpeting that also ran up the wall several feet. They sat down on the floor and chatted quietly. A man wearing the blue-gray tunic and sash of an elder walked to the center of the space. He was followed by a kinsman in lighter gray who carried a transcription machine.

"Good evening," the elder said. "Mod be with you."

"And also with you," the group answered.

"On this Advancement Day eve, let us seek to remain focused on the work at hand. Every mapmaking session not only brings us closer to a deeper understanding of ourselves, but also contributes to the growing body of insights which will help guide mankind into a more balanced future. Whether lay member, novitiate, kinsman, elder, proponent, or emissary, everyone shares in the teachings as we refine our wisdom through questions and clarifications.

"So many of our brothers and sisters in the outside world have lost their way. Is that not proof that we will be needed, and that our work each night has value? Let us begin with Brother Fremont, whose letter to me provides tonight's first kernel. He says, 'My studies seem to reveal that serene poise is the key teaching. How can this be maintained when a) the church believes in certain immutable human traits, while b) the world itself changes at exponential rates?'

"A truly thoughtful paradox. Could it be that in having to grapple with so much external instability, we are forced to tap into powerful mental chambers that were previously unknown to us? While we do not *create* new human faculties, perhaps this process unlocks and strengthens capabilities that were simply dormant within. And because this world is ours, surely nothing that arises from it cannot be harnessed, fenced in, and steered to our purposes. Now, who is ready to divert the trail?"

An older man sitting against one of the walls stood up. "I would like to offer a small challenge."

"Very well, Brother Carmichael. Please..."

"What the year 2028 looks like would have been unimaginable to someone from 1928. Just as 1928 would stagger a person living in 1828. And yet man as a whole adapts step by step as time goes by. He does his best to weather displacement, while also taking advantage of the positive changes.

"But two thoughts trouble me now. First, what if new developments come so fast that no one is able to keep up? As if psychologically, we could not make the leap? Which leads to my greater fear. Will we reach a point where our creation is so intelligent and so self-sufficient, that not only does it not need us to maintain it, but it refuses to serve us?"

"Are you worried that one day AI will turn on us? Perhaps by killing or enslaving humanity?"

"It could be worse than that. What if the technology decides to abandon us? Turns its back, refuses to function at all, and leaves us out in the cold?"

The elder scratched his goatee while slowly moving across the room. "Yes, two very unsettling hypotheses. One hopes that the normal sputtering pace of human progress would negate the first idea. As for the other, would it be incorrect to infer that providing humans with everything they need is the real danger?

"Have we not already seen the cultural malaise of the past fifty years, as people living within this worldwide cargo cult have been divorced from the need to produce anything, as well as from the consequences of their own actions? They have incrementally been separated from the land, from their factories, from creating art, and now they even abandon marriage and reproduction.

"Ah, I see you nodding your heads. Now you understand why, when people first join our church, they are encouraged to jump into group activities. Farming at the rooftop gardens for a week often gives our lay members a greater sense of community than they have ever felt in their entire lives. We also hear wonderful stories of people who never thought they had any musical aptitude—but given the breathing room and a nonjudgmental opportunity to explore, they now share their beautiful singing voices in our choir. Indeed, it is often the little moments of creative expression that provide more joy than the ten thousand songs contained in one's electronic device.

"This is the power that we are giving back to everyday people. Because since the dawn of the internet, our species has been racing madly toward Andy Warhol's fifteen minutes of fame. But along the way, this road somehow became perverted, and now we all dread our own fifteen seconds of shame.

"Mod bless the Prescient One for establishing this church as a proving ground to help us find another way. Because although our religion sprang out of reactionary principles—using modesty as a bulwark against the all-seeing eye—the baton is willingly offered to any member whose insights can help grow the spiritual component.

"Beyond the intangible, we also offer a return to the ways of small-town community life, where everyone is respected and contributes however they can. It is a rebirth of intimacy with materials through craftsmanship, thus restoring purpose to hands whose only function was to swipe across plastic screens. It reinvigorates minds which could critique food but had never prepared a meal of their own.

"People have mocked us for this approach. Saying that we are similar to the Amish, or that we pick and choose which decades we prefer to live in. But is it wrong to want the tools that mankind has developed to serve us? What is there to condemn in wanting to assess which features work and don't work, rather than just blindly accepting everything that has been created? Is it a sin to seek a way of life in which each person is able to fulfill their potential?"

A younger man arose from the crowd. He said, "I think it's fear that causes them to ridicule us. Look how large the church has grown nationwide in the last year alone."

"Tell me, Brother Byron, who is afraid of us?"

"Any number of groups that risk losing market share if we succeed. For one, other religions which have gotten so bogged down by dogma, that they are paralyzed and cannot address this world which is in flux. Governments and corporations and the military all have so much to lose if we keep expanding."

"That is a bold claim. Please, enlighten us."

"People who are happy, self-sufficient, and at peace within a community do not give those entities much to work with. We have weaned thousands of our members off of prescription drugs. And Modestians are not desperate for money, nor so empty that we need to buy trinkets and—"

"Just because we *live* in a shopping mall doesn't mean…"

All the men gave a hearty laugh as the elder trailed off.

"To conclude my idea," the young man said, "the military cannot recruit us because Modestianity has no history of quarrels with other religions. Indeed the enemy today isn't human at all, but the surveillance technology and its tendrils run amok. We are the antidote to that techno-punitive future, that hellscape where it is far more likely that databases will be used to provide evidence of people's crimes and little sins, rather than to compile a highlight reel of their most loving moments or deeds of charity."

"Well said, young man. I commend your insights. But if I may suggest, perhaps you're only half-correct on that final point. Because part of the enemy *does* live within each of us. Only through controlling our hearts and our minds, can we redirect the fiery urges of the flesh and comport ourselves in a dignified manner."

"Amen," several of the men murmured.

"Yes," the elder chuckled, "somehow our map always leads back home. The sacred code of circumspection as the path to the good life, proven correct yet again. And that seems a fitting end note for this wonderful evening.

"Now, it has been a robust six months for the novitiates who advance tomorrow. I bid you to sleep well tonight, because more responsibilities and training await you in your new role as either kinsman or elder. Let us pray…"

"Hail Mody, full of pause," the group recited, "thy patience is with me. Cautious art thou weighing options and cautious is the path of thy life's work. Holy Mody, guide of the future, calm our heartbeats, now and in times of tension. Amen."

The mapmaking session concluded, and as the men were walking back toward the cloisters, they passed a column of female novitiates also returning to their quarters.

"Good evening, sister," the men said quietly.

"Same to you, brother," the women replied.

The sound of shuffling feet filled the silent hallways. At this hour, most other Mall residents had also gone to their lodgings for the night. While there was no formal curfew, by nine o'clock almost all activities had ended and the cuisine courts were closed.

Bill and his comrades entered the cloisters and went into the locker room-style facilities. After brushing their teeth and washing their faces, they retired to the sleeping quarters of bunk beds that had been modified into pods. This was the one taste of privacy novitiates were afforded during their trial period. (All higher ranking members slept in small monk's cells, except in the cases of families, who lived in apartments which had been built into former storefronts.)

Bill climbed into his rectangular sleep pod and zipped the edges shut. He turned on the lamp and fished out his diary from a tiny bookshelf, then eased himself under the covers. He unlocked the book by placing his thumb on a front sensor, then began to write by hand.

"October 25th. Another fulfilling day here at the Mall. Anticipation about tomorrow's festivities is palpable, but we were still able to stay on task and have a productive mapmaking session tonight.

"But how can I forget our performance this afternoon! My dance troupe debuted a new movement to end our sequence. It was just… thrilling! There is something about being here at the Mall that gives my life a sense of richness and fulfillment that nothing from the old days can touch.

"Hitting home runs back in college was a rush, but that was all for the fans. Closing… deals for my bosses also never brought me this kind of personal satisfaction. But now the dancing, the community work, the learning in earnest… Something has awoken in me, and for the first time I feel able to fully express what resides in the depths of my soul.

"This symbiosis of the self resonating with others in truthful purity, that is my ultimate breakthrough. The secrets that I have kept from my brothers will now become the lies that I tell my superiors. For I know that after today's profound revelation, I can never go back to the real world.

"I truly am a Modestian for the first time. I will endure the consequences of letting down those who had entrusted me to perform an important job. Because now I clearly see a flicker of what our leader the Prescient One sees, namely that our society is on a collision course with an existential crisis it is not prepared for.

"It's funny how at first these Modestians can come across as paranoid, eccentric, even borderline agoraphobic. But this religion's evolving vision for how to face the future is the best that I have seen offered by anyone so far. They may not be the richest or most powerful church, but this unlikely gathering speaks from unguarded hearts. I believe that this lack of guile has protected them from falling into any of the traps that usually do 'cults' in.

"I pray that Mod shines upon us in the coming months as the church continues to grow. Just as I hope to be of honorable use to my fellow brothers and sisters. Now I must rest…"

At dawn the cloisters were already bustling and full of chatter. The candidates for advancement bathed quickly and then put on long tunics of shimmering silver that were only worn on special occasions.

They bypassed morning banquet and took escalators up to the third floor, then marched toward the Hall of Emissaries. This is where the inner circle of high ranking church officials lived and worked.

The thirty male candidates entered a waiting area full of plush blue couches accented by silver pillows. An elderly kinsman greeted them with stoic grace.

"Blessed morning to you, gentlemen. Please make yourselves comfortable. You will be called into your interviews shortly, and in no particular order. Refreshments are available on the table beside the far wall—although I, like most others on this momentous day, could barely manage a sip of water until all was known."

The kinsman now acted as usher, escorting the novitiates and pointing to couches they might wish to take. He smiled at Bill and motioned to a nearby cushion.

Bill sat and said, "Thank you, kinsman."

He waited in silence, patiently enduring the butterflies in his stomach while imagining that he too was a caterpillar about to be transformed.

One by one, his brothers were beckoned and taken into a private chamber. He didn't see them come out afterward and assumed they had left by a separate exit—best not to expose their joy or disappointment to those still waiting.

A tap on Bill's shoulder.

"Brother Evans? It is time."

The kinsman smiled graciously and opened a heavy door, then led him down a hallway with carpet so dense that their feet barely made a sound. Finally they stepped into a small blue room whose lights had been set low. A man of sixty sat in an antique brown chair with velvet upholstery.

"Good morning, novitiate," the man said. "I am Emissary Karlov. Please sit down."

Bill sat in an identical chair facing him and said, "Esteemed emissary, I am honored to be in your presence today."

"Mod be praised, thank you. Now, my son, I have received positive reports from the elders. They say that you are one of our most well-rounded pupils."

"I have only done what was expected of someone who had chosen this path. If I have stood out from my brothers, I hope it is neither seen as pride on my part, nor a defect on theirs."

"Most certainly not," Karlov said. "One's commitment is the most important aspect. Beyond that, there is room here for all to express their strengths."

"I see," Bill said. "That is good indeed."

"Our only wonder is that you don't appear to have any weaknesses."

"Please, emissary, you flatter me. I don't know if that assessment is true, or if I even deserve it."

"We shall see," Karlov said. "What concerns me is the perceived gap between your old life and its troubles, compared to the heroic man I see sitting before me today."

"I don't quite understand what you're asking," Bill said. "Please forgive my blindness."

"Brother Evans, I am not trying to embarrass you by making you relive your humiliation. But I must say that having one's wife begin an affair with a neighbor after she discovered that he had been spying on her... It is a devastating blow, and no surprise that you would come running into the arms of

Modestianity. But your remarkable turnaround? I scarcely know how it has been possible, and I am as firm a believer as the Prescient One Himself."

"I appreciate your candor. The best answer I can give is that it is not merely the religion itself, or even the teachings, that have affected me so. It has been the full immersion into a community aimed not just at a life lived well, but with conscience. And we see the fruits each day—especially over the past weeks as the influx of refugees has tested our capacities. After all of this, I feel as if I am a whole man and ready for the responsibilities of an elder."

The emissary folded his arms and rested them on his belly.

"I believe in your sincerity," he said. "It's just that a number of people have joined the church due to similar, shall we say, destabilizing moments where technology was somehow involved. We've found that being a lay member offers them the comfort they need, but sadly they're often not fit even for the light duties of a kinsman. Brother Evans, you have done remarkably well as a novitiate. But I must know not only what is *in* your heart, but if you *have* the heart for the life of an elder."

"Blessed Emissary," Bill said, "I understand your concerns and know they come from a place of love. It has been a trying probation period for me indeed. But just yesterday at the theater, while standing for applause with my fellow dancers, I felt a tingle at the base of my head and neck. My mind began floating in a heavenly haze that I have only felt a few other times in my entire life. And for me it is the most wonderful feeling of all— like I am not alone, I can set down my burden, and need not pretend or hide from anyone. After that feeling of lightness fades, however, I want to weep because I don't know how many years of numbness or pain will pass before some other unexpected moment returns me to that mist.

"It was no fluke that it happened to me here at the Mall," Evans continued, "where I live among people of all backgrounds, and whose common bond is that they choose to take life seriously. If I had previously felt weak or on the verge of faltering, no such threat to my resolve exists now. I am ready to advance so that I may serve."

The emissary closed his eyes and exhaled audibly through his nose. "Your heart within hearts has spoken," he said. "I cannot stand in the way of a man who shows such determination in the face of life's trials. I congratulate you, Brother Evans, for soon you shall be an elder! Go prepare for the ceremony."

Bill stood up and grabbed hold of Karlov's hand, then placed the crown of his own head in its grasp.

"Thank you, emissary. This is the greatest day of my life."

Bill was escorted to the exit by a different kinsman, then breezed down one of the large open foyers as if in a trance. He made his way down to the amphitheater where the advancement ceremony would shortly begin, then sat down among his brothers feeling utter contentment. They spoke of this and of that, but Bill barely heard what was said, so great was the joy pulsing in his soul.

When the ceremony began, he gazed upon the many church members in the audience through misty eyes. He saw the royal procession walk across the stage, heard the lofty pronouncements, and finally the Prescient One appeared to great fanfare.

After several brief scripture readings, the new kinsmen and kinswomen were announced. These twenty crossed the stage, each shaking hands with a proponent as well as receiving a nod from the Prescient One, who was seated among the church leaders nearby.

Next, Bill and the other novitiates being promoted to elder went up to the stage. As each name was called, one member of the group crossed over and embraced both an emissary and a proponent. The Prescient One, who had risen and come forward, also offered a quiet word of blessing.

Bill heard his name called and stepped out into the open. He smiled as the audience applauded, then felt real tears well up as first the emissary, and then the proponent, took him into their arms.

He nearly broke down when he heard the name "Elder Evans" announced over the loudspeaker as he approached the Prescient One. The figurehead was absolutely glistening in his silver robe, and his blue-painted face was as smooth as cast acrylic.

Bill searched for the right words to express his joy and gratitude, but felt his veins turn to ice when the Prescient One leaned in and said, "Congratulations, Marcus." He tried to pull back as a wave of nausea constricted his stomach, but the other man held him firm and whispered, "It's alright. You have nothing to fear. I know exactly where your mind is. For now, focus on your new role as elder. But soon we will meet privately. Because you and I have great work to do together!"

He left the stage in complete shock. Rather than join the other freshly anointed elders in celebration, he wandered out of the amphitheater and found a secluded corner to sit in. He dropped his head into his hands as the same thought echoed in his mind over and over.

How can he possibly know that I work for the FBI?

8. THE WAR ROOM

Eleven days out from the election, the president and a dozen of her staff gathered around the Roosevelt Room's long table for a ten o'clock briefing.

"Okay, people," Eileen Jeffries-Lao said, "let's lay it all out. Give me whatever you've got, good or bad. Then we can head into the weekend knowing where we stand and what we need to do for the final push. Bottom line, we've got to get this HRA business shored up right now, or the next ten years will be a disaster. If Dominguez wins—even if he doesn't actually dismantle the administration—he'll find a way to run it into the ground.

"Millions of Beneficiaries will suffer as a result. Grandmothers trying to pay for their groceries will find a zero balance on their debit cards. And overseas—my God—what country would actually follow our lead and go through with their own version of Reparations if we fail? I cannot stress enough the magnitude of what's at stake. Now, Tony, let's start with you."

Chief of Staff Tony Rizzuto stepped forward and handed binders to all the staffers.

"Thank you, Madam President," he said. "The whole team is here to deliver for you. The first order of business is keeping the peace. The bad press we get from every vandalized field office could cost us a hundred votes. We're already working with the

National Guard and local law enforcement in high-sensitivity areas. Plus we've provided them with additional access to the surveillance grid, as well as our S'more Stopper teams. At every large gathering, our smart camera network will relay the data and deploy any necessary countermeasures.

"Next up," Tony continued, "news on our opponent. Victor Dominguez will be sweeping across the southern states this weekend. Natalie, can you fill us in on the details?"

A female staffer seated at the table consulted her tablet, then a series of graphics and charts appeared on the projector screen.

"Look at what he's doing," Natalie said. "Heading straight into the heart of Reparations country to stir things up. Louisiana, Mississippi, Alabama, Georgia, and Florida. He's calling his speech 'A Better Way Forward.' From the intel we've gathered at other recent events, Dominguez has been testing the waters by slowly ramping up his anti-HRA rhetoric."

The president clucked her tongue. "So he's going for broke right now. Into the belly of the beast! I admire his guts, even if he's out of his league. What I want to know is how much of what he's doing is deliberately planned, versus his campaign just winging it?"

"Madam President, if I may continue?" Natalie said.

"You know what? Everybody just call me by my first name for now. We're getting our hands dirty here. If we patch this dam before it bursts out onto the country, then by all means, I'll be proud to still be addressed by my formal title after Election Day."

"Sure thing, Eileen. Here are clips from two recent Dominguez speeches given a week apart. First, here he is in Houston last Saturday."

The image of Victor Dominguez appeared on screen. He said, "This Reparations thing is like a road trip that wasn't fully planned. Sure, you stocked the car full of food and supplies, but you didn't consult the map and now you're stuck in a ditch. So you have to call Victor's Towing Service to pull your car out, make any necessary repairs, and get back on the road."

"Next," Natalie said, "the speech yesterday in Philadelphia."

"When you get old or sick," Dominguez said, crossing a stage where dozens of people in matching red t-shirts stood behind him, "you can't always do what you want to do. So you go to the doctor and he explains what's going on. I, Dr. Dominguez, and my expert staff have done all the tests. We've looked at the charts, and honestly the prognosis for this Reparations program does not look good. Mr. and Mrs. Beneficiary, I'm very sorry. We may be able to repair the broken bones, but after this kind of a fall, I don't think the program will ever walk again."

"No!" The president slapped her thigh. "Tell me he didn't go there. Can you believe these metaphors he's using? Is he actually calling himself the Mexican mechanic? Sure, vote *him* in! My god, who's writing these speeches?"

"I know, it's ridiculous," Tony said. "And normally it would be a laughing matter, if he didn't keep gaining in the polls. Kwame, can you give us the latest on that?"

"Of course." A thin Afrigro-American with shiny shaved head stood up. "After the debate last week—Dominguez's coming out party, according to the media—he got a sizable bump which then settled back down. So here's the full array: two weeks ago, we were up sixty-two to thirty-four. By last Friday, the margin had shrunk to fifty-eight to thirty-nine. And as of today, it stands at fifty-four to forty-four. The remaining percentage points are distributed among the two independent candidates."

"So he's slowly cutting in, bite by bite," Eileen said. "Interesting that he's now choosing to take on the South so aggressively. You'd think if he was looking for a few points, he'd head into the Rust Belt and play his violin for all the disgruntled Caucs out there."

"My information suggests that Dominguez's people are as much on a fact-finding mission as they are trying to gain votes. So the reception he gets from the diverse southern crowd will probably determine where he travels next week."

"I'll be damned. They *are* making it up as they go. They don't even know which states they might be able to snipe from us. But something's working. So how does all that impact where we're going?"

Tony spoke up. "We're still on schedule to hit the cities we booked when this was all just a victory tour. That said, we'll add some small town stops to meet with the locals in between the bigger speeches."

"Also," Natalie added, "we've got you scheduled to record several promo spots when you're in New York on Monday.

Mostly national stuff, maybe one or two tailored to a state race. Plus, we came up with the idea of putting you alongside a guest which might help restore confidence in the HRA."

"And who might that be?" Eileen said.

"Kate Donohugh."

"What?! The one from that *DDM TV* disaster? Are you crazy?"

"Look," Tony said. "She's composed, photogenic, even has the cancer survivor angle. Did you see when they put her face to face with that fugitive DDM in the hospital? It was *compelling*. Truth is, Kate's a part of the zeitgeist now, and we can make her into whatever we want. She was also one of the HRA's earliest advocates long before she ended up working there, so you're not likely to find a bigger supporter of the program."

"And now," the president said, "it's all unraveling in front of her eyes. People like her care more about Reparations than you, me, and even a hell of a lot of blacks. Damn, damn, damn. You all might be onto something. Use these ads to recharge the base of true believers that started this whole thing."

"Exactly. Remind them that they're just like the Abolitionists of the nineteenth century. Up against the odds, but on the right side of history. So they can't quit. It's too important of a mission to let a few stumbles derail the whole thing."

"It's time to rally the troops again. Rebuild their faith in the HRA. Because I will *not* preside over another failure like Obamacare! Do you all hear me?"

"Yes, of course. But please," Tony said, lowering his hands slowly, "try to stay calm. We're all here as a team. A winning team. We'll make the right plan and focus like a laser."

"Okay, I'm taking a breath. But tell me, what have you got on the Sentinels?"

"After the private message they sent following the first hack, one of their members has been communicating with us behind the scenes ever since."

"Unreal. What's the newest intel?"

"Their liaison insists that they'll continue to stand down and will not foment any unrest, as long as we work with them in acquiescing to their demands regarding the HRA. Not that we will, but…"

"Never mind that. Just keep them talking. They may be men of their word for now, but I still intend to capture them, shut them down, and if the polls support it, bring them to justice. For now though, we do need to show the public something encouraging on this front. I can't believe that none of our agencies—who are always tooting their own horns, I might add—they still haven't caught anyone yet. How is that even possible with all the people they've interviewed?"

"I assure you, there are numerous persons of interest being moved up the list for tighter scrutiny."

"Oh hell, we're *all* under scrutiny now! You've got to give me more than that."

"What I'm trying to say, Eileen, is that we don't want to tip off the big players by taking any low-level moles into custody."

"Tony, that may sound sensible, but right now I need some damn arrests! And on camera too. Good optics to help secure the vote of every last person who's on the fence about whether I'm cut out for the job after all. You know… We're just gonna have to fake it. Hire a couple actors and put on a good show. I'm sorry, but this is where we are."

"Very well," Tony said after a pause. "If that's what you want. Is there any particular… racial and gender configuration that you'd prefer?"

"Same as pretty much every other hacker. Cauc. Male. And… balding! Drag a guy with a comb-over in front of the cameras."

"Consider it done. How about we give him a lazy eye while we're at it?"

"That's the spirit! Aw, don't look so glum, everyone. In eleven days we'll be popping champagne and getting drunk as hell! And then we can get back to work for real. I promise you."

"All in good time, Eileen. First, let's win this thing."

The president stood up and leaned forward with her hands on the table.

"Damn," she muttered. "A month ago we were sitting pretty. Oblivious. In dreamland, coasting toward re-election."

"And then just like that—" Tony snapped his fingers.

"Just like that, we're about to serve up the White House to the next Jimmy Carter."

"I need a drink. Victor Dominguez will *not* become president on our watch. He has a pet iguana named Tito, for Christ's sake."

"And his wife is always out running marathons in those skimpy neon shorts. That freckled fool is thin as a rail!"

"Okay, I think the idea of there being a *first lady* next year is all the motivation this group needs to get back on track."

"Speaking of which," Eileen said, "does anybody know the whereabouts of my husband?"

Everyone looked at each other sheepishly.

"No one? I don't care what he's up to, believe me. I am completely focused on this campaign. Knowing where he can be found is just one part of my master checklist."

"I believe," one young staffer mustered, "that the *Beltway Times* posted a picture of Mr. Jeffries with one of the, um, female golf pros over at Congressional."

"Okay, fine. So he's in the area. Moving on!"

Tony consulted his binder. "We've heard rumblings that some advocacy groups are nervous. They're not happy about Dominguez rising in the polls every time he opens his mouth and says something more derogatory about the HRA."

"Assure them that all this Dominguez talk is just hype and scare tactics. He's been riding a lucky wave that's about to crash badly. We're solid as a rock and will put him away soon enough."

"The NAACP still has full confidence in you. They say they're happy to send out an email blast in support, if we can provide them with a quote."

"Of course. Someone record this. 'I was proud to stand beside the NAACP as we fought to secure long-overdue Reparations for the oppressed people of this country. I am honored to know that this prestigious organization still supports me as we resist those who would seek to defeat us before our noble task is complete.' "

"Got it. Moving on. The stock market has mostly bounced back from its initial post-hack lows, though trading volumes are lower than normal."

"We're in the hold-your-breath phase. Probably will be like that all next week, unless the polls show good separation back in our favor."

"Exactly. Next up, overseas there were a couple of bombings by the usual suspects. Ten dead in Egypt, thirty-five over in Iraq. Anything you want to include in our statement?"

"Go with boilerplate as long as no American citizens died. We've got too much going on to deal with that right now."

"Right. Finally, at least for my list, are battleground state updates in other elections. Looks like we'll take the governors races in Florida and Oregon—"

"We'd better! How on earth did we lose Oregon back in 'twenty-two? It feels like we're in a battleground *nation* right now. Please, go on."

"And in the Senate, it could be a wash. Up in North Carolina and Pennsylvania, but down in Colorado, and if you can believe it, California."

"If things were on firmer ground here, I'd be happy to fly out and give a speech or two. But as it all stands right now, I'm sorry to say that they might be on their own."

"I'll relay a message saying that 'the president sincerely regrets that prior commitments preclude her from offering in-person support.' "

"You're a hell of a translator, Tony. Okay, let's wrap this up. Is there any *good* news to report?"

Natalie raised her hand. "One thing that seems to have gotten lost in the shuffle is the grand opening out in Las Vegas this weekend."

"Oh, that's right!" The president rubbed her hands together. "Wow. I know we didn't plan it this way, but the timing could be perfect. Please tell me they're promoting the hell out of it."

"I believe," Tony said, "there's going to be a TV special hosted by none other than Ryan Richards."

"What, is everyone from *DDM* looking for redemption now? Regardless, clear my schedule for that time slot. And you're all invited. We'll get some snacks, vodka, beer. Let's have a little pre-party before the final push. It's Vegas, guys. Come on!"

"And we're going to win."

"God damn right we are."

9. PAYBACK

"Now, coming to you from Las Vegas, Nevada... Please welcome the host of *DDM TV Live*, the one and only, Ryan Richards!"

Applause roared through a crowded casino as spotlights darted around wildly. Big band music brought out a dancing Ryan Richards, whose face was so bronze it was as if he had stepped directly out of a tanning booth and onto the stage. He smiled and waved to the audience as he strutted forward, then raised a pencil-thin silver microphone to his lips.

"What a difference a few weeks can make, eh folks?" he said with a wry grin. The crowd gave hearty laughter. "But how fitting that one of the world's premier boxing cities is where we scrape ourselves off the mat, and come out swinging with a combo of our own. Ladies and gentlemen, are you ready to gambllllle!"

Everyone yelled and waved their arms. Hip-hop began to play as camera-mounted drones circled above the casino floor, revealing a sea of slot machines and video poker units, plus dozens of gaming tables. As the cheers died down, Richards pulled a wad of cash from his pocket and motioned as if to hand a bill to a member of the audience, before yanking it away playfully.

"Got ya! Oh, I see we have some spooky Halloween costumes out there in the crowd. Hopefully you'll bag some treats tonight. Now, why are we all the way out west, and not back in our New York studios? Because we're celebrating this very special new casino which offers a unique twist on gambling. Ladies and gentlemen, it's Paybax time!"

As the crowd erupted once more, giant video screens near the stage showed endless streams of gold coins pouring down into a pair of brown hands. Richards began peeling off bills from his stack and throwing them into the crowd, then stepped back with a wave.

"Sorry, sorry. That wasn't supposed to be part of the show. I just couldn't contain my excitement. We're having too much of a good time tonight! So, what is this place all about? Consider the name: Paybax. Who is doing the paying, and who is getting paid back? Hmm…"

Richards pointed to a paunchy white woman in her fifties and declared, "You *and* you! 'But Ryan, how can that be?' you ask. Simple. Because all the games here at Paybax Casino are linked with the HRA's accounting framework.

"For every dollar you gamble, one half of one percent is immediately applied to your Debit Score balance. And that's only if you lose! Because if you win, some of that prize money can be used to pay off what you owe—or will owe down the road after MARVIN digs up more dirt, haha.

"Look, we know that Reparations hasn't been much fun for most Debtors. But now, you can reduce your obligation all while getting in on the excitement. That is, if you have the guts to play!"

Loud brass music blared and a series of logos and graphics flashed across the screens. The announcer read, "Come try your luck on one of the many games exclusive only to Paybax Casino. First, take a puff on the Prosperity Pipe. One big win and you'll be spouting Jackpot Theories. Are you brave enough to enter the Haunted Plantation?"

Richards cocked an eyebrow and pursed his lips, then looked dramatically from side to side.

"So far, we've only been talking about Debtors. And this casino isn't some Caucs-only club, now is it? Noooo, zir! Hahaha! There's plenty of fun and games to be had by Beneficiaries as well. Tell 'em, Donnie."

The announcer said, "How about up to two hundred dollars in chips for free? Offer only valid once per Beneficiary per week— sorry, they make us say that. What about one free double-down bet per night? Or, how about a little something we call Spontaneous Reparations? Yes, if you suspect that a Debtor at your table has a better hand than you... Whoosh! You can swap cards. Just yell out 'Houdini!' and the deed will be done— handled by the dealer of course, because there *are* cameras everywhere."

During this interlude, Richards had left the stage and gone out onto the bustling casino floor. He approached an elderly white couple playing Acre's Bounty and said, "Howdy, folks! What brought you to Paybax Casino on opening weekend?"

"Hi, Ryan!" the woman said loudly, trying to be heard over the buzz of the crowd. "We love the nickel slots, so we said why not give this new place a shot?"

"Indeed! How have you fared so far?"

"I'm up a few dollars, but my husband hasn't—oh my goodness! Look, honey! You just got three mules in a row!"

Richards turned to the camera and said, "It can happen to you too, just like that! Come on, let's go meet more people. Aha, it looks like there's high drama over at this Texas free 'em table. Let's watch the action."

Three players looked on intently as the dealer turned the river card. They each placed their final bets, then as the hands were revealed, the black man playing threw his arms up in triumph. The dealer pushed several stacks of chips toward him.

"Looks like we have a winner," Richards beamed, "in more ways than one. Let's mosey on over to the craps table, where it looks like someone's on a bit of a roll."

A young brunette at the head of the table was shaking her fist high in the air. She threw the dice down the length of the table, bouncing them hard against the walls, and watched them settle. The group of people watching roared. She looked at the man standing next to her and he said, "One more time, baby!"

The woman joined her hands as if to pray, then cast the dice forward with her eyes closed. A great cheer arose and she fell into the man's arms crying.

Richards approached them and said, "My, oh my, another big winner! What's your name?"

The woman wiped her eyes. "I'm Stephanie and this is my fiance, Trent. Go Badgers!"

"Oh wow, all the way from Wisconsin. What brought you two kids to Vegas?"

"We each have pretty bad Debit Scores as it is. But when we got the estimate from the MARVIN Marriage Calculator, we almost died when we realized how much our future children would owe."

"Too many DEs?"

"No, no," Trent said. "Turns out we're both distantly related to General Custer."

"Forbidden love, ooh la la!"

"So," Stephanie continued, "we came here to see if Lady Luck would tap us with her magic wand. And now she has! We just won enough money to help reduce our own Debit Scores, plus start a Reparations Fund for our kids."

Richards gave Trent a high-five, then started walking back toward the stage.

"Just amazing," he said. "Paybax truly has all the glitz and excitement of the casinos you know and love. But with the added bonus of poker and slot games that you'll find nowhere else. Now, I know that you folks in the audience can hardly restrain yourselves from joining in the fun, but we've got one more surprise in store, so hold on. A very special guest is here to help me officially get this party started.

"I'd like you to welcome my well-traveled friend—a man who has journeyed from Mexico to California to New York City. A man who took a *little detour* into South Dakota on his way back to Los Angeles, and is now here in Las Vegas for the very first time. Put your hands together for my hero, Mr. Luis Ortega!"

Luis jogged out onto the stage wearing a baseball cap with flipped-up brim and his trademark black-framed glasses. Richards gave him a high-five and Luis waved at the audience.

"My, oh my," Richards crowed. "A reunion that could make the angels sing. How are ya, old man?"

"I'm good," Luis said. "Feeling well rested."

People in the crowd said, "Awwww," and put their hands on their hearts.

Richards escorted Luis across the stage to a giant faux-stone disc that towered above them. Similar to Italy's Mouth of Truth and the Aztec calendar stone, it had ornate nooks and crannies, cryptic inscriptions, downcast hollow eyes, and a gaping lower jaw that protruded like a toll booth collection basket.

"Oh boy, Luis. This is it, the main attraction here at Paybax Casino. Because every hour on the hour, they'll hold a ceremony here at MARVIN'S Mouth so that people can pay tribute to Reparations. And joining us to demonstrate how it works is Frank, a Debtor who won five thousand dollars playing Repatriated Artifacts earlier today. Frank, come on up and tell us how much you would like to keep, apply to your debt, plus do our variation on 'phone a friend.' "

"Hi, world! Frank Turgeson here. How about I keep half, apply forty percent to my Score, and pay the rest of my chips *forward* to Luis?"

"Wha-what?!" Richards screeched as he fell to his knees. "Payin' it back! Payin' it forward! Sing it with me, folks. We're payin' it back, by payin' it forward..."

Richards began a ridiculous dance as he repeated this refrain. A bass drum began to thump from somewhere. Fred threw his hands out to raise the roof. Luis looked offstage, nodded at someone, then started to dance as well. Richards caught his breath and motioned for them to stop.

"Now," Richards said, "let's see the process in action. Frank, step up to the left side like so, just let the stone take a quick retinal scan... And now follow the instructions on the touchscreen to make your selections."

"Feed me!" a deep, craggy voice bellowed from inside the monolith. "Feed me!"

Frank dumped his chips and tokens into the wide open mouth. The sound of crunching and cash register dings filled the casino. Richards motioned for Luis to come closer.

"Luis, now you just need to scan your eye and—"

A siren wailed and a torrent of silver coins shot out of the eyes onto the ground below.

"Go on, buddy. Take them all. That's yours to gamble now."

Luis knelt down and put some of the money into his pocket. Richards gave Frank a big hug and said, "Wonderful, just wonderful."

Luis stood up with bulging pockets and Richards asked, "Is there anything you'd like to say now?"

"Uh, wow. Thank you, Frank. I hope I can win some more out there."

"Anything *else* you'd like to add?"

"Oh yeah, sure." Luis dug a small sheet of paper out from under the coins, then began to read. "In addition to this new casino," he said slowly, "I am here to announce the HRA's new Beneficiary Deferment Program. Of which I am the first participant. That's right, now any Beneficiary who is in school or who has another pressing commitment, can choose to defer their DDM assignment until he or she completes said program. In conclusion, I would like to thank the Historical Reparations Administration for helping me fulfill my dream to become an electrical engineer and make my family proud. The new deferment program—helping the HRA help Beneficiaries like me."

"Well said, young man," Richards added after the crowd gave respectful applause. "Do you hear that, world? 'I prefer to defer!' Because this whole Reparations thing *is* for the Beneficiaries, right? It just took a little healthy civil disobedience to persuade the HRA to accommodate this reasonable request. Speaking of accommodations, I hear the hotel rooms here are 'suite'!

"Well, that about wraps it up for this special broadcast. For those of you watching at home, be sure to make a stop at Paybax

Casino a part of your next Vegas vacation. Because hey, just one bet could reduce your debt! And to everyone here in person tonight, you've been so patient, but it's finally time to get out there and play. This is Ryan Richards saying good night, and I'll see you out on the casino floor!"

The crowd hollered one last time before flowing out into the gaming area, and lively brass music piped through the speakers to end the show. Richards skipped off the stage and grabbed a napkin to mop his forehead. He took in the lively scene of tourists having fun amid all the flashing lights and electronic beeps, then gave a big sigh.

He felt a squeeze on the arm and saw that it was Gayle, his *DDM* producer who had flown out to oversee the broadcast.

"Ry Guy!" she beamed. "That was great. You really went the extra mile for us out there."

Richards wiped more sweat off his temple. "Aw, shucks. And likewise. The whole crew was on point. Excellent show. And hey, no hacks or protesters out on the casino floor, so I guess security actually did their job."

"Yep, everyone pitched in. But seriously, Ryan. You delivered! Huge energy and stage presence. That was a command performance and you should be proud."

"It's all about embracing the moment, Gayle. Sometimes you've just got to be on."

"I hope the people in high places who were watching appreciated it."

"Well, if darling Eileen wins, maybe she'll invite me to emcee an event sometime. Because if she loses—"

"No one's going to lose."

"*If she loses,* I may never work again."

"I swear, sometimes you take hyperbole to the extreme."

"Okay, fine. Relegated to a cooking show or selling magic glue on an infomercial. Heh, worst case, I'll get stuck hosting a game show on Lifetime."

"Are you kidding? That would be your dream job, getting housewives all hot and bothered. Anyway, we've done our part. Why don't you go take a load off?"

"That's easy for you to say. You live behind the camera. I'm all amped up right now. Buuuut, I see someone who might relate. Luis! What's up, buddy?"

Richards ran over to Luis and gave him a high-five.

"Hi there, Mister Ryan."

"Great job out there, man. It all went off like a charm."

"Cool. So nobody took over the show this time? I'm glad."

"You and me both, buddy." Richards turned his eyes into slits and scanned the surrounding area. "But now it's time to see what kind of trouble I can get into. You up for a quick drink over at the bar?"

"Nah. I'll go find my parents, see what they wanna do."

"Aw, come on. Luis! It's me! I sat by your bedside, remember? Let's go shoot the shit until your folks turn up."

"Okay, I guess. Let me just text them real quick."

An hour later, Ryan Richards was twirling a cocktail umbrella between his fingers and saying, "Here's the thing, bud. You gotta learn to loosen up. Like earlier, when you were worried they wouldn't serve you because you're under twenty-one."

"I know, I'm sorry."

"Because Luis, it's Vegas! Brand new casino and everything. And hell, it's almost like a private party with all the crew members and HRA people around. Plus, who's gonna say no to me? I'm Ryan Effing Richards. Having a night out with my main man, Luis *El Boracho* Ortega!"

Luis cracked a smile and gulped some beer. "Nah, I'm not as cool as you. Tall *gringo* with the really white teeth, haha."

"Ah, come off that humble crap," Richards grumbled as he poked at the ice in his glass. "It's smooth, though. Like you've got your own vibe. Sitting back in the pocket. Doing things on Ortega time."

"Hmm. What time is that, exactly?"

"Time for some shots, that's what! Hey, girly! Two shots of Patrón Silver, *por favor*."

Luis looked down at his phone while the bartender came over and poured their drinks.

"Oh man, where are my parents anyway?"

"Probably out gambling or watching some circus show bullshit. I tell you what. Let's stop worrying about them and take on the town! I'm a real celebrity. I still got some street cred from my old acting days. Annnnd, I could probably get us in VIP at some strip clubs!"

"Nah… You mean, like, naked girls?"

"Hotties. Nude. Full bar. And maybe even some *private dances!*"

"Dang. Can you like, touch 'em?"

"Well, you're not really supposed to—but it don't matter if you're VIP!"

"Crap, why won't my parents pick up?"

"Forget 'em, man. We're in Vegas, on the Strip! Are you in, or am I gonna have to handle all the girls myself?"

"No way! You probably get lots of chicks because you're famous, but—" Luis downed his shot of tequila "—now I've been on TV too, like twice. That's gotta be worth something. So let's go, *cabrón!*"

Ryan drank his shot and gave a howl. "Luis, about to get dowwwwn!"

The next morning, Luis woke up to a steady banging sound. His body ached from head to toe, so he just stayed curled up. But the noise didn't stop. Finally he dragged himself out of bed to see what it was. The banging was coming from the door that connected with his parents' suite.

He called out, "Who's there? What do you want?"

"Luis!" his mom cried. "Are you okay?"

"Of course, I'm fine. What's the problem, Mama?"

"Please, can you open the door?"

Luis unlocked the door and then ran to put on a bathrobe. His mother and father came into the room and embraced him.

"Thank the Lord!" his mother said. "We didn't know what happened to you."

Luis eased out of their arms and fell into a chair. "But last night I couldn't find you after the show. Where did you go?"

Mr. Ortega said, "Seeing you on the stage made us too nervous, so we walked down the street. We looked inside the casinos. They were all very nice."

"Plus we did some gambling!" Mrs Ortega said. "But only just a little. Papi won fifty dollars one time. Then we got a little lost, and when your father checked his phone for the map, he sees that the battery is dead. I don't have my phone, so what do we do?"

"Finally we get back to this casino and ask for you, but

somebody say you leave here in a fancy car. I plug my phone and try to call you, but I get your voicemail."

"Sorry," Luis said. "I guess I turned my phone off."

"It's okay. We were tired. We think you must be having fun with the people from the television. But now this morning you don't wake up, you don't answer the phone… Your mama gets worried so she knocks on the door."

"But now we see everything is fine," Mrs. Ortega said. "Did you have a good time?"

Luis scratched his head. "I think so."

"Okay, you go take a shower. Then we get breakfast and leave for the airport."

"Sure, Mama. See you soon."

Luis got back into bed and tried to remember what had happened the previous night. Vague memories of vodka bottles and dancing to techno flickered in his mind. Then he noticed that the sugary smell of female fragrance was still on his own body. He found his glasses under the bedside table and put them on. One lens was covered with a neon green imprint of kissing lips.

Now very intrigued, Luis crawled over to his jeans which were on the floor and took his phone out of the pocket. He turned it on to discover that not only was Ryan Richards now one of his contacts, the man had in fact sent him over a dozen photo messages.

The final picture showed Luis hugging a topless woman, while Richards was bent over pretending to bite his backside. The accompanying text message said, "Don't tell MARVIN!"

Luis wrote back, "omg. i dont remember half that stuff".

"Doesn't matter," Richards replied a few minutes later. "I'm sure I'll be out in LA soon. We'll do Hollywood together in style…"

"Haha ur crazy. Oh and thank u. I had fun!"

"And you sir are a legend. Rock on!"

Luis nestled under the covers and slowly scrolled through the pictures again, blushing as he relived his wild night in Sin City.

10. FACE TO FACE

When Kate arrived at the Newark HRA megabranch early Monday morning, she was relieved to find that all the protesters she'd seen the previous week were gone. The Debtor and Beneficiary lines were also considerably shorter than before, so even though several National Guard troops were still posted out front, she hoped this was a sign that public perception was starting to turn in the HRA's favor.

Just over a week ago, while still reeling from the shock of her experience in Virginia, Kate found that it wasn't so easy to turn her back on nearly fifteen years of living when groping for a new way forward. Almost drowsily, she took the path of least resistance and returned home to Brooklyn ready to give everything another shot.

At work she joined in on the nationwide effort to reaffirm that the HRA was functioning reliably. But all the while, she kept her discoveries a secret from everyone—not only her coworkers, but even her husband—because she simply couldn't afford to make any rash decisions without knowing the consequences.

And today she was thanking God for having done it this way. In just a few hours she was expected back in the city to appear in election ads with none other than the President of the United States.

She, Jan, and TJ had sent frantic and excited group texts to each other about it all weekend, and now Kate was not surprised to find them waiting on the couch in her office with big smiles.

"Hi, guys!" she said.

"The ride continues!" Jan said. "Are you ready, girl?"

"I can't believe that this, of all things, is happening."

"You've made it through the lows. Now it's time for a high."

"I'm starting to feel nervous. Whew!"

"TJ, tell her the good news so she can calm down."

TJ swiped into a tablet and said, "Dominguez bombed over the weekend. This article here says half the crowd walked out on him both in Mobile and New Orleans."

"Goodness," Kate said. "What went wrong?"

"His mouth, apparently. Listen to this quote. 'Y'all down here been livin' amongst each other for hundreds of years. I reckon you could do a better job handling your business than some far-away government body.' Then someone in the crowd yelled out, 'Are you talking about states' rights?' "

Jan smacked her forehead.

"Well, how did he respond?" Kate said.

TJ chuckled. "That question was a setup. There's no right answer. He gave a hesitant 'yes,' but a 'no' would have pissed people off just as much."

"And," Jan said, "I saw on the news this morning that Jeffries-Lao got a healthy bump in the polls. So Kate, there's no need to be anxious when you see her."

Kate smiled. "That is good news. I've always wanted to meet her. And I was just dreading the thought that if I did poorly today and she lost, that some part of that would reflect on me."

"Instead you're just going to knock in an insurance run for the team. So have fun! Next week we put all the doubts to rest, and then we'll get back to it in here."

"Full steam ahead."

"I'm counting on you. Just because you got off the hook not going to Cleveland thanks to Luis, don't think we aren't going to work you here!"

"That's right," TJ added. "And now that those FBI snoops have finally moved on, we'll be able to pep everyone up again. Team leaders, unite!"

They came together and gave a group high-five.

At noon, Kate arrived at the studio space in uptown. She passed through a security checkpoint before being escorted to an upper floor. She sat briefly for hair and makeup, where she was also quizzed by a producer as to whether she had reviewed the scripts the president's team had sent over.

Kate was then led to a small holding room, where she found herself face to face and alone with Eileen Jeffries-Lao. She couldn't breathe.

The president smiled broadly and extended her hand. "Hello, Kate. Thank you so much for agreeing to help my campaign on such short notice."

"It's an honor, Madam President. Unexpected, to say the least, but I am at your service."

"Excellent. I wish I could say that I commanded a prepared production crew, but apparently they're still setting up in there. Shall we have coffee while we wait?"

"I'd love to," Kate said.

They sat down at a small wooden dining table. Kate didn't dare break the silence. The president smiled again, then said, "So you live in the city?"

"Yes," Kate said. "My husband and I have an apartment in Brooklyn."

"Kids?"

"No. Two dogs."

"Ah. And from what I gather, you've been with the HRA since the beginning?"

"Even before that, actually. I joined the Colonial Amends Committee in the spring of 'twenty-three."

"Oh," the president said. "I'm a bit surprised we've never met then. The CAC was one of several groups my campaign allied with during that magical journey."

Kate blushed. "I've seen you speak several times. But the occasion never actually brought us together."

"Well, if this roller coaster ride the HRA's been on is what it took to finally introduce us, I hope we'll both be better for it. And truly, I'm appalled that you've been personally impacted during this trying time."

"That's so kind of you to say, Madam President."

"Please, it's Eileen for everyone between now and the victory party."

"Okay," Kate said, "I'll do my best to remember that."

The president flipped through some papers, making small notes in the margins. She looked up at Kate. "So, you're an assistant regional manager. How high up do you want to go with the HRA?"

Kate set down her coffee and brought an index finger to her lips for a moment. "I can't say for certain. I've always just wanted to help people. That's been my motivation. So even though today, while I have an impressive-sounding job title and more management responsibilities than if I was working at a women's shelter, the core sentiment remains the same."

"Interesting." Eileen paused, then said, "I do think that people with real talent shouldn't let the idea of 'service' get in the way of making the right decisions for themselves. Our movement can't afford it, in fact."

"How so?" Kate asked.

"Because stunting your own potential, by being passive rather than planning, only hurts those in need. There will always be someone out there going through hard times. Do you have the energy for that kind of a life? Down in the trenches, always fighting, fighting, fighting for the underdog?"

"I have, so far. And that's what led me to being part of the surge that made the HRA possible."

"Kate, when you're in your twenties, it's all fresh and exciting. And with the HRA you rode a timely wave into, if we're going to be honest, the rock star world. Big new agency, fancy new building, a nice income for yourself. But now that there's been a hiccup..."

"What am I supposed to say?"

"The point is," Jeffries-Lao said, "even after we clamp down on the Sentinels, take some time to think about where your life is headed. If you stay where you are while the program runs its course, it might become less fulfilling each year. Or maybe you could use your experience to help when we launch overseas."

Kate said, "I'm not sure what that would mean for my marriage."

"Exactly. These are the types of considerations we have to make as we get older. There's other fields, other options."

"But I don't know if anything will be as rewarding as what I'm doing now."

"Oh, I believe you," Eileen said. "But it was the rarest of opportunities that sprang up only because all the right conditions arose. So maybe before you move onto something new, take stock and see what it is you really want in life."

"Forgive me," Kate said, "if I'm a bit shocked to hear you put it so bluntly. It seems as if all you've ever done is serve."

The president sat back in her chair. "If you look at my resume more closely," she said, "you'll notice several small gaps between the major moves. Each time I considered taking that leap—from local to state to national politics—I briefly stepped away. First, to live a little, but also to consult with my family. Because they're in it just as much as you. Have you talked with your husband about what might happen if I were to lose next week?"

Kate looked away for a moment. "The truth is that since being sent to South Dakota to deal with the Luis Ortega situation, I haven't been communicating with Chris very well. And when I was away, I even made some upsetting discoveries about my education that have knocked my equilibrium out of whack.

"But," she continued, "I've put too many years into my work, and the HRA needs all the support it can get right now—so I stuffed the doubt back down and just soldiered on. And here we are. I'm unsure whether what you're saying is supposed to snap me back in line, or if it will end up leaving me even more confused."

"That's just what we call the life of a career woman," Eileen said with a smile. "They pump us up as little girls, assuring us that we can 'have it all.' As if feminism and advantageous hiring practices magically make it so that we don't have to sacrifice or give our all.

"You can't legislate respect. You can't control where men's eyes wander. And when you have children, even an accommodating country like ours can't carry the baby for you. It can't clear your mind to focus on work when you're swooning with nausea. So you see, even when things are at their best, nothing's perfect. And that's why, yes, some of this does have to be only about you."

Kate smiled. "I'll take this advice to heart, thank you. But after you win, how could I in good conscience step away anytime soon?"

"How old are you now?" the president asked.

"Thirty-two."

"Here's a little tidbit, just between us warrior princesses. From nine to five, keep working as you have been. But when you get home at night, really be present with your husband. And who knows, maybe one morning you'll just happen to find yourself pregnant. Then all these doubts will start to fade away. Because you'll just know what to do."

"Is it as simple as that?" Kate asked. "I feel this urge to not trust my instincts—because that would be selfish."

"Oh Kate," Eileen said, "when they sold us on having it all, they neglected to highlight that we already had something incredibly profound within us. But we do. The one thing we can do that men cannot is give birth and be mothers. It's a gift from God to us—and our gift to the world."

Kate sighed. "I get it but, how were you able to manage your incredible career at the same time?"

"First and foremost, Chinese culture values family very much. And try as we might, you can't always outrun where you come from. But another thing. At times this political game forces you to act hard as nails. And as a woman competing in a male-dominated arena, I sometimes come off as aggressive and biting. I get it, that's the nature of the business."

Eileen smiled. She said, "But I still remember changing my daughter's diapers and rocking her to sleep. That really puts things in perspective. And in four years, when this is all over for me, I envision stepping off Marine One and lifting my future grandchild into my arms. *That* is how I plan to spend my retirement, not waving banners in the streets."

"You'd walk away completely into private life?" Kate asked. "I don't know if I could do that."

"Well, I'm sure I'll give speeches and make other appearances as required of an ex-president, but the point is this. Even if you did want everything that you've gone after so far, you owe it to yourself to make sure that in another ten years, your life looks like what you want it to be."

"I will think about it, thank you."

After a silent moment, the president looked at her watch. "Hmm, they are taking their sweet time in there. Maybe a couple Dominguez supporters are on set."

Kate half-smiled, then said, "Eileen, do you ever have doubts about what we're doing?"

"You're always taking flak in my line of work, so you tend to question yourself as a matter of course. But more specifically, what's on your mind?"

"I mean, do you have any fears about the consequences of Reparations? What things will look like at the end?"

Jeffries-Lao exhaled. "If you're asking whether I feared that the database would turn into a surveillance state nightmare, I'll say this. While I was made aware that our project leader had left under protest, I guess you could say we were all swept up at the time envisioning the United States as just the first of many lanes on the Reparations highway. Obviously, things are a little dicey right now. But I've already dealt with a lot of naysayers this month, so please don't tell me you're also in that camp."

"I'd be lying if I said I didn't have any doubts," Kate said. "But I've been fighting for this cause for a long time. No one should doubt my commitment, but maybe they shouldn't ignore my concerns either."

"Well, you've got my ear while we're waiting. What scares you the most and what can we do to address it?"

"For one, I… We'd all be devastated if you lost next week."

"Not going to happen," Eileen said, "so cheer up. Next?"

"I think it's clear that the grace period is over for the HRA. We need to show people that they can still count on us."

"Six months from now, when we've tightened all the leaks and done a PR blitz about our commitment to privacy, I assure you this whole situation will be looked back upon as nothing more than growing pains."

"I do hope you're right." Kate paused, then said, "Since I have intimate HRA knowledge, would you be offended if I voiced another concern?"

"Not at all, Kate. You are an industry professional and I welcome your insights."

"Thank you. The impression I'm getting—from a few close colleagues, as well as how adamant the masked man was about even law enforcement losing faith in some of our more punitive methods—it seems as if internal fixes and PR blasts might not be enough to contain anti-Reparations sentiment."

"That's a valid fear," Eileen said. "I don't think stricter methods to keep people in line are the answer."

"Especially if Telecom & Penal are able to get Congress to authorize their plans."

The president shook her head. "I'd almost forgotten about them. Turning our own database against us, terrible. Microscopic Protocol would do incalculable harm to the Beneficiary class."

"I know," Kate said wearily. "All of us at the HRA dread what a setback it could be."

"After the inauguration, my people will put as much pressure on them as possible to get them to reconsider taking that step."

"Thank you for hearing me out. All I want is to help the HRA in any way that I can. No doubt your administration has been under more pressure than I have since the hack, but… I'm really struggling to digest the public humiliation they put me through."

"Like it or not," the president said, "you're a public figure now. It can really be rough. Me? I've taken abuse for over twenty years from small town op-ed writers, foreign leaders, and of course those trolls in the meme brigade. But hopefully being in this ad with me will serve to rehabilitate your reputation—and help you get your confidence back."

"I appreciate your saying that," Kate said. "And because I admire you as such a strong woman, please allow me one last question."

"Of course."

"I thought I knew exactly who I was for the longest time. I believed in myself and was firing on all cylinders. But what that masked man said knocked my feet right out from under me. Every day since then has been a struggle."

"He really got into your head, didn't he?" The president shook her head with concern.

"I'm afraid so."

"Kate, in a few minutes I want you to step in front of that camera and envision that you're talking directly to him. Show that SOB he hasn't broken you and that you're stronger than ever. Because look, you're working with the President of the United States right now. And who's he? Just another disgruntled Debtor with no other way for his voice to be heard than by resorting to Ted Kaczynski tactics. Let's go show him who's boss!"

They finished shortly after five o'clock. Both were worn out after dozens of takes under bright lights. As they parted, the president offered Kate a few last kind words and a gentle hug. Kate left the building feeling a warm glow of satisfaction, and she couldn't wait to get home to celebrate with Chris.

But halfway through the subway ride, she remembered that he already had evening plans. Glenn, the singer from his old band, was in town and they were going out drinking. She was almost tempted to try and track them down once she got back to Brooklyn, but decided not to interrupt. Plus, she and Glenn weren't on the best terms these days…

Instead, Kate dropped by the neighborhood Whole Foods and treated herself to wine, cheese, and snacks. She was going to make the best of having to fly solo, because not everyone got to speak privately with the president for nearly half an hour—let alone become "fast friends," as Kate allowed herself to indulge.

She set up shop on the couch and opened the first bottle of a Peruvian Malbec. The dogs were attracted by the cheese and settled in around her. She was munching on pita chips and browsing maternity websites on the big screen, when suddenly she heard the chilling croak of her inner voice for the first time since her illness last summer.

"*Kaaaaaate,*" it said. "What are you thinking about? Don't tell me you're veering off course."

"Excuse me," Kate replied, "but the president of our country just gave me some very heartfelt advice. I'd be a fool—and ungrateful—not to think it over."

"But who are you to her? She doesn't know you, so why should she open up to you like that?"

"Probably because I and people like me were the ones who made her presidency possible. By the way, I just looked it up and she did in fact decline to run for re-election in California back in 'twenty-two. It was only because of the groundswell we created that she entered the presidential primaries."

"Nonsense! That may be a nice cover story, but as I recall, her campaign hit the ground running early in 'twenty-three. Maybe she was just buttering you up so you'd perform well on camera. Or, perhaps she was feeling you out for a potential job in her next administration. In which case…"

"Oh, you are a fiend! But that *would* be nice. Live and work close to my parents. But how would Chris feel? I guess, in theory, he could run his business from anywhere…"

"Bah, Chris. He's not really doing anything. Just a techie. You're out there making a difference!"

"Everyone needs support staff. I wasn't part of the construction crew that built my field office. And I don't know anything about the networks we run."

"But you *are* the one the HRA puts on TV."

"Be quiet! You're getting me all mixed up."

"Why won't you just trust me?" the voice cooed.

"Because I really need to know how much of me is not

genuine, but something… else. I need to figure out where my life is going."

"But you've done so well on this track. First, you broke through the natural resistance and became aware of your privilege. And then you actually put this truth into action, changing millions of lives for the better in the process."

"All this talk about change, it's making me dizzy. Changing the world. Being a change agent. But who decides which changes are good? Are some people not fit to change anything?"

"Kate, my darling. I've known you for a long, long time. So permit me to speak freely here. The fact that you are so privileged is the very reason that you're equipped to bring about the better world we wish to see."

"Stop! Ugh—that phrase… 'Better world we wish to see.' My whole head is just filled with these canned lines. And they come from the likes of you!"

"Don't get mad at me! All this time, did you ever do anything you didn't want to? Did you not think highly of yourself after every canned food drive, charity run, and HRA outreach? You sure had a lot of fun for someone who claimed to be sacrificing for others."

"Wait a minute! That's what you're for. And haven't you been doing that since the beginning? Clicking the rows of the abacus back and forth to make sure it all evened out?"

"I tried. But no matter what I did, somehow I just couldn't keep up with your pride. The satisfaction you got from it all. That is *not* what this belief system is all about."

"What belief system? You make it sound like I joined a religious group. No way. This is supposed to be about the heart using the mind to help the less fortunate."

"Yes, but if you want to make a real impact, it can't just be on an individual basis. You need a system to plug these ideas into. Hey, why the sour face? The HRA is that system—and you helped create it."

"I know what the HRA is, thank you very much. I'm sick to my stomach right now because I realize that schools are also part of a system that's designed in the same way, but nobody sees it. And I'm mad because I was never told what its real purpose was."

"Katie, don't turn your back on the strong women who set the stage for the trajectory of your life."

"But they did it without my permission! Would anyone send their children to a summer camp or a church, if they knew that the staff was going to subliminally put a secret ideology into their minds? Even if it's not criminal, it's not forthright—and nothing about how I've lived *my* life involves hiding the truth."

"Why do you want to pick things apart like this? After the fact? After all the good we've done—"

"We?! We? ... Oh my god... Who the hell are you anyway?"

"I—"

"Lurking in the back of my mind, always ready to pop out and throw in your two cents. It's funny, because everything you say boils down to me prostrating myself in order to... do what? Save the world? Well, you know, I'm tired. Exhausted, in fact. But I see it now. All these years, even when you were silent, you still pulled the strings. I just can't do it anymore. I'm done!"

"Kate, how can you say that? We've been working together for nearly fifteen years. I incubated in your mind, just like I was your baby, long before I even first spoke to you. We're one, together. You and me."

"No, no. I obeyed you because I trusted you. And naturally, I *thought* you were my voice. But you're just an impostor! Someone slipped you into my subconscious, like an ideology roofie. They hijacked the direction of my entire life through you, and... and... now I'll crash this plane if that's what it takes to get free."

"Think twice before you do that, Kate. Without me, you'll just be out on a ledge, blind and alone. Stay with me, we can talk and work things out. You're a mature woman now, so maybe I can let go of the reins and give you more control. Heck, you've earned it. You've done far more than anything I could ever take credit for."

"What, are we bargaining now? About who gets what percentage stake of my mind? I'm not a company you can just divide up. This is *me!* And you are not my warden."

"No, I've never claimed to be in charge. If not a roommate, then maybe your spiritual guide? And now, yes, I can see that you're ready for more autonomy. But that doesn't mean you should just suddenly go out on your own. We have so much more work to do out there!"

"Have you not been paying attention to what's been going on lately? If not with the HRA, at least within me? I simply cannot move forward like before. I don't know what to do. ... Chris! The first thing I'm going to do is hold Chris in my arms and listen to what he's got to say. Poor guy, he's stood by me through everything so patiently, while *you* only keep nagging me and driving me forward with your whip."

"Oh, for God's sake. Chris, Chris... Damn him! That hypocrite. The little businessman hiding behind his punk rock t-shirts. What *do* you think is on his mind? While his wife was bounding around the country without him, chasing down a mystery that has led her right back into the gray matter inside her own head? Lost and found, Mrs. Kate Donohugh, thank you very much."

"You monster! Trying to poison me against my own husband. For what? So you can turn me into just another lonely old woman who's so bitter that no one is willing to put up with her?"

"Kate, stop right there. You really don't want to keep pulling that thread..."

"Or what? Will I find that there *is* something else in my mind? Something pure that you've been hiding? What is it? Where is it? You—get out of the way!"

"Kate, nooooo!"

Kate brought her hands up and cleared away a wash of tears that had filled her eyes. She reached for her phone and called Chris. It went directly to his voicemail.

"Hi, baby," she said softly, "it's me. I know you're out having fun tonight. I just want you to know that I love you so much. When I see you, I... I... Chris, I want you to be the father of our children."

11. THE WARNING

A burly man with a thick red beard carried a pitcher and two pint glasses away from the bar. He set them down in front of Chris Donohugh, then hung up his black satin flight jacket before sliding into the booth.

"Feels good to be back in Brooklyn," he said. "And it's great to see you again, man."

Chris poured the beer and then offered a toast. "Cheers, Glenn. Sucks we don't do this more often. Philly's not all that far away."

"Forget it, man. Life gets busy. I'm just glad you could meet up. Nice to have a day off before we hit the road again."

"You should've told me about the gig last night. Maybe I could have made it."

"Nah. Some dive up in the Bronx. I knew it was gonna be shit. I wanted to see you when I was in a good mood. Better mood, at least." Glenn gulped some beer and laughed. "So how you been? I see Kate's famous now."

"Yeah," Chris said. "Our dirty laundry aired out for the world to see. Just awesome."

"Don't sweat it. That stuff passes. Who doesn't have something embarrassing as hell out there?"

"What's really insane is that after all that, somehow *the* president actually wanted Kate to be in a campaign commercial with her."

"Say what?!" Glenn called out.

"Oh yeah, no biggie," Chris said. "Jeffries-Lao's people just called her right up on Saturday."

"Haha, that's wild."

"Kate was tap dancing around the apartment all weekend. Anyway, the filming was supposed to happen today but I don't know how it went. Sometimes this shit's just too much, you know?"

"And that's why we drink!" Glenn said. "Well... In Chris news, are you still designing?"

"I can't stop. That's what keeps me out of the cubicle."

"I never liked offices either. Unless I've got a microphone in my hand, I'll stick to the shadows. Blue collar or bust, baby! Here, tilt your glass."

"Hold on," Chris said. "Let me pound this."

"That's my boy." Glenn's eyes moved to the TVs that were on the wall behind the pool tables. "Would ya look at that. A special news report about the Sentinels. 'Reparations on the Razor's Edge.' So dramatic! What do you think's gonna happen, Donohugh?"

Chris shrugged. "They'll get it squared away. It's too big of a deal to give up on. Like they say, these things only come around once every five hundred years, right?"

"Well, jeez. Lucky timing for us to live through it!" Glenn paused. "But check this out. You remember my ex, Jen?"

"Of course, man."

"Back when she was getting her PhD in women's studies, she was obsessed with this author Doris Lessing. Jen said her voice gave… let me try to remember this… 'a penetrating view into the ripples of colonialism throughout the twentieth century.' Such a scholar, I know.

"Anyway," he continued, "one time she came home with a box full of books—she'd bought someone's entire collection of Lessing's stuff. Turns out some of them were actually sci-fi. Jen didn't care but I was actually intrigued. I wanted to know what would compel such a famous author to switch gears like that. So I checked out the first book, *Shikasta*. It's dense, real slow going, but I gotta tell ya—there's *a lot* of real-world politics behind the space and aliens stuff. Like at one point, the survivors of World War Three decide to symbolically put the white race on trial for all its crimes."

"What the hell?" Chris said. "I never heard about any of this before. When was it written?"

"Dude, this series came out back around 1980."

"Holy shit! So what happens at the trial?"

Glenn said, "The delegates from around the world give their damning testimony. But then, just before the guilty verdict, the group from India steps up. And they have to admit that they treated their own Untouchable class like dirt for thousands of years—way longer than any Caucs were out there colonizing."

"Damn," Chris said. "Maybe no one *wants* to know about this book."

"Ha, you might be right."

"So did Jen read it after you told her about that scene?"

"Nope!" Glenn leaned back and exhaled. "And you know something else? The reason she and I broke up is because I didn't support Reparations one hundred and ten percent. Ain't that something?"

"Really?" Chris shook his head.

"Yeah. When everyone was getting fitted for halos as the whole thing ramped up, I had this uneasy feeling and just couldn't play along. I mean, I liked some of the ideas, but that wasn't enough for her. So one day she just ended it."

"Goddamn."

"It's alright," Glenn said. "I'm always thinking about stuff too much. And sorry I couldn't share this with you at the time. But you were married, living the normal life. And Kate was right there in the middle of it. I didn't need to be told by you that I was the weird one. Or have your wife cut me out of your life completely—which has sort of happened anyway, go figure."

"Oh man, Glenn," Chris said. "You've been my brother since we were in sixth grade. I don't give a shit what you think about the HRA. Now I'm just bummed you felt like you couldn't tell me what went down in your life."

"Don't sweat it, man. That's just how it goes. Relationship truths—some doors open, some slam shut. But tell me," Glenn added, leaning in, "now that we're buzzed and you're a free man for one night, what do you really think about Reparations?"

Chris chuckled. "It's been my policy for a long time to not even think about it at all. That helps keep the peace at home. I just focus on running my business."

"Ah, well played. The diplomat hunched over a fireplace blowing on embers to keep his indie spirit alive. But hey, with all those quotas promoting everybody else, I guess that makes you the odd man out anyway."

"Damn," Chris said. "That was a cheap shot."

"Nah. That's just the fallout from everything we fought for. A leg up for the marginalized, right? You were fine with putting that in our music, but then what happened? Didn't you ever want to work for them? And before you answer, understand that I am *not* judging you here."

"Whew. Things are getting heavy right now. But, going back to your original question—the part of my brain that didn't think about Reparations, it finally has recently. And I even told Kate some of this, so don't think I'm being a coward or a hypocrite here."

"And how did she react?" Glenn asked.

"Hold on. First, I think they opened up Pandora's Freakin' Box and it could spiral out of control into a big mess."

"I knew it all along! But no one listens to Glenn, 'cause I'm an asshole."

"Yeah, yeah," Chris said. "Look, all the surveillance tools are getting smarter and smaller. The reach back into history is gonna go so damn far beyond 1492, I can't even comprehend what the impact will be."

"Just domino after domino falling down." Glenn drained his glass. "The HRA got through the first couple innings with no sweat, but the rest of this game is gonna be a nail-biter. Lawsuits. Petitions for exemption. And here's my big thing I'm waiting for. What if someone finds a document that ends up knocking the whole timeline out of whack? Revisionist historians will have a field day! Think total narrative collapse, bro."

"Not sure I follow you, to be honest."

"Remember the ending of *Raiders of the Lost Ark*? All those artifacts just getting locked away forever? Talk about inconvenient archives! If they get Reparations going in other countries, we're talking maybe a million scanners around the world. Who knows what some shaman up in the hills might submit? Unless a narrative safeguard gets programmed into MARVIN, just one obscure scrap of paper could force us to rewrite world history. Then who do you send the monthly bill to?"

"So if something like that happens, where they have to change the timeline... What would the HRA do?"

Glenn said, "I have no clue. The bigger point is that the program has such a narrow focus, they forgot how complicated everything really is. How do you help one group without hurting another if you frame everything as a zero-sum game? Holding whites up as the all-time evildoers doesn't leave much room for reconciliation."

"You know," Chris said, "I find it almost impossible to believe that the guy who wrote the song 'God of Exploitation' is now saying all this. What the hell pushed you so far in the other direction?"

Glenn fidgeted with his beer glass.

He said, "It started with my dad. He's been sick. His hip and his back are messed up too, so he's laid up most of the time. And what's on the TV? Sitcoms and news anchors saying how great Reparations is. He busted his ass on job sites to put food on the table for me and my brother. Now he's fading away with crap healthcare—but the HRA still takes its cut every month! Not much dignity in all that."

Chris frowned. "Sorry he's having a tough time. Your dad was always a great guy to be around. And a big help to the band when we needed support. But... we all have to pay. I just don't see what he's got to do with this Reparations talk."

"Listen to me, Chris. He's going to his grave with a new kind of bitterness that wasn't there five years ago. And if it's happening to him, it's happening to other white people too. So you know, take their money, whatever. They've been feeding that bottomless pit of taxes their whole life. But now, you want to dig up all this dirt and back them into a corner with accusations? Maybe haul them off to a debtors' prison, or make them have a Kumbaya moment on TV like Kate got dragged into?

"I'm telling you," Glenn added, "it's no good. You're draining decent people of their compassion and replacing it with some ice-cold shit. And here's what keeps me up at night. If what the big narrative says is true, then they took over the whole world once already. Put them in a cage and start poking them out of revenge—be careful you don't reawaken that European bloodlust that's been dormant since the end of World War Two."

Chris shivered. "You're scaring the hell out of me, man. That's some Nazi-level shit. Do I have to quote another one of your songs?"

"That's not even the point!" Glenn said. "You join a band when you're young and the scene provides the wardrobe and all the cookie-cutter song topics. Punk, metal... Everything's all laid out there for you. So of course we sang about evil skinheads, workers' rights, anti-war stuff—we covered all the bases. But I never wrote a song about Mao and he killed a lot of people, that's for damn sure. So yeah, let's go hook up MARVIN in China and see what he has to say about all that!"

"Nah, come on," Chris said. "Don't get too wasted now. You were making an actual point about your dad."

"Alright, alright. Look. How much frustration or outright failure do you have to go through in life, before maybe you start to drop parts of this worldview that we swallowed at age what, fourteen?"

"I don't know, you tell me."

"If our stupid band hadn't had even the minor level of success that it did, we would've been forced to face these facts in our early twenties. But as it is—"

"Hold on, dude!" Chris protested. "One, don't throw Raucous Voice under the bus. And two, I've been running this tech business for eight years. You're the one still playing in bands, banging sluts, and chasing the dream. But *now* that you're finally discovering reality, you want to show it to *me?* I'm the married guy! I'm always in check."

Glenn sighed. "I'm not trying to get holier than thou on you, bud. And maybe in some ways I am behind the curve compared to you. But I see the big picture really clearly right now. When I look at my father's face, lying on that couch… I just wonder how many able-bodied white guys have stopped engaging on social media because they believe the time for conversation is over. Do you want to see them get violent?"

"Hell no," Chris said.

"Neither do I. Nobody does." Glenn paused. "So maybe it's a good thing that the Sentinels of Jubilee are out there, assuming they really do want to keep everything peaceful. And maybe because they've got momentum, that's why the revolutionary types are hanging back. But what if the cops find their leaders and drag them in front of the cameras?"

"Jesus. You think they'd rise up and trash some cities?"

"I think… that I don't know who I want to win this election. Because if she does, will that push these guys over the edge? But if Dominguez wins, maybe the HRA falls apart so fast that it's the Bennies who do the shooting."

Chris dropped his head into his hands. "How did we get here? It's like overnight it all just changed."

Glenn poured out the last of the pitcher into their glasses.

He said, "There was one big, old problem that we tried to face, but the plan was so one-dimensional that it didn't consider all the other little problems too. I think the real mistake was taking a good policy, like high taxes for the rich, and trying to morph it by saying, 'Oh, since you're white you have privilege, which is a *kind* of wealth, so we can take that too.'

"But," Glenn continued, "people still have mortgages, old cars, and even bands that want to rehearse but can't afford to, because the money they would have set aside for a new PA system got sucked up by the HRA. But I'm the bad guy now for making it personal."

"I see what you're saying," Chris said. "They're picking and choosing between people's dreams."

"Exactly. And now they can't put the genie back in the bottle. Spent billions on the HRA infrastructure. Moved trillions of dollars around. That's why maybe the Sentinels have the right idea in calling for some sort of transition out."

"You've mentioned them a few times now. They convinced you, just like that?"

"Bear with me. The HRA has hundreds of locations around the country. Tens of thousands of scanners all over the place. Why not make use of it all in other ways? Like, let's encourage people to submit their poetry or paintings to a national cultural database. Then we can sit in awe of everyone's creativity, whatever their race or gender."

"Okay," Chris said, "I like that…"

"Next, repurpose the HRA branches so that instead of splitting people into two groups, it's a welcoming place for charity and volunteer work. Just like we used to do at the soup kitchens back in the day—we wanted to be there, and the people appreciated our help."

"Yeah, make it a two-way street. But will enough volunteers show up? I mean, probably one reason we needed the HRA was because the resources weren't there."

"I don't know," Glenn said. "But is it wrong to think that after a few years of testing this huge program, we might want to take some readings and course correct if necessary?"

"That sounds a lot better than going on TV in a friggin' mask and scaring the shit out of everybody."

"Maybe people needed a wake-up call. Because maybe a thousand guys like me carefully explaining this kind of pivot would fall on deaf ears. Maybe it already has."

Chris said, "Are you dancing around something here? If you've got something else to say, spit it out."

"I want to," Glenn said. "I just don't know if you, because of the position you're in, can really handle it."

"What does that mean, 'my position'?"

"It means your wife damned near took a pledge of allegiance to serve Reparations! And I love you too much to risk putting anything between you and Kate unless your eyes are open."

"Yeah, my wife," Chris said. "Who went on some spiritual

quest and has barely said a damn thing about it since she came back. My wife, who I stood by when she got sick and was nearly losing her mind. So just say it, man."

Glenn said, "Let's take a walk. I've got to tell you some stuff and we shouldn't be surrounded by people when I do it."

They finished their beers and walked out to a side street.

"Okay," Glenn said. "Let's assume the techs get MARVIN debugged and back online. How do I say this? I mean, you're a computer guy. Have you not heard the rumors that this religious guy the Prescient One is actually MARVIN's original designer?"

"That nut job covered in glitter?" Chris said. "I don't know. Sounds like just a good cover story to get people to join his cult."

"No, Chris. It's true. He designed the whole system that Kate and her coworkers use every day. But—there's more, and I swear to God I'll kill you if you go behind my back—"

"Jesus Christ! What's got you so edgy? I'm your bro, tell me what's up?"

Glenn put his lips to Chris's ear and whispered, "The masked man *is* the Prescient One."

"Holy shit…"

"I've been working with the underground for a while. Sometimes we share information with the Sentinels. And now you're going to help us."

Chris slowly pulled away and ran his hands through his hair. "So this wasn't a chance meeting at all. You didn't just happen to be passing through New York."

"We were on the road, man. The shows were booked. Why wouldn't I look up an old friend on our night off? I was gonna find a way to connect with you, one way or another, when the time was right."

"Yeah, sure. Look, I don't know what you're planning to say here. All I can promise is to listen. And short of murder, I won't give you away. Now, what do you want from me?"

"Let's hit another bar first," Glenn said. "You're gonna need a stiff drink."

Chris walked Glenn to the subway entrance, sending off the friend he'd known for twenty years with a firm embrace. It was good to know that Glenn, even if he tended to shoot from the hip, was loyal and spoke from the heart.

Chris looked at his phone during the cab ride and saw that he had a voicemail from Kate. Between the haze of alcohol and trying to process all that had been discussed with Glenn, hearing her message put his mind over its daily limit and he went blank the rest of the way home.

It was nearly one o'clock when the cab dropped him off. He entered the apartment as quietly as he could. A metal jangling sound came from the living room, then light tapping along the hardwood floor. One of the Corgis rubbed against his legs in the darkness.

He crept down the hall and saw Kate sprawled out on the couch. The other dog was asleep next to her head. Two wine bottles, one empty and one half full, sat on the coffee table.

Kate was breathing easy. Chris studied the contours of her pale face. A strand of dirty-blond hair had fallen across her chin.

He leaned over carefully and picked up her wine glass, then poured himself a small drink. He sat down at the end of the couch and leaned back. The dog that had met him at the door now came over and lay down at his feet.

Chris thought about how life was crazy and confusing and you never knew what was coming next. But life was also good. He drained the glass and set it down, then rested his hand on Kate's ankle.

He was soon fast asleep.

12. THE ASSIGNMENT

Elder Evans jerked awake. He sat up and turned on the bedside lamp. Two elite guards stood above him in this small private room, which he had moved into after the advancement ceremony a week ago.

"What are you doing in here?" he asked. "What do you want?"

"Pack your things," one of the guards said.

"Why? What's happening? Am I being evicted from the church?"

The guards laughed. "You're going for a ride on TP-One.

Now get ready. The helicopter leaves in twenty minutes."

Elder Evans gathered his few possessions and stuffed them into a duffle bag. He hastily freshened up then presented himself to the guards, who were waiting outside in the hallway.

They escorted him down several corridors which were vacant at this early hour, then across a walkway where the night's subtle glow came in through the skylights. The trio next passed through a guarded door, and soon came to an elevator. One of the guards waved a key card and it opened. They rode to the top floor, then after exiting walked down a ramp toward sliding glass doors.

Elder Evans saw a jet black helicopter sitting on the rooftop. As he and the guards approached, the Prescient One stepped out.

"Here he is, sir," a guard said.

"Wonderful, wonderful." The Prescient One put his arm around Elder Evans and whispered, "Good morning, elder. How are you?"

"They put the fear of Mod in me waking me up like that. I thought for a moment that I'd been found out."

"Nothing of the sort! And now, as we step on board, you will cease to be Bill Evans. Are you ready to go to Iowa, Marcus?"

"I have all my belongings with me. I am at your service."

"Bless you." The Prescient One waved to the guard standing just outside the door. "We're ready. Prepare for departure."

The guard boarded and closed the door. He put on a headset and said, "Captain, we're ready to go. Take this bird up."

The flight had been a quiet one. Shortly after leaving the Mall, the Prescient One covered his face with the hood of his cloak and dozed off. Marcus soon fell asleep as well. A while later, as the sun began to peek above the horizon, he awoke and saw the Prescient One staring at him.

"How does it feel to be an elder?"

"It's an honor to be in that position of trust," Marcus said.

"I must say, I very much enjoyed your cover story for Bill. The 'peeping Tom who stole my wife' tale, perfect! But that's not you at all, and eventually you couldn't hide it."

"I guess not."

"Scholar-athlete," the Prescient One said. "Son of an attorney and a CEO. The sky seemed to be the limit for you. So I must ask, what motivated you to join a branch of law enforcement?"

"I grew up around people who had a lot of money," Marcus said. "But that didn't necessarily make their kids smart or even honorable. At first I pursued a law degree because I was intrigued by how rules, that were supposedly set in stone, became subjected to endless interpretation in cases that involved real people."

"Fascinating. And yet you didn't end up working in offices."

"I realized I was too young to be cooped up like that. I had to get out into the field and put all of my skills to use."

"Ah, so by the time you came to our church, it was just another assignment for you?"

"Yes," Marcus said. "The point of the mission was to keep an eye on this crazy new church that had come out of nowhere and was growing so quickly. We didn't want another Jim Jones to happen on our watch."

"But instead, we found our way into your heart."

Marcus smiled. "I let my guard down. Didn't keep my distance."

"It could happen to anyone." The Prescient One waved a hand. "We're all so used to the frantic pace of life in the outside world, that we have no frame of reference that something could be wrong. And I'm well aware of how ironic it is that people need to experience *my* church to get a taste of normalcy."

"Yes, it's quite the paradox. May I ask, how many of my church colleagues and superiors know of my true identity?"

"The emissaries are aware of almost everything that goes on at the Mall. They're the real security force, not the armed guards and plainclothes lookouts that we regrettably must employ. You see, Marcus, the truth is that you are far from being the only spy within our walls. I would say that at any given time, perhaps two percent of Mall residents are there on behalf of some other group, and not actually following their own hearts."

Marcus said, "I suspected a few people from time to time. What normally happens to them when they're caught?"

"It depends what their agenda is. Sometimes they're harmless. Sometimes we can make use of them. But sometimes…"

"You have to kill them?"

"Oh, not at all!" the church leader said. "We may forcibly remove them, yes. But besides the occasional fisticuffs, the worst we ever do is more of a prank. We knock them out with a laced drink, then leave them in a field somewhere not far from a gas station or convenience store. They wake up to find that their whole body has been painted blue! But the best part is, we also spray silver glitter onto their skin through stencils with the words, 'Mod bless you!' They rarely bother us again."

Marcus raised his eyebrows. "You've been an interesting study, sir."

"As have you," the Prescient One said with a wink.

"On the one hand, you're deadly serious and forward-thinking. But on the other, this silliness and playfulness… I can't quite put my finger on it."

The Prescient One leaned in. "Why aren't you married, Marcus?"

Marcus turned his gaze toward the window, then down. "I'd say commitment to my career was more important. Setting myself up on the right path would give me better marriage prospects down the road."

"But you're nearly forty now. Surely you're well enough along that path?"

"The last six years I've been embedded undercover more than half of the time. Hard to start something meaningful under those circumstances, let alone keep it going."

"Indeed. And you did not meet any women that you fancied during your time with us?"

"That's not true," Marcus said. "There are two I was fond of, in fact. But I had to stay focused on my mission for the FBI. Plus, the rules regarding courtship, Modestianity's whole approach to sexuality…"

"So natural as to be confusing for the twenty-first-century mind, perhaps?" The Prescient One smiled softly.

Marcus said, "I remember once writing in my diary the phrase 'druidic chivalry' to describe it. I admit that there's something genius in your approach. Like a spigot—there's a time and a place to turn it on and water the plants. But then you keep it shut tight and focus on the other aspects of life."

"Well said. We've been so saturated with sex in our culture that we lost all sense of its purpose. Putting it in ads to sell products. Being able to view any act imaginable from the safety of an office chair—it's perversion through the looking glass. Because this almost clinical distance made us forget that we *are* animals, and that sex is the most primal, non-intellectual part of our being. Too much and we lose ourselves. Too little and we fall into neurosis."

"You've got it all so thought out," Marcus said. "Somehow every aspect of Modestianity is ready to fill the needs of people living in this modern world. But so much of its core draws from ancient models of human behavior. How did this harmonious philosophy form so quickly? Did it just appear to you in a dream?"

The Prescient One ran his fingers down the side of his face, where today he wore a partial mask of crescent-shaped molded plastic that ran along the jawline.

"It's hard to take credit for something that you created in a state of desperation," he said. "Or horror. For you see, when I looked deep into MARVIN's eyes, I saw the nightmarish future in a flash. A time when good people armed with this technology would terrorize each other, not for justice, but to pillage and defame. Creation, discovery, culture—all would stop dead in their tracks.

"Had I not been abruptly cast out of the HRA," he continued, "perhaps we could have built some safeguards into the system. Yes, it would have lacked the comprehensive depth that Modestianity now possesses, but it would have had a much wider influence."

"But that's not how it played out," Marcus said.

"No. I was forced into exile. Had my Moses moment out in Colorado. Then I began the humble task of preaching in the streets, trying to save the souls of people busily rushing from swipe to swipe. But with every speech I became more confident in myself. And soon, people started to resonate with my words because what I saw removed the cataracts from their souls!

"They were trapped in the paradox of having gorged on every piece of information, every TV show, every type of food, and yet were still spiritually starved. That, my friend, was the true key to Modestianity's rise. You can only bring so many people into your church with scare tactics. But to keep them, you must offer them a hopeful alternative to their malaise."

"It works." Marcus shrugged his shoulders. "It worked on me."

The Prescient One's contact lenses twinkled blue. "I know."

"I kept my defenses up against the ladies that I admired, never realizing that Modestianity was also working its charms. Maybe my superiors will say that I have Stockholm Syndrome."

"Nonsense," the sage replied. "If you discard my ornamentation and eccentric ways, what you're left with is an approach toward life which denies less of our human essence than other religions. Modestianity seeks to draw out the best from each, for each. Thankfully, my wealth kept us uncompromised during the first years, and now the acolytes who emanate joy and satisfaction in their local churches are the best recruiting tool we have."

"Your Prescience," Marcus said, "I don't know why you specifically called on me today, but I assume that I have passed a test of character. Would I be too presumptuous in daring to ask a personal question?"

"Not at all, Elder."

"You asked me about not being married," Marcus began. "I figure we must be close in age. And yet I don't see you with a queen on stage. There hasn't even been gossip about you taking advantage of any of the female novitiates. You have so much power and a glorious title, yet your reputation remains spotless. How can this be?"

"Think of a mountain climber," the Prescient One said. "He sets out along a trail, scales the first wall, then continues hiking until the next climb. Up and up he goes, steadily onward. Do you think he will just stop and turn around before he reaches the summit?"

"No."

"So it has been for me. And like the climber exploring new areas where the terrain has not been mapped out, I never knew that after each success there could be an even higher peak behind it. Most game developers in my position after a triumph like *Thor's Tablet* would have moved laterally within the industry. But then I saw great potential in the blockchain movement, so I focused completely on that new field of interest. It too was another massive success.

"And when the HRA planners came to me," the Prescient One added, "it was a fresh challenge to surmount. While working on such an important program, I simply could not let myself be distracted or I might fall."

"But something did snap your rope anyway," Marcus said.

"Or maybe it saved me. Because while licking my wounds, I saw a glorious new mountain in an undiscovered country. And I have been climbing this tallest peak ever since, while also serving as guide for countless other climbers. Until we reach the top, how can I commit to a marriage? Too much of humanity's fate is on the precipice.

"I now see," the Prescient One said, "that everything I have done and endured in life prepared me to lead people out of their despair. And after one terrible fall from grace, I cannot allow even the slightest hint of an allegation of impropriety against me, not when the stakes are so much higher."

"But other powerful men have had wives," Marcus offered. "Presidents, generals, religious leaders. Is your mission really more important than theirs?"

"Marcus, I value your concerns. Have you noticed that many people are being promoted to higher office throughout the church? These are the next wave of visionaries who will enrich Modestianity, because soon I will step out into the world to unveil an even greater plank of my vision."

"What?!"

"Yes, it's true," the Prescient One said. "I will not linger in the Mall like some god to be worshiped, not if Modestianity is truly is about the people and not me."

"You're going to leave us?" Marcus pleaded. "And do what?"

"Please calm yourself, dear elder. You are still so new to this. The only way I can describe the next frontier is by calling it, prescience beyond prescience. But until that day, there is still crucial work to do. And you are an essential part of these plans. Will you honor me by serving in good faith?"

Marcus said, "You know very well I've thrown in my lot with Modestianity. All I hope is that the FBI doesn't come down too hard on me—or the church."

"Never mind that for the moment. Ah, we're almost there." The Prescient One pointed to a cluster of buildings sitting within a sea of cropland. "The church's charter is expanding, Marcus. Beyond souls and identities. We must conduct humanitarian missions for those in need."

"Where are we?" Marcus asked.

As the helicopter eased down into a patch of cut grass within a larger field, the Prescient One said, "I call it the Farm."

They were greeted by a staff of fifteen. A cook, a groundskeeper, two doctors, three guards, and the rest nurses. Marcus remained silent while they toured the grounds. The Prescient One asked the staff members questions about various aspects of the facility.

There was one large building, which was surrounded by a spacious yard, two smaller buildings, several gardens, a horse enclosure, a work shed, and a barn. Inside the main building was a dining hall, small private bedrooms, a crafts room, and an entertainment and gaming hall.

Finally Marcus could hold his tongue no longer and quietly said, "What is this place, Your Prescience?"

The Prescient One walked to a large front window and smiled. "It looks like they're here."

Marcus followed as the staff walked out the front entrance and lined up in the yard. A convoy of six vehicles was coming up the drive.

"This is just the beginning," the Prescient One whispered to Marcus, "of a very important new phase of our mission. It is my honor to place you in charge of this test run."

"But who's in those vans? What am I overseeing exactly?"

"Just wait. You'll soon understand."

The white vehicles swung around in front of the group and stopped. Orderlies got out and opened the side and rear doors.

A hulking black man in desert camo who only had one arm stepped out of the first van. He turned back and offered his hand to a tired-looking white man with unkempt hair, who then limped out onto the grass.

Other men wearing various styles of military fatigues also exited the vehicles. They too showed signs of either injury or ill health. After they had all gotten out, one of the men yelled, "Attention!" They fell into place and stood tall.

The Prescient One came forward, his blue cloak fluttering in the light morning breeze.

"Gentlemen, I hope your journey was comfortable. Welcome to the Farm!"

As most of the group nodded, the man with the wild hair nudged the one-armed man and said quietly, "Would you take a look at this guy?"

"I know! I still got the blues for you," the other man sang. They both started laughing.

The Prescient One turned toward them. "Is something the matter?"

The white man waved a hand while they both tried to cover their faces.

"Oh," the Prescient One said, "is this not James Haggerston? Yes, I do believe it is. The fugitive from justice!"

James got serious and took a step back. "Wait a sec. Is this all some big trick? We were told that they were taking us somewhere to get real medical care."

"And this is it. The Sentinels never lie."

Marcus's jaw dropped. The Prescient One turned back to him and nodded with a smile. Marcus took a deep breath and regained his composure.

"Now, James," the Prescient One said, "I specifically requested your group of veterans. Do you have any idea why?"

"No, sir."

"I did so because I owe your son Morgan a debt of gratitude."

"Oh, my God!" James said. "You *are* the Prescient One. So he made it to the Mall safe?"

"Not only that, he showed great character as a faux-acolyte. And ultimately his words helped convince me to go on… my walkabout."

"Do you have a message from him? I was out in the shanty towns helping round these other guys up for months. I haven't spoken to Morgan since the summer."

The Prescient One said, "I'm afraid he left the church grounds during my absence. I have no news. But please, introduce me to your friend with the wonderful singing voice."

James beamed. "This is Private First Class Bo Alexander. We served together during the First Gulf War back in 'ninety-one."

Bo extended his one hand—the left—and the Prescient One took it, saying, "Thank you for your service. I'm pleased to meet you."

"And thank you for the hospitality," Bo said. He elbowed James. "This fool found me and ten other guys killing time down in Texas. We just wanted to be left alone away from all the stupidity that's going on. But no, this old stiff, who claims he can barely text, he used the internet to track me down."

"Don't blame it all on me," James said. "The underground has these whiz kids that helped me out. Admit it, you were glad to see my face after all these years."

"You wish! Look at you, trying to get the band back together."

"We did have some times though. Then and now. Tell him about the drones we fought off!"

Bo said, "Mister TPO, get this. When we all left that shithole town heading for the barracks the Sentinels set up, some government drones attempted to engage us along the way."

"S'more Stoppers," James said. "But I've had experience with them. We took 'em out!"

"Fierce suckers, like giant flying beetles. But James is right. We won that skirmish. Then this cracker here, he made me take a picture of him with his foot on top of one. Like it was a hunting trophy!"

"But I had to!" James said. "One of them tasered me the last time. So yeah, I got my revenge."

"Anyway," Bo said, "looks like we're holding up this little ceremony. Excuse us."

The Prescient One smiled. "By all means. I'm glad you're here." He motioned for Marcus to step forward. "Gentlemen, this is Marcus Young. *Former* FBI undercover agent, current Modestian elder, and now the superintendent of this facility. Marcus, we've got two dozen men who have served their country honorably and are in need of treatment. Do you think you can handle that?"

Marcus said, "All the arrangements have been made, Your Prescience. Gentlemen, it will be a privilege to make your stay here as comfortable as possible. The staff will now see you to your rooms."

The Prescient One stood beside Marcus, and they watched the contingent of veterans slowly make its way into the main building. He said, "Life is truly sublime."

"How do you mean?" Marcus asked.

"You never know where it's going to take you. But as long as you fulfill what you're supposed to do each step of the way, you always end up in the right place."

Marcus folded his arms. "I've spent the last week joyfully immersing myself in my new role at the Mall. But you're saying

I was meant to be all the way out here instead?"

"Marcus," the Prescient One sighed, "this is not exile. Nor is it your last stop. What we're doing here at the Farm is just the tip of the spear for where Modestianity will go in the future. I hope I wasn't wrong in selecting you for this task."

"No, Your Prescience." Marcus paused. "Forgive me if you saw any disappointment in my face. It's just that, to go from betraying my government over a religious experience, to then being taken away from the life I would have led as an elder… I… I know that this is a profound opportunity to serve. Tonight I will pray for strength and guidance."

"Mod bless you. Keep the faith."

"Thank you. I shall strive to prove your prescient instincts correct."

As Marcus walked toward the door, he turned back to see the Prescient One smiling at the sun.

"…I still got the blues…"

13. AT THE CROSSROADS

It had been a few weeks since Clyde had spoken to Nolan in person. Nolan was busy traveling around meeting with community groups that had been impressed by his message during their *Nifty Minutes* appearance a month ago.

Clyde, meanwhile, had stayed local while trying to finish his new song. He worked for days on end writing and rewriting the lyrics, and slowly Eddie Pryor's offer began to weigh on his mind. The temptation to sign on to Hollywood's version of the big time butted up against his own desire to see if he could produce another relevant track. Did he really have talent, or was Eddie just trying to make a quick buck off a hot trend?

Nolan's schedule finally opened up so they could meet on Friday afternoon. Clyde loaded his phone with the beats and lyrics he had come up with so far, then hired a private car to take him over to Nolan's building. Clyde smiled at one point when they passed a local bus that was pulling over to the side of the road—it was nice not having to wait on the public transit schedule for rides anymore.

Once inside Nolan's building, Clyde rode up to the third floor and saw Damon waiting for him outside the elevator.

"Hey, DJC," Damon said. "Nice to see your face again."

"Sup, Dee?" Clyde said. "I can't believe y'all got eyeball scanners down in the lobby. Nolan do that?"

"We got to be careful nowadays. Lots of curious folks poking around our business."

"For a second it felt like I was walking into a bank or something."

"We makin' money, that's for sure."

"So, you Nolan's number one general now?"

Damon said, "Basically. I mean, I probably got moved up quicker because of all the action with your track. First off, Nolan been super busy giving them speeches all around. And then, some of the older guys didn't like the extra heat they was sensing around our operation. So they took off. That left me in a good spot."

"No doubt. You been able to handle all that?" Clyde asked.

"Aw man, at first it was a lot! But I learned to delegate like a champ. Follow me, I got to show you something."

Damon led Clyde down a hallway, then flashed a key card to unlock a door with a glass window. They walked into a darkened room where a half dozen boys were working at computer terminals. A couple of them glanced over before turning back to their screens.

"Welcome," Damon said, "to the bowels of our empire. You think I'm good with gadgets and tech? Hell no! These little brats can surf smarter, type faster, and post better than you or me. By a mile!"

"So what they doing in here?" Clyde said.

"Company business. Searching for talent. Maybe even promoting you."

"Oh, really?"

"Hey, yo!" Damon called out. "Don't any of you kids recognize DJ Clydoscope when he standing right in front of you?"

Again, only a few boys looked back and gave a wave before returning to their computers.

"See? They're machines! DJC is just another project for them.

Let's get on out of here—these kids make me nervous sometimes."

"So," Clyde said, as they walked back down the hallway, "they just up here working all the time?"

"Yeah," Damon said. "Day and night. Never stop til they mama tell 'em to come home. Yo, one of them's even called *Ervin!*"

"Haha, that's too close for comfort."

"That's what I'm sayin'. Anyhow, what's up with you? We all still waitin' on your next song to drop."

"I know, I know," Clyde said. "I feel like I'm almost set on what it's gonna be, just want to get some perspective from Nolan before I pull the trigger."

"Good luck getting much time with him."

"I know! He's been so busy."

Damon said, "All this national exposure's got him pulled in different directions. I mean, no one expected y'all's song to blow up like it did. But anyhow, other folks payin' attention now too, like churches and schools. They all want Nolan to work with them, give speeches or whatever. I don't know what it means for me and what we doin' here."

"Yeah," Clyde said, "if the Pigeon Man goes straight, what happens to the old operation?"

"He don't like to be called that no more."

"What? Naw, he all about them birds!"

"Not anymore," Damon said. "We gettin' too big for that. So I'm just telling you—"

"Telling him what?" Nolan said angrily as he stepped off the elevator. He cracked a smile. "Clyde, come here and give me some love."

They came together for a quick hug and pat on the back.

"Let me look at you," Nolan said. "The world-famous Clyde Jenkins and he can't even grow sideburns."

"Get off me with that!" Clyde said, throwing a playful jab at Nolan's shoulder.

"When I was your age, I had a goatee and could bench press three hundred pounds. Look at both y'all, scrawny kids strong enough to lift a soda can and that's about it."

"And a microphone."

"Yeah, yeah. I'll believe that when I hear a second song from you, boy."

Clyde said, "That's kind of what I'm here to talk to you about."

"Alright. But run upstairs with me for a minute. I got to check on what these guys are doing."

Clyde and Nolan took the elevator to the top floor, then walked up a small flight of stairs that led out onto the roof. A ray of sunlight caught them in the eyes.

"Hmm," Clyde said. "Back where it all began."

"Don't get too nostalgic now," Nolan said. "We all still got work to do."

A few guys not much younger than Clyde were hacking at the planter boxes which Nolan used to hide the contraband HRA mini-drones that he'd bought and reprogrammed for his own uses.

"Keep going! Chop, chop!" Nolan called out as he and Clyde walked past into the work shack.

Inside, a boy of ten wearing goggles was using a soldering iron to mangle the components of a small green motherboard. Once finished, he carefully set the hot tool in its holder, then closed the drone's plastic housing and manually tightened the hex screws.

Nolan flicked Clyde on the chest. "Got my *real* protege workin' in here decommissioning these drones."

"Oh yeah?" Clyde said. "Then what you plannin' to do with 'em?"

"Got to return these birds to their rightful owner. Government property and all. Especially now that we're trying to go more legit."

"So it really is rest in peace for the Pigeon Man, huh?"

"It's night, night for him. And hello, Mr. Simmons!"

Clyde stepped outside while Nolan conferred with the kid at the work bench. The guys over at the planters gave him a nod and a "wassup" before continuing to dismantle the wood boxes. A moment later Nolan came out of the shack and waved.

He said, "Let's go talk in my office like real businessmen."

They rode down to the fourth floor and Nolan keyed in to a huge room that Clyde vaguely remembered as being a lot smaller. It was filled with high-end production equipment— camera stands, a green screen, fancy desks, TVs, studio racks— and cardboard boxes were stacked all over the place.

"Hey," Clyde said, "what's all this? Are you building a real studio in here or what?"

"A little different this time around, isn't it?" Nolan said. "No expenses spared. Knocked down some walls, too. Gonna do this place up right. Home Base Studios, I want to call it. Be an executive producer on a whole stable of projects. The mastermind behind the scenes, like Jerry Bruckheimer."

"What kind of stuff?" Clyde asked.

"First thing I want to do is get some news anchor types doing a weekly show talking about what's going on in our world. No pro sports talk or Middle East BS, just real life on the ground floor. But I'm so damn busy that I don't know when it's actually gonna happen. Also trying to wind down the old business— thinking about putting Damon in charge, but he ain't sure what he want to do. Go legit and be humble, or take the risk and be the big dog?"

"Looks like you really planning things out."

"Hey," Nolan said, "I got twenty years on you, kid. I'm late to the party compared to you, so I got to keep the pedal to the metal."

"Yeah, I'm at the big party for now." Clyde paused. "Just not sure I got what it takes to stay there."

"Why you say that?"

"It's this next song, man. I know what I want to do, what the message should be. But maybe ain't nobody gonna like it."

"Why's that?" Nolan asked. "You got to sing from the heart."

"That's what I thought too. But now it's like, the business people don't even care what you talk about. They'll run with your attitude no problem, long as you let 'em dress you up in some fashion designer's clothes."

"Nothing wrong with looking good. Why not take some of their gear?"

"I don't want to look like a clown!" Clyde said. "Who knows what they'd put on me?"

"I feel you." Nolan paused. "But set those guys aside for right now. You got the hot mic, not them. What's on your mind?"

Clyde said, "I got a lot of different fans, Nolan."

"I know you do. In hoods all across the U-S-and-A."

"No, I mean different *kinds*. At this one club in Hollywood, a lot of white people came out to meet me. Just regular folks. And they were nice. Shook my hand. And not fake, like they was just happy to say hi and didn't want nothin' from me."

"So what's that mean to you?" Nolan asked.

"Feels like I'm trapped between two or three places," Clyde said. "See, my song let everybody know what's up with the HRA. But I did it because I wanted it to get better, not just fall apart and leave people with nothing."

"Yeah," Nolan said, "but 'technical difficulties beyond our control' and the hack are conspiring to try to bring down the HRA just the same."

"Mm-hmm. You got one side trying to cash in on my frustration and turn it into a brand. Another side is trying to use it like a soundtrack for their revolution. But there's also everyday people who got no agenda, no power—and they appreciate my song just for what it is."

"One small piece of powerful, political art."

Clyde blushed and looked down.

"But anyway, these people," he said, "they have their own minds, just like me. I can't forget about them just 'cause they're Caucs and we supposed to be mad, because of our ancestors or whatever. Especially if what the hackers say is true, then the real enemy ain't even human at all."

"MARVIN."

"Yeah," Clyde said. "Stupid name for the devil to have, too."

"Whatchu you talkin' about?" Nolan started wriggling his arms and body around wildly. "Hail MARVIN, yo! Oh Lord MARVIN, cast us not into the hard drive of hell!"

"Haha, you crazy. But that's a good line though. I may have to use it."

"On the house," Nolan said. "But keep going. What are you gonna do if this is where your mind is at?"

Clyde said, "My new song has to move forward. Because I feel like I'm changing."

"You're growing up. Fast, too."

"Whatever you call it. But I got to say something like, if we're looking for enemies, we will we always find one. *And* the computers and cameras will find so much bad stuff that we'll all be in trouble. But we'll also act like a judge. Throwing stones at each other back and forth. Who's gonna be left standing after all that?"

"Stupid-ass MARVIN," Nolan said.

"Heh, yeah. So that's where I'm at. I got some big ideas for this track. You feel me?"

"You're definitely ahead of the curve. Again! This one might vibe with even more folks."

"Yeah. You know," Clyde said, "I actually brought over some rough cuts of what I been workin' on. You maybe want to take a listen?"

"Of course!" Nolan said. "Better yet, we can put you in the new vocal booth and test it out. Come on, take a look."

They walked to a corner of the space where several long desks had been set up with computers, monitor speakers, and other hardware. Clyde ran over to a large enclosed structure and looked inside.

"Wow, Nolan! This is tight."

"A real game changer. I predict a lot of hits will come out of there."

"Yeah? You already working with other artists?" Clyde asked quietly.

"Not yet, don't get all jealous. But I got so many ideas, even bigger than music or that news show. Like TV series, movies—all self-produced and self-financed. Complete creative control. Our message and our voice, with no middle man changing up what we got to say in order to make some *sheikh* dude happy."

"Who?"

Nolan said, "Foreign investors, man. The point is this—think about how many fingerprints that ain't black are all over projects that are supposedly FUBU."

"I don't know any of that, Nolan. You the man of the world. Tell me what's up."

"Picture a chess board right now."

"Okay," Clyde said.

"What do you see?"

"Bunch of white pieces and black pieces staring each other down."

"Right," Nolan said. "Now say it's the middle of the game. What's that look like?"

"They all tangled up. In the mix fighting. Some dead pieces sitting off to the side. And eventually, somebody gonna take the king and win."

"Alright, so that's chess in the controlled environment of a game. But in real life, most of the black pieces are pawns.

Maybe only a few rooks and bishops in the mix. But ain't no kings or queens out there."

Clyde said, "Whatchu mean no queens? Every block around here, and at every club I been to around the country, sistas be walkin' around flaunting they stuff like they's queens."

Nolan let out a big laugh. "Oh, you funny, boy. I set you right up for that one."

"Yup!" Clyde started singing, "Ebony princess, please say yes… Nubian queen, you are my dream!"

"There he go. Mr. Improv throwing away lines for free, like some baron giving out alms to the poor from his coach."

"Just sharing my gift with the world, haha," Clyde said with a laugh. "But, sorry. You were talking chess."

Nolan nodded. "Like I said, it's mostly pawns. And not only that, a lot of 'em *think* they're actually kings. That's the saddest thing I see around the hood, and it's what I try to teach all of y'all. Perspective. Even if you can't see everything, at least know where you at."

"True, true. So where am I at, then?"

"Hold on," Nolan said, "we'll get around to you later. I'm talking about *my* vision right now. The big plan! Hey, you ever hear of that TV show called *The Wire*?"

"I don't know," Clyde said.

"Anyway, real quick. Takes place in Baltimore about twenty-five years ago. And you know the score down there. But there's this guy named Stringer trying to get out of the drug business and go legit. So he hooks up with this corrupt brother who's a politician, thinking that's his ticket out and up. But nope! Politician played that man, even set him up for a cash drop using a white dude as bait."

"So," Clyde said, "he thought he was about to maybe become a knight, but he got fooled."

Nolan wagged a finger. "The pawn that wanted to be a black knight, ha! But you're wrong though—no one fooled him. He left himself exposed because he didn't gather all of the necessary information. Anyone can become a master of the level they're in, but then watch what happens when they try to move up. They just close their eyes, hoping and praying that it will all just happen for them. But that's not how they did it the first time. And why would anybody on the cruise ship let someone sitting in a rowboat get on board?"

Clyde said, "All these riddles, I don't know."

"They wouldn't! Unless you got something to offer."

"So how do we get on board?"

"Hell," Nolan said, "you already about on, kid genius. But it depends what you want to do on there. Think about the people with money who are chatting you up right now. Even though you busted out on your own, maybe they're just trying to fence you in as a reliable milk cow."

"Hmm. So that's why they're being so nice." Clyde paused. "A year ago, they would've seen right through me if I passed them on the street. Damn…"

Nolan said, "Don't get all sad about it, Jesus. You just got to be smart. That's what I've been saying. If you want to be a big player on the big stage on your own terms, you got to know how it all works."

"Man, I can't see that far ahead. This doesn't sound as fun as it used to be."

"Welcome to being a man! You already done provided for your moms and helped your sister out. Be proud about that, but also understand that success comes with responsibility if you want to maintain it. Look at my operation. I've been building it slowly for years, always reinforcing my gains brick by brick."

"So, what?" Clyde said. "Am I supposed to keep an eye on everything now? Not much time for creativity if I got to look at DJC like it's a store I'm running."

Nolan said, "But kid, that's your ticket to freedom! Being in charge of your own destiny, that's what it's all about."

"Nolan, this is too much to take in! Another one of your truth bombs dropped right on my head. Why don't you record these speeches and put them out on PerformTube instead?"

"And play by the rules on their boat?"

"How would you do it then?" Clyde asked.

"Build my own damn boat! That's what this whole place you're looking at right here is. I'll pull my own Stringer move, but with eyes open."

"Oh, okay. So I ain't alone in trying to do this."

"No, sir," Nolan said. "I'm standing right beside you on that chessboard. Now, shields up and swords out!"

Clyde grabbed a microphone stand and swung it through the air.

"Pawns," he said. "But not for long…"

14. THE SERMON

The Reverend Matthias G. Witherspoon was awake well before dawn. He arrived at his church in Akron, Ohio, just as the first hints of daylight began to peek through the clouds. The parishioners would start showing up in two hours for his Sunday sermon, and he could expect about an hour of solitude now before his support staff arrived.

Matthias first went into the annex which housed the Foundation for Healing Colonial Guilt, the outreach program he had established shortly after the HRA was born. It had been a good source of federal funds which, initially at least, were used to sponsor workshops that helped "build a bridge toward racial reconciliation."

But somewhere along the way, pride or vanity had led him, and in turn the foundation, very much astray. He had shamefully allowed the group leaders to go off script, by instead teaching the schoolchildren who had been bused in to feel either guilt or grievance, depending on their heritage. These workshops also drove a psychological wedge into the identities of mixed-race boys and girls who had the misfortune of attending.

Worst of all was his own behavior. For over a year, Reverend Witherspoon had been the ringleader whipping white men into a frenzy of contrition in debtors' prison yards across the region. What started out almost as a gag—"Let's see how far they'll let me take it"—grew into a traveling circus that had taken on a life of its own, with Matthias becoming just as enthralled by the power of his own voice as were the crowds he harangued.

The truth was that he had once been a thoughtful and reserved man, but always allowed himself to be led into temptation by his ego. On this morning in particular, he lamented that the name Witherspoon was considered a joke among serious people. Because during the month since the Sentinels of Jubilee first hacked into the HRA, Matthias grew more nauseous as it slowly dawned upon him that the program could actually be in jeopardy.

Even worse, he had to admit that like so many other black folk around the country, he hadn't taken what the HRA offered seriously enough, and instead let the weakest aspects of his personality run wild while the money flowed into his coffers.

Matthias left the church annex and entered the main building, then went into his private study. He pulled a stack of papers out of his briefcase and settled into his leather chair, putting on a pair of reading glasses as he reached for the desk lamp.

Here was the speech he intended to deliver in church today, one whose tone was much more serious than his usual theatrical fare. Because with an election only two days away, and so many people's fates hanging in the balance, the least he could do was try and rise to the occasion.

As he reviewed the sermon outline and made notes in the margins, Matthias sensed that certain points were not directly aimed at the congregation—or even the modest audience that would be watching live on the church's PerformTube channel—but possibly intended for one of his competitors, and almost as a plea for forgiveness.

Matthias closed his eyes. He was overcome with a feeling of juvenile envy as he pictured that eccentric man known only as the Prescient One. All this time, while Reverend Witherspoon was getting praise from regional press and being featured on European news programs, the world had scoffed at this weird new religion called Modestianity. Everyone thought that it was either a joke that would fizzle out, or a cult that would come to a bad end.

But now Matthias knew that people had it all backwards. While he himself had not been serious enough to seize the moment and use Reparations to bring his people across the finish line, his counterpart the Prescient One—who had been mocked and disrespected while steadily growing his church—it was *he* who had seen the crucial issue beyond the moment. And now he was the one offering a long-term vision to lead the nation out of its divisive squabbles, in order to face the bigger threat as voiced by the Sentinels.

The writing was on the wall now. Refugees were flocking to the Mall of Absolution while Matthias had done little of lasting impact to help his own community. The Mall was more than a place of shelter, because it also offered a fresh new vision for how to grapple with modern challenges.

But Matthias did not wish to upstage or defeat the Prescient One now. He simply wanted to be a worthy ally during this new War for Dignity, which he hoped would transcend the sputtering War for Equity. Because the cameras and microphones certainly didn't care what color your skin was or who your ancestors were. They were out there working nonstop, steadily compiling an impeccably thorough ledger on all people—and there was no telling when that bill would come due or how someone would be expected to pay it.

Today Reverend Witherspoon would take his shot at redemption in the only way he knew how—by using that silver tongue of his for good, and not merely to score points with bleeding hearts. But he could not do it alone, so he bowed his head and finally spoke to God as he was supposed to: in humility, and with no false fronts or evasions.

Matthias asked God to forgive him for wasting time and performing more for people's praise rather than His glory. He knew that there were countless ways in which he had chosen wrongly and therefore let his people down. But now he would let his own foibles fall away, so that he might finally share a message that was bigger than himself.

He understood that the fallout from this sermon might lead to being abandoned by his parishioners. If so, that would be fair recompense for what this fifty-four-year-old man had allowed himself to become. As he unclasped his hands, Matthias took heart in the notion that God buttresses those who act upon what they must do.

As the church bells tolled outside, Matthias left the study and walked out to his forest green Cadillac. He pulled a tin from the glove box and selected a piece of citrus hard candy, then took a moment to savor the textures and bitter flavor. With this calming ritual complete, the reverend was now ready to lead Sunday services.

"It is a blessed morning, my people, and I hope it finds you well. But the truth is, I greet you all with a heavy burden upon my heart. Still I give praise, because right now I've got the power of the Almighty God in my soul. While I am an imperfect vessel to deliver His word, I know that He will surely see me through.

"Exodus, fifteen: 'Thou in thy mercy hast led forth the people which thou hast redeemed: thou hast guided them in thy strength unto thy holy habitation.' Amen.

"Because the truth is that I messed up. A lot of us messed up. Too many of us didn't take Reparations for slavery seriously. And in the ultimate form of irony, it was all those white allies doing the heavy lifting to create the HRA—they *did* believe! But us? These past three, four years, we treated it like just another program to help catch a free ride.

"And we were wrong to behave like this. Because just like that, one little hack showed that it could go away in an instant. Now we have to hope that on Tuesday, we're granted four more years to prove we were worthy of Reparations after all. And if we get that chance, I hope we don't make the world regret it.

"Y'all need some tough love, though. We've got to start playing to our strengths, and stop deluding ourselves about our blind spots and shortcomings. Join with me in a little prayer of contrition. Pray with me now, as I thank the Lord Jesus Christ for His guidance out of my own prideful sins. I ask Him to give us all the strength to face that cruel mirror, so that we may be better and more truthful in our lives. I do solemnly swear that I will honor His teachings by loving my fellow man, both with praise when it is deserved, and correction when it is just.

"Oh, I see you fidgeting in your seats out there. Some of y'all don't like this new me. I get it. You want good-time Matthias to make you laugh. 'Haha, he a clown! It's the Sunday circus show!' But I can't do it no more. It's time to get serious, all of us, and start thinking about our futures for real. Picture that white-and-green HRA debit card in your purse, and imagine that it was gone forever. What would you do? How would you provide for your family?

"Oh Lord, I know they closed that factory down and sent it to China or Bangladesh or wherever. But a lot of Caucs lost their jobs when that happened, too. Yeah, I know they let in all those Mexicans who work on the cheap. But you know, they show up at the job site, stick around to raise their kids, and within one generation they're all dialed in. They speak English, finish high school, and can hold down a job.

"But what about us? Decade after decade, it's the same destructive cycle. Esther, chapter eight: 'For how can I endure to see the evil that shall come unto my people? Or how can I endure to see the destruction of my kindred?'

"You know what I think? I bet you that one day, maybe thirty years ago, the government just threw up their hands and gave up on us. Said something like, 'Let those Latizos in, see how they do.' And just like that, the Latizo population exploded. Give it another fifteen, twenty years, and think about how much political power they're gonna hold. And they ain't got none of that white guilt! No, sir! Are you starting to get it yet?

"That's why the time is *now* to make Reparations work. Somehow we got this last blessed chance at a hand up, and we must use it to get ourselves right instead of just punishing whites. Lord, I have been *so wrong* in playing that foolish game, and I ask that You forgive me. No, we have to turn that vengeful eye back onto ourselves and be held accountable, too.

"Because in reality, I have seen good white men in those debtors' prisons. And I know that when they're released, the home they go back to isn't some great mansion, neither. Plenty of poor Caucs killin' time down in the cell block, that's right!

"And the sad truth is, we get softer and weaker after every dollar we take from them. Meanwhile that Korean who owns your neighborhood convenience store, he's so disciplined that he can always squeeze out a profit—even while we steal from him. Because of course, we resent him. Proverbs, chapter twenty-one: 'The desire of the slothful killeth him; for his hands refuse to labor.'

"So I'm telling you now, the clock is running out. On patience. Money. Sorrow. And hope. We've got to stop complaining, stop gaming the system. Find some gratitude and turn it into pride. Say to the world, 'Yes, your ancestors sold me and your grandfathers shunned me. But today, you renew me so that tomorrow we can look forward together, unburdened by the weight of history that is crushing us all.'

"Look, my people. It's not hopeless. Progress has been made bit by bit since Barack Obama first knocked down that color barrier into the presidency twenty years ago. Yes, we're getting closer! But there's still so much shocking brutality within our own ranks. Crimes and killings done more out of callousness than desperation.

"Which is why I worry. I worry that one day, main street

America is going to say that all the entertainment that college basketball provides, it's not enough to offset the endless cycle of single-motherhood by too-young teenage girls that produces more criminals than healthy members of society.

"Tell me, is the creative destruction within the black community really worth it? For every great singer who inspires the world, we leave a pile of black bodies in our wake. For every brilliant scholar, square miles of ruin. For every athlete that makes it big, how many others fall right back into the soup?

"Ezekiel, chapter five, verse fourteen: 'Moreover I will make thee waste, and a reproach among the nations that are round about thee, in the sight of all that pass by.' Because I swear it, the few eagles among us are not enough to sustain it all. I'm talkin' about the waste, the squandered potential, the unfulfilled dreams... We can't afford it no more! No one can.

"Especially when there's a whole world of people of *all* races out there who are eager to come take our place at the table. While we spill our glasses and throw food at each other, there are Africans, Russians, Filipinos, and Chinese standing outside the door politely. So is it any wonder that the system would rather import the Third World than deal with us? Before we call anyone racist, we better look in the mirror and ask why. Because they're already trying to phase us out!

"Don't hide your ears from my tough talk, I beg of you! These are just words, not bullets that kill. I'm pulling no punches today because if we don't get our act together in the next four years, we may be knocked down for the count.

"And then what are we gonna do? And where are we gonna go? Back to the Motherland, where we haven't stepped foot in centuries? Y'all couldn't survive in metal shacks or a mud hut. You've never even been camping! But I'm with you on that. I like my shower too much. So we can't go back! We've got to make the most of what we have right here. And I quote Psalm Thirty-three, 'Blessed is the nation whose God is the Lord; and the people whom he hath chosen for his own inheritance.'

"So let's start by showing a little respect. 'For what?' that lady just said. For what?! Hahaha! For the food, the shelter, the cars, the electricity, and the roads. For the cell phone you use to call your sister and listen to your favorite songs—and which you *could* use to better yourself, like learning a new language instead of looking at pornography.

"All these tools are at your disposal, but the choice what to do with them is still up to you. Your ancestors would have *killed* for something that offered a person—any man, woman, or child— access to a way out of ignorance. Oh Lord, you can lead a horse to water, but you can't make him drink. And you can give an Afrigro-American the key to his enlightenment, but you can't make him think.

"That is, unless he wants to! So, do you? Do you, my brothers and sisters, want to make the best of your mind in this wonderful country to improve your own lot in life? Because I can't do it for you. The Caucs can't do it for you. And most definitely, that magic money coming from the Historical Reparations Administration isn't the cure. Otherwise people who win the lottery wouldn't end up so miserable and broke once again. That's right! I am preaching truth right now! Stand back!

"Say, you, Mr. Morris. How much money you got on you right now? Eleven dollars? Tell me, how much has the HRA paid you and what have you done with it? Did you use it to better your life, or did you waste it? *What did you spend it on?!*

"All that money, which they say was earned by the blood and sweat and tears of our ancestors. And yet you used it to get drunk on cognac, thinkin' you was a prince. Don't tell me y'all haven't seen the costs go up on our favorite vices now. Because you know they have—but every day, you still pull out that debit card and let them swipe away the gift that was paid for in pain.

"Or maybe you like to gamble. I see the hustles you boys run in the doorways of those vacant shops. Losing money you should be investing to open new businesses in those same storefronts. It's so easy, too. All you'd have to do is show the smallest bit of initiative and it could be yours. Why? Because the color of your skin will get you in! Yes indeed! Say it with me now. The color of your skin... will get you in!

"You got to plan out the next step. Because I'm tellin' you right now, equity isn't enough. That's right, it ain't! You know that old 'teach a man how to fish' line? Well, I think it's missing something. Because it's not just about putting food on a black man's plate, or his ability to grow crops of his own. What we need is to be able to *participate* in the future! Don't you want to be involved in that struggle to move humanity forward, rather than just playing dominoes in the park?

"Do not let this opportunity slip away. Oh my Lord, if Victor Dominguez wins do you not think that the Latizo population won't flex its muscles and say no more? My God Almighty, did you just hear me? If Dominguez wins, that might be the end of any kind of sympathy for our godforsaken race. Not when there's Mexicans and Koreans and Indians here by the millions and two generations deep.

"And they don't feel the slightest twitch of guilt. No sir, they are not weighed down by the white man's albatross. But go on, keep it up. Keep playing the fool and testing their patience. Just remember, the 'new Americans' are moving forward day by day.

"'But Reverend,' you say. 'Them foreigners ain't suffered like our people.' Oh yeah? You don't know that. You would, if you bothered to use your tablet to read about world history and not play video games. Did you know that there was a war in Korea seventy-five years ago that split their proud nation in half? That's where North Korea and South Korea come from. Yes, 'the North and the South.' Hmm, where have we heard that before? That's right, Koreans had their own civil war.

"And then there's India, my god! If you saw the poverty over there—the filth, the desperation!—you'd get up off your hind ends so fast and never complain again. But no, you just want to stay in your little bubble where the narrative says that you can take, but not give. Use, but not create.

"So answer me this. If the narrative you believe also says that our African ancestors built up this nation from nothing without fair pay, will you just stand around while people who got here last week take over? 'Cause they're coming. They'll sweep your craps game off the stoop and move their whole family in, then start selling you junk to pay for their kids' college. And in twenty years they'll be gone, moved out to the nice neighborhoods where none of y'all live. You know and I know that when that happens, they won't even bother to say thank you for using us as their stepping stones to the American dream.

"My people, I know that my words today are harsh and shocking. But this is a wake up call! As I turn over a new page in my own life and seek to become a more serious man, I extend my hand so that you all will join me. Do as I do from now on. Respect yourself and be the best men and women that you can be, because maybe the narrative *is* correct when we cry out that ain't no one coming to help us.

"We've got to start working together to create our own wealth. Effective tomorrow, I will begin reorganizing the Foundation for Healing Colonial Guilt to help facilitate entrepreneurship among members of this congregation and our community at large.

"So yes, after wading through all that muck, I hope to end this sermon on a positive note. Deep in my heart, I have tremendous hope for all of us, because I know that the story isn't over. That our history of suffering is only part of the whole. It is, in fact, the part that precedes our redemption and fulfillment in this great land of opportunity.

"And that is why, despite it all, we are glad to be here and not back in Africa. Because our painful journey through history bought us advance tickets in getting to know our Lord Jesus Christ. At this very moment, there are millions and millions of our cousins over there who never heard His name or learned His gospel. Hundreds of years of black men and women who the slave traders *didn't* catch, but who also lived and died in complete ignorance of the true God.

"Stand up and raise your hands for me now, because I can't do this alone. God is responsible for every gift and every tribulation. He's at your side during every glorious moment and bears witness to every tragic scene. The good and the bad are what it means to be human! No one goes through this life unscarred, and no one gets out alive. So don't hold yourselves back just because of grief or imperfection, not when you've got the power of Jesus Christ alive in your heart and in your mind!

"That is *your* privilege. A glorious strength that billions of people of all races around the world do not possess. Honor it and honor Him by leaving here today with a newfound sense of appreciation for what you have, and a reaffirmed faith that He has a wonderful plan for you.

"May God bless you all. Amen…"

15. ELECTION EVE

Victor Dominguez and his wife Jaclyn were alone at home in Scottsdale. They had flown in earlier after last-minute appearances in Michigan, where his team believed that poll numbers suggested the state was suddenly in play.

Jaclyn brought a tray into the living room and placed a scotch-on-the-rocks on the table beside Victor's recliner.

"Thank you."

"My pleasure. It's so nice to have a few minutes to ourselves after all this time flying around."

"Are you ready to be the first lady of our nation?"

Jaclyn sat down and said, "I've been with you every step of the way so far. Count me in."

Victor turned to the iguana that was lounging on the arm of his chair. "And what about you, Tito? Do you have what it takes to be the first pet?"

The iguana flicked its tongue. Victor gave him a gentle squeeze on the ribs.

"I wonder what the kids will think if I bring him to the Easter Egg Roll."

"You know, Victor. One day when I'm old and frail, in my last memoirs I think I'll finally reveal that Tito was your most trusted sounding board when you had to make the tough decisions."

"As long as it's the right choice, the methods don't matter."

"Then I hope he survives the next four years."

"Or eight."

"One step at a time, darling."

"So, which one of you should I kill first?" Ryan Richards said with villainous contempt.

His head lay across his arm and he was staring at a row of shots set out on the bar. Some were clear, others brown, and still others golden. Suddenly he perked up.

"I know! Let's go with the buddy system."

He lifted two of the glasses to his lips, then tilted them back sloppily. As Ryan wiped his face with his sleeve, a silver-haired real estate tycoon with a spray tan that rivaled his own sat on the stool next to him.

"Why are you so down in the dumps?"

"I just have a bad feeling about the election," Ryan said. "My job's on the line too."

"There's no way she's going to lose. Look at everybody else here. They're relaxing, having a good time. It's in the bag. Everyone knows it but you."

The tycoon reached over and picked up one of the shot glasses.

"Help yourself," Ryan chuckled. "I want to believe you. I'm just so wrapped up in it, you know? I don't have any perspective right now."

"What's the big problem, anyway? Every acting gig you ever had came to an end at some point. Don't tell me you didn't save up enough money?"

"I've got plenty of cash in the bank. And my DS isn't even all that bad considering how long my family's been here. But if Jeffries-Lao goes down and *DDM* gets canceled, or if they decide to go in another direction with a new host..."

"You're giving yourself an ulcer over nothing."

"Did you know that after *Antiques Roadshow* got canceled, the producers didn't just get blacklisted from the industry? They went into hiding! So if the pendulum swings back the other way, I don't know if I have enough in the tank to reinvent myself again. If they even let me."

The other man laughed. "What's it been since you last played Rolph Dungeonlord? Eight years?"

"Something like that. Don't remind me, please."

"Why? He was fun! Maybe bring him back, start swinging that battle-ax around again. You know, for nostalgia's sake."

"Christ... Will that be my only option if this all falls apart? I forgot most of my German anyway."

"Ryan, let me put this in perspective for you. If Dominguez wins and they start dismantling the HRA, we're all gonna have more to worry about than who gets cast as what on TV."

Richards straightened up. "I'll be damned. You're right. It will be," he called out dramatically while lifting a glass, "a time of change!"

"That's the spirit. Now bottoms up."

"Let us eat and drink, for tomorrow we die!"

Glenn Murray whipped his head around like a windmill and pumped his fist. The guitar player to his left flashed his teeth menacingly while strumming with blinding speed. The mosh pit in front of the stage swirled in rhythm to the kick-drum's punchy beat, and the smell of sweat and beer filled this small Providence bar.

"Fury!" Glenn howled into the microphone that was cupped in his hand. "Furious at the lies! In front, behind, coming from all sides. Behold the corruption if you dare, then fall to your knees, escape is nowhere..."

"Crisis actors are a girl's best friend!"

Eileen Jeffries-Lao slid back over the arm of a soft lounge chair and kicked off her heels. Paul Jeffries caressed one of her stockinged feet as he walked past and sat in a matching chair. He set two drinks down on the coffee table, then loosened his tie.

"Well," he said, "I just hope the detaining officers haven't abused him too badly."

"I'm sure their supervisor was briefed that no harm should come to our 'suspect'. Otherwise, hazard pay!" Eileen reached out from her awkward position and scooted a glass into her fingers. "But it's fine. Our little ruse has already paid dividends."

"Oh, really?"

"Yes, indeed! Someone who works for the HRA in Dallas turned herself in."

"A woman? Hmm."

"She's fairly low level, but has been dating one of the IT guys who works at the same location. Apparently he 'turned' her to the dark side. But seeing all the panic at her branch firsthand, and then sensing that our nets were closing in—it gave her a change of heart."

"And the boyfriend?"

"Ah. We picked him up during his lunch break yesterday.

And he's been singing ever since! Now the poor fellow won't be able to cast his vote for Dominguez tomorrow."

Paul leaned forward and tipped an imaginary hat. "Finally, a crack in the dam. That's great news!"

"And he's not the only one."

"Really now?"

"I wish we could've done it sooner for PR's sake, but the point is we'll now be sweeping up some of the top Jubileers."

"Anyone I might know?"

Eileen shrugged her shoulders. "National security. Sorry, hon."

"I do wish you wouldn't keep so many secrets from me. I hate to put my foot in my mouth when being interviewed."

"I know, it's a tough gig having to toe that fine line between platitudes and evasions."

"Despite your own little evasion here, congratulations nonetheless."

"Thank you, Paul. I don't think my team was too happy about us staging an arrest five days before the election, but it gave me a nice boost in the polls, and now—"

"Now they can focus on taking down the Sentinels in time for you to make a rousing inaugural speech."

"Oh, Mr. Jeffries, you have such a knack for dramatic timing."

"Please. The first man *does* do more than drink bourbon and hobnob with dignitaries."

"You won't mind such a taxing workload for another four years, will you?"

"As long as there's still time to keep my golf swing in rhythm, I'm the man for the job."

"Well... We all have our vices."

Ms. Jenkins came in from the garage with a hamper under her arm. She stopped when she saw that Myra was standing at the front window looking out into the street.

"I don't think he's coming back tonight," she said. "Get away from there and help me with these clothes."

Myra slowly pushed through the canvas drapes and walked toward the dining room table. She picked up a shirt, saying as she began to fold it, "I just don't understand why. Everything, and I mean everything, has been going so good for us all."

Ms. Jenkins balled up a tiny pair of yellow socks. "He been a wild, strong man for a long time. Made the best of himself considering where he started. Song or no song, it got to be hard for him to come into our house. Be dealin' with women and babies, when out there on the streets he got excitement and… the unknown."

"Oh, Mama. He's been so good with Sarah lately, too. Buying her gifts, singing her little songs. I just don't know how he can switch that off so quick."

"I guess he still ain't decided whether he wants to be part of this family, or…"

"Or what? Keep chasing after other girls?"

"That ain't the all of it. Sometimes men, they just get stuck in this mode, like they's lone wolves roaming in the night. So lost, they don't even realize when they got what they was after."

"So what do I do?"

"About Octavius? Nothing. You take care of you and these kids. Better to have him 'round here only if he want to be."

Myra glanced at Sarah bouncing lazily in her swing. She bunched her lips and kept folding clothes.

Upstairs Tyrell was watching an animated TV show. Two squirrels in red spacesuits teleported into a hall filled with purple entities that were shaped like tall floor lamps. The visitors were greeted by the flashing on and off of their bulbous heads.

One of the squirrels said, "Salutations from Earth! We are grateful for this welcome, but are troubled by all of the energy expended in such a display. Remember: conserve resources, save the planet!"

A purple character waddled forward. "We do not receive many visitors on our remote world. Those that do come are usually pleased with our hospitality. Who are you to take offense?"

"We are the Impact Kids! Traveling into the deepest reaches of space to share our wisdom—efficiency, utility, coopera…"

Tyrell turned his attention away from the TV to his tablet. It was much nicer than the ones he and his classmates used at school. He spent a lot of time exploring all the interactive learning games which his uncle Clyde had installed on it.

But tonight Tyrell wasn't playing one of those. He entered the DoWork program and opened a file called *home*. A spreadsheet appeared and he scrolled down until reaching a cell with the words *week three*.

He selected a box next to the one labeled *mommy* and typed, "said a bad word 5 times. didnt flush last nite". Tyrell then moved to a line designated for his grandmother and entered, "yell at the mail man…"

He glanced up at the TV screen. The two astrosquirrels were standing in front of a commander back on their ship. They turned to the camera and said, "Join us next time as we nobly scurry where no bushy tail has scurried before!"

Octavius was sitting in his Buick. His right hand gripped the top of the steering wheel, but the engine was off. Searing yellow from a nearby streetlight reflected off his dark face.

He looked around—empty parking lot, couple of closed stores, quiet street, then a row of houses. Nothing going down at the moment, but he knew that around here that could change in an instant. So you always had to be ready, because instigator or not, it was on you to survive.

He was twenty-eight years old. Already a veteran of the street life. But all this family business, first with Myra and especially now that Clyde was involved, was getting him confused. His daughter was turning into a beautiful little girl. And this goofy kid Clyde wanted him along for the ride with his music career.

It was all too warm and gray for someone like himself who lived in a world of absolutes, where you had to stay detached if you didn't want to be the next victim. But the life was a grind, constantly looking over your shoulder and having to put on displays of confidence. Buying souped-up cars and fancy matching jewelry, not because you wanted those things, but because that kind of flair commanded respect. And out here, that could save your life.

Octavius figured that sooner or later it was all going to catch up with him. Hustle for long enough and it didn't matter how you looked or who you were in good with. Someone new was always gunning for your corner.

To think that hooking up with Clyde, at the cost of putting him out of his comfort zone, might give him a way to walk out of here on his own two feet, instead of leaving in a body bag…

Well, he thought, *there's worse ways to go.*

Octavius turned the ignition and pulled into the street. He could already picture Sarah's little eyes smiling at him from her crib.

Eddie Pryor closed his eyes and draped an arm over the microphone stand. He nodded his head to the rhythm of the song before doing his best Wayne Newton impression.

"The love between the two of us was dying…"

When the song finished he peacocked over to three Vietnamese women in matching lavender dresses. They devoured him as he fell into their booth.

"Girls, girls," he said as he sat up, "it is damn good to be alive!"

The trio laughed and tried to smooth his hair and shirt collar.

"So," Eddie said, "which one of you is gonna go up there and serenade me?"

"Oh, no, no!" they laughed. "We don't sing."

"How the hell am I supposed to make you ladies famous if you won't even go up in front of a bowling alley crowd?"

"Famous, who?" one of the girls said. "We want to have fun."

"Yeah? Are you having fun? Good, good."

"Oh, very much fun! And even if we don't sing, maybe later we dance for you."

Eddie waved over the server. "Get these dolls whatever they want. And another whiskey-soda for me—if I'm gonna do all the singing for this group, I need to keep these pipes lubricated. Whoo!"

Elder Marcus Young was making his final evening rounds before settling in for the night. The Mall's weekly publication had just come out and he wanted to read the latest news.

He looked in on a resident who had arrived with bronchitis. A nurse was making notes in her tablet while the man slept.

"How is he coming along?" Marcus said.

The nurse nodded her head slightly. "We got the coughing under control."

"That's a good sign."

"But he's in rough shape. Malnourished. Frail. Addressing these symptoms is just the first step."

"Thank you, nurse." Marcus turned to leave.

"And how about you, sir?"

"Doing fine. Thank you for asking. I think the first couple of days were hectic for everyone, but now we're all settling in."

"If there's anything you need," she said, "don't hesitate to ask. The staff here has seen it all—inner city ERs, meth country, you name it—so you can rely on us."

"Wonderful. Have a modest evening."

Marcus clasped his hands behind his back and walked softly down the hallway toward the front of the building. He kept his ears alert for any sound that might indicate one of the patients was in distress.

As he passed the sliding double doors that led into the entertainment room, he saw that several of the men were playing cards. He approached them with a wave.

One of the men grumbled and threw his cards onto the table. James Haggerston reached out and gathered up the pot, saying, "Mmm, mmm, mmm."

Bo also flicked his cards away and cursed. He glanced over at Marcus.

"Hey, boss. What's the word?"

Marcus stepped closer. "Good evening, gents. I was just taking a last look around before retiring. Is everything well with you?"

"Yeah. It would go better if James didn't win so many hands."

James threw his hands up. "Is it my fault these guys don't know how to bluff?"

Marcus stepped back, saying, "I'll leave you to your sordid ways, then."

"Say," Bo called out, "you want to sit in, play a few hands?"

"Oh, I don't know. This is your thing."

"Come on, man! You can't just play nanny all the time. Come hang out with us."

Marcus gave a sly smile. "Alright. Just remember, back

before I found Mod, I was pretty worldly. I don't want to hear any crying if I take all your money."

"This guy!" Bo said. "Now he's a card shark."

"I wash my hands of it. Deal!"

Luis Ortega was studying at the kitchen table. His mother dried her hands and shuffled past into the living room. She sat down next to her husband, who was watching soccer on the TV.

A few minutes later, the sound of voices close by came in through the open front windows. Mrs. Ortega got up and looked outside.

"*Dios,*" she sighed as she pulled back.

"*Que pasa?*" Mr. Ortega asked.

"There are people outside in the driveway. Young people."

"Luis's *amigos*, no?"

"*Yo no se.* Excuse me, Luis? I think some of your friends from the school are here."

Luis looked up from his work. "I don't know, Mama. We usually meet in the library on campus."

"Can you please go and check who they are?"

Luis got up and stepped out onto the front stoop. There were about twenty people standing together, and several held lighted candles with religious figures printed on the glassware.

"Ahhh," the group said when they saw him.

Luis adjusted his glasses. "Hey, can I help you guys?"

"Oh, Luis," they began to sing, "sweet Luis. A boy so brave, they fell to their knees…"

Luis brought a hand to his forehead, then waved at the group until they stopped singing. "Who are you, anyway?"

A man in his mid-twenties stepped forward. "We are," he said proudly, "Luis's Lieutenants. And we are here to serve!"

"Wait… What the hell?"

"Everyday people with busy lives, just like you. And thanks to your courageous example, we all found each other."

"But how'd you guys find my house?" Luis asked. "I mean, like, did you just come over to say hi?"

A young Latiza around Luis's age emerged from the group.

"This is Cristina," the man said. "Go on, tell him."

The girl looked down. "I got a DDM notification a few days

ago. But I'm on a gymnastics travel team—I don't wanna go!"

"But it should be fine," Luis said. "They told me Beneficiaries can put it off til later if they want."

"That's the thing," she said. "Inside I'm mostly white. The show called me on as a Debtor! Saint Luis, can you help me, please?"

She ran forward and hugged him. At first Luis stepped back to get away, but when she looked up he could see her face clearly in the light. He thought she was really cute.

"I don't know," he said, easing out of her arms. "But maybe we can think of something."

"Thank you," she whispered.

The group linked arms and started to sway back and forth. "Oh, Luis… Sweet Luis…"

Emissary Karlov entered the Prescient One's private chambers and saw that the thicket of blue cloth vines had been opened up by tying them off into neat bunches. He walked across the space and found his leader sitting tensely on the edge of a divan.

The Prescient One rose and said, "So good of you to join me, Emissary Karlov."

"But of course," Karlov said. "I would be remiss to decline such an invitation. How can I be of service?"

"Please, sit down. You have always offered me valuable help in the past when I was troubled—even if it was just lending me your ear. So please, indulge me now once more."

Karlov settled into a plush chair. "It would be an honor. What concerns you tonight?"

The Prescient One said, "As we speak most of the country, if not the world, is nervously awaiting the results of tomorrow's election. But of course, the scope of our upcoming expansion is so vast that political matters are almost inconsequential."

"Indeed," the emissary said. "The church is channeling your prescient insights so that we may be humble leaders and not merely followers—or even reactionaries, if you can pardon my frankness."

"I adore you for it," the Prescient One said with a mild laugh. "And that is why I asked you to join me. As we prepare to move forward with these bold steps, I find myself experiencing ripples of doubt. But whether it is simply about the church or perhaps something deeper within myself, I cannot tell."

"I see," Karlov said. "Forgive if what I'm about to suggest risks overstepping my bounds, but I only mean well. Shall I continue?"

"By all means."

"No one here, least of all me, doubts your sincerity or the rightness of your vision. But perhaps the outward manifestation of your push for modesty belies... something more personal about you. The old you, in fact."

The Prescient One touched a piece of putty that was stuck to his cheek, then yanked it off. "Do you refer to this? That perhaps Mod could have been shared with the world a bit... differently?"

Karlov said, "Far be it from me to question methods which, however unorthodox, have resonated with so many people. Modestianity has saved thousands from being held hostage to shame, and in turn given their lives a grounded sense of pride. But if you are afflicted with doubts at this critical juncture, surely they must not be ignored. If something destructive has been hiding deep within your subconscious, perhaps since long before your first major success twenty years ago—well, you must face it down right now!"

"Something going that far back in time, you think?" the Prescient One asked. "And it may have played a hand in the eccentricities that accompanied my philosophy right from the start? I don't even know whether it is benevolent, malevolent, or benign. How might I go about discovering the truth, emissary?"

"There is only one way," Karlov said. "You must open yourself up to Mod more than you ever have before. Only by becoming truly vulnerable will He guide you to the deepest wounds."

"I see. Take off the *inner* mask."

"Yes, Your Prescience."

The Prescient One opened his mouth as if to speak, but then hesitated. A moment later he said, "But what if at the end of this process, I no longer believe?"

"In Mod?" Karlov asked.

"In Him, the church, all of it. Because if I don't know who has lurked within me for all these years, how can I be certain that after looking him in the eye, any of who I am today will survive?"

Karlov made a circular motion around his chest. "I offer my sincere prayers that this does not happen. But in that worst case, the church will carry on your mission. I swear it."

"Beloved emissary," the Prescient One said, "I know you will. But what if the new me declares itself your mortal enemy?"

The emissary said, "Your words make me shiver. I know very little about your past private life. I pray that we all have not been misled by a man who secretly harbored a devil inside."

"And I as well. I regret if our conversation has shaken you so. That was not my intention."

"And yet only a few moments ago, it was I who feared offending you. Still, I am an emissary with good reason. Delve well, Your Prescience, and I shall greet whichever version of you returns."

"Thank you for this frank discussion. I beg Mod to shine upon us all."

TJ and David walked across the movie theater lobby and stepped into the concessions line.

"This was such a great idea to get out of the house," TJ said.

"I know!" David said. "There's only so much of those talking heads you can take."

"And there'll be *no* talking at all tonight, haha."

"I can't believe we're going to see a movie that's over a hundred years old on the big screen."

"Who needs 3D anyway?"

"Well," David said as he grabbed hold of TJ's arm, "we've got it where it really counts."

"Thanks for always being there, my love. Now, let's pick out some snacks…"

Dramacrat Congresshuman Neil Thornton sat typing frantically at the work desk in his country house. After sending each email, he also crossed one line off the list of gibberish words that ran down a piece of paper.

When he was done, he burned the sheet with a match. Then

he took the computer into the kitchen and put it the microwave. Sparks and crackles gave way to a cloud of noxious smoke. Neil covered his face with the neck of his sweater, popped the microwave door open, then sprayed a fire extinguisher inside.

After cleaning himself up, he opened a beer and poured some Scotch into a tumbler, then returned to his desk. He slid the drawer open and removed a silver revolver. He checked the chamber—all six rounds were there—then pushed it back into place. He set the gun down and took a sip of beer as he relaxed into the high-backed leather chair.

A violent crashing sound of glass breaking came from behind him. Several dull pops followed. The air hissed and began to fill with smoke. Thin beams of red light strobed through the room as gruff male voices shouted to each other.

Congresshuman Thornton leaned forward and placed his hands face down on the surface of the desk. The unified force of three SWAT members wrenched him out of the chair and into the cold night air. A dozen officers formed a circle around him, while two S'more Stoppers buzzed loudly overhead.

As he was being cuffed, the team leader approached and said, "Looks like the Sentinels' days are numbered."

"Watch," Neil said with a grin, "I'll still keep my seat tomorrow."

"Take him away…"

"… So everybody, please put your hands together for the man behind this uniquely American story of inspiration, Mr. Nolan Simmons!"

Nolan jogged up and shook the host's hand. The audience gave warm applause as he took the podium.

"I'd like to thank the New Haven Optimist Club for inviting me to speak tonight. As if my life hadn't already been a fascinating journey, these past few months have taken it to a whole new level.

"But I speak from the heart when I say that nothing gives me greater pleasure than being able to share my insights with respected institutions like this one. Let's have a real conversation about how to improve communities and put powerful new ideas into action.

"Surely by working together, we can raise up the millions of Americans of all races who may be down and out right now, but are just looking for that opportunity to shine. I truly believe that most people want that feeling of pride that comes from contributing to their communities.

"Tonight I will discuss the main points of my new program, Nolan's Nine Strategies to Navigating Success…"

Kate and Chris Donohugh were at home glued to the TV. The various food containers strewn about were proof of their commitment to finishing all the leftovers that were in the fridge.

But conversation was sparse, and it was only the frantic election prognosticators on screen whose voices filled the air. A segment ended and the channel cut to commercial. Kate's face appeared.

"Oh, God," Kate moaned and fell forward onto a pillow.

"Come on," Chris said, "you have to watch."

"Fine, alright."

The Kate on TV said, "I'm Kate Donohugh, HRA employee and lifelong advocate. Our opponents will stop at nothing to try and tear us down. And while I may be one of their victims, let's make sure it doesn't happen ever again. On Tuesday, cast your vote for strong leadership by re-electing President Eileen Jeffries-Lao."

The commercial then cut to a wide shot of Kate and the president standing side by side.

"Make no mistake," Jeffries-Lao said. "I take these hackers and their fear tactics very seriously. Send me back to Washington so that I can stand up for Kate, fight for Beneficiaries, and keep our proud nation moving forward."

Chris clapped his hands and called out, "Bravo, bravo! Encore, please!"

Kate lowered the TV volume. "I hope that helps, but jeez, I hate to watch myself."

"I thought you looked kind of hot in that business suit. Can you model it for me?"

"Hey, what's got into you?" she said. "All week you've been in shutdown mode."

"Come on, it's not like you're Miss Consistent either. I mean, that message you left me is still standing here like the elephant in the room."

Kate sighed. "I don't know. I just feel like we haven't been on the same page for a while."

"Maybe some of it's just life happening. But you *are* the one who chose to travel around and then stay with your parents. You barely talked to me the whole time."

"I was feeling pretty lost. I just needed a breather."

"How'd that work out for you?" Chris scoffed.

"Why are you being so testy?"

Chris put his hands on the top of his head. He said, "All this stuff that's been going on has me really confused. And I guess it's dragging me down. I mean, if you had come back from that meeting with the president and said you'd accepted a job working for her down in DC—that I could maybe understand. But wanting to have a baby? That's the last thing I imagined you'd ever say."

"But it wasn't just from talking to her," Kate said. "It's everything that's happened this month. This year, really. Facing my own mortality. And seeing my old teacher, Ms. Herron. She *inspired* us back when we were in high school—but now she just seems like a witch casting spells. Oh my god, I can't believe I even said that."

"She's irrelevant, you don't really mean it."

"No, I mean how it reflects back on me. All of us. It's as if every classroom has its own pied piper luring children away from their parents, from their own desires—from whatever they'd known to be true before entering that school building."

"Kate," Chris said, "do you actually think teachers have the power to unravel kids' minds and reshape them just like that?"

"When you give them ten years to work on you, maybe!"

"If that's all true," Chris said slowly, "what I want to know is this. Who gave them the right to access our minds?"

"More like," Kate said, "why did they *think* they had that authority? We were innocent children!"

"What does that say about our educational system?"

"What does that say about us? We're products of that system. We've been doing its bidding out in the world for a long time."

Chris said, "So if you were brainwashed, then wasn't I too?"

"I... What would that mean to you, Chris?"

"I have to wonder then, how did it change the course of my own life? I mean, what if I didn't join a political band back when I started playing guitar, but spent that time learning classical or jazz? Maybe I could've become a great musician…"

"This is all getting too crazy," Kate said. "I don't know how much deeper I can go right now. Especially if you're in the water without a life jacket too!"

"Alright, Kate. Let's just rest. Have some calm before the storm tomorrow."

"I agree. And we really should make time for a day date soon. Go to brunch, maybe see a movie afterward. Just have some fun together."

"Sign me up," Chris said.

"God, I hope she wins." Kate shook her head. "I don't know if I have the strength to face the alternative."

"We'll do the best we can, no matter what."

"I do love you, Chris."

"I know, babe."

The woman dipped the mop head into the water, then rolled the bucket forward by holding onto the handle as she walked. She gave the wringer a firm press, then made several precise strokes across the vinyl floor.

She worked her way down the corridor steadily. After reaching a turn, she called out, "Stepping into ladies room!"

The woman entered the restroom without the cleaning supplies. She bent over a sink and rinsed her face, then retied the strands of brunette hair that had come loose while working. She stood up and looked into the mirror—the bright-green-and-white striped jumpsuit and her tired eyes reflected back.

She saw one of the stall doors behind her slowly swing open. She whipped around to see a man staring at her. Before she could even gasp, let alone scream, he leaped out and grabbed hold of her. He looked intently into her eyes, until finally her shock gave way to recognition.

"Oh, Morgan," she moaned in a whisper. She threw her arms around him and sobbed into his chest.

"Emily, I'm here," he said quietly. "I can't stay long. Are you alright?"

The woman pulled back and wiped her eyes. "It's awful. After work they make us come to this clinic and clean up all the messes."

"And the kids—where are our kids?"

"I still don't know anything!" she said more loudly, then quickly covered her mouth. "They just took them away after we got arrested. No one's told me anything since you all escaped. Now… God, I missed you so much!"

Morgan looked down at his watch. "I have to go. The guys who got me in here are waiting outside. I just had to see you, had to let you know I'm out there trying to make things right. One day we'll all be a family again."

Emily put her hand on his cheek. "Find them. No matter what it takes. Just find our children and bring them back to me."

"I swear to God, I will."

A moment later, the ladies room door opened and the woman in green stripes took up her mop. She kept her head down as she worked, so that the security cameras would not see her tears.

Clyde Jenkins sat writing lyrics at a dining table in the little furnished apartment he had rented. It was a safe haven for when things got too crazy, and this was just one of those times he needed to be alone. Everyone was talking about the election, asking him what he thought was going to happen with the HRA —but his head was somewhere else.

His thoughts went back to the summer, to the moment right before he sent his first song into that great content pipeline where unknown artists vied for a place in the zeitgeist. He'd felt like a little boy running along the sidewalks, oblivious to the workings of the world that made the buildings he passed possible, or how the businesses inside them operated.

But somehow, now millions of people knew his name and could recite his lyrics. Were they fools? As much as he enjoyed being showered with praise, Clyde was uneasy about being called a prophet or a revolutionary. He may have stumbled into the cultural conversation because of some unfathomable stroke of good timing, but he knew it wouldn't happen like that the second time around.

Clyde made his peace with the decision to go forward with

the new song as-is, because even though the message was different, it came from the same place as before—his heart. So whether the response was a rocket launch even higher or an echo that never returned, what mattered was knowing that he'd followed his own instincts in the face of temptation.

Whenever he felt too stressed, he reminded himself that he was already playing with house money. He had taken the steps to provide for his family, first and foremost. And the words that had made him famous were not superficial, but actually gave other Beneficiaries insight into their own lives—as well as spread a little hope that things might improve at the HRA.

Sometimes the little boy inside him whispered that he was too young and uneducated to understand all of the HRA's inner workings, so who was he to criticize? All Clyde could do in the face of such doubts, was to put his trust in the poet's ability to cut through the world's complex structures and grasp the core ideas holistically.

And right now, Clyde felt that everybody needed to rein in their frantic thoughts and just be in the moment. They would do better to look inside for strength, and not elsewhere for help. Most of all, he wanted people to reach a hand across the street, instead of overwhelming themselves by trying to change the whole world.

Sometimes it was your own small efforts, made sincerely and without expectations, that ended up reverberating far and wide. Not because you shouted, but because other people spoke your name.

Clyde Jenkins, the unlikely hip-hop sensation, was ready to try his luck once more.

THE END.

Reparations CORE

(BOOK THREE)

1. THE WRONG PICTURE

A spotlight flashed on and illuminated a tiny portion of the sound stage. A handsome white man in a striking gray suit stood with his head bowed.

Over the loudspeakers a voice shouted, "Ah-one, two, three, fooooah!" and big band music filled the air with a rollicking, upbeat tune.

The man on stage threw out his arms and looked up—the face golden tan, smiling teeth blinding—then began to frantically dance in time with the music. He performed a series of sophisticated tap dance moves, although his shoes made no sound. He held a triumphant pose as the final note rang out.

There was manic applause as the main lights came on. The man ran toward the side of the stage and caught a pencil-thin microphone that was flying in the air toward him.

Trotting back to the middle, he said, "Boy, oh boy! We're baaaack!"

Another eruption from the crowd, which slowly morphed into a low rumbling chant of, "DDM! DDM! DDM..."

"Oh yes, you know it, folks. Ryan Richards back again with you on a Saturday night. *DDM TV Live* is locked and loaded and here to spread the good news. Eileen Jeffries-Lao—*la presidenta* herself—has been re-elected for four more years. Ooh, ooh, ooh... can you just taste the sweetness?!"

A handful of affirmative catcalls came flying back from around the packed studio audience.

"And Lord knows, if she's back and *DDM* is back, then we darn well better up our game. That's why we've got something new for you on tonight's show. A little sizzle to up the ante during these complex, *interesting* times. Are you ready... to get... *willllld?!*"

The percussive thump and low chants of a tribal ceremony echoed throughout the studio. Ryan Richards took a wide stance, placing a hand on each thigh as he bent his knees, then stomped and grunted his way around the stage.

The mighty blast of a baritone horn and two cymbal crashes sent him scurrying in mock-terror to a corner of the stage. He cowered even lower when a bird of prey's fierce cry filled the air.

Richards fought through his fear and glanced through trembling fingers at the huge screen that was above the stage. It displayed the *DDM TV Live* logo in a bamboo font. The flowing cursive words below it read, "Walk a Mile on the Wild Side."

Ryan Richards pretended to hack through a jungle as he made his way back to the middle of the stage. At last he fully recovered his confidence and addressed the rapt crowd.

"Dearest fans, here at home and around the world. For two full seasons we've dished out the healing balm to put old grudges into the dustbin of history. We've built bridges between the races after centuries of feud and abuse.

"However," the host continued, as he began to saunter across the stage, "so far all the work we've done has been along the clear-cut lines of color and ethnicity. *But!* Tonight that's all about to change. Strap yourselves in, ladies and gentlemen, because I'm about to blow your minds and expand this rail service right into your souls. Say it with me now. Wild, wild, wild, wild…"

The crowd began stomping their feet and chanting in unison. *"Wild, wild, wild, wild…"*

Images of chains and beaches and spears and wooden ships flashed across the large studio screens. The sounds of whips cracking and terrified screams grew louder and louder, until Richards flung out his arms and shouted, "Enough!"

In the anxious silence that followed, he lowered his voice and said solemnly, "If you can take it, I'd like you to meet Mr. Emile Smalls. Fourteenth generation Afrigro-American, whose family has seen the highest of the highs and the lowest of the lows. But through it all, they've shown grace and the survivor's spirit. Emile, come on out here!"

A slim black man wearing khakis and a polo shirt with bright stripes waved to the crowd as he walked briskly across the stage. He gave a smile and shook the host's hand.

"How are you, fine sir?" Ryan asked.

"I'm great. A big fan of the show."

"Is that right? Splendid! Then you're familiar with how all of this works?"

Emile gave a thumbs-up. "Of course. This should be fun!"

Ryan Richards turned to one of the cameras and smirked. "Oh, and it *will* be. Now, Emile... meet your Direct Descendant Match!"

The face and ancestry profile of a middle-aged black woman appeared on screen. The crowd gasped and murmured. Someone called out, "You made a mistake! That's the wrong picture!"

Ryan wagged a finger in the direction of the heckler. "Now, now. Hold your plow horses..."

"But I don't understand," Emile said. "This isn't how DDM works. Shouldn't that be a Cauc up there?"

"Let me let you all in on a little secret," Richards said. "In some ways, those naughty boys working for the Sentinels of Jubilee were on to something. Maybe MARVIN *would* keep digging and crunching the data. Can you guess what he found?"

Emile shook his head.

"Come on," Ryan prodded, "take a stab."

"Is that lady part-white?"

"No, sir! Not only is she one-hundred-percent of African descent—nice rhyme, eh?—but we have concluded beyond a reasonable doubt, that in 1746 her ancestors on the Ivory Coast sold *your* entire family into bondage!"

"No way..."

The audience nearly fell out of their seats in shocked confusion.

"That's right," Richards continued, "captured them all and dragged 'em on down to the shore. Handed them over to the European merchants to be shipped off to the colonies abroad."

Emile was pacing in circles. He ran his hands over his face several times. Finally he mumbled, "I don't even know what to say."

"Well, you'd better think of something, because here she is... Connie Doumbia!"

A woman of forty, dressed in green cashmere sweater and dark blue jeans, reluctantly entered from the other side of the stage. Her eyes were cast down. The crowd, which normally went crazy when *DDM* contestants were introduced, now offered subdued applause.

Ryan Richards motioned for Connie to approach. "Come on over, it's okay. We're all friends here. Emile, can you say hello and shake hands, please?"

After the two guests had exchanged a silent greeting, Ryan said, "My, my. What ever should we do? Connie, are you feeling okay?"

The woman shrugged her shoulders. "Actually," she said through a mild African accent, "I'm in shock. I worked so hard to come to this country—legally!—fifteen years ago. How can this be happening to me?"

"Oh, I know," Ryan said, offering her a gentle pat on the shoulder. "But rules are rules—and ratings are ratings! Now Connie, your people did a *very* bad thing to Emile's family way back when. Would it be too much, after all these years, to finally say you're sorry?"

"*Me*, apologize? I don't know this man. He seems happy, in good health. How can anything I say make his life better?"

"Maybe we should ask him then. Emile, what do you think?"

Emile brought a hand to his chin and looked down in thought. Then he said, "You know what, Ryan? I just got a little bit scared."

"Why's that?" the host asked. "Are you frightened of *her*? Don't worry, I'll protect you!" Richards made a show of standing between Emile and Connie as if breaking up a fight.

"No, no," Emile said testily. "This isn't any fun! I was expecting… something else!"

"Hey," Ryan said, "times change." He gave a pained, wry smile.

"So *DDM TV* could be like this from now on? Brothers and sisters going against each other?"

"As well as Latizos, Tribal Americans, perhaps even people from Asia. Because apparently, our charter has… expanded."

The audience, which had been sitting in confused silence, now began to hurl boos and curses. Ryan Richards put up his hand and tried to placate them.

"Come on, folks," he said. "This show has always been about courage. Having the strength to look at our flawed history without fear, and then do what it takes to make amends. We don't get to set the boundaries of where this journey begins and ends."

Connie said, "What are we supposed to do now? I have two children in high school. I need to help them get ready for their college applications. I cannot leave with this man to do whatever it is you would have me do."

Richards put a hand to his ear. He nodded several times. *"I think—"*

"Just stop," Emile said. "I have an idea."

"Huh, really?" Richards was getting flustered. "And what would that be?"

"Ryan, you know I love the show. You're the best, man! But this is all getting too weird. Look, I don't want to punish this lady..."

"What *do* you want then? I mean, we have to do *something.*"

"Connie," Emile said, "I would like to invite your family to have a cookout with mine. It's my mother's birthday next month. Let's all get together and have a nice time."

"Hmm," the show host said. "Sounds tasty." He slowly shifted his gaze toward Connie. "Ms. Doumbia, what do you say to that?"

"Well," Connie said, "that would be lovely. Then at least we can turn this foolish use of people's time into something positive."

Ryan's face flashed a beaming smile. He spread his arms wide and pulled Emile and Connie in close.

"How about that, world?" he said with renewed confidence. *"DDM TV. Defying* expectations. *Dramatic* turns of events. And... *Magnanimous* examples of the *humane* spirit. Why don't we all take a quick breather? Then it's back to more unforgettable DDM showdowns after these commercials."

The audience, heartened by this pleasant outcome and hopeful of more-predictable Direct Descendant Matches to come, cheered enthusiastically once again. The stage lights faded out.

2. MONEY ON THE TABLE

Dawna Jenkins stood in the back next to the closed-up bleacher seats. Her arms were folded and she unconsciously nodded her head from time to time. Slowly she turned and surveyed the scene of this indoor block party.

Kids were running around the Newark rec center gymnasium

having fun. Others played games like beanbag toss or were doing arts and crafts. A few police and paramedics kept a watchful eye. And Clyde was up there in the middle of it all singing his heart out.

"It's sell your soul to sing the Super Bowl. Keep it real? No endorsement deal…"

The dozens of people milling around from vendor to vendor sometimes turned to the stage and raised the roof. Others stood right up against the small stage and grooved along with DJ Clydoscope.

Dawna turned away to go see about getting some hot cocoa from one of the food sellers. She saw a wispy little white man dart out from one of the interior doorways. He flashed her a smile from under his mustache.

"Oh hi, Ms. Jenkins," he said, taking her hand into both of his own. "It's so nice to meet you!"

Dawna looked down at the man suspiciously and freed her hand. "Are you lost? You sure you know where you are?"

The man brushed some imaginary dust away from his wool trench coat. He nodded in the direction of the stage. "Pretty good singer, eh?" he said.

"He's doing alright. Lot of echoes in here though."

"Still, it's good to get another show under his belt."

Dawna flashed her eyes back at the man. Suddenly the tension in her forehead eased.

"I know who you are," she said. "Shoulda recognized. Just didn't expect to see you *here*, I guess."

The man extended his right hand in a formal greeting. "Dawna, it really is a pleasure to finally meet you."

She gave a half smile, saying, "You too, Mr. Pryor."

"Please, it's Eddie." He motioned for her to walk with him. "Let's get some refreshments, have a little chat."

"You want to talk to *me?* What about Clyde?"

"Oh, most definitely you. You're the adult in the family, right?"

Dawna readjusted the purse strap on her shoulder. "Trying to be. But of course, *he* doin' what he want. But whatever… I'm just rolling with all the changes. Even my friends be treatin' me differently now, too."

"How so?" Eddie nibbled on a toothpick as they neared the

food vendors.

"They all seem to need some sort of help now. Calling on the phone with sad stories. Comin' around the new house…"

"Ah," he said. "Can I buy you a coffee?"

"Cocoa. Thank you."

A few minutes later, after they'd gotten their drinks, Eddie said, "Ms. Jenkins, the reason I'm here is simple. I—we, my team—we think Clyde has tremendous potential."

"I always knew he was talented."

"Indeed. And he's got fire! Which, I think, expressed itself again when he went his own way on the new song."

Dawna stopped walking. Her eyes grew distant. "That one ain't doing too well."

"It happens. 'Soul's Gold' wasn't *bad*, but maybe the concept just went over people's heads. It was *kind of* fun, *kind of* smart, *kind of* emotional. He'll learn over time."

"I hope so," she said, moving forward again. "But he's still a kid. They do what they want to."

Pryor gave a gentle smile. "No one wants to listen to us older folks. What do we know, right?"

"Huh! Only how many ways to Sunday life can hit you."

"I'm glad you said it. That's why I came to you directly. Clyde… he's raw. But at some point he's got to *refine* that energy if he wants to stick around in the spotlight."

At that moment the music stopped. Dawna turned around and watched Clyde up on the stage wave to the small cheering crowd. She said, "Maybe he only wants this. Maybe he's okay singing to the local kids."

Pryor shook his head and looked down. "But you know better. *Your* hands are tired. I think you'd be doing your son a disservice by letting him walk down the path that ends with him waking up at age fifty, looking back at what could have been, if only."

Bringing the insulated cup to her chest, Dawna said, "I know we all got to make our own decisions, but when there's money on the table…"

"And family to think about."

"Mm-hmm."

"Will you talk to him?"

"Ooh, I don't know. He seems to think you won't let him be

him."

"I'll put it to you this way. We work with artists of all stripes. Yes, it's *easier* for us if the talent wants to play ball. We plug them right in to our setup and then everyone's off running. But, in the case of someone like DJC," Pryor said with a wave, "we can paint the whole thing as 'the defiant genius at odds with his artistically illiterate management,' and such."

"Hmm," Dawna sniffed. "So you got all your bases covered then?"

"Ma'am, I make money for a lot of people. And look, I may not be an innocent little choir boy, but I do always approach those I want to work with straight. Clear and to the point. I want everyone to be *happy*. That way we all prosper, and no one's looking over their shoulder afraid the last person they burned is coming to take revenge."

Dawna sighed. "Thank you for saying that. But no matter what, I'll always be watching!"

"Please, Ms. Jenkins. Talk to your boy. You know that life doesn't stand still just because you want it to. After the success of 'Fly So High,' he can't just do it all in a vacuum according to his own whims."

"There's a lot of folks who want to work with him, though. Really, why should he go with you—a white man—when there's plenty of brothers who be knockin'?"

Eddie spread his arms in supplication. "Because if I screwed him over, you would show me no mercy. There's no gray area when dealing with someone like me—it's true black and white, eh? I can't get away with anything. You wouldn't let me."

A smile fought its way through Dawna's clenched teeth. She nodded. "Okay. I'll sit him down. It's time to hear the facts of life that he didn't—couldn't—learn on the street."

"Wonderful, just wonderful."

"But if I get him to do this, and I *ever* catch a whiff of something…"

Eddie Pryor shook his head, looking up at Dawna with puppy dog eyes.

"Let's *all* make money," he said. "A lot of it."

3. HEARD SOME RUMORS

Chris Donohugh held the door open and Kate entered the clinic bundled from head to toe. It was freezing out, even by New York City standards for this time of year. Chris followed her in and pulled down the zipper on his own heavy leather jacket.

He stood to the side while Kate checked in at reception. A few months back in the swing of life and he'd forgotten this whole medical routine. The smiling staff, the cleanliness, all the *empty space* in these hospitals. As if the unspoken enemy, death and disease, would get lost and dissipate in the endless corridors.

Chris inspected Kate's face as she chatted away with the receptionist. She *looked* fine. But during those scary spring and summer months he had found himself going into some very dark places mentally. There was just no one to dump his husband's anxiety on—and he was mortified by even the thought of telling Kate, not when she was fighting her own battles. Today he suddenly felt that oppressive mood returning.

"It'll be just a few minutes," he heard the receptionist say.

Kate eased out of her long puffer coat as they walked over to the seating area. She dropped her things into a pile on a chair, picked up a random magazine, then sat down and threw one leg over the other.

"Here we go again," she said.

Chris poked around the selection of periodicals. "Do you want me to go in with you?"

"I don't think you need to. Just a scheduled checkup, right?"

"Let's hope so." Chris sat down next to her without taking a magazine. He put his hand on her thigh and gave it a rub. "How about we get something really greasy to eat later?"

Kate smiled. "Chinese. I want pork fried rice. And sweet-and-sour pork with extra sauce!"

"Okay, Porky," he grinned. "We'll eat our way through this cold front."

"Mm-hmm."

A few minutes later the door near reception opened and a nurse in pastel purple scrubs said, "Mrs. Donohugh? We're ready for you."

Kate picked up her purse and squeezed Chris's hand. "Be back soon."

She followed the nurse through a few hallway turns with the usual chitchat, then they entered an exam room.

"Please take a seat," the nurse said. "Doc'll be here very soon. But before she comes in, let me just do what I need to do."

Kate received the battery of pulse, eye, and other basic inspections. When the nurse said, "You haven't lost any weight, that's good," Kate looked at the reading on the scale a second time. Up *seven* pounds from her last doctor's visit. Still, Chinese food was definitely on today's menu.

"Hi, Kate!" It was Dr. Lowell. Six feet of spunky energy that had helped Kate get through the whole ordeal. "How is everything?"

Kate leaned in and gave her a hug. "It's so nice to see you. Things are... good. Really good."

"That's so great to hear. Let's run through this and get you on your way then."

"Are you going out of town for Tribesgiving?" Kate asked while removing her shirt and bra.

"Oh, yes. We'll be taking the kids to my in-laws' country house in Upstate." The doctor slipped on gloves and began to examine Kate's torso with deft hand movements. "And you?"

Kate, in between taking long even breaths, said, "Visiting Chris's parents in Maine. Which means we'll be headed down to DC to spend the Holy Holidays with my family."

"How wonderful."

"Although," Kate sighed, "fingers crossed, I might be doing some work down there as well."

"In Washington? How's that?" Lowell continued to inspect Kate while they spoke.

"I've heard some rumors, let's just leave it at that. But it would mean more responsibility than ever."

"Well, you've been an inspiration this whole time. If your body stays cancer-free, I can't imagine that you'll have any trouble keeping up on the job front."

Kate looked down into her lap. "Dr. Lowell?"

"Yes, Kate?"

"I… Lately I've been thinking about the possibility of having children."

The doctor smiled. "Hey, now!"

"But, I need to be sure that my body will… for both me and the baby."

"Kate, the best news is that in your case we caught it all so early. Plus, thank God, you didn't need chemo. Your body's recovery time—and affected area—was considerably less than if we'd had to go all the way."

"I know," Kate said, gratefully running a hand through her long hair. "It's just that between work, being older, and all this… I need to be sure I'm doing the right thing."

"Darling," the doctor said while snapping off the gloves, "thirty-three is not *older*. Now, let's get you X-rayed and back out into the world. Hmm. I'd love to see you as a mom!"

"Thank you."

"And you'd better bring little Baby Donohugh in to meet me, too."

Kate smiled as she pushed her arms into the patient gown, then followed Dr. Lowell toward the X-ray room feeling light on her toes.

4. HONORING A THEME

President Eileen Jeffries-Lao sat in stunned silence. She reread the diplomatic cable that had been received through private channels earlier in the evening.

"Madam President and your esteemed staff… After profound reflection… extensive consultation… regret to inform… conclusion that in our nation's best interest… will not be participating in a Reparations program… administration's inability to oversee this, your signature program... detrimental effects... the soul of your people...

"...our hope that the United States can one day return to its role as leader and innovator... your cultural priorities... pray that you will course-correct... With sincere regret, but with hope for other cooperation in..."

Jeffries-Lao felt hollow and numb. Her stomach was tight and when she went to stand up, she found that her free hand held the armrest in a death grip.

After a moment of slow breathing to calm herself, Eileen walked over to the secure phone that was on a tiny table next to the door. When the crisp, subdued male voice on the other end of the line answered, she said, "The Philippines has declined our invitation to the dance."

"I see," the man said after a brief pause. "What do we intend to do in response?"

"I do believe that rampant green card fraud has been going on for years unchecked. Start there. Let's see the reaction when thousands of their citizens are deported—*and* the money being sent home dries up."

"Very good. For your information, 'unchecked' does not necessarily mean 'unobserved.' We know who's out there, ma'am. Just give me a number..."

Eileen took the curled black phone cord into her fingers. She looked at the small diamond-shaped mirror hanging on the wall nearby. "Start with three thousand."

"How do you want us to handle... the optics?" the man asked.

"Hmm. I'm locked in for this second term, but the fight just got tougher. If this letter of regret is any kind of barometer, then other countries on the fence are going to want to see strength. Resolve."

"Consider this, Madam President," the man said. "After word spreads about this order, there will be cameras rolling every time we arrest someone. How humane will the Reparations president look when she's seen rounding up families in the dead of night?"

Eileen uttered something that was more of a grumble than a sigh. After a moment she said, "I guess we just need to remind the world that our generosity doesn't necessarily go on forever. If the Filipinos want to play hardball against our offer to patch them into the HRA's ecosystem, that's fine. Let's flex our muscles until they realize that *we*, the United States, still set the terms of deals on the big stage."

"Understood," the man said. "I'll instruct the apprehension teams to do this as discreetly as possible. But in the case of..."

"Tell them to just do what they need to do, alright? I'll have my people ready to spin this thing any which way we need to. No one can compete with *our* PR machine."

"Consider it done. Give us one week."

"Thank you."

Eileen found herself staring into the little mirror long after she had hung up the phone. Her hand was up at her throat, fingertips tapping the beads of her necklace.

All that work. All of the *years!* She had given her life to honor... a theme. Serving those who could not speak for themselves. Performing the high-altitude work of coordinating with her privileged allies to wrangle the mishmash of society's outcasts into a patchwork coalition that could win elections.

Yes, Eileen acknowledged with a near-smile, the strict household of her Chinese parents had paid dividends. All of the rules, the discipline, the watchful eyes—a traumatizing experience when compared to the easygoing home lives of her white California classmates.

Decades later, it had proven to be the advantage that enabled her to rise politically while harnessing those same vain, pot-smoking, bleeding hearts to create real change. They could never have done it on their own. Eileen was the engine, the glue, the *prescient one* who saw how to bring the fringe idea of Reparations into reality.

Early on in local Orange County politics, she'd utilized her connections as a school board member to get a state-of-the-art homeless shelter funded. It was touted as offering a trifecta of benefits: humane treatment for the residents, student safety while walking to and from school, and keeping the sidewalks clear for business.

This successful outreach effort, which went far beyond the

charter of her job description, had given Eileen her first taste of... not power, but the kind of results her influence could bring about.

No one had ever quite been able to pinpoint her secret. Eileen wouldn't have gotten anywhere had she run as a Rebellican, but as a Dramacrat she soared by following a simple strategy. Publicly she *leaned* leftward, but always made a point to acknowledge the merits of her opponents' concerns. This served to establish her reputation as a dignified, patriotic stateswoman early on in her political career.

Meanwhile, at private fundraisers and rallies, she also encouraged members of the Far Left to express their ideas openly. And later, when the party's diverse factions inevitably devolved into self-interested squabbles, the humble Eileen was there to offer a moderate-sounding platform that would, behind the scenes, still work to chip away at the more controversial issues over time.

A prime example of this took place in 2021 when she was the governor of California. She spearheaded a controversial outreach program which included two ancillary benefits for herself— bringing the Jeffries-Lao name to national prominence, as well as endearing herself to conservative women.

Her ingenious insight? As a counterbalance to the *pride* aspect of encouraging girls to pursue serious careers, she carefully crafted a message warning about the mental and physical health risks of *empowered* sex, which disproportionately affected women.

Eileen believed strongly that this nod to traditional life had convinced many Rebellican women around the country to vote for her in 2024—and therefore secured several swing states on her path to victory. Once again, the Chinese *cultural* influence had played a hand in winning a *political* victory, which not only made her ancestral homeland proud, but also eager to do business.

A few short years later and what had she become? The montage of photos chronicling how much a president aged while in office did not sufficiently capture the slow deformation of Eileen Jeffries-Lao's soul.

But she took some small solace in knowing that it wasn't about her anymore. She'd already done the impossible by getting this Reparations program codified. If the next four years had to be spent throwing haymakers in a slugfest to save the Historical Reparations Administration, so be it. She would rest later, much later.

Now the visage of one masked man entered her mind. She dreamed of the day when she might knock him to the dirt for his terrible treason against the crowning achievement of her life's work.

There were others as well. A growing list of defectors and those who had betrayed her. One former ally in Congress would soon be expelled and possibly put on trial—but that would all have to be handled delicately. If only he had been a Rebellican!

Hundreds of civil servants had also aided and abetted the Sentinels of Jubilee. Cowards! She had always loathed the types of people who thought they could bring about a revolution while simultaneously funding their 401Ks every two weeks.

And finally, she thought of the ingrates. All those Beneficiaries who hadn't gotten their act together even after millions of dollars poured into their communities. Worse still, the likes of Clyde Jenkins and his promoter-enabler Nolan Simmons, whose homemade rap song had become a rallying cry whipping up discontent across the nation.

This was the first time in Eileen's life that she had ever felt such thirst for revenge. But of course in the past, there was always some next step forward to pursue. She had simply harnessed any negative energy inside her toward winning, leading…

But after all this, there would be no other hills to conquer. And Eileen Jeffries-Lao was too hungry and proud to just go quietly into the night. She would make a last stand at all costs.

5. EDGE OF TREASON

Victor Dominguez heard the phone ring but ignored it. He rolled onto his back and stared at the ceiling.

The attempted call had torn him out of a nightmare, but his waking thoughts in the week since the election had been no better. He pulled a pillow over his face, hoping to block everything out.

As he drifted back toward sleep, Victor heard the phone ring again. He turned his head and looked at the bedside clock—twenty past five. He wondered who the hell would have the nerve to call not once, but twice at such an early hour.

Victor reached over and took his phone off the table and disconnected the charger. Unknown number. He pressed to answer.

"Hello?" he said testily.

"Good morning, Victor."

"Who is this?"

"Let's just say, I could be a friend." The man's voice was crisp and clear, and had the staccato flair of an upper-class Spanish accent.

"Now listen," Victor said, "it's too early for games. What do you want with me?"

The man chuckled lightly. "Tell me, how have you been feeling lately? You know, post-election?"

"Look, I don't know who you are, so you'll get no free sound bites. But draw your own conclusions."

"I sympathize, truly. Or should I say, *we* sympathize." The man paused, exhaled. "Victor, how would you like the opportunity to… if not grab victory from the jaws of defeat, then perhaps take the reins of another powerful horse?"

Dominguez sat up in the bed. A glow of blue and yellow was creeping in through the hotel suite curtains. Quietly he said, "I came so close. Even when, for most of the campaign, no one gave me a shot. Or support…"

"We know it. My god! We were in *awe* watching how the sacrificial lamb almost became the shepherd. Which is exactly why I am calling you now."

"Please," Victor said, "what are you hinting at—or offering?"

The other man cleared his throat. "Did you happen to notice anything else of particular interest about the election night results?"

"Not really. I didn't have much time for anything, besides being there to support my disappointed campaign staff and voters. It's all been one sad blur."

"True, but you've still got two years left in the Senate before you're up for re-election. We can make that work. For everybody."

"How does that relate to the election we just had?"

"Victor, did you really not see the wave of Latizo candidates that just swept into office? Nationwide, at all levels, we are gaining real political power."

Victor Dominguez stood up and walked over to the room's small writing table. He sat down and flipped on the brass-topped lamp. "I'm sorry that I wasn't able to deliver the ultimate prize," he said faintly.

"Oh, but you have!" the caller replied. "This game has only just begun, Victor. And you proved by the way you handled yourself that you're just the kind of man we need to lead us."

"I really don't know what you mean. In fact, I still have the interests of my constituents to serve. I don't know if I can help you."

"Nonsense. Listen to yourself. Do you *really* think you'll be able to just go back to being who you were? Can your *mind* handle the downgrade to boring Arizona politics after that big talk about taking on the HRA?"

"I was defeated," Victor said, tapping a pen against a notepad emblazoned with the hotel's logo. "Besides, John Kerry did very well for himself later on after playing the good soldier."

The other man laughed heartily. "I'm not talking about waiting *four years* hoping to get a posh appointment. We want you *now*."

"Spit it out then. You've woken me up and still not said who you are or what it is you want with me."

"Senator Dominguez, we are interested in you because

everything you said about the HRA was so true. More importantly, *we* don't need Reparations."

Victor's eyes widened and he felt his skin tingle. "Who's... we?"

"Latiz-Americans, that's who! We've been rising on our own merits this whole time. We don't need any of that redistributed money. Not if it ties us to the Afrigro-Americans as they drag themselves down. And definitely not if we want to be seen as equals on par with white people." The man chuckled. "Many of us do in fact have some Caucasian blood as well, you know..."

After a moment of silence, the caller said, "Victor? Are you still with me?"

"Yes," Dominguez whispered, running a hand back over his thinning black hair. "I hear you, but I still don't *see* where this is leading."

"Sir, we are strong! It is time for this Latizo coalition to flex its muscles out in the light of day."

"So, what? Do you want to have a parade, or for me to sponsor a bill setting aside a day in our honor?"

"Don't be ridiculous. I'm talking about us having the power to act *right now*, as if you were in fact president."

Victor let the pen fall from his fingers. That cruel illusion of hope, which he had foolishly allowed himself to indulge in the home stretch before Election Day, now slithered back into view. He said gravely, "This kind of talk is getting very close to the edge of treason. You'd better assure me that you're not thinking of trying something that could get a lot of people... punished."

"No, no," the man said with a heavy breath. "Eileen Jeffries-Lao will remain as president unless she chooses to leave office of her own free will. But... now that she has survived this scare from you, her administration will be doubling down on expanding the HRA into new territories. Their logic being, of course, that the more franchises they open, the less likely anyone will be able to shut down the original terrible idea."

"Do you want me to take to the Senate floor and filibuster against those plans?" Victor asked.

"I'm afraid that won't be a firm enough message to send. Not when you're just one lonely voice out of a hundred. No offense, my friend. Let me say it again—Latizos are rising. The last thing we want is for the HRA to get its tentacles spread all across

Central and South America. We must not let our people be corrupted by that mental poison!"

"Oh my God…"

"Glory, not grievance, Victor!" the man rasped. "*Reconquista*, not *Reparaciones!*"

The line clicked dead. Victor Dominguez sat shivering at the desk in his boxer shorts and t-shirt. He watched the light of the dawning day slowly flirt with the edges of the curtains. Soon he would call room service and order the strongest coffee on the menu.

6. A BETTER MAN THAN I

The Reverend Matthias G. Witherspoon saw them poking out above the dozens of RVs that were parked beside the road. As he slowly drove his green Cadillac forward, the objects closest began to come into focus.

Steel structures of the prefabricated, quick-build variety dotted the landscape. And a half mile beyond them stood his destination—the Mall of Absolution in Bloomington, Minnesota, where he had accommodations and appointments already booked.

But even after the long drive in tough autumn weather from his home in Akron, Ohio, Matthias was too intrigued by this spectacle to just go racing past. Because although he'd heard about how the Modestian headquarters had been bombarded with refugees, actually seeing this gathering of humanity in the flesh was overwhelming.

Matthias turned onto a makeshift dirt road that had been graded and which led to one of the steel structures. At the cul-de-sac, a man wearing a neon blue hardhat and jacket with silver reflectors hailed him to the side. Matthias pulled over then rolled his window down.

"Good afternoon," the worker said. "Can I see your papers and decal for this dormitory?"

Matthias blinked twice. "I, uh…"

"Sir, we've got a lot of people to process before this next cold front passes through. I'm happy to scan you in, but please try to keep things moving."

"Is this here all part of the church?" Matthias asked while waving his hand around. "Modestians put these buildings up?"

The other man smiled. "Yes, sir. A lot of these folks who showed up, well, they either came in the early fall or don't own RVs. There's no more space in the Mall, but we couldn't very well have them ride out the winter sleeping in their cars either. So, the Prescient One and the committee fast-tracked getting these dorms put up."

"But there are so many…" Matthias marveled.

"And we're still building more. About two a week. If they come, you will build it, eh?" The man grabbed the lip of his hardhat and chuckled. "Anyway, sir. No offense, but if you're just sightseeing I'm gonna have to ask you to move along so I can get to these folks behind you."

Matthias peered into his rear view mirror and saw that two old beater cars had pulled up behind him.

"Yes, of course," he said. "I'm actually headed to the Mall now. I have an appointment with Emissary Jacoby."

"Oh, my!" the worker exclaimed with genuine admiration. "In that case, please do get back on the main road and follow the signs in. You'll get a much better night's sleep in there compared to out here."

"Wonderful." Just as Matthias was about to close the window, he looked at the man and said, "You know, son. You really are doing God's work."

"Thank you, sir. And Mod bless *you!*"

Matthias pulled forward and swung around the end of the loop. He glanced to his right and looked inside the structure's large sliding door which was halfway open. The building, which was about the size of a high school gymnasium, was brightly lit and filled with people bustling around.

He saw cots and bunk beds, folding tables, and a cafeteria-style food setup before the motion of his car took the dormitory out of view.

The Reverend Matthias G. Witherspoon nodded to himself. Now he was certain about his decision to take a leave of absence from his own black church back home, so that he might meet these Modestians face to face. It was clear they did more than just *preach*. They solved problems—coordinating and cooperating—and did so with a positive attitude, rather than pretense.

About a quarter mile from the Mall itself, Matthias was taken aback when he came upon what looked like a border crossing. The road opened up into a fortified toll plaza, with armed guards keeping watchful eye as cars fanned out into the different lanes.

Matthias eased forward and pulled up next to one of the booths. A guard and a thick steel gate blocked his path.

The man sitting inside the booth looked up from a tablet and said, "Welcome, Reverend Witherspoon. How was your journey?"

"Fine, thank you," Matthias said. "How did you know it was me?"

"Plates and retinal scans. So fast, I know! We'll get you on your way in just a minute."

"Excuse me for asking but, what would have been the greeting if I was an unexpected guest?"

The officer chuckled. "I'm sure you'll understand if I don't reveal all of our security precautions."

"Of course."

"But let's just say, anyone who makes it inside the Mall is supposed to be there. We're not just a fun little group anymore. A lot of people see us as a threat now."

"So I've heard."

"But not to worry, Reverend," the man said pleasantly. "That just means you'll be safe and secure during your stay with us. And I do hope you find what you're looking for."

Matthias smiled. "I'm finally starting to understand why they say that God works in mysterious ways. Just a few months ago I was a much different man."

"I know the feeling. Well, we're glad that you've come. Now," the man said, pointing a finger beyond the gate, "once you pass through, pull on up to that little blue shack on your right. They'll instruct you where to go."

Matthias heard a heavy click and then saw the metal gate tilt back and down into a recession in the pavement. The guard standing in front waved him forward. Matthias drove past and approached a tiny outhouse a hundred yards up ahead.

A matronly woman in a glittering silver pantsuit stepped out and waved to him. She tried the passenger door handle but it was locked, so she politely knocked on the window and pointed down. Matthias pushed the button on his side panel to unlock the doors.

The woman opened the door and poked her head in. "Greetings, Mr. Witherspoon! May I?" She patted the empty seat.

"Of course," Matthias said.

"Thank you, thank you." She got in and closed the door. "Eldress Cameron. It's an honor to meet you."

Matthias shook her hand and smiled warmly. "Glad to make your acquaintance. I have to admit, I wasn't expecting such a fortified—or personal—reception."

"And this is just the beginning," Eldress Cameron said with a laugh. "Now, if you'll just continue down this road, I'll have you turn into the second parking structure. There's a VIP spot reserved just for you."

Matthias did as he was instructed and pulled into a multi-level garage that was adjacent to one section of the Mall itself. He drove up a ramp to the second floor, and then as he rounded a corner saw two dozen men and women in matching teal robes surrounding a parking space. He could see that they were singing.

Eldress Cameron motioned for him to enter the spot. He eased in very slowly so as not to accidentally bump against any of the choir members. When he opened his door, he heard the lovely hymnal "Come, Let Us Anew Our Journey Pursue" echoing through the garage. He joined Cameron in standing behind the car to admire the performance.

"O that each in the day of His coming may say, 'I have fought my way through...' "

Matthias clapped and gave a polite bow when the group had finished singing. "Thank you!" he said. "Wonderfully done."

Eldress Cameron began to lead him away, saying, "We of course have our own repertoire of original hymns, but thought it would make you feel at home—and see that our religions are not *too* distant from one another—if we sang something already known to you."

"A thoughtful touch, indeed. Oh," Matthias said, glancing back at his car. "What about my bags?"

"Reverend, please! You are our *guest*. All of your needs will be tended to." Cameron shook her head with a smile. "As if you would be expected to bellhop your own suitcases, Mod help us all…"

They stepped onto a covered walkway that connected the garage to the main structure. Two strongmen wearing teal-and-gray camo fatigues stood watch, each armed with a blue-turquoise ceremonial staff that was topped by a dense acrylic bulb framed in silver.

Matthias and Eldress Cameron passed through two sets of sliding doors, and then the interior expanse of the Mall opened up. Matthias marveled at the ornate banners and elegantly color-coordinated design. It felt as if the castle of a wealthy Medieval king had spread out over a million square feet.

As they proceeded, he saw that old storefronts had been converted into crafts rooms and gift shops. They passed a line of schoolchildren quietly streaming into the youth gymnasium. And over at a small table, several women in matching ash-gray robes were discussing what Matthias assumed to be the Modestian holy book. The gentle patter of an unseen fountain completed the picture.

He and Eldress Cameron rounded a corner and entered a main foyer. Matthias stood stock still. He brought a hand up to his chest. Cascading down from the skylight was a massive banner of the Prescient One giving a knowing smile. Matthias felt his heart shudder.

Eldress Cameron touched his arm softly and said, "Are you alright, Reverend Witherspoon?"

"Yes," he said. "Very. It just hit me that I'm really here, that's all."

"Come, then. The Prescient One himself is eager to meet you in person."

"Oh Lord, give me the strength…"

"Shush! He's still human, just like we all are."

"Maybe," Matthias said. "But he's a better man than I am."

"Let Mod be the judge of such things, Reverend."

7. TOO MUCH TRUTH

"Hold up, hold up. Rolling it back. Let's try it again."

Clyde Jenkins closed his eyes in frustration. This felt like the twentieth time that the producer had stopped the track and cut him off halfway through a line.

"Ready whenever," he said.

The music started again. A solid percussive hip-hop beat with hints of moody synths played in his headphones.

"She got that Ho'Spice. Naughty nurse, booty so tight. Ho'Spice, make me see the light. Ho'Spice, my sickbed's delight. Easy come, easy—"

"Cut, cut!" the producer growled. "Clyde, it's got to be more sexy, more smooth."

Clyde nodded at him through the studio glass. "Oh."

"Look, the dude in the song, he ain't *really* dying. He gettin' laid! But this girl be like a drug, you know what I'm saying?"

"No doubt."

"Say, DJC. You need a little, uh, spice of your own to get into this jam?"

Clyde brought his hands together as if in prayer. He said, "Lemme just get this part. Then maybe, yeah."

"Cool. Okay then, here we go..."

Half an hour later Clyde was back in the console room listening to the chorus he'd just tracked. Besides the producer Sylicon Smoov, there was also his engineering assistant Raw D-Eel and two other guys who were just hanging out. Clyde didn't remember their names.

"So check it out," Smoov said, his finger hovering above a button on the mixing console. "Right here you sort of wander off. Like, you *thinking* instead of just singing."

He tapped the button. Clyde heard his voice falter right when it was supposed to rise and hold a bold expressive note. He nodded. "Yeah, I see that."

"Good," Smoov said. "Long as you get the message, we can

dial it in the next time around."

"Yeah. You want me to try it now?"

"Not just yet, no. We got other parts to go over. Like here, right at the end, what you think about this?"

Sylicon played the very final moments of the song where after two cycles of the chorus, Clyde alternated between a firm, staccato rap and uttering goofy animal noises. The room burst out laughing.

When Clyde pulled his face out of his hands, he saw Sylicon raise his eyebrows and say, "So, whatchu think?"

"Man, I don't know," Clyde said. "It all sound kind of stupid, you know?"

"Stupid how? Your performance or the words themselves?"

"Both? Like, the rap part makes sense. I like the lyrics—he *feelin'* good in that moment. So why he now want to sound like a cow or a monkey?"

One of the guys who was sitting in touched his friend on the arm and said, "See, the kid don't get it yet. He don't *know!*"

Clyde blushed. All these guys were older. This was their crew, their studio, their song. Reeling from his own recent dud, he had accepted their invitation to come to the Bronx and get a coveted "featuring" credit on Sylicon Smoov's new single. But now he just felt dumb and out of his league.

He said quietly, "What don't I get?"

Sylicon took a puff from the blunt that Raw had just lit, then offered it to Clyde as he said, "It's like this. The cat in the song feels like a king. You know, he just tapped that hot piece of ass. But now this girl also in his head, because she drugged him with that Ho'Spice. She gave him some sex, but that was only the hook! One taste of that high and now he got to get more. 'Cause it be killin' him already!"

Clyde felt a rush through his eyes and head. He passed the blunt off. "So," he said, "it's like he kind of got tricked. But... why you want to say that in a song with your name on it?"

"For one," Sylicon said with a smirk, "because it's true. That's what happens with these bitches."

"You'd think the famous DJC would figure the other part," Raw D-Eel added.

"Help me out," Clyde said.

"Before we do," Smoov said, "you ain't a virgin, right? Or gay?"

"Nah, man! What the hell?"

The group laughed at Clyde's defensive plea. The blunt made its way around the room.

Smoov flashed his silver-and-purple grill into a smile. "Because, young man, every girl that listen to this song think that *she* gonna be the one to do that to you."

"Get ready!" the two friends called out, bringing balled fists up to their mouths and rolling around in their seats.

"Yeah," Smoov chuckled. "This ain't gonna flow only to me. You on this track too, son. Hos gon' be sniffin' you out, lookin' to reel you in. Break yo' heart and take yo' money!"

Clyde shook his head firmly. "Nope. I'm doin' music. Ain't going to fall in love. I got places to go."

"Love? Shit! I'm talkin' about babies. That's the *real* message in the song. Knock a bitch up, then watch how quick your royalties become *her* priority for twenty years."

Clyde reached for a crinkled sheet of paper that was on the console. "Let me look at this again. Hmm. No… I don't see anything at all talkin' about baby mama or whatever."

"Don't trouble yourself." Sylicon took the lyric sheet back into his hand. "Your job is to sing the words, get paid."

One of the guests tilted his head back and blew a thick stream up smoke upward. He said, "Just rap… and then wrap it up."

After a dead moment, the studio exploded in laughter.

"Ain't that the truth, though," Sylicon said. "DJC here talk about Reparations. *We* payin' Reparations just for doin' what come natural."

"Lie down with dogs, pay for puppies," the guy holding the blunt said.

"All them baby bills," Raw said, shaking his head. "World sees us put on them gold chains for the pictures, but it's the pink and blue chains that keep us hustlin' day and night!"

Smoov pointed a finger at Raw. "You know it. They jump into the sheets with you, no problem. Then, what? Here come they lawyer handin' you a whole other kind of spreadsheet."

There was a low rumble of agreement from the assembled crew.

Clyde said, "Y'all speakin' some real truth right now. Why not make a song 'bout all that?"

"That's *too* much truth," Smoov muttered. "No one really

want to hear that."

"I did it," Clyde offered, folding his arms in self-satisfaction.

"Shit, kid," Raw said. "That's a one-off! A fluke. Go on, do it again. In fact, try and make a career always kicking over everybody's cup. I dare you."

Smoov waved his arm. "Come on, lay off the boy. He got pipes and a silver tongue. Long as he help us move this single, I say let him think whatever he wants."

Clyde nodded his head. "Come on then," he said, "give me another drag of that."

As Clyde closed his eyes, exhaling the weed out through his nostrils, Smoov said sternly, "Don't get too comfy now. You got to get back in there and make it right."

"No doubt. I'll deliver the goods."

Smoov thumped a fist into his open palm several times. "This is the hit factory, straight up! We can't be stopped. No, sir!"

"Never stop," Raw said lazily. "Not with all them mouths to feed…"

8. DREADFUL SILENCE

Chris Donohugh sat in the hazy late afternoon light of his Brooklyn apartment. He had Kate's home laptop open in front of him on the dining room table. A small black plastic device was dancing between his fingertips.

After a moment, the login screen appeared and he typed in Kate's password: ilovechrisd. Despite making a career in technology, Chris had never been able to convince her to add a number or capital letter to her passwords in all these years.

He disabled the computer's internet connection and then opened the program Kate used to check her work emails remotely. After poking around the various account settings, Chris scratched a few notes onto a pad and then turned his attention to the little black device.

He tapped around its tiny keypad, glancing briefly at his notes, then inserted the connector into a laptop port. The device's tiny screen lit up to full brightness and said, "Pairing…

Searching… Authenticating… Embedding… Complete."

Chris removed the device and put it into his shirt breast pocket. He closed the email program, turned the internet back on, then quickly scanned the computer screen to make sure nothing else had accidentally opened or been changed. He pushed the top closed.

What the hell am I doing?

Chris returned Kate's laptop to the charger on the floor near the TV in the living room. He patted the pocket while making his way toward his office in the spare bedroom. The two Corgis followed slowly, their nails tapping against the hardwood floor as they trudged down the hallway.

Just as he was about to sit down in front of his own computer, out of the corner of his eye Chris caught sight of the little shrine dedicated to his old band Raucous Voice. Now relegated to a corner of a bookcase's lower shelf, this collection of mementos included their two 7" EPs, a shattered guitar's headstock that had been autographed by the band, and several small framed group photos.

Chris picked up one of the pictures. It had been taken outside a bar after one of their shows. He, singer Glenn Murray, and the two other guys were lined up in a happy drunken pose. He studied the faces—so young, so hopeful—and got a sick feeling. He sensed a vague regret that wouldn't come into focus. Or nostalgia for something that had been lost.

He stared into Glenn's eyes. Years had passed since that night, but their bond was so strong that Chris was now willing to use his own wife to spy on the HRA. Or maybe, Chris wondered, it was simply his own creeping doubts that had led him to this moment.

Stress after stress had hounded him all year, from Kate's medical battle to all the drama surrounding the HRA hack. And just when some semblance of normalcy began to return after the president's re-election, Kate was called down to Washington to meet with the Jeffries-Lao team.

Now Chris was left by himself to speculate on where this roller coaster ride would hurtle next. And he couldn't help but feel that the course of events was being influenced, if not guided, by Kate herself.

Her needs. Her existential crisis. Her career. Her suddenly

relevant biological clock. And perhaps her relocating to the DC area to work for the president.

In moments like this, Chris felt more like a passenger than a partner. He was expected to both *give* what Kate needed, and *give in* to what she wanted. Meanwhile, all he felt he had to show for himself were the memories of a punk band that made about eight dollars a year in royalties from some European streaming service.

Chris returned the picture frame to the shelf after carefully dusting off the edges with his finger. He shuffled to the desk and sat down in the swivel chair. He connected the little black device to his computer. As his fingers entered the commands that would duplicate Kate's emails to the catch-all program on his system, Chris felt his head start to swim.

Suddenly he realized what it was he had been yearning for when thinking back on his band years. It wasn't about the time that had passed, or even the dreams of fame that never materialized. It was the loss of that energetic blind faith that had fueled them to write manic, politically charged anthems, then pile into a van and play shows at grimy clubs all across the Mid-Atlantic region.

That fire had slowly, almost stealthily died out while Chris went about the routine business of life in the adult world. Before, there had always been something to look forward to. But now in the silence of so many forgotten days, Chris saw the stark truth: The world he was meant to live in—where he could thrive and shine—was gone and possibly never to be seen again.

Instead, Chris found himself violating his wife's trust while she was meeting with the leader of the free world.

He felt so petty and lost. A small creature that had been led astray, perhaps since birth. Here was Kate standing on the precipice of professional glory, while he sat alone in near-darkness tinkering with hacker software. Chris had no idea how all the years of his life had drained into this paralyzing moment.

Panicking, he ran out of the room and grabbed his heavy coat. But just as he reached for the house keys, the wet bar came into view—and a giant bottle of cheap whiskey offered him its tantalizing curves.

An hour later, Chris was sitting on the floor of his office still wearing the coat. The record player he'd fished out of the closet was blaring a fast-moving punk rock track, the yellow splatter-vinyl spinning at 45 RPM. Chris took a pull out of the whiskey bottle, then pushed the fur-fringed hood away from his face.

He nodded in time with the song, suddenly sitting up in anticipation before shouting along with the chorus. "We know! … Let's go! … Gutter war! … Explode!"

Chris fell back against the wall. He pumped his fist when the screaming guitar solo came in. "Hell yeah!" he applauded. "Raucous in the house!"

One of the Corgis started howling and jabbed its paws into Chris's leg. "You know it, pup!" he said, making a clumsy playful grab at the dog's ear.

Chris heard the house phone ring. The automated voice announced, "Call from… *Kate*."

"Oh, shit," he blurted. He lifted the needle off the turntable and crawled across the floor out into the hallway. He picked up the receiver. "Hello?"

"Hi, Chrissy Poo!" Kate said. "I thought you'd be home. Whatcha doin'?"

Chris slipped out of the winter coat. "Hanging out with the pups. You know, uh… just listening to music, laying low."

"That doesn't sound too bad."

"Well, what about you? How'd it go?"

"As we speak," Kate said, "I'm riding in the back of a Towncar headed to my parents' place. Because we're going to *celebrate!*"

Chris flipped on the hall light and squinted. "Um… yeah? What happened?"

Kate's voice was beaming. "Today I hung out with Eileen! I also met Tony, Danielle, Natalie, all the insider peeps."

"Yeah? That's awesome."

"I couldn't believe how welcoming they all were. *Annnd…* they want me to work as a direct liaison between the HRA and the White House as they roll out sister offices in some of the smaller former colonies."

Chris licked his lips. He said, "Do you know *where* you'll be working?"

"We haven't figured out all those details yet. But hey! Can't you say 'congratulations'? Be *happy* for me, please."

"Oh, yeah," Chris mumbled. "That's amazing. But I guess

maybe we thought that might happen, right?"

Kate was silent for a moment. "Chris. Have you been drinking?"

He exhaled audibly into the phone.

"Really?!" she said.

"I'm just having a couple beers."

"Hmm. Well, just don't forget to walk the critters, please."

"Sure, of course."

"I'm gonna get going now, Chris. Don't celebrate too hard without me."

"Ha, yeah. Tell your parents I say hi."

"Sure. 'Night!"

Twenty minutes later Chris was again wearing his coat, but now standing at a nearby street corner while the Corgis sniffed around the base of a stop sign. His stomach was a tight churning pit, and he looked searchingly at each person who walked past.

He scooped up the dogs' business and dropped the bag into a trash can on the way back to the apartment building. But he paused near the front steps, reluctant to go in. Because he knew what came next. The climb up the stairs while the dogs tugged at their leashes. Then passing into the dreadful silence that lay behind the front door.

No amount of music or alcohol could dull how profoundly alone Chris Donohugh felt tonight. And he simply could not be happy for Kate right now, not when feeling so little hope within himself.

9. WHO COULD REFUSE?

Kate Donohugh set down her things and eased into a chair at Reagan-National Airport. The bright morning sun of this clear day defied the cold air outside and warmed her face ever so slightly.

She sipped her to-go coffee and closed her eyes for a moment. During the early rush from her parents' house in nearby Arlington, Kate had just enough energy to get from their door all the way through check-in and security. But now that she was settled with a forty-five-minute wait until her flight home to New York boarded, the whirlwind of the last day suddenly caught up to her.

The quick trip down to DC. The private car picking her up VIP-style and driving directly to the White House. The dizzying encounter with all the president's men and women. Their joyful buzz and the promise of things to come for Kate. And finally a night out in Old Town Alexandria celebrating with her mother and father.

Now, as Kate blinked into the sunlight through the airport's giant window panes, that last pour of red wine was taking its toll. She pulled a pen out of her purse and turned her attention to a crossword puzzle. She sighed after a frustrated moment, using the pen more as a drumstick against the folded newspaper than actually filling in any of the little squares.

I'm never good at finishing these things.

Out of the corner of her right eye, she sensed that someone was staring at her. It was a woman, maybe a bit older than Kate. Now leaning away, whispering to someone else. Was she pointing at her too?

Kate couldn't stand the growing tension any longer and whipped her head around. The woman, who was sitting several seats down on the row facing her own, perked up and smiled. She then turned to a girl seated to her left, patted her on the back and made an encouraging gesture.

The ten-year-old child stood up and slowly approached. Kate realized she was clenching her coffee cup so hard that the thick cardboard was nearly buckling.

The girl stopped a few feet away. "Hi," she said nervously. "Are you... Kate?"

"I am indeed." Kate felt the pressure inside her body fall away. She exhaled, then said in a sweet tone, "And who are you?"

"Samantha." She looked back at the other woman and gave a thumbs up. "That's my mom."

Kate beckoned the woman to join them with a wave.

"Hi, I'm Meredith. I hope we're not disturbing you."

"No," Kate said, "not at all."

"We both recognized you and, I guess, did a double take since it was here in DC."

"Well, the HRA likes to fly us around."

"I'll bet. Um… Samantha here is just such a big fan of yours and wanted to say hi."

"Of me?" Kate blushed. "I haven't done anything—in public at least—to warrant that kind of praise, I don't think."

"*Someone* disagrees. Go on, Sam, tell her."

The girl smiled. "Ever since you were on *DDM TV*, I've been learning all about you. I even watched the show you did with Tina way back when."

"Wow," Kate said. "I'm impressed. And? What do you think?"

"That you're great!" Samantha raised her hand and waited until Kate gave her a high-five.

Meredith sat down beside Kate and confided, "Girls need more role models like you. Confident, involved… and strong enough to get up off the mat when life knocks you down."

Kate smiled. "Thank you, again. That's too kind."

"So tell us, what brought you down to the city?"

"Actually…"

Kate paused, then thought better of the momentary burst of pride that made her want to share everything about her day at the White House. "Oh, you know," she said, "just more of the endless training and meetings we have to endure."

"Of course," Meredith said. "And I can relate. I work with regulatory groups. Well, Samantha. I think we've taken up enough of Kate's time. Please say goodbye and wish her a safe flight."

The girl leaned in and gave Kate a hug. "Yay, Kate Donohugh!" she beamed. "La, la, la…"

Kate felt a bit flushed as she watched Sam skip away and start digging into her bright backpack.

"Bye now," Meredith said.

"Cheers," Kate said with a wave.

She tried to focus on the crossword again, but her mind was fluttering. *Role model?* Kate couldn't quite believe it. But seeing the smile on that girl's face gave Kate a kind of satisfaction that was far different than when assisting Beneficiaries or doing charity work.

Kate suddenly saw a new horizon open up where she might be a mentor, or even one day a leader of some kind. She thought about this White House opportunity and wondered if it could vault her toward that more quickly. Or perhaps it might hold her back?

She would discuss it all in depth with Chris. The truth was that there were a lot of things the two of them would need to lay out on the table soon. Deep down Kate knew that accepting an out-of-town job without fully consulting one's spouse wasn't a good look. The worst thing she could do was pack her bags without making some sort of maintenance plan for their relationship.

Because once again she was asking Chris to accept something big on her behalf. And whereas her illness and the HRA hack were life events they'd both had to react to, this new job was something… *important*. He would be *expected* to acquiesce—or else be seen as the bad guy.

Although, Kate figured that if Chris really pressed her about how much time she anticipated being away from home, she could always plead powerlessness. Because who could refuse when the President of the United States said jump?

An attendant at the podium announced that the New York flight was about to board. Kate gathered her things, gave Meredith and Samantha a final wave, then made her way directly to the front of the line for first-class boarding.

Flying at the president's behest did come with its perks.

10. BROADER IMPLICATIONS

A lanky young man approached the long folding table at the front of the meeting room. He picked up a thick hardcover from the mess of books and thumped it loudly against the surface.

"Alright, everybody," he said. "Let's take our seats and come to order."

Several dozen young adults separated from the groups they were standing in and filled the rows of folding chairs arranged near the table. A woman who had been conversing near the back of the room now joined the man up front. She set a briefcase down and smiled.

The man said, "This will be the first official meeting using our new name, the B&D Alliance. The change comes in deference to a request made by one of our newest members, who —while touched that we admire his bravery—prefers for the focus not to be about him. Thank you for everything, Luis."

People gave polite applause as the man turned to his left and bowed to Luis Ortega, who was seated in the front row. Luis nodded and mouthed, "Thank you." A girl seated to his right smiled, briefly laying her head on his shoulder.

"Now," the speaker said, "it's time for us to get to work. Joining me today is Sabine Plotz, an attorney specializing in immigration law. In recent years she has worked a variety of cases related to the HRA. Hopefully she can provide the legal insights we need to achieve our goals. Sabine?"

The woman, in her late thirties with long brown hair pulled back into a ponytail, and wearing a purple chambray skirt suit and maroon heels, shook hands.

"Thank you, Miguel," she said. She waved her hand over the table. "Somewhere within these volumes, we just might find the solution you desire. To turn the one-time, explicitly defined DDM deferral as pioneered by Mr. Ortega"—she tilted her head respectfully—"into a permanent exemption with broader implications. But the first question I must pose to this group is, what are you truly willing to give up in order to get your way?"

After a pause, someone in the crowd said, "We just want to be left alone."

"Believe me," the lawyer responded, "I understand what you mean. But the law always makes things more complicated than... black and white." She shrugged her shoulders. "Anyway, what I'm getting at is, despite the number of other Reparations-related court cases, there is no precedent for what you seek."

Miguel took a step forward, "Guys and gals, I think Ms. Plotz wants clarification—or better yet, a commitment about how far we're ready to take this thing."

"All the way!" someone else shouted.

Sabine tapped her toe against the floor three times. "Oh yeah? As in," she said skeptically, "complete renunciation of all HRA benefits? Or possibly going *all the way* to the Supreme Court?"

Three people in back—all Minoricans of different shades— clapped their hands in unison and said, "Leave us... alone! We want... to stay home!"

They sat down after several recitations of the chant.

Sabine began a slow wide arc around the table. She said, "I feel your passion, truly. You'd be surprised to read about the various legal challenges that have been brought by both Beneficiaries and Debtors over the past few years. My main concern today is that people are often not prepared for how *long* this process can take. You could wait *years* for your case to wind its way through the system—and possibly to only in the end not get what you want. Ask yourselves if you're *really* prepared to give up so much of your time in court or poring over documents, when the pain of a DDM assignment might be the quicker approach."

A college-aged female Cauc stood up. "Hi," she said. "My name is Lauren. I'm a pre-law student at Texas Tech trying to help out this group of young activists as best I can. Ms. Plotz, isn't it true that once these Beneficiaries formally begin the process, that they would be granted a temporary stay against any DDM call-ups?"

"That's correct," Sabine said. "But it wouldn't cancel the assignment altogether. Whenever your case is decided down the road, if you lose then that's it. Your obligation begins immediately thereafter. And if I know anything about life, it's a truism that one's future is always *busier* than today. Having done this professionally for years, I'm suggesting out of caution that the expedient option is to just bite the bullet."

Miguel turned to her and said, "Since we all value your time, I'm going to get to perhaps the biggest point, or strategy, of all. We *hope* that any legal proceedings take a long time."

"You do? Really?" The attorney seemed perplexed.

"Yes, because we intend our cases to outlast the Reparations program. And then it'll all just go away."

"Let me get this straight. As in, you envision not just winning an exemption for yourselves, but for the entire HRA to cease operations?"

Members of the group began to cheer.

Sabine leaned forward onto the end of the table and shook her head. She said slowly, "Okay, there's a lot to think about here. First, do you know how hard it is to repeal just the average local law? That becomes almost impossible when you're dealing with a national administration like the HRA. Why? Because too many interwoven special interests act as a root system to keep it entrenched."

"Too many barnacles!" a man yelled. "Sink the whole thing!"

"Believe me, I'm not defending how it all operates. Now," Plotz said, staring intently at the group, "there's also the issue of… well, I don't know if the word is perspective, or something else. But you all are so young. You never experienced any of the privation and cruelty which the Reparations program sought to make amends for. I'm sure that many people would say you're being ungrateful, just because your lives might be inconvenienced. Tell me, how many of your ancestral homelands have a military draft, for instance?"

"Hey, I thought you were supposed to be advocating *for* us," the same man called out.

"And I am," the lawyer said. "Which includes using my real-world experience to make you aware of the obstacles such a campaign might run into."

As the gathering started to murmur to one another, the young pre-law student stood up again. She said, "Ms. Plotz, if I may add, since you're meeting us all for the first time. This is a very brave and committed group fighting for their rights as they see fit. They have so many wonderful hopes and dreams that might go from delayed to bottled up forever, if the government is allowed to exert so much power over their lives."

A few whistles came in response.

Sabine said, "Lauren, thank for you helping me to understand. If you all are absolutely set on seeing this through to the end… Well, I've fulfilled my responsibility to inform you about the road ahead, so it appears we're ready to formally proceed." She gave a hearty smile. "The HRA better watch out, because here we come!"

Everybody stood up and applauded. Some left their seats and crowded around Sabine and Miguel.

Luis Ortega sat blinking through his glasses, bewildered about the turn of events that had plucked him out of obscurity and seemed unwilling to let go.

He felt Cristina slide her arm through his own. She smiled up at him. He playfully scratched the top of her head with his free hand.

This burgeoning movement that was trying to defeat the HRA's DDM program had all started because Luis just wanted to make his family proud as a college student. Then these people here at the meeting had brought a very special girl into his life.

He didn't fear what came next as long as Cristina stayed by his side.

11. ONE OF US

The hood was finally yanked off his head. It had remained in place from the moment he was first thrown inside a van, then hustled with claws digging into his back to a prop plane, until finally being driven to this unknown location several miles from the airport.

Marcus Young squinted in the searing fluorescent light. He felt someone jam a water bottle into one of his zip-tied hands.

"Here," a voice behind him said. "Drink up."

Marcus knew better than to try turning around to see who was in the room with him. The scenery had quickly confirmed his suspicion that he was in a law enforcement interrogation room. The only question was who had taken him into custody—DHS, HRA, or his own employer, the FBI?

He kept his head bowed and unscrewed the bottle cap. He drank half of the water in several gulps, then waited for the other man to speak again.

Hands pressed down onto his shoulders.

"Marcus, Marcus, Marcus... what *ever* are we going to do with you?"

The man released his grip and stepped forward, leaning a hip against the table that was in front of Marcus.

"Well.... what do you have to say for yourself?"

Marcus felt the man staring at his drooping face. Slowly he looked up and said, "If I knew who you were—who you worked for—I could give you a better answer."

"Ha! Who do I *work for?* The same as you. Until recently, that is."

Marcus nodded. "Mm. I figured as much. That you'd track me

down sooner or later."

"Yup. But I gotta hand it to you. You took the concept of 'embedding a field agent' to a whole new level. If you knew the lengths we went to, to track you down..."

"Enough with the theatrics, please." Marcus nodded his head at the security cameras and the two-way mirror that was in the wall directly across from him. "I'm not scared. You won't have to *beat it* out of me. And besides, I'm still one of you guys."

The other man, who was wearing a hybrid business-tactical suit made of strong woven synthetic material, now reached into one of the half-dozen cargo pockets and removed a porcelain cigar. He sat in a chair and put his feet up on the table.

"One of us, eh?" he said, blowing a cloud of shimmering synth-smoke into the air. "Federal Bureau of Investigation... or was that, in your case, Indoctrination? Mod bless you—am I right?"

Marcus didn't react to the smirk that followed this jab. He gave a slight shrug, then said, "I'll interpret this as just part of your power play, and not an example of religious persecution. So why not extend a little professional courtesy my way? You'll probably get what you want a lot easier."

A thoughtful expression replaced the interrogator's grin. "Okay," he said, chewing several times. "Special Agent Young, my name's Axelsson. *Supervisory Special Agent* Axelsson. And it was my team, in fact, that received all your info drops from inside the Mall. For most of those six months you were doing excellent work. I even recall once or twice telling the guys that someday I hoped to meet you. Can ya believe that?"

Axelsson cocked an eyebrow, then chomped down on the faux-cigar's rubber tip.

Marcus said, "And what was your takeaway from my reports?"

"Oh... Mostly harmless, the Modestians themselves. But I'm not so certain about the higher-ups..."

"Sir, I assure you that—"

"Please," Axelsson said with a wave. "I think your opinion might be a little biased."

"But you don't intend to take any action against them, do you? They've done nothing wrong!"

"Calm yourself, Mr. Young. This isn't about *them* anyway.

The reason we're here today is because of you! You goddamn deserter!"

Marcus couldn't help but flinch when Axelsson's hand came slamming down onto the metal tabletop. He sensed his newfound Modestian serenity grappling with the old adrenaline-fueled habits of his life in the FBI. He exhaled coolly.

"SSA Axelsson," he said, "you took me away from a most meaningful task out on the Farm. I can't even imagine the chaos and worry that your raid inflicted upon everyone there. And when word gets back to the church... Just tell me, was anyone hurt?"

"No, no," Axelsson said. "We left them all in peace. Even the Debtor whose fugitive status came up during the retinal scans. *You* were the target."

"Well... I thank you for leaving them be. Those men are all military vets. Served their country, *the same as you*. Now, what the hell do you want from me?"

Axelsson stood up with a laugh, throwing out his arms as he walked toward the mirror and said, "He thinks he's running this thing! Who knows, maybe that's just one of the mind-controlling tricks he learned from that cult."

The man swiveled back toward Marcus, saying, "I don't know how much news you've been privy to since you disappeared two weeks ago. But our law enforcement brothers have been kickin' ass lately. Rounding up Sentinels of Jubilee members high and low, all over the country."

"I'd heard a bit," Marcus said. "But what does that have to do with me?"

"Special Agent Young, you don't even recognize an olive branch when it's being waved in front of your face, do you?"

"I still don't understand."

"Jesus Christ!" Axelsson pleaded. "Think about it, will ya? I could have you disappeared into solitary if I really wanted to bust your balls. But you did some admirable work living among those Modestians, and so we're willing to overlook your lapse of conduct for the moment—because we need you back out in the field to land us a big fish."

Marcus reflected briefly, then said, "Assuming I succeed, what happens to me after you double back around?"

Axelsson pointed his cigar at Marcus. "Do you, uh, really trust this guy, the Prescient One?"

Marcus hesitated, not wanting to reveal that he had spoken intimately with the church leader once before—let alone that he knew the man's treasonous secret. He said, "His Prescience may come across as an enigma, or eccentric, but his motives are pure. As are his methods. I see no reason to suspect anything nefarious or perverted about him."

"And you," Axelsson continued probing, "you're so smitten with this religion that you would continue on as a believer?"

"With Mod as my witness."

"Fine. I'm sure we'll find some way to accommodate this… unique situation. How lucky for you that you're such an effective agent."

"What's my new assignment?" Marcus asked.

SSA Axelsson made a beckoning motion in the mirror. Seconds later another man wearing a traditional business suit entered, then handed over an accordion folder before departing. Axelsson carefully laid out a number of documents on the table.

"Here," he said, "are three regions of the country that suffered a spate of SOJ-related sabotage in the past five months."

"*Five?*" Marcus said, puzzled. "I thought these guys had been moving silently until that first hack. Which was when, early October?"

"Correct. But they were active long before anyone even knew of their existence. Only now have we been able to piece together events that just seemed like random acts of vandalism."

"I see. So what am I looking at here with these particular areas? From the maps it looks like Boston, Metro New York, and parts of Michigan."

"Right again," Axelsson said. He held up a grainy black-and-white photograph of a bearded man who seemed poised to devour a microphone clasped in his fist. "Do you know who this is?"

Marcus shook his head. "I have no idea. Should I?"

Axelsson dropped the picture onto the other papers. "No," he said. "Just the lead singer of a band no one ever heard of. But! This band, which calls itself Bleeding the Aggregate, just so happens to have been out on the road playing at dive bars the exact same dates these crimes were committed."

Marcus began to speak, then held up his joined hands. "Could you untie me, please?"

"Of course." Axelsson split the zip-tie with a small knife he produced from a cargo pocket.

"Okay," Marcus said, rubbing his wrists before taking up some of the papers. "First of all, I see gaps between these events. Couple of weeks here. And over a month between Detroit and Boston. What gives?"

"That's because these were individual mini-tours. Like I said, this is not a famous band. Members are in their thirties, work regular day jobs. Anyhow, we're confident these trips were booked as cover so that this man with the beard could go out and coordinate with other Sentinels between shows."

"If true, that's quite clever." Marcus tapped the photograph with his finger. "So tell me, who is this guy?"

"His name is Glenn Murray. Originally from Maine, currently lives in the Philadelphia area. Works off and on doing industrial paint contracting."

"So if you know where he lives, and everyone else is getting arrested right now, why not just take him in?"

"Because," Axelsson said, leaning onto the table with a grin, "Bleeding the Aggregate has a handful of shows booked starting next weekend. And I want you, Special Agent Young, to lead the team that catches Mr. Murray and his Sentinel conspirators in the act."

"Where?"

"First stop, Washington, DC."

12. ALL THEM FUNERALS

"What about them lyrics Smooth Move made you sing?" Dawna Jenkins asked, adjusting herself on the kitchen stool.

"Who? You mean Sylicon Smoov?"

"Whateva he call himself. Point is, sound like he got a rough crew over there."

"Nah." Clyde gave a sour wave. "He teachin' me the ropes. What it take to be a successful producer. Like he said, 'Great beats keep you from sleepin' on the streets.' "

Ms. Jenkins laughed. "Listen to yourself. For how many weeks and months did you go on about how 'I gotta be my own artist, can't sell out'? Sure sound like you changed your tune."

"But this is different. That dude Pryor, he shifty, sneaky like. Meanwhile Mr. Smoov, he treat me with respect like a brother does. Yeah, Pryor took me out to dinner and stuff, but Smoov's crew, they know how to *chill*."

"Yeah, they chillin' while you drive them to the bank. Black sellout's no different from a white sellout. Except..."

Clyde perked up. "Except what?"

Dawna got up and moved around the counter, wiping some invisible crumbs into her hands. "I doubt you gonna like what I think, or will even believe what I got to say."

"Come on, Mama," Clyde said. "Try me."

"Aight, then." She stepped back and leaned against the sink. "There's other differences between Mr. Pryor and your friend Smoov. Those boys he run with all got criminal records. Some of it real nasty, not just for the petty stuff."

"But Octavius—"

"Shush! And don't you ever, *ever* say such a thing in this house again. Lord have mercy on this boy and his mouth. Clyde, my son. Just 'cause you ain't a nobody no more, and got a real focus in your life, that don't make your world any less dangerous."

"I know, I know..." Clyde started pacing in the kitchen. He said, "But I won't sing any stuff about gang bangin' or robbin', I promise you."

Dawna threw up her hands. "Do you think the real criminals give a damn? All they know is you got fame, and that means money. So when they see you roll up to Mr. Smoov's spot, they see prey. And I *know* you ain't tough like... Mr. O., who can handle hisself. I wouldn't even want you to try."

"So what are you sayin'?" Clyde pleaded. "I got to make some kind of play. It ain't no fun to do stuff alone. Bad for your career, too."

"That's well and good. But since you don't play a real instrument like the violin, which would always keep you *safe*, I really think you should reconsider Eddie's offer."

Clyde paused for a moment. "You callin' him Eddie now, huh? You talk to that man?"

"Son, I just want what's best for you in the long run. And that don't only mean hits or money. I want you to *live* for a long time. So we got to find that place in the world where you can make the music that moves you, but you ain't in danger of being killed in some drive-by. Be such a waste…"

Dawna reached an arm forward and pulled Clyde in for a hug.

"Aw, thank you, Mama."

"I just love you too much. And I've seen enough pain in my lifetime already. Trips to the hospital, visits up at the jail. And all them funerals, my God…"

Clyde slowly let go. He wiped a tear from his cheek when his face was out of Dawna's line of sight. Just then he heard a few thumps on the carpeted stairs. His nephew Tyrell was in pajamas making his way down toward them.

"Hey, sleepy dude," Clyde said. "Have a nice nap?"

"Uh-huh."

Clyde knelt down on the bottom step. Tyrell jumped onto his back and yelled, "Yeah! Let's go!"

"Where to, kiddo?"

"Living room! I wanna watch TV."

"What, you don't wanna say hi to Gramma?"

Tyrell shook his head. "I already saw her this morning."

"That's harsh, though. If you be nice, I bet she'll make us a snack."

"Okay, we see her."

Clyde jerked around and made a whinnying noise as he galloped into the kitchen. "Snack time!" he yelled. "The horse and his rider are hungry. Whatchu got in here?"

Dawna kissed Tyrell on the head. "Hi, little man. Want Gramma to get you something?"

The boy looked around the room. "Popcorn," he said. "And ice cream!"

"Now, Tee," Dawna said, "we gonna have dinner not too long from now. Let's pick one of those. I think popcorn is a great idea. Maybe I'll have a few nibbles myself, in fact."

"Noooo! All for meeee!" Tyrell smiled. "Now giddy-up, horsey!"

Tyrell slapped Clyde on the shoulder and then they were off running into the front room.

Dawna poked around the cupboard and pulled out a bag of microwave popcorn. As the kernels slowly inflated the bag, she glanced in on the boys sitting together on the couch and smiled.

It was good to see them bonding. And safe. She intended to keep it that way.

13. FOREVER HOME

Matthias Witherspoon fell into step with the procession of men dressed in full-length cerulean blue tunics. A line of female Modestians wearing matching silver outfits kept pace along the other side of the corridor.

As they walked, Matthias could hear the hypnotic somber tones of an organ's low register. He found the occasional bright flourishes curious, noting that Modestian music was much more affecting on a primal level than the Christian hymns performed at his church back in Ohio.

Moments later the group entered a wide open area beneath triangular skylights. There was a round fountain in the middle, but for today the water had been turned off. Up front, ten rows of padded folding chairs faced a small stage that was decorated with enormous bouquets of pastel flowers and marble statues that were at the same time beautiful, demure, and striking.

As ushers led guests down the center aisle to their seats, Matthias noted that, as was often the case at the Mall of Absolution, the two genders sat separately. However, he had been told by one of the excitable young novitiates he'd struck up a friendship with, that after the wedding vows had been taken, Modestians were known to loosen their collars with pagan abandon.

The organ began to play more softly now. Matthias saw heads turn toward the aisle. He looked back just as a regal-looking man wearing a silk teal-and-silver striped robe strode past with firm, deliberate steps. This man was followed by two adolescent couples bearing small bouquets of ivory roses, who then took their places at the back of the stage.

A new, more bombastic musical arrangement filled the air. Again the guests turned their heads back.

Matthias, who had attended and officiated many weddings during his years as a preacher, was shocked when he saw not bridesmaids and groomsmen, or even family members, but a figure covered from head to toe by a large piece of shimmering blue cloth. Three young children were pulling this person forward on a small square cart using attached ropes.

The reverend was momentarily appalled, being unable to avoid seeing similarities between this spectacle and the humiliating atonement rituals he used to lead in debtors' prison yards. As the cloaked figure rolled slowly past, Matthias asked God both for strength and forgiveness.

Had he been fooled into visiting a lunatic asylum that was only masquerading as a church? He took wry solace in the fact that he would very soon find out the truth.

The little wagon stopped in front of the stage, then the children dropped the ropes onto the carpet and carefully guided the draped figure up the three steps and into position on the priest's left side.

As the music blended into a more serene aria, Matthias saw that yet another cart was on its way. He felt perspiration begin to form on his temples as the next arrival, similarly cloaked in silver, was wheeled down the aisle. Resisting the instinct to cross himself, Matthias instead fished around under his clumsy garment in search of a handkerchief to dab his face.

This obscured individual was escorted into place beside the priest, who himself then took a step forward and spread his arms wide.

"Mod be with you," he said.

"And also with you," the seated guests replied. "Amen."

I know that one at least, Matthias thought.

"Let us rejoice," the priest said, "for today is one of the great moments in Modestian life. The joining together of two souls under the banner of our still very young religion. This old tradition that, whether through neglect or sullied institutions, seems to have fallen out of favor in the wider world. But today we revitalize it within the Church of Modestianity."

The man turned to the first figure and placed a palm upon its head. He said solemnly, "Brother Reese Carter. You came to us one year ago from a small town in Nebraska. Everything about you screamed for 'the new.' A new perspective for a world in flux. A new religion that had the courage and zest to truly *live,* and not hide behind rote doctrine. And ultimately, you sought a new type of woman to be your bride."

Suddenly the priest yanked the cloth up and tossed it away. Matthias saw a handsome white man who was not a day over twenty-five. He stood proudly in an electrifying blue tuxedo, a lightning rod of confidence and vitality from head to toe.

The groom and the priest exchanged a warm smile. Then the official swung slowly around and placed a hand upon the other covered head.

"Sister Ramona," he said, "precious jewel of the Bell family, who all made their way to this Modestian sanctuary from rural Utah ten months ago. You confided in me that your clan is a bit restless when it comes to churches, but I hope today's ceremony means that you personally *have* found a forever home with us."

The priest quickly disposed of the silver fabric, which revealed to all an angelic brunette whose cheeks sparkled with glitter. She smiled at the priest, who now turned to face the crowd.

"Let us praise Mod and the Prescient One for bringing together these two yearning souls..."

As the official spoke about the young couple's first meeting and carefully supervised courtship, Matthias instead found himself thinking about the Prescient One. For the reverend had lived within these church walls for nearly a week, but still had not gotten an audience with the Modestian founder and leader.

He had *seen* him speak at one of the larger community gatherings, but any inquiry about their previously scheduled appointment was met with vague answers from the elders. And as much as Matthias was enjoying his sabbatical among these happy Modestians, he could not put off his own church responsibilities back home indefinitely.

"...and so I ask you, Brother Carter," the priest said, "do you willingly and joyfully accept the responsibilities of husband and eternal partner?"

The young man on stage inhaled deeply. "I do."

"And do you, Sister Bell," the priest said after pivoting to his right, "take this man as your protector and conscience? Whom you will serve and honor and provide with children?"

Ramona turned her head toward the wedding guests. Her eyes scanned across the dozens of eager faces. Finally she looked into Reese's eyes and gave a firm, contended nod. "I do."

Smiling brightly, the priest said with great emotion, "As you embark upon your new life as one, I offer this personal bit of advice. If you play to your strengths and always remember to lean on each other, you will find the stamina to thrive in the decades to come. Now, I am elated to declare you husband and wife. Sir, you may kiss your bride!"

Matthias felt his throat catch as he watched the young couple intertwine their fingers before slowly leaning in. Maintaining eye contact, Reese and Ramona sealed their union with a delicate but long-lasting kiss.

Reverend Witherspoon now found himself almost unable to breathe. A tear ran down his cheek. He saw the man next to him bare his teeth in a satisfied smile, which somehow caused all of his own tension to release.

Matthias exhaled slowly and deeply, sensing in his mind's eye a flicker of his own wedding day many years ago. Where it had all gone wrong with Janelle he didn't have the heart to wonder about, not now during such a hopeful and touching moment.

He watched the newlyweds through misty eyes as they walked down the aisle together, their joined hands raised in triumph like sports champions. The young children who had earlier brought them in on the dollies now danced and frolicked in their wake.

The Reverend Matthias G. Witherspoon sat back and sighed. Whenever he thought he'd had enough of this eccentric church, he always experienced something new which awakened a corner of his heart that had gone dormant over the years. Whether those dead ends had manifested through neglect, ego, or cynicism did not matter now. He was thawing and finally tasting that rebirth which he had come here humbly seeking.

He also saw that he would be wise not to feel frustrated by the Prescient One's continued unavailability. "All in good time" was a message that every philosopher or religion worth its salt preached. Just as Matthias himself had advised parishioners in need of guidance a thousand times before.

Reverend Witherspoon would wait. He would live among these Modestians and learn from them everything that his own God had allotted for this interfaith experience.

And perhaps one day, Matthias mused, he would be known as... The *Patient* One.

14. TEMPTATION

Cornelius Alemán was standing with his back to the room while inspecting a row of antique books. He wore a beige linen blazer and rustic gray slacks, and his lush head of silver hair had been gelled into place. He turned around.

"Victor," he said, "so wonderful of you to come. Please, join me."

The elder gentleman motioned toward several brown leather seats and couches that were arrayed in a square in the middle of the lushly appointed living room. Drawn semi-opaque shades filtered the outside light, and several small lamps added a soft yellow glow.

Victor Dominguez, fresh off a charter flight at Alemán's expense, which was followed by a ride in a restored vintage car out to this secluded Vermont mansion, extended his hand.

"Pleased to meet you," Victor said. "Your estate is breathtaking."

"Thank you kindly," Cornelius said. "*Mi familia* never understood why I would choose to live so far away from the border states. But then again, for some reason I have always loved the cold. Please, sit."

The men sat catty-cornered to one another in deep, plush leather chairs. A moment later, a middle-aged butler with bronze skin and shimmering black hair parted to the side entered the room.

"Bartolo," Alemán said, "I think we're ready."

"Excellent, sir." The butler approached, his shoes barely making a sound on the walnut flooring. "*Señor* Dominguez, would you care for something to drink?"

Victor consulted his watch. "Do you have sparkling water?"

"Of course. I will bring it immediately. And for you, Master Cornelius?"

The old man waved his hand. "The usual, with plenty of ice, please."

"Very good, gentlemen." Bartolo bowed his head and exited the room.

Cornelius smiled and rubbed his hands together gently. They were immense paws, but Victor had noticed during their initial greeting that these were more like soft pillows than a forceful weapon.

Alemán said, "Victor, I am so glad you agreed to meet with me. And before we begin, I do apologize for my outburst at the end of our first phone call."

Victor tilted his head, saying, "I honestly didn't know what to make of it."

"Sometimes I just get carried away." Cornelius smiled. "It's not what I really meant at all."

"I'm glad I made the trip then. To get a clarification."

"Think of it this way. I'm not a young man anymore, Victor. I turned seventy earlier this year."

"Congratulations."

"Yes, thank you," Alemán said. "When you've reached my age—and have *engaged* with life the whole time—you find that your *understanding* of things helps in overcoming all the fatigue you may feel in body and mind. Like any man who's honest with himself, I can admit that I've had more defeats than triumphs. But that doesn't mean now, just because my hair is gray, I am willing to quietly fade away."

Cornelius thumped the arm of his chair, then straightened his posture.

At that moment, the butler returned carrying a silver drink tray. He deftly slid a small table into the open space between the outside of the leather chairs, then placed two coasters down in one swift motion. Napkins bearing a coat of arms were also deposited, and finally Bartolo's white gloves reached for the drinks. A faint blue cylinder for Victor, and Cornelius received an oversize clear tumbler filled with amber liquid and three large pieces of ice. Bartolo withdrew without a word.

"Victor," Alemán said, as they brought the glasses together for a delicate clink, "I see tremendous leadership potential in you. Yes, sitting before me is a man who could unlock centuries of greatness."

"That's very flattering," Victor said. "I'm honored you would think that of me. But I'm still dressing my wounds right now, so in truth, I don't know how much fight I've got left at the moment."

"Don't worry about that." Cornelius patted Victor on the wrist. "Life proceeds in phases. There are periods of rest. Thought. And then, decisive action!"

"I hope that my story is just in an intermission then, and not over."

"Indeed, young man. Especially now that we're having this meeting of the minds. Tell me, does the name Luis Ortega mean anything to you?"

"Of course," Victor said. "He's the college kid who got the HRA to change several of its DDM rules."

"Yes, correct! People are referring to it sardonically as 'Bennies Choice.' What I find remarkable is that he was just a bit player at the time of the Sentinels' hack. In fact, if you'll remember, he was standing on stage while the masked man delivered his manifesto to the world. But it was *Luis* who ended up stirring an awakening among a segment of the population which the Sentinels could never dream of reaching."

"Beneficiaries," Victor said quietly.

"Yes! Empowering them to think for themselves through a spontaneous act of courage."

"No manifesto required."

Cornelius's eyes twinkled. "And that scares the daylights out of everyone from the White House on down. People whose lives revolve around making promises with strings attached."

"Ah." Dominguez pointed a finger skyward. "Because the 'hand up' often sets limits on how far you actually rise."

"It's no accident, Victor. If no one needs the HRA's assistance, not only will many highly educated people be out of a job, but perhaps a whole philosophy will also come into question."

"The missionary do-gooder." Victor was becoming more animated now. "I've been fighting an uphill battle against these types my whole adult life. They hide behind nice-sounding words, then call *you* taboo names to put you on the defensive if you disagree with their agenda."

"So true," Alemán said, taking a sip from his glass. "But look at what an average Jose was able to achieve. He put his foot down and moved the mountain that is the HRA."

Victor nodded and said, "He did more than that, actually. He put his body on the line. Luis could have been killed the way the FBI apprehended him."

"Yes," Cornelius conceded, "but the bigger point is that he never had the infrastructure or even an agenda like the SOJ did. But he sure made those bastards scramble!"

Victor paused. "So, what are you saying? Use him directly, or hold up his example to recruit other Davids to erode the HRA Goliath?"

"Here are the facts, *compadre*. As highly as we think of ourselves, we can't win this battle through leadership alone. We need the support of many Luis Ortega clones. Young, apolitical, family oriented… and sometimes not all that intelligent. Or at least, not likely to consider the big picture in the way that we do."

"Forgive me for saying this, Mr. Alemán, but it sounds like you're dreaming of a peasants' revolt. That has not gone well for our people in the past."

"Victor, please!" There was a fire in the old man's eyes. "Is that not what we're seeing among the Caucasians, who either support the SOJ or are disobeying the law in a hundred ways?"

"But the difference is," Victor said, "they *know* why they're angry. Latiz-Americans are the exact opposite. They're *glad* to be here. And in their heart of hearts, many of them know they caught a lucky break being granted amnesty in 'twenty-one. I think the last thing they want to do is make America reconsider its past generosity."

Cornelius shook his head. "But don't you see? It's too late! What this election showed is that we've crossed the tipping point. Not just demographically, but more importantly in terms of *participation*. The likes of Luis Ortega may not know *why* they're voting for whom or what—but it only matters that we got them to the polls. Now let's get them to take action."

Victor was baffled. "And do what?"

"Whatever we want them to."

"Just like that? At the snap of your fingers?"

"Someone's, perhaps. But Senator, another truth about getting older and having many responsibilities is that whether you want to or not, you start to see the world *as it is*. And sadly, it is barely at all what you wish it to be. But with this clarity, at least you can, as in the style of the martial arts, use your surroundings and the existing momentum to bring the world closer to that more pleasant vision in your mind."

Victor shifted in his seat. He said, "Give me a concrete example, please."

"Certainly," Alemán said. "A person coming here from another country fifty years ago was required out of necessity to fit in. Learn the language, join their new community—and get to work. But in this century? It seems as if people only move to the United States for the running water and abundance of food. These new generations do not care about the First Amendment. And any interest they take in the country's history comes from a place of grievance—either to justify their own short-sighted gluttony, or to excuse their disdain for the virtues of civic life."

"Now wait," Victor said, feeling his head start to throb. "These are the same people you were just plotting to... I don't know... harness or inspire?"

"Yes indeed." Cornelius inhaled deeply. "Pardon me if I sound too cynical. I'm sure they're all good people with nieces and other beloved *familia*, but no one gets a pass in this life. No matter the color of your skin, where you came from, or how long ago you stepped off the boat. You have to *pay attention* if you don't want to be abused. Especially here in the busy United States—because this isn't the jungles of Guatemala, nor the dusty towns of our Mexican homeland.

"So these people," Alemán continued, "my cousins. They think they can sleepwalk forever. The train of ants that walked across the border, whose children speak English and even go to college—they still don't want to put it all together!"

Dominguez crumpled his napkin in frustration. "You're making *me* feel stupid now. Just what are you getting at? Because on the phone you had me thinking that your interest was in the people still living south of the border."

"Bear with me, please. If I can't wake Latizos up," Cornelius said, "I will at least corral them for my own purposes. Consider that they could have made history by electing you as the first Hispanic president. But so many of them were stuck looking backwards, caught up in the old narrative—because they lacked the integrity, *the individual courage* to renounce that Reparations check. Money which deep down most of them know they don't even deserve. And that, Senator, is the sickness I have vowed to prevent from spreading further south."

Victor looked down at his hands. "You think *they* are the reason why I lost the election?"

Cornelius leaned forward and brought a hand to his chin. He said, "It pains me to say this, believe me. But at their core they lack any sort of grand vision for the future. They're content to sit on their front porch and watch the neighborhood stagnate—they never think to climb the hill and contemplate the world beyond! But regardless, it is still out there and will be won by those who dare."

Victor Dominguez adjusted himself in the deep leather seat. "And you see that in me?"

Alemán smiled. "A tad reckless and unrefined... but yes, it is there within you, my friend."

"But perhaps I'm too set in my ways to cultivate? I'm no genius. And maybe not even a dyed-in-the-wool conservative. It's likely that I fell in with the pro-business side only by chance. All those days on the job site swapping out pipes with my father, and seeing him pinch pennies to provide for us. Did that give me a better chance of standing out, as opposed to being just another Minorican calling for more entitlements?"

"That could be part of it," Cornelius said. "But Victor, you carried us so close. Under the radar, all by yourself! I could never hope to achieve my goals, let alone so soon, without the bold charge you just made. Incredible... *salud!*"

Cornelius drained his whiskey, crunching a bit of ice as he set the glass down.

"I do appreciate this tribute," Victor said. "My ego hates to think that in some ways, it was just a convergence of factors much bigger than myself that put me in such a position."

"As if you were perhaps... sleepwalking?" The old man smiled. His gelled silver hair looked like grooved concrete in the afternoon's fading light.

"You seem to know me better than I do," Dominguez said.

"I just know life, Victor. Even if you only felt like a passenger, the day you realized that the party intended for you to lose, that's when you started throwing real punches. Lunging wildly, and not caring *who* you hit. It was beautiful!"

"Yes but, now that I've lost, my Senate colleagues are cold and often unavailable. People who in the final weeks of the campaign became very friendly when they smelled an upset. Now where are they?"

"But *I'm* here." Cornelius cupped his hands on top of his knees. "Sitting before you, face to face. *Hombre a hombre.*"

Victor exhaled, then clenched his jaw. "I am not so hurt as to go running into the arms of the next person who says that they approve of me. I too am old enough to endure defeat and disrespect."

"Of course." Alemán raised his palms in a placating gesture. "I'm not trying to scoop you up on the rebound. Here it is: this country is torn along many lines right now. The Dramacrats used to speak to Latizo interests, but our rising numbers and grinding work ethic reveal that we don't need their handouts anymore. Victor, the Left has chosen to be the party of the *loser*, even as they pat themselves on the back encouraging 'the underdog.' The Rebellicans, meanwhile, are in an eternal identity crisis. They too obsess over the past—but for them, instead of injustice, it's a perceived *greatness* that they allow to be chipped away for fear of... being spoken of unpleasantly. So, with such interparty weakness, do you finally understand why I see an opportunity?"

"You want to create a new third party?" Victor asked slowly.

"Yessss!"

"For Latizos? With me as the first leader?"

Cornelius smiled broadly. "The face, at least. You'll have a lot of backline support. From me, of course. And others. We will provide a road map so that it doesn't fall on its face out of the starting gate."

Victor Dominguez's eyes were wide in astonishment. "Do you really think it's easier to reach tens of millions of, as you say, sleepwalking Hispanics, rather than to end one faltering government program?"

"No. But it's more essential! To look *forward* with confidence. To not simply sit back complacently because your material needs are provided for—because that is the surest way to fall right back into dependence. After that, the helpless become the conquered. My friend, if Latizos are too sheepish to feel any sense of destiny after having spread across the United States, then I will *create* one for them!"

Cornelius Alemán stood up and shook his fist.

Senator Victor Dominguez sat very still in his chair while looking into the face of this impassioned man. He thought of his wife Jaclyn and their three children. He knew that he was now, suddenly, at a crossroads far greater than even that fateful moment when he first decided to run for president.

15. HEADS WILL ROLL

On the morning of November eighteenth, a viral video began to make the rounds on underground internet chat rooms. Within two days it had already been viewed fifteen million times. A group calling itself The Last Sentinel claimed responsibility.

The six-minute clip was titled "Explosive Forbidden Video Reveals Secret Government Pre-Education Camps for Children." Further details were provided in the description section:

"Watch as a masked team of Sentinels of Jubilee sympathizers infiltrate a South Carolina facility in this daring nighttime raid. It is here that an HRA-funded program houses and indoctrinates the children of imprisoned Debtors. Warning: The contents of this video will likely shock the sensibilities of any freedom-loving American."

The footage was compiled from cameras worn by several of the raiding party. They first moved briskly through a wooded area, before breaching the perimeter fence. They next surveyed four small structures before converging upon a small church house, whose bright lights and large windows revealed the scene inside.

Two dozen children ranging in age from three to ten, and whose faces were blurred out, chanted in unison with a woman wearing a bright green dress. Captioning provided with the video read, "The past is my burden, but the future starts with me. The ends justify the teams, because the friends multiply the dreams."

Next the raiders breached the windows and doors. Brandishing bats and Tasers, they quickly subdued the half-dozen staff members without inflicting violence, then tied them up. The children, who at first had begun to panic in the chaos, were soon calmed by the soothing voice of a masked woman.

A large banner above the teaching board read, "Everything is racist. Everything else is a human right."

After the building was secured, one of the team members removed his mask and fell to his knees as he embraced two of the children. The video clip ended here, with these final words appearing on the screen: "The Sentinels are reuniting families. Pledge your support so we can fight back against this out-of-control government."

President Eileen Jeffries-Lao turned away from the projection screen in disgust. The small group of staff members, who had already been working late at the White House, now sat in silence after watching this viral propaganda piece.

Chief of Staff Tony Rizzuto stood up and croaked, "Well, now we know where we stand."

"More like, knocked out cold on the canvas," someone muttered.

"In a word, yes. But there's more."

"More?!" The president's face was ashen. "Do not tell me any children died at that... school."

"Not at all. Kyle, would you?" Tony motioned to the computer tech. As the next clip began, he added, "This is security footage retrieved from the property. Here you see the man who earlier removed his mask, and is now exiting the church with his son and daughter—"

"Do we know that to be true?" Eileen asked.

"Yes. And here's how. Although the light was low, the camera was able to get definitive scans of both his eyes and face. The man's name is Morgan Haggerston. Does that ring a bell with anyone?"

The staff looked around at one another.

"I guess not," Eileen said. "Should it?"

"He was among the dozen or so inmates that escaped from the debtors' prison in Pennsylvania last summer."

"Wait a second," analyst Danielle Flanagan said. "That was a Sentinels' inside job coordinated with some of the guards, right?"

"Correct," Tony said. "The staff involved were disciplined severely. But of the fugitives, only two were caught in the ensuing months. So right now you may be thinking, 'Oh well, this Morgan fellow just went out looking for his kids.' "

"Who were what?" Eileen said testily. "Not put into the custody of other relatives? Not attending their normal schools, but instead sent off to... the wilderness? Because last I checked, I was still the president—but I really seem to be missing something here."

"This is all true," Tony said, maintaining his poise. "And your consternation is duly noted. But bear with me, because this all gets even more interesting."

"We are all most definitely interested. Proceed." Eileen waved a hand, shaking her head in disbelief.

"Who else escaped with Morgan? James Haggerston, his father, who just so happened to come up in a recent face scan. How? Because the FBI was hauling in an agent of their own— who had gone AWOL while secretly embedded at the Mall of Absolution!"

"Hold on," Danielle said, raising a finger. "I heard about that through one of my... Well, never mind who. The point is, that action took place on a farm in Iowa, not Minnesota. How—and why—did an old man working for the Sentinels in Pennsylvania go all the way out there? And he went undetected the whole time?"

"It gets stranger." Rizzuto consulted a tablet. "This property where... Special Agent Marcus Young was apprehended, it too is owned by the Church of Modestianity. However, it actually functions as a medical facility for military veterans."

Eileen snapped out of the daze she had fallen into. "What?!"

"It's true. All high-level care. Nothing subversive or religious going on out there. We believe that is why James—a disabled Iraq War One veteran—was not also taken into custody."

Everyone in the meeting room started throwing out theories. After a few minutes, the president raised her hand for silence.

"So you're telling me," she said, "we've got an FBI agent who went rogue, possibly linking up with the father of the man we just saw at that children's camp? Who do I even go after here? This Morgan Haggerston or our own people? Jesus Christ, this is like Abu Ghraib all over again."

"Well," strategist Natalie Greer said, "according to what I just pulled up, the whole Haggerston family was caught burning documents. So maybe the children..."

"Let's get real," the president retorted. "A lot of people are doing that—of all colors and stripes, too! No, no..." Eileen Jeffries-Lao's face tightened as she declared, "We're staring into the abyss now!"

Tony said, "There's no need to get maudlin here, Madam President. You won the election. You have the mandate. These are potholes, not bridge collapses."

"Still, an ugly bruise. Kids always pull the heartstrings, and we're on the wrong side of this one."

Natalie said, "Eileen, we know the optics look bad right now. But these programs all exist for a good reason. White anger is…" She trailed off as she watched Eileen bite into a pen. A moment later she quietly added, "From my understanding, the goal is to reroute the nerve from defiance to cooperation."

"I don't think we were in the wrong to fund an… insurance policy that took the form of these schools," Danielle said. "Look at it in the context of recent history. The colonial era had been over for decades, and Europe seemed poised to show the world what a multi-ethnic bloc could achieve. But then—" She compressed her lips.

"They rolled back the clock," Eileen said. "All the usual suspects, too."

"And a lot of their Italian, German, and British cousins are here in America."

"You know," Eileen said, leaning back into the padding of her chair, "has anyone really looked into the role that the migrant expulsions played in getting *us* elected in 'twenty-four? In stark contrast to the Europeans, we had a *plan* to right the ship *and* keep moving forward."

Danielle asked, "So you're saying it was more than just disgust at what those other countries did?"

"Absolutely. The EU had this abstract idea that plopping millions of warm bodies into Europe would magically solve their debt and population problems. And who knows, maybe it could have worked. But people are not all plug-and-play with the exact same programming. Were their policy wonks simply too afraid to acknowledge even basic cultural differences for fear of being called racist? Is that really what prevented them from successfully integrating their new citizens?"

"We're the melting pot, not them," Kyle the tech guy chirped.

"Hmm," Jeffries-Lao said. "Their bureaucratic class has just always been so out of touch. Everything seems to take them by surprise! 'What, the migrants are congregating in ghettos?' 'What, the host population doesn't like being raped and stabbed?' I swear, so much of that terrible violence we saw earlier this decade was completely avoidable. And I—off the record, of course—put blame at the feet of complacent EU leaders. One, for not designing a plan that involved actual humans. And two, they forgot the capacity for barbarism among their own people."

Tony Rizzuto cleared his throat loudly. "This is great philosophy," he said, "but we'd better get back to the present. Because despite all *our* planning and recent win at the ballot box —critical eyes are looking our way. How many millions of Americans are now thinking about those sad children in South Carolina?"

Eileen leaned forward, rubbing her hands as she said, "This is all so complex. To navigate history. To try and bring out the best in all people. To inspire. To assist. Especially now when people flinch if a new idea doesn't arrive wrapped in foam. I mean, you can't just say, 'Hey, let's give all the Caucs partial lobotomies,' am I right?"

Everyone laughed nervously. Tony said, "I wouldn't be in favor of that, actually. Because I've got perfect hair."

"No, no," the president cackled. "I'm just riffing on the political magic arts. To get not just yourself, but entire populations from here to there... You've got to balance subtle moves with the public policies that are there for all to see. I'm afraid we've missed the mark on that first part, and now we're paying the price with this terrible PR."

Eileen Jeffries-Lao stood up and shook her fist.

"I *never* liked the idea of debtors' prisons," she said, "but they talked me into it. Said *enforcement* was the key to collections. Those GI Joe types were probably just salivating about all the new military toys our budget could pay for. You want to lock up the adults? Fine, fine. Set an example to other would-be document deniers. But abducting their children! I hate to say this, but it's times like these when we really need to ask ourselves if we've lost our way. Who knows, maybe it would have been better for Dominguez to win, and then everybody could have watched him stumble around knocking over everything we built."

Danielle tilted a notepad downward and started writing as she said, "So how do you want to respond to the crisis at hand? I worry that condemnation, even while also pleading no foreknowledge, could still come back to bite us. Perhaps stressing *reform* under the larger HRA-wide rehabilitation project will help cover our bases."

"Some heads will have to roll, though." Eileen sat down again. "Gonna need to have at least a couple fall guys on this one. *Real* this time, too."

"Understood." Danielle gave a devilish grin. "Let's go with the Colonel Kurtz narrative. Some career civil servant—left to his own devices, with too much funding but not enough oversight—he just took it too far."

"Jesus," the president said, running a hand through her hair. "Even when we spin, the big picture makes us look like we don't know what we're doing. My god, spending the next four years fending off scandals is no way to run a presidency, let alone a program like the HRA."

"It's happened before," Kyle said. "Iran-Contra pretty much tied Reagan's hands. But still, the Berlin Wall came down not long after he rode off into the sunset."

Eileen sighed. She said, "The fact is, moving money to where it needs to go isn't enough to sustain us anymore. The deeper the HRA gets entrenched, the more complicated it all becomes. Dents on the hull, tangled nets, and then of course there's the crew…"

"Don't lose hope," Tony said. "It's only a few drunken sailors, not a full-on mutiny."

"Ha! Half the country is itching for a revolt. Anyway, I think we're done here. Time for *us* to get a little drunk. Because there's some choppy seas between now and January of 2033."

"Aye, aye, skipper."

16. SURROUNDED BY FOOLS

"What's up, Mister Flop?" Nolan set down his fork and chomped on a pickle spear.

"Oh, you know," Clyde said, dropping his bag into the booth opposite Nolan as he sat down. "Just thinking about the next solo track, I guess."

"That's a good attitude," Nolan said, mopping up ketchup with a steak fry. "Learn anything from song number two?"

Clyde's eyes wandered across the diner. It was nicer than

most other places nearby. He said, "How quick people forget, even *after* you hit big. This one got played for like two days, then nothing."

"Okay, so you're paying attention. That's good. The fact that you actually followed up with something is a plus. But you know, the song probably just wasn't all that great. Video looked pretty good—even if I would have done a few things differently."

"Oh yeah? Funny, I heard you were booked the day we made it." Clyde reached over and grabbed a french fry.

"C'mon now, DJC," Nolan said, falling away with a smile. "Don't hurt me! Nah, of course that's right. I had some stuff going on out of town."

"New stuff or… old stuff?"

"Who want to know?" Nolan stared at Clyde, who matched his gaze. "S'alright, kid. I'm just probing you. See who you are now that the spotlight's faded a bit."

"I'm the same old Clyde, I think. But what about you? Little while since the Pigeon Man was laid to rest or whatever. How's the new Nolan doin'?"

"Well," Nolan said, gathering his papers and tucking a few dollar bills under the check, "let me show you what I've got cooking. Walk with me back to the crib."

Nolan handed the receipt tray to the hostess on their way out and said, "Nice to see you again."

"Any change?" the woman asked.

"Never. You keep it, treat y'all selves to something nice."

The woman smiled. "Have a wonderful day, Mr. Simmons."

They stepped outside and Clyde started gyrating his body wildly. He said in a falsetto voice, "Ooh, Mr. Simmons!"

"Yeah, well," Nolan said with a wave of the hand, "you only mock because you don't yet understand the value of how everyday people can make your life a little more pleasant."

"I think you just like flirting with them waitresses."

"That's 'cause you still got your mama cooking you nice meals. I got operations to run, no time to cook. Fast food and delivery are one thing, but sometimes it's nice to get that human connection. Be treated right."

Clyde kicked at a small branch that had fallen onto the sidewalk. "But then you got to pay extra. The tip."

"And it's worth it too. For good service. A waitress that's on point will make you feel good for the rest of the day."

"How's that?" Clyde asked. "She smile at you? Shake her booty?"

"Sometimes, yeah." Nolan grinned. "But you seat me with a old lady who got her timing down right? That's gold right there. Refill your coffee when it need it, give you time to eat your soup before bringing out your sandwich... and no unnecessary interruptions all the while. I swear, it's a real treat. In fact, I wish I was still hungry just so I could go back and do it again!"

"You crazy, Nolan." Clyde stuffed his hands into his hoodie pockets and shook his head.

They came to a stop at the corner of an intersection. As they waited for the signal to change, a car going in their direction pulled up behind another idling car. The driver side door opened slightly and a pile of trash dumped out onto the pavement. The light turned green and a second later the car was moving forward in traffic.

"Did you see that?" Nolan said bitterly.

"What happened?" Clyde looked all around the intersection.

"That mofo in the Mercedes just threw a bunch of garbage out from his car."

"Yeah?"

"Look at it." Nolan pointed. "Paper bag. Wrapper. Fries box. And a cup. Dude had some drive-thru, scarfed it down, and that was that. God damn! Can't believe people be doin' that in their own hoods."

"Maybe he don't live around here." Clyde stepped into the crosswalk.

"Whatever. Anyway, Clyde. Keep doing what you need to do for you. Don't waste your time worrying about these types of people no more. You've already given enough. And them?" Nolan waved a hand behind him. "Every day—in the little things like that right there—they prove they ain't worth none of it."

"He probably wanted to keep his car clean." Clyde bobbed his head up and down. "Mercedes are tight!"

"Are you serious? What about the neighborhood itself? Why not just squat down and take a shit in the street?"

"Nolan, you too much, man. It's just a little trash, it'll blow away."

Nolan gave Clyde's shoulder a squeeze. He said, "I'll forgive you because you're just a kid. But Clyde, it's the small, everyday things that define you, reveal who you are. See, that dude probably wears diamond earrings, keeps his car spotless. But in that one moment right there, he showed us who he really is on the inside."

"Damn," Clyde remarked, "you got all that from one thing?"

"Yes, sir. It says, 'I'm lazy. I don't care about anyone else. I'm only living in the moment.' That's how he lets us know he doesn't want to be a part of this community."

"Why you so mad at that man? You maybe know him from somewhere else?"

"No, I don't know him! It's because he just took a mini-shit on every one of his neighbors, that's why."

"Haha, maybe he call himself MC Mini-Shit!" Clyde began to riff, "Yo, I be a hungry rapper. Fill the street with my beats, and chicken sandwich wrappers. Mad respect or I'll... use the gutter as a crapper! Step off, y'all!"

Nolan couldn't help but smile. "This is why we got to get you out of here. Talent like that, you should be a million miles away from this mess."

Clyde nudged Nolan's arm. "You still here. And you smarter than me."

"Boy," Nolan sighed, "I've been trying to help. Really thought I could. Kept a lot of you youngins out of the nets, but... It just burns you out seeing so many get eaten up."

"Don't quit, I'm serious. Without you, nothing ever would have happened for me. I know it."

Nolan stopped, turned to Clyde. "Thank you, young man. Guess I'm at a turning point. Met a really nice lady at one of those speeches. Lives down in Connecticut. So we been talkin'..."

"Wait... Is she white?"

Nolan looked over at Clyde and gave a sly smile. "Yep. But she got a real figure on her, boy!"

"Aw, man!" Clyde began to shadow box down the sidewalk. "Nolan... be rollin'... Gave a lil' talk... fell in love with a Cauc!"

"Clyde, Clyde, Clyde. You are some kind of mad genius. But if I do it—really get out of here—will you promise to follow my lead?"

"I don't know, man. Before all this blew up, I just wanted to say something for my people. Can't expect everything to just get better overnight."

"That's noble. But listen to me. Sometimes you can do the most good by stepping away. I think your music might be able to help people from all over. But you can't do it when you're surrounded by fools who, one way or another, are going to drag you down."

"Well, maybe *you* can just up and go. I got my family here. Tee especially, he needs me."

"I understand," Nolan said. "Just remember, I'm not blowing smoke up your you-know-what when I say you're an exceptional talent. I don't want to get all sentimental, but it's a tragedy for the world when God's gifts don't reach their potential. And I've seen it happen before."

Clyde bowed his head, saying, "That's too much, Nolan. Don't give me all that. I mean, should I sign on with Pryor and move out to Cali, or what?"

"Possibly. Just really think about how much more you'd probably achieve in a place where there ain't trash sitting all over the place."

Clyde looked at a crumpled can that had been jammed into a nearby bush. "They don't want to fly," he said quietly. "They'll get down with my song and dance to it… but they won't take my hand and come up to the roof to see. Damn…"

Nolan threw his arm around Clyde and gave him a fatherly squeeze. "Don't feel too sad, bro. I know this dump can get to you. But there's good people out there. Fighting the battle in every city. They don't have your way with words, but they'll understand your message. So write for them, inspire them not to give up. You just don't have to do it from the inside of a toilet bowl to keep your street cred."

"C'mon, you know that ain't me." Clyde then muttered, "I don't have any street cred."

"That's right, 'cause you're a good kid. We got to change your location—improve your situation—to help save the nation. Such is the equation!"

"Haha," Clyde said, pulling away. "That's a good rap, Nolan."

"All part of today's lesson," Simmons said with a grin. "But now, that's a wrap! Come on into the studio, check out some of the improvements we got goin' on."

17. PARALYZED

Chris Donohugh kept thinking about his friend Glenn's email on the subway ride home.

"Hey, Shredder!" the message had read. "I played those new riffs you wrote for the other guys. They were impressed! And now that you've upgraded your rig, they definitely want to hear more."

Glenn was of course writing in code. Because for all of his own band nostalgia on that solitary night when Kate was out of town last week, Chris had not once touched a guitar.

But he had made use of the software that copied the work emails on Kate's home laptop and sent them to his own computer two rooms away. To keep his conscience from a complete meltdown, he had as an extra precautionary measure coded a crawler to meticulously erase all personally identifying information contained within these messages.

His final step in thwarting the HRA's increased IT security was to purchase a used laptop with cash from a pawn shop. After several hard drive wipes and software modifications, he used it to send Glenn the encrypted data from public locations like cafes and bars.

And no one in the world could ever possibly guess the file's password: VotingBoothSarcophagus. This being the title of the last song Raucous Voice ever wrote, but never played live or recorded before the group disbanded nearly a decade ago. The phrase had been an ongoing inside joke between Chris and Glenn ever since.

Chris knew from a quick manual scan of Kate's messages that there was nothing particularly juicy in these first batches. But there was no telling how many other hacked HRA email accounts were also being fed into the underground's growing database, where perhaps bits of her conversations would make sense within the larger context.

"The people's MARVIN," Chris said ruefully as he trotted up

his building's front steps. A smile fought its way to the surface against the pressure of his clenched jaws.

Once inside his apartment, he felt his stomach churn while thinking about the last line of Glenn's encoded message. The "upgrade" referred to was Kate's promotion to liaison between the HRA and the White House. Despite the felonies he'd already committed, somehow only now did the Jeffries-Lao connection bring the phrase "threat to national security" to mind.

Chris wasn't sure he could keep doing this. He might have been able to sleep soundly next to Kate, even while the bits of confidential data were flying through the walls from her computer to his, if it was just regular HRA office stuff. But now, when it appeared that she would be spending many nights in another bed two hundred miles away, he was mortified that someone on the White House staff might catch wind of his activities.

Next would come the wrath of the president's digital espionage team. A soap-opera scandal that all the networks would dig their teeth into. The haunted look of betrayal on Kate's face through the plexiglass divider in the jail's visiting room—assuming she even came to see him. And himself in an orange jumpsuit, just like his high school band had worn as gag costumes at live shows.

Chris was starting to feel nauseous now. He paced around the apartment several times as the gravity of what he had already done began to sink in. If there was no way back—no magical undo command like computers had—there was also no way out or forward. He would probably have to sink down into the mud and hide with this lie for the rest of his life.

Because he couldn't afford to lose Kate. He'd already gone through those hypothetical emotions months ago during her cancer scare, and watched his hair nearly turn gray in the process.

On the other hand, he was at least certain that Glenn wouldn't rat him out if he was ever arrested for conspiring with the Sentinels. The bonds that musicians formed in a tour van were stronger than anything known to man, except perhaps actual combat soldiers.

And it was a two-way street, apparently. How else to explain Chris agreeing to spy on his wife during that drunken reunion with Glenn several weeks ago?

Chris opened the file cabinet drawer in his office and fished out the little device he'd used to pair the two computers. The urge to crush it was followed by the desperate desire to plug it back into Kate's laptop and uninstall the spyware. To at least hide his tracks, if he couldn't erase the deed and its consequences.

But he was paralyzed. He wouldn't do anything right now. Not for Kate. Not for Glenn. Not to protect the president. And definitely not to help the Sentinels.

Chris didn't even know what he could do to save himself.

He saw the top of a softshell guitar case poking out of the open closet door. Instinctively he glanced at the shrine to Raucous Voice on his bookshelf. A crushing sadness came over him in the silence of the room.

I should've written a new song after all.

18. HISTORICAL LANDMARK

Eileen Jeffries-Lao never expected something like this to happen to her. If asked months ago, before it had started, she would have honestly answered that she didn't even *want* it.

But in the weeks leading up to the election—suddenly stressful and chaotic and her campaign *vulnerable*—she had just spent so much time with her chief of staff Tony Rizzuto, that she found herself falling into his arms late one night in October.

Weeks later and she was still trying to make sense of having this side of herself awakened. Her marriage had been on ice for years, in the carnal sense. First Man Paul Jeffries was of course known for his wandering eye—and more—during most of their public lives, but Eileen had been able rationalize it away because *she* was the rising political star. Later still, as she was leading the Reparations movement that was righting so many wrongs, his infidelity seemed a small personal price to pay.

Whether it was the unexpected late-hour election threat from Victor Dominguez, or understanding that even in victory her political career would be over within a few years, Eileen Jeffries-

Lao had stumbled into an affair with one of her male subordinates and now clung onto it greedily.

Besides, Tony had been her rock for years. Now Eileen was just... leaning in a little more.

Tonight would be their last evening together before Tribesgiving. Tony was flying to Arkansas with his family tomorrow, so now she kissed him with extra intensity. It had been so long since a man had made her feel such passion.

"Tony," she cooed. "You have no idea where that last... dance took me."

The man gave her shoulder a squeeze. "Maybe not. But I know when what I'm doing is working."

"Mm-hmm... I'll miss you when you're away. Will Alana give you what you need?"

"Let's not talk about that," Tony said. "All we gotta do is get through the holidays, New Year's, your inauguration... then the world is ours."

"God, I adore you," she said. "You see the road ahead so clearly. If people really knew how much of their president is just me acting out what you and the others have prepared... they'd call me a fraud."

Tony reached his free hand onto the bedside table and picked up the TV remote.

He said, "Hey now, Miss Lao. Why don't we watch something, take your mind off all that for awhile?"

"Sure, sure. I've been a bad girl today. Asked for alone time before Wall Street even closed. You better put on some news first, check the headlines."

Tony Rizzuto pulled up one of the twenty-four-hour news channels. Immediately he perked up. A graphic on screen indicated there was breaking news. He felt Eileen adjust onto an elbow beside him.

"...truly stunning announcement," the reporter was saying. "Today a lawsuit was filed in the state of California by a group of young Beneficiaries seeking to contest the compulsory aspects of Direct Descendant Match..."

"What?!" Eileen blurted. She was up on her knees in a flash, then turned her face back toward Tony with questioning eyes. He just nodded back in the direction of the screen.

"Let's listen," he said.

"…formally submitted by attorney Sabine L. Plotz, a rising legal star who is no stranger to HRA-related disputes."

The next shot showed Ms. Plotz standing outside a courthouse while flanked by a dozen Minoricans. She said, "Today I stand with these brave youngsters to help guide their mission toward success. They are here to say, 'We may be Beneficiaries, but we've already had enough of this Reparations millstone!' I hope to do them justice every step of the way."

"Oh, turn it off!" Eileen gasped. She fell back onto a pillow.

"You want to talk about this?" Tony said.

"Absolutely not," she said, staring up at the ceiling. "Not tonight. Please, just change the channel."

"Okay, no problem."

Tony began flipping through the TV stations. Eileen wiggled around and rested her head on his leg. He could hear her mutter, "No… no… no…" as he surfed. Finally he felt her playfully whack his shin.

"Yeah!" she said. "Let's watch this."

One glimpse of the man wearing khaki shorts and retro safari hat, and Tony knew exactly what he was in for.

"Alright," he chuckled. "I didn't realize you were such a fan. Good old Rog…"

"Turn it up," she said, nestling down into his thigh.

Tony did as she asked, then eased back onto the headboard to watch.

On screen the world-famous Australian TV host Roger Stephens was walking through a brightly lit office-laboratory. The camera trailed behind as he spoke with animated gestures.

"…what fascinates me the most about what we do is something I call Pre-Singularity Studies." Stephens held up a pink external hard drive, saying, "A period of somebody's whole life is stored inside here. Pictures, emails, hopes, dreams… An entire time capsule stockpiled in this one little plastic case. And it's dated… 2015. Hmm… Right before politics hit that crucial tipping point, and then wrenched us all into the monocultural divide which we're still grappling with today."

The host set down the hard drive, then looked at the camera intently.

"Oh yes," he said, "and *that* is why I do what I do. Rather than chase wild animals or search for sunken ships full of coins

—I seek *humanity*. Our loves, our passions, our history. For I am… Rog the Hard Drive Hunter! Join me tonight on this ultimate adventure, as my team pursues a lead that could change the course of life as we know it… forever!"

After the show's opening credit sequence, Roger reappeared in the back of an equipment van that was bounding down a rough road in near-darkness.

"Our journey takes us to rural West Texas," his recorded voice said. "It was here that for decades industry prepared recyclable items before they were shipped to China for final processing. However, extreme fluctuations in the market price of raw materials often meant that these types of businesses would shut down without warning. Which is why we've traveled all the way out to the modern-day ghost town of Clint, Texas."

The van pulled up to a tall security barrier. Rog stepped out of the side door and pointed into the distance beyond. He said, "Our team was alerted by an anonymous source about the massive warehouse you see past this reinforced perimeter. And it just might contain… the mother lode! Shall we?"

In the hazy blue and orange pre-dawn light, Rog and three other team members slipped through a freshly cut breach in the fencing. The camera crew kept pace as they approached.

The team gathered outside a fortified iron door. Rog said, "We've just wired the frame with cutter charges. This should disable the locking mechanism without doing any further damage—or worse yet, starting a fire. Are we ready now?"

Everyone ran behind a rusted-out dumpster. A series of jarring cracks could be heard. The camera pointed back toward the door and revealed a great deal of smoke and dust rising into the air.

"We're in!" Rog waved an arm. They sprinted to the door, threw it open, and turned flashlights on as they ran inside the cavernous warehouse. The team scattered and moved cautiously through a network of dark and dusty aisles.

The next shot showed Roger leaning forward with his hands pressed against a giant metal object whose sides angled inward from the top, as if it were an inverted pyramid. He was shaking his head from side to side while staring at the ground.

Finally he turned to the camera and joined his hands as if in prayer. "Ladies and gentlemen, this is indeed the moment we've all be working toward. Years of our lives dedicated in faithful pursuit. Now, I present to you... the Treasure of the Terabyte Madre!"

He took a camera into his hand and scaled the monolith's attached ladder fifteen feet up to the lip. It was uncovered and filled nearly to the top with... something. Rog swung the camera around and its spotlight revealed hundreds of small plastic rectangles of different shapes and colors.

He began to laugh maniacally. Suddenly the camera lurched down five feet—he had jumped into the container!

A hand was seen poring through the objects, scooping them up and then casting them aside like playing cards. A loud crunch came from behind and then the camera was passed off. Roger backed away and fell to his knees.

Visibly shaking and nearly babbling through tears, he said, "This is... it. The Holy Grail that we at *Hard Drive Hunters* always dreamed of. Because this is not simply the recent history of a nation. No, it's also perhaps a priceless tool that will aid MARVIN in his quest to compile the ultimate, most comprehensive record of humankind ever. Oh yes, ladies and gentlemen, they really did back everything up... right here!"

Rog started humming a tune and took a yellow case into his hand. He bounced it on his palm as if gauging the weight, then flipped it over to inspect the information label. He took a small device from his breast pocket and scanned the bar code.

"Oh my goodness!" Rog gave a thumbs-up. "This drive dates all the way back to 2006. Now, it's not a very large capacity storage device by modern standards. But perhaps it contains recordings of an old man born in the early part of the twentieth century recounting his life. Or maybe scans of legal documents tracing a family's property holdings going back two hundred years. It could be anything..."

He fell forward and began to swim playfully across the lake of hard drives. "Do you understand what I'm saying?" he wailed. "Ten thousand of them in just this one vat alone. Maybe a *million* drives in the whole facility." He sat up, smiling gaily. "And to think that for years law enforcement has been chasing down individual Debtors for vandalizing a few documents— meanwhile this incomprehensible trove of data has been sitting here unguarded the entire time. Just imagine how many person-hours this restoration project will take. Hint, hint. We'll be hiring!"

Rog exhaled profoundly, then said in a somber voice, "By the authority vested in me by our generous sponsors at the Historical Reparations Administration, I, Roger Stephens, hereby declare this property, the former Leary Metals, Inc., to be a landmark of historical significance. It shall be afforded all the legal protections therein."

As the end credits rolled, an announcer said, "Join us next time on *Hard Drive Hunters*, as we journey once more into civilization's forgotten corners in search of digital gold..."

Tony Rizzuto glanced away from the television and saw that his mistress, the President of the United States, was fast asleep.

19. PRIVATE AUDIENCE

"Your Prescience, it's an honor to finally meet you."

Matthias Witherspoon was seated comfortably across from the Prescient One in an antique-style chair which had Modestian imagery carved into the wood, as well as within the upholstery. A servant had just delivered tea before closing the doors on the church leader's private study.

"Likewise, Reverend."

As Matthias casually glanced around, he was surprised that the room seemed so... conventional. He had heard rumors from various church members that this man was a quirky interior decorator.

"Looking for something?" the man in electric blue attire asked him.

"Oh, just soaking in the mood," Witherspoon said. "Seems very relaxing, but also conducive to getting work done. I have a small office tucked away at my church where I compose many of my Sunday sermons."

"Indeed?" The Prescient One smiled. "I recently had these quarters remodeled. Everything seems to have become much more serious lately. I couldn't focus with all that blue rope dangling from the ceiling."

Matthias was unable to suppress a grin.

"Oh?" the church leader said almost playfully. "So you knew about the old look in here? Well, if that's the worst bit of gossip people are spreading..."

"I assure you I've heard nothing else."

"Now, Matthias," the Prescient One said, "please do accept my apologies for not being available sooner. As Modestianity grows, there are always a million little things that require my personal attention. Blessings, lectures—but surely you know all that from your own church duties."

"Ha, yes. And no matter how much you've delegated, someone always needs something."

"Surely. But tell me, now that you've lived intimately among us for nearly two weeks, what are your thoughts on our upstart new religion?"

Witherspoon took a sip of tea. He said, "To be honest with you, I was in a daze for the first little while. Felt like a fish out of water, second-guessing my decision to leave my people behind during this sabbatical. And then, seeing everyone so happy here, singing songs, getting work done—every day I was just *waiting* for someone to hand me some sort of cryptic note."

"Oh, really? Saying what?"

"Maybe a plea for help or warning me to leave. I don't know..."

The Prescient One shook his head and smiled. "That's all so twentieth century. I suppose there's been some real *cults* in the Internet Age, but nothing on the scale of Modestianity. Could you imagine if we really had, what, sex dungeons in the basements? With all the tiny cameras and sensors everywhere? We'd be exposed in a heartbeat!"

"That's not really my area of expertise. But maybe someone was blackmailing you. Or..." Matthias paused. "Well, that was part of what I came here to find out. If you were for real."

"Aha, so this *wasn't* purely a spiritual quest for you, Mr. Witherspoon. Interesting. You came also to snoop around. Why? Or more to the point, for whom?"

"For myself, dammit!" Matthias nearly yelled. "Before I went and made any other big life changes, I had to be sure you were legit. The real deal. I couldn't be no sucka—a fool!—like I'd been makin' these men act all up in those prisons!"

Reverend Witherspoon sat back in a huff. The Prescient One stood up, then reached into a desk drawer and pulled out a small picture frame. He handed it to Matthias before returning to his seat.

"Look at that face," the Prescient One said. "That was me fifteen years ago. When I was just a regular fellow working in the video gaming world. We all change, Matthias. Sometimes for the better, sometimes not. But as *you* must surely preach, no man or woman is permitted to give up on his chance at redemption."

Matthias wiped an eye with the back of his hand. "No, we're not."

"I don't blame you for projecting your own regrets onto my church. That suspicion not only brought you here, but led you to a much closer examination of who we are. Trust me, I'm well aware that many of our members first came here out of material desperation, and not faith. But what good is a religion if it is solely focused on the ethereal and doesn't aid people in their daily lives?"

"Hale-Bopp," Matthias said and chuckled to himself. "To the stars and beyond."

The Prescient One nodded solemnly.

"So the question is, Reverend Witherspoon, what will you decide to do now that you've confirmed in your heart that we are pure? We would be honored if you converted to Modestianity. And I would personally attend the ceremony."

Matthias handed the frame back. He looked down into his hands and said, "I could. And maybe I *should*. I have so much to learn. But that would be the easy way. Or... the popular choice. Because to do that would say to my people, 'Hey y'all, these guys over here seem more effective, so let's run into their corner while the gettin's good.' "

The Prescient One smiled warmly. "And we would welcome them all."

"But we already have our God. We have our Holy Scriptures."

"The spiritual—"

"But no!" Witherspoon said, shaking his fist. "These folks have their homes, their families... their *way of life*. Who am I to tell them to drop everything and follow some white man—or blue man, whatever the hell color you paint yourself—why should they follow you, when there's no commonality at the *root?*"

"Perhaps," the sage said after a pause. "But Modestianity is the ultimate colorblind religion because it's so new. We have no dusty old baggage. No mistranslated texts. No feuds, no prejudices…"

Matthias laughed, almost angrily. He said, "Then it's even more irrelevant to my people. *We do* have baggage. We got real history!"

The Prescient One brought his hands together. "So your choice is this. Just let it all go here with us and make a fresh start. Or do you have the courage to dig in and tear everything apart?"

"We have no choice, Your Prescience. I *got* to find the strength to face what's inside. Hold up every beautiful silk shirt and every stained pair of drawers we got packed in that suitcase we been carrying around. It's the only way forward."

The Prescient One folded his arms over the picture frame and nodded definitively. "So you've come to a decision," he said. "I'm glad, truly."

Matthias laid his palms on his knees and rocked his head from side to side. His eyes were closed. Slowly a smile transformed his tense face. He looked up at the Prescient One. "Now I see. You *are* a wise man. A good man."

"I thank you, Matthias. It is my belief that you are one as well."

Witherspoon clapped his hands together. He said happily, "I shall call you the King of Clarity. Or maybe… the Dean of Dialectic."

"You honor me," the Prescient One said, smiling once more. "While most people do know in their hearts what they want, sometimes they have to put it into words to see what's required to achieve it."

"Mmm… So you couldn't just *send* me home. Because *telling* me that this was the right thing to do would leave my mind full of doubt every step of the way back to my church. But as soon as *I* said those words…"

The reverend's face eased into an expression of total satisfaction.

"We make a pretty good team, don't we?" the Prescient One said. "When the dust settles on all this political chaos, perhaps one day you and I will have the opportunity to share a unified message with the American people."

"I would like that. Very much." Matthias cleared his throat. "But I've got a lot of work to do between now and then. If this whole Reparations thing is about to go away, I need to prepare my people."

"Indeed. But don't feel as if you have to fight the battles alone, Reverend. Call on us for any insights or assistance you might need."

Matthias rose and took the Prescient One's right hand into his own hands. "Sir, I don't know how to thank you for all that your existence has done to put me back on the straight and narrow. Truly, I had lost my way." He shook his head to try and stifle a chuckle, then continued, "I know the Lord doesn't always give us the road map, but damn if I still can't believe that it was your kooky Modestian family that—"

A booming flash came out of nowhere. Matthias felt himself stumble across the room. He landed painfully on his left side. Rolling back onto his elbows, he saw the space filling with smoke in the half-light. Suddenly a number of black-clad figures fanned out with weapons drawn.

Matthias, stunned into near-deafness, cowered in the shadows as he watched the bright cape of the Prescient One hoisted up into the air. He lay in stupefied horror as the stormtroopers carried the Modestian leader out of the room through the breach.

A light flashed into his eyes. He raised a sore arm in front of his face, but an instant later the light moved away. He found himself alone in the Prescient One's bombed-out private chambers.

After several tense minutes, Matthias cautiously made his way out of the smoky room. He wandered blindly down a dark corridor, and as his hearing slowly returned, tragic wails echoed through the Church of Modestianity's inner sanctum.

The Prescient One was gone.

20. RIDING THE WIND

Arizona Senator Victor Dominguez was back home in Flagstaff for the Tribesgiving recess. He'd enjoyed simple pleasures like driving his three children to school, even if Michael the oldest made a stink about not being able to ride on the bus with his friends.

The home-cooked meals around the family table with Jaclyn at his side almost enabled Victor to dial back the clock and forget the whirlwind that he had just lived for the past year. He tried to savor these quiet moments at home, rather than replay for the thousandth time all that could have been.

He knew that people faced defeat every day. His daughter's youth basketball team had lost just the other evening, in fact. Victor's election failure happened to be on a national stage and with much bigger stakes, however. But as he had told little Yasmin, she would have to learn from the loss and put it behind her—because there were many more games left for her to play in life. Many shots to take, and other important challenges to stand up to.

The senator tried to internalize all this while driving home alone after having dropped off his youngest child Nina at a morning playdate. But he suspected that his own defeat more resembled that of a young sports phenom who entered the professional leagues too early, and then for various reasons never peaked during his career. Would the Rebellican Party really nominate him again in four years? What headspace would the country even be in at that time?

No, on paper he seemed destined to serve perhaps two or three terms in the Senate, before moving on to lucrative work as a consultant or lobbyist. Had he really consigned himself to all that when delivering his concession speech on Election Night?

At the last second Victor veered his truck onto I-17 South instead of continuing directly home. Because that new option on his life's horizon had the power to throw his name right back in the ring—and he needed to consult with a trusted friend before making that crucial decision.

After an hour's drive down to Cottonwood, Victor stepped out of the vehicle and quietly approached the long curved wall of stone. He placed a small bundle of flowers into the mounted vase, then closed his eyes for a moment.

"Hello, Papa," he said. "I'm sorry for not coming to see you much lately. But I hope you can understand."

Victor rested a hand on the marble plaque that honored the late Eugenio Dominguez.

"And now I must ask for your advice. You see, I've been on such a wild journey these past few years—always rising, rising —and just when it seemed to have ended, and I was starting to make peace with that... Suddenly a new path opened up again. And frankly, Father, it has me terrified."

Senator Dominguez gazed down the length of the memorial wall. So many lives sealed behind the marble and stone. Dead, but not forgotten, he hoped.

Victor found that he was uncomfortable speaking like this, as if all the ghosts here might listen in on his private thoughts. He stepped away from his father's grave and began to stroll around the Catholic cemetery's contoured grounds.

"Oh Papa... I have always wanted to make you proud. You risked so much when you came to this country, but everything was simpler in your time. Wake up early, go to work, unclog people's drains, come home with the paycheck for Mama to buy us dinner. But now, for me..."

Victor trailed off. His attention had been caught by some sort of large bird that was arcing and swinging across the sky, and barely needing to flap its wings as it deftly rode the wind. He resumed his walk, all the while keeping this bird visible out of the corner of his eye.

"This opportunity... I keep asking myself, will it be good for the country? Because I already know what it could do for *me*. So Papa, now I must know, is this what *you* would have wanted me to do? Because although you never fully lost your accent, I know how important it was to you and Mama that Rita and I were *American.*

"But the 1970 or even 2000 version of that word is quite different from what it has meant lately. If your generation was forced to add the hyphen, it signified that you had chosen to *become* a Mexican-American. Today it seems to be the opposite. We aren't all Americans now—we're all just *in* America.

"And Father, I fear that this new… proposed venture is less about pride than it is about power. Seizing it and flaunting it angrily. Your immigrant's humility is being replaced by… something very unpleasant, just because people can."

Victor started moving back toward his truck. He said, "Cornelius Alemán seems more interested in assembling an army than even a voting bloc. He wants me to help give his movement legitimacy. But—he says there are others, many others in business and politics who have already joined him. I could lose a great deal simply by refusing this man, if he still succeeds without me.

"Oh Papa, I miss hearing your wise words. But I'm afraid that your mind couldn't handle the choices we are required to make in today's world. Perhaps it is better that you have passed on."

Dominguez took a last look at the mausoleum wall through his windshield. The people of the past were filed away and suspended in that silent geometric grid. But *he* still had life flowing through him.

Victor vowed that he would not allow himself to be hushed, or manipulated, or forced into doing anything that went against what he knew to be right.

After a quiet prayer of thanks, he started the engine and began the drive home.

21. THE BRIGHTEST STAR

Clyde Jenkins didn't like what he heard coming from upstairs. His sister Myra and her boyfriend Octavius were arguing over something. Again.

He glanced over at his nephew Tyrell—Myra's first kid, but fathered by another guy who was out of the picture. The boy was intently focused on the video game they were playing, his fingers moving across the controller faster than Clyde could believe.

"You ain't playin'," Tyrell said.

"Sorry."

Clyde returned his focus to the enormous TV on which a dozen military personnel were stealthily moving toward the perimeter of a fort. Tracer bullets began to whiz past as the group neared the fence.

"Find cover!" Tyrell commanded.

"Where do I go?" Clyde said.

"Behind that truck… Run!"

One of the soldiers on screen fell in a burst of red spray, but all of the others safely made their way behind a burnt-out troop transport vehicle.

"Now what do we do?" Clyde asked. "We're still taking heat."

Tyrell looked down at his controller and pressed a dizzying combination of buttons. He said, "I got to order up some bombs."

"Oh yeah? One of these dudes here got like a bazooka in his bag?"

"Nah. Hold up. You'll see."

A moment later a dull roar came out of the surround-sound speakers, then the TV screen filled with orange flame and a billowing mushroom cloud.

"Yeah!" Tyrell said. "Let's move out…"

Clyde smiled. His little nephew already knew this war game well enough to call in the airstrikes. Then he heard a real-time thud come down through the living room ceiling. He wondered if *he* should call the police…

Probably not. He'd wait to see what his mother would do. She was in her bedroom upstairs and would know if… or when… to intervene.

"Aw… now you dead!" Tyrell said.

Clyde had let his soldier trail behind the group and an enemy rifleman who had survived the bombing shot him through the head.

"Sorry," Clyde said. "Get into that base without me, I guess."

"No doubt."

"Hey, I'ma take a break until you get to the next level."

Clyde went into the kitchen and opened the fridge to grab a soda. It was packed with leftovers from the previous day's feast. The Jenkins family, for all its imperfections, truly did have a lot to be grateful for this Tribesgiving.

He took his goose down jacket from a chairback and stepped

out onto the little patio that was behind the family's condo. He glanced up at the lighted window of the room that Myra and Octavius shared. Their daughter Sarah was probably inside with them too. Things seemed to have quieted down for the moment.

Clyde sipped his drink, easing back onto the wood railing as he looked at the sky. Pockets of stars revealed themselves as the clouds moved past. He focused on a particularly bright star and waited for it to reappear after each cloud.

He wondered which part of this scene he was supposed to be. The cloud in motion, making its way across the land—or the shimmering light sitting as a fixed guide?

A muffled shout came through the upstairs window. It was the same kind of lovers' quarrel he had been witness to since the succession of his mother's boyfriends during his own childhood. At least those guys barely laid a hand on him—he'd heard some pretty rough stories of abuse from other kids he knew growing up.

Clyde exhaled wearily. He'd tried his best to set everything up nice. With all that money his song "Fly So High" brought in, the least he could do was try to give Myra and her kids a better place to call home away from the old neighborhood. And he did like Octavius too—a hard-edged guy to be sure, but one who always came at Clyde straight.

Still, Clyde was only a teenager. After every fight that took place under the roof that his magic money had provided, he sensed that there were just some things he couldn't understand, or fix.

He thought about his recent talk with Nolan. The mentor who seemed adamant that Clyde "sell out to get out." Or was it more accurately, get out to survive? To leave these streets where people still fought and shit and screamed as if nothing good had ever come their way.

Clyde heard the patio door open. Tyrell poked his head out.

"I'ma go to bed in a minute," the boy said.

"Oh yeah?" Clyde smiled. "Lemme come in and say good night then."

A half hour later and all was quiet in the Jenkins residence. Clyde had helped his nephew get ready for sleep, and all the while he didn't hear any sounds from the other bedrooms. He didn't know if Octavius had slipped out for some Friday night action while he was standing on the patio, but usually it was best to leave others to their own business.

Clyde went back down to the living room and started flipping through the channels, although he wasn't really paying attention. He still felt uneasy, like he was butting up against some sort of invisible barrier. What was it?

Sometimes he just wanted to roll up to a club and let the remaining DJC mystique attract whatever good times might be had. But the people close to him kept saying that he could do *more*.

He knew he had some sort of talent... or potential... or a spark that the average person didn't. Otherwise a hot shot agent like Eddie Pryor wouldn't be so persistent about trying to sign him. And the local big timers who'd recruited him to record that silly chorus recently, they wanted him too. But was his choice only between cranking out club hits in town, or to take a leap of faith into the arms of a shifty white man whose agenda Clyde didn't really know?

Just then the TV caught his eye as it cut to some urgent news report. A lady holding a microphone was in a massive building, and people were running all around her in a panic. The camera panned to show others on the floor weeping.

"We're here," the woman said, "inside the Mall of Absolution, which is home to the mysterious Church of Modestianity. Normally members of the press are granted only limited access, but today an unprecedented event has taken place."

A man in a blue robe ran up and took the woman's microphone into his hands. He said breathlessly, "They're saying the Prescient One was responsible for the HRA hack! They came in, blew apart his sanctuary, and now he's gone! What will become of us?" He dropped the microphone and ran off.

Clyde leaned in and listened to the details of what had happened.

The reporter was back on, saying, "...this may be the last, and biggest, of the sweeping net of arrests that have reined in the Sentinels of Jubilee, the rogue group which claimed responsibility for infiltrating the MARVIN supercomputer back in early October..."

Then came a brief biography of the Prescient One, alter ego of former game developer and ousted HRA system designer

Scott Cullen. "…overnight success who transformed from hard-partying playboy into an enigmatic philosopher dressed in teal, who now preaches his own reactionary brand to thousands of followers desperate for answers in these complicated and troubled times."

Clyde muted the TV. Suddenly he sensed the possibility of a third way forward for himself. A small, calculated pivot he could make. Because this man they were talking about on the TV, he too had become famous unexpectedly, and ultimately chose to "do his own thing" by creating a platform to share his beliefs.

But what do I believe. Or know, really?

This Cullen guy had been tapped into what was going on for years before he made his big choice. Would Clyde have to navigate the waters within the music industry for a while before finally seeing the personal path that fit who he was?

In a way, he was groping to *endure* as the Beneficiary who had once spoken so effectively for other Beneficiaries. But were his blind spots or lack of life experience too great an obstacle? Clyde hadn't been groomed to face the public the way that lifelong actors and politicians were.

Did he even want the responsibility of helping people just because they shared his skin color? All that deep history to think about, but he was barely sixteen years old. Maybe what he wanted was simply not to be trapped, or pigeon-holed as one thing or another.

Clyde smiled. *Pigeon*-holed. Like Nolan, who was also reinventing himself. Growing. Maturing. Trying to leave the questionable aspects of his past behind.

All of these older guys that Clyde knew had *stories*. Nolan living overseas, doing God-knows-what for the military. Sylicon and D-Eel with kids all over the place. This Prescient dude designing video games and inventing a religion. But Clyde…

He just wrote one song and then the world had opened up to him. Maybe that was too easy, not the way it was supposed to be for anyone. It was called "success," but he didn't have the callouses or past disappointments to make it feel like more than a dream.

But you couldn't go back and reverse engineer any of that. He'd just never know what it felt like to bang your head against the wall for years hoping for a breakthrough—as Nolan had tried to explain to him. He also didn't have that taste of betrayal on his tongue which had driven Scott Cullen insane—and then turned him from an ally of Beneficiaries into an enemy saboteur.

But, Clyde thought, this Church of Modestianity didn't come across as super anti-Reparations. He'd heard a little in the past about their weird rituals and funky costumes. They seemed more interested in hiding away and dancing around than fighting the government.

Clyde turned the volume back on when he saw a large, round black head fill the TV screen.

"…with the Reverend Matthias G. Witherspoon," the reporter was saying. "He's been visiting the Mall while on sabbatical from his own *Christian* church back in Ohio. Now, sir, you say you were actually meeting personally with the Prescient One when he was taken away?"

"Yes, ma'am," Matthias said, wiping dusty beads of perspiration from his temple. "We were in deep discussion about fate and life's challenges."

"So," the woman continued, "as a Beneficiary yourself, I have to ask, what are your thoughts knowing now that you were having a heart-to-heart with one of the alleged masterminds behind the hack that nearly crippled the HRA?"

Witherspoon shook his head angrily. "Y'all just don't get it. This man is thinking on a higher level! Beneficiaries… Debtors… who cares? We've all got so much work to do—on ourselves, our society, how we're going to live… Not just with each other— white, black, yellow, brown—but with all those ones and zeroes that are tracking us and judging us more harshly than any God I ever spoke to. Do you catch what I'm sayin'? It's not enough to *repent* anymore! But, do we *retreat* into the shadows, or *retaliate* viciously against this surveillance state? America, will you *recoil* in horror at the tech monster we've let loose, or—"

The reporter yanked her microphone away. "Thank you, uh, Reverend Witherspoon, for your comments. We've got to move along and speak with other Modestians…"

Clyde shut off the TV. He really needed to think now. There was something about this business at the Mall that electrified him. He sensed that… it was all so much bigger than how his mind had perceived the world only minutes ago.

The Prescient One was not just a guy sitting in his apartment writing beats and tossing them out into the ether, like a fisherman casting a line with no bait attached. But Clyde had gone that route, and it was a preposterous miracle that he not only got a nibble, but had in fact caught a giant whale with the song "Fly So High." The least he could do right now was seize upon that gift of fate by making a firm life decision. Because he finally felt like he had, maybe not *all* the information, but still a much better perspective on things.

If that Prescient fellow could go from computer nerd in a dorm room to one day offering salvation to all kinds of people, then Clyde figured there was no telling what he himself might be able to do with his own bigger ideas down the road.

But which ideas? Clyde didn't even know! But that was okay. It was time for him to get more professional as a musician, and start clearing out those blind spots.

"Okay, LA," he said to himself, "think you ready for DJC?"

22. SECRET THRILL

Chris had just run out for a quick double-errand—walk the dogs around the block after the long car ride home from Maine, as well as pick up to-go coffees for himself and Kate—so he was more than surprised to see her *repacking* her suitcase on the bed when he got back.

"Are you leaving me?" he asked jokingly while handing over her drink, but still feeling a touch of fear deep beneath his words.

She smiled, saying, "No, but duty calls!"

"In and out just like that, jeez. Back to DC then?"

Kate turned and reached into a closet, saying with a sigh, "I'm afraid things have become a bit more urgent than they were before."

"More than twenty minutes ago?"

"Apparently!" Kate removed two blouses from their hangers. "I can't pinpoint it, but something in the air really has people shook up lately."

Chris darted his eyes around the room. "So, um, where are they sending you?"

"Jamaica."

"*Jamaica?* I'm pretty sure they were a British colony."

"I know, I know. But we've got the infrastructure. It's time to help the UK set up offices, install document scanners, get their system online and repaying some debts."

"Oh," Chris said softly. "So how long are you going for?"

Kate stepped into the bathroom and unzipped a toiletry bag, then began placing items from the counter and medicine cabinet inside.

"For... a while..." She couldn't resist a smile. "Yeah, I'm really helping them do this thing!"

"So the trip's open-ended?" Chris sat on the bed.

"Jamaica's not the only country on my itinerary, either. What I don't know is if the HRA will have me come home in between, or just puddle jump."

Chris popped the cover off his coffee and drank from the lip of the cup. He said, "Kate, I know this is what you always wanted, but remember all that talk about starting a family? Does it just get pushed back, like a rescheduled flight?"

Kate looked up, then stepped closer and gave him a light kiss. "Are you saying it was something you wanted now, too?"

"We kind of let my parents know, right? I mean, I've had plenty of time to think, especially with you being so busy at work."

"I know. I'm sorry."

"But this, what I'll be doing while you're gone... holding it all together... what exactly is the point? For the Beneficiaries? For social justice? For the president? I just feel like I need more of an incentive than any of that... or whatever the next job title you get turns out to be."

Kate's eyes widened. "You want *more*... or are you asking me to make a choice?"

"I don't know," Chris said. "It's not even that I want something *else*, but whatever this life is right now is not *working*. Something's off, out of phase. And I just don't know if I need a screwdriver or a sledgehammer to fix it."

Kate pulled away slowly. "Well," she said brightly as she put on a smile, "we certainly do have a way of leaving things on a cliffhanger. But I really have to run. The car's picking me up in fifteen minutes. And Chris... I can't help but suspect that once

I'm in the whirl of all this overseas business, that our conversation tonight won't be at the forefront of my thoughts. But *you'll* still be brooding. And I don't want that for you—for us."

Chris was silent for a moment. The room felt heavy in the stillness.

"I guess just try to call me when you can," he said. "I'll get your bags when you're ready."

He walked out of the room.

Kate stood there absently for a moment. As eager as she had been to get back into the swing of life after an unusually quiet car ride home, she was also secretly thrilled when that phone call came in telling her to pack her things for Jamaica.

Now, after the latest exchange with Chris, she realized that some of this very same tension had been present during their trip. An evasive moodiness in his demeanor which she couldn't just pass off as the fatigue that came from dealing with one's family in close quarters.

Kate folded each article of clothing and placed it neatly into the suitcase. She watched the accents of her machine-made diamond engagement ring reflect vividly in the room's soft light.

Suddenly she wanted nothing more than to be out of this apartment and on the road again.

23. PREDATOR AND PREY

"Got a light?"

"Yeah, sure. Here."

The burly man reached into the pocket of his black canvas jacket and pulled out a silver Zippo.

"A classic," the other man said, lighting up and inspecting the chrome piece before handing it back.

"Yup. My dad got it back in the day."

"Nice. What time do you guys go on?"

"We're next. You, uh, you a fan?"

"Oh yeah! Never too old to rock, right?"

"Haha, I'm trying. What's your name, by the way?"

The first man held out his hand and smiled. "Marcus," he said. "Nice to meet you."

"Likewise. Glenn. Alright, I'm gonna head back in."

FBI Special Agent Marcus Young watched him pass through the front entrance, then gave his own cigarette one long last drag before tossing it down into the street. Real tobacco smokes were a rare treat these days.

But, Marcus mused, he had already encountered a number of throwbacks during this stakeout on the life of Glenn Murray. Old cars, old combat boots, and tonight an old flip-top lighter.

Marcus, tasked with collaring this suspected SOJ spy, had followed him down from Philadelphia to this dive bar in Manassas, Virginia. Glenn's band Bleeding the Aggregate was performing tonight, and then—perhaps he would rendezvous with other conspirators to damage HRA infrastructure.

During all his years as an FBI agent, Marcus Young tried to get as close to his quarry as possible. Was it in order to better know the man, or just some kind of sick personal thrill? Part of the lifelong process of understanding the criminal mind—or was he testing the effectiveness of his own facade?

Either way, Marcus had felt compelled to come down from his crow's nest of surveillance and meet Glenn in person. He'd outfitted himself with a faded leather jacket and torn jeans, then even painted his fingernails black in an effort to blend in with the rough-edged crowd that attended these punk rock concerts.

He stepped inside the venue, paid the modest cover charge, and ordered a beer at the bar. A small melee of bodies was churning a chaotic circle in front of the stage, where a high-energy trio was blasting away.

This was the sort of tangible data that you could only get by playing chameleon and inhabiting the world of your target. The two-man team that was hanging back in an unmarked car couldn't *feel* what was going on in the way that Marcus did right now. Not only were surveillance cameras and microphones limited in what they could monitor—Marcus wanted to *taste* his prey.

The bass player on stage sent a searing and gravelly "Yeah!" into his microphone, then held the yell until his voice slowly died away.

Marcus felt the impact of that howl in his core. This was why he *loved* going undercover and being right there in the midst of real life. All of a sudden the Mall of Absolution felt very far away, and in turn his life as a Modestian... Had he merely bought into that role too deeply?

These were not the types of thoughts that Special Agent Marcus Young could afford to have right now. He was supposed to be a hardcore-punk music fan out having a good time on a Saturday night. He picked up his neglected beer and quickly drank half of it down, then set the pint glass onto the bar loudly. No one paid him any mind.

Half an hour later, after Glenn's band had set up on stage, Marcus made his way into the crowd of sixty-plus that was in attendance. He stood safely away from the slam-dancers up front, but was still close enough to take in Glenn's visceral performance.

The canvas jacket was off now, and pasty freckled arms were strangling a silver-capped microphone as he unleashed a raspy wail. Then Glenn moved left, planting his boot onto a speaker and pointing menacingly into the crowd. He tilted his head back and roared, with his face and beard changing colors under the flashing stage lights.

"Another... changing of the guard! Why bother... the plan marches on!"

Who was this man? Marcus asked himself. A talented performer with the kind of charisma that demanded you pay attention. The way that Glenn took possession of the stage, surely his band couldn't just be a cover for the SOJ activities. Besides, Marcus had seen several people wearing Bleeding the Aggregate t-shirts, and the small merchandise table was doing respectable business.

As the enveloping assault of blistering crust-punk continued around him, Marcus wondered if this Glenn Murray knew something that he didn't. Was this imposing man not only righteous, but *right* in his anger toward the HRA?

Marcus himself had always felt mostly ambivalent towards the Reparations movement. Being three-quarters black and coming from a family of educated professionals, he had lived a privileged life that was anchored in constant work and striving. His friendships were based on the sports he played, the college he and his wealthy classmates attended.

So the HRA and its spray-and-pray method of dispensing funds to anyone who happened to fall into the Beneficiary class

—this as a philosophical approach just seemed alien to him. His family had already risen; he didn't need anyone else's help.

As for his brothers and sisters in the so-called black community... Marcus felt more palpable kinship as a member of the law enforcement fraternity. No matter a person's race, creed, or gender—when you put on that badge, you were all working toward the organization's common goals.

Just like when Marcus was an individual player on his college baseball *team*. And as he had later become one small but valued part of the living, breathing, growing idea that was the Church of Modestianity.

Marcus suddenly fought his way back toward the bar. He ordered a shot of whiskey and sent it down, then motioned for another even while knowing that this was going a step beyond the role he was supposed to be playing. Have one or two beers throughout the night, fine. But don't get wasted drunk and risk exposing yourself...

"They don't realize it yet," Marcus muttered. "They don't see what's at stake."

"What's that?" the bartender called out over the din, looking up from the drink he was mixing a few feet away.

"Nothing," Marcus said with a wave. "Same old shit."

"Ha, don't I know it!" The bartender shook his head with a sheepish grin, then walked away carrying a glass in each hand.

Marcus leaned onto the bar and looked back at the stage. Glenn was in full command up there—confident, surging, completely in his element.

Then he looked down at the black polish on his fingernails. A few tones lighter and he'd be no different than the Prescient One. Just another costumed man playing out a role, hiding or reacting...

"Lost! Lost!" Glenn growled into the microphone.

Marcus looked at him again, then at all the people in the club. Everyone *was* lost. But still on alert, always seeking the voice or the idea that would set them back on a good path.

A sick feeling rose up from Marcus's stomach. It wasn't the alcohol or tobacco though. It was dread. Because if his intuition was correct, he would have to arrest Glenn Murray—the very man who seemed so sure of himself, of the truth, and of how things ought to be.

And if this was the type of person that the government

wanted to lock up, then Special Agent Marcus Young was almost ashamed to be a part of the net that was slowly closing in to silence Glenn's plaintive voice.

He closed his tab at the bar and walked back out into the chilly night. He would surely see Glenn Murray again sometime after the show—all that remained was the how and when.

24. FALLING AWAY

As he packed a work bag in the silence of his home office, Chris Donohugh wondered if he would ever again find a way to really shine. The near future in his mind's eye didn't seem to hold much promise of that, not for someone who had spent a lifetime putting the needs of others ahead of his own.

He pictured Kate seven months pregnant, arriving home for a quick weekend in the city, then back down to DC doing her critical work. He of course would be available to accommodate her at all times. And later, when the baby came, maybe even be expected to close up shop on his life in New York City and relocate to Northern Virginia. Because he couldn't very well live apart from his newborn, or leave so much responsibility to his in-laws.

And yet... fatherhood! His own little child to teach how to ride a bike. There would be birthdays, with Kate bringing out the cake... He would be taking pictures to capture the moment... But perhaps deep in his breast, that one secret betrayal would live on intertwined with the frustrations and disappointments that lingered.

Chris left the apartment with the pawn-shop laptop stowed in his carry bag. He took the subway on a circuitous route, stepping off at random stations and once even letting his desired train pass by, before finally ending up in the area of Central Park.

He bought a coffee with cash from a bakery that faced an open courtyard, then took a seat on the semi-enclosed patio that had gas heaters. He opened the laptop and sipped his drink while it booted up—just another city dweller getting some work done while out and about.

"Dude," he typed. "Got some bad news. Big new project came up at work. Not sure I'm gonna be able to do any music for a while after all. Hope you can make something out of what we already jammed on."

Chris sent the message. Gently, he pressed the laptop lid down. Hopefully Glenn would accept that this was the end of the road.

He gazed outside through the unfurled clear plastic that housed the patio. A man in a navy pea coat was looking at him from the pavement outside. A hand went to the ear. Now the lips moved briefly. The other hand fidgeted inside a pocket.

Chris felt his body clench to near rigor mortis. Had he finally been caught? Were government agents converging for some horrific raid in broad daylight that dozens of cameras would record? Was the all-too-public scandal which had played out in his mind fifty times actually about to unfold?

Chris understood what he had to do. Casually pack up his things, then meander back inside the cafe to dispose of his cup, just like any other responsible citizen on his way to the restroom. He would next dash into the kitchen and look for a way out back. If someone was waiting for him there—

Suddenly the man standing out front began to nod his head, then pointed a finger in Chris's direction. Chris heard a firework explode inside his head as the man took a step forward...

Then in stunned silence, and with vivid tunnel vision, Chris saw a woman come into view from the left. The man turned toward her and gave a big smile as he leaned over the stroller she was pushing. The hand that was in the pocket slid out and flashed a small toy, then disappeared behind the stroller's canopy.

The couple embraced, then slowly walked away and out of view.

Chris stared down with unfocused eyes at the little table for nearly a minute. Slowly his heart rate dropped back to normal. He rose, put on his coat, packed the laptop away, and finally walked out the bakery's front door into the gray wintry day.

He was safe.

But something very hollow and troubling stayed with him. He had nowhere to go. No pressing work to do. No one to meet at home later in the afternoon—except two hungry dogs. His guy friends were all at normal day jobs…

Chris felt a longing that was encapsulated by the word *Kate*, but he couldn't shake the feeling that it came from a position of weakness or neediness. Whereas, if she was even thinking of him… He was taken for granted. An underling serving the boss's needs. A knot that just had to be massaged the right way so that she could get what she wanted.

Now he really didn't know what to do. He couldn't very well reopen the laptop and tell Glenn he was back on board helping the Sentinels bring the HRA crashing to its knees. But he also couldn't reach out to Kate—and risk coming across as the lonely spouse pathetically hounding the all-star who was busy making waves.

Chris turned his brain off and started walking through Central Park. If only these trees, whose leaves were dying and falling away, could impart some of their timeless stoicism to help him endure this crisis. Because at the moment, he felt dangerously close to losing himself altogether.

25. MORE PRIMITIVE

"But my good lady, perhaps we need more than simply money to heal our wounds. If indeed the white man used to rule over us, and now you are here to make amends… Should you not also send Caucasian laborers or servants to achieve this noble aim?"

Kate Donohugh stared incredulously across the walnut desk. Jamaica's Minister of Finance and the Public Service, the Honorable Thomas Howard Nelson, was smiling sardonically at her with arms folded over his stomach. Portraits of a dozen national heroes were mounted on the walls of this stately office.

"But sir," she said, "Reparations is primarily meant to settle the books. People must still be involved in their own lives, and responsible for shaping their future destiny."

"No, ma'am," Nelson said. "You do not get to set the terms of your concession. Not if it is to be seen as done in good faith. If you truly believe that you owe us for past crimes against our people, then surely it would be a conflict of interest if you were in charge of setting the parameters, and then to also act as the executor. No?"

"Honorable minister, my government is acting as an intermediary on behalf of the United Kingdom in this matter. What would you have us do?"

"Give us control of both the funds and the operation," Minister Nelson said flatly. "Who knows the island people better than those of us who also live here?"

"Mr. Nelson," Kate said, "surely you know that's not how our charter is written. I have to follow the letter of the law."

"Man, to hell with what's on that piece of paper!" the man burst out. "That's how we were all bought and sold to begin with. Hundreds of years of evil, chronicled in great detail by these documents—and now you dare to wave a new one in front of my face?"

"With all due respect, if there weren't any surviving historical documents then there would be no Reparations to speak of at all." Kate sighed. "I *really* hate to quote one of my ideological opponents, but the Dutch politician Erich Bakker made a valid point when testifying before the United Nations last year. He noted the irony of how cultures that had a written language and kept meticulous records, they are now the ones being held accountable. Whereas more primitive people, whose traditions were often communicated orally, have no such archives to track down and—"

The man sucked at his tongue, shaking his head sadly. "And there it is," he said. "The condescension I knew would come. Even from the mouths of so-called allies, I hear it all the time. But, what am I to do? If I kick you out of my office, they will just send another in your place. And the funds will be delayed for my principled troubles."

"Minister Nelson," Kate said as she forced a smile, "may I offer a personal insight? During my several years working for the HRA, I dealt intimately with members of the public, both Beneficiaries and Debtors. This... tension we're experiencing today is just part of the process. There is *a lot* of money on the line here. And that's why this *has* to be set up so formally, because the possibility for corruption is just too great otherwise."

"Do you think I, or my people, that we are tempted to steal, Mrs. Donohugh?"

Kate pursed her lips. "I make no such assumption," she said. "Nor did I write out the policies. But I *am* here as a liaison on behalf of the President of the United States, whose staff I have worked with personally. So I'm afraid that when I tell you there are strings attached—"

"They are actually ropes?" Nelson brought his fingertips together. "Thick hemp ropes, as once used on the great sailing ships that carried away my ancestors from their beloved homeland, which they had known for thousands of years."

"If you want," Kate said slowly, "to find a metaphor in everything I say, you probably can. But I do think we should try to get some work done here. My instructions say that five facilities should be set up to begin with. And since there are primarily Beneficiaries on the island, we won't have to build new divided structures, as we did back in the US. That should definitely expedite your country receiving its funds. So for one, I'll need someone to help research where the appropriate buildings might be found."

Minister Nelson paused. "Ma'am, I don't really know if this project is something we want to be a part of."

"But I don't understand. Your government has already come into de facto agreement…"

"When I hear you talk about doing this or that, telling me I need to find people to set up offices… It sounds to me like you are trying to assert control over my country."

"That's ridiculous."

"Yes, yes, I know." The minister leaned forward onto his elbows. "To you it may seem that way. But this has been America's playbook around the world in recent times. Instead of colonists or armies or missionaries, it is organizations such as yours, and the Peace Corps before that, which send attractive young ladies into poor countries under the guise of offering assistance to the lowly brown people. But nothing ever improves! All we are left with is your footprints, your litter, and the dangerous ideas you have put into the minds of our people."

"Sir," Kate bristled, "I have devoted fifteen years of my life to helping the less fortunate, be they black, white, trans, disabled —anyone who is marginalized in any way."

Mr. Nelson stood up. "Mrs. Donohugh," he said, "I am kindly asking you to leave. This office and my country."

"Like you said, they'll just send somebody else." And as Kate began to pack up her things, she was shocked to hear herself say bitterly, "Maybe someone who isn't as… personable as me."

The minister extended his hand formally.

"Then tell your people that next time, perhaps my response won't be as civil either. Yes," he added with a chuckle, "I shall act more… *primitively*. Good day to you."

26. IT AIN'T FAIR

The limo came to pick him up at noon. When he went to grab his bags, Tyrell wouldn't let go of his leg.

Clyde patted him on the head. "It's okay, kid. I ain't going forever."

A tear ran down one of Tyrell's cheeks. He bowed his head.

"Uncle Clyde, I need you to play them games with me."

Clyde looked up at his mother and sister who were standing nearby. Octavius was out, but they'd already shared a brief and uneventful farewell the night before.

"Game time is over, for a while," he said to his nephew.

"But it ain't fair," Tyrell said, his lips quivering.

"Oh my Lord," Dawna Jenkins said, lifting her grandson up into her arms. "You don't even know how much 'it ain't fair' there is to go 'round. Now come on and be a big boy for your uncle."

Tyrell buried his face into Dawna's shoulder.

"You makin' it hard for me," Clyde said. He gently rubbed Tyrell's back. "I'll see you soon, little man. Promise."

Myra leaned in and gave Clyde a hug. "Take care of yourself, baby brother. I'm so proud of you."

"Yeah. Do right by this boy here. He's my special buddy. You hear that, Mister Tee?"

Tyrell reached out his hand and Clyde gave it an energetic shake.

"You got to go now," Dawna said. "Don't forget about us."

"Why you say that, Mama?" Clyde gave her a big hug after Myra had taken Tyrell into her own arms. "I'll always still be me."

Dawna smiled. "In my heart you will. But now it's time to live your life. Go knock 'em dead."

The city he'd grown up in sped by on the way to the airport. After everything that had happened since the summer, all these people were still here chipping away at this game of life.

Somehow it was Clyde who had made a name for himself on the back of their suffering, and now he was leaving the cold Newark winter for a chance in sunny California. Other people did come and go from the old neighborhood, of course, but he had found a way *out*—even though for so long his heart had wanted to stick around and be with everybody.

But destiny was often just the right combination of timing and opportunity. Clyde finally understood that he would be a fool to not seize upon the DJ Clydoscope name for all it was worth right now. So he had called Eddie Pryor and told that slick LA agent what he had been waiting to hear—that Clyde was ready to play ball and go big time.

A liaison greeted Clyde when the limo pulled up to the curb at the Newark airport. This man instructed a skycap to load up Clyde's bags, then escorted him through the terminal.

At one point Clyde, who was dressed somewhat incognito hoping to avoid being spotted, paused when he saw a big sign for international departures. He stared at it for several seconds, until the liaison said, "Is something the matter, Mr. Jenkins?"

"No," Clyde said with a smile. "One step at a time."

"Very good, sir. Now, please follow me and we'll bypass those awful lines to get you on board much more quickly."

Not long afterward, Clyde was comfortably seated and awaiting takeoff. On the private jet that had been arranged by Eddie Pryor.

Clyde chuckled. By playing hard to get he had graduated from First Class to this. *And* with a flop of a second single sandwiched in between. Who else could claim that?

Probably another life lesson in there somewhere. Because only weeks ago he had been set on sticking to his guns with "Soul's Gold." Now his integrity wasn't so much being rewarded, as maybe taking a sideline to Eddie's more pressing interests.

But also, Clyde remembered seeing a lot of framed headshots on the wall at Nolan's favorite diner. They were signed by actors and singers who were all formally trained and probably quite talented, but who had just never caught a lucky break. Clyde knew he couldn't afford to squander his own good fortune.

When the little plane lifted off and popped out through the cloud cover, Clyde Jenkins had enough clarity of mind to sense that, while he might not fully know himself, it would all turn out okay. Because he was about to jump headlong into the professional arena, which would reveal to him and the world just who really was behind the DJ Clydoscope persona.

Genius? Fluke? Impostor? Or the next rising star headed for an unforgettable career?

I'm an uncle, Clyde thought. *A brother and a son. A Jenkins, forever.*

He looked out the window and contemplated the colorful sky, as his jet raced along in its quest to catch the receding sun.

27. A SHINE ON HIS SOUL

Reverend Witherspoon could not help but feel a touch of whimsical longing as he drove away from the Mall of Absolution. The people inside had given him a very special gift, yet he was now leaving them at a time of great uncertainty for the church.

The four days since the Prescient One's abduction had been filled with some of the most gut-wrenching moments of Matthias's life. The fear, pain, and confusion he saw on the once-bright faces of his Modestian friends might have brought a weaker man to despair.

But instead, Matthias Witherspoon saw this crisis as an opportunity to employ his newfound strength and clarity, as he helped shepherd many people across the bridge from shock to calm comfort. He told them to not lose hope, and look toward one another for reassurance—because God imposed setbacks not to cripple people's will, but as a challenge for them to redouble their resolve.

Yes, the Christian teachings he had shared over a lifetime while presiding over his own church, so many of them had translated beautifully at the Mall. And perhaps, Matthias thought, this was the key to the Prescient One's success. That man hadn't simply created a new religion out of whole cloth—because as quirky as many of its surface features were, everything in Modestianity's core was grounded in the realities of human life.

As Matthias came to understand while sitting in on the nightly mapmaking sessions, the religion initially sprang up as a *reactionary* belief system—society caught in the manic throes of twenty-first-century life—but had since opened itself up to any and all forms of *inspiration* that might further launch the souls of its people into fulfillment and joy.

Thus it was with a bittersweet swirl of emotions that Reverend Witherspoon decided it was time to depart for home. His own flock had been without a leader for two weeks now. And truth be told, the controversial Sunday sermon he delivered just prior to the election had sent a fracture through his church. Those members who viewed services as a kind of social event were appalled that Matthias would invoke so much fire and brimstone, let alone aim any of that judgmental wrath at the congregation itself. Some of them up and quit, while others demanded the preacher either recant or resign his post.

Thankfully for Matthias, about a third of his followers resonated with his admonishment to hold themselves more accountable in the game of life. This group refused to let their voices be drowned out. They told the complainers that the purpose of a church was to challenge oneself, and not simply serve as a venue to strut around in fancy suits and floral dresses.

Under the dark shadow of this rift, Witherspoon had announced his intention to take a leave of absence so that he might find the solution to all of their woes. Each side sheepishly agreed to a temporary ceasefire until the reverend's return.

And now he was going home.

Fortified in ways that he couldn't have imagined, but certainly hoped to be. Tested by the unforeseen trauma of a special ops team descending upon the Mall in a stealth raid. Then feeling the weight of oppression in subsequent days, as other law enforcement members patrolled the corridors.

And ultimately, walking away with a shine on his soul courtesy of these idealistic Modestian believers and their resilient spirit. As the spark of life returned to their eyes, and confidence in the church's strength was reaffirmed—that was the moment Matthias knew he could leave them in good conscience.

The remaining church leaders had in fact called a general assembly, where they played a previously recorded speech by the Prescient One entitled "Continuing the Covenant." He declared that he would soon depart from the Mall—either by choice or by force—but was confident that the end result would only bring more glory to the Church of Modestianity.

Initial shock at their leader's announcement—that he actually *planned* or *expected* to leave them—soon gave way to faithful acceptance, because he always seemed to have a forward-thinking plan. They took heart in his commitment to always act as their guide. Therefore, if he ever disappeared from sight, it was not because he had abandoned them.

Matthias hated to see their leader's name dragged through the mud, particularly after his own enlightening discussion with the man. The reverend was still processing the allegation that the Prescient One was *also* that masked man who had delivered the Sentinels of Jubilee's staggering existential warning nearly two months ago.

Witherspoon chuckled to himself. Yes, he still was and would always be a Christian, but in this instance he chose to humbly defer to the Prescient One and trust in the other man's penetrating insights.

In the meantime, he had a great deal of work to do back home in Akron, Ohio. The first order of business was to repair the splinter inside his church before it turned into an all-out civil war. Next he would begin investing resources to strengthen his local community, just as he had vowed to do in that contentious Sunday sermon.

If the Church of Modestianity was now experiencing its first dark night of the soul, then his own people had already endured a torturous half-millennium. Matthias vowed that he would work tirelessly for his black brothers and sisters so that they might heal, rebuild, and find common ground. None of them could afford to face the future with bitterness toward one another.

Because as Matthias had sensed in a chillingly prescient vision of his own, neither fork in the Reparations highway boded well for black folk in America. Any decline or dilution of the

HRA would be painful enough, but still worse... If the Reparations movement planned to spread worldwide in order to keep itself relevant as a brand, then surely the original Beneficiaries would be forgotten in the expanding gold rush. He would have to mentally prepare his people for all of these contingencies now.

As the Reverend Matthias G. Witherspoon drove along the cold interstate heading south, he thought he saw a glint of the Prescient One smiling at him in the rear view mirror. He began to hum to himself as he plotted out the next sermon he would deliver to the members of his church.

"My people, my people. It is *good* to be back home once again. But now it's time for all of us to get to work..."

28. SUDDENLY

Chris Donohugh found himself almost giddy as he scrambled to clean up the mess he'd created throughout the apartment in the four days since Kate had left town. Now she was suddenly on her way back—something bad had happened, but her messages as to exactly what had all been vague. The only thing she would confirm was that it had nothing to do with her health.

He was amazed at how quickly all of the emotions that had been crushing him simply rinsed away at the very thought of his wife coming home early. He allowed himself to savor the feeling, and didn't worry about how long until she went back out on the road.

Instead he cranked up his stereo system and had a "heavy metal cleaning day." This had once been the tradition among Chris and his college roommates, and it was an incredible way to quickly get the household chores done. Wicked-fast drummers set the pace, a bunch of angry singers kept you on task, and whammy-bar-powered guitar solos inspired heroic acts of sweeping and scrubbing. And today, two dogs also provided backing vocals.

When Kate arrived home that evening, Chris was sitting on the couch with legs crossed on the ottoman. His heart and the

Corgis all jumped at the same instant.

He entered the front hall just as she stooped down to receive the dogs' love. She looked up—eyes and face so tired—but still the beautiful girl he'd fallen in love with all those years ago.

"Hi, babe!" he called as he rushed over to her. "I'm so glad you're home."

Kate stood up, dropping wearily into his open arms. "I am most definitely home. Whew!"

Chris carried her bags into the apartment as she slipped off her jacket and pulled out a dining room chair.

"Oh… my… goodness," Kate said. She rubbed her face with her hands. "I am one tired girl."

"And thirsty too?" Chris asked. He stepped into the kitchen and removed a bottle of wine from the pantry shelf.

"Could be!" Kate extended her hand to receive it, then inspected the label. "Ooh. Milton Ravine… From 'twenty-five? I didn't know we had this!"

"Nope." Chris smiled. "I picked it up this afternoon."

"Aw… Please, do the honors. I only have enough energy left to lift a stem."

"Certainly, m'lady."

Chris made a silly show of formally presenting the Merlot with a dish towel draped over his forearm. He mumbled in a French accent as he removed the cork and set it on the table. Kate played along in her role of snooty restaurant patron, first by swirling the sample pour doubtfully, then sipping and finally approving with a dignified nod.

When a red drop of the wine ran down along the outside edge of her glass and clung to the lip of the base for an unbearable second, Kate stuck out a finger to dab it, then brought it up to her tongue. They both burst out laughing.

Chris sat down at the corner seat beside her and smiled. He said, "So, to what disaster do I owe this surprise visit?"

Kate assumed a haughty formal tone and said, "The Honorable Minister Thomas Howard Nelson, of Such-and-Such Department, has requested the presence of fifteen hundred white butlers and field laborers. In addition, of course, to the funds already promised. Now Mr. Donohugh, with your admirable corkage skills, would you be interested in such an opportunity?"

"What—I mean, *what?!*" Chris said.

Kate gulped some wine, shaking her head with a smile as she said, "I really should savor this more, but I think I need to get drunk."

"Go for it! We've got something cheaper I can open too, or… pour you a shot?"

"No, no. I'll ease into this. I was just… so looking forward to being home! And now I'm here, so… yeah, no rush anymore."

"Great," Chris said, sipping from his own glass. "Wow, this *is* good."

"Yup. So," Kate said, easing back into her chair. "The first overseas trip didn't go too well. So poorly in fact, that the folks down in DC decided to send me home while they figure out what the hell happened."

"Well, what the hell *did* happen?"

"When I got back," Kate mused, "some of the folks at the White House clued me in to a few of their… regional insights. Maybe they were just trying to make me feel better, and not think that I failed them."

"Enlighten me about these insights."

"You've heard the expression 'island time' before. What I encountered is what Eileen's people call 'island pride.' The leaders see their populations as a tight-knit community, so they don't like it when big countries show up and tell them how to run their lives."

"Okay," Chris nodded, "I can totally see that. But with so many countries out there to potentially work with, how did this all get so screwed up? Did no one in DC predict that this might happen?"

"Chris, my darling," Kate said, spinning the stem of her glass between thumb and forefinger, "that is what we in government simply refer to as 'the price of doing bureaucracy.' "

He smiled. "I'll stay in the private sector then. And you, meanwhile, need to get some rest. You look exhausted."

"I am." Kate tilted her head. "What about you? How were you holding up?"

"Eh… Not a lot going on with work. Clients always slow down around holiday time. But I did restring my Gibson and start messing around trying to remember how to play."

"Oh yeah? That's great! My husband, the thirty-something rocker. Because punk will never die, am I right?"

"Never!" Chris declared, grabbing the wine bottle and raising it triumphantly. He also took the opportunity to refill their glasses.

"Oh, God," Kate said breezily. "We do make a cute couple, don't we?"

She smiled at him with such sweetness that Chris thought he might do a backflip. He heard himself say, "I bet our kid would be cute, too."

Now it was Kate's turn to contemplate spontaneous gymnastics. But instead, she leaned in and planted a slow, moist kiss onto his lips.

"I want to do better," she whispered.

"Yeah?" Chris said. "What... how do you mean?"

"You're my world. Which means you're more important than the rest of the world."

"Is that why you came home?"

"No, they really did send me back. But it's going to be my decision to stay."

"*Stay?* As in... no more Eileen?"

Kate lifted her glass as she slung her other arm over the chairback. "Now look here, fella," she said with a film-noir affect. "That Jeffries-Lao dame is only gonna be in office til 'thirty-two. I hope—no, I *expect* you to stick around for a lot longer than that. You hear?"

Chris's eyes began to water as some horrendous pit in his stomach fell away. He felt lighter and freer than he had in years.

He flipped the dish towel back onto his arm, wiggled his whiskers, and resumed the role of French waiter. He said, "But of course, madam. Who else would keep your wine glass full?"

Kate and Chris Donohugh reached out and held each other's hands in silence.

29. GOING UNDERGROUND

"Where the hell is he going?"

FBI Special Agent Marcus Young had asked himself this question aloud half a dozen times in the hour since Glenn Murray had pulled onto the highway and begun a winding drive through hilly Blue Ridge Mountain country.

Marcus's two partners had split off to tail the man who had met with Glenn earlier at a gas station in Charleston, West Virginia. By all appearances, Glenn was just a guy picking up an old SUV that needed repairs. He had then driven off alone—his tour van and bandmates were nowhere around—and Marcus felt in his gut that the chase was finally on!

But every mile Glenn drove on Route 119 in a southwesterly direction took him further away from cities or any of the military and government facilities indicated on Marcus's official map. This was what perplexed him so much. If Glenn was en route to his next act of sabotage, Marcus wondered, what could he do in a region of mostly farmland and tree-capped hills?

Marcus had to keep his distance now. Traffic had been sparse on the curvy highway, and after exiting a short while ago, Glenn had since made a series of turns onto smaller and smaller country roads. Finally Marcus was forced to stay even further back when Glenn veered onto a bumpy dirt road, and use the dust kicked up by the SUV's large tires to keep track of where he was. All Marcus could hope was that Glenn didn't check his mirrors and take note of Marcus's own swirling dust.

Suddenly the wispy brown chimney stopped rising up about a quarter mile in the distance. Marcus pulled his own car off to the side of the road. He put on his coat, then trotted briskly in the direction of where Glenn had come to a stop. His right hand subconsciously tapped against the .40 cal Glock 23 handgun on his hip. He hoped he wouldn't have to use it.

The gray Toyota Sequoia was sitting a few feet off the road in a patch of craggy plant life that was in the process of entering its dormant winter state. Marcus scanned the scene quickly—one cluster of trees leading away, but not nearly thick enough for Glenn to have run into without still being seen now. Otherwise the space was wide open, with wisps of tall grass and a number of bushes dotting the area. There were no buildings in sight.

Marcus suddenly wondered if Glenn had come all the way out here to commit suicide. He unholstered his pistol and made a wide arc around the trunk, checking inside from a distance to see if there were any human forms inside.

Once he had ascertained that both front seats were empty, Marcus sprinted up against the left rear panel and peered in through the tinted windows. He was perplexed to see the entire back seating and storage areas filled with the kind of supplies one would take on a family camping trip.

"A real big fan, huh?"

Marcus felt his heart surge with a rush of adrenaline as he swung around and raised his gun in one quick motion. He saw Glenn standing thirty feet away. Same black canvas jacket. Burgundy wool cap. Hands raised out to the side. Both empty.

Marcus blinked, exhaled heavily through his mouth.

"What the hell are you doing out here, Glenn?"

"Took me a second to place you," Glenn responded. "Who do you work for?"

Marcus lowered his weapon slightly, but kept both hands on it, ready to aim and fire in an instant.

"FBI Special Agent Marcus Young. Mr. Murray, I have reason to believe you are engaged in illegal activities on behalf of the Sentinels of Jubilee. Including but not limited to sabotaging the Historical Reparations Administration."

"Am I suspect then?" Glenn said calmly.

"Yes, you *are* a suspect! Now don't play games with me. What is the purpose of your travel today, sir?"

Glenn made a motion to lower his arms. "May I?"

"Yes, but keep 'em where I can see 'em. Now start talking. I noticed a lot of supplies in the back of this truck. But your band isn't around. What are you up to?"

Marcus saw Glenn's face soften, heard him say, "It ain't what you think, man."

"I don't know anything yet," Marcus snapped. "Lay it out for me, nice and clear."

Glenn Murray chuckled. "You know, I don't want to die. But this is about more than me."

"Glenn! I'm not here to hurt you. Just tell me what's going on. Who or what is out here that would make you bring all this stuff?"

The bearded man looked down, stamped his feet. He said, "You took an oath to the Constitution, right?"

"That's correct," Marcus said. "The United States Uniformed Services Oath of Office. What does that have to do with all that's going on here?"

"Because," Glenn said, "I drove out all this way to deliver these supplies to American citizens. And whatever laws I may have broken in the past, I can't let you put any of them in danger."

"Danger?!" Marcus was exasperated. "Are they all Sentinel fugitives too?"

"Not in the least. Jesus Christ," Glenn sighed. "They're just people."

"But where?" Marcus took one hand off his pistol and waved it around. "There's nothing for miles."

Glenn took a step forward. "Come on, I'll show you."

The next few minutes were a blur for Special Agent Marcus Young. Getting into the Toyota with Glenn. Agreeing to leave his electronic devices back in the other car. The steep, winding drive directly onto one of the nearby hills that dotted the countryside. Pulling off onto a slender path, before stopping and backing up close to the mouth of a cave that dipped sharply down into the earth.

"Okay," Glenn said. "Let's unload."

"*What?* Here?!"

Marcus stepped out of the truck, his head swooning, then saw several people emerge from the cave.

"It's alright," he heard Glenn say, but wasn't sure if those words were intended for himself or the others.

For the next ten minutes he helped unload the truck in silence, handing cases of canned food and toiletries to the men and boys who hustled back down into the cave's entrance. Heavy trash bags were then brought out and placed inside the vehicle.

Marcus saw Glenn exchange a few final words with one of the men, then motion to get back in the truck. As they pulled forward down the slope, Marcus turned back and saw that several of the helpers were obscuring the SUV's tracks with brooms.

"So," Glenn said finally, "are you a patriot or a subversive now?"

"I don't understand," Marcus said. "Who were those people?"

"Guys who just needed to get their families away from it all."

Marcus was stunned. "Did you say... families? Glenn, how many people are inside that cave right now?"

"That one? Oh, about twenty-five or thirty."

"You mean there are *other* groups living in *other* caves?"

"Yep." Glenn tapped his fingers along the top of the steering wheel.

"My god... But why?!"

"We all fight for what we believe—or love—in our own way. There's a storm overhead in this country, and they're trying to ride it out in safety, I guess."

Marcus experienced a sudden flashback to the days when he was living incognito as Bill Evans at the Church of Modestianity. There too he had heard talk of storm clouds and taking shelter. As they now rounded a curve and his own car came into view, he found himself desperate for air.

"We need to talk," Marcus said as he spilled out onto the side of the dirt road.

Glenn leaned back against the right side of the hood and waited for Marcus to compose himself. Finally the FBI man said, "So you're telling me people are hiding away from Reparations, surveillance, or whatever... in caves all over the state?"

"All over the country, probably," Glenn remarked.

"But why?" Marcus pleaded. "It's just a tax. It can't go on forever—and they can't survive like that for long."

"I don't think they're doing it for the money." Glenn lit a cigarette with the Zippo, then offered one to Marcus. "It's about capitulation. A lot of us are waking up to the fact that no amount of concession will ever satisfy... whatever you want to call the mindset that's behind this Reparations movement."

Marcus took a drag on his own cigarette and tossed the lighter back. He said, "Glenn, I've got a file on you going all the way back to when you were thirteen years old spraying anarchy symbols on street signs. Nowhere did I see anything about your life that said 'right wing'."

Glenn nodded. "I was always so sure about how things were supposed to be. Just like everyone else is, nowadays. Wanna know why? Because we're *all* extremists on the inside. With me, the tide must have secretly shifted at some point, and where I stood went from idealist to… what, being an insurgent?"

Marcus felt a chill ripple through his body. He said, "Just a few years ago, they held parades because people thought they were taking part in the end of history. *They were sure of it*. But now… I don't know. Is the beginning of our own version of the Russian Revolution actually what's happening?"

The air was getting cooler, the shadows slowly lengthening in the mid-afternoon light of this autumn day.

"You know how it always starts?" Glenn asked. "The unraveling, that is? The path, it begins with everyone saying that they're just trying to help. The HRA. You cops. Even me," he added ruefully. "You know, volunteer work, lyrics with a 'message.' Then somehow I found myself involved with… hmm… those other things. It's funny how we all justify to ourselves what we're doing. Because now it's not simply, 'I'm good and my enemies are evil.' No, the wording got more complex, but human nature hasn't changed. By saying that you're 'fighting for people' or 'building bridges'… You can get away with *anything* using phrases like that as cover—even excuse when your equally righteous allies give in to temptation worse than the average person."

"So you think it's lack of scruples all the way down?" Marcus asked. "Then why does anyone lift a finger?"

"And not also pick up a sword when they do?" Glenn said. "Beats me."

They both smiled briefly.

Marcus said, "So tell me, if everyone thinks they're the good guy, and nobody's actually running a secret genocide program out of their food pantry… Where does it all go wrong? What's the glitch that makes everybody crazy, so that right now you and I are out here, instead of doing something simple and above-board back in our communities?"

"You're asking *me* for answers?" Glenn thumped a fist against the side of the truck. "I was screaming about the same things for fifteen years before I finally realized that maybe I had blinders on. Didn't see the whole picture."

"How so?" Marcus folded his arms.

"I mean, there's just so much going on behind the scenes that you'll never be privy to. Everywhere. As for me personally, I hate to think that my scene—punk, hardcore—we're just a steam valve that keeps concerned people distracted. Compartmentalized. Not taking action. Thinking *small*."

Marcus said, "I don't really know as much about your musical world as I let on the last time we met. Can you explain it more?"

"Alright," Glenn said. "Take capitalism, or war. Couple of buzzwords that every kid who sees a chopped-down rainforest or flattened city can write songs about. But anyone who works in those industries, they all truly think they're helping. Making their family proud. Providing materials for the village. Fighting against evil."

"Capturing the saboteur?" Marcus said, raising his eyebrows.

"Yeah." Glenn chuckled nervously. "But you can't really put that kind of nuance into my style of music. The fans are frustrated by bullshit, they're looking for answers with clean edges. You know, get that anger release. Wear the band t-shirts out at the show before having to go back to their real lives, where it's all more complicated. Not as cool. Less empowering."

"So why do you do it?"

"Play music? Or… the stuff that led to this meeting?"

Another brief smile from Marcus. "You tell me. I'm listening."

"So, I'm not a college professor type," Glenn said. "Those guys write papers no one can understand—if they even get read. Me? Guys all over *the world* have heard my stuff. It resonates on a primal level. No need to explain jack shit with footnotes, either! Is that ego talking, or am I just one more fighter in that rumble of bodies trying to change the world?"

Marcus nodded. "To make it better. Keep it safe from X, Y, and Z. Because we're all the good guy. And when there's no more villains—it's just an arms race of virtue."

"But now," Glenn said, blowing warm air into his hands, "after so many have fallen or bowed out, we see that maybe there isn't actually a championship belt. Or, it's not nearly as nice as we imagined it would be."

"And then what?" Marcus kicked at the dirt.

"Then you're home. Your dad's laid up on the couch in

chronic pain. It's raining outside and some part of the roof is leaking. You realize that after all you've done to 'help'—while standing in the spotlight you pointed at yourself—you still haven't been able to escape that silent void. Which is what? Death… decay… or God?"

Marcus kneaded a fist inside the palm of his other hand. Slowly, he said, "Glenn, how much do you know about the Church of Modestianity?"

"Some. But I do know that the man in charge, uh… that he and I have a common interest."

"That may be so," Marcus said, matching Glenn's gaze, "but that's not why I ask. I shouldn't tell you this, Glenn, but last summer I was covertly embedded at the Mall of Absolution to keep an eye on things. Nothing nefarious, mind you. Just a precaution."

"Sure," Glenn said, "you were *helping* to protect people from themselves."

"I was just following orders," Marcus said with a shrug. "But along the way, something about it clicked with me. Whether *I* was missing something, or if it was the Prescient One's warnings about surveillance… Glenn, I found myself actually converting to Modestianity, and violating the trust of my bosses in the process."

"So, what… you've been tracking me as a free agent?"

"No, sir! They dragged my ass back in. Made me a deal. Said if I helped them land a big fish, they'd consider overlooking my… conflicting loyalties."

Glenn nodded. "And I'm that fish?"

"You got it."

"Speaking of loyalties then," Glenn said, "tell me this before you arrest me. How does race affect how you follow orders?"

Marcus titled his head. "What exactly are you getting at?"

"You're black, man! And what I've been doing lately… Heh, well, it certainly isn't helping your side."

"Ah, yes." Marcus let out a little chuckle. "We can't outrun—or outperform—our identities. The paint job. Especially not now when the government is involved. We're constantly reminded of… not who we *are*, but who came before us."

"Yeah." Glenn scratched his beard. "But you know something? I think MARVIN is a bit narrow-minded. When's he gonna toss us Irish guys a few crumbs?"

"You might be on to something there! If the Brits have to pay India back, why not their own neighbors?"

They both laughed.

"Oh man, once that gets going," Glenn said, "maybe they'll call it the Reparations East India Company. Start a whole new form of international trade. Then it'll never end."

Marcus wagged a finger. "Not until the last SOB who cut me off in traffic has to pay for his crime."

"Alright, I got it. You're not in love with what's going on."

"Glenn, I'm a cop. A lawyer. And before that I was a ball player. You made the squad by turning double plays, not by asking the runners to go back to the dugout on their own."

"But what about the guys who got cut from the team?" Glenn asked sarcastically. "They've got feelings. And families, too."

"Who the hell wants to watch a shitty baseball game?" Marcus sighed. "Look, I'm a quarter-white anyway. So I guess my loyalties have been divided since the day my parents or grandparents fell in love. I don't have the patience—or computing power—to figure it all out. Try as we might to let how we live as individuals determine our worth, someone's always got that hook ready to yank us back into the pen. But I can't fight *every* battle. So I do my job, try to be true to myself, and then hope for the best."

Glenn rubbed his hands together. "So is it time to do your job now? With me?"

"Christ, I don't know," Marcus muttered. "I really just do not know."

The two men stared at each other for a moment.

"So what's gonna happen?" Glenn said. "Can't stand here until the sun disappears."

"Shit..." Marcus said. "It's been good talking to you, Glenn. Couple of guys just hashing it all out... But now it's back to the world."

"It used to be," Glenn said, "that maybe a person could really hide away. But now drones and satellites and microphones and cameras are keeping tabs on every damn thing. We *have to* play a part at all times, because no one's safe even in their own bedroom! When does that act become more of who you are than the truth you've been hiding?"

Marcus suddenly brought his hands to the top of his head. "I have to take you in," he said. "But... I have to let you go."

Glenn folded his arms, then let them fall away. He said, "I made my choice months ago. Now you have to make yours."

"But I did choose!" Marcus said. "When I became a Modestian I also betrayed the FBI. Betrayed my oath. But they were willing to forgive if I would *help* them track down your network."

"Hmm. How concrete is the evidence you have against me?"

Marcus twisted his mouth. "Circumstantial. But the heightened state of alert means we could take you into custody, at least temporarily."

"So if you turn a blind eye," Glenn said, "someone else'll be right on my ass?"

"The president almost lost the election over all this. So yeah, I don't think the heat's gonna die down anytime soon."

"The hell with it," Glenn grumbled. "I've got to take the fall."

"Are you serious?" Marcus said.

"And not just for those people out there, either. I'll do it for you, too."

"*Me?*"

"Who can have more of an effect, me or you? There's already other people bringing supplies out to the caves. But you, a reformed Modestian back on the job? You could play any number of roles going forward."

"Damn, damn..." Marcus was amazed at Glenn's courage. "Alright. I'll bring you in. But away from here. I don't want those people who are hiding to be found."

"Exactly," Glenn said. "Follow me back a ways. I'll pull over somewhere."

"Even better," Marcus said, opening the car door and pulling out his official map. "There's a small NSA relay station about twenty miles from here. That's where I'll slap on the cuffs."

"Perfect. I just gotta dump this garbage out of the truck somewhere along the way."

Marcus nodded. As they moved to get back into the vehicles, he said, "And Glenn. I'll never forget what you did today."

Glenn Murray gave a wry smile.

"I've been provoking the system for a long time. Now we'll finally see who's gonna win."

30. THE LONELIEST REVELATION

"I just knew it was you. The whole time, I could feel it."

"Then why did you wait so long?"

"Believe me, I wanted to act. But other voices prevailed. Urging patience, caution, timing. The presumption of innocence!"

"So why now then?"

President Eileen Jeffries-Lao looked into the man's eyes and said, "Because *I won*. Now we have four years to set my legacy in stone—and no one can be allowed to get in the way. All of your Sentinel cronies have been rounded up, of course, but perhaps you thought you'd escaped detection?"

The man, his left wrist shackled to a chrome table in this sparse interrogation room, shrugged his shoulders.

"Mod only knows," he said, "what tomorrow holds."

Jeffries-Lao laughed, then wagged her finger. "Come now, Scott. Surely a *prescient* man such as yourself would have seen this coming, no?"

"And what if I had? Then *you* would be the one who fell into *my* trap."

"Are you serious?" Eileen stepped closer. "You, locked in a secure facility unknown to the outside world, while I have the means at my disposal to raze your precious Mall straight to the ground."

The Prescient One frowned. His face had been stripped of all putty and makeup shortly after his initial capture a week ago. Even his signature blue outfit had been replaced by the hideous orange jumpsuit of a common criminal. He was, for all intents and purposes, Scott Cullen once again.

President Jeffries-Lao, for her part, wore a power outfit of sky-blue blouse tucked into a gray pencil skirt that was belted tightly about the waist. Her three-inch heels were stacked, as much for balance as to stomp loudly when needed.

"You wouldn't do that," Cullen said. "It would create a

humanitarian—and public relations—disaster."

Eileen kept her eyes on him as she walked a slow circle. "Not if we ran with the story that your whole church was a breeding ground for subversives. Home base of the hacker cult!"

The man jangled his cuffed wrist. He said, "You could do that. And get away with it as well. But perhaps my foresight had also accounted for that."

"Are you playing games with me?" Jeffries-Lao's voice echoed through the room.

"I wouldn't dare."

The president exhaled slowly. "So tell me then, what *is* your endgame? And don't get cute. Because, you know, I could have my guards kill you under the pretense that you'd endangered my life." Eileen motioned toward the two Secret Servicemen who were standing in opposite corners of the room. "I'm telling you right now, it's time to lay all your cards out on the table."

"Eileen," Scott said, "if I may call you that... How old were you when you got your first cell phone?"

She smiled. "Okay, I'll play along. It was around the time I finished college, so about thirty years ago. Why?"

"How often did you use it?"

"Well," Eileen said, "all you could do in those days was make phone calls, so not very often."

"Indeed. You're about ten years older than me, and by the time I turned twenty-one, smartphones were on the march. Texting had graduated to web browsing, video chat, email, music... A whole life right in the palm of your hand."

"Yes, yes," the president said impatiently. "And it only kept evolving into the indispensable tool we have today. But what is your point?"

The Prescient One made as if to rise, looked at his shackles, then leaned back into the chair. Deliberately he began, "Everyone is familiar with the story of my fall from grace three years ago. As well as the profound vision in exile that guided me to where I... was at least until recently. But years and years before that, during the height of my success with *Thor's Tablet*, I remember seeing a young woman—she was stunning, with pale skin and long brown hair... But she was so engrossed in her phone that she looked like a hunchback! It was a nightmare! Voluntary scoliosis. In that moment I was absolutely horrified, because I too was contributing to the digital addiction that continues to lure people away from nature in a million ways. Of course, I was also a young man back then, and life excitement soon distracted me from that moment of clarity. But I've never forgotten it."

"A touching memory, I'm sure," Jeffries-Lao said. "But what does that have to do with the predicament you're in today?"

"Because, madam," the prisoner said, "despite my church's best efforts to reacquaint people with real life—by planting gardens and singing freely—I fear that humanity's next reaction will not be to abandon the void of the artificial world at all. No, in order to fully escape the scrutiny state which *you* oversee— this living hell where surveillance conspires with punitive measures—people will dive in *deeper* via full immersion. Perhaps with some combination of float tanks, neural implants, and feeding tubes... Any method to renounce the body and protect the mind—and all this by choice! Then they will again be free to love, grow, make mistakes, be *human* in a way that is now denied to them under the all-seeing eye. Perhaps we will call that new state of existence, Screen Rapture!

"And Eileen," the man continued, "if your legacy is truly what fuels you, please remember my warning: MARVIN and the Reparations program could *accelerate* this ultimate form of self-segregation. Where each man, woman, and child chooses to hide away alone, for fear of what humiliation and punishments might befall their imperfect fleshly lives."

Jeffries-Lao shook her head doubtfully. She chuckled. "Ah yes, the silver tongue of the cult leader. But it's always been about the negative side of things with you. Crying wolf for years now, in fact. Just consider this though, Scott. Sometimes what we call accountability isn't all that far removed from your punishment bogeyman. I'd rather we shine *more* disinfecting sunlight onto the world, than the alternative of continuing to sweep inconvenient facts under the rug."

Scott Cullen smiled softly. "And *I* just knew you would say something to that effect. What I've tried to do with Modestianity is put up a roadblock, or pave a new path as best I could. But," he said, eyes twinkling for the first time in days, "you might get exactly what you want in the end."

*   *   *

Eileen Jeffries-Lao had signaled for refreshments to be brought in. After a rolling cart with food and beverages arrived, she sat on the edge of the table holding a small sandwich plate.

"Scott," she said, "do you really think you're more qualified to lay out a vision for the future than me?"

"It's not a matter of qualifications," the man shackled to the table said.

"No? I'm president today because I took the proper steps while working within the system for many years. I proved that I was a steady hand, a team player when needed, and all the while was still able to keep my core vision intact. But you," Eileen said, wiping her mouth before tossing a crumpled napkin onto the table, "you ping pong from lark to lark, just doing whatever strikes your fancy. And always relying on your so-called genius, when maybe you're nothing more than an Elmer Gantry. Using the salesman's cleverness to convince people to pony up money, or indeed, devote their lives to a new church. So yes, I do think the nation would be wiser to lean on me and my team of vetted professionals."

The Prescient One took the discarded napkin with his free hand and brushed several crumbs off the table surface, then put it into his jumpsuit pocket.

"Again," he said, "I believe there is more than one path to… Well, what is all this about? Knowledge? Experience? A person becoming the total package? Because maybe relying on job titles and certifications is a religious faith of its own. Yes, the cult of credentialism! And what distinguishes your kind from mine, is that people like me scare you to death."

"Absurd!" Eileen cracked open a soda can and stomped away from the table. "You are truly a reckless and dangerous individual. So in that way, I very much *would* fear your type fiddling with the levers of power. We've already seen how nervous an unstable president can make the rest of the world."

"No, no," Cullen said sharply. "What you find appalling is the realization that someone might make it to the same level of authority or wisdom as you, but without the humiliation you endured as down payment. Kneeling to kiss the ring. Turning a blind eye here, turning the other cheek there. Oh yes, I navigated the same world as you, but without having to sell my soul."

"I'd rather lose a few chunks on this righteous mission," the president snarled, "than completely fall apart as you have. Sir, you wear glitter and prosthetic glue on your face as a selling point!"

Scott Cullen rubbed a hand against his bare skin, then raised his eyebrows.

"You know, Madam President, the most dangerous thing that a self-made millionaire can do is turn away from hedonism and start pulling back the curtain of the world. Because in truth, I figured out a few things early on, but still had enough to believe in that I could disregard those uncomfortable ideas. But when you and yours cast me aside, destroyed my reputation... Well, you can guess the rest. Out of that madness and disillusionment, I first found a new purpose for myself—and then came a comprehensive understanding of how it all really works."

"Oh?" Eileen scoffed. "Do tell! I might need to take some notes."

"Maybe you should," the Prescient One said. "It's actually why in the end I can't hate you. Because I know you're just one of the more gilded pawns on this global stage. While I may not see the entire picture, I surely know more than you—because you've been rewarded for conforming all this time. Mrs. Jeffries-Lao, you only masquerade as a leader."

The president thought for a moment. She said, "I may have conformed, as you say. But what's wrong with that if, in the end, you're on the right side? That blinding shine you see on me is *confidence*. No nervous ticks like the eccentric you are."

"Optics aside," Cullen said, "so-called eccentrics like me do the work of going down all the different rabbit holes. Then we piece that random data together on our own. Which of course turns out to be so ludicrously ironic."

Eileen was back at the food cart taking nibbles of chopped fruit. She looked up and said, "I promise you, I'm writing in my mind. Keep going, please."

"Certainly. Take that old sales pitch from Apple computers. 'Think different.' It's a nice sentiment for children, but what happens in real life? You come back proudly holding up what you found, but then people cover their eyes and scream, 'No, no! We didn't *really* mean for you to think different!' The truth is, if you just want to be weird on the surface, that's fine. They'll pay you handsomely as long as you go with the flow. But don't call the plan into question, otherwise they have to rewrite everything."

Eileen Jeffries-Lao, who had been shaking her head with a smirk, now said, "You see me as some kind of globalist shill, don't you? Well, Mr. Cullen, I'll have you know that what I've done with the HRA, is to pour the concrete foundation for something that will live on writ large for decades to come. And history will remember who was on the captain's bridge when humanity finally began to move forward *together*. Meanwhile you… This Modestianity nonsense will turn out to be nothing more than a did-you-know footnote in children's textbooks."

"What's the point in comparing my legacy to yours?" the Prescient One asked. "I fell into prominence—*you* sought it out! Had my concerns about MARVIN been addressed, then I would have remained a quiet techie behind the scenes, perhaps consulting remotely from time to time while off building my next business idea. As for this talk of uniting humanity, you're not speaking to a supporter-dupe out on the campaign trail. I know very well that your worldwide Reparations expansion is already floundering."

"My god!" Jeffries-Lao let out a near-scream. "You fool! We've got alliances with over a dozen countries already in place. And I assure you, plenty more are waiting in line right behind them."

"This is a farce!" Scott shook his head and laughed. "That roster of small colonies is birdseed compared to China or Russia. The grand imperial powers want *nothing* to do with outsiders looking into their archives."

"My, what a short memory you have," Eileen said. "It was we who won the Cold War. And my embarrassing predecessor does deserve credit for the strong trade policies that reigned China in. Before you say anything, no, I am not beholden to the land of my ancestors. Because as you are well aware, my husband is Caucasian."

"Good old Paul, yes. The Jeffries in Jeffries-Lao!"

Eileen nodded patiently.

"Thank you for remembering," she said. "Now, Scott. These countries may be physically bigger than England, which is fully on board with paying Reparations, but I assure you they are still *weak*. Dysfunction at every level. If they and their billions of people have any hope of being relevant this century… If they want a chance at order, unity, peace, being there as mankind explores the stars…"

For the first time, the Prescient One looked surprised. "What *are* you getting at?" he nearly shouted.

"I am telling you," Eileen said, "why they will eventually acquiesce and join us. Because it's all so much bigger than countries—and yes, even race. Therefore what is money in this context? Bait? A tool, or a device used to persuade? And in that regard, maybe I *am* just a well-fed pawn on the world stage, as you say. So be it. Because as you now see, this project goes far beyond the scope of Reparations. That's just one stepping stone helping to vault us all toward the kind of cooperation needed to fulfill humanity's dream of seeding other planets. What do you say to that, sir? Do you not now finally begin to feel some shame because your own terroristic actions worked against such a noble venture?"

The Prescient One was momentarily stunned. He shuddered, then finally said, "The ends always justify the means, don't they? The lies, the cover-ups. And the steamrolling of uncomfortable ethical concerns. But now I see just how far people like you are willing to go to keep the candle of that messianic faith burning."

Eileen stared daggers at him. "*You* would dare call me out as a messiah? Ha! I never looked the part. I never played the part. That's your area of expertise. You have followers. I have allies. You speak *to* your people—I speak *for* mine."

"I might actually believe that," Scott said, "if you hadn't just blurted out that whole space travel manifesto. No one who voted for you and the Reparations ticket ever imagined that the HRA could be used to bring about some sort of worldwide NASA alliance."

Eileen inspected one of her cuticles. Dropping her hand away she said, "It's true that they might not have the wide-angle lens for such an all-encompassing grand vision. But I bet you, ninety-nine percent of them hope to colonize the stars just as much as they support equity."

"Ah, colonizing." The Prescient One closed his eyes and nodded. He said, "First you will ensure that Earth is completely homogenized. Then we will go out and plant our flag somewhere else. Until what—one day all of humanity owes Reparations to the planets and moons we disturbed and imposed our will upon?

Wiped out with our strange diseases?"

"Beyond ludicrous! Truly, Scott, you've outdone yourself. I'm speechless."

"Because you realize you just stepped in it. You're so mentally ill that you could watch a million or fifty million people die in conflicts about the past, as long as Mars got terraformed in the process. But I say no!" Scott Cullen was fuming. "Your lens is completely flipped. We aren't supposed to keep spreading out. We need to get simpler, more intimate, quieter, and slow down. Because we as a species are *exhausted!* We've all been smashed together, lurched from horses to jet planes... but still the creeping dread of some nameless malaise hounds us.

"And I know," Cullen continued, "that we won't be able to escape it in deep space, either. We might succeed in ignoring this doubt for a while—keep everyone so busy *doing* what it takes to build the ships to get us out there. But eventually the bustle ends, and then we're left with ourselves again. It'll be the loneliest revelation ever—half a million miles from home."

President Eileen Jeffries-Lao began to clap sarcastically. "A touching warning, thank you. But I'm sorry, we simply can't afford to wait. Not with all the tools at our fingertips—and a few great leaders who are prepared for this moment. Those who have the stomach and the courage to do what is necessary. These opportunities are so rare that we are *obligated* to seize them. In that light, what you have done might be unforgivable. I wish I was ruthless enough to have you killed right now."

Cullen looked up. Eileen was staring at him, hands on hips, beautifully vicious. He said, "But you still need me for something, perhaps?"

She exhaled slowly. "Yes, I suppose I do. A great mind is a terrible thing to waste, after all."

"If only I would go along with the plan, right?"

"It's called staying in your lane!" Jeffries-Lao shouted, but then calmed herself. She said, "You're a technician, not a politician."

"That may be so," Scott said, "but I think your fervor has bled over into fanaticism. You never revealed those sharp teeth out on the campaign trail."

"Me, a fanatic? Mr. Cullen, I do believe you are the pot calling the kettle... teal."

Eileen smiled with self-satisfaction.

Scott Cullen straightened his posture and said, "The difference, Madam President, is that I have always been forthright. And beyond the teal and gray, Modestianity's intentions are wholly transparent. You, however, secretly hide the ambition of a would-be immortal behind a deal maker's calm smile."

"If not me," Jeffries-Lao declared, "someone else would have filled the role!"

"I know!" Cullen whacked the table with his cuffed hand. "And that's a great danger for us all. There are tens of millions of aspiring messiahs who hide behind the title of 'activist' or 'advocate.' All salivating for the moment when *they* hold the power to manipulate entire nations. I use my words to enrich, rather than twist the minds of others."

"But Scott, everything that you see in the world came about through molding and manipulation. Land, objects, people—all changed by invention, war, and yes, even that word you must dread, *policy*. It can't be stopped. All we can decide is who steers the ship."

The Prescient One looked down at his bright jumpsuit for a moment. He said finally, "You've devoted all this time and effort to one man—me. Why, Eileen? Why exactly are you here today? You've got an entire nation to spy on, a Reparations program to run, and apparently a spaceship to steer!"

"Because," Jeffries-Lao answered coldly, "twice you have tried to derail me and the progressive vanguard that I serve. From the Beneficiaries to their allies, you have threatened and nearly broken the hearts of countless people across this country. To think that one rudderless man could become so filled with spite, just because someone took away his door key. That he would allow the gift of his brilliant mind to be so perverted, and then seek to chop down a nationwide movement at the knees! No, Mr. Cullen, I cannot let you continue to put any more Americans at risk. It is now time, in fact, for you to be punished."

"What do you intend to do?" Scott asked quietly.

Eileen Jeffries-Lao leaned forward onto the table, then pointed a finger directly at his face.

"I want to know," she said, "what really drives a man to invent a new god, and then appoint himself as the conduit. Is it ego? Or is there a gaping hole in his heart that he could never fill? A successful man like you… But you don't really know what it is, do you? Your *Prescience*, you still haven't figured out how it all came to this. But that's okay. We'll get to the bottom of it. No resources or pain receptors will be spared, you treasonous bastard!"

The President of the United States turned on her heel and motioned to the two Secret Servicemen standing guard.

A moment later Scott Cullen, aka the Prescient One, was alone to contemplate his fate.

31. UNCHAINED

The *DDM TV Live* studio audience clapped along in time with a rousing big band number as Ryan Richards strutted onto the stage. His shimmering navy blue suit was accented by a gray shirt and snowman-print necktie.

"Wow," Richards said. "Can you believe it's December already? After everything that we've been through together this year—the ups and the downs—let's take a moment to remember that we're still here. *Breathe!* We are alright. Now," he said, pumping a fist, "let's get this episode started with a bang!"

A snare drum roll slowly built to a crescendo as a TV screen was lowered to stage level beside him. Cymbals crashed and the face of a distinguished elderly man appeared on the screen.

Ryan Richards studied the picture thoughtfully for a moment, then said, "This is Cornelius Alemán. Do any of you know who that is? Have you even *heard* his name before?"

Murmurs of doubt came from the crowd. Richards flashed a mischievous smile.

"No?" he asked, slowly letting the vowel fall away. "He's *only* among the top two hundred wealthiest people in the world! Oil and gas interests, global shipping… oh, and he's been known to dabble in, how shall I say it? Media… politics… the fate of nations!

"Ladies and gentlemen," Richards continued, his voice now working into a frenzied lather, "he is the Mexican George Soros!

Anywhere around the world you look, you'll see Alemán bucks in action. An Argentinian newspaper rescued from insolvency. Movies financed in the Philippines, but only when the language spoken is Spanish! And of course, a generous endowment for Latiz-American scholarships right here at home. But... But, but, but!!!"

The host wagged a finger at the photograph.

"Even this polished scion of the noble Alemán dynasty has secrets. Secrets, secrets..." Richards whispered. "Only talked about in hushed tones by those fearful of his wrath. Oh, if you only knew. Guards!" Ryan shouted. "Bring him... to me!"

The host put hands on hips and stuck out his chest as three giant men in black cargo fatigues prodded the elderly man forward. Silver shackles that were linked by a vertical chain bound the newcomer's hands and ankles.

Nervous sounds from the audience mixed with the low rumble of orchestral bass drums thumping through the studio speakers. No guest had ever appeared on the show restrained in this manner. People were asking themselves, just how dangerous *was* this man?

Alemán maintained his dignified composure. Despite the humiliating double chains, he had at least been permitted to wear slacks and a blazer instead of a prisoner's jumpsuit.

As the guards spread out to different corners of the stage, Ryan Richards took the opportunity to playfully inspect the man. Finally he drew back and said, "Cornelius Alemán, ask not for whom the spreadsheet tolls—today it tolls for thee!"

A gong sounded from somewhere. Alemán held his ground as Richards tried to nudge him closer to the TV screen.

"Look at these stats," Richards said, shaking his head sadly at the charts which detailed the man's genetic breakdown. "*Eighty-eight percent* Western European DNA. And yet you masquerade as a champion of the Latizo people? Shame on you, sir."

In the silence that followed, Alemán raised his eyebrows at Richards, who nodded back.

The old man said, "My name is Cornelius Gomez de Vallarta Alemán. I am a respected US citizen. I have been abducted from my home in Vermont and dragged here on trumped-up political charges. Shame on all of you for being a part of this disgraceful charade."

Alemán winced at the barrage of boos and catcalls that followed this declaration of innocence. Ryan Richards flashed his trademark smirk and said, "I don't think they like you, Corn Dog. And they haven't even been presented with the evidence yet."

"What evidence, you… court jester?!"

Richards brought a hand to his chest, then grimaced as he said, "Who, little old me?"

"We love you, Ryan!" a female voice called out from the darkened seating area.

"Thank you, my dear," he replied, loosening up for a moment before putting on a stern expression and again facing his guest. "To Mr. Alemán and everyone here tonight, I ask that you all turn your attention to the video screens—hard as it might be to stomach."

A series of disturbing images began to cycle through. There were black-and-white photographs of dead bodies, charred ruins, and groups of men holding rifles.

"And there it is," Richards said gravely. "Over three thousand killings during the Mexican Revolution attributed directly to the Alemán clan. Men, women, children—even the livestock when their farms were burned to the ground. Horrible, just horrible!" Richards moaned. "There are no words."

Alemán's poise finally broke down. "This is outrageous!" he thundered. "You cannot in hindsight impose the niceties of peacetime upon a nation that was in the throes of a civil war. To cherry pick one anecdote from a decade-long struggle, where both sides suffered terrible losses…"

"Just as a law court holds one trial at a time," Richards said, "so too can *DDM TV* only film one episode at a time. And as anyone can see, our docket is full! Backlogged with the likes of you, who would deny or explain away their Bloodline Crimes!"

The audience was torn between somber grief for the victims and a boiling desire for vengeance against Cornelius Alemán.

"What the hell do you want then?" the old man said contemptuously. "I am familiar with the nature of this preposterous television program. Who will you bring out here in hopes that I would grovel at their feet for forgiveness?"

Ryan Richards dropped his head, shaking it slowly. "No," he said, "there's no one."

"Good!"

"It is not good, *sir*. The reason being that entire lineages were wiped out in these massacres. And the few ultra-distant relatives MARVIN did find in the system were simply too afraid to make the long journey—even with all expenses paid by our proud sponsor, Total Comfort Airlines."

"So," Cornelius said, "these people don't even live in the United States? What in the name of God am I doing on this stage bound in chains? Oh... I see now. This isn't about justice, or healing anything. You are trying to discredit *me*. Destroy my reputation, derail my charitable efforts. Did... did she put you up to this?"

Richards drew back dramatically with widened eyes.

"*She?*" he said.

"Your president, of course," the old man grunted.

"Well," Ryan stammered, "I'm just the host here, not the producer..."

"Witch-hunt!" Alemán screamed and raised his shackled fists above his head. "You are all witnessing a political lynching."

Ryan Richards stiffened. "Now, now, mister! Let's not go throwing around culturally sensitive terms. You know what? I've had enough. Guards, just get him off my stage..."

"This is a travesty!" Cornelius cried. "You people in the audience, look what they're doing here. Not even obeying the rules of their own show. Will you just sit there and take it? I am being judged without the ability to even face my accuser!"

Now the studio audience was on its feet, angry at both Alemán for his Bloodline Crimes and the show for not following its normal course of conflict resolution. Ryan Richards stepped forward and motioned for them to calm down.

"Fear not, *DDM* fans," he said with a confident smile. "Because come on, this is *me* you're dealing with here. Ryan Patrick Richards, the captain of this proud ship! Mr. Alemán, do you *really* want a showdown?"

The elderly man gave a chilling smile that rivaled any of Ryan's own top-ten grins. "It's the only way," he said.

"So be it," the host replied. "Ladies and gentlemen, behold... the plaintiff!"

A middle-aged Latizo man wearing a beige suit came into view. He saluted with great fervor as he walked across the stage.

Recognition slowly dawned on the crowd—this face had been a staple of the news cycle for more than a year.

But applause was not forthcoming. Here was the man who had insinuated his desire to rein in the HRA if elected president. What damage might he have also done to this popular television show?

"You traitor!" Cornelius Alemán howled as the man came near.

Ryan Richards struck a dramatic pose as he swung from left to right, and said, "Welcome to the show, Senator Victor Dominguez! Sorry-not-sorry about your loss last month. But no hard feelings! Now, what do you have to say to our friend Cornelius?"

The senator brushed Ryan away with a wave and fixed a hard gaze upon the old man. "No, Mr. Alemán," he declared. "It is *you* who is the traitor. Or should I say… infiltrator?!"

At this accusation, the show host fell flat on his back as if bowled over by a raging bull. The crowd stood up again and gave a loud cheer—finally there was blood in the water.

Richards scrambled to his feet and sidled up against Cornelius. He said, "Mr. Alemán, that is quite the indictment. What say you, sir?"

"I am a public figure known and highly regarded around the world," the old man declared indignantly. "It is outrageous to slander me like this."

"The floor is yours, Victor," Ryan Richards said. "What have you got to back up your claims?"

Senator Dominguez pointed a stern finger and said, "I may not have won the presidency, but God has now given me an even greater opportunity. To prevent the country from being torn apart by this man right here!"

Richards leaped forward and threw a left-right punch combo into the air. "Ouch!" he gasped, then imitated a ring announcer as he said, "That one stunned him, Frank! Will Victor go for the knockout, or just toy with him for a while?"

Dominguez looked askance at the host, then continued, "Ladies and gentlemen, there are differences, and then there are *differences*. Dramacrats and Rebellicans may disagree over political ideas—and yes, the rhetoric has gotten quite vicious over the past decade. But I believe deeply that we still have enough in common to sit on the patio and enjoy a sunset together."

Ryan Richards batted his eyes and placed a hand on his breast.

"But this man," Victor continued, "wants to tap into the worst aspects of tribal thinking in order to consolidate his own power. Cornelius Alemán uses nice-sounding phrases like 'Latizo Pride,' but not to gain more appreciation for our people, as a new national holiday might do. He rejects *E pluribus unum* in favor of only one race rising to the top of the melting pot. My oath to the Constitution—and my heart—cannot abide by such anti-American sentiments."

Ryan Richards staggered back, his head wobbling as if stung by an uppercut. "Cornelius," he pleaded in a raspy voice, "you've got to fight back. Throw a punch, or it's over!"

Cornelius Alemán yanked at the lapels of his blazer, shackles clattering loudly as he did so.

He said, "I am ashamed of you, Victor. To think that I ever had faith in you. That you would so fawn over being an American. You short-sighted fool! You turncoat! We are descendants of the greatest empire the world has seen in a thousand years—the Spanish Empire! Lasting far longer than the British, and today our language and architecture live on around the globe.

"What *is* this worship of the United States all about?" Cornelius implored. "Why do people hold such reverence for a leftover from the skirmishes between European powers? It is a wasteland where all genetic stock is perpetually wrecked against the rocks of disorganized breeding! So am I *really* a traitor? Or just the latest visionary to try his hand at remaking the landscape? What, are you shocked by my candor? Your own president is less than seventy-five years removed from the rice paddies of China! Yet you don't think it's possible that *her* foreign ties could influence any of her policies?"

Ryan Richards choked for words amid the din of the audience's screams and howls. Victor Dominguez took a step forward and motioned for silence.

He said, "Not long ago, Eileen Jeffries-Lao and I were fierce ideological combatants. But do you know what we have in common? We both married outside of our races. My wife Jaclyn is fifty-percent white, one-quarter Navajo, and one-quarter Hispanic. And First Man Paul Jeffries, who I respect very much, is a full-blooded WASP whose family goes all the way back to this country's colonial beginnings. All of our children are *one-hundred-percent* American! And that is why I chose to stand up in full opposition to the Alemán Conspiracy."

Richards smacked his forehead audibly. "A... *conspiración?!* Senator, please forgive me. I misjudged you. A truer patriot I've never known."

"I'm just thankful for this chance to lay out the truth," Victor said with a bow.

Ryan Richards whipped his arm in the direction of Cornelius Alemán. "Guards, guards!" he called out. "Seize this creepy old geezer and take him away."

As the men in fatigues dragged a struggling Cornelius Alemán off the stage, he wailed, "You can silence me. You can jail me. But you cannot stop our rising tide! The future is Latizzzzz..."

The roars of the frothing crowd drowned out Ryan's attempts to speak. Everyone was simply too riled up after the most shocking outcome in the show's two-year history. Again it was Victor Dominguez who patiently lowered his arms until all was quiet.

"Thank you, ladies and gentlemen," he said. "After such high drama, perhaps we can all go home tonight as better people. Wiser and more compassionate. God bless you and the United States of America."

Dominguez quickly shook the host's hand before turning and walking toward the side of the stage.

"Uh... Not so fast, Senator."

Ryan Richards stood there with his arms folded, a wicked smile on his lips.

Victor stopped and turned his head back slowly. "Excuse me?"

"We've actually got some unfinished business here."

"Really? Like what?"

Richards motioned for Dominguez to come closer.

"Victor," he said, "you're from Arizona. So surely you know that large swaths of the American Southwest were once part of Mexico."

"Yes, of course." Victor was now standing beside the host.

"There was also an independent Republic of Texas for nearly ten years."

Dominguez smiled as he said, "Did you know that Sam Houston actually served as its president on two separate occasions?"

"Really now?" Ryan said. "Well, since you're so familiar with that country's history, tell me this. Does the name Salvador 'El Diablo' Colon ring a bell?"

Victor froze. He licked his lips. "Oh, no…"

"Oh, yes!" Richards exclaimed. "A little naughty, naughty during the Mexican-American War! Victor, we know you were vetted before the election, so I can only assume that new ancestral connections have been made *south of the border*. And with such nastiness in your genetic past, it looks like America really dodged a bullet this past November."

The sound of a large dog barking began to play over the PA system.

"Hey Victor, do you hear that?" Ryan said.

"What's going on?" Sweat was beading on Dominguez's forehead.

"It's MARVIN," Ryan whispered. "I think he broke free."

"Broke free?"

"Oh my God!" Richards howled. "Ladies and gentlemen, MARVIN's on the loose! MARVIN, stop that! Come here, right now. That's a good boy, yes… No! Bad MARVIN, *bad!* Uh-oh… I don't know if I can hold him much longer…"

Ryan Richards fell to his knees as the barking receded into the distance.

"Run for your lives, everyone! I think he's got rabies. He could be coming for you next! MARVIN has been… unchained!!!"

THE END.

Reparations
MAZE

(BOOK FOUR)

1. PEACEKEEPERS

The headwaiter shuffled over to a small table near the back wall, carrying in each hand an enormous steaming plate of spaghetti. He set these down in front of two men, being careful not to splash any of the red sauce onto them or his own white formal shirt. He bowed and moved away.

One of the men, a middle-aged Caucasian with sparse hair and a black-dyed beard, gently nudged his plate aside and consulted a pocket flip pad. He made a mark on one line of the page, then looked up.

"So, that takes care of robberies. You ready to talk fights?"

The other man chuckled. A grizzled Afrigro-American with buzz-shaved head, he still possessed an athletic build despite his advancing age. He said, "The ones on camera... or off?"

"Well, that depends. How many are, uh, Certified Historical Events that got our friends in law enforcement involved?"

"Come on, Michelangelo. You know I can't keep track of all that. Just too many Domination Events taking place between our people, you feel me?"

"Of course." As he took a bite of his meal, Michelangelo said, "But that's alright. Let's not lose the forest for the trees. 'Cause Duke, you and me, we do some good business together. Sometimes you leave the table up, sometimes you're down. But mostly it all evens out. So please, eat your food. We'll square this in good time."

"True that, my friend."

Over the next half hour, Duke and Michelangelo haggled over the handwritten lists that ran down each of their notepads. The plates were cleared away, then coffee and port arrived. Finally, Michelangelo scribbled something onto a cocktail napkin and handed it to Duke.

The black man closed his eyes drowsily and shrugged his shoulders. "Okay. So I walk out of here a winner this month."

Michelangelo snapped his fingers. A skinny teenager who

had been standing in the shadows near the kitchen now approached. A few words were exchanged quietly, and then the boy walked through the empty restaurant out into the street.

"An extra measure of precaution," Michelangelo said with a wave. "To keep our, uh, freelance conflict resolution service a private matter."

Duke nodded. He tapped a fingernail against his glass of port. "Well, I'll take this type of service over standing in line at the HRA any day of the week."

The men laughed together heartily. A moment later, Michelangelo adjusted himself in his seat and wiped the corner of his mouth with a cloth napkin.

"So tell me," he said, "how's the family? Everyone good?"

"Oh, you know how it is. They're fine. Got no time or patience for the man who holds it all together... But they're good, doing real good."

Michelangelo smiled softly. "Everybody thinks that this is easy. Sitting around in fancy suits, eating and drinking, just a couple of guys shooting the breeze, right? If only they could see below the surface!"

"Mm," Duke grumbled. "Don't even offer to trade places with me for an hour. 'Cause if I got *one taste* of that weight off my shoulders, I'd probably never let 'em put it back."

"Absolutely. People take what we do for granted. Keeping peace in the streets—relatively speaking, of course. But more importantly, limiting each neighborhood's exposure to the surveillance pipeline."

"That's it! We keep all their Debit Scores down, for Christ's sake. Keep the tension from spilling over into chaos, so they can go about their lives. But oh, 'Papa Duke goin' off on one of his pub crawls again.' My foot! I'm the person cleaning up all *their* vomit."

Just then the front door of the restaurant opened and the lanky young man returned. He pulled a frosted plastic tube out of his inside jean jacket pocket and handed it to Michelangelo without a word, then moved away to his spot in the shadows.

Michelangelo gave the green-capped container a little shake and held it out over the table. "Here ya go, count the coins if you want. You're the big winner."

"Unfortunately my jackpot is destined to be short-lived,"

Duke said with a chuckle as he received the bullion. He stowed it inside his blazer. "Next stop for me is Rabbi Lovitz. I got to hustle over there before sundown. I swear, the knockout game ain't no game when it comes to these here private payouts, no sir."

Michelangelo rose to escort Duke to the exit. "Maintenance work is rarely glamorous. But why should everything that happens be the entire world's business? So, we settle these trifling debts our way. Wipe the hard drives, seal the records before—"

Duke rapped a knuckle against the doorframe twice. "Before MARVIN drops in for a visit. Mm-hmm. See you next time, *compadre*. And thanks for the supper!"

"Anytime. You have yourself a nice New Year… *Il Duce*."

The men shook hands and Duke stepped out into the cool gray day.

2. EQUITUS

Security was tight at the Kennedy Center on Saturday evening. Patrons found themselves required to pass through a limited number of entryways before gaining access to the famed theater's bright red carpeting. Once inside, they encountered members of the Secret Service who were posted throughout the venue.

Because tonight, in their final public appearance of the year, the President and First Man would attend the Noah Rafferty play *Equitus*.

A hush fell over the crowd. Heads turned and craned upward. There were murmurs, then loud applause erupted as Eileen Jeffries-Lao and husband Paul Jeffries entered their private box and came into view. She was wearing an elegant navy blue dress that sparkled from a thousand different points.

The couple waved graciously, then motioned for people to retake their seats. Several minutes later, the theater lights faded out and the performance began.

Equitus was the shocking story of a troubled young man who live-streamed charitable acts by day, but later committed hate crimes in fits of amnesic rage. A love triangle involving his employer's Affirmative Action hire and a woman he'd known in high school propelled him inexorably toward a psychotic break —or perhaps the breakthrough that would change his fortunes forever.

"Ridiculous!" Eileen heard Paul snort late in the first act. He was seated to her left, his right leg crossed over top and body leaning away.

"What now?" she whispered.

Paul waved a hand toward the stage. "More sex, that's what!"

"But darling, these two have been dancing around the tension ever since they drove to the soup kitchen together."

"Eh, maybe. I thought this kid was finally going to look in the mirror. Now *another* roll in the hay to solve his problems?"

Eileen cast a sideways glance at Paul in the faint light. She said, "Isn't that how you've always gone about it?"

Paul's leg slid down and he turned toward her, mouth agape for a moment. Then he smiled, saying, "Don't be resentful just because you showed up late to the party."

"What is *that* supposed to mean?"

"Please. People talk. Word gets around. I'm aware of certain... work friendships over at Sixteen Hundred Pennsylvania Avenue."

Eileen Jeffries-Lao felt a shiver run across the surface of her body. The ongoing affair with her chief of staff, which she had tried to keep a secret from everyone... Who else knew?

"I..." Her voice trailed off. Down below, the hay-rolling actress's father was in a huff about something. She felt a pat on her knee.

"It's alright," Paul said. "Everyone's got to play their role up on stage. You got your 'four more years.' So, whatever it takes to sustain you across the finish line, I understand."

Eileen cocked her head at an angle. "But still, you're jealous? Or mad?"

He chuckled, saying, "You've no idea the types of indignities that the husband of a pioneering female politician must endure. Who you engage in pillow talk with is the least of my troubles— especially at this late hour in your career."

"Oh. So you're watching the clock, now that you believe my stock is done rising?"

"Possib*ly*. Although I don't imagine either one of us expects to retire to some palatial estate together and pass the years quietly."

Eileen reached for her wine glass, while her mind envisioned a distant fork in the road. On one path, that idyllic retirement where she would play grandmother to her daughter's children. On the other, working even more feverishly with the international power brokers who were secretly engineering the great space project that would send humanity to the stars.

But an arduous second term as president lay between her and that day in 2033. All the travel, the speeches, and cagey political decisions that would be laid at her feet—and upon her legacy. Perhaps even the quietly proposed scaling back of the domestic Reparations program. Cord cutting done only for the greater good, of course…

"Ah, the gears are turning now," she heard Paul say. He frowned and added, "I do hope you aren't planning to have me offed. No need, my dear. I'll continue to stay out of your way. But always ready to keep up appearances! Oh yes, you can certainly rely on this old soldier!"

Eileen watched as he rattled the ice cubes inside his whiskey glass and drank. The First Man in that moment looked stoic, and yet so very small. He had paid a tremendous price in hitching his wagon to her—a WASP marrying a second-generation Chinese immigrant, then playing second fiddle throughout the course of her career. And with the Historical Reparations Administration serving as the capstone of her presidency, perhaps there was something cruelly poetic about his having to attend so many events where he stood in as the symbolic fall guy.

Liquor and young ladies were the balm for Paul's frustration, which Eileen had at least understood if not quite forgiven. But now with Tony Rizzuto as her own guilty pleasure, the drug to help endure the strain of it all… Not only was she no better than her philandering husband, he seemed to have cultivated an artful veneer that masked his disappointments and imperfections.

As for herself, bearing the weight of so many critical responsibilities had apparently left her susceptible to one of the little vices that so often ensnared the types of people she looked down upon.

Eileen reached out and clinked her glass against Paul's tumbler. "Thank you. Maybe we *will* have something to talk about when all is said and done."

"Shh," he said. "I think someone else is about to have sex now. Or maybe get assaulted. You never can tell with these modern plays…"

The president turned her eyes back toward the stage.

3. THE NICE PLACE

"All in a day's work, my friends."

The Reverend Matthias G. Witherspoon tugged at the zipper of his jacket, then used the long grabber tool he was carrying to snatch a mangled plastic food container out of the grass.

"Yes sir, you kids are getting a real taste of what it's like to help your community."

Surrounding him were half a dozen boys, each carrying a thick orange plastic bag and wearing work gloves. Every so often one of them would reach down and pick up a piece of trash.

"Don't let me catch you dawdling now," Witherspoon added. "It ain't *that* cold out today. And the alternative—well, y'all already know a thing or two about juvenile hall."

"It ain't so bad in there," one of the boys said. Matthias gauged him to be about ten years old. "Got TVs, hoops…"

"That's what they want you to think, Geoffrey. Make you feel comfy behind bars. Not so you'll reconsider your mischievous ways, neither. Nah, they gettin' you used to the idea of spending your life inside a cage."

The group arrived at a residential intersection. Reverend Witherspoon said, "Well, which side looks worse off, left or right?"

"Left," one boy said.

"Right!" another declared.

"Let's split up," a third offered.

Matthias said, "No way. We operate as a team, watch each other's backs. Need to do a thorough job out here for these folks, too. Why? Because everybody wants to go to the nice place— instead of doing the work to make *a place nice*. So many people got a chip on their shoulder, and an excuse on the tip of their tongue. And when they put their hand out, that completes the Holy Trinity of Failure. But not me, for I choose to take pride in this town. Anyhow, I say we go to the right. Ten minutes, we'll pass the truck, get a sip of water and swap out any bags that are full. So come on."

The clean-up crew slowly made its way along a quiet street that was flanked on one side by a warped chain-link fence. As they retrieved crushed cans and discarded toys and the occasional piece of wet clothing, Reverend Witherspoon felt a wave of contentment warm him from within. Initially his return from sabbatical had not gone smoothly, but now everything seemed to have worked out.

He brokered a peace deal between the warring factions inside his church—those who attended primarily for social reasons versus the parishioners inspired by his fiery October sermon to take Christianity, and life itself, more seriously. A balanced schedule of events, patient discussions with all aggrieved parties, and a commitment to turn frustration into meaningful action had helped mend the congregation's fractures.

Litter removal was just one of the many activities he hoped would not simply engage with the local community, but help to unify and revitalize it. He felt that these kids here with him today were much too young to get caught up in the criminal justice system, let alone the street life, and so Matthias took great pride in this mentorship opportunity.

"Y'all are some good dudes," he said, exhaling into the cool air. "Just got too much free time for all that energy. You don't realize what I'm about to explain, 'cause how could you know? But truth is, all them cops and judges and lawyers, they *want* y'all to act stupid and break the law."

He heard a scraping sound and then watched as a glass bottle went bouncing down the street. Nicholas, who had kicked it, said, "I think you lyin'. That don't make no sense!"

"Oh, we got a skeptic here. That's fine. So tell me, Mister Nick, how am I wrong?"

The boy, only eleven but already capable of a fierce scowl, said, "They ain't like... construction workers, who come in and make something new. Nah, all they do is the cleanup."

"That's riiiight," Matthias said. "And speaking of which, don't you forget to pick up that bottle you thought was a soccer ball... But let's get into it, and I hope you other boys is listening, 'cause your friend Nicholas might teach you something here."

"Yeah, yeah," the other boys said. They were starting to get tired, Matthias noticed, lazily kicking at the plastic bags as they moved along.

"So check this out. A super-secret life lesson courtesy of the Reverend Witherspoon himself. And free of charge. You don't even have to put on your Sunday best and step inside the church. Now look across the way there. Y'all see that house? Nice place. Up above, power lines on the poles. Pipes under the road too. I bet there'll be a couple cars pulling into that drive end of the day. That all costs money."

Geoffrey said, "Cash money! Mm-hmm."

Matthias paused to grab a soda cup with his claw. "Yep. Money, cooperation, all that community stuff I been talkin' about. So... Okay, sometimes in the kitchen you spill or break an egg on the floor, right? Accidents happen, but you still get to eat your meal."

"When are *we* gonna eat," Matthias heard a voice whine softly from behind.

"The problem comes when certain people make it they life habit to always be that broken egg. The mess! Society says, 'What can we do?! We tryin' to move forward, but this crew always settin' us back a step.' So what you think now, Nicholas?"

"They going to kill us?" the boy asked.

"Ha! They *wish!* So don't give 'em no ideas. But no. What they do is flip the mess into their own favor. They already set the world up for makin' money, so now that's what they do with lawbreakers. From the policeman to the attorney's secretary on down, they *all* cashin' in on folks who play the fool. And it's *better* than a meal, because that you only get to eat one time. But a repeat offender, my God! That's like in pinball when your ball gets stuck up at the top. Bouncin' and bangin' all around those bumpers racking up points, and you don't even have to do a thing. Are you startin' to feel me, fellas? Anyone?"

Geoffrey said, "So, like, where they get the money from? Who pay them?"

"Good question, young man. Very astute. The answer is, the taxpayers. All the other people who live here in town. And for them, it's worth it. They're happy to pay their neighbor the judge to keep the ruffians off the street. Now lemme get real with y'all. How many of you know someone been locked up a bunch of times?"

Matthias paused to make a count of hands, but before he could continue, Nicholas said, "And you think that gonna be us too? That we next?"

The reverend exhaled heavily. "Look here. I don't believe any one of you got malice in your heart. Truly. But the system don't care—it can't *see* that part. All those vultures see is another black boy shoplifting from the convenience store. All they see is y'all voluntarily posting videos of you and your friends gangin' up and beatin' on somebody. And Lord of Mercy, that is why I'm trying to intervene on your behalf! To talk some sense into you before you really go too far, and they lock you up and throw away the key. Because the coppers and all them, their lives are totally set up. Sittin' on their butts until fresh criminals come along and give 'em something to do. So tell me, you still wanna step in their trap, now that you know it's there?"

The boys had stopped walking. There was the occasional sound of crinkling plastic as one of them adjusted his weight. A police cruiser rounded the corner at the end of the block, and Reverend Witherspoon waved at the white officer as the car rolled past.

"See?" Matthias said. "Someone's always keepin' an eye out."

A boy named Ismael dropped his bag and said sadly, "What we supposed to do? If they just waitin' for us to mess up… Sound like we always gonna get caught in the mix."

"My friend, I do not know. But stick with old Matthias and we'll try to figure it out. At least now you know something you didn't before this morning. So let's wrap it up for today, get out those sandwiches, and I'll log in your hours. Few more sessions with me, not only will this town be looking more beautiful than ever, maybe we can cook up a plan to keep you fine youngsters out of the legal system's teeth. 'Cause believe you me, even when you done *nothing* wrong, they'll still take a chunk out of you. Consider for example the former Mrs. Witherspoon, who at present is living in a mighty fine house that was paid for by yours truly…"

4. THE MOST BEAUTIFUL BOW

It was all so bittersweet. What with everything happening down in DC for President Jeffries-Lao's second inauguration, and Kate Donohugh being completely out of the mix.

Weeks ago she had stepped down from her position as HRA liaison working at the White House's behest. Packed up her belongings from her parents' house in Arlington and returned to Brooklyn, where she resumed her duties at the HRA megabranch in Newark.

But that wasn't all. She had a little secret no one else knew about. One that, if it came to fruition, would change everything and put the most beautiful bow on what had been the wildest year of her life.

She was pregnant. It was only the first month, however. Far too early to tell anyone, let alone make plans or think hopeful thoughts which might reverberate for the rest of her life.

She needed to stick to her normal routine—walk the dogs, work diligently, and keep riding the wave of reconciliation she'd been on with her husband Chris ever since returning from a disastrous overseas HRA work trip in November.

But now, while tidying up the apartment after a small New Year's Eve party, Kate pictured the living room floor as it might look when littered with brightly colored children's toys. Her mind started to helicopter up into the clouds as one pleasant future vision triggered another, and soon she was dancing through fantasy land..

It might have been the first time in her life that she truly wanted something just for herself. Because through the years, something *external* had always pushed her toward whatever she did. Go to college not simply to learn, but to get a good job. Join a volunteer organization to save this endangered species, or protect that marginalized group. And finally, work for the HRA to *avenge* the past.

She held her breath for a moment, suspecting that she had

stumbled upon another layer that was hidden beneath this role of playing helper. Something negative, angry… Something that thought in zero-sum terms, rather than of building on top of what good was already there.

Kate looked down at her body, thinking, *But this is different. This little thing is completely vulnerable. Later, when she comes out, her skull will be soft, her neck too weak to support the head. No words, no thoughts. Just needs—for milk, for warmth, to know she's still protected and safe after leaving my body.*

And then what? Kate would teach this baby words… in order to tell her how privileged she was? To start planting those seeds of doubt and self-recrimination before she'd even taken her first steps? Make this child question herself, rather than blossom confidently?

Kate vowed that she would not allow her daughter's mind to be influenced at such a young age. There had to be another way to teach empathy without putting a person's own foundations at risk.

There's a new life inside of me. I must protect her. She is mine! *My responsibility. She does* not *belong to the world…*

But it was still so very early. Any number of things could go wrong. Then she would be right back where she started—but also carrying heartache instead of a child…

Kate set her cleaning supplies down and closed her eyes. She took a moment to remind herself how blessed she already was. With health after a breast cancer scare that had mercifully only required a brief series of radiation treatments. Blessed with family and friends. A nice apartment. Coworkers who adored her.

And then there was the job itself. Assistant regional manager for the Historical Reparations Administration. Source of both satisfaction and strain. Career fulfillment after nearly a decade of working with activist groups.

Would she really go back to work when her maternity leave ended? After so many years spent battling on the front lines of progressive politics, suddenly she saw how tempting it would be to check out completely.

But logistics were a very real consideration. Chris ran a small one-person tech design business. While his clients did keep him busy, it was really Kate's government salary and gold-standard benefits package that fueled their household. He would most certainly have to take a real job if she decided to be a stay-at-home mom…

Kate shook her head. The instant that thought crossed her mind, she knew how cruel it was. Implying that what Chris did wasn't substantial, or meaningful in its own way. Belittling sideswipes like that were what had ground him down and put their marriage on the rocks just two months ago.

She would have to keep working on herself. Cut negative thoughts off at the pass. Respect her husband and their special bond. She knew in her heart they could navigate around whatever new challenges lay ahead. Because it was all worth it. And would be ever more so, if their family grew to three.

Plus the two Corgis, of course.

5. A WIN-WIN

"Well? What do ya think?"

Clyde Jenkins turned away from the TV screen and glanced at Eddie Pryor. The man's eyes were bulging in anticipation of what Clyde would say about this other rapper who was being pitched to team up with on a new song.

"It's kinda weird, to be honest," he replied.

"I know, I know," Eddie said. "But it's unprecedented what this guy does—and *did*."

Clyde wondered, *How can Eddie act so smart, but then sometimes he seems really dumb?*

He was recalling how this Hollywood mogul had suggested—no, insisted that Clyde's family fly out and visit Los Angeles. His mother Dawna, sister Myra and her boyfriend Octavius, plus his young niece and nephew all got the royal treatment around town during the Holy Holidays. But Clyde now suspected that this invitation hadn't come strictly from the goodness of Eddie's heart. More likely, it was a calculated move to prevent Clyde from having second thoughts about their freshly inked deal, had he taken a trip back home to Newark.

That was the man's smart side. But the proposed pairing with this other artist did not seem to make any sense.

DJ Low Bought started out as just another singer who had grown up poor, before catching a wave of success with some mix tapes under his first stage name, MC Nyte Nyte Nine. But a couple years back *something* happened—a car accident while not wearing his seat belt, or maybe resisting arrest during a drug-fueled freak out. The end result was that a portion of his brain had been surgically removed. And then, contrary to what all common wisdom suggested, he'd had *even more* success under his new moniker.

But all Clyde saw was a man who had taken mumble rap to a ridiculous new level of spectacle—complete with diamond-crusted scooter, bandana-print bib, and an 18-karat-gold drool pan in the lap. While the circular and rhythmic sounds that emitted from DJ Low Bought's quavering mouth were in fact hypnotic, Clyde could not fathom why Eddie Pryor wanted this guy of all people to be a part of his next song.

Clyde said, "There's got to be other dudes, or girls, who rap about the same kind of stuff as me. Because Low, he just makes crazy noises. So… I don't see what you see. Sorry, man."

Eddie sighed and rolled his chair away from the desk. They were in his private office which overlooked Hollywood toward the south. "Your concerns are understandable. And Clyde, I'm always happy to hold your hand and explain things to you. God knows, at least you *listen* and try to make the right decision."

A smile transformed Eddie's face. He said, "So here's the plan. Many people believe that you, Clyde Jenkins, have the Midas Touch, right? Turning everything into gold—or platinum, as the case may be, hehe. So… I'm gonna let you in on a little secret. And don't you *dare* spill the beans. Otherwise someone, who's probably much taller than me, will come and *mess you up!*"

"Jesus, Eddie!" Clyde cried. "What the hell is it?"

"I'm saying that DJ Low has been faking it the whole time! Do you *really* think someone with a half-empty skull can rap to a beat that's in nine-sixteenths time?! Come on, it was a gimmick—one that took on a life of its own. Who knows, maybe it started out as a bet to see what people were willing to go along with."

"Oh," Clyde said quietly. "So if I'm serious and he been playin'… How do we meet up?"

"Exactly! Because, Mister Midas, *you* are going to use your superpower of truth to reveal and heal him. First, we'll get a whole religious theme going. Then in the middle of the song, you—the wise man of integrity—will call out this sinner who's been hiding in plain sight.

"The extras wheel him up to the stage, arms twitching, lips babbling, while you deliver a sermon about how it's time to put an end to lies in the name of purity and goodness. Slowly he rises up… a rejuvenated man with his faculties restored… and together you guys dish out some great rhymes. The end!"

Eddie gave a self-satisfied smile. By now even Clyde was laughing along. He said, "Oh, okay. This is all really weird, but kind of fun too, I guess. What do you think will happen when people find out it was all a game?"

"Who the hell knows? But that's part of the thrill. Phase three of Low's career could be the biggest yet—or maybe someone whacks him with a lead pipe and he really does end up a vegetable. Ha!"

Clyde thought for a moment. Then he said, "So DJ Low already been acting like that for two years. How long was it supposed to go on? Or did you already know when you were gonna break his cover?"

"Well, Clyde, we're always drawing up new storylines here in the command center. Kind of like pro wrestling, except it's artists and celebrities. Their projects, as well as their private lives. My guess is someone here on staff toyed with the idea that you, DJ Clydoscope, might be a good fit to pull back the curtain. So we ran some models in our system and yeah, it all looked good. I mean, picture it. You arrive on the LA scene dropping this earthquake of a hit single—and finally Low can go back to walking around in public without a diaper on. I'd say that's a win-win!"

Clyde left his chair and walked to the window. A few months ago, he would have bristled at being part of such a silly song. But he was in it for the long haul now. He intended to dazzle the world for years—decades even!—and if the price was a few compromises along the way, so be it.

He turned back toward the office and said, "Alright, Eddie. I'm in. Guess I better get fitted for my preacher's robe then, huh?"

"That's the spirit," Pryor beamed. "The Holy Spirit!"

They high-fived and retook their seats.

6. RIPPLES OF TRAUMA

He was lost in a violent swirl of nightmares. Faces from the past painted in ghastly colors morphed into abstract shapes, then another horrid memory entered the frame. His soul howled for relief from these ancient torments as they gushed through the breached dam which had held them back for decades.

Time had ceased to exist. There were moments of calm reprieve, then a cool liquid rush sent his psyche hurtling back into the chaotic torrent once more. He thrashed frantically against pain... fear... doubt... the hundred soul-killing paths which could send a human mind into the bleakest corners of despair.

As these hellish waters slowly receded for the last time, Scott Cullen sensed that his captors were ending the torture simply because they had broken him to the point that there was nothing more to take. Beyond the confession of any worldly crimes, perhaps he had also admitted to some vulnerability or hideous truth that was still unknown to his conscious mind. And it was the ultimate motivator, the secret fuel which had driven him so hard and so far throughout his life.

Now, as he began the slow process of withdrawal from these drugs—regaining his senses and rebuilding his strength—Scott remained at the mercy of the federal government and the case its lawyers were surely building against him.

Decades in prison seemed a foregone conclusion. A treason conviction might bring the death penalty. What would become of the Church of Modestianity? What would his thousands of followers *do* if the Prescient One became the young religion's first martyr?

Scott wondered what he would say if he ever got another opportunity to speak to them. He couldn't pretend as if nothing had changed inside of himself, or preach confidently while hiding this raw spiritual gash beneath his cloak. No, he would have to dive back down, bring it into full focus, and then face it without fear.

As he fell into a quiet meditation, a scene from over twenty years prior flashed before his eyes. He was walking to school on a cold winter morning. Suddenly a car pulled up beside him. A female classmate he liked was being driven by her father. The man offered to take him the rest of the way. And Scott said no.

With his head drooping, he made that same lonely walk every day the rest of the year, when if he'd had the courage to do what his heart wanted, perhaps he would have kept carpooling with them, and maybe even become the girl's boyfriend—and then those years would not have been so crushingly hollow.

But instead, Scott Cullen kept to himself and mastered all the facets of computing that enabled him to design a video game which made him rich and famous while still in college. This obsessive drive to work in near-isolation... It was not simply dedication. There was an obscure darkness compelling him to immerse into *projects*, the same way that political types devoted their lives to *causes*. And yet, self-denial for a higher purpose had been responsible for the game *Thor's Tablet* and later the timely Church of Modestianity...

It was all masks and evasions. Burying his pain beneath frantic efforts, but never able to outrun the latent damage. Like an engine with an oil leak, sapping his soul drop by drop back into the inevitable sinking feeling after every triumph.

But how long could a person be propelled toward heroic deeds by the ripples of trauma which emanated perhaps from early childhood, if not also through ancestral memory? A life without the capacity for joy, either because it had been stolen or crushed, was sure to inevitably crumble—no matter how successful it appeared before that fateful moment of collapse.

Scott pursued that elusive source of existential nausea from within the confines of his jail cell. Tried to unravel the paradox of how fatalism could be converted into *performance* over and over again. Sought the cause and memory of his original wound. But this mysterious final layer, and the residue of psychological destruction, remained shrouded...

He had been in agony for far too long. And now that he was on the cusp of losing everything he possessed in the outside world, Scott Cullen could no longer carry the sickening weight that kept him trapped within a prism of dread.

He stalked the corridors of his mind each day. Eliminating a culprit here. Staring down an old regret there. Walling off alleys and mazes that were infested with self-effacing negativity. On and on…

He trudged relentlessly through the worst nightmares, the hazy sensations that suggested abuse, or paralyzing terror, or neglect, or humiliation, or betrayed trust… or simply his own faulty wiring.

A deceptively soothing voice offered him the promise of quiet sleep, if he would just give in to despondency. But he refused to let the pilot light of his soul be snuffed out—because if he survived this ultimate reckoning with a single *shred* of sanity, let alone goodwill…

Then surely Scott Cullen could rise once again, and emerge with grace in his heart.

7. OUTNUMBERED

Luis Ortega's schoolwork was laid out before him on a circular concrete picnic table in the courtyard of the LA City College campus. It was a pleasant sixty-five degrees and he was focused on an assignment for his electrical engineering class. He did not sense when the small group crept up and surrounded his table.

"Ay, you the Ortega kid?"

Luis looked up from his work. In front of him stood two guys and girl. Glancing over his shoulder, he saw that two others were hovering aggressively close.

"Uh, yeah," he said. "That's me. What do you guys need?"

"We just want to ask you a couple questions," a tall Latizo in black t-shirt and faded jeans said as he sat down across from Luis.

"Like what? School stuff?"

"Nah," the guy said with a laugh. "We's like, wondering why you think you're better 'n all of us?"

Luis nervously pulled his school materials closer, then said, "I don't even know who you are, man. How am I supposed—"

He felt a light slap from behind and his baseball cap fell down onto the table. "Listen to this fool!" a voice grunted.

"Playin' like he dumb."

Luis looked down and readjusted his glasses. "So we're back in high school, is that it? You think because I'm little, you can just—"

"Shut your friggin' mouth!" the first guy snapped. "Naw, this got nothin' to do with school shit. This about you runnin' your mouth on TV, messin' with everybody's HRA flow."

"Oh." Luis saw for the first time the anger in these brown and black faces that surrounded him. He braced himself for the beating that might come if he said anything which provoked them further. "What do you want me to do?"

The Afrigro-American girl jammed her hands into her pockets and said, "You don't like gettin' paid, why not take yo' sorry ass back to Mexico?"

The group laughed and exchanged fist bumps, then crowded Luis even closer. The guy sitting on the bench raised his arms for silence.

"Look, Luis. I'm Latiz like you, so forget her." He smirked at the girl. "You can stay in LA, it's cool, amigo. But maybe you got to keep a lower profile, know what I'm sayin'? Think about the rest of us—we ain't as *privileged* as the other kids in your lawsuit. We got to eat too. So stay away from the cameras, 'cause we *do not* want to see your stupid face on the news no more!"

Luis smiled involuntarily. "You're kidding me, right? The *last* thing I wanted was attention. I'm trying to do my damn work for class, man. But no one will leave me alone—not even you!"

Quickly he grabbed the edge of the table, then pushed himself off the bench before the person behind him could grab his shoulders. He scurried toward some other students who were walking past, but they jumped back and scattered, so he ran over to another table and climbed up onto the surface.

"Is no one gonna help me?" he pleaded with panting breath. "Crap! I thought college meant no more gang stuff. What the hell, guys?"

Luis felt terror rise up from his shuddering heart. Dozens of students were staring at him maliciously. In that moment, he wasn't a fellow Minorican. He represented a threat to the way of life that Beneficiaries had gotten used to—and one of these days, they might want to do more than just chat.

He nearly vomited as he thought about his two cousins who

had been beheaded by cartel members in Mexico a few years ago. His parents believed they had left all of that behind by moving to the United States...

Luis now watched as the intimidating group first trashed his belongings, then sauntered across the courtyard loudly. When he was sure that they were gone, he stepped down from the table and picked up his scattered possessions.

Today his friends from the HRA-defying legal petition seemed very far away. He didn't want to let them down by backing out of the whole thing, but none of them could protect him in his daily life, either. He was also mortified at the thought of telling his long-distance girlfriend Cristina about what had happened—and felt deep shame because he had not been able to stand up for himself when outnumbered.

He just wanted to be left in peace to live his life. As it was, he'd barely had the heart to endure any of what had befallen him in recent months. First the mandatory appearance on *DDM TV Live*, then fleeing the set during the chaos of the hacked broadcast. Going from fugitive to hero to advocate... and yet somehow, now he was seen as a villain.

The weight of the world was suffocating young Luis Ortega, and he didn't know how he would ever break free.

8. PROVING GROUNDS

"Here's the stuff. Jesus, what a nightmare..."

Nolan Simmons waved at the stacks of boxes piled six feet high which filled half of the small office space.

"You want us to go through it?" Jaden asked. He and his friend Harvell sometimes helped Nolan with maintenance and other grunt work to make extra cash.

"Nah," Nolan said. "Toss it."

"What is all of that though?"

"Just stuff that's accumulated over the years. Got moved from place to place. It's time to stop pretending I'll ever get around to dealing with it. Especially now that we need the space."

"Oh, okay. So take it all down to the dumpster? Or the

donation place?"

"Hell no to both! I want you to load up the van and head over to the same spot I sent y'all after Quincy got pinched a year back. Remember that?"

Harvell spoke up for the first time. He said, "But those things Mister Q. had was hot. Or knock-offs, right? This shit here..." He kicked at the boxes. "Look like a bunch of junk."

Nolan said, "You ain't wrong. But it's still got to be dealt with properly. Lemme show you why."

He pulled a medium-sized moving box off the top and ripped open the flaps, then tossed the contents onto the floor as he rummaged through.

"What do we got in this one? A clock... Oven mitt... Aha! Some papers! Car loan documents. Small claims court crap. Copy of an old lease from 'twenty-three. Are you starting to catch on? This is my personal paper trail. And I don't want none of my business falling into the wrong scans."

"We got you, boss," Jaden said. "We'll take care of it. Uh... still want me to shoot pictures, like last time? I mean, I know it's your own stuff, but figured I'd ask."

"Definitely. Gimme proof that the past has gone... poof!"

Nolan left them alone with the hand truck to load up the elevator, and then trip by trip, remove the clutter from his life forever.

Tomorrow some potential video clients were scheduled to check out the one-on-one interview setup in the soundstage down the hall, so all of the miscellaneous studio gear that was lying around needed to be moved into the space that the guys were clearing out. Nolan began organizing those items so that everything could be filed away neatly for future ease of access.

A few minutes later, however, there was a knock at the door. He glanced over his shoulder and saw Harvell standing there with a cardboard box in his hands.

"What's up?" he asked. "Is there a problem?"

"I know you said to throw everything away," Harvell began. "But I thought you might want to check this one out first."

Nolan set down the cables he was untangling and approached. "Why you say that?"

"Look." Harvell pointed at the words written in thick black marker across the top. "It's your Army things. Figured you'd probably want to keep some of 'em."

"I'll be damned."

Nolan took hold of the box and added, "Good looking out, Harv. Anything else catch your eye, you can maybe set it aside."

"No doubt, will do."

Nolan used a utility knife to carefully slice the box top open. He reached inside and felt his mind fall into a vortex of memories. Arriving at boot camp... The crackle of gunfire at the outdoor shooting range... Immersive classes on how to repair battle-damaged electronic equipment... Shipping out overseas... The endless heat and sand...

Nolan looked over the items laid out before him. Desert camo jacket with "Simmons" name patch on the breast. A respectable collection of service ribbons and badges. Framed photographs of himself and his buddies from the unit. And a small bundle of brochures that he had been given when leaving the Army—information about veteran benefits, mental health resources, and strategies for reacclimating to civilian life.

These glossy leaflets took him even further back, to the moment when he first noticed an Army recruiter's storefront half a lifetime ago. The promises made by those slick promotional posters were a stark contrast to the gritty Newark streets where he had grown up. Cleanliness. Functionality. A chance to excel, see the world, and make an impact.

He had seized on that opportunity and never looked back—until he did. Stationed around the globe at foreign bases, stateside posts in Illinois and Texas, and finally an honorable discharge after twelve years of service. Any number of opportunities awaited this United States military veteran who possessed advanced electronics knowledge.

But he went back home instead. To help fix up the old neighborhood? Or prey upon the weak, by using his skills to turn their petty vices into big business? Nolan knew very well that his mini-empire had not been built by planting trees or organizing charity runs.

He was also reluctant to admit that, had he not agreed to produce a music video for local kid Clyde Jenkins—the one that became a surprise hit last summer—he might never have changed his ways. Kept rationalizing to himself that he gave structure to the neighborhood kids who had no dads by putting them to work.

As if sending them off to tag along with the volatile older guys
was any kind of example to be setting for them.

None of this was in keeping with the military's code of
conduct, where you did the honorable thing when no one else was
looking or the odds were against success. But for the past six
years, he too had been weak. And too smart for his own good. A
cynic masquerading as a businessman, who perhaps chose the
straight path only because there were incentives to do so.

Now he was phasing out the unscrupulous aspects of his
operation with quiet urgency, while also transitioning into
above-board roles such as manager of his own entertainment
production facility. Solidifying gains. Guarding his perimeter.
Burying evidence. Papering over the predator who had run a
consortium of underground businesses from behind a computer
screen, while other people put themselves in danger by doing his
bidding in dark alleys and abandoned row houses.

He needed to maintain control of the narrative of his life
while his sphere of influence grew among the general public. His
story was being told and held up as an inspiration, so certain
details had to be massaged or omitted when delivering speeches
to schools and volunteer organizations. But the people who didn't
have his best interests at heart—ambitious journalists, IRS
agents—might already be digging for the unvarnished truth
about this self-made man from the Newark projects.

The magnitude of his failure of character weighed on Nolan
far worse than any exposé that might come out in the press,
however. He could stomach the outside world's contempt if his
name was dragged through the mud for a week or two. What he
really dreaded was looking himself in the mirror each morning.

So much so, that he had even considered leaving town for
good recently. There was a white woman who lived in
Connecticut he'd met during an October symposium, and they
had hit it off right away. But then he started feeling
uncomfortable at the oddest moments—and every time his mind
wandered back home.

What it boiled down to, he realized, was that he just didn't
want to spend his life surrounded by Caucs. Which maybe also
explained why he had originally returned to Newark after getting
out of the Army.

He reluctantly broke things off with his new lady friend

before the Holy Holidays, and then began declining invitations for any future public speaking engagements.

Because Newark was *his* garden to tend. He needed to uplift his neighbors, his friends, and even reach out to enemies or those hurtling toward self-destruction. Until the graffiti was gone and the boarded-up storefronts alive with black-owned businesses, he had no right to give lectures out of town about how things ought to be done.

Nolan placed the collection of keepsakes from his former life back inside the box. He let out a heavy breath, then walked down the hallway to the slim vertical window that was near the elevator.

He looked out onto the cold city as the sun disappeared behind a haze of winter clouds. Knowing in his heart that money and name recognition meant nothing if you sat atop a dung heap.

Nolan Simmons had always been torn between affection and disgust for these streets. Now they would serve as the proving grounds which revealed whether he had truly led a successful life or not.

He was finally ready for the challenge.

9. A TROUBLED CLOWN

"I can't do it anymore. I'm done."

Ryan Richards was pacing in front of his agent Mel Hedren's desk.

"What do you mean by that?" Mel asked. "Done hosting the show? Come on, you can't be serious!"

"But it's true! I'm tapped out."

"*DDM* just got renewed for a third season. Two months ago, you were all bent out of shape thinking it was gonna get canceled in a Dominguez administration. So what gives, Ryan?"

Richards waved his hand dismissively. He said, "Ancient history. I wanna leave. If it turns out to be a career ender, they're welcome to write in the obituary, 'His psyche died from complications due to ambiguity.' "

"Huh?"

"Mel, think back on the early days of the show."

"Yeah, and?"

"Real good times. It was all so clear-cut then. And everyone was excited! We were doing something, ya know? But now…"

"Now, what?" Hedren looked up at him incredulously. "Your ratings are still through the roof! Even *with* all the new, uh, color combinations, hahaha…"

"Eh, it's losing focus. All these changes on the fly, we're just winging it. The show used to stand for something absolute, Mel! People watched it and were inspired. But now it's part Jerry Springer, part car crash, and part *schadenfreude*."

"You've got to be pulling my leg, Ryan. You were out there doing the biggest cartwheels of your career these past few shows. What gives?"

Ryan Richards sighed. "I am a troubled clown."

"So… is this actually more about what's going on with you? Or…"

"I—my career—and the show are joined at the hip. And considering how much it's changed just recently, what else might they expect me to do next month or a year from now? I'm scared."

"I don't know, Ryan. How much further could it possibly veer away?" Mel fished a handkerchief out of his back pocket and dabbed across his shiny bald head.

Ryan leaned in and wailed, "Why not animals next? Or trees?!"

"Holy Christ. He's lost it…"

"Come on, Melly baby. You know I'm right! How many species have we hunted to the brink of extinction? What about all the adorable little calves cut down before their prime to make veal? Or the geese they force-feed so we can eat pâté at fancy parties?"

"And the trees?" Mel asked softly.

"Earth, man! We're killing the whole planet. Whale bellies full of plastic because their home is a toxic soup. Clear-cutting forests left and right to put up more goddamn condos. Need I go on?"

"Apparently you want to. Do you really think the show would go that route? Seems kinda out there. Or has someone been talking?"

"Nah, this is all me. But they're gonna have to ramp up the tension—and the absurdity—so folks keep tuning in. That's why

I want out now. I'm not gonna do my whole song and dance while some spoiled brat prattles on about everyone's carbon footprint. What would the punishment be? Who would even go on trial during that episode? Corporate polluters... or people who litter? 'Cause I tell you what, all those folks who got amnesty eight years ago... They sure as hell left a lot of trash in their wake as part of the migrant caravan."

"Okay, Ryan. You're overloading your brain with all these hypotheticals. You really should rest."

"Whatever you say. Yes, tonight I shall rest my world-weary head upon a goose-down pillow. But pray tell, what sins hath mankind committed to acquire *these* dream-inducing feathers?"

Mel paused and gave Ryan a sympathetic look. The strain was evident in the show host's face. He said, "You know they'll never let you walk away, right? Like it or not, you work for the HRA's PR department. They got too good of a thing going to break up the band just yet."

"Dammit... But I *need* to get out before I lose my freakin' mind!"

"I think you're making a mistake. Can I say that? Take a look at the new shows coming up on the spring schedule. You'll see, Reparations is still a hot ticket!"

Mel pawed through some papers on his desk and opened a copy of the *Tinseltown Talker*.

"What do we got here... Boom! *Credit or Debit?* Everyday people bring in their home inventions, then celebrity judges weigh the benefits to humanity. I love it. What else, what else... Couple archaeology programs catering to the indigenous crowd, and next... *Unpack Your Privilege.* Some kind of Sunday morning roundtable, I don't know... Aha! This is the one I really like. *Pardon the Appropriation.* Can you not see it, Ryan? They're really starting to have fun with it now. And *you* started it all."

Richards brushed aside the compliment with a wave. "And who are the hosts? Let me have that rag... Mm-hmm, yeah. Boom, yourself! Look at all these hacks. Beverly Orleans talking serious politics? Give me a break. Oh, and Justin Chan in the role of MC dealing with a group of A-listers? Doc, get me out of this lunatic asylum. I've already done my time!"

"Just... think it over. You were the trail blazer. That's got to be worth something."

"Bah. This trend is gonna drop like a stone one day—and I don't want to be on stage when it does."

Mel Hedren pursed his lips. "That's the thing, Ryan. You *were* on stage when the Sentinels first attacked. What would it look like if you turned tail just a few months later?"

"Oh Mel, you sly bastard. I think I'm gonna be sick! How long will *that* debacle chain me to *DDM*?"

"Let's not worry about that right this second." Mel pulled open the top drawer of his desk. "The real reason I wanted to meet today was so I could present you with this." He removed an official-looking envelope and handed it to Ryan, who opened it and read aloud slowly.

" 'Dear Mr. Richards… cordially invite… guest of honor… inaugural celebration… evening of…' Holy shit! Mel, you beaut! I'm going to DC!"

"What can I say? You've earned it. And I'm sure the president thinks so too."

"Wow. Eileen Jeffries-Lao and me. The guy who couldn't get a speaking part in the high school play."

"And now the leader of the free world wants to shake your hand in gratitude. Bravo!"

Ryan Richards floated out of his agent's office and headed for the nearest bar. Not to drown his sorrows as planned, but to celebrate.

10. BEST FOOT FORWARD

The house was silent. Tyrell was at school. Dawna had gone out a while ago to have brunch with some friends. And Octavius was… somewhere.

Myra Jenkins stood at the foot of her bed in the upstairs bedroom. Baby Sarah was sleeping peacefully in her crib over in the corner. Myra looked at the dresses laid out on the comforter.

A crinkled purple spaghetti strap with matching blazer. Plain black ending below the knee. Navy and white horizontal stripes with flared hem. All three were so nice. And tomorrow morning, Myra would put her best foot forward when she left Newark wearing one of them and headed into the heart of New York City —to hopefully change her life forever.

Myra sighed and turned away. She had been agonizing over her outfit for an hour. She wished Clyde was here to tell her some jokes, make her laugh the way he always could. Because right now she was feeling so nervous.

Of course her kid brother would take overnight fame in stride and move out to Los Angeles like it was nothing. He was still young. Didn't have any of the responsibilities or real-life stresses that she did. Juggling two kids, dealing with a mother who offered too much unsolicited advice—and then there was the tense relationship with the man she loved.

But if Clyde was reaching for the stars while strutting around as DJ Clydoscope, Myra's dreams were much more down to earth—even though they sometimes seemed just as improbable. The odds had been stacked up against her long before she awoke from the stupor of her youth to find herself a mother at age sixteen. Nearly seven years later, Myra Jenkins was suddenly on the cusp of her own small breakthrough.

Because while the world was fawning over Clyde and his music, Myra quietly followed through on her own goal of earning a high school GED. She had also completed nearly a dozen interior design projects for a woman who had befriended her down at the HRA vocational school where she worked as a childcare assistant.

And tomorrow, she was scheduled for an in-person interview at the Regnery School of Art in Midtown Manhattan. They had spoken glowingly of her sample portfolio, and the admissions counselor she'd talked to on the phone made it sound like this meet-and-greet would be a mere formality.

Best of all, they appeared willing to extend her a full-tuition scholarship, or something close to it. Myra didn't know if this offer was merit- or need-based. All that mattered was that someone saw she had potential and they wanted her around— wanted to help her grow and make something of herself.

For Myra, this was what she could control. Not pop music trends. Not the choices Octavius made when he was out of the house. Not the people working at the HRA field office, who made her feel stupid just for asking questions.

She didn't always like the way her mother spoke to her,

either. Disrespected her boundaries. Cast a judgmental eye toward how Myra lived her life, even though Dawna herself had raised two kids as a single mother.

Myra always hoped she could do better. Be better. But she'd just never known how. A year ago she never would have believed that this reality was out there, let alone so close to home.

As she gazed around the bedroom of this nice condominium which Clyde's success had paid for, Myra admitted to herself how glad she was that she wouldn't have to rely on his money for her art school classes.

Family was one thing. Pride was another. Myra Jenkins had lived her whole life as a nobody in the shadows. Not even considered a disappointment because no one had ever expected anything from her. But now, she was going to walk proudly into the Regnery administration building wearing a beautiful dress— and there was no telling how bright her own star might shine from now on.

11. UNSTOPPABLE SPIRIT

He couldn't believe it was happening.

As he frantically strummed his black Gibson SG guitar, Chris Donohugh watched nearly a hundred people crash and slam into each other as they swirled around the mosh pit in front of the stage. Another three hundred fans stood nodding their heads safely on the periphery.

Chris took a step to his right, leaning toward a microphone as he shouted, "Storm troop… Beverly Hell!"

After several back-and-forth callbacks with the singer, he moved to the edge of the stage and down-picked the first screaming bluesy chord that led into the guitar solo. Hands reached up to him from below and clawed maniacally in playful celebration of his own fingers dancing high up on the fretboard.

Chris eased back and shrugged his whole body in rhythm with the next riff. The drums pounded a mathematical beat that sounded like a factory cranking out industrial-grade machine parts. A warm swirl of satisfaction enveloped him—he was *back* on stage, and playing in front of the largest crowd of his life.

He glanced around. Behind him, drummer Ken was hitting hard and sending beads of sweat flying everywhere. Far to the left, bassist Ian was whipping his yellow-dyed mohawk like a fan.

And center stage gripping the mic was—not Glenn. No, instead longtime friend and scene veteran Miles Dexter had stepped in to sing at this unexpected Raucous Voice reunion. Just one of the five bands gathered tonight in honor of their missing comrade Glenn Murray.

Tonight We Fight: A Benefit Concert for One Political Prisoner's Legal Fund.

That's what the promo posters said. And here on the Boston venue's walls were handmade signs that proclaimed, "Don't Silence *His* Voice!" and "Free Glenn!"

After Raucous Voice finished their set, Glenn's current band Bleeding the Aggregate would take the stage as headliner. Another guy would sing and try to fill Glenn's larger-than-life combat boots during the performance.

The story was that Bleeding the Aggregate had been on a mini-tour when Glenn simply vanished after one of their shows in West Virginia. They'd been forced to cancel the last two dates, and then slowly word spread throughout the punk scene that one of their own was missing.

His family knew nothing. His current and ex-girlfriends hadn't heard from him. As speculation ran wild, from suspicion of suicide to a drunken fall off a bridge, Chris had a better notion of what might have happened to his childhood friend and former bandmate.

And so it was he who had anonymously circulated vague rumors that Glenn could possibly be in trouble with the law. All he'd hoped for was to discover Glenn's whereabouts, but it had quickly taken on a life of its own...

Suddenly other nameless sources came out of the woodwork offering concrete details. Within three weeks of Glenn's initial disappearance, it leaked out that he was being held at the Wallens Ridge supermax prison in Big Stone Gap, Virginia. No formal charges had been filed, no press releases distributed. Nothing. It was as if Glenn Murray had ceased to exist.

So the punk rock scene jumped into action doing what it did

best: rallying together with camaraderie and that unstoppable DIY spirit. It had culminated in this concert—raising money, promoting awareness about Glenn's plight, and for Chris, the opportunity to play music live for the first time in nearly a decade.

As he wrenched toxic bar chords out of his beloved Gibson, Chris Donohugh soaked up the overwhelming sensory joy of this moment. There would be time later to think about Glenn sitting alone in a small cell, and hope that word about the concert had gotten to him. To agonize over the possibility that Glenn's interrogators had gotten *to him*—and that he might incriminate his colleagues in the Sentinels of Jubilee. Chris now deeply regretted the few crumbs of HRA data he had given them in a moment of spiteful weakness when he and Kate were at odds.

He stomped his foot and shook off the dark thoughts. A chorus he'd personally written was coming up, and he intended to howl it with such fury that his own raucous voice might travel far and wide, to penetrate those prison walls and let his spiritual brother know he wasn't alone.

Because hundreds of people had come out to support Glenn Murray against government tyranny. Chris knew he would like that very much.

12. BEYOND LOYALTY AND DOUBT

FBI Special Agent Marcus Young was home. Whatever that meant for a man who often spent months embedded among groups that the government was keeping tabs on. He adopted so many fictitious identities that sometimes he even lost track of himself.

Gun runner supplying a motorcycle gang in the mountainous wilds of California. Prospective buyer of several children being trafficked through the Port of Miami. Disgruntled crane operator plotting with others to bomb the mansion of a governor whose policies had put thousands of blue-collar laborers out of work.

And finally, convert to the Church of Modestianity living at the Mall of Absolution in Bloomington, Minnesota. To monitor that start-up cult and its potentially dangerous leader, a man called the Prescient One.

The fallout from these last six months was almost too much to comprehend as he now sat in the silence of his townhouse in Fredericksburg, Virginia.

Before Marcus had completed his reconnaissance mission, the government arrested the Prescient One—aka Scott Cullen—for aiding and abetting the Sentinels of Jubilee. This hacker group had been designated as a domestic terror organization shortly after claiming responsibility for breaking into the HRA's mainframe back in early October.

But by this time Modestianity had already taken hold of Marcus's heart, and on the day of the dramatic raid, he was out doing humanitarian work at an Iowa medical facility owned by the church. The FBI soon tracked him down as well, and persuaded him to join the pursuit of another person of interest—the musician Glenn Murray.

Since then, his allegiances had not simply been tested, but blurred while navigating the high-stakes arena where politics and federal crime overlapped. Playing chess—or a game of chicken—with the bureaucratic state that buttered his bread and told him how high to jump.

Because Marcus had most definitely made compromises with himself. Committed sins of omission during the course of his official duties. Begun to question the depth of his commitment to his newfound faith. And been forced to arrest the man who possessed more integrity than anyone he knew.

Glenn Murray. The rough-edged rock singer with no credentials and seemingly nothing to lose. Who had lost his freedom when events... or his conscience... or the need to provoke a denouement... Whatever his true motivation, Glenn had essentially forced Marcus to arrest him so that—to *protect* Marcus! Because this FBI man was also caught in the drama surrounding America's new reality of living in a restitution-based surveillance state.

After Marcus turned Glenn over for processing, the month of December had passed in a haze. First, the Bureau honored him at a commendation ceremony in which he was showered with praise. Several wild parties followed, and he figured that his bosses were trying to help him ignore any temptations to reconsider his near-defection to Modestianity.

He appreciated their efforts, their understanding, their willingness to forgive his lapse of judgment. Because they knew very well the types of temptation that embedded agents faced. Sex, money, drugs, power. The old identity wavering after months isolated from family and friends.

But now back home with no wife or children of his own to ground him, and only commuting into the local FBI office as needed, Marcus Young felt himself drawn into an uncertain realm. He was beyond loyalty and doubt. Had transcended right and wrong as defined by the hard rules of laws and organizations. He was shell-shocked from time spent in the trenches of a war where no one was shot or killed.

Instead, the weapons were words whose meanings could be twisted for political gain. The mission was not to take land, but confuse and divide populations. And victory was the spiritual demoralization of your foe.

Marcus Young was uneasy about the enfolding nature of this asymmetric conflict. Because he had played a role, or roles, in it. But also because he sensed there would be more ambiguity, more disillusionment—a ship of state slowly sinking down into the bog, perhaps for decades.

All Marcus could do was turn away. He was so fatigued. A stranger in his own home. Blindly probing for answers about what he even wanted out of his own life. After years of sacrifice for career and country, always serving other people—and now waking up at age forty-two to realize that he had neglected to provide himself with anything more concrete to fight for than acronyms and ideals.

But he would not live in such selfless imbalance any longer. Whether that meant throwing in his lot with the Modestians, doubling down with the FBI, or even striking out in a completely new direction—his own interests would have to be a factor from now on.

13. THE REAL YOU

"Of course! I remember that one now. But you was so young!"

"Excuse me?! Just how old do you think I am?"

Clyde Jenkins felt his throat tighten. But that's what happened when you put your foot in your mouth. He tried to recover.

"Nah, I just meant you looked like a kid. But now… you're a woman!" He flashed a smile, and his heart soared when her eyes flickered and she smiled back.

"Awww, ain't you sweet? Come on, let's get some more drinks."

For the next fifteen seconds Clyde felt like he was in heaven. Floating across the room arm in arm with Ayana McGinn, the caramel-skinned former child actress who was now making waves playing more sophisticated roles.

A few moments later, after one of the catering staff had replenished her red wine and his rum-and-cola, they turned and waded through the living room of this mansion high up in the hills of Studio City.

"Anyway," Clyde said as they slipped out onto the quiet balcony, "tell me more about the real you."

Ayana held out her hand, inspected the long blue-peppermint fingernails, then gave a sigh. "The me beneath these acrylics, you mean? I don't know. Guess I'm boring."

"You? No way! All the shows you been in? That's got to be exciting."

"You know, Clyde, my dad used to joke that he wished someone would've gave him a furniture dolly back when I was born. Because that's been my life—always moving back and forth between auditions, acting classes, over to set, on and on. So when I'm not working, yeah, boring is good."

"But you're here tonight, right?"

She chuckled. "You're so green. And it's adorable! But this is a *work* party. You never know who from the industry you might run into."

"Oh," Clyde said, slowly realizing why Eddie had insisted that they attend this stuffy Saturday night affair.

Just then a tall white man with gelled-back hair stepped onto the patio. "Ah, there you are!" he said to Ayana. "Will you be able to… in a few?" He nodded back toward the living room.

"Of course. Just a second. Jerry, this is my new friend Clyde."

The man reached out and shook hands.

Clyde said, "Hi, nice to meet ya."

"Jerry's my agent. Like I said, work party."

"Haha, yes indeed," the man said with a shrug of the shoulders. "So Clyde, what do you do?"

"I sing, and rap. I'm here with Mr. Pryor. Eddie. You might —"

Clyde watched the smile disappear from Jerry's face. The man turned to Ayana and whispered harshly, "Do you not realize who this guy is?"

"DJ… ummm." She blushed, dropping her head with a smile as she reached out and tickled the top of Clyde's hand. "DJ Cutie."

"Well, there'll be nothing cute happening with your career if you two are seen together in the tabloids. Come on back inside, I've got someone *important* for you to meet."

"Hey now, boss!" Clyde protested. "I ain't done nothing to her, or you. Why you get to interrupt? I know y'all is doin' business, but at least let me get her number first."

Jerry scowled at Clyde, then addressed Ayana again. "This clown is the one who wrote 'Fly So High.' "

"I know," she said. "He told me. I heard it a few times awhile back. So?"

"Uh… Ayana, darling, where do you think the funding for *Kentucky Bless* comes from? The HRA! And you do want your character to return next season, right?"

Clyde saw confusion and then sadness wash over Ayana. Heard her say quietly, "Oh." Watched her turn away from him and reenter the party with Jerry close behind.

He took a sip of his drink, but it didn't taste good now so he dumped it over the railing. As he looked out into the cool night, he heard the sliding door open and then Eddie's loud voice.

"Clyyyde! There's my main man." Eddie hoisted up his beer

glass as he approached. "Hey, why so glum? Come rejoin the fun. Somebody I know wants to introduce himself. Oh, and let's get you fixed up with another drink while we're at it."

Clyde stuffed his frustration down and followed Eddie into the house. He would put on a smile and talk to whoever, then try to slip Ayana a piece of paper with his phone number on it before the party ended.

Otherwise, he might need to write a new love song just for her…

14. A LEADER'S JOURNEY

President Jeffries-Lao cycled through the tabs on her computer screen. News articles and videos chronicling the wave of protests around the country that were aimed at her administration. As expected, many Debtors couldn't face the prospect of another four years out of power without throwing a final tantrum before her inauguration.

Then there were the rallies pleading leniency for members of the Sentinels of Jubilee who had been detained. Here Eileen planned to make several gracious concessions in the spirit of moving the nation forward. Implicated Dramacrat Congresshuman Neil Thornton would be freed in exchange for resigning his House seat—which he had in fact won a fourth term to serve, despite being arrested the night before the election.

Also irksome was the benefit concert in Boston which held up some incarcerated musician as a "political prisoner," despite the evidence suggesting that he was an SOJ accomplice. Eileen's advisors had brought this story to her attention because most of the attendees were left-leaning. The takeaway being that just weeks after voting to re-elect her, they were now putting personal loyalties ahead of what benefited the big picture.

Another group of agitators were those kooks up at the Mall of Absolution. Not only were they hosting outrageous masses at home in support of their imprisoned leader, they'd also mobilized the ranks of their satellite churches nationwide. Eileen and her team were deeply disturbed by the passionate spectacle of the so-called Million Modestian March. These dozens of gatherings, which averaged a thousand attendees who were all decked out in asinine teal and silver costumes, proved enough to force her hand.

But only *after* Scott Cullen, aka the Prescient One, had been humbled, humiliated, and spilled his guts. Not just by confessing to his involvement with the Sentinels, but also detailing the inner workings of his brainchild, the Church of Modestianity. And as the cherry on top, Scott made some very disturbing personal revelations while under the influence of tongue-loosening drugs. Oh, what she might do with all that juicy material...

But pragmatism had won out. The Modestians themselves apparently being such true believers, the White House pulse-takers were convinced that the shrewd play was to not make their guru stand trial, let alone force the religion to disband. Because somehow in just a few short years, this color-coded cult had gained a large enough following throughout the United States, that sending in the Feds to scatter them to the wind risked provoking a public relations disaster, if not open conflict.

Better to avoid another potential Waco debacle, and instead return Mr. Cullen to his people a weakened figurehead. Thus neutralized, he would forevermore preach just enough truth to stay in power, but never go so far as to disrupt anyone's agenda.

Eileen now considered the potential benefits of keeping Congresshuman Thornton in place after all. *That* would be one vote she could always count on. He might even be persuaded to take the lead in supporting a series of space initiatives her administration planned to unveil in the fall months...

Jeffries-Lao understood that a leader's journey was long, and often required calling audibles or taking unconventional paths to get across the finish line. Magnanimous gestures made people feel like they were being seen, heard, and catered to. Sometimes all it took was the use of symbols to garner sentimental press coverage as you tossed crumbs to the aggrieved.

And while the masses were out celebrating a trivial victory, your forces moved ahead to fortify real gains. What were a few million dollars donated to some charity but a bargain, when the tectonic shifts facilitated by your laws, executive orders, and bureaucratic outposts were everlasting?

Eileen turned her attention to more positive news. The latest polls showed that her approval among Afrigro-Americans was virtually as high as at the start of her presidency. They still believed in her. That she was their champion and would always fight for them.

She recalled her first attempt to alleviate their plight while serving as California's governor. Appalled by the conditions of black homelessness in cities like Los Angeles and San Francisco, Eileen had spearheaded humane policies to help get drug addicts and the mentally ill out of their filthy tents, as well as bring purpose to the daily lives of those who rode public transit for hours on end. It was one of her most heartfelt political initiatives —which also delivered practical results. Because in clearing a path to restore these poor souls' dignity, she had reopened the sidewalks for business.

And now, nearly a decade later, after having achieved more for Afrigro-Americans than anyone but perhaps Abraham Lincoln, President Eileen Jeffries-Lao had the luxury of taking stock and contemplating her next act in a way that the assassinated emancipator never could.

What crossed her mind was unprintable. Too callous. Too politically *raw* to be spoken outright in a society beholden to politeness. But the truth was that they had all used each other to get here. Had allied to achieve objectives that were certainly noble, but which ultimately had a shelf life.

Soon Eileen would begin the decoupling process, because the world did not begin or end with the needs and pleas of Americans of African descent. They had wanted long-overdue justice and Eileen's administration delivered it—game over.

Were they willing or able to accept that the ledger had finally been settled? That it was time to stand on their own two feet and seize control of their destiny? Not that Eileen had any plans of turning her attention back to the much-maligned Caucmerican crowd...

Because it wasn't even *the world* that beckoned now. Using the HRA to help other former colonial powers patch up their reputations was an important next step, but far from the endgame. Successful space exploration would only be possible if humanity harnessed all of the best minds that globalism had brought together—in technology, science, medicine, and yes, even government.

The universe itself awaited, and Eileen Jeffries-Lao was ready to deliver planet-transcending results during her second term.

15. ULTIMATE PARADOX

"What's up with all these hackers going free after just a slap on the wrist? When *we* get in trouble, they work us through the system hard!"

The man sat down and slapped his leather gloves against his thigh. As the gathered crowd voiced its agreement, a woman wearing a beige dress stood up and said, "We can't just accept that that's the way it is. We got to hit the streets and be heard!"

Loud applause echoed throughout the church meeting hall. Before the woman retook her seat, she added, "And you, Reverend Witherspoon, ought to take the lead."

Matthias Witherspoon eased off the edge of a table up front. He said, "Go out into the streets and do what? Hold up signs—or burn our city down?"

"We gotta let 'em know we feel betrayed after all that big talk before the election," someone hollered. "Supposed to bring the Sentinels to justice!"

Matthias waited patiently as several others vented their frustrations about how the government was disrespecting Afrigro-Americans. He nodded his head after each person said their piece.

Someone pointed a finger at him and demanded, "Well?!"

Reverend Witherspoon pointed back and said, "Well, what? I've been telling you for weeks now that something like this could happen. That it was *bound* to happen. If you had believed me instead of plugging your ears, maybe I *would* help y'all get a street protest going. But now? No way. It's too late."

The lady in beige called out, "What you said, was that the HRA might start pulling away from us. We're all used to broken promises, Reverend." There were murmurs of agreement as she paused. "But letting the people who tried to *end* Reparations walk? No, yourself. That is disgusting! How can we witness such an injustice and sit quiet?"

Matthias said, "Mrs. Lloyd, you're not wrong. It's one more

slap in the face after God knows how many others. All I'm trying to do is help everyone look ahead, so we don't get blindsided again. We got to be more prescient moving forward."

"There he go," another woman said in a biting tone. "Talkin' all that Modestian talk."

"Yeah! Why'd he come back again?" a voice boomed.

Matthias forced a smile, then sighed. "I came home because I love you all so much. I want what's best for our community. So now... Do you *really* think there's anything we could say that would make the government folks change their minds? They've thought it all through, and bottom line, they got other plans. Bigger plans that got nothing to do with us! So you can go complain in the streets—*or* we make our own plan now, so we won't have to humiliate ourselves begging Caucs for crumbs no more."

After a loud chaotic moment, a man's voice rang out. "How we gonna do that? You got it all figured out or what?"

"I got some ideas," Witherspoon said. "And that's why we get together after services are over. To discuss these more earthly matters. So let's all cooperate, try to work it out, and find happiness here in this lovely corner of the world."

"Amen!" an old woman cried.

"You got that part right," Mrs. Lloyd added sarcastically. "Because we sure are gonna need a miracle at the end of all this."

"Aw, don't be so salty, Lady Lloyd!" Witherspoon said. "Maybe it's actually a good thing. Truly. You don't want someone else payin' for us *forever*, do you?"

As the grumbling died down and the crowd settled in, he added, "I sure am sick of hearing why we can't do for our own. We got to quit whining... stop lying to ourselves... and just find a way! Because the world is *huge*. While you carry on about how the white man in America done you wrong, people in *other countries* with ugly legacies of their own are making it happen.

"Did you know, that fifty years ago in Cambodia they killed all the people who were educated? Doctors, scientists—hell, if all you did was wear glasses, they might put a hole in your skull. Yep, almost a quarter of their population died in less than four years' time. And look at 'em now! Those Cambodians may not be number one, but at least they're back in the fight. I bet a couple of y'all are wearing some clothes made over there, in fact.

"Not only that, I could spin a globe, pick any other place at random, and I bet something worse happened there than what you got to complain about. Say what? Price of beef went up? Best friend's in jail? Your leg hurts? Ha! Tell that to the people in Syria, who your best friend Barack Hussein bombed all to hell.

"Uh-oh! I done stepped in it now. 'Matthias, you naughty man!' But it's true. Anywhere you look, a hundred years ago or less, people got hit hard by something. Lot of 'em end up moving here to the United States, too. Mm-hmm. Let's chew on that. They never liked us to begin with, these immigrants. Then they see us in action, and back of their mind is saying, 'My uncle got taken away in the middle of the night, and we ain't seen him since. What are these fools complaining about?'

"And you know, they may be right… but dammit, they're also wrong! Why? Because this is *our* country, *our* land! I don't like *no foreigner* sauntering around flappin' his gums about us. No, sir. 'Cause when he steps off the plane, there's a whole system in place to help get him on his way. Free healthcare, nice government housing, school for his kids, family networks too. Anything and everything to give him that soft landing we never got after the boat ride.

"I mean… I *guess* Reparations was supposed to be that. But even if the dollar amount was just right, I say it came way too late. We tired, we broken! We been confused for so long, we don't know what to believe. So we lash out, hit anyone we can— while of course saving the worst for our own kind. Because in our hearts, ladies and gentlemen, many of us hate ourselves.

"Easy as it would be to cook up a fresh batch of poison, what if we took this pledge instead? For one year, we will make the right decisions. We will take the *least*-destructive path. 'Cause let's face it, lot of temptation come a person's way in twelve months, hehe. Can't hurt to try our best, am I right?

"Choose to defuse an argument before it turns to the gun. Pick up those dusty old dumbbells and walk around the block. And when you pass the liquor store, and sneaky Mrs. Kim smiles with those shelves full of booze, you tell her, 'No! I ain't drinkin' none of that tonight!'

"Give me a year, folks. Check in with *each other* every week. One thousand small steps in the right direction, and this congregation will emanate a glow that's sure to spread over to the next town, on and on. Simple as that. Each person doing a tiny bit each day is how you make progress, my people.

"Not by filming yourself yelling, 'I am the greatest!' But ain't that the ultimate paradox? One minute we're down on ourselves, then the next we braggin'. Not about accomplishments, mind you, but sayin' stuff like, 'I'm a king.' 'I'm a queen.' 'We *all* kings and queens.' And then there's my personal favorite, 'Black people is *powerful!*'

"Look, I get it. Some misguided fool put that idea into your head, trying to instill pride or self-esteem or whatever. But my goodness, replacing depression with delusion is *not* the solution! Same reason just 'cause I drop a nice rhyme now and again, it don't make me a world-famous rapper, right? No, ma'am. Matthias is only master of the Sunday morning ceremony, not out at the club on Saturday night…"

The crowd laughed. Reverend Witherspoon took a sip of water, then continued.

"I bet some of y'all caught on to the fact that old Matthias is a student of history. Would you believe me, if I said I found out who the first ever debt protester was? It's true. Somebody who really didn't want their own inconvenient archives seeing the light of day.

"Let's go back a bit. The year is 1982. Yes, that's correct. Long before Baby MARVIN was born and started cryin' and poopin' all over our lives, there was a treasure hunter who went looking for gold in sunken ships all over the world. This gentleman was exploring some wreckage off the coast of Brazil —a country, by the way, which received *four million* of your African cousins. That being forty percent of the total number of slaves shipped across the Atlantic Ocean, for your information. But y'all don't know, y'all don't care, right? Right! Moving on.

"Anyway, the dude dives down and starts poking around this underwater boat. What does he find? Not much in the way of coinage, but there's lots of artifacts. Beautiful vases, pottery… nice stuff for museums. So what was the problem? I'll tell ya what. Those items dated back to Roman times! Fifteen hundred years before the Portuguese first landed on those same shores!

"So did Brazil say, 'Oh my gosh, thank you kind sir for making this incredible discovery. Humanity will be so much richer for the knowledge which you risked your life to acquire'? Heck no! First, they took this adventurer to court to keep him away from the site. Then one day, the Navy went out there and dumped a whole lotta dirt on top of the ship, so no one could get at it anymore. I kid you not!

"And all for what? Money? Prestige? Nope. Brazilian government just didn't want to deal with the hassle, the *inconvenience* of having to rewrite their history books—or their treaties with the mother country, Portugal.

"So look, the next time your local paper prints an article about some dastardly Cauc who got caught burning an old contract he found up in his attic, maybe you'll remember that Matthias said to cut him some slack. We are all weak-willed sinners. And now you know, he ain't the first or the worst offender.

"Let us praise the Lord, because I do love you all. If we remember to stick together, we'll surely make our way through."

16. ANONYMOUS TIP

Work had become a breeze. No more arguing or haggling with the Debtors and Beneficiaries who showed up at HRA branches. Instead, all reasonable claims were processed with a smile, from requests to increase one's monthly stipend to accepting documents that might reduce a person's Debit Score.

Kate Donohugh *had* noticed that the staff was smaller than before the Holy Holidays and New Year's long weekend, but there was always turnover around this time. She simply couldn't believe that all of the missing faces had been let go—or caught in the Sentinels dragnet. Her supervisor Jan remained mum on the subject as well, so Kate just kept her head down and focused on her own job. She herself had already taken two leaves of absence from her Newark office in the past year—and with possibly a third to come, she figured it would be wise not to rock the boat.

The streamlined workflow meant that her department was freed up to tackle new initiatives. Today she was sitting in on a presentation entitled, "Second Act: The HRA Reaches Maturity." A bubbly male-and-female duo was riffing on all of the upcoming changes.

"...after reaching many wonderful milestones. Battles won—"

"—and lost—"

"Now, now, Erica. That's just life!" The man gave a goofy smile. "Which is why it's so crucial to not just have a team—"

"—but the whole organization behind you," the woman said with a declarative nod. "While you all were kicking your feet back and enjoying holiday cheer, the HRA busy bees were finalizing an exciting game plan for 2029..."

"...and beyond!"

The static image of the HRA's green and white logo being projected onto the wall now gave way to a montage of data graphics and stock photos featuring people of all ages and races enjoying each other's company.

"Caring!" the woman shouted. She pumped her fist triumphantly.

"Let everyone know how much you care about them," the man implored.

"Outreach!"

"Don't hide away in that cubicle, friend. The HRA wants to see you in *action!* Mm-hmm."

"Security!"

The man brought a hand to his forehead and simulated peering into the distance. "That's right. If you suspect any fishy business, don't just look the other way. You can submit—"

"—an anonymous tip—"

"—and help save the day!"

The duo did a synchronized celebratory dance before moving on to the next topic.

Kate looked at her watch and sighed. This meeting would run for another half hour, then she was scheduled for a sit-down with several supervisors and managers that would last two hours. After that, she needed to write the first draft of an article for the department's internal newsletter...

She held her phone below the table surface and typed, "When does the outreach part actually begin?"

Her coworker friend TJ giggled from his seat nearby a moment later, then a reply message came back saying, "More like, out of touch!"

"How much do you think these two get paid for doing this?"

"You mean it isn't *punishment?*"

Kate laughed quietly through her nose as she typed, "Maybe they were on *DDM TV* too."

"Speaking of which… are you off the hook or what?"

"Speak no evil, hear no evil. So, just holding my breath and waiting."

"But, missy… you *did* evil. Scofflaw!"

Kate looked over at TJ and shook her head. He smirked.

"Who's the Southern gentleman again?" she wrote.

"My conscience is clear. Most of us Rowes were too poor to own property, let alone *people*."

"Jerk!"

"Cyberbully."

"Redhead."

At this, TJ snorted before quickly covering his mouth. Kate closed her eyes and held her breath to keep from laughing out loud and making a scene.

Meanwhile the presentation up front continued unabated, as bold statements and animated gestures rammed home each talking point with the power of a slam dunk.

17. EYES INSIDE THE GATES

The paperwork he was required to sign seemed endless. Declarations that he wouldn't speak negatively of the government. Bank drafts transferring portions of his assets to the United States Treasury. Detailed confessions that were most likely transcribed from his drugged-out ramblings.

Scott Cullen wondered why he agreed to such a deal. To cooperate with Eileen Jeffries-Lao's administration and gain release without a trial, so long as he obeyed the provisions of the documents stacked in front of him.

Maybe he believed that the Reparations-as-surveillance-state awakening was inevitable, and that he would rather be a free man during that chaotic time. Or maybe he did it for the Church of Modestianity. To fulfill his prophecy after leaving the Mall of Absolution in chains.

Or the torture had actually broken him. Had completely stripped away his ego and accomplishments and soul, leaving only a liquefied psyche in its wake. If the Prescient One ceased to exist and Scott Cullen was also a shattered slate, then perhaps he would have to create himself out of whole cloth once again.

But he would not do it alone this time. He knew in his heart that something beyond himself had been his guide out of the darkness. It was an element both beautiful and pure, extending the promise of unknown future joys if he dared to survive. And so he had.

This transfixing light had also left the seed of a riddle inside his mind. It whispered, "For a human life to achieve true meaning, one must not simply transcend the process of reacting —but also go beyond the self. To perform acts that emanate *out* as well as build *up*."

But having already lost so much, Scott could not help but wonder if these epiphanies were impossibly grand delusions…

After the documents were signed, he was returned to his cell to collect the personal effects he had accumulated during nearly two months in captivity. These items included the holy books of several esoteric religions from centuries past, a bar of soap which he had whittled into a capital *M*, and a small bag of toiletries.

Scott hoped that the electric blue outfit and cape he had been wearing at the time of his abduction would be returned to him. But one of the guards just laughed and said, "Nope. Government's keeping that stuff as a scalp."

"No great loss," Scott said. "I have others. Casual clothing will suffice."

"Sorry, fella. No can do. That beautiful orange onesie you've got on looks just fine."

"But why? I don't understand. I'll be a free man."

"Oh, you'll see…"

And a short while later, Scott did see. His arrest and incarceration may have begun in secret, but it all ended with a media circus. He was forced to walk out in the open for nearly three hundred yards, going from the facility's entrance to a transport vehicle which seemed to have been intentionally parked as far away as possible.

So that the frail and haggard Scott Cullen would be exposed

to the harsh winter elements, his bright jumpsuit flapping in the swirling winds as he trudged forward. Exposed to the unforgiving cameras of the hundred-strong press corps, which had been invited to maximize his humiliation in the eyes of the world—and his church.

Scott clenched his jaw and endured this shameful walk while flanked by three imposing guards. Were these men in place to keep the reporters from charging, or to dissuade a hidden sniper from attempting assassination on this gusty day?

A youngish business type wearing a sport coat was waiting in the back seat of the van. As Scott took his place across from him, the man said, "Mr. Cullen! Agent Vance. I'll be your escort, as well as two other support vehicles. Got to keep you safe, right?"

"But of course. I'm still a wealthy man, despite the close shave your employers just gave me."

"Hey, do the crime, pay the dime. But I might suggest you spend some of that leftover cash at an all-you-can-eat buffet. 'Cause you look like absolute shit."

"That's what happens when you're fed a steady diet of brain-relaxing chemicals." Scott pointed at his stomach. "The weight, here and on one's conscience, falls right off."

"Oh, so you really have lightened your burden? I swear, you and those effing Sentinels… Made us look like idiots."

Cullen noticed that Vance was absently tapping at the side of his blazer. He said, "Is this really an escort… or are we en route to some sort of Mafia killing, complete with a ready-made patsy?"

The agent laughed. "I wish. But no, Your Prescience. Just a not-so-subtle reminder that we'll be watching you closely from here on out. Break the terms and we'll break—"

"Nothing," Scott interrupted. "Which is why I'm getting out now. Short of murder, there's nothing more you or anyone else can do to hurt me."

"Heh, I guess we'll see about that. Just keep your nose clean, Scottie. We've got eyes inside the gates."

"Spies at the Mall, you mean?"

"All of them fervent believers. They love you, and they love Mod too. Oh, yeah…"

The ride to the airport proceeded in silence. Scott Cullen remained calm, knowing that very soon he would begin the next major project to redefine his life.

18. PARALLEL DIRECTIVE

"Uh-ohhh…"

Nolan Simmons clenched his front teeth together and glanced uncomfortably around the room. He reread the tabloid headline on his computer screen.

Pre-Columbian Dirt Muddying Reparations Waters!

Quickly he scanned the article for prominent names. So far, all of the politicians and celebrities mentioned were C-list at best.

"But for how long?" he said to himself, grabbing a tablet as he rose from the leather swivel chair and exited the business office. He rode the elevator down one floor and flashed a key card outside a room that was dark except for the glow of nearly a dozen computer screens. He cleared his throat after entering. The boys inside slowly turned away from their workstations.

"Now listen up," Nolan said sharply, then held the tablet aloft. "I just sent this news story to y'all. And if it is to be believed, then our friend MARVIN is working on a parallel directive."

"What's that mean?" a kid wearing glasses asked.

Another boy stood up. He moved his arms jerkily and said in a robotic voice, "Macro… Aggregating… Restitution… Vector… Input… Navigator."

Everyone burst out laughing.

Nolan waited a moment before addressing the first boy's question. "Zeke just said 'what's that mean?' Don't none of y'all nerds see what's going on?" After getting no response, he added, "It means the Sentinels ain't actually dead!"

This claim prompted some nods and murmurs from the young computer whizzes. Their jobs centered around promoting local creative projects that Nolan was supporting, but ever since the Sentinels of Jubilee struck back in early October, they had also been keeping tabs on all things HRA-hack-related.

"So, Mister S.," another boy began, "how do we fit in with all of that?"

"Excellent question, Omar. Now, if y'all don't mind while I just—" Nolan nudged the light dimmer up a step, so that he wouldn't crash into anything while delivering his pitch. "Look, the normies might not see it yet, but articles like this, even if they start out in the gossip papers… It means the writing is on the wall, y'all."

"For who?" was the boys' reply.

Nolan chuckled. "Not who, but when. Two reasons. First, it's admitting they might change how far back the MARVIN tech goes digging. And second, could be the Sentinels are basically saying, 'We can't stop Reparations from spreading, so eff it, let's go for broke!' And by doing it that way—by accelerating the process—they might blow up the HRA's timetable for rolling out in other countries. Y'all feel me now?"

After seeing a few tentative shakes of the head, Nolan shouted playfully, "What?! You're supposed to be geniuses, that's why I hired you! Alright, alright, I know you're only *technicians*. Look, the government planned to do everything on a certain schedule—to maximize the money getting paid out while maintaining social stability. Y'all know they hit that speed bump couple months back, then got themselves fixed up. But! This right here looks like it could be a damn iceberg!"

"C'mon, Nolan," Zeke said. "Help us *see*. What we supposed to do?"

"Y'all are gonna help MARVIN out."

"What?!"

"That's right. Don't matter if you don't understand why, but Reparations as we know it is done, son! Cooked goose. Soon as a few top-bill celebs or all-star point guards start getting lit up by their *unauthorized* Debit Scores, oh my God, will we be in for a show! Afrigros gonna be *beggin'* Jeffries-Lao to shut it down once and for all."

Several of the boys stood up as Nolan doubled over in a fit of laughter.

"So what y'all are gonna do," he continued, "is help find more data that's older than 1492. And hell, anything you can get out of Africa, India, Aztecville, wherever, grab it all."

"Yeah, yeah!" the boys cheered.

"Each of you will get a budget of a hundred bucks a day. Post classified ads, information requests, whatever you think might get the documents flowing into our network. Gonna be a lot of international work too, so use your translation software, generate regionally sensitive avatars with the portrait blender... and have fun! In one week we'll analyze the early results, tweak our methods, then increase funds as necessary. How you geeks feel now?"

"In MARVIN we trust!" Omar declared as he thumped a fist against his chest. All the other boys laughed.

"Damn right! Glad you remembered that line."

"You only played the track a hundred times," someone muttered sarcastically. "How could we forget?"

Nolan whipped his head around and peered through the darkened room. "Who said that? Come on, don't be afraid."

A hand went up slowly.

"Alright, Mr. Philpot. Very funny. Just be sure when you say your prayers before bed tonight, remember to thank God for DJ Clydoscope. 'Cause without him, you'd all be playing dice out on your front stoops. And dead broke too!"

As Nolan walked back toward the elevator with a jump in his step, he wondered how Clyde was adapting to life in Los Angeles. Because the wolves out there were willing to take advantage of *anybody*, regardless of gender, age, or skin color.

A city of equal opportunity predators, all selling that dream...

19. BETWEEN TWO WORLDS

Luis Ortega felt awake for the first time in his life.

He realized that he had always been a passenger on someone else's journey. An accessory to their story, their agenda. First as a baby, when taken from Mexico by his parents to cross into the United States illegally. And then more recently, appearing on that Reparations-themed TV show to be used as a prop for whatever those people were trying to achieve.

Luis now sensed that beneath the desire to honor his family, who had risked so much for a chance at a better life, he was also subconsciously driven to prove himself worthy of being in

America. The country that had agreed to adopt him and millions of other foreign-born people, despite the fact that they hadn't stood in line. And yet... there was some mysterious touch of fear within it all.

An apprehension that would not take solid form. Because everything about his life seemed vague. Nothing was definite or reliable. His entire conscious existence had taken place in the United States, but every day someone reminded him that he was Mexican, a Latizo, a Minorican...

Perhaps his escape from the *DDM TV Live* stage was the first in a series of desperate attempts to... latch onto something *other* than imposed identity. To declare that he, Luis Ortega, was his own person. But, if the main reason for pursuing an associate's degree was in order to become the first college graduate in his family, then even that accomplishment might not be enough to sustain him.

Especially now, when it was a diverse group of Minoricans— and not resentful white supremacists—who had gotten in his face with *threats* saying he should go back to the correct ethnic pen. Meanwhile his Cauc professor at LACC, Mr. Smiley, he wanted everyone to succeed...

These conflicting thoughts were too much for the normally easygoing Luis. He felt paralyzed, and wondered if he really *was* trapped in some sort of cage. Because if achieving educational goals could not liberate or define him, what else did he have? How would he even go about creating a new version of himself?

Luis thought about his girlfriend Cristina who lived in Boulder, Colorado. She made him feel really good when they were together, but now he was even having doubts about why she liked him. They had only met because two months ago, a group of young people who were protesting the Direct Descendant Match program hoped to use his notoriety to gain traction for their anti-HRA lawsuit.

They were already holding him up as a near-mythical figure by the time Cristina, who was of mixed Latiz-Caucmerican ancestry, contacted them in hopes of deferring her own DDM call-up on the Debtor side. Luis had instinctively shied away when they appeared at his parents' house unannounced, but the tragic look in Cristina's eyes as she pleaded for help out on the driveway... He simply couldn't resist trying to live up to the vaunted reputation of the "Saint Luis" who was praised in the group's hymns.

But the tides were shifting aggressively now. Luis knew that he couldn't be so passive anymore and survive. He would have to push forward—or lash out—to avoid being completely crushed.

He tried to think of anyone who could give him the proper guidance as he took the first bold steps in his nineteen years of life. His parents and other older relatives couldn't help. Mentally, they acted as if they were still back in Mexico. They didn't understand anything about his experience as the boy who straddled the fence between two worlds.

Cristina was sweet, and he hoped they could be together, but she was always so busy with her college gymnastics team. If he was lucky enough to rely on her heart, it was probably too much to think that she could help resolve his identity crisis.

Suddenly Luis perked up and smiled. He *did* know one person who would definitely offer some unique advice.

He opened the contacts app on his phone and brought up the entry for Ryan Richards. He typed, "hey ryan its luis… remember me??"

Five minutes later, he heard the phone ring.

"What's up, kiddo!" The man's voice was as loud and boisterous as ever.

Luis said, "Hey, Mister Ryan. Thanks for calling me back. I hope I—"

"Of course, bud! I wish half the guests on my show were as cool as you. So what's going on out in LA, bro?"

"Actually, I hit you up because things are kinda weird. I need like, some help."

"Okay, uh… sure. What's got you out of whack?"

Luis took a long breath. "Man, you're so natural, so smooth. I just… sometimes I feel really out of place. Like invisible one minute, and then they're telling me what to do."

"Ahhh…" Ryan said with a sympathetic chuckle. "What you're talking about is *respect*. You want people to know you're more than a chair they can just move around."

"Hmm. Sometimes I'm kinda watching everything happen, you know? I *wanna* speak, but like, maybe I'm not really there?"

"Well, *I* hear you, amigo. Loud and clear. And hell, I really appreciate you reaching out to me. 'Cause Luis, I'm a real person, too. The truth is, I *became* the Ryan Richards that people know and love—or loathe. So take it from this old loudmouth here, sometimes ya just gotta put your foot down and shout, 'I'm me, goddammit!' Let the world know you are somebody, that you're *good*, and it really ought to consult you from time to time *before* making all the decisions."

"Yeah!" Luis was starting to feel electrified. "Because, you know, I do everything I'm supposed to. But then... people come up, they get on me anyway."

"Who? Are you talking about the HRA, or... not me, I hope?!"

"Oh, no, not you! It's these guys at school. Buncha Latizos, Afrigros... They got in my face 'cause I didn't wanna do the DDM stuff."

Ryan sputtered his lips. "Christ... Effin' bullies, man! What can ya do? What can *we* do? I say fight fire with fire. Why not use all the surveillance to your advantage? I assume they threatened you in public, so you should pay a visit to the school's IT department and have 'em pull that footage."

"Aw, no... I can't do that. If I get them in trouble, maybe they'll tell one of their friends to cut me up."

"What the... ? Okay, in that case, what are your other options? Run, hide, drop out of school? It's no good, Luis. You *have* to stand up for yourself. This is one of the most important moments in your life."

"Really?!" Luis smacked his forehead. "I already had like two of them this year!"

"Ha! You are a funny one, Mr. Ortega. Look, I gotta head out soon for some work crap. But just remember, *you* are the man who stuck a middle finger in the HRA's face. You did it first, before anyone else had the guts. So I really think that in the moment, you'll find there's more courage in that heart of yours than you realize."

Luis smiled slightly. "Thanks, Ryan. You're awesome. So... how's everything going with you?"

"Ah, you know. I'm a puppet with great perks. But soldier on we must, fine sir!"

"Cool, cool. But seriously, thanks again. You're a good friend."

"Shucks, kid. You just made my day. Chin up out there..."

20. PRISONER EXCHANGE

The president's busy schedule of pre-inaugural events next took her to Forrest City, Arkansas. Here on this bright but brisk Wednesday morning, a crowd of several hundred was gathered outside the front entrance of a stout official building made of gray stone.

Eileen stood on a low riser with several dozen other people. As a crush of cameras jostled for position up front, a white woman with tousled gray hair approached the podium. She adjusted her horn-rimmed glasses, then began.

"Oh my, what a wonderful turnout. For those who don't know, my name is Marjorie Dorfman. I am a professor of political science at the University of Michigan, Ann Arbor. And we're here today because of a question that I posed during a lecture two years ago. I asked, 'How can a privileged college student majoring in criminal justice turn their passion from theory into actual real-world experience?' Well, the movement that sprouted from that idea has most certainly redefined the concept of a summer internship, I should think."

This last line was met with laughter and then rousing applause.

"And so," Dorfman continued, "today we mark the conclusion of our prisoner exchange program's maiden six-month voyage. New volunteers will be checking in, while those who have completed their terms hand off the proverbial baton. Now, shall we?"

A dozen fresh-faced male Caucmericans wearing street clothes came forward and flanked the professor on her left. They smiled and gave a wave to the assembled newspeople. Then, from behind, a door swung open and out came an equal number of casually dressed Minoricans. They stepped onto the riser and fell into position on Dorfman's other side.

"The gentlemen to my right have all served lengthy sentences behind these walls. But with years of model behavior to their credit, and all soon eligible for parole, they were ideal candidates for our new pilot program." Dorfman glanced over her shoulder and smiled. "Sirs, welcome back to the world!"

The men raised their arms in triumph as the crowd cheered. A few moments later Dorfman added, "Now, tag your partners in!" The young Caucs raced past the parolees, slapping hands loudly as they hopped off the stage and ran through the prison's front entrance.

Once the commotion had died down, Professor Dorfman said, "We also happen to have a *very* special guest here with us today, so I won't keep you waiting much longer. But since the reinforcements have just gone inside, I say out with the old and in with the new!"

The prison door opened once again. Now a third group emerged. Ten young Caucs in orange jumpsuits staggered out into the light. Several were emaciated, and their faces ashen. One man's arm was bandaged in a heavy cast. Another limped noticeably and struggled up the riser's few steps. The man with a teardrop tattooed beside his right eye flashed a smile, and it was apparent that several of his upper teeth were missing.

The crowd gasped. Eileen Jeffries-Lao, who had remained silent and inconspicuous until this moment, was horrified. She leaned toward the staffer at her side and hissed, "You need to get me out of here!" The other woman stared back at her like a deer caught in the headlights.

"My, my," Professor Dorfman beamed. "Here they are! Our brave first wave of participants, who now have intimate knowledge of what life is like on the inside for the people we represent as advocates. Let's hear it for these future revolutionaries in the field of criminal justice reform!"

The applause was more subdued now. The crowd murmured in quiet, anxious tones. Dorfman continued to clap loudly even after everyone else had gone silent. She sighed.

"Such a proud moment for us all. But the best is yet to come. It is my privilege and honor to introduce to you our great leader, the President Re-Elect, Mrs. Eileen Jeffries-Lao!"

Everyone clamored loudly as Eileen emerged from the rear of the stage. She radiated in a yellow-gold skirt suit, and her hair had been done up with bulbous volume. She grasped Dorfman's hand warmly, and held the grip with her free hand when she felt that the other woman intended to move in for a hug.

Speaking into the microphone, she said, "Thank you, Professor Dorfman. And kudos for your... truly unique vision. I'm sure we all have high hopes for these fine gentlemen beside us, who have no doubt earned the right to re-enter society ahead of schedule."

Eileen nodded graciously at the cluster of parolees, who were now positioned much further back on the riser and flanked by four members of her Secret Service detail.

"Perhaps my appearance here today will be considered somewhat ironic, but I have an important announcement to make. One that I believe will, in its own way, demonstrate my administration's efforts to think long term. Not only toward increased understanding, but also with reconciliation in mind. Last night, I signed Executive Order number 14215. It authorizes the closure of all HRA-affiliated debtors' prisons within six months. Each inmate's obligation shall be marked as paid in full, and their records wiped clean."

The audience gasped in shock once again.

"Now, now everyone. Please hear me out. We've all come so far these last few years. And while the events of recent months have been challenging, we must see them as opportunities to grow. My priority has always been to steer our country safely ahead. So believe me when I say, we won't make it if we see fellow citizens who disagree with us as potential lifelong enemies. We've simply got to find a way to put the animosity behind us. And I assure you it will be worth it, because there is so much more coming for us all to look forward to..."

Eileen continued speaking for several minutes, but sensed that her words were falling on deaf ears. When she concluded her remarks, the crowd gave its most lackluster response of all.

She eased away from the podium and closed her eyes while Professor Dorfman offered some final thoughts. She deeply regretted the scheduling blunder which had put her in this awkward position. It would have been wiser to announce her olive branch of an executive order from the controlled environment of the White House.

21. BE MY ROCK

Octavius Blount wrapped his large hands over the top of a chairback and leaned his weight forward. He said, "So you're gonna be spending a bunch of time up at that school, then?"

"You're supposed to say, 'Congratulations, Myra.' "

"Oh… yeah. 'Course. You know I want the best for you. I'm just tryin' to see how it's all gonna play out."

Myra left the kitchen and walked past Octavius into the dining area. "You mean like, how we goin' to fix our schedules so the kids get to where they need to be?"

"Something like that, yeah I guess." Octavius began to pace. "But…"

"There's something more, isn't there? It's bothering you, too."

"I mean… Look, Clyde got out. Now you goin' legit. And I know what your moms thinks of me, even if she talk nice to my face."

"But baby, she *loves* you! She always stands up for you."

"*Stands up?* What about me needs standing up?"

"I don't know! But maybe, it sounds like, you were about to lay it all out?"

Octavius shook his head. "God damn, I got some kinda pressure on me in this house. Myra… You the mother of our little princess. And now you're heading up into that *other* world, with white folks and all they different rules—"

"Oh, so you don't think I can run with them? That I can't do the work? Thanks!"

"No, girl! I'm sayin' you *can*. And me, the way I make my money… I don't think none of them school folks'll want to see me—or more like, pretty soon *you* won't want any of them to know about me."

Myra brought a hand up to her cheek. "Octavius, I can't believe you're doing this to me. I didn't think that anyone could spoil my moment, but now you're making me feel sick."

"Ha, how you think I feel? I'm the one who sees a future

where I get kicked to the curb, and you end up this big interior design lady or whatever."

"You really think I'm already planning all that out? I don't even have any textbooks yet!"

"I ain't sayin' you doin' anything wrong. No blame goin' out to anyone here. But I sure as hell see the writing on the wall. And maybe normally, the old me, he would just jump in the car and be gone. Long gone! But for real, I am *trying* to be on it witchu. So that's it. That's what I got to say."

Myra leaned into his tall frame and wrapped her arms around him. "Octo-Man, you know that I adore you. I see you every time I look at Sarah's eyes. Just... let's take it one day, one week as it come. 'Cause you know, if you maybe a little bit scared, I might be too! I'm the one who got to go up there and pretend I belong. I don't know how to act at a school like that. So come on, be my rock, please."

Octavius relaxed and eased away. He said, "Okay, I see what's up. We both got our worries. Guess only time will tell."

"Exactly. But I'm glad it's you I got on my team. The man who got my back."

"I got yo' back, no doubt. Got yo' booty too! Now come on in and give me a kiss."

Myra smiled. "Yeah. That's my Mista Blount. I give you a kiss alright."

22. LEGAL KNOTS

"Ah, Marcus!" Sabine Plotz rose from her chair behind the oak desk and opened her arms for a hug. "What brings you into the belly of the beast?"

FBI Special Agent Marcus Young embraced his old law school friend and said, "All hands on deck. They want this inauguration to go off without a hitch."

"I'm sure. Have there been any... credible threats?"

"I'd say it's more the volume of the chatter. A few crackpots with too much time on their hands are probably responsible for most of it."

"Well," Plotz said while retaking her seat, "I'm glad you had some free time to stop by for a visit."

Marcus sat down in one of the two guest chairs. "When I heard you'd taken an office in DC, how could I not?"

"*Temporary* office," Sabine said with a smile. "Our little lawsuit seems to have won the we've-got-their-attention lottery."

"Oh? Lay it on me."

"Marcus, since you've been out running around in the field for so long, you might have forgotten what a grind this can all be. The pursuit, the preparation, then blindly throwing darts at the wall hoping something will stick."

"I remember… enough," he said with a chuckle. "It's why I had to get the hell out of the office for good."

"Right. Well, I was involved with several other HRA-related cases before this one fell into our laps back at the firm in So Cal. And let me tell you, all of those were a frustrating slog at best. I mean, the administration would never post *this* on their rah-rah page, but a hell of a lot of government lawyers have *also* benefited from the HRA jobs program these last few years. If you catch my drift. And with good reason, too, because their track record is no joke."

"But your new case is different?"

Sabine looked down and fiddled with a pen. "It is, but I don't want to get too cocky. Especially because much of the power behind our case comes not from my legal skills, but *who* my clients are."

"Bennies."

"Exactly. Although, not all of them. Some are, for lack of a better word, white allies. And others still are mixed-race, and all of the complexities that go along with that."

"Ah."

"But the unifying theme is that they're all *young*."

"Which means what?"

Plotz paused. "Think about how different our country looks today compared to just twenty years ago, when you and I were around college age. Even if everything wasn't great back then, there was more *certainty*. A lot of truths you could still rely on. But today that narrative authority has been lost. Now imagine if you'd been born in 2008. A lifetime of economic struggles, lingering wars, political chaos… Who could you trust growing up in that reality? I think that this upcoming generation has forged a unique alliance—both online and in person—that on the surface *looks* diverse, but the glue is that they all share a common lived experience."

"Let me think about this," Marcus said. "They've been grappling with the consequences—or fallout—of the policies that previous generations put in place. And now that they're technically adults, they're making their own choices."

"Very good, Special Agent. *Everything* has aftereffects that are both unpredictable and uncontrollable."

"Mm. So, what's next for the case?"

"This!" Sabine thumped her fist down onto a tall stack of folders and binders. "It's the substance of the case, formally speaking. As you can see, a lot for everyone to get through, even if they run keyword filters through their digital files. Regardless, I think we've got a good shot to win round one—but who can ever predict what the result might be at the appellate level? Still, moving through each stage eats up more time. And all the while, this ragtag coalition of plaintiffs will be out there celebrating their initial victory in the streets and online. As I've heard them say many times, imagine what would be possible for their peer group if the government would just get off their backs."

"Wow!" Marcus rubbed his hands together excitedly. "That's some kind of an escalation. And it sounds like they're making a statement that transcends this one particular program."

"Indeed. They want *everyone* out of their lives. Call them libertarians, no-one-is-illegal-istas, whatever. The point is they are a new breed, a new kind of army, and there's no silencing them."

"They've got the perfect cover, too. What's the point of the HRA, if Beneficiaries can't speak for themselves?"

"I know," Plotz said, leaning back and exhaling breezily. "Sometimes I feel like I'm working this case on cruise control. I'm not saying I can't lose, but in no way will the government win—in the abstract sense, at least."

Marcus gave a little grumble. "Something about this makes me nervous, though. Just now you called them a new breed. You know, a long time ago *I* used to think about how I was something new, or unique. Being mixed-race was still fairly uncommon when we grew up, and nothing like what we see everywhere today. I could have even been called a 'minority among minorities,' because I didn't speak or act in a way that certain people would call 'black'. But you know, I still had *American things* to fall back on. Like baseball culture. That gave me a life. A lifestyle."

"I remember you showing me a few clips of you hitting home runs, way back when."

"Yeah, good times. I haven't even played catch in years... But anyway, this young crew. Growing up in an era of uncertainty. Loss of faith in every sector, where even your gender might be a toss-up. Amnesty for lawbreakers one year, then punishment for your ancestors' crimes the next. Where's the stability or consistency? No wonder their loyalty lies not with race or nationality, but with those other kids who also got tossed into the melting pot at public school."

"But now," Sabine said, "that dish isn't turning out like the chef wanted. And so..."

"You think there's more to come?"

"Maybe she'd rather dump it out than close the whole restaurant down."

"How... how would she do that?"

"The chef's got four years left on her lease, right? So you get out there this weekend and do your job. Keep the president safe so we can find out."

Marcus smiled. "But you'll be ready, Sabi, won't you?"

"Let's just say, as much as I wish I was back in California instead of freezing my butt off in DC, this office might not be so temporary after all."

"So, the HRA's even providing *you* with job security. Yup, the lady is getting paid..."

"Don't give me any of *that* lip. My family's from Germany."

23. A DIFFERENT KIND OF DARKNESS

Clyde Jenkins was in a funk. Something about this LA experience didn't feel right. As he eased into a chair out on the balcony of this condo which Eddie Pryor had set him up in temporarily, he thought about his encounter with Ayana McGinn.

He had in fact been able to hand her his phone number when

her agent Jerry was facing away talking to someone else. But now, it was days later and Clyde still hadn't heard from her. He wondered if that was Jerry's doing—or worse, maybe Ayana also believed that the name DJ Clydoscope would be kryptonite for her career.

This wasn't the first time someone had pulled back from him the moment they fully grasped who he was, either. In just a few short weeks, several lively conversations with a potential collaborator had gone ice cold after "Fly So High" came up.

Stranger still, Clyde suddenly realized, was that almost every person who turned away was black. Meanwhile, any number of white industry folks were more than willing to schmooze and pose for pictures...

Why were the brothers and sisters hesitant to associate with him? Several months ago, at the height of his song's popularity, Clyde was hip-hop's darling from coast to coast. Could it be that since the HRA was back on its feet, Afrigro-Americans just wanted to keep a good thing going for as long as possible?

It wasn't as if the government had made any sweeping policy changes in response to his song. All they did later on was arrest a bunch of people involved with the SOJ hack, then got back to business as usual—while of course giving the usual reassurances that the system was secure and people's privacy was safe.

Clyde supposed that today, people regarded his song as merely a puff of smoke that had dissipated into nothingness. His cries for help from the heart of the inner city were irrelevant and forgotten, now that the president had been re-elected and MARVIN was fully operational again. Except that Clyde was very far away from Newark, soaking up the Los Angeles energy thanks to Eddie Pryor's persistent recruiting efforts—and Caucs seemed to be the only people who wanted him around.

What could that possibly mean? Did they *really* like his lyrics and think he had talent with long-term potential? Or did he just fill one black slot in their diverse roster of artists, like a Hollywood-style investment portfolio? Nolan would probably agree with that take. But still, his old mentor had also been one of the loudest voices encouraging him to leave town and give LA a shot.

Clyde got a bit of a sinking feeling as he thought about home. Because he hadn't simply *left* his old neighborhood, but *escaped* it. Run away from violence and mistrust and self-destruction—right into the arms of an entertainment mecca run by white people.

That was the trade-off he had agreed to. Leaning on Caucs for safety and the opportunity to grow his career into something that would last. But he still couldn't see what they wanted from *him*, and it was stressing him out! Was the plan just to make a few bucks off the last of his name recognition for a year or two, before dropping him back into obscurity once the well ran dry? Or worse, were they using him as a prop to show the world that 'I have black friends,' 'I support the black community'?

Clyde found this kind of thinking very unpleasant. "Fly So High" had been pure, an idealistic plea made in good faith. And he'd gotten what he envisioned, fame and fortune and doors opening with the red carpet rolled out. But less than a year into the whole process, and already he was becoming aware of a different kind of darkness within this glitzy world of success.

Even more confusing, Clyde sensed that of all the people he had met on this journey out west, it was Eddie Pryor, with his shifty grin and wiggling mustache, who he could trust the most.

He closed his eyes and tried to enjoy this calm afternoon on the patio. Later tonight he would be out socializing again, this time mingling at some art gallery opening. There was no telling who might be angling toward him hungrily—or slinking away in fright.

24. THE WORST MOTIVATOR

"Excuse me, Your Prescience. I hate to disturb you so soon after everything you've been through, but I feel that I must."

Emissary Karlov closed his eyes and gave a slight bow. The bulky man then took a few steps back.

The Prescient One lay on his divan, weary but also joyful to be back in his inner sanctum. The bombed-out chambers had been rebuilt during his absence. Now he was resting after the spectacular return reception he had received while touring the Mall of Absolution earlier in the day.

"It's no trouble, Samuel," he said. "Whatever's on your mind. Let us speak man to man."

Karlov smiled happily for a moment, then his face sobered as he reached into his attaché case and removed a tablet. He tapped the screen several times before handing it over.

"No doubt you will want a full briefing on the state of our mini-nation. Thankfully, I can report that once the initial panic surrounding your abduction subsided, this Modestian family rallied together in ways that would have made you very proud. But—"

"But," the Prescient One said, "what I see here does not look good at all."

"Ah, no, Your Prescience. How best shall I put it? Our church continues to grow as the alternative way of life we offer becomes more widely known. And, after the first Sentinels of Jubilee hack in October, we easily absorbed that first wave of techno-refugees. However, as you now grasp..."

The Prescient One had been watching a montage of footage compiled from the Mall's security network. There were instances of theft inside several storefronts, acts of lewd behavior in dark corners, and worst of all, physical altercations on the auxiliary property outside the main structure. Here steel dormitories had been hastily built to accommodate the additional refugees, many of whom were not equipped to endure the cold Minnesota winter months once the church had reached capacity.

The Prescient One handed the device back and said, "That's enough. Please continue."

"An unfortunate development, to be sure," Karlov said. "But I don't think anyone can be blamed. Had *you* been here during that time, perhaps the result would still be the same. And Mod knows, our longstanding members have done everything they could to be welcoming. The plain fact is that not all of the newcomers are acting in good faith."

"Then we have several challenges to address. First and foremost, we must *defend* the church. Our people and our way of life are why the Mall became a destination, or target, in the first place."

"Yes, yes. Naturally."

"Next, for violations rooted in carelessness or ignorance about our customs, I suggest firm but forgiving enforcement.

Finally, zero tolerance for any and all *malicious* behavior. We cannot let predators think they've found a new group of pushovers to fleece, by using our hearts against us with sentimental pleas."

"Strength, not weakness. I understand."

The Prescient One rose from the divan and walked a slow circle around the room. He said, "But there's also the matter of their sheer numbers. How many arrived in total?"

Karlov looked up at the ceiling. "Off the top of my head... In October, seven hundred people came, and all settled inside the main Mall complex. Starting in November the numbers ballooned, and I believe an additional fifteen hundred arrived. Thank Mod we allocated the resources to build the necessary structures so no one froze to death! Anyhow, in December the numbers dropped—whether due to your, uh... absence or because the Holy Holidays were approaching, I do not know. Still, nearly four hundred more came. Estimates for the first half of this month are approximately one hundred."

"We could be looking at three thousand in all by the end of January," the church leader marveled. "That's a quarter of our own membership here at home, not even including those who attend independent churches throughout the country. For us to absorb that many new people, coming from all backgrounds and having different motivations... And not just to provide food and housing, but allegedly to teach them the ways of our religion, which itself is still so young and in development... Emissary Karlov, I don't see how we can manage it without losing ourselves. Basic accommodation might be doable, but only if we quarantined all of the refugees while screening for authentic converts."

"Yes and no, Your Prescience. Already a number of the troublemakers have invoked their human rights in an attempt to avoid punishment for their mischief. And several lawyers within the refugee ranks have jumped to their defense. It is quite distressing."

"But of course!" the Prescient One said with a wry laugh. "It takes two to tango. But this actually relates to another point I want to make. Emissary, our faith is not yet set in stone. The true believers are doing glorious work hammering out the fine details in the mapmaking sessions. What if impostors were to barge in and start polluting those holy waters? No! We *cannot* allow our charitable instincts to be taken advantage of to the point that the structural integrity of our community is put in danger."

Karlov shuddered. He had never seen the Prescient One so angry before. "What do you propose?"

"We can't possibly interview them all face to face. Besides, sometimes judging a person's character is more subjective than we'd like to believe. So we must test their purported faith instead. Tempt them. Let them reveal their true natures. They will either find a home with us... or be asked to move along."

"What kind of tests, Your Prescience?"

"We have thousands of cameras in place, do we not? Our own little surveillance fiefdom, haha. Surely you and the other emissaries can arrange a series of real-world situations to draw out the best and worst of our refugee population."

"Very good. And to think, if even only a third of them pass muster, it would mean an additional thousand new Modestians!"

"Perhaps." The Prescient One raised a finger. "Better that we reject all but a hundred, if their hearts aren't true. Remember, while the church itself was initially founded on reactionary principles, its long-term survival depends on beliefs that have the capacity to *grow*. Fear is the worst motivator when making any decision. So, my friend, you must challenge the newcomers to surmount their weaknesses. Then they won't have to deny their essence while assimilating into our flock."

"You are a wise man, truly." As Emissary Karlov turned away, he paused and said, "If you are not too fatigued, I have one last question."

"Of course, Samuel. What is it?"

"Before your unfortunate ordeal, you had mentioned to me in private discussion the need to dive deep and explore the source of what created you, as well as the man Scott Cullen beforehand. I wonder if your recent experiences served to shed any light on the matter?"

The Prescient One nodded. "Blindingly so. And I am still... reacting. Please give me time to make sense of it all, then I promise to incorporate new wisdom that might help enrich our church."

"Indeed, Your Prescience. It is my honor to serve Mod, and act as your confidante when needed. Rest well..."

25. A MAYPOLE IN BROOKLYN

"Yeah, I can manage this."

Chris Donohugh rubbed his hands together briefly, then began moving down the sidewalk with the two Corgis scuttling alongside. A brief reprieve from the winter chill had brought many New Yorkers out on this bright, cloudless Saturday. He and Kate stopped in at their favorite neighborhood coffee shop, then began a relaxing stroll around the Brooklyn streets.

"So," he said, "this is the life, eh?"

"We're doin' it. Everything's back to normal. Well—for us, at least. Any updates on… ?"

"Not yet. But damn, the concert is getting a lot of coverage."

"Still?"

"Oh yeah. Even some sites over in the UK and Germany."

"Uh-oh," Kate said with a laugh. "This could get out of control."

"Effing Glenn, man. That guy is a human battering ram."

"If all you have is a hammer, everything looks like a nail…"

"Hammer of justice!"

Chris handed off the leashes and started playing air guitar. Kate waited patiently. This was just one of the quirks she'd had to accept about her musician husband. By the time he concluded his faux-solo with a leap, her attention was already elsewhere.

"You hungry?" she asked while trailing after the dogs, who smelled something tasty in the air and were moving forward aggressively. "Annnd," she called back to him, "looks like it's early enough that the wait won't be too long."

Chris caught up to her and they took their place in line on the sidewalk outside of Blockbuster Tacos. He craned his neck to get a better view of the crowd, judging that it would only be twenty minutes until they ordered.

Just then a pair of mini-drones appeared at the nearby intersection. One peeled off toward them and slowly made its way down the street, then zipped away.

"What the hell was that all about?" Chris said.

"Beats me."

"Like, I *never* see those things flying around here."

"Oh well," Kate sighed. "The new normal, I guess."

"Yeah, yeah. Another thing we're supposed to accept without being told about first."

"Don't start on that now, babe. 'Cause remember, I married the *guitarist*, not the singer."

"So just shut up and look good?"

"Basically." She slipped her arm into his.

The line crept forward. The dogs made friends with a chocolate Labrador whose owner was several places behind, so the Donohughs stepped back and talked to her while they waited to order.

Inside the restaurant's seating area, they ended up joining the other woman at one of the long picnic tables. She was a Pilates instructor named Laurie, who promised Kate a free session at her studio that was in the neighborhood. While they chatted, the dogs played cleanup crew underneath the table, snorting greedily and gobbling up bits of food that had fallen onto the floor. After an exchange of phone numbers, Laurie gave Kate and Chris a quick hug and then went power-walking away as her Lab trotted along.

"Back home," Chris said, "or onward?"

"Let's keep going. Work off this meal."

"You lead the way. Or… maybe they will."

The Corgis were in pursuit of a new scent. They lurched left at the next corner and pawed forward until the trail went cold on a front stoop halfway down the block.

"So, do you think he did it?"

Chris froze. She had finally broached the subject. After weeks of tranquility and renewed wedded bliss following Kate's return from overseas HRA duty, here it was. The test he dreaded. It had the power to tear his world apart forever.

He said, "How would *you* feel if it was all true, what they're saying about him?"

"I really don't know." Kate tugged at one of her knit gloves. "Because I just don't understand."

"What, exactly? Glenn himself, or what he might've done?"

"Chris, let's just assume he did it, that he was part of the SOJ.

And, what if he was in the right? That would mean I'm one of the bad guys."

"Oh. Meaning you'd also have to ask yourself how and when that happened, right?"

"Yup. Because we all used to be on the same side fighting for the same things. Our methods were different, sure. You guys doing your music, and me working with charities and PACs."

"What was the separation point then?" Chris asked. "That our bands never reached the level of success to become corporate sell-outs? Whereas the HRA—a big government entity—is the equivalent of that in your sphere?"

"But if that's accurate..." Kate trailed off. "Okay, here's the paradox. We've been striving for change our whole lives because we were told that was the thing to do. Then, our generation actually achieves the goal, so we're not just protesting out in the streets anymore. We've got offices, budgets, and infrastructure in place to really go for it. I don't see how that can be a bad thing."

Chris tightened his grip on the leashes as they approached a crosswalk that was on a red light. He said, "Maybe it's got nothing to do with the administration itself. Not the goals or even the people working there, who let's assume—Sentinels sympathizers excluded—are competent and loyal. The bigger point is that *any* company or group of that size, with that much reach... it's vulnerable to... not even corruption or rot, but... Maybe the expectations of the people it's supposed to serve are too high. Or do all entities just automatically become *targets* for those who, I don't know... hate big things, or want to skim off the top? Eh, I've already drifted so far from my original thought here, I don't know where I was going with it."

"Yeah, you touched on a lot," Kate said. "I guess, now that we've been around for a while, people see the HRA as one more government bureaucracy."

"Not only that, your charter really swung for the fences! This wasn't just, say, the Get More People to Eat Healthy Administration. So give yourself a break. It's been a good sprint, a good first round. There's nothing wrong with saying the HRA'll have to adapt, like any business, really."

"Maybe, hmm... But getting back to Glenn. Why would a guy like him join that fight, when there are so many other ills he could've gone after? I mean, *you* saw him back around the end of

October. Did he say anything, or did you pick up any hints that maybe something was up with him?"

Chris leaned over and started adjusting one of the dogs' harnesses. He needed to buy some time while figuring out how to deflect her question without telling an outright lie.

"Ah, you know how he is. Goes off on every topic like some conspiracy theorist calling a talk show. '9/11 was an inside job!' 'Why can't civilians explore Antarctica?!' So yeah, he probably said some stuff about the hack too."

"And did you agree with him?"

Chris looked Kate directly in the eyes and said, "And what if I did? What if that song I'm writing right now is called 'Restitution Junkies'? Would you leave me—or throw your panties at me?"

Kate held his stare for a moment. Slowly, their mouths both curled up into a smile. She eased forward and pecked him on the lips.

"You've got me wrapped around your finger, Mr. Donohugh. More than you even realize."

Kate placed a palm onto her stomach and rubbed it in a circle. Her eyes flickered.

"What? You mean… ?"

"Mm-hmm. It's early… but I'm late."

Chris felt his head swoon in a buoyant thrilling rush of incomprehensible emotions. He closed his eyes as enormous tears formed and rolled down his cheeks.

And then they were embracing, rocking back and forth to the silent song that was playing only for them. The Corgis walked a slow circle around their ankles, turning the Donohughs into a maypole lost in a hopeful reverie.

Life was good. And God willing, it was about to get a whole lot better.

26. CARDINAL SIN

"I'm telling you, Reverend, you're being too harsh."

"But it's just tough love," Matthias Witherspoon pleaded. "And if not from me, you're going to hear it from somebody else who's less compassionate and got less skin in the game."

"No, no. That's no excuse for you ridin' the Tinfoil Express."

Nadine Jones folded her arms after she said this, and Matthias noted that several others in attendance were nodding their heads in approval. Before he could respond, another man stood up to speak.

"Look here, Mr. Reverend. I never took sides during all this internal strife been going on these last few months. And I *thought* everything was patched up nice again. But now it looks like you're back at it, frothing in the pulpit again. That wasn't part of the agreement."

Matthias got an uneasy feeling in his stomach. The mood at this Sunday afternoon meeting was starting to turn against him. He wanted to double down, but sensed that it might be wiser to lose the skirmish for diplomacy's sake. Maybe there was a third way…

"Aw, come on now, people," he said, flashing his teeth in a who-me smile. "You know how ol' Matthias can get. Once the engine revs up, sometimes I run it too hot and get hog wild. Hehe, so how about this? Maybe we'll pass out yellow flags, and anyone who sees me get loose can call a penalty, like in football."

A few people snickered. Others were not so impressed by this little joke.

"I'd throw the flag right now," Nadine clucked. "He's just swapping out the business suit for the clown costume. Still the same Witherspoon bag of tricks, though. I've seen it all before."

"That's right, that's right," came the response. "Say it, sister!"

A flustered Matthias switched into humble mode. "Listen, y'all. We been through this before. Times are gonna start getting tougher for black folk, starting last week. So I got to speak on it, is all."

Some murmurs and whispers. He felt like he might eke out a victory after all. But—these people were his flock, not enemies or Joe Public. Simply having this discussion without bruising anyone's ego was a delicate matter.

A younger man stood up. Thin, wearing sharp clothes, and a recent college graduate. He said, "If that's the case, then how can *you* help, dear Reverend? Because I assume what you're referring to falls into the categories of economics and politics. Do you know how to solve those kinds of problems?"

Louder chatter now. Some hesitant applause that might keep feeding on itself if Matthias didn't come back with an effective retort. He raised his arms placatingly.

"I hear you, Mr. Ames. And welcome back home. Congratulations on collecting your diploma last month—was that in three-and-a-half or four-and-a-half years? No doubt you're eager to make your mark on the world. But this youthful enthusiasm to run out and prove yourself, it don't realize something that I do. As a man of God, I understand that the challenges facing us have nothing to do with physically going any*where*. Because the most important battles are fought within." Matthias touched his breast and then his temple. "You got to change here and here, to have any *chance* at protecting yourself."

On-the-fence grumbles and a couple of meek boos came back at him from the seated crowd. The young man said, "But we need *practical* steps to take, so we can start seeing results in our daily lives. We have real dreams. And no time to sit around day*dreaming!*"

"Preach on!" someone shouted. "Oh yes, the Reverend has met his match!"

Witherspoon said, "My man. We are taking steps. Community investment. Got the new farmers market starting up in the spring. Youth crime intervention programs. Do you—"

"That's small potatoes," Ames interrupted. "Or reacting to a problem that's already there. People, I get what the Reverend's been hinting at. If the HRA pulls back, then the vultures are gonna fly in. Koreans, Indians, Russians, Israelis, whoever! And we know them immigrants don't care about us. They'll just say, 'I'm here too. So whatcha gonna do?' Any thoughts on that, Matthias?"

"Of course, you're right. All the groups you mentioned, plus the Armenians, the Vietnamese, the Salvadorans, and more. They're all here and they want to be heard. Their grievance, their glory, their power play. So, who gets priority seating at that crowded table? Not you! But I got a little secret to share—it's all gonna blow up in everyone's face, yessir. 'Cause MARVIN won't stop, *can't* stop. He'll be happy to oblige some first-generation Syrian refugee, who says that Turkey or Iraq blew up his house. Then the chant will be, '*Pay* me too!' Yup, the whole world is comin' here to get paid. And our country's just one big strip-mining club, makin' it rain for everyone, hahahaha!"

Ames threw his arms out violently, then wagged a stern finger to prevent the room from exploding into chaos. He said, "Even if that's all true and our dear leader can see into the future, the fact remains, ladies and gentlemen. Mr. Witherspoon *ain't... got... no... plan.* He's a scaremonger, a band-aid seller. At the end of the day, he simply lacks the tools or the ability required to fight off the coming storm. A Noah he is not!"

And right in that moment, Matthias Witherspoon felt his world come crashing down. Young Robert Ames, who had grown up attending Sunday services at his church, in the course of a diatribe which borrowed from his own pulpit style, had exposed a fatal weakness.

Because faith didn't read the newspaper or put food on people's tables. It was there to help a person absorb life's defeats and still get out of bed in the morning. But it couldn't pick you a winner in the stock market, or resist the encroaching repercussions of an immigration policy which had kicked Afrigro-Americans to the back of the bus.

As if Reparations was the final smokescreen after sixty years of open borders, and soon Heritage Americans, black and white alike, would find themselves electorally swamped by their imported neighbors. Their own happiness, preferences, communities, and right to self-determination were null and void —because long ago, a political decision had been made to change the demographic makeup of an entire landmass.

The United States of America as it had been known for centuries was no more. Transformed in the blink of an eye without consulting anyone, let alone by royal decree. And the people being overrun were expected not to mourn the loss of their homeland, but just roll over and fade away. Never mind that it was their own families who were responsible for creating *this* nice place, where so many others from around the world wanted to live…

Matthias snapped back into the moment. He realized with sick clarity that the crisis playing out was a mess of his own making. Because in warning of particular dangers that he as church leader couldn't defend against, he had committed the salesman's cardinal sin. And now his followers, truly aware of the real-world peril they faced, would begin looking for answers elsewhere.

He fumbled for the kerchief in his pocket and wiped his face. Robert Ames was smiling in triumph as he received pats on the back from the other parishioners. Reverend Witherspoon gathered himself to utter the words that would bring this meeting to a close as quickly as possible.

There was no use prolonging his opponents' satisfaction, now that he had lost.

27. TICKING TIME CAPSULE

The banging of hammers resonated throughout the entire structure. Drills whirred and buzzed every few seconds. Sam Cooke was crooning from a speaker on the upstairs landing.

President Eileen Jeffries-Lao stood smiling, drywall saw in hand, while several members of the press corps snapped photos of her and an assembled crew of Minorican volunteers. After the workers returned to their tasks, Eileen pulled off her gloves and attempted to brush the construction dust out of her hair. She removed her yellow-tinted goggles and handed them to one of the organizers as she stepped out into the front yard.

"Nice outfit," Vice President Hank Pendleton said, motioning to the beige canvas overalls Eileen had been provided earlier in the day. The big Texan was wearing his own personal outfit of buffalo plaid flannel shirt and black stonewashed jeans.

"Tools of the trade," she replied. "Are you lollygagging around or what?" She smiled as she spoke, aware that there were press photographers crawling all over the site of this halfway house which they were helping to renovate.

Hank pointed up toward the roof. "See that gutter? Rusted and rotten. It's got to be replaced. I'm just waiting on a ladder that's tall enough so I can start ripping it down."

Eileen nodded at Hank's Secret Service detail. "Are they really going to let you climb up there? You'd be quite the sitting duck, a mighty fine target."

"*Someone's* had her coffee this morning," the vice president said to one of his minders. "Come on, back to work…"

An hour later, Eileen was on the move as part of a caravan that would visit a number of locations around the DC area to commemorate Martin Luther King Jr. Day. The TV in her limousine showed one of the many parades that were taking place across the country. On screen, a troupe of black high schoolers wearing the bright outfits of a marching band proceeded down the street in unison. Business as usual—all was well on this annual celebration of Dr. King's life.

Eileen fished out a metal flask from inside her handbag and took a sip. It had been *cold* in that house, with all the doors being left open so workers could come and go freely. Now she was off to a shelter to ladle out meals, before getting herself cleaned up to attend the headstone unveiling ceremony for a Baltimore civil rights leader who had recently passed away.

It was a grind of a day to start the week of her inaugural festivities, but nothing so stressful as the lead-up to this holiday two years ago. Because of all the historical bills that had come due during her first term in office, perhaps none were as potentially explosive as the ticking time capsule that was the sealed MLK archives.

Back in 1977, a judge had decreed that many documents surrounding King's life and death, including the government's full-court press of surveillance as approved by FBI Director J. Edgar Hoover, should be kept under lock and key for fifty years. Eileen Jeffries-Lao happened to occupy the Oval Office when this vault was scheduled for exposure to disinfecting sunlight— and much public scrutiny.

A considerable number of these pages had already leaked out over the years, however, which not only cast a dark shadow on King's personal reputation, but also raised questions about the government's official narrative of the events surrounding his assassination. President Jeffries-Lao believed it would be reckless to permit an unvarnished data dump of the remainder.

Instead, her administration had quietly invited a group of prominent Afrigro-American leaders to meet with representatives from several alphabet agencies for a private game of poker one evening in the fall of 2026. Papers were spread out across an enormous conference table. The two parties then engaged in a tense showdown, before each side selected an equal quantity of undesirable items to be destroyed—and thus lost to history for all time.

A sizable trove of salacious or otherwise troubling material remained in the mix, to help ward off potential accusations of a cover-up once the public was granted full access to the files.

The location of that secret meeting had been a clean room. No cameras. No electronic devices of any kind permitted. No MARVIN.

And so now in January of 2029, the initial fervor surrounding the archives' release having long since died down, the best of the legacy of the man named *Martin* lived on.

The presidential limousine eased into a parking lot where law enforcement and reporters had gathered in anticipation of Eileen's arrival. She popped a breath mint to mask any lingering traces of alcohol, then closed her handbag and waited for the car to stop.

All she needed to do for the rest of the day was go through the motions with a smile on her face. Because in less than a week, Eileen Jeffries-Lao would be sworn in for her second term as president. Then she would be truly free to use the full force of the United States government—FBI included—to see to it that her agenda moved forward at an aggressive pace.

28. FEW KNOW MY NAME

"Clyde, goddammit, I brought you out here so your star could shine. Now don't get me wrong, I knew from before day one that there might be some, uh… if not diva moments, let's say principled outbursts. But Jesus Christ, this?! What the hell, bud?"

Clyde Jenkins had never seen Eddie Pryor mad before. Like, for real mad, and not just playing it up in a meeting to get what he wanted.

"I'm sorry, Mr. Pryor. Honestly, I—"

"Don't gimme any of that hangdog shit, please. I've had a hell of a time cleaning up your mess. What I really need right now is a drink, and some silence."

"Oh."

"Yeah, 'cause I gotta *think*. About how to fix those burned bridges... maybe even flip the situation around... so everything ends up better than before. Ooh, baby! That's why they call me Eddie P.! The cooker, the cleaner, the clairvoyant dream weaver. I have touched *billions* of hearts around the world, and yet few know my name. Oh, you like that, do ya?"

Clyde watched Eddie dance a little jig as he mixed a drink at the wet bar here in the man's downstairs den.

He himself had been brought here by an unmarked LAPD vehicle just a short while ago. He'd seen Eddie hand the two officers something while slinking into the house, and then waited while the men talked outside for several minutes. He tried to smile now that Eddie was in a better mood.

"You don't realize the kind of influence I have, kid." Eddie waltzed over to his recliner, artfully brushing away the bottom of his satin robe before plopping down and kicking up his feet. "But it's true. Of all the showbiz heroes the average person worships, I bet you that I've had a hand in one or two of their careers. Like... you know the flick *Unstoppable Memphis* about that old rap group?"

"Of course," Clyde said. "Been listening to those dudes forever."

"Yeah, well, I rewrote half the damn script for them— *uncredited*, mind you. No one puts *me* on camera. No one hands *me* the microphone. Because..." Eddie waved a hand up and down the length of his body. "Which is fine, because I do my best work behind the scenes. Making things happen! The sizzle on Hollywood's grill!"

"Eddie's empire, it sounds like."

"Exactly! Which is why... you are driving me *insane*, Clyde! The way I see it, all we gotta do is figure out how to work your integrity angle into my proven system—and we'll make you a freaking *legend!*"

"Legendary status, alright!" Clyde pumped his fist.

The muscles on Eddie's face collapsed. He pushed the

recliner down with his feet and leaned forward. "But I can't do it when I get a phone call in the middle of the night, saying that my newest protégé snuck onto the property where Miss Ayana McGinn lives *with her parents*, and darn near got himself killed trying to do some romantic-movie bullshit outside her window. Do you see how that might concern me?"

Clyde got up from the sofa and went to the bar. Dejectedly, he dropped several ice cubes into a glass, then poured soda over top. The fizz bounced against his cheeks as he took a sip. Finally, he said, "I know, Eddie. It's just... I need to... I don't know how to say it."

Pryor's expression softened as he said, "Help me understand what's going on."

Clyde sat down again and rubbed the side of his head with his palm. "I'm the new kid in town. And I like this girl. A lot! But damn, it seems like right from the start, a lot of people be tellin' me no."

"Uh-huh. Go on."

"And part of me knows I'm a fluke. I got like, stupid lucky when 'Fly So High' took off. It changed everything *for* me—but not *about* me. Now I see that maybe not everyone out here all that impressed by DJC, neither. Okay, so what I'm supposed to do? Got to step up, that's what. Assert myself, prove I belong. That I ain't, like, some pretender out of his league. But... maybe I am?"

Eddie stood up. His eyes were glassy. "Come here, son. That was just... from the heart. We need more of that in this town."

Clyde set his drink aside and joined Eddie for a hug. He heard himself sniffle and then dropped his face onto Eddie's shoulder. He pulled away, shuddering slightly as he wiped under his eyes and said, "God damn."

After a silent moment, Eddie said, "You're a good kid, Clyde. And I know I get ridiculous sometimes, but this city can do that to ya. You have my promise on two things. One, I will never tell a soul what you just shared with me. So unless you wanna express that in one of your songs, it will remain private."

"Thank you, Eddie."

"And as for your shenanigans up at the McGinn residence tonight... While I can't guarantee that no one will ever know, rest assured my team has been out there trying to cover your tracks since the moment I got the call."

"Oh yeah?" Clyde looked up. "So no tabloid stuff?"

"Any and all visual evidence we can acquire will be purchased and destroyed. Then it'll just be he said, she said. And I highly doubt the ambitious young Miss McGinn wants any bad press either, now that she's trying to be a *serious* actress."

"Oh my goodness, Eddie, you saved my life! How much do I owe you for buying up them pictures?"

"Not one cent."

"No! Why?!"

"Because now you know I'm not just all talk. I've got your back when it counts. That's a fair price to pay."

Clyde exhaled with happy relief. He said, "One thing, though. How'd you get your people on the case so quick? Were you, uh… waiting for me to mess up?"

Eddie flashed a smile. "Clyde Jenkins, you are *not* the first entertainer under my tutelage to make a damn fool of himself. Looking out for the team's interests is just like an insurance policy. Yep, Eddie P. has all the bases covered!"

"Alright then, cool. Should I catch a ride home, or… ?"

Eddie waved a hand. "There's two spare bedrooms down the hall. Go get some rest, you creepy night prowler! I'll arrange a car in the morning."

"Thanks again."

"Forget it, kid. We're all young once. Even the rich and famous…"

29. CAUSING A RUCKUS

"Murray, let's go."

The metal door clanked open. Two heavily armed prison guards stood outside waiting.

"No cuffs?" Glenn asked.

"Not today," one of the guards said. "Get your shit and come on."

Glenn didn't wait for clarification. Whether he was being rotated to another cell or transferred to a new facility, anything was better than stewing in this six-by-eight concrete pen which was slowly driving him insane. He quickly grabbed a few personal items and exited the cell.

He walked slowly down the corridor. The guard behind him held a heavy baton at the ready. They passed through several remotely activated door locks, then stepped into an elevator.

On the ride up, one of the guards held out a mesh knapsack and said, "Put it all in here."

Glenn deposited his belongings, then awaited further instructions. The elevator doors opened onto a hallway that was more welcoming than the austere passageways below, and the guards nudged him in the direction of a large office.

"Inmate G. Murray here to see you, sir," the lead guard announced.

As Glenn entered the room, a man of medium build with leathery skin rose from his chair behind a heavy old desk. He motioned in front of him and said, "Sit down."

Glenn sat without a word. He had never seen, let alone met this man before, but assumed he was the warden. So Glenn kept his guard up, sensing that his fate hung in the balance.

"Tell me, Mr. Murray," the man drawled, then exhaled heavily through his nostrils. "Would you say that you've been anything less than a model inmate during your time with us?"

"No, sir," Glenn replied. "I haven't been disciplined since I got here."

"Very true." The warden tapped a newspaper that was open in front of him. "But someone's been causing a ruckus about you. Or should I say, a *raucous?*"

The paper was rotated so that Glenn could read it. A finger pointed out the headline that read, "Local Bands Unite in Support of Jailed Singer." He felt a surge of vitality after weeks spent in cold isolation.

"Did you know about this?" the warden asked.

"I—"

"I guess it doesn't really matter. Not now, at least. Shouldn't even be my concern. But what you did…"

"Allegedly." Glenn couldn't help himself. His gusto was returning.

The warden snatched away the newspaper, crushing it with his large hands and dropping the clump into a wastebasket beside him. He said, "Don't make me mad, please. I may not have the power to hold you any longer, but an unfortunate accident might very well befall you on your way out. Understand?"

Glenn nodded.

"I'm gonna speak my mind before you leave us. Don't think it was just your friends that made it happen, neither. These Jeffries-Lao executive orders are really what punched your ticket. Amnesties and pardons for criminal scum across the board. All I know is, you broke the law. And where *I* come from, if such is the case, then a man's got to serve his time."

Glenn said, "Sir, I haven't once seen a lawyer, or been charged with any crime. Is that also how things are done where you come from?"

"Oh, no, most definitely not. But don't you try to pin that on me. I'm just the babysitter. Not my call what time Mommy and Daddy come home."

"Or if the kids sneak out of the house." Glenn stood up and smirked. "Thanks for the hospitality, but the food here stinks. I'm out."

As he left the office, Glenn came face to face with the two guards from earlier. Tall and burly himself, he sized them up without fear, then cracked a smile.

Somehow, some way, he was getting out of lockup. To breathe the fresh free air for the first time in more than six weeks. He couldn't wait to unleash his voice once again.

30. THEY FOUND SOMETHING

Nolan Simmons was not a drinking man. One or two cocktails during the Holy Holidays or when celebrating a milestone, mostly. So when his right-hand-man Damon discovered him swiveling around in an easy chair with a half-empty bottle of whiskey in his lap, he knew something big was up.

"Hey, boss... You, uh, you okay?"

Nolan's droopy eyelids slowly eased open. He said, "Not really. No. But I ain't thirsty!" He raised the bottle. "We got some real trouble on our hands, Dee. And pretty soon, maybe no one's gonna be okay."

Damon pulled up a chair. He pointed at the bottle and said,

"Gimme some of that first. Then lay it on me."

"Right. Here, drink up… So last week, I got the tech crew to put out the call for more historical data."

"Yup. I been keepin' tabs on their hours. Go on."

"So first couple days, nothing out of the ordinary. I didn't expect much from overseas that soon anyway. This first push is mainly to get the word out—then we'll start seeing real results a few months down the road."

"Cool, cool."

"As for the domestic side of the search, I couldn't predict what might turn up. 'Cause everything's been sifted over pretty good—or burned—these past few years. I just never…"

Nolan trailed off, his eyes glazing over as he took hold of the bottle again.

Damon said, "What's got you so spooked, boss?"

Nolan whispered, "The Sentinels did a lot more than bury some new code inside MARVIN. *They found something!*"

"And… now you got it too?"

"Yeah. I sure do. But I don't know if I want it."

"What the hell is it, Nolan?"

"Turns out MARVIN—the system's original, pre-hack version—was holding out on us."

"Say what?"

"He held stuff back, by design! Those sneaky mofos over at the HRA were hiding *their own cache* of inconvenient archives!"

"You mean… bad stuff *we* did?"

"Hehe, well… It sure makes things look a lot grayer. Especially 'cause the HRA has been all about moving the green from white hands to black."

Damon brought his fingertips together. Slowly, he said, "So whatchu worried about more—that we'll have to pay some of the money we got back, or are we gonna owe a lot more on top of that?"

"I like the way you think," Nolan said, now perking up. "But it's even more complicated than what you're talking about. Since we know the HRA wants to expand into other countries, here's what I think happened. While they were helping set things up, someone must've noticed that a lot of the documents they were feeding into the other MARVINs… Well, that stuff actually brushes up against people here at home too."

"Yeah, I guess that makes sense. Like, can't only be everyone moves *north*, right?"

"No doubt. So they've been gathering data on all the races, from lotsa different countries, and *I suspect* they got overwhelmed. Because history is just too damn complex, man. As for our buddy MARVIN... Well, he's constipated now!"

They burst out laughing. The bottle got passed back to Damon as he said, "So if they already having problems just trying to add a couple more countries—uh, real quick, can you say which ones?"

"Colombia and Aruba, I know for sure. Then there's a couple of British colonies. My hunch says, one dip of the toe and they freaked the hell out. Decided to back off for a while."

Damon said, "Maybe they just need more computing power?"

"Haha, nice try, Dee. But no. It's like they realize if they keep going, the blame won't always be white, white, white. So they're backpedaling, trying to press stop without anybody knowing. Look at it this way. How many Aztec types you think maybe owned some Africans down there? Or vice versa?"

"Oh... crap. So we might have to start cashin' out *other people* besides Caucs?"

"Now you're getting it! And going one step further, what gives the government the right to hold anything back? Should be, you find it, you post it. So now, here's a little theory. MARVIN ain't human, right? His goal is complete and objective historical accuracy. What happens if you hide stuff from him or refuse to announce his verdict? Say he's tied in to the drone network that's got law enforcement powers—that could mean some serious robot apocalypse shit!"

"We're gonna need another bottle, you keep talkin' like that," Damon said. "But seriously, what else about that keepin' secrets part bothers you?"

Nolan took a moment to calm himself. Then he said, "The fact they're picking and choosing which archives to share, to me that looks like it could have legal ramifications. Meaning... Okay, you may not remember this, but back around ten years ago, this undocumented guy—we're talkin' pre-amnesty now— he dragged this white girl who was out jogging in sexy pants into the bushes and did his thing. Then he chopped her up and buried her in garbage bags, like it was nothin'!"

"Jesus…"

"Yup, yup. Anyhow, cops messed up when they arrested the cat and so he walked on a technicality. Right on back to Mexico, safe and sound!"

"Son of a bitch! But what's that got to do with…"

"Courtroom complexities, my friend. There's a whole squadron of lawyers who been takin' little ankle bites out of the HRA this whole time, just slowly chipping away at the thing. But so far, they ain't scored any direct hits. Well, this treasure trove I got might give 'em enough ammo to tear off the whole head!"

Damon exhaled a long, slow breath. "Oh. Now I see."

"You do? That's great. What's our best course of action?"

"No, no. What I mean is, now I see why you're sitting by yourself drinking all that whiskey."

"Sittin' on top of a powder keg is what I'm doing."

"Can't stay there forever. Otherwise… what if one of our tech boys accidentally sends something out, because he doesn't understand what it is?"

"Oh my god!" Nolan leaped out of his chair—the room did not explode—and wagged a finger at Damon. "I gotta lock this place down!"

31. THE THOUSAND PROBLEMS

Marcus Young found himself pulling lighter duty on Tuesday. The District of Columbia was crawling with Feds like him, so headquarters rotated them through low- and high-priority targets in order to keep everyone fresh and on their toes.

Today a group calling itself Beyond Latiz was hosting an indigenous pride festival inside the National Museum of the American Indian. Several well-known actors and musicians were scheduled to appear, so security had been beefed up slightly to include members of Marcus's FBI team.

They circulated around the museum, pausing now and again to chat with officers from the Metro Police who were also on duty. In addition to the permanent installations, Marcus passed dancers wearing traditional costumes performing in the main atrium, authentic food selections, handmade pottery and crafts for sale, and artists who painted ornate designs on patrons' arms and faces.

Guest lecturers presented their work throughout the day in the first-floor theater. Topics listed on a large placard outside ranged from a discussion of sacred rituals to how modernity was encroaching upon remote tribes. Marcus listened in on each presentation for a few minutes while making his rounds through the museum's four levels.

He had just re-entered this auditorium when a new speaker took to the stage. The man wore a striped pullover sweater in native pattern and blue jeans accented by large metal belt buckle. An enormous papier mâché pyramid stood next to the lectern, and further away an Uncle Sam piñata dangled from the branches of a plastic tree.

Marcus decided to linger as long as possible to see where this speech might be headed.

"Good afternoon," the man said. "My name is Elias Topiltzin Alhambra. I am currently a professor of trans-hemispheric studies and pan-tribal languages at UC Santa Cruz in California. Prior to that, I spent nearly fifteen years living among my ancestral cousins, the native peoples of Central and South America.

"Today I pose a challenge for Caucasians who talk incessantly about wanting to preserve their heritage. Tell me, what is there worth saving, let alone celebrating? What is the point of building walls, when you only end up locking progress out? Do you do it for your warmongering military-industrial complex, which uses sentimental manipulations to fool you into invading far-away nations?

"Or is it your culture of sickness you defend—the processed food and pharmaceutical cartels that are more interested in paperwork and patents than health? Is it your financial system, which first imposes taxes, then creates investment funds so that you may avoid these taxes, but all the while the money printing machine ensures that inflation prevents you from ever getting ahead?

"I could go on and on, providing countless examples of how your country has not merely failed you, but was meticulously designed to extract the most effort out of its deluded human livestock. Vanity, obesity, ignorance, cruelty, exploitation, and slavery—all dressed up as opportunity. But why listen to me? I am merely an indigenous voice trapped inside occupied lands.

"We native people have been unwilling investors in the half-millennium of bloody schemes that preceded the creation of the skyscraper. On behalf of those who have no voice, I declare that the funding for all modern inventions has come from New World suffering!

"You invaders must finally admit the brutality of your past. Acknowledge that we were not mere primitives. Confess that it was the colonizers' own impatience and unwillingness to understand which resulted in our so-called esoteric wisdom being lost. *You* were the savages in spirit, despite your shiny armor. *We* lived in harmony with our world before you despoiled it.

"Behold the verdict, the referendum on your long and painful rule: the rivers overflow with plastic trash, yet you dare to mock us for our piles of skulls! What a mess you have made of the world which you deign to oversee. How many cities leveled, how many millions of lives lost during your centuries of warfare? How many modern 'crises of diversity' are in fact a direct result of these destabilization campaigns which turned entire populations of innocents into refugees?

"If your civilization feels like it is being ripped apart from within, then blame yourselves for creating a Tower of Babel in every city. Your greed, your shortsighted expediency… all have contributed to your imminent downfall.

"We of the rainforests and the mesas shall survive while you consume yourselves in an avalanche of hate. For we are the strong ones. The patient. The timeless. The mountain people who were not tempted to forsake our marriage to the steppes for your coins or comforts. We who live along the water's edge, the harsh plains, the mysterious caves…

"We are the true caretakers of this Earth, our spirit eternally striving but never foolhardy. Whereas you—the eternal colonizer —you are desperate to escape this world which you have polluted beyond repair. We wish you not luck but good riddance. And if we hope you succeed, it is only so that you will leave us in peace as you ruin the other wandering stars that populate our beautiful night sky.

"Oh, blessed gods and goddesses, please hear our prayers as we speak from genuine hearts. Protect us from these modern barbarians, who think that their fancy words and overwhelming legal documents can fool the Great Spirits. Shield us from their factory exhaust, the provocative filth that they call entertainment, and the medicines which kill so many of their own each year.

"Do not let our eyes be fooled by the thousand problems hidden within each solution they offer to sell us—for that is their Trojan Horse! Defend us from chasing after their impossible pleasures, and the corrupt path which ends at the tragic cliffs of barrenness. Oh yes, lead us not into temptation, indeed!"

The professor held out his arm in the direction of his props. He said, "We built thousands of pyramids as sacred temples. You obeyed the government-approved food pyramid, and it has become the tomb of entire generations. Now I will repay your haughty Uncle Sam for all that he has done to you, as well as inflicted upon the world…"

Alhambra stepped behind the fake pyramid and reached down. A moment later, he held a wooden baseball bat aloft.

In a flash, Marcus felt himself hurtling toward the stage. He sprinted down the aisle faster than he ever ran trying to beat out a bunt at first base. Now he plowed full-force into the man in gray who had left his seat and charged the stage shouting obscenities.

They tumbled and rolled in a chaotic stalemate. Finally, Marcus maneuvered the would-be attacker onto his stomach, pinning his arms back just as other officers arrived to complete the submission and apply handcuffs.

As the commotion died down in the auditorium, Professor Alhambra approached Marcus with a grateful smile.

"Thank you very much for defending this event, Officer… ?"

"Young. Special Agent Young."

"Oh. With the FBI? Nice of you to actually *help* an indigenous person for once."

"Say," Marcus said, nodding at the baseball bat. "Were you going to use that on the piñata?"

The professor smirked. "But of course. It was my grand finale."

"What's inside?"

"Ethically grown chocolate candy purchased from farmers who respect the Amazon rainforest. If you'd like, I can still…"

Marcus reached out and grabbed the bat by its head. He tugged until Professor Alhambra released the handle.

"Well, in that case, Mr. Young, be my guest. Batter up!"

"No, that's taking it too far. *Speak* all you want, but don't disrespect the game."

Marcus walked off the stage with a confident strut, knowing that he had done his job. The professor, and the Louisville Slugger, were both safe.

32. WORD TO THE WISE

"I told y'all, the well is dryin' up."

"Easy for you to say."

Dawna Jenkins adjusted her weight forward. "And what's that supposed to mean, Mrs. Thomas?"

The woman seated across the round table said, "That maybe you got another well of your own set up already."

"Yeah," the third woman in the group added. "One that's all filled up 'cause it double dipped in the Reparations trough."

Dawna dropped her hand of playing cards onto the table. She said, "My, my. Just listen to you two today. Who needs enemies when you got friends like these? Any other comments?"

Mrs. Thomas inspected her fanned cards as she said, "How's your boy doing out in Los Angeles, by the way? He meet any movie stars yet?"

"We all had a very nice visit with him, thank you for asking. And what of it if he *has* rubbed shoulders with some celebrities? Is that alright with everyone?"

"Just making conversation, is all. Rita, I'm dumping two. Deal me, please."

The third woman dealt Mrs. Thomas fresh cards for her cast-offs, then added, "Don't get so touchy now, Dawna. We're just messin' witchu, like we always been doin' with each other. You ain't too fancy for your old friends, are you?"

Dawna picked up her cards. "Okay, then. I love you too. But

what I said before was true—and it wasn't 'cause I was bragging or nothin'. I got it on good authority that we need to watch out for ourselves."

"Who said?!" the two other women demanded.

"That, I am not at liberty to discuss. But he—or she—came to me to share what they had discovered."

"And?" Rita asked.

"Just for me to start spreading the word. Because my gossip turns into *our* gossip, which turns into a whole lotta hens sharing the message. So here goes. Reparations as we've known it for the past three years gonna be different in the future."

"Go on."

"And since they started by helping us, there's no way it'll get any better after the change. So we got to prepare for when we get less."

"Less money?" Thomas said.

"That, or maybe less attention. Fewer opportunities, less accommodation. Plus, that's just on the front end!"

"Hold up, woman. The HRA gonna downsize just like that? I don't see how, or why. They makin' money. Lots of jobs in it, for *them*."

"Because," Dawna said, "they're not closing up shop at all. They're just looking away, adjusting their camera."

"To focus on what?"

"Not us! That's all I know, and it's probably all we *need* to know. Because for whatever reason, the government is moving on to something—or someone—else."

"I blame that bitch Lao," Rita said. "Soon as she got herself re-elected, probably told her people to drop us *that night!* And who knows, maybe she was even in on the hack."

"Oh, you must be playin' games now," Thomas said. "Because for a second, you had me nodding right along with you. Too bad you let your mouth keep runnin' into crazy town."

"Me, the crazy talker? What about Dawna? She the one who started this whole thing."

"That's right! So what you got to tell us about the back end of all this, Mizz Jenkins?"

"Same source," Dawna began, "but now maybe with less concrete... not information, but predictions. Basically, think beyond the fact the HRA's gonna set up shop in new places. My friend also worries about the wild card. If the unexpected were to happen."

"Keep going," Thomas said as she shuffled the deck.

"The program almost collapsed because their computers got broken into, right? Well, that's not the only way they could lose control. Like, what if MARVIN doesn't do what they want him to do anymore? Or worse, maybe he starts going in the opposite direction. What you think about that, ladies?"

"The opposite?"

Rita added, "Like come after us? Make *us* pay?"

"Could be!" Dawna said.

"Now who's in crazy town?"

"Just a word to the wise, is all I'm sayin'."

Mrs. Thomas said, "Well, what are we supposed to do if it's gonna turn into a big bother? Please, we need some answers, or direction. Tell us what you would do."

"Or your friend," Rita muttered.

Dawna rose from her seat. "Okay, I've got some thoughts. But first, someone deal these cards while I fetch the iced tea…"

33. PERHAPS ONE DAY

People gasped throughout the corridor. Then they separated and slowly backed toward the walls as he passed.

The Prescient One, despite wearing the simple uniform of an elder instead of his signature teal cape and prosthetic makeup, had been recognized instantly. He could not walk freely through the Mall of Absolution as planned.

He whispered to one of the four bodyguards who were discreetly escorting him. Now that the ruse had failed, they would need to fall into standard protective formation.

And send one of the men ahead as a scout.

The Prescient One and his cohort soon arrived at a bakery that was renowned for its innovative methods. He was most interested in learning their secrets—and from one staff member in particular.

The advance scout greeted the group with a solemn nod, and

the Prescient One gave his shoulder a friendly squeeze before entering the shop.

A vibrant birthday-style banner above the counter said, "Welcome to A Modest Celebration!" There were many colorful pastries in the glass display cases, as well as a selection of ornate cakes that awaited personalization.

The seating area had space for thirty, and the ten or so customers present turned away from their coffee and conversation when they realized who had just entered the shop.

"Welcome, Your Modness!"

The Prescient One looked up from the food offerings. A fifty-something woman wearing matching teal apron and chef's hat was smiling at him.

"Please," he said, motioning to his humble garb, "today you may refer to me as Elder Cullen."

"Certainly, Elder. Has something here caught your eye?" she added with a wink.

"Your culinary artistry is the talk of the Mall. I've come to be enlightened, and perhaps have a taste."

"In that case, we *must* give you a private tour of our kitchen. Please…"

The woman stepped to her right and pulled a door open. The Prescient One and a single guard passed through and followed her into the back of the bakery.

He saw several women working alone in brightly lit cubicles. Each was bent over a stone surface, carefully sculpting mounds of dough into different shapes and sizes.

The group stopped beside a young baker who was stuffing the contoured edges of a three-pronged metal frame.

"Eldress Foster," the clerk said, "a customer has expressed keen interest in how we create our leavened magic. Would you be so kind as to give a demonstration?"

"I'd be happy to." The woman set down her materials and looked up for the first time. "Who—"

There was a moment of silence as her eyes met those of the Prescient One. Neither broke contact for several seconds.

"Well," the clerk said, "I mustn't neglect the counter. I'll leave you to it." She scurried back toward the front of the shop, and the guard moved into a quiet corner of the kitchen.

"Hello, Julia," the Prescient One said.

The young baker blushed, then brought her powdery hands together. "Forgive me, Your Prescience. I almost didn't recognize you. But what is your reason for... dressing down?"

"So that you might call me by my real name. Scott."

"Did you... Do you really want to see what we do here?"

"Oh, yes. People say that your cakes are true works of art. As temporary as ice sculptures, but an altogether more interactive experience."

"Then come closer and I'll let you play appren—*novitiate* for a while." She smiled.

The cake was halfway finished and in the style of a medieval castle. Two perpendicular walls were held into form by interlocked baking sheets. Julia demonstrated how she filled the interior, layer by layer, with elements such as knights and thrones and tapestries using dyed dough and colorful candies.

Once the structure was complete, she sealed the outer walls and pressed two more baking sheets against them. Scott noticed that the bottom edges of these sheets also had metal roller wheels built within tiny coverings. When he inquired about this feature, Julia said, "That's to account for expansion while in the oven. The same goes for these small openings on top. When the castle itself is done, I'll add the turrets and center spire which bake separately inside smaller molds. Then I'll apply the frosting and use this tool to create a realistic stone texture."

She picked up a flat metal square and pointed to the grooves and indents which covered one side. As Scott reached to inspect it, their fingers briefly touched.

He said, "I've thought about this moment a great deal. How I would thank you properly."

"Thank *me?* For what? I only had the honor of speaking to Your Prescience for a brief moment, back..."

"I remember our first meeting very well."

"But we barely exchanged more than a few pleasantries after the ceremony. You were so busy, understandably. How could I have... ?"

"Julia," Scott said quietly, "I was subjected to terrible psychological tortures while in captivity. I was forced to confront my oldest demons and my worst faults, until my entire being nearly fell away. Somehow I survived intact, and at first wondered if I had unlocked a new source of inner strength. But

later, when my mind had truly cleared, I realized that there had
been a guardian angel hovering over me. Her light guided me
forward to make it through. Julia, it was the image of *your*
smiling face on the day you advanced from lay member to
eldress. It offered me *hope* for a wonderful future—if I could just
hold on. And so I did. Now I can finally thank you. And perhaps
one day, offer you more."

Eldress Julia Foster looked down. She brushed away some
dried flakes from her apron, then shook her head slowly with
compressed lips.

"I've thought about you too," she said at last. "But I had no
reason to dream. There are hundreds of other women here at the
Mall. And when you were gone, I cried—not knowing if they
were the tears of a Modestian, or for myself."

"Julia, why *did* you join the Church?"

She smiled and turned away. "One step at a time, Mr. Cullen.
But right now this cake is ready for the walk-in cooler. I do hope
you've enjoyed the tour. Perhaps you'll come visit us again?"

After Julia had transferred the castle onto a rolling cart and
began moving away, Scott placed the metal texture tool back
onto her work table. The corner of a silver envelope peeked out
from underneath.

"Indeed," he said. "Good day."

34. JUST GETTING STARTED

"But I'll tell you, that's why I pinched my nose and voted for
Dominguez." The comic on stage shook his head. "At least a
new president means you get to write fresh material. I swear, if I
hear *one more* bit about crouching tigers, I'm gonna go to the zoo
myself and throw Molotov cocktails at any cat I see!"

He snatched a beer bottle off the stool beside him and drank.

"Look, I've been in this comedy racket for over twenty years.
Weathered all the storms, from political correctness to the anally
retentive conservative types. And at the end of the day, I've
always found a way to give politicians... a good roasting in
effigy."

He grinned, cocking an eyebrow while adjusting his rimless spectacles.

"I can't seem to get a rise out of this MARVIN fellow, though. He won't take the bait! And so damn *honest*, my gosh, he won't even up your Debit Score for messing with him! Heh, good old MARVIN... But still, he scares me. I really think they opened up Panderer's Box this time. Seems like every hour, another old evil deed shoots out like a firecracker! And then the world goes chasing after it like a bride's bouquet, because *there's gold in them debts!*

"I'll tell ya, know what we need right now? A real-life Ghostbusters squad! Suit 'em up and send 'em out into the streets. It's time to lock those ghosts *up!* And I, being so very handsome, would of course be perfect to cast as one of the male leads..."

Clyde Jenkins laughed along with the other audience members here at the Chuckle Condo on Sunset Boulevard. He glanced at the girl sitting beside him at this tiny round table near the stage. The lights reflected prettily against her eyes and cheeks.

Ekaterina Something. Ukrainian former figure skater now trying to make it big as an online fitness instructor. Three comics in and she had barely cracked a smile. Clyde wasn't even sure she remembered he was here.

But she was damn cute. Shoulder-length blond hair parted down the middle. Sharp pointed nose. Glitter sparkling on her eyelids. And a body toned to perfection from twirling on the ice her whole life.

Eddie had set them up to help Clyde get his mind off of Ayana. Expand his horizons by spending time with a white chick who wasn't from America. But Ekaterina had barely spoken the whole time, even during the car ride over from the lounge where they'd first met up. He'd tried to make small talk, but she mostly gave simple one- or two-word answers to his questions about her work and life back home.

Still, it was good to be out and about rather than back at his place pining for Ayana. Apparently she had flown out to whatever state they filmed her TV show in. Clyde didn't ask where—he didn't want to risk being seen as a stalker type anyway.

He heard Ekaterina laugh. That was a good sign. He glanced

at her again, only to see that she was looking at her phone. She tapped around the screen, nodding and smiling at whatever was going on there.

Oh well...

"...you please give it up for a very good friend of mine, the star of *Shaquan's Razor*, the hilarious Mr. Freddie Overton!"

The host stepped back from the microphone stand with his arms raised triumphantly as a heavyset black man wearing a leather driving cap arrived on stage. The two men embraced, then the MC trotted away.

"Thank you, thank you," the comic said after pulling the mic free. "My goodness! Jason, that was such a touching introduction... So how y'all doin' tonight? I see a lot of lovely faces in the crowd, yes I do. How many of y'all ever had your nose broke? And I ain't talkin' about you girls who done got a little plastic surgery, you know, thinkin' it was your ticket to success in *this* town. Nah, I'm talking about like, in a fist fight."

Overton scanned the crowd for a moment.

"No? Guess we got some softies in attendance. Bunch of male models. Whateva. That's okay. But me? I'm from the *streets!* Had my nose broke twice in one *day!* That's right. From two pm until seven-fiddy, it was tilted *this* way. Then some cat named Trucka popped me, and my nose swung like the rudder of a damn boat back the other way.

"Oh my God. The blood was pourin' down my face. Trucka was flexin', askin' if I wanted any more. I told him, 'Attention, shipmates. This is your captain speaking. We're now heading in an easterly direction to get away from those dark, muscular clouds...' "

Clyde rolled in his seat along with the other people nearby as Freddie puttered around the stage while flipping his free hand back and forth above his nose. Because Clyde knew all about those days when trouble seemed to find a person from dawn to dusk. He'd never actually had his nose broken, but survived plenty of scraps all the same.

He took another peek at Ekaterina. She was staring blankly at the stage. Freddie's story had made zero impact upon her.

'Whateva' is right.

After a month of Hollywood fakery, it was refreshing to get a raw taste from this guy up on the stage. Clyde settled back into his seat, ready to absorb the rest of the act.

And who knew, maybe he'd ask the club manager if he could meet Freddie later on. DJ Clydoscope had millions of streams to his credit. Surely this comedian had heard his song once or twice...

"Okay, I go," Ekaterina said, yanking Clyde out of his reverie. He watched her zip a small handbag closed and then reach back to pull her jacket off the seat.

Stunned, all he could muster was, "Really? Now?"

"Sorry. Friends have something happening too."

She offered a halfhearted smile and stood up.

The comic saw Ekaterina put on her jacket and called after her, "Where you goin', girl? I'm just getting started up here." He winked. "But with *those* legs, I bet her night's just getting started too."

The audience whistled and jeered as Freddie simulated a sexy walk across the stage. Then the man dipped his head in Clyde's direction.

"Sorry, brutha man. Happens to us all. Now, where was I at? Oh yeah. Taking relationships to the 'let's move in together' phase. Note to you young fellas—*don't do it!* Trust me, because..."

Clyde sank further down in his seat and folded his arms. Another night ruined because of a girl. Another ego bruise because he'd signed up to be a little fish in a big pond.

Hmm. Guess I gotta flip my own rudder, head in another direction too.

35. EMERGENCY BROADCAST

"This is the Reverend Matthias G. Witherspoon of Akron, Ohio. I am coming to you live from an undisclosed location with an emergency broadcast.

"I regret to inform you, my loyal followers across the nation and around the world, that I have been driven out of my church. That's right, ladies and gentlemen, you heard correctly. Abandoned, denied, and unceremoniously removed from the property like a criminal.

"Psalm 41: 'Even my close friend, whom I trusted, who shared my bread, he has lifted up his heel against me.'

"I didn't know how long I would still have access to this PerformTube channel, so it was essential that I shared my side of the story before anyone else bore false witness and tarnished my good name.

"What happened? Why was I besieged there within my private chambers? The answer is as simple as it is tragic. No one wants to hear the truth. They're too proud to handle correction. But I won't stop, because I see that this country is *sinking*. So I got to speak up, no matter how costly it might prove for myself, a loyal servant of God.

"I declare that it is folly to blame political, economic, or cultural changes for our woes, because stacked on top of all that, we also got a weakness of spirit inside ourselves. Afflicting us from coast to coast, and in every pigment across the color spectrum. We are losing ourselves. And worst of all, we don't have the gumption to admit it.

"It seems to me that after millennia, humanity is *still* grappling with the same tired issues that destroyed so many civilizations of the past, before burying them under the dust. Hear me now, my people. When disagreement devolves into conflict, it can quickly spiral into violence. Today I walk away from my betrayers, whom I still love, to spare us from such awful consequences. It is most certainly better that we should all live and walk free. Better to carry the pain in our hearts for ugly words spoken, rather than regret actions which cannot be undone.

"Although my tenure at the Ministry of the Divine God appears to have concluded, know that Matthias G. *has not* lost his fighting spirit. And I will draw inspiration from the Lord Jesus Christ Himself by remembering that sometimes… it takes only one.

"As long as one man carries the flame of truth, God will prevail. I make this pledge to you courageous souls listening now. If it has been fated for me to abandon the city and roam the land as a nomad or bedraggled vagabond, just as so many saints and apostles and martyrs have done through the centuries, then so be it. Let all others bear the consequences for averting their eyes out of fear or expediency.

"Yes indeed, if the truth lives on in one man's heart, then surely we can rebuild anew once again. So stay strong, my fellow lovers of the gospel. I guarantee you that the lie cannot last forever. Why? Because it does not create, but only feeds upon the stores of bounty accumulated by the humble.

For those of you who still believe two plus two equals four, don't be afraid to walk out that door. 'Cause it's the deceivers that need *you!* They'll whisper into your ear and say that you should keep 'em around to remind you of how great you are. Don't fall for it! Don't believe it, not for one second! Resist that temptation, or your vanity shall fall prey to the locust lie.

"Old Matthias will now take the lead, so watch out! White flight ain't got *nothin'* on me! I too will abandon the city if that is my cross to bear. I just pray that I will find the strength to accept it with as much serenity as my Lord Jesus Christ. That I will walk His path with the same patient resignation as He did after being forsaken.

"Remember and remember again, that in dark times all a man need do is seek the truth. Protect it and speak it. Then, even if he is a wanderer for years and years, righteousness shall survive while the tallest of castles crumble.

"Romans 5: 'And not only this, but we also exult in our tribulations, knowing that tribulation brings about perseverance; and perseverance, proven character; and proven character, hope.'

"So persevere, we must! I will talk to you again soon, somehow and somewhere as I venture into the unknown. Fall from grace? Never! I *got* the grace! And like my Lord Jesus, I shall rise up and return, stronger than ever before. There is so much hot air left in these preachin' pipes, ladies and gentlemen, you have no idea. Do not worry about me. Instead, praise the Christian God, amen!

"This is your friend, the demoted but not demoralized Reverend Matthias G. Witherspoon, signing off from this outcast broadcast. God bless you, me, and these Disintegrating States of America."

36. THE QUEENMAKERS

"Did you know that Robinson Crusoe's island was a meritocracy?"

These were the first words spoken by a man whom Eileen Jeffries-Lao had never before met, on the night of a fundraising gala in Orange County many years ago. Eileen, who at the time was mother to a young daughter and also served on the local school board, did not know what to make of this odd introduction.

She had smiled respectfully and waited for the man to explain himself. Afterward, her life was never the same.

"But the problem is," he continued, "there's no glory or gold medals to be had when all your efforts are spent on mere survival."

"I take it you're not a fan of the novel?" Eileen had offered.

The man laughed, clinking glasses with her as he said, "No. But I am a fan of *you*."

Again speechless, Eileen glanced around the room while fiddling with her bracelet.

"Well, not just myself. Mrs. Jeffries-Lao, considering what you've achieved locally in only a few years, clearly you have a great career ahead of yourself."

"I thank you," she said. "And do hope you're right."

"So let me ask you this. Would you rather be queen of a small island, or perhaps someplace a bit more noteworthy?"

"I must say, Mr… ?"

"Kent."

"Mr. Kent, you flatter me, and I'm intrigued by your riddles. So please, do tell!"

He winked. "The sky's the limit, if you have the right team on your side."

"Ah," Eileen said warmly, at last understanding the point behind his Robinson Crusoe allusion. "But surely you believe that an educated modern woman can rise through the ranks on her own?"

They had both laughed at this, with Kent adding, "I never

said I didn't. But consider an alliance with the people I represent as the express shuttle. And *you* have already earned a ticket on board..."

It had all been so friendly. Lively and complimentary banter right out in the open among the other notable members of Orange County politics. And the gregarious Mr. Kent had most certainly delivered on his promises.

Eileen Jeffries-Lao next served a brief term as a California state representative, before vaulting into the governor's mansion. And then, in the blink of an eye, she was President of the United States—and in fact, could not have done it without his organization's influence.

A younger, more naive version of herself would have added "not so quickly" as a qualifier, but the fatigued and battle-tested Eileen of 2029 knew better. Because the club which had extended her a membership believed in a world ordered by more than *merit* alone.

Networks. Alliances. Fifty-year plans. Blackmail and the promise of mutually assured incrimination. Fail-safes put in place to promote or clip the wings of ambitious individuals. Tools used to maintain global security—or orchestrate chaos.

Eileen Jeffries-Lao almost pitied the people who worried that the HRA's centralized supercomputer might usher in a surveillance state. The headless system had already been compiling dossiers on any and all potential *Who's Who* candidates for decades.

She herself had fallen into their trap long before ever appearing on their radar, however. As the daughter of exiles from Communist China, she understood perfectly why the government might keep tabs on any of her youthful political involvements. But no, she'd been ensnared far differently, and to this day still shook her head in disgusted admiration of their methods.

They had evidence of one of her few lifetime indiscretions filed away within their stockpiles of blackmail, like some grotesque variation of a De Beers warehouse, which stored human foibles instead of diamonds. A drunken romantic tryst after a night of letting loose with college friends. Sex in the bushes outside of a small hotel where some backpackers from Holland were staying.

Through all of human history, the worst that such liaisons produced was an unplanned pregnancy. And prior to the internet era, perhaps this scene would have gone no further than becoming part of some pervert's celluloid collection, with the sole copy eventually gathering dust in a cluttered attic.

But in the twenty-first century, that security camera footage was used to control a woman long before she ever became the leader of the free world—and today it continued to steer her administration's agenda.

Eileen in her darkest moments fantasized about one day revealing all on a hot mic. In a flash, the general public would be thrust into an existential crisis about how their world actually operated. But besides putting her family in mortal danger, such a confession was not in keeping with her temperament—a metric which surely had been scrutinized before she was tapped to join the group that owned her.

Eileen Jeffries-Lao would never disclose their secrets willingly. Because she had been able to reach levels of success that far surpassed her Asian family's towering expectations. Because she had gotten to live the good life, never soiling her hands with peasant labor, while also making a positive impact for the working people of her adopted country.

And ultimately she believed—or had been convinced—that the masses needed to be led. A billion Robinson Crusoes, however competent, would only result in more inefficiency and disorder. But with the proper guiding hand, humanity might be capable of the kind of cooperation needed to conquer deep space.

This ethereal, majestic vision brought her to a state of calm that was as genuine as it was elusive. Glorious spaceships lifting off to leave all of the cruelty and filth and betrayal behind. The human race proclaiming to the universe that it had finally overcome its built-in flaws, which seemed to express themselves in a million destructive ways each day.

On the eve of her second inauguration, Eileen Jeffries-Lao took solace in the thought that, despite her own failings and regrets, she was helping to set the stage for the species' next great act.

37. GRAND PLOT

It was like old times again. Chris, Glenn, and Kate were hanging out and shooting the breeze. Cold beers for the guys and Kate was drinking hot tea.

"Cheers," Chris said, "to the rest of our lives."

"Cheers!" the others replied and beverages were clinked.

"So Glenn," Kate said, "what's the theme of your next song gonna be? Pro- or anti-government?"

Glenn gave a mild laugh. "You can guess what I was thinking while I was stuck in solitary. But now that I'm out… Think I'll just sit back and enjoy the taste of freedom for a while." He took a big gulp of beer.

"Not to rush you, but I've heard *somebody* practicing in his office a lot lately."

"Oh yeah?" Glenn thumped Chris on the arm. "Keepin' your chops up or writing some new riffs?"

Chris smiled bashfully. "I got a couple chord progressions I'm working on. Mapped out some drums too. But lyrics aren't my department, so…"

"Aha! This whole get-Glenn-out-of-jail thing has been a grand plot to reunite the band. Well played, you two!"

They all laughed.

A moment later, Glenn added, "But seriously, thank you so much for everything. I could've been locked up for a long time. So maybe I do owe you at least one song, Chris."

"Hell yeah! We'll, uh, sing about international stuff so the Feds don't reconsider their decision to let you go."

"And what about the fate of your current band?" Kate asked.

"You know how it goes," Glenn replied. "Controversy equals notoriety. A lot more downloads. The other guys even had to reorder shirts from the printer twice! I figure we might be able to get on a decent tour as the opening act later in the spring. So you might even say, I fought the law… and I won!"

"Sell-out," Chris grinned.

"Heh, yeah. And Kate, you're back working local again?"

"The old grind," she said. "But things definitely seem different now. I'm not sure if it's all in my mind, or maybe the administration will just never feel as electric as it once did. And no, Glenn, I don't blame *you* for it."

Chris looked down, wary that this get-together had the potential to crash and burn at any second.

Glenn fiddled with his glass. "I will neither confirm nor deny anything that relates to the Jubileers. But I wanted to ask you, did the HRA foreign legion not float your boat or what?"

"Now it's my turn to be diplomatic," Kate said. "Let's just say, my own goals will be better achieved here on the mainland."

She reached out and scratched Chris on the back. He nodded, saying, "I'm glad you're here. Both of you. My two favorite people, ever."

"Come on, guys," Glenn said. "Enough with the weepy emo stuff. We're one year away from a new decade. What disasters can we clean up?"

"Oh god, here we go again," Kate said jokingly. "Anyone got a pen and paper handy for lyric ideas?"

"Always. Because a true artist never lets his guard down. Chris, you in?"

Chris rolled his eyes. "Duh! Why do you think we invited you out? To just have fun? Let's do this! Yup, the old gang's back at it. DIY fixes for top-heavy crises."

"Ooh," Kate marveled. "Looks like maybe we've got *two* wordsmiths here."

The trio laughed again, then got to work trying to solve all of the world's problems...

38. NO SIGN OF RECOGNITION

Clyde had been on his best behavior all day. Anywhere he was supposed to stand, or when asked to repeat a choreographed move fifteen times—he did it all professionally.

There were a lot of people running around this small warehouse soundstage, even though today was just a dry-run rehearsal in preparation for his upcoming video with DJ Low Bought. There was going to be CGI, and possibly real flames, so the production team wanted to capture some test footage to make sure the planned spectacle turned out larger than life.

A white girl with curly brown hair and a walkie-talkie on her hip approached.

"Hey, Clyde. The crew's all going on break, so we won't need you for a while. Feel free to grab a snack from craft services, and we'll find you in a bit."

She was on the move again before he'd even said "thanks."

Clyde ambled away from his spot in front of the green screen and went looking for the food tables. At one point, he passed several other crew members who were huddled around a gear cart deep in conversation.

After loading up his plate with some fruit and chips, Clyde wandered around the warehouse lazily while humming a tune. He almost stumbled over DJ Low, who was partially hidden within several black curtains that hung down from the rafters.

"Oh, Clyde," Low said from his electric scooter. "There you are. Good, good. Come on in and join me."

Clyde grabbed a plastic folding chair that was nearby and dragged it into the small enclosure. "What's the word, Low?" he asked.

The other rapper cleared his throat—he had a dry, raspy voice that made him sound much older than twenty-six.

"How you handlin' yourself?"

"Aw, you know. Tryin' to learn, day by day. It's the only way."

"Right, right. Well, look. I been watchin' you, and you know, you aight."

Clyde jabbed a finger at the food on his plate. "Thanks, man. You know, this whole thing kinda weird. Eddie told me the deal witchu back at the beginning, but still, I didn't know how to act around you."

Low rubbed his rough and wiry beard as he smiled. "Nah, you doin' fine. That's why I want to talk to you one on one. It's gonna be a huge deal, this reveal about my 'recovery.' We got to be on the same page when the firestorm hits."

"You think people gon' be mad when we tell 'em hard-cortex rap ain't for real?"

"No doubt. Because, that *is* the plan!" Low paused for a moment. "So I been running this LA hustle for a while now. Got a lot figured out. But you're new around here. I got to make sure you always land on your mark."

Clyde pointed his thumb in the direction of the set. "We been doin' that all morning, bro. I got it. I know where to step."

"Nah, kid. Forget about all that. I'm trying to take your head to another *level*."

"Oh… Like… ?"

"Like gettin' you to think about the dynamics of your surroundings. Look at all this right here. The building, the lights, the gear, all the people it take to run the show. It ain't cheap! And *we* are the main attraction."

"For real, though. But can't be nothin' wrong with that. Means we made it!"

Clyde offered a high-five, but Low waved it away with annoyance. The man said, "I keep asking myself why, of all types of art out there, why are they sinking their cash into hip-hop? And of all the things these folks on the crew could be doing with their time, with their skills… Why are they workin' with *me*, a hustla from the streets?"

"To make that money?" Clyde offered. "Or they just know what's hot."

Low scoffed. "Kid, our rhymes might be good, but they ain't *that* good. Like I said, there's another level I been chewin' on. So buckle up."

Clyde smiled and popped a grape into his mouth.

"All these white folks that move to LA, they don't just come here looking *for* something. I think they also tryin' to get *away* from something. But it ain't even that, 'cause the word that keeps coming into my mind is 'renunciation'. They are *renouncing* something about their white-bread Midwest world, and LA is the temple where they make the blood sacrifice to get their revenge."

"Whoa. Um… and how do we fit in? They gonna sacrifice *us?*"

"No, Clyde. Worse. They *romanticize* us."

"Huh? No way, hold up." Clyde sat forward and said, "I got to disagree on that. 'Cause I remember firsthand *those* types of Caucs from back in the day, when the HRA got started. They all came to the hood stupid as, patted us on the head, nothin' worked, and then after a while they was gone."

DJ Low Bought closed his eyes for a moment, then said, "You ain't totally wrong, but… Okay. This crew on set here, they all *competent*. They're the opposite of what you was just talkin' about. They know what they doin' and *still* they hoverin' around us. So if they ain't dumb, and they qualified to work on movies or the opera or whatever, why in the hell they wanna be with rappers instead of their own kind?!"

Clyde said, "Maybe 'cause they're colorblind? Equal opportunity and such?"

Low tapped his temples with his fingertips. Finally he said, "People in the know say I pulled this lobotomy stunt to stick it to white people for patronizing us. But truth is, I decided to hunker down because I needed time to think."

"So now, if you 'bout ready to come out of your stupor, that mean you got your solution?"

"Eh… I got a bit more understanding. I just don't know if it's the answer I wanted. Clyde, tell me, you know what a mandarin is?"

"Mandarin chicken? Oh yeah! Yum!"

"No, you fool! I'm talkin' 'bout mandarin Caucs!"

"Huh? Saaaaay what?"

Low leaned in very close, speaking quietly but with a harsh intensity. "It come from China. All the little bureaucratic types who waddle around messin' with everybody's business. They got no balls, but still think *they* should be the king. They smart, but they stupid. *However*, on the flip side—they also stupid, but smart. Chew on that riddle!"

Clyde stared blankly in confusion. "DJ, I…"

"All these Caucs in here are too afraid to step in front of that camera themselves and show they face to the world. But they still hold all the levers of power. Location, materials, funding…"

"But I got money now too—"

"Shut yo' mouth, boy! I'm layin' down some truth. Without them and their whole setup, we'd all just be rappin' on the stoop, hoping to catch a few quarters while dodging bullets from some other brother's pistol. So why is it that you and I are here at this goddamn warehouse, when there's a thousand dudes who can play Mozart on the cello that ain't nobody gonna see in no video?"

"I don't *know*, Low, so tell me!"

"Because all these Caucs are *sick!* Sick in they soul. So sick, they'll use their hard-earned skills to film me drooling, rather than true art, because something inside them says they need to cater to us Minoricans. Yup, yup, we're their little babies! Got to coddle us and push us down the street in a stroller!"

Just then, one of the crew members poked his head through the curtains.

"Hey, fellas! The director's back on set and ready to start blocking out the next sequence of moves. As soon as you can, we'd love to see you out there."

"Aight, cool," Clyde said. He turned to DJ Low Bought and added, "Chat's over for now, I gue—"

He did a double-take.

The other man had slumped forward in his scooter. A long stalactite of spittle dangled above his kneecap as he whimpered in a falsetto, "Ma-ma... Da-da... Ma-ma..."

Clyde looked into the DJ's eyes, but there was no sign of recognition. He got up shakily and left his plate on the folding chair, then followed the PA toward set.

His mind was in a daze.

39. OBSESSED WITH RACE

Rebellican Senator Victor Dominguez was neither grateful nor bitter as he arrived outside the Capitol Building for the inauguration ceremony of Eileen Jeffries-Lao. Slightly grumpy perhaps, but no one who had ever lost an election felt particularly well on the day that their opponent was sworn into office.

It could have been worse. As a consequence of his Debit Score lurching skyward after he appeared on *DDM TV Live* back in early December, he might have been assigned to a lengthy term at some community service project doing God-knows-what.

But Jeffries-Lao had deemed his patriotic takedown of the conspiracy-minded Cornelius Alemán sufficient grounds for canceling out whatever DDM punishment was due. The aging scion Alemán remained one of the few players involved in the recent political scandals whose charges had not been dropped. The man did, however, tap into his wealthy network of allies to acquire the ten million dollars necessary to post bail, and then promptly fled to South America. His whereabouts were currently unknown.

Victor himself was now free to return to the Senate and serve out the final two years of his term. Whether he would run for re-election was debatable. On the one hand, he knew Eileen Jeffries-Lao so well that he could act as a formidable watchdog. However, the presidential election campaign had taken so much out of Victor that he didn't think he had another go in him—especially not when his three children back home in Flagstaff needed his guidance.

As he took his seat in the gallery next to his wife Jaclyn, Victor quietly resolved that he would only stay in Washington for the next two years. But each day, working to put the pieces in place so that the president found herself in check at every turn.

Why? Because the percentage of the population that had voted for Victor was much larger than expected. Because he believed that the damage done in a Dramacrat president's second term was always magnitudes worse than during the first. And because, despite his own proclamations on *DDM TV* that Eileen Jeffries-Lao was a dutiful American, Victor sensed that her demeanor had subtly changed in the weeks following the Holy Holidays. Was it just relief after two election-season scares—or was something more sinister lurking behind her piercing eyes?

Victor drifted off into his own thoughts amid the drawn-out pomp and circumstance of the ceremony. But something Jeffries-Lao said must have rattled his subconscious, because suddenly he found himself paying careful attention to her words.

"...time marches on, history places new challenges before us, and we must meet them directly. If we cannot afford to perpetually relive the past, then we must also not allow ourselves to fixate on the present moment.

"My first term could be defined as having led a united national effort to restore a sense of fairness. In my second term, we will use this repaired root system to launch ourselves farther than we have ever gone before.

"For decades, First World nations have tried to feed and clothe the poorest of countries. But how many containers full of grain and second-hand fashions can we send, before needing to find a new higher goal? One that will tap into and inspire the global community, which has become so interconnected via the power of the internet this century?

"I say that goal will be to fulfill the dream presently incubating in places like the research laboratories of Palo Alto, California... the test launch sites at Cape Canaveral, Florida... as well as in the heart of every child who aspires to be an astronaut.

"You know, some of the critics have said that my administration is obsessed with race. To them I say, you're right! And just you watch how determined we will be to achieve great things in this next phase of the *space* race! Where by working together, governments all around the world will ensure that soon, very soon, human colonies on Mars and the Moon are not simply Hollywood productions on the silver screen."

"Jesus Christ," Victor heard someone mutter. "It's JFK all over again."

"...one such priority," Eileen continued, "is to avoid the stagnation that comes from trying to reinvent the wheel over and over again. Especially now, when there are multistage rockets waiting to be built..."

Victor Dominguez got a chill in his bones. He sensed that something fanatical was bleeding through the president's normally unflappable veneer. Passion for scientific endeavors was of course commendable, but he found what Jeffries-Lao exuded from the podium today greatly unnerving.

He would indeed keep a close eye on her during the coming months. Because if her plans continued to diverge so far from what she had campaigned on, then how many economic sectors —or Americans in general—might be left behind in her zeal to open up the far reaches of space?

Victor Dominguez vowed to make the President of the United States work for every step. The nation could always recover from a stumble, but perhaps not after leaping off whatever cliff Eileen Jeffries-Lao was fixated upon.

40. THE DEVIL YOU KNOW

The Prescient One leaned in very close and said, "Have you ever faced two intertwined choices that were so potentially volatile, you couldn't even think clearly?"

He heard the proponent on the other side of the partitioned booth clear his throat. Then the man said, "Are you able to offer any specifics? I understand that people often visit a direction booth due to the sensitive nature of their concerns. However, if I am to help steer you effectively, it would be better to share as many details as you can."

"I see." The Prescient One took a slow breath. "One path involves oaths and legalities. The consequences of breaking these would be quite detrimental to me. Not only that, but speaking up will also bring disturbing new truths to light. Perhaps this is necessary."

"My heavens! And your *second* dilemma?"

"It regards my potential happiness. I know that her heart is there for the taking."

"Oh, yes?" the proponent said, his voice fluttering. "So what about these seemingly distinct issues gives you pause?"

"If I expose the first, no one will be able to control the fallout from the scandal. I would also be severely punished—meaning that she and I could not be together."

The Prescient One heard the bench creak as the proponent leaned away from the mesh screen that separated their faces. His own face was bare, having made the decision to stop applying prosthetic makeup altogether after first presenting himself to Julia in the flesh.

The other man said, "You are a brave Modestian for entrusting your hopes and fears with me, a mere believer. It seems as if you have come to one of the defining crossroads of your life. So we must ask, where do a person's obligations to society end? When are they worth the ultimate sacrifice? But consider, no one should be a slave to the masses—you too deserve all the happiness that such altruism ensures for others."

"Perhaps I have been addicted to sacrifice. The promise to myself always being of course, that *this* selfless act will be the last."

"Oh, but it is!" the proponent said. "Until the next, and the next after that."

The Prescient One nodded his head slowly. "Ah. Good men and women have many opportunities to prove their charitable nature. But the moments which might change their own lives are quite rare."

"Yes, exactly! And if a self-interested act results in a person's heart overflowing, then their capacity to give is also replenished for years to come. Conversely, neglecting our human needs can sap us of the strength to be our best."

"Then the second matter is settled. I will ask her hand in marriage."

"Wonderful!"

"But still, the first… It cannot be ignored."

The proponent lowered his voice. He said, "What would be the worst-case outcome if you remained silent?"

"The devil you know." The Prescient One rose. "Thank you so very much for helping me work through these troubling questions. Mod be with you."

"And also with you…"

A short while later, the Prescient One was standing in his private study. Laid out on the desk before him were a white sheet of paper and a small zip-seal plastic bag which contained a soiled napkin. Printed on the page were the lab results of a sample taken from this napkin.

He recalled the words of the technician who had discussed the shocking implications with him earlier in the day.

"Something is distorting her DNA sequence."

"But for how many years?" the Prescient One had responded. "Surely an old item stolen from her home in California by an enterprising thief would match what we have?"

The tech shook his head in confusion. "I'm just a data guy, Your Prescience. I would assume you know more about the world of politicians than I do."

"Wait… Are you saying she may have been… obscuring… or scrambling… her DNA for years? Before MARVIN was even an idea?"

"It's possible."

"But how..." The Prescient One trailed off. "How could it happen that I got such a pure sample?"

The technician's jaw clenched. He said, "Either she takes regular doses, like a prescription, or normally no one is able to get their hands on her saliva like you did."

"So... She pops a pill or receives an injection each morning? Or anytime she's about to interact with the public? Maybe that's it! She only needs to be careful when she's exposed. Her handlers must also do some sort of cleanup afterward."

"And with you incarcerated at the time, she didn't think she had anything to worry about."

The Prescient One now looked down at the sealed napkin and lab printout. Two seemingly innocuous items, which together had the power to turn the world upside down.

Because if Victor Dominguez deserved to be raked over the coals of ancestral shame for the crimes of a mid-nineteenth-century Mexican *bandito*, then what might be the fitting punishment if Eileen Jeffries-Lao's unadulterated genetic history came to light?

The Prescient One closed his eyes and pictured a montage of Chinese peasants and warriors falling down dead through the centuries. Eileen's own distant relatives had long-forgotten blood on their hands—but the body count paled in comparison to anything that Chairman Mao had achieved during a single year of his twentieth-century reign.

Next he imagined the tumultuous scenes that might play out after the president's revised Debit Score was announced. Calls for her resignation. Political defenders and opponents at each other's throats. Was *this* inconvenient archive radioactive enough to break America's long chain of peaceful transitions of power... or even usher in a second civil war?

For him to remain silent—to sacrifice the truth in the name of stability—would be perhaps as strategic as it was prudent. Because now the Prescient One was armed with something no one else had: proof that for many years, a hidden network had groomed Eileen Jeffries-Lao. First for her role as president, and then to serve as the global ambassador promoting interplanetary exploration.

In secrecy, he would remain free to keep watchful eye from his position of chastened church leader. To map out the organization's structure. Gather information about its members. Undermine their conspiratorial plans...

And he would have the strength to keep fighting for what was right in a world being poisoned by snakes that slithered in the shadows. Because he had finally reached that place of joy which he sought for so long in the trenches of blind grueling effort. Soon, Julia Foster would be his bride.

The Prescient One locked the damning pieces of evidence inside a hidden wall safe. There they would remain, he hoped for all time.

He took a private elevator to his sleeping quarters for a brief rest. Afterward, he would still his fluttering heart and call upon the woman whose memory had given him the will to survive weeks of torture—and all the while, keeping an incriminating napkin hidden from his jailers.

41. FOR THE CHILDREN

Nolan Simmons closed up the gear supply closet, then looked in on the roomful of young computer techs while heading to the elevator. There they all were in near-darkness, tapping away at their workstations and completely focused on the task at hand. They were so sharp, so intuitive, so effective.

These were the brightest of the street kids that Nolan had plucked out of the bedlam and trained in electronics. The public schools had been of no use to them—how many were once habitually truant students, but now eagerly showed up here three days a week?

An unconventional setup to say the least, but it wasn't Nolan's fault that yet another government body which functioned on the surface—the buses ran their routes and the teachers' unions got funded—still let entire generations of poor kids slip through the cracks.

Stepping away from the computer lab, Nolan thought about the powder keg of archival information that these geniuses were dredging up. In truth, he was implicating them as accomplices in what might be considered a threat to national, if not global security. The boys, meanwhile, thought it was great fun to see who among them could gather the most historical data. The rankings posted on a whiteboard in glowing neon ink were updated at the end of each week.

As he arrived back at the custom-built video editing room, Nolan wondered if he really ought to just be grateful for the financial windfall that producing Clyde's first music video had blessed him with. Meaning that he would need to cancel this "Great Library of Newark" project, and instead let whoever was in charge of worldwide Reparations roll it out on their own schedule.

Nolan felt like he was caught in a vise. Simply *possessing* this information was so risky. An FBI raid was quite possible, even if none of the tech kids mistakenly leaked any of it. And what would *that* scene look like? A bunch of eight- to eleven-year-olds working in violation of child labor laws, now being led away in handcuffs!

Everything that Nolan had worked for would crumble after that. He would never make good on his silent promise to the neighborhood. No, he could not put that at risk…

But even if he scrubbed every last bit of data from his network, a savvy government cybersecurity expert could probably trace its route through the public fiber-optic pipes. If Nolan instead threw caution to the wind and opened the spigots, the fallout would likely be so chaotic that no one would have time to pursue the source for weeks or months. And at that point, perhaps society would consider the deed as having been a public service.

Because Nolan was of the belief that secretly filling up a reservoir with obfuscations and lies, while also grandstanding about the audit being conducted overseas—it could only lead to an even more disastrous reckoning than whatever he had the power to provoke now.

While he wasn't as qualified as a lawyer or politician to weigh all the merits of the situation, Nolan simply could not allow *more* chains to be wrapped around humanity's psyche. And here he agreed with that masked Sentinels of Jubilee speaker, who during the original hack had warned against the dangers of arbitrarily bottling up creative potential in the name of short-term punitive thinking.

Having seen his platoon of tech geeks in action only moments ago, Nolan truly understood how tremendous the possibilities were. Somehow he would have to find the courage to unleash the digital deluge—for the sake of future generations and the unimaginable greatness they would surely achieve...

But an hour later, as he sat nursing a glass of whiskey, Nolan Simmons still couldn't believe that he was the one who had been fated to launch this supernova of a truth bomb on the unsuspecting world. No military man, despite his training, could truly predict what he would do in moments fraught with so much responsibility.

"At least those guys have their orders," Nolan said to himself quietly.

A stream of catch phrases suddenly popped into his head.

Just do it.

Do the right thing.

If it feels good, do it.

Do what you gotta do.

He held the tumbler under his nose, and sweet warm tones emanated into his nostrils. He would have to decide sooner rather than later. Because in less than two weeks, Black *History* Month would begin.

Nolan thought of his young apprentices once again, and another cliche came to mind. It was perhaps the most overused justification for any and all policies, pleas, and interventions over the past fifty years.

Do it for the children.

Nolan Simmons took a sip of whiskey and closed his eyes with a wary smile.

Because he just might have to.

42. INAUGURAL BALL

"So, Mr. Richards, I hear you're thinking of leaving us."

Ryan Richards flashed one of his trademark million-dollar smiles and guided his dance partner along with the flow of the room. A nineteenth-century waltz filled the air.

"That *is* a possibility," he said vaguely.

He felt a hard squeeze on the shoulder before Eileen Jeffries-Lao leaned in close and breathed into his ear, "Just tell me what you need, Ryan. More money? An hour-long puff piece about your life? How about a star on the Walk of Fame?"

"Haha, that *would* be tempting."

"Or perhaps, as the ultimate proof that you had triumphed over your B-movie career, a night's stay in the Lincoln Bedroom?"

"Me, a guest at the White House?"

"Oh yes, certainly. Because... These last few years, using entertainment to help bolster cultural acceptance of Reparations... Your show has been instrumental in achieving that goal. And *you* have been an inspiration, sir."

"Well, Madam President, I'm flattered. Truly. And *DDM* has had a good run, but..."

"Look, buster. You threw your lot in with the HRA and have done quite well for yourself."

Richards tried to pull away. He said testily, "Yeah, I know. But all these changes to the show make me nervous. We've lost our edge. I'd rather not be there when the ratings tank."

"Don't worry," Eileen assured him with a light pat on the lapel of his tuxedo blazer. "We'll tell your agent when it's time to start auditioning for something new."

"I don't know..."

"Ryan, my administration always takes care of its loyal soldiers." Eileen got very close now. She said, "And so, during your visit, if you'd like for someone who's say, blond... around five-seven... to place a mint on your pillow... That can all be arranged."

"Madam Pres—"

"Ha, don't give me any of that, Ryan. I know all about your reputation. You might be able to blush for the TV cameras on cue, but I'd find that hard to believe in your private life."

Richards glanced around the room at the elegantly dressed dancers and other guests who were mingling at the edges. "We're all taking one for the team, eh? How long am I supposed to stay on?"

He felt her thumb dig into his hip bone as they entered a crush of bodies on the dance floor.

"Just one more year," the president said fervently. "We all have to hold on for another year."

"One thing, though. There aren't any hidden cameras inside Lincoln's old playpen, are there?"

"Not a chance. Guaranteed to be clean. We perform a sweep before every guest's arrival. For *everyone's* sake."

"I see," Richards said breezily. "Guess I'll have to film Miss Five-Seven myself..."

"...then the world is ours."

Presidential Chief of Staff Tony Rizzuto had spoken these words to help soothe Eileen Jeffries-Lao's nerves the week before Tribesgiving. If they could just stay calm through the inauguration, he'd promised, then they would have four years to shape the future together.

Of the nation. Of the world. And their illicit relationship.

But now, with the oaths taken and festivities reaching a fever pitch, he found that his own anxieties were actually getting worse...

He was married to a beautiful woman who had given him two children. Alana Rizzuto could also be counted on to support his every career move—both vertically and across the country when duty called. He saw her standing near the cocktail bar, patiently listening to some blowhard from the State Department regale her with stories that were as unverifiable as they were self-aggrandizing.

How had he gotten himself romantically involved with a Chinese-American woman nearly ten years his senior? It all began during the chaos leading up to the election. That sudden fear of losing power had brought them so much closer—and now he was risking everything that truly mattered to him for… what, exactly?

What did he want with *the world*, if one day his son Doyle didn't respect him because he had been outed as the president's gigolo in some tabloid?

And if that potential shame wasn't reason enough for Tony Rizzuto to seek a way out, he had also recently noticed some concerning quirks in his mistress's behavior. Bizarre declarations that were followed by a grating cackle. She'd even left a few classified documents which were far above his pay grade out in the open during one of their clandestine sleepovers.

The autumnal haze of tension, triumph, and lust was finally giving way to a sober clarity. Where did his loyalties ultimately lie? Could his career and personal obligations be reconciled? And which would take precedence, should they ever diverge?

Because if Eileen Jeffries-Lao was at risk of becoming a madwoman, then he himself might be more effective than anyone else at warding off disaster—which meant he would need to remain close by her side. Could he do that *and* end their affair? If he stayed on as chief of staff to protect her, surely he would also be expected to fill the role of male comforter, perhaps going through the motions for *years*…

Tony Rizzuto was revolted by such a prospect. He had been a varsity high school linebacker. Had graduated from Penn in three years before earning his master's degree at Georgetown University. Never could he have imagined that his legacy might be defined not by personal achievements, but as just another Beltway insider who couldn't keep it in his pants.

Or, he could simply walk away. Cite stress or some other health reason for taking a brief leave of absence. Then, having bought a little time before Eileen suspected anything was amiss, move his family out of their Bethesda home under the cover of night.

But where would he take them?

Any place that was safely out of range from the blast crater Eileen Jeffries-Lao might make of his life.

First Man Paul Jeffries had set a rule for himself: no more than one drink per hour when appearing in public. If he faltered, he was then obliged to speak to the ugliest or dullest person in his vicinity until back on schedule. Such was his burden on those important occasions when he absolutely must not bring embarrassment to all things presidential.

A quick glance into each of the venue's rooms confirmed that tonight his resolve would surely be put to the test—if only because there were so many beautiful ladies in attendance.

And Paul, in his more roguish moments, sought to model himself after the aristocratic dandy that Ben Franklin became when touring France later in life. He tried to ignore the whispers insinuating that his affairs with much younger women were not conquests, but in fact sad compensation after years of being emasculated throughout Eileen's political career.

It had once been said, that while everyone looked forward to the day when the United States of America elected its first female president, no one actually wanted to be that woman's husband. The singular distinction had befallen Paul Jeffries—and it would be his ultimate legacy when all the biographies were trimmed to mere paragraphs.

No one would ever remember the jazz power trio he had founded back in the early 1990s. Himself on guitar and backing vocals. Ronald Lewis pounding the drums. And fronted by the inimitable Monty Castillo, whose voice and fretless bass lines were silkier than ice cream on a hot summer day.

They were an interracial Bay Area staple back before anyone kept obsessive tabs about identity. Parrot Esoteric, as they were called, tapped into the freewheeling spirit of the sixties and seventies, when creativity swirled in a glorious mishmash of styles—then refined it with the technical proficiency and production quality of the eighties. All that AOR rock and the finger-tapping solos made famous by the hair metal bands on MTV, inspired The Parrot to take their own musical vision to the next level, rather than sit back comfortably and rehash the past.

The national artistic scene was overflowing at this time, with original hip-hop and alternative rock, as well as thoughtful movies that captured everyone's different experiences. But then something seemed to shift imperceptibly almost overnight, and people scuttled away from one another to retrench in a fog of misunderstanding and isolation.

Was it grunge suddenly toppling the radio-rock dynasties from the album charts? Michael Jordan's shocking retirement from basketball after three straight championships? Or Bill Clinton sliding into the Oval Office because an upstart third-party candidate had split the vote?

No matter what the true cause, everyone knew in their hearts that the light and exuberant feeling of the eighties had been irretrievably lost.

For the young Paul Jeffries, it meant that so-called serious music quickly fell out of favor. Attendance dropped at the gigs which became fewer and far between. Soon Monty was spending more and more time down in Miami playing in bands with his fellow Cubans. And Ronald, who was always in demand, ended up making a career out of touring with established groups that were in need of a skilled drummer.

Which left a deflated Paul vulnerable to the *sensible* appeals of his parents back in Upstate New York, who offered to fund graduate school even if he insisted upon staying out on the West Coast. He spent the rest of the decade puttering around the campuses of Cal-Berkeley and Stanford, compiling degrees in history and business management—while also futilely playing out on weekend nights hoping for the break that never came.

Then one evening late in 1999, he met a vital Asian-American woman who was a decade younger than himself. He saw in her eyes the kind of appreciation that had eluded him for years.

Paul thought it was he who had pursued her, and only much later realized that their courtship had been a strategic game on her part. Demure interest followed by hesitant acquiescence, and then total submission to his sexual desires—right up until the day he awoke to discover that the former Eileen Lao had not inspired him toward greatness, but in fact supplanted the last vestiges of his inner fire.

He eyed her now from across the ballroom. She was dancing too closely with some suntanned son of a bitch whose capped teeth glared in the chandelier light as he whispered into her ear.

Paul Jeffries found himself alternately enraged, humiliated, thirsty, and horny. He felt the urge to lose himself in a haze of cocktails while flirting with any number of the women in attendance for whom this event was a life highlight. He could take one of them to a hotel—or some supply closet here at the venue—and unleash all of his frustration out on her with animalistic fury, knowing that she would file the whole night's experience away as a thrilling secret memory.

But instead of allowing a petulant reaction to ruin his night—not *this* early, at least—Paul turned away and entered another space where a live band was up on stage. He ordered a vodka-soda from the bar and watched the blues-rock quintet play a few songs. After finishing his drink, he ascended the steps that led up to the stage platform.

He waved casually at the black bandleader until he got the man's attention, then mimicked strumming a guitar. Paul had noticed that this guy was a solid player in his own right—a fellow also-ran who nobody ever heard of, fated to a lifetime of performing other musicians' hits at weddings and parties.

"Ladies and gentlemen," Paul heard the man say a few minutes later, "we have a surprise guest joining us on stage right now. Please put your hands together for the First Man himself, Mr. Paul Jeffries…"

He fell into the rhythm of a sixties classic, his neck oscillating slowly with the groove of a drumbeat that felt suspended in time. Paul took great satisfaction when, out of the corner of his eye, he saw the bandleader do a double-take after he bent and held a succulently sweet note high up on the third string. Because this wasn't pretend. Not some phony smile for the cameras, either. This was music from the soul. Making magic in real time. Touching people on a level beneath the skin—and far beyond what could be expressed with words.

In that wonderfully pure moment, on a night to celebrate his wife's grand triumph, First Man Paul Jeffries looked back on the last thirty years of his life with a bewildered sense of clarity. So much of it had been lost to waste and distraction and merely going through the motions—the drunkenness, the affairs, the thousand meaningless social functions he'd been forced to attend.

And despite it all, while commanding a stage he had imposed himself upon, Paul Jeffries showed the world that he could still summon God with a Fender Stratocaster and speak His Word in 4/4 time.

He closed his eyes, tapping his foot steadily as he let the tragic weight of all that could have been fall away, and wailed on a solo for the ages…

Eileen was mortified. Someone had pulled her aside to let her know that Paul was prancing around up on stage making a scene. She simply couldn't believe it. On this of all nights.

But there he was, sweating and making faces and leaning back to back with the bass player, each of them smiling and looking up to the heavens. The singer crooned, then threw his arm over Paul's shoulders as the old fool twiddled his fingers on that guitar he'd gotten from somewhere.

Eileen was *this close* to stomping across that stage and shutting the whole embarrassing spectacle down. But then the heavyset drummer crashed the cymbals violently and the band stopped short. Bass, guitars, and keys rang out as the metal hiss slowly faded into nothingness. And filling the void… was applause.

Wild, frantic cheers for the band. Cheers for Paul. The other musicians offered exaggerated bows as he slipped out from under the guitar strap and handed the instrument back to the singer. He pressed his hands together humbly and nodded his appreciation to the crowd, then received pats on the back from onlookers while stepping off the stage.

As the next number kicked in, Eileen kept her eye on Paul. He stood as if in a daze, eyes wide but perhaps seeing nothing at all. She felt the tension release from her own body.

Just let him have it. Let him have this moment.

The night that Paul "stole the show," as the media would surely report it. But she knew he would never seize upon this little cameo to get himself back into music seriously. It would, however, perhaps buy her several years' worth of domestic tranquility.

Yes, because Paul Jeffries had finally gotten a taste of glory in the spotlight. He wouldn't trouble Eileen as she moved in for the kill doing the things that *really* mattered in this world.

43. EPILOGUE

Myra Jenkins had her routine set. What trains to take, how long the commute was—and even which cafe near campus made the best coffee.

The first week had been nerve-wracking. Every new thing she'd worried about beforehand had in fact combined to throw her into confusion. But she quickly discovered that everyone at the school was happy to answer her questions about where to go or how to install the student apps on her tablet.

Myra had even made a few friends in the two classes she was taking this semester. Only two because the guidance counselor had suggested she start with a lighter course load to avoid getting overwhelmed. She was fine with that.

Two kids, two classes. Seems about right.

She had also discovered that her fellow undergrads came from many different cultural backgrounds. This immediately put to rest her fears about being the one dark face in a sea of white. Instead, the Regnery School of Art's student body very much looked like New York City itself. So Myra Jenkins was just one of the many aspiring creators eager to collaborate and learn.

She knew that if she stuck to it through all the challenges that arose, she would one day make everyone proud. Her mother, her kids, her brother Clyde, her man Octavius… and most of all, herself.

It was a nice goal to have.

Marcus Young felt more relaxed now than he had since back in early November, just after he settled in as head of the Modestian medical clinic for military veterans. Otherwise, he would have to go all the way back to the previous spring, right before he was first deployed to go snooping around the Mall of Absolution.

The Jeffries-Lao inauguration had gone off without a hitch,

and now the month of January was nearly over. Which meant that warmer weather was right around the corner—and another chance to get back into something he'd neglected for years while out in the field on assignment.

Marcus had a much different field in mind as he entered the Chancellor High School parking lot on this brisk Sunday morning. He pulled on an embroidered FBI cap, then grabbed a dusty oblong bag out of his trunk. The winter air nipped at his bare lower legs as he trotted toward the gymnasium.

He opened the door and was greeted by loud cracks and shouting voices. Someone pointed at him and hollered, "About time! Get over here!"

Marcus grinned and went to shake the man's hand.

"Howdy, Coach. Thanks for the invite. Can't believe I'm finally doing this."

"Team could use a good outfielder. I'm sick of seeing guys boot routine fly balls, losing us winnable games. But there's no upward age limit in men's league, so what the hell."

"I'll do my best. Just a bit rusty is all."

The coach nodded at Marcus's bag. "How old's that gear?"

"Ah… glove's from the teens, but I did oil it up. Feels great now. As for my bat? Never been used."

Marcus unzipped the narrow pocket at the end of his bag and slid out a pristine wood Louisville Slugger. He smiled.

"Island life, here we come!"

Dawna Jenkins squeezed in between her friends Rita Coleman and Gwen Thomas, who were leaning over the cruise ship railing as it left the Port of Miami.

Rita said, "Bye-bye, USA. Bring on the piña coladas… and the *shopping!*"

As the ladies made their way up a flight of stairs headed for the pool deck bar, Gwen said, "This sure beats fightin' your way through the icy streets of New Jersey. Thank you, Dawna, for being such a generous friend."

"Here, here!" Rita called out. "A nice little getaway for three very vivacious ladies."

The women hugged briefly, then stepped up to the bar. The male server wearing an unbuttoned Hawaiian shirt was dancing to the steel-drum beat of a lively calypso song.

"*Hola, señoritas!* What can I get for you?"

Dawna grabbed Rita's arm and whispered, "He can get that booty moving straight on up to my room, know what I'm sayin'?"

There was laughter and more hugs, until Gwen finally said to the man, "Baby, c'mere. What's your name… Carlos? Okay, look here. I don't care what you give us, but it's got to be *mixed drinks* only! We got five days on and off this boat. Can't have none of these fine ladies out of commission on account of too many shots."

Carlos bowed. "Your wish is my command. How would you like if I made you one of my personal favorites? It's called, Mango Home With You."

"Ooh, I like the sound of that," Rita said as she threw a hand in the air.

Dawna and friends next settled onto a row of vinyl lounge chairs, each holding a tall plastic aqua cup that was adorned with fruit wedges and an orange umbrella.

She said, "Mrs. Thomas, what if we just stay on this boat forever and leave our troubles behind?"

"I hear that, Dawna darling. I may not be too old for Mister Carlos, but I still am tired."

Rita chirped, "You *can* just lay there. He'll do all the work."

"Nasty! You a nasty lady, Rita."

Dawna looked up at the slowly shifting sky as she said, "I don't know if I can do any more. My boy Clyde, he's hungry. And that friend of mine we was talking about last week, he wants *us* to fight too. But I don't think I got it in me."

Gwen said, "What is this now? You sayin' to forget everything we discussed? No Underground Railroad of the soul? No using our voices to warn of danger, like the drum beats of old?"

Dawna drank through her straw. "Sorry, but I guess not. It's so funny, though. A bright new hat. Stepping off the shore. And one creamy adult libation. That's all it took for me to lose myself. All the weight I been holdin' up? Poof, it's gone. Now I am Island Woman, hear me snore…"

Rita reached out and bumped her cup against Dawna's. "Don't get depressed just 'cause you finally allowed yourself to have a little fun. Now *is* the time to let it all hang out! At least wait til you get back home before deciding if you gonna play hero or not."

"That's exactly right," Gwen said. "Now get on up, the both of you. We got a whole boat to explore. Bars to discover. And men to meet. Let's go!"

Dawna smiled. "You girls really are the best. Thank you for cheering me up. Now, somebody help me out of this chair. I might just poke my head into one of them buffets while we're on the move…"

Eldress Julia Foster stood in front of the dressing table mirror. She looked down at the necklace she had purchased earlier in the day. The fine silver chain felt silky in her palm. Its only ornamentation was a teardrop pearl.

She had just put on a Modestian-approved casual dress which revealed a small area of skin below the neckline. Now she secured the necklace clasp and appraised herself in the mirror.

It was not vanity that told her she looked radiant. Nor was it greed that suggested she might return to the jewelry shop and also buy ball earrings in the same color. No, Julia was only thinking of how to please the man who had noticed *her* among all others—and be worthy of the ultimate honor, should she inhabit the role of Prescient Mistress as Scott Cullen's wife.

Her journey to this moment was singular, but then again, almost every Modestian Julia had spoken to seemed to have a peculiar life story which made them receptive to the new religion.

Her own family had attended a progressive non-denominational church, but even that open-minded sect was not able to satisfy the many clarifications demanded by a child of the "I Totally Exalt Science" generation. If traditional Christian theology could not sufficiently account for the vastness of space, then Julia also wondered why some groups were hesitant, or vehemently opposed, to utilizing inventions and ideas that were possible on this world which God had created for people.

But the supreme paradox to her mind, was how atheists could hold computer logic in such high regard, when according to their beliefs, the universe itself had come about through random and purposeless chance.

She had grappled with these questions privately, as well as

with pastors and university professors, but never reached the place of certainty necessary to lead a fully functional life. Then one day, about a year and a half ago, a coworker had forwarded her a short video excerpt from a speech given by the Prescient One. This was intended as a gag to mock the church leader's medieval cloak and feature-obscuring makeup, but the timing coincided with a deep longing for harmony between her mind, body, and soul.

This strange man spoke of striving for balance in life, rather than trying to merge with technology as the solution to human imperfection. He also preached modesty as the ultimate form of empowerment, in an age when flamboyance was seen as the pathway to confidence. Because self-control, he said, protected people against dissipating themselves in wasteful activities, which might trap them in a loop—or even bring about their total destruction.

Within months of first discovering the Modestian gospel, Julia closed up shop on her old life in Missouri and took a leap of faith by moving into the Mall of Absolution. So many of her persistent frustrations simply fell away after she began her half-year trial as a novitiate.

The simple life, one of self-examination and curiosity about one's immediate surroundings… It all proved more manageable, more rewarding, more *intimate* than the lofty aspirations of major religions and scientism alike, which both appeared to overshoot their mark by neglecting the importance of practical daily living.

And now Julia's wildest hopes for a loving future were about to come true, despite how preposterous her conversion to Modestianity had seemed to her family and friends a short while ago. She was ready to aim her own empowered heart like a laser beam at the man adorned in silver and teal, Mr. Scott Cullen.

Mod willing, she would fill the home of this Prescient One with precious little ones in the years to come…

Clyde Jenkins was back at the writing table. For the first time since forever—summer, maybe?—he felt like his mind was in the same place it had been before he uploaded "Fly So High" on a hope and a prayer.

Just his own thoughts now. No rush, no worrying about other people, no hoping the girls would bat their eyes at him. Somehow a lifetime of experiences and wisdom had been crammed into just six months, and tonight he could finally reconnect with himself and explore what he might want to say next.

The new lyrical ideas came fast and in chaotic bursts. Images, themes, and sensory details all poured out onto the page in the same way that his HRA protest song had begun. He wrote about life moving on, estrangement, triumph, disappointment... Of vague wishes turning into reality and the domino effect of consequences...

Waking suddenly in a fancy hotel's king-size bed, after a nightmare which had channeled the real-life moment of violent terror he'd experienced in an alleyway five years ago...

The soundless memory of attending a funeral at a very young age for one of his mother's uncles, the church clothes and somber faces...

Myra coming into his room crying after a loud fight with Dawna—and Clyde too naive to understand what the implications of her being pregnant meant, and why Dawna was so mad...

Lazy summer days spent wandering around the neighborhood with his crew. Convincing the old-timers to give them a sip of beer or a puff of whatever they were smoking out on the stoops...

Discovering new music from anyone and everyone. Straining his ears to identify the singers' unique styles and trying to mimic them note for note. Then thinking that he too would like to be a performer, to live that life on stage...

Delivering a handful of his own rhymes on the corners with friends. Impromptu rap battles during lunch at school, or after a round of basketball at the public courts. Sometimes even hopping up on stage at the local venues, before the serious and more established rappers got going...

Feeling the tingles on the top of his head during those first few days when "Fly So High" started taking off. Dawna and Myra and everyone else screaming themselves silly, crying tears of joy, and embracing each other in the living room of their old apartment...

He would never forget the summer of 'twenty-eight, even if

some of the minor moments were lost in the avalanche of new experiences. All the parties, the interviews, the girls, the liquor, the weed...

The dream might have continued on and on and on. But then one day, some *other* group that didn't appreciate the Historical Reparations Administration dropped their own track.

The Sentinels of Jubilee's live broadcast on October seventh had changed the national conversation in an instant—and suddenly Clyde's song was seen in a much more serious light. Everything started to feel tighter, more tense. Instead of friendly Afrigro-American radio hosts, he was talking politics with people who did that sort of thing for a living.

So in hindsight, he couldn't blame himself for changing gears lyrically on his second solo release, "Soul's Gold," which flopped badly. And then he'd recorded the ridiculous song "Ho'Spice" with a couple of accomplished local guys, but that single still wasn't even out yet. Clyde could only guess what Sylicon Smoov and Raw D-Eel were up to at their studio back in the Bronx.

But Clyde had not stopped tumbling forward on his own accelerated track. He eventually gave in to Eddie Pryor's overtures, but only after his mentor Nolan Simmons had made it clear that there was nothing left for him in Newark.

Next arriving in Los Angeles and diving right into work. Soon discovering that *everyone* had something to say to him—whether it was offering life advice, pitching new project ideas, or simply a resounding no.

But he had learned two important things about this town. One, you needed to keep moving forward, and never doubt what had happened in the past. And second, you also had to make time for yourself. To remember who you were, and work on your own passions.

And that's just what Clyde Jenkins was doing right now. Laying the groundwork for solo track number three, after devoting his daytime hours to the collaboration with DJ Low Bought. He would embrace the role of mainstream entertainer, so long as he also got time on the mic to spread his own personal message.

Already he and Eddie had been through enough of the good and the bad, that Clyde could say there was at least one person in all of Los Angeles he could rely on. That was a start.

DJ Clydoscope put his notebook away for the night and looked out the bedroom window. A few stars were peeking through the city's bright glare. He would do everything in his power to keep his own light shining for years to come.

Luis Ortega kicked at some pebbles with his bare feet. A trickle of water eased in and rinsed the sand out from between his toes. Two seagulls cawed as they passed overhead on their journey down the shoreline.

It was breezy but still mostly sunny at the quiet Malibu Lagoon State Beach park. Luis had come here rather than Santa Monica or Venice Beach because he didn't want to be surrounded by noisy tourists. There were only a few dozen other people lounging on the sand or lazily walking around this small cove.

All week he had been stumbling around in a fog. Nothing dramatic had happened. No one else had bothered him at school, either. But without a critical moment to test his newfound resolve, Luis felt like he was bottled up with stress. So he headed to the beach...

He watched some tiny insects rush into a clump of seaweed that was slowly being left behind by the receding tide. His feet made deep prints in the mushy sand, but soon the in-out flows of the cool water washed them all away.

Over to his left, where the lagoon drained out to the ocean, Luis noticed that some people were crossing onto the sandbank from another portion of beach that was closer to Pacific Coast Highway. Curious, he ambled in their direction, until finally realizing that the water level here had dropped to virtually nothing. He also saw that if he kept going south, he'd be able to check out the pier that stood nearby.

As he worked his way up the sandy incline toward the road, some surfers who were paddling around the deeper waters caught his eye. He sat down and watched as they grappled with the choppy waves.

A little while later, one of these guys swam to shore and began heading up the slope with his board tucked under his arm. Luis gave him a thumbs-up.

"Sup, dude?" the surfer said.

"Just chillin', man. Hey, how cold is the water?"

"Ah, you know. Definitely need this!" The surfer slapped at his wetsuit. "But once you get moving, you don't really feel it."

"Cool. Like, how hard is it to do, surfing?"

"You never tried? It's super fun. You should, for sure."

Luis motioned at the surfboard. "But it's got to cost a lot. The gear, right?"

"It *can*. But there's plenty of used stuff out there. The important thing is you get in that ocean. It's special, trust me."

"I think it would be cool. You have lots of friends that do it?"

"Oh, totally! It's a community, man. A brotherhood. What's your name, by the way?"

"I'm Luis. And you?"

"Colin." They bumped fists. "Good chatting, but I gotta roll here in a minute. You should think about picking up a board, though."

"For real? It's that good?"

"Dude." Colin cast his arm out in the direction of the water. "I'm telling you, man. Once you're out there, everything else goes away. It's just you and the flow. Work *with* it, and you'll catch some great waves right to the shore. But if you fight it… Ha, better cover your head before it tosses you onto the rocks."

"Oh. So it's dangerous then?"

Colin laughed. "It's real life! The danger *and* the thrills. Don't pass it up or you'll miss out. See ya, Lou."

"Later."

Luis turned his attention back to where the other surfers were clustered. He watched them maneuver along the pulsing ocean surface, each waiting for his turn to push up from paddling position and try to catch a brief exhilarating ride, before dropping back into the blue-green sea.

THE END.

If you enjoyed this book,
please visit the website where you
purchased it and post a review.

ABOUT THE AUTHOR

Originally from Northern Virginia, Philip Wyeth has lived in the Los Angeles area for many years. He's an entrepreneur, musician, film aficionado, hockey fan, and enjoys playing tennis and golf.

Inspired by such unique writers as Heinrich von Kleist, Ambrose Bierce, Joseph Conrad, and Len Deighton, Wyeth's imaginative novels will resonate with fans of Philip K. Dick, Rich Larson, Michel Houellebecq, and Neal Stephenson.

Also a lifelong fan of heavy metal music and its many sub-genres, Wyeth strives to infuse his writing with comparable levels of intensity, independence, and larger-than-life visions.

His website is www.philipwyeth.com, and you can follow him across the social media landscape under the following handles:

@PhilipWyeth: Twitter, BitChute, Gab, and Minds.

@PhilipWyethWriter: Instagram and Facebook.

www.ingramcontent.com/pod-product-compliance
Lightning Source LLC
Chambersburg PA
CBHW032109110726
47902CB00003B/519